Ghost-in-Law Omnibus #1

Ghost-in-Law Omnibus #1

Jana DeLeon

Published by Jana DeLeon

ISBN: 1940270154
ISBN 13: 9781940270159

Trouble in Mudbug

Chapter One

"I still can't believe she's gone," Maryse Robicheaux murmured as she stared down at the woman in the coffin.

Of course, the pink suit was a dead giveaway—so to speak—that the wearer was no longer with them. For the miserable two years and thirty-two days she'd had to deal with her mother-in-law, Maryse had never once seen her wear a color other than black. Now she sorta resembled the Stay-Puft Marshmallow Man dressed in Pepto-Bismol.

"I can't believe it either," Sabine whispered back. "I didn't know evil incarnate could die."

Maryse jabbed her best friend with her elbow. "For Pete's sake, we're at the woman's funeral. Show some respect."

Sabine let out a sigh. "Maryse, that woman gave you holy hell. And her son was worse. I don't even understand why you wanted to come."

Maryse stared at the casket again and shook her head. "I don't know. I just felt compelled to. I can't really explain it."

And that was the God's honest truth. She'd had no intention of attending Helena Henry's funeral. Yet after her morning shower, she'd stood in front of her closet and pulled out her dark navy "interview" suit and matching pumps instead of her usual work clothes of jeans, T-shirt, and rubber boots.

Looking down at Helena, Maryse still didn't know why she was there. If she'd come for some sort of closure, it hadn't happened. But then, what had she expected—the dead woman to pop up out of the coffin and apologize for bringing the most useless man in the world into existence, then making Maryse's life even more miserable by being the biggest bitch on the face of the Earth?

It wasn't likely when you considered that Helena Henry had never apologized for anything in her entire life. It wasn't necessary. When you had a pocketbook the size of the Atchafalaya Basin in Mudbug, Louisiana, population 502, people tended to purposely overlook things.

"I think they're ready to start," Sabine whispered, gesturing to the minister who had entered the chapel through a side door. "We need to take a seat."

Maryse nodded but remained glued to her place in front of the coffin, not yet able to tear herself away from the uncustomary pink dress and the awful-but-now dead woman who wore it. "Just a minute more."

There had to be some reason she'd come. Some reason other than just to ensure that Helena's reign of terror was over, but nothing came to her except the lingering scent of Helena's gardenia perfume.

"Where's Hank?" Sabine asked. "Surely he wouldn't miss his own mother's funeral. That would be major bad karma, even for Hank. I know he's a lousy human being and all, but really."

Maryse sighed as Sabine's words chased away her wistful vision of her wayward husband in a coffin right alongside his mother. If her best friend had even an inkling of her thoughts, she'd besiege her with a regime of crystal cleansing and incense until Maryse went insane, and she was sort of saving the insanity plea to use later on in life and on a much bigger problem than a worthless man.

"Hank is a lot of things," Maryse said, "but he's not a complete fool. He's wanted on at least twenty different charges in Mudbug. This is the first place the cops would look for him. There's probably one behind the skirt under the coffin."

Sabine stared at the blue velvet curtain for a moment, then pulled a piece of it to the side and leaned down a bit. Sarcasm was completely lost on Sabine.

"Cut it out," Maryse said and jabbed her again. "I was joking. Hank wouldn't risk an arrest to come to the funeral, karma or no. The only thing Hank liked about Helena was her money, and once the estate is settled, Hank's bad karma can be paid in full."

Sabine pursed her lips and gave the blue velvet curtain one last suspicious look. "Well, it's going to be hard to collect the money if he's playing the Invisible Man."

Maryse rolled her eyes, turned away from the Pink Polyester Antichrist, and pointed to a pew in the back. "Oh, he'll be lurking around somewhere waiting to inherit," she whispered as the music began to play and they took a seat in the back of the chapel. "Even I would bet on that one. With any luck, someone will grab him while he's in close range."

Sabine smirked. "Then he'll collect momma's money and work a deal with the local cops through Helena's friend Judge Warner, and everything will be swept under the rug as usual."

"Yeah, probably. But maybe I'll finally get my divorce."

Sabine's eyes widened. "I hadn't even thought of that, but you're right. If someone grabs Hank, you can have him served." She reached over and squeezed Maryse's hand. "Oh, thank God, Maryse. You can finally be free."

Maryse nodded as the song leader's voice filtered through her head. What a mess she'd made of her life. She hadn't even been married to Hank thirty days before he disappeared, leaving her holding the bag while numerous bookies and loan sharks came calling. If they'd lived in any other state but Louisiana, she would have already been divorced, but Louisiana, with its screwed-up throwback to Napoleonic law, had only two outs for a marriage—either you served papers or you produced a body. No exceptions.

She'd had no choice but to ask Helena for help. Hank hadn't exactly borrowed money from the nicest of people, and if Maryse wanted to continue to live in Mudbug, she had to pay them off—pure and simple. That was two years ago, and despite the efforts of four private investigators and several angry friends, she hadn't seen Hank Henry since. Oh, but she'd seen Helena.

Every other Friday at seven A.M., Helena appeared like clockwork at Lucy's Café to collect on the debt Maryse owed her, along with the 25 percent interest she was charging. Now the old bat had the nerve to die when Maryse was only two payments short of eating breakfast in complete peace and quiet.

She turned her attention to the pastor as he took over at the front of the chapel. He began to read the standard funeral Bible verses, meant to persuade those in attendance that the person they loved had moved on to a better place. Maryse smirked at the irony. Mudbug was the better place now that Helena had exited. She cast her gaze once more to Helena, lying peacefully in her coffin…

That's when Helena moved.

Maryse straightened in her pew, blinked once to clear her vision, and stared hard at Helena Henry. Surely it was a trick of the lights. Dead people didn't move. Embalming and all that other icky stuff that happened at funeral homes took care of that, right?

Maryse had just about convinced herself that it was just a lights and shadows trick when Helena opened her eyes and raised her head. Maryse sucked in a breath and clenched her eyes shut, certain she was having a nervous breakdown that had been two years in the making. She waited several seconds, then slowly opened her eyes, silently praying that her mind was done playing tricks on her.

Apparently, it wasn't.

Helena sat bolt upright in the coffin, looking around the chapel, a confused expression on her boldly painted face. Panicked, Maryse scanned the other attendees. Why wasn't anyone screaming or pointing or running for the door? God knows, she hadn't been to many funerals, but she didn't remember the dead person ever sitting up to take part.

She felt a squeeze on her hand, and Sabine whispered, "Are you all right? You got really pale all of a sudden."

Maryse started to answer, but then sucked in a breath as Helena pulled herself out of the coffin.

"Don't you see that?" Maryse pointed to the front of the chapel. "Don't you see what's happening?"

Sabine cast a quick glance to the front of the chapel, then looked back at Maryse with concern—no fear, no terror…nothing to indicate that she saw anything amiss.

"See what?" Sabine asked. "Do we need to leave? You don't look well."

Maryse closed her eyes, took a deep breath, and dug her fingernails into her palms, steeling herself. Even though it was the last thing in the world she wanted to do, she forced her gaze to the front of the chapel.

Yup, her nightmare was still there. And, just as in real life, she didn't want to stay silent for long.

"What the hell is going on here, Pastor Bob? For Christ's sake, I'm Catholic," Helena ranted. "If this is some sort of weird Baptist ceremony, I don't want any part of it." Helena paused for a moment, but the pastor continued as if she'd never said a word.

Maryse stared, not blinking, not breathing, her eyes growing wider and wider until she felt as if they would pop out of her head.

Helena turned from the pastor and surveyed the attendees, narrowing her eyes. "Who dressed me like a hooker and shoved me in a coffin? I'll have you all arrested is what I'll do. Damn it, someone drugged me! What are you—some kind of weird cult?" She paced wildly in front of the coffin. "I'll see every one of you assholes in jail, especially you, Harold." Helena stepped over to the nearest pew and reached for her husband, Harold, but her hands passed completely through him.

Helena stopped for a moment, then tried to touch Harold once more, but the result was exactly the same. She frowned and looked down at herself, then back at the coffin. Maryse followed her gaze and realized Helena's body was still lying there—placid as ever.

Helena stared at herself for what seemed like forever, her eyes wide, her expression shocked. The pastor asked everyone to rise for prayer, and Maryse rose in a daze alongside Sabine, but she couldn't bring herself to bow her head. Her eyes were permanently glued on the spectacle at the front of the chapel. The spectacle that apparently no one else could see.

Helena began to walk slowly down the aisle, yelling as she went and waving her hands in front of people's faces. But no one so much as flinched. As she approached the back, Maryse's heart began to race, and her head pounded with the rush of blood. She knew she should sit down, but she couldn't move, couldn't breathe.

All of a sudden, Helena ceased yelling and stopped in her tracks about ten feet from Maryse's pew. Her expression changed from shocked to worried, then sad. Maryse tried to maintain her composure, but the breath she'd been holding came out with a whoosh. Helena looked toward the source of the noise and locked eyes with Maryse.

Helena stared for a moment, her expression unchanged. As the seconds passed and Maryse didn't drop her gaze, Helena's face changed from sad to puzzled, and she started walking toward the pew. Maryse held in a cry as Helena drew closer. A wave of dizziness washed over her. Her head began to swim. One step, two steps, and then the apparition was right in front of her.

That's when everything went dark.

Maryse came to surrounded by a circle of black. For a moment, she thought she was in a tomb, but then her vision cleared, and she looked upward to the concerned and curious faces of the other funeral-goers. Helena's funeral, she remembered instantly. She was at Helena's funeral.

"Maryse, are you all right?" Sabine leaned over her, worried.

Maryse sat up on the floor and felt a rush of blood to her head. "What happened?"

Sabine shook her head. "I don't know. The pastor was praying, and the next thing I knew, you were on the ground."

An elderly lady standing next to Sabine handed her a Kleenex and chimed in, "It looks like you fainted. It's probably the heat."

Maryse took the tissue, wondering what the hell she was supposed to do with it, and nodded. It was a more diplomatic response than pointing out that the chapel was air-conditioned, so that theory didn't exactly hold water. Maryse rose from the floor, wobbling a bit on the uncomfortable high heels, and perched at the end of the pew. Deciding there was nothing more to see, the other funeral attendees drifted out the door and away to the cemetery for the interment.

Maryse rubbed her temples and looked over at Sabine. "I swear, I don't remember a thing. What happened?"

Sabine frowned and gave her a critical look. "I'm not sure what to tell you. You started looking kinda weird in the middle of the service and asked me if I saw something, but I have no idea what. When we rose to pray, you were white as a sheet, and while the pastor was praying, you must have passed out. By the time I opened my eyes, you were already hitting the ground."

"It must be stress," Maryse said. "That's the only explanation."

"Maybe," Sabine said thoughtfully, then placed one hand on Maryse's arm. "Are you going to be okay to drive?"

Maryse nodded. "Yeah, I'll be fine. I was a little dizzy at first, but now I feel fine."

Sabine narrowed her eyes. "Are you sure? I have an appointment in twenty minutes or I would do it myself, but I can call Mildred if you'd rather someone give you a ride."

Maryse waved her hand, rose from the pew, and gave her friend a smile, hoping to alleviate some of her worry. "No use bothering Mildred while she's working." Maryse glanced down at her watch. "Speaking of which, did you close the shop for the morning?"

Sabine shook her head. "Raissa agreed to cover for me until noon. Mrs. Breaux's coming in for her tarot reading right after lunch. That's the appointment I can't miss.

Mrs. Breaux absolutely hates getting a reading from Raissa."

Maryse stared at her. "But Raissa has real psychic ability. You're just shamming."

Sabine rolled her eyes. "I know that, but do you really think these people want to know the truth? If they did, they'd drive the hour to New Orleans and see Raissa for a dose of reality. The only reason Mrs. Breaux keeps coming back is because I tell her what she wants to hear."

"But how long can that possibly last? I mean, sooner or later, she's going to figure out you're never right."

Sabine shrugged. "Doesn't matter. Raissa says she'll be dead by year-end anyway, so the charade doesn't have to last much longer. Her soul's fine though—very clean, actually—so she should do well in the next round." Sabine took a step closer and gave her a hug. "Give me a call later. And think about taking the afternoon off, please."

Maryse nodded, not even wanting to consider how Raissa knew when Mrs. Breaux would expire, then made a mental note to avoid running into that psychic anytime soon. Death was definitely one of those things where ignorance was bliss. "Thanks, Sabine. I really appreciate you coming with me on such short notice. And don't worry. I'll be fine from here on out."

Sabine didn't look convinced, but there wasn't much she could do. She gave Maryse an encouraging smile and turned to leave.

Maryse gave her retreating figure one final glance and looked back to the front of the chapel. What in the world had happened? There was something in the back of her mind, but it was fleeting, like a movie on fast forward. Something important that she needed to remember, but it was flashing too fast for her to lock in on it.

What could cause a young, healthy woman who spent most of her time outdoors to faint in an air-conditioned building? The answer hit her all at once and she gasped.

Helena!

The image of Helena Henry crawling out of her coffin and yelling at everyone in the chapel made her shudder all over again. And that look in her eyes when she'd seen Maryse watching her...

But how was that even possible? Helena Henry was dead. There was no mistaking the bitter-looking woman in that casket for anyone else—despite the hideous pink suit and Vegas-showgirl makeup.

The only explanation Maryse had was that she must have imagined the whole thing. All the strain of trying to find that idiot Hank and paying off his ridiculous debts to that devil-mother of his must have caused her to break. That had to be it. The dead didn't show up to their own funerals and call people assholes.

She paused for a moment. If they could, though, she'd have bet Helena Henry would have been the first to volunteer for the job.

Certain her current line of thought had gone way too far, she left the chapel and made her way to her truck, anxious to get away from the overwhelming feeling of death. It was barely noon, but it was definitely time for a beer. Maybe she'd pick up something from the café on the way home—like a bag of boiled crawfish—then take a shower and a nap. Just a bit of a refresher.

After that, she needed to contact her attorney and make sure he was prepared for a Hank appearance and was ready to serve him the divorce papers. She pulled into Mudbug, all eight buildings of it, and parked in front of the café. Turning off the truck, she stared out the windshield at her reflection in the café window. She didn't even want to think about having to face Hank. She wasn't even sure it was possible without trying to throttle him.

Maybe she'd have fries, too—fries and *two* beers and forget she'd ever known Hank and Helena Henry.

Maryse awakened mid-afternoon, surprised she'd slept so long. But napping any longer was a luxury she couldn't afford. She'd already lost almost an entire day of work. If she hurried out to the bayou, there might be enough daylight to take some pictures and satisfy the state's latest request for images of bayou foliage.

Just as she was about to crawl out of bed, she felt the hair on her arms prickle as if she were being watched. Her cat, Jasper, stiffened and let out a low growl. Before she could figure out what had upset him, he leaped from the bed and shot out the cat door built into the window beside the bed.

Shaking her head in amusement at his antics, Maryse caught a flash of bright pink out of the corner of her eye and looked up to find Helena Henry standing in the doorway of her bedroom, studying her like she would the fabric on designer sheets.

Maryse felt her back tighten from the tip of her neck all the way to the base of her spine. This couldn't be happening—not after only two beers.

"Well, hell," Helena said finally. "That solves it." She took a few steps closer to the bed and looked Maryse straight in the eyes. "You can see me, can't you?"

Maryse nodded, unable to speak, unable to blink.

"I thought for a moment at the chapel that you'd finally lost your mind, but I should have known better. You're far too practical to let something like a funeral take you down. Especially *my* funeral." She blew out a breath and plopped down on the end of the bed. "This is certainly unexpected but will probably come in handy."

"Handy?" Maryse managed to croak out, her mind whirling with confusion. There was a dead woman sitting on her bed. Weren't they supposed to float or something? "But you're…I mean, you are…"

"Dead?" Helena finished. "Of course I'm dead. Do you think I'd wear polyester in the summer if I were alive? And don't get me started about the color, or the low-cut top and the skirt that is way too short." She stared down at the offensive garment. "Makes me want to puke."

"But how…why…" Maryse trailed off, not sure where to go with the conversation, not entirely convinced she was actually having the conversation. Finally, she pinched herself, just to make absolutely sure she was awake.

Helena gave her a grim smile. "Oh, you're awake, honey. And I'm really dead, and you're really sitting in your bedroom talking to me." She scrunched her brow in concentration. "Although, I suppose it's not really me but the ghost of me. Hmmm."

"But at the funeral, you looked confused, surprised…"

Helena nodded. "It was a bit of a shocker, I have to admit. Waking up in a coffin in the middle of my own funeral service.

Took me a couple of hours to sort it all out, but once the memories came together, it all made sense."

"But why me? Why in the world would you be visible to me?"

Helena shrugged. "Just lucky, I guess."

Lucky? Lucky! Good God Almighty! Maryse could think of plenty of words to describe being haunted by her dead Antichrist mother-in-law, but lucky sure as hell wasn't one of them. "Please tell me you're going to go away and haunt a house or a cemetery or something."

Helena shook her head. "Can't do that just yet. I have a bit of unfinished business here. And much as you may hate it, it involves you. Plus, there's that nagging problem of letting my killer get away, and as long as I'm hanging around, I figure I might as well do something about that, too."

Maryse jumped up from the bed. "Your killer? The newspaper said it was respiratory failure from your asthma."

"Respiratory failure, my ass. My lungs may have given out, but it was only after I drank whatever the hell was put in my brandy snifter. I collapsed right afterward."

Maryse absorbed this information for a moment. Certainly what Helena implied was possible, but if she was right, that still left a huge question unanswered. "Who did it?"

"I don't know, but they were clever. I haven't had a drink of brandy in a long time. Could have been there for a day or a month for all I know." Helena shrugged. "Guess I'll just have to figure out who wanted me dead."

Maryse stared at her. Was she kidding? A shorter list would be people who *didn't* want her dead.

"I think that might be a bit difficult," Maryse said finally, trying to be diplomatic. After all, she didn't know anything about ghosts. Maybe they could do curses or something. This *was* Louisiana.

"You weren't exactly the most popular person in town," Maryse continued and braced herself for the blow up.

Helena surprised her by pursing her lips and considering her words. "You're right," she said finally. "There are probably plenty of people who weren't sad to see me go. The question is which one was desperate enough to take action?"

Maryse thought about this for a moment and began to see Helena's point. When one really boiled down to the nitty-gritty of the situation, there was an enormous difference between preferring someone was dead, or even wishing them dead, and actually killing them. Still, the word "desperate" brought her missing husband to mind.

"You're thinking of Hank," Helena said, and gave her a shrewd look. "Of course I thought of him, but I don't think that's the answer."

Maryse started to open her mouth in protest, but Helena held up one finger to silence her. "I'm certain he won't be sad to hear I'm dead. But quite frankly, Hank lacks the brains to carry out something like this. If he ever tried to poison someone, he'd never think to use something the coroner wouldn't detect. He'd probably go straight for rat poison or whatever was closest."

Maryse studied Helena's face carefully, trying to discern whether she was being sincere or sarcastic. She couldn't find any evidence of sarcasm. Well, that hung it all. If Helena was talking trash about Hank, the woman was most certainly dead.

Oh, how a little murder changed everything.

"Okay," Maryse said, chasing away the great visual of Hank Henry rotting away in a prison cell. "What about Harold?"

"Hmm." Helena scrunched her brow in concentration. "It usually is the spouse, especially when there's money involved. But as far as Harold's concerned, I was worth more alive than dead. With the bequests I left to various people and organizations, he actually comes out on the short end of the stick, and he's probably known that for a long time."

Maryse threw her hands in the air. "Well, if you've got a logical reason for why Hank or Harold aren't guilty, then I don't know why you bothered to come here. I obviously don't have the mentality to think like a killer." She took a deep breath and rushed on before she could change her mind. "I don't think I can help you, Helena."

There. It was out in the open. She bit her lower lip and looked at Helena, hoping she would politely agree and go away.

Helena gave her a withering look and shook her head. "Sorry. You have something I need."

Maryse felt her breath catch in her throat. Helena already had something in mind, and Maryse knew with complete certainty she didn't want to hear a word of it. "What in the world could I possibly have that you need?" She waved one hand around the one-bedroom cabin. "This is all I have in the world besides my truck. A camp in the middle of the bayou."

Helena looked at her with sad eyes that seemed to go straight to her soul. "That's not true. You're alive. You can touch things, move things. I can't. And you're the only one who can see me."

Maryse narrowed her eyes at Helena. "What do you mean you can't touch or move things? You got here, and the only way to get to my place is by boat."

Helena's eyes lit up. "I know. That's been the only interesting part about death so far. I stood at the bank thinking about how to get over here. Finally, I decided to borrow one of the small aluminum boats parked at the dock, but no matter how hard I tried, I couldn't get a grip on anything. My hands just passed right through everything like it wasn't even there."

"So how exactly did you get here?"

Helena beamed. "I walked on water. I finally figured what the hell, if Jesus did it, I would give it whirl. So I stepped off the pier onto the bayou and voilà—I could walk on water."

Maryse stared at her in dismay. This was the start of the Revelation…she was positive. If Helena Henry could walk on water, Maryse was absolutely sure He was on His way back to claim His own.

Well, that sealed it. Church this Sunday was no longer an option. She had some serious praying to do.

Chapter Two

Maryse stopped at the office with the intention of making a quick in-and-out stop. The state was trying to determine if the orchid cypripedium kentuckiense, known to regular folk as the Southern Lady's Slipper, was reproducing as a poisonous hybrid. All she needed to do was get the picture the state had sent her and head for the bayou where things were safe, sane, and normal.

Except that the office wasn't empty.

A man sat at her desk, his back to the door. A man she'd never seen before. A man with a lot of nerve, since he was trying to log in to her computer.

Apparently, the hacking effort had him totally engrossed because he didn't seem to hear her come in. Maryse pulled the door shut with a bang and got a small satisfaction out of making him jump. "Who the hell are you and what are you doing in my office?" she asked.

The man turned around in the chair, and Maryse felt her breath catch in her throat. He was gorgeous. Long black hair pulled into a ponytail, dark eyes, and skin with that deep brown coloring that implied Creole or Native American. He smiled at her, and she blinked. Even his teeth were perfect.

He rose from the chair and extended his hand. "I'm Luc LeJeune."

Maryse stared at him a moment more, then shook his hand. "And you're doing exactly what in my office, trying to break into my computer?"

Luc glanced back at the computer, then looked back at her. "Oh, that. Well, you see, I'm a zoologist for the state. I'm going to be working here with you for a while…maybe a couple of months, and this is the only computer in the office I could find."

Maryse's head whirled. "Working here? There's barely room for me." Technically, there were two offices, but one was her lab, and by God, she wasn't giving it up. "There's only one bathroom."

Luc smiled again. "I don't mind sharing as long as you leave the seat up."

Good looking and funny too. God help her. "This is not going to work," Maryse said. "There is one desk in here, one computer. There's no way we will both fit."

Luc shrugged. "Guess we're going to have to. I have a job to do, and this is where the state sent me. Based on the time you showed up here today, I assume you spend most working hours in the bayou. Either that or you're really not a morning person."

Maryse bristled. "I'm fine in the morning, Mr. LeJeune. *This* morning I was attending a funeral for my mother-in-law. Not that it's any of your business."

Luc glanced at her bare left hand. "You're married? That's a shame. This assignment was starting to look interesting."

"No, I'm not married. Well, technically, I'm married, but not really."

Luc looked at her in obvious amusement. "You're not really technically married? I'm fascinated. What's the story?"

She paused for a moment, deciding on an answer. "I'm getting a divorce."

"You don't sound convinced."

Maryse sighed. "Look, Mr. LeJeune, I don't really care to discuss my personal life with you, I don't care to share my office with you, and I sure as hell don't care to leave the seat up on the toilet. Now, if you don't mind removing yourself from my desk, what I do care to do is use my computer so that I can manage a bit of work today before the daylight is gone."

Luc slid the chair to the side and grinned, aggravating her even more. "All yours."

Maryse pulled a metal chair up to the computer since the rude zoologist apparently had no intention of giving up her comfortable leather chair. First thing tomorrow morning, she was calling the state about this. There was no way she was going to have that man snooping around her research, using her computer, looking over her shoulder.

Like he was doing now.

Luc LeJeune had rolled his chair back toward her and now the arm of her leather chair was almost touching the arm of the cheap metal thing she currently sat on. In the cool, air-conditioned office, she could feel the heat from his body as he shifted toward her, his arm and shoulders not even an inch from hers.

She lifted her arm away from his warmth and leaned forward in her chair and slightly to the side in order to block his view of the keyboard. Then she tapped in her password. The screen flickered, and she opened her mailbox and started scanning for the picture she needed. Leaning back again in her chair, she clicked to open the e-mail she'd been searching for.

"So who was your mother-in-law?" Luc asked. She could feel his breath on her neck.

Silently willing her hormones into submission, she frowned. "*Ex*-mother-in-law. And why would you want to know? You're not from Mudbug."

Luc shrugged. "My grandparents used to live on the bayou in the next town. They have friends in Mudbug. I figure your mother-in-law might have been someone they knew."

"*Ex*-mother-in-law, and her name was Helena Henry."

Luc let out a laugh. "You're the one who married Hank Henry? Wow, that sucks. No wonder you're not technically married. Hank's been gone for, what, a year now?"

Maryse gritted her teeth and worked to control her voice. "Two years actually, but I'm sure that's about to change."

Luc studied her for a moment, then frowned. "So the wicked witch is dead. Ought to make things interesting."

Maryse clicked on the picture she was looking for and sent it to print. "What do you mean?"

He shrugged. "She was filthy rich, right? Always interesting when someone with that much money dies."

Damn. His words brought her right back around to Hank's likely reappearance and Helena's definitive one. She grabbed the printout from the printer and was about to shut down the computer when the office phone rang. She reached for it, but Luc got there first, sliding the headset just out of her grasp.

"Luc LeJeune," he answered and gave her a lazy smile.

Maryse turned back to the computer, determined to ignore him, but his next words caught her attention.

"Yes, sir," Luc said, his voice the epitome of respect. "She just walked in. Can I ask what this is concerning?"

Maryse jumped out of her chair and grabbed the phone from Luc. She covered the headset with one hand and glared at him. "When I need someone to screen my calls, I'll hire a secretary." She moved her hand and turned her back on Luc. "This is Maryse Robicheaux."

"Ms. Robicheaux," an ancient, very proper-sounding voice spoke. "My name is Randolph Wheeler. I'm the attorney for Helena Henry's estate."

Unbelievable. Helena was planning on collecting Hank's debt even from the grave. Maryse gritted her teeth and tried to modulate her reply. "If you'll give me your mailing address, Mr. Wheeler, I'll be happy to mail the last two payments to you tomorrow."

There was a pause on the other end of the line, then Maryse heard the attorney clear his throat. "I apologize, Ms. Robicheaux, but apparently there's a misunderstanding here. I'm not calling to collect anything on behalf of the estate. Quite the contrary, actually. My call is to notify you that you've been named in Helena Henry's will and your presence is requested at the reading tomorrow."

Maryse sank into her chair, stunned. "Helena named me in her will? What the hell did she leave me—more debt?"

There was another pause and Maryse could feel the attorney's disapproval coming across the phone line. "Ms. Robicheaux, I'll be happy to cover all of that tomorrow. The reading will begin at one o'clock at my office in New Orleans. The street address is 115 Morgan. Do you need directions?"

"No," Maryse said, her aggravation slowly giving way to disbelief. "I'll be there."

"Then I'll see you at one o'clock." The lawyer disconnected.

Maryse dropped the phone from her ear and sat completely still. What the hell? Life had offered her far more surprises lately than she'd ever asked for, and none of them the pleasant kind. Whatever Helena had left her couldn't be good.

"So," Luc said, "the old bat left you something. Cool."

Maryse stared at Luc, momentarily surprised that she'd completely forgotten he was in the room. "I seriously doubt anything to do with Helena Henry will ever be called cool." She reached for her mouse and closed her e-mail.

She'd been given more to worry about in this single day than a person should have in an entire lifetime, and more than anything, she needed to get out in the bayou and away from people. If there was any chance of getting a grip on her racing thoughts, the bayou was the only place it would happen.

She grabbed her printout off the desk, shut down her computer, and jumped up from her chair before Luc realized he still didn't have access to her PC. "I've got work to do," she said as she headed out the door. "We'll settle this whole office thing tomorrow afternoon, but I wouldn't get too comfortable if I were you."

Luc LeJeune watched as Maryse slammed the office door shut behind her. Things hadn't gone exactly as he'd planned. He had intended to waltz into the office, charm the woman who worked there, get the information he needed, and get the heck back to DEQ headquarters in New Orleans before he remembered why he hated small towns.

But Maryse Robicheaux might prove to be more of a problem than the Department of Environmental Quality had originally thought.

He turned to the computer, his fingers poised to start an intensive search of her personal files, when he realized the password box was flashing at him again. Damn it. She was sneaky. He'd give her that. And if he hadn't been pressed for time on this case, he might have even been amused. He yanked his cell phone from his shirt pocket and pressed in a number.

"Wilson," the man on the other end answered.

"Hey, boss, it's LeJeune."

"Yeah, LeJeune, you romance that botanist into giving up her secrets?"

"Not exactly."

There was a pause on the other end. "What...you losing your touch?"

Luc counted to five before answering. Given his reputation among the bureau as a ladies' man, he probably had that one coming. "No, I'm not losing my touch, but our research department needs a swift kick in the ass. This is no lonely, single scientist living like a hermit on the bayou."

"No? What part's wrong?"

"For starters, she's married—to the local cad, no less—and he ran out on her years ago. To top it off, the cad's mother died recently. The woman was filthy rich, and the reading of the will is tomorrow. Which means this town is probably about to be a clusterfuck of money-grabbing relatives—the least of which is going to be the disappearing husband, since he was an only child."

"So what's the problem?"

"The problem is this woman is so distracted she barely noticed me, except to be angry about my being in her space. She doesn't want me in the office and made that perfectly clear. I don't think this is going to be as easy as we originally hoped."

"Well, easy or not, it's still your job. We need to know if that woman's up to something. Do what you have to—pick locks, read diaries, whatever—just don't put it in your report. Either she's part of the problem or she's not. We need that information sooner than later."

Luc looked across the tiny office to the locked door. "There is another room here that's locked. I guess I need to get in there and see what she finds so important that she'd deadbolt an interior door."

"Sounds like a plan," his boss said. "And, LeJeune, don't take rejection so personally. Even a guy like you can't have them all."

Luc flipped his phone shut and glanced at a photo on the desk of Maryse and some other woman standing in front of a bar in downtown Mudbug. Her wavy brown hair was longer now, but the body was still the same—toned, tight, and tan. He knew he couldn't have them all. Hell, he hadn't had them all, and apparently this was going to be another one of those times.

But damned if he wasn't going to try.

Maryse rolled out of bed the next morning wishing her life belonged to anyone but her. She fed Jasper before he started wailing for his morning tuna, then walked over to her closet and peered inside, wondering what the heck you wore to a will reading. Business, casual, formal wear? Knowing Helena, and from the pompous sound of her attorney, it was probably somewhere between business and formal. And since her only good suit was still at the dry cleaners, courtesy of cleaning the funeral home floor the day before, her choices were seriously limited.

She sighed as she flipped through T-shirt after T-shirt and realized her wardrobe needed some serious updating if she ever planned to do anything but toodle around the bayou in her boat. God forbid she ever had a date. She would be one of those women who "didn't have a thing to wear."

At the thought of dating, Luc LeJeune flashed to mind. Oh, no. She blocked out the thoughts of his tanned skin and muscular build and dug into the back of the closet for something, anything but ratty old jeans. No way was she allowing any thoughts of Luc

LeJeune to leak in, especially while she was standing in her bedroom, half-clothed.

Luc LeJeune was the hottest guy she'd seen in forever, and her body's reaction to him had confused and scared her. Sure, it had been a long time since she'd been with a man...okay, more like two years since there hadn't been anyone since Hank...but that was no cause to go jumping on the first good-looking man she saw. Especially when she couldn't afford distractions. Especially when a good-looking man was what had gotten her into the situation she was in right now.

Which brought her back to Helena.

She hadn't seen the ghost since her visit to the cabin, and Maryse hoped things stayed that way. Maybe there was a delay in transitioning to the other side, and she'd simply gotten the raw end of Helena's transfer. Surely God wouldn't let Helena roam the Earth alive *and* dead. He was supposed to be benevolent.

She frowned and yanked a cocktail dress from the back of her closet. Okay, so a will reading probably didn't rate a party dress, but she simply didn't have anything in between. Sighing, she tossed the dress onto the bed. At least it was black. It was as close as she was going to come to business attire and would have to do. She dropped down, dug around the back of the closet floor, and pulled out a pair of shiny black satin shoes. Yuck. But the only other options with heels were her rubber boots or her funeral pumps, and they were navy.

She rose with the shoes and tossed them next to the bed, then threw on a T-shirt, jeans, and tennis shoes. She figured she'd have just enough time to send off the samples she'd collected yesterday and still be able to rush home for a quickie shower before changing for the will reading. With any luck, Luc LeJeune would be out in the bayou studying rat droppings or whatever else he was there to do.

Ten minutes later, she was in her truck and headed to the office. She always drove just a little too fast down the windy gravel roads back in the bayou, but there were rarely other cars on this particular stretch, and the gravel certainly wasn't going to hurt her well-worn-in truck. Usually, her speed wasn't a problem.

Until today.

As she approached a sharp turn in the road, she pressed the brakes, but there was no response. Trying not to panic, she lifted her foot and pressed again. Nothing. The pedal just squished to the floorboard as the truck kept hurtling toward the ninety-degree turn.

Now frantic, she turned the wheel, hoping to make the turn, and threw the gear shifter into park. The truck lurched, and, despite the seatbelt, her forehead banged into the steering wheel. The truck tilted to one side at the very edge of the road, and for a moment, Maryse thought she had pulled it off. Finally inertia won out, and the truck slid off the road into the bayou.

Huge sheets of water splashed up and over the cab, making visibility nil. Maryse covered her aching head with her arms and hoped like hell this was a shallow section and not inhabited by any of the bayou's more aggressive creatures—particularly the meat eaters.

It only took seconds for the water to clear, but it seemed like forever. Almost afraid to look, Maryse lowered her arm and surveyed the damage. The truck was submerged in the bayou almost up to the hood. From the groaning of the metal and the increasing water level, Maryse knew immediately that the truck was sinking further in the thin bayou mud.

Water began to spill in through the cracks in the floorboard and the door, and Maryse figured now was as good a time as any to make her exit. As she cranked down the window, she was grateful she hadn't been able to afford the fully loaded truck with power everything. Sometimes the old-fashioned way is the best way, she thought as she grabbed her keys and her purse and crawled out.

She cautiously moved into the water, hoping she wasn't stepping on anything dangerous. As it took her weight, her foot sank into the mud up to her calf. She tugged on the foot to remove it from the vacuum created by the mud hole and took another step with the same result.

By the time she got to the bank, one shoe was missing—lost forever to a bayou sinkhole—and the other was so full of the stinky, gooey muck that it felt like her leg weighed a hundred pounds. She flopped onto the bank and groaned when she felt the jolt through her head.

"Ouch," she said, and gently rubbed her forehead. There was definitely a knot, but a quick body inspection didn't reveal anything bleeding profusely. Just minors cuts and what would probably develop into some lovely bruises over the next couple of days. She looked over at her truck and sighed. The water was over the hood now and pouring into the cab. Definitely a total loss. Her insurance rates were going to go through the roof.

What in the world had happened? She'd just had her truck in for its scheduled maintenance a couple of weeks before. If there had been a problem with her brakes, the dealership would have let her know. Hell, if there had been a problem with the brakes, the dealership would have been delighted to charge her more money.

She tugged her cell phone from her wet jeans pocket, but it was just as she'd feared—totally fried. Looking back at the road, she considered her options. It was probably five miles or more back to her cabin, which put her around two miles from the office. Maybe Sabine could give her a ride into New Orleans. She pushed herself up from the ground, swaying for a moment as the blood rushed to her aching head.

Unbelievable. She'd totaled her car and had a raging headache, and she hadn't even had the pleasure of being drunk to accomplish it. Disgusted, she shot one final look at her sunken truck and stepped onto the road with one muddy tennis shoe and one muddy bare foot. The gravel immediately dug into the sensitive skin on her bare foot, and she grimaced. All this and then a will reading—probably complete with a ghost.

The day just kept getting better.

Luc pushed his Jeep faster down the gravel road to the office. He had planned on arriving early, hoping Maryse might make a stop in before her appointment in New Orleans, but a faulty alarm clock put him thirty minutes later than he had hoped. He tried to tell himself that his desire to catch Maryse at the office was part of the case, just doing his job, but the truth was the woman intrigued him.

How in the world had such an intelligent, attractive woman allowed herself to get hooked up with the likes of Hank Henry? It simply boggled the mind.

As he approached a large curve in the road, sunlight glinted off something ahead of him, and he squinted, trying to make out where it was coming from. As he neared the turn, it was all too clear. Maryse's truck was buried in the bayou just off the curve, the sun bouncing off her side window.

He slammed on his brakes and threw his Jeep in park before it had even come to a complete stop. Panicked, he jumped out and rushed to the edge of the water, trying to make out whether a person was inside the truck, but he couldn't see a thing. He was just about to wade in when he saw a trail of flattened marsh grass followed by muddy footprints.

Thank God. Maryse had definitely made it out of the truck. His tension eased a bit now that he knew she was alive, but then his thoughts immediately turned to injury. The truck was totaled, and any number of things could have happened to Maryse during the wreck or wading through the bayou afterward.

The office was a couple of miles away, and since he hadn't passed her on his way from town, he had to assume she'd started walking in that direction. He rushed back to his Jeep, threw it in drive, and tore down the road to the office, scanning the sides of the road as he went, just in case she'd stopped to rest, or worse, collapsed.

He'd gone about half a mile when he rounded a corner and saw her walking on the road ahead of him. She turned around to look, and the relief on her face was apparent, even from a distance.

"I thought I'd scared you away yesterday," she said, as he pulled up beside her.

Luc shook his head. "I love a challenge. I thought I'd head in to the office early—practice putting the seat down on the toilet."

"Well, three cheers for work ethic," she said. "I was beginning to think I'd be walking the rest of the day."

He stepped out of the Jeep and gently gripped her arm with one hand, checking her up and down. "Are you all right? Are you hurt?"

"I'll be okay," she said. "I banged my head on the steering wheel, so I have an enormous headache, and walking on a gravel road with a bare foot wasn't exactly fun. But I don't think there's anything serious."

He reached up to her face and moved her bangs to the side. She definitely had a goose egg, and from the size of it, he didn't doubt the severity of her headache. It was going to take more than Tylenol to fix this one.

"What happened?" he asked.

Maryse shrugged. "I don't really know. The brakes just failed, and I couldn't make the turn."

Luc felt his heart beat a little faster. "Have you had the truck serviced lately?"

"Yeah, that's the weird thing. I just had it in for a sixty-thousand-mile service. They checked everything." She paused for a moment. "Or at least they said they did."

Luc nodded, trying to keep his facial expression normal, but his senses were on high alert. This accident sounded fishy. "We need to get you to the hospital," he said. "Someone should take a look at that knot. Just to be safe."

Maryse shook her head, then put on hand over her forehead and groaned. "No time. I have to be at this will reading this afternoon. I still need to send some samples to the state, change clothes, and pick up my spare cell phone. The old one took a dip with the truck."

"The samples can wait. I'm pretty sure this rates a sick day."

"Maybe, but the reading won't wait, and I can't exactly go looking like this. If you'll just drop me off at the dock to my cabin, I'd really appreciate it."

"It's not a contest, Maryse. You don't have to be present to win. I'm pretty sure the attorney can tell you about it afterward."

Maryse gave him a withering stare. "Can you arrange to have my wayward husband served with divorce papers, too? I have to find Hank, and Helena's death may be my last chance. There's more at stake here than some inheritance. Besides, knowing Helena, she probably left me more debt or a pig farm or bubonic plague."

"Fine. But as soon as you've showered and changed, I want to take you to the hospital."

Maryse frowned. "I've already told you there's no time. It's a headache. I'll have it checked out after the will reading."

"What about your truck?"

"It's not exactly going anywhere. It can wait until this evening."

"You've got insurance?"

She gave him a dirty look. "Of course I have insurance. I also have smoke detectors and contribute to my 401(k)."

Luc held in a smile. "If you give me your insurance card, I can take care of the tow."

"I can take care of the tow myself. I'm fairly certain no one's going to steal it."

Luc threw his hands up in exasperation. "Are you always this stubborn?"

"Are you always this bossy?"

He stared at her for a moment, then grinned. "Yeah, pretty much."

"Well, you've just run into a brick wall."

No shit. He looked at her and shook his head. "At least let me drive you to your appointment in New Orleans. I need to run an errand there today anyway, and you can pick up a rental car in the city a lot easier than getting one delivered to Mudbug."

She narrowed her eyes at him and stared for a couple of seconds, and Luc knew she was wondering what his angle was. He hoped to God she didn't find out until he was gone, because if Maryse was this prickly when she thought he was trying to help, he'd hate to see her reaction if she knew he was actually in Mudbug investigating her.

"Okay," she said finally, "you can drop me off at the attorney's office."

Luc nodded, and she pointed a finger at him.

"But I want to be very clear," she said, "that the only reason I'm accepting your offer is because I'm down to one source of transportation and I don't think I can get my bass boat all the way to New Orleans—at least not by one o'clock."

Luc couldn't hold back a grin. "You make me feel very special, Maryse. I'm so glad you're going to allow me to chauffeur you around."

Maryse shook her head. "Don't get any ideas. Just because I'm catching a ride with you doesn't mean I've changed my mind about sharing an office."

"Now, what in the world makes you think I would get any ideas?"

Maryse frowned and walked over to the passenger side of the Jeep. "I know your type, LeJeune. Technically, I'm still married to him. Guys like you are always full of ideas."

As she climbed inside his Jeep, Luc took a peek at her firm, round bottom, every curve clearly outlined in her wet jeans. Maryse was dead wrong about him. He wasn't full of ideas—he was overflowing with them.

Chapter Three

Maryse stepped carefully out of her bass boat, making sure one of her shiny, satin heels didn't slip between the boards of the dock. Luc sat at the dock in his Jeep and stared at her with a mixture of amusement and disbelief. Okay, so it probably wasn't an everyday sight, but did he have to laugh? She glared at him as she climbed up in his Jeep. "What? You've never seen a woman in a dress before, LeJeune?"

Luc shook his head. "Mostly I see women out of dresses, and I've absolutely never seen a woman wearing fancy clothes in a bass boat."

"You would if you lived in Mudbug."

Luc smiled. "Aren't you a little overdressed for a will reading?"

Maryse shrugged. "It was either this or jeans."

"You need to get out more."

"Just drive," Maryse said, and reached over to turn the radio on—loud. Then she leaned back in her seat and closed her eyes, shutting out all images and sounds of Luc LeJeune. God knows she had enough to think about. She was about to come face to face with Hank Henry for the first time in two years. It was probably a good thing she was wearing a dress. It wouldn't be as easy to kick his ass in high heels.

Luc pulled up in front of the attorney's office fifteen minutes early, and Maryse felt her back stiffen as she picked up her purse and prepared to step out of the Jeep. Turning to Luc, she gave him what was probably a grim smile. "I really appreciate you giving me a lift. And I'm sorry if I was a big bitch earlier."

Luc smiled. "You weren't that bad."

Maryse felt a momentary burst of disappointment. "I'll try harder next time."

Now Luc laughed. "I don't have any doubt about that. Now get inside and claim your pig farm and your divorce and anything else you've got riding on this reading."

Maryse smiled for real this time, stepped out of the Jeep, and glanced over at the attorney's office. Luc pulled onto the street, waving as he drove off. Maryse sighed and tore her gaze from the Jeep, trying to refocus on the will reading and everything that went along with it. Luc LeJeune was Hank Henry all over again...good-looking, charming, a professional flirt, confident beyond belief, and probably had a list of conquests that rivaled Alexander the Great. He was everything she was trying to avoid in one neat, gorgeous, well-defined package.

Taking a deep breath, she turned and walked to the attorney's office, hoping the will reading would be quick and painless. She was due a break after the horrific funeral, and besides, locating Hank was the most important thing on her mind. She pushed open the door to the office and stepped into a cherry-wood nightmare. Antique furniture covered every square inch of the tiny lobby. The place was so stiff that even the threads in the Persian rug were rod straight. Chintz pillows graced the corners of every chair, the narrow couch, and the loveseat. The only plus was the room was empty. Apparently she was the first to arrive.

At the reception window, Maryse checked in with a pinched-faced elderly woman wearing horned-rimmed glasses. Once the woman confirmed her identity, Maryse turned to consider her options and decided on a chair in the far corner of the room with a clear view of the doorway. That way she'd be sure to see Hank, just in case he showed up to collect his bounty. She'd put her attorney on speed dial in her spare phone, and he had a deputy waiting nearby ready to pop in and serve Hank the all-important papers. Everything was in place except her missing husband. As usual.

She removed the chintz pillows from their perch at the back of the chair, arranged them in the middle of the seat, and sat on top of them. Probably not what the decorator had intended, but she didn't really care. The chair was bound to be uncomfortable as hell, and she'd already put her body through enough strain today. She glanced at her watch for at least the tenth time in so many seconds and heard the office door open.

She sucked in a breath, wondering who was going to walk across the entryway, and did a double take when three women walked in—one of them a nun, in full habit, robes and all. The other two were in their sixties and wore the dark clothes and bad makeup of Helena's generation, so she figured they had to be family.

But what was the deal with the nun?

Surely she wasn't a relative. Being related to Helena Henry would be enough to convert a religious person to atheism. The other two women presented their IDs to the receptionist, then proceeded to cackle over the reading.

"She better have left me her porcelain angels," the first woman said. "I've been wanting those for years."

"Well, I don't give a rip about those angels," the second woman said, "but I desperately want her family quilts. Do you have any idea how much those quilts are worth? They're practically a part of history."

The other woman nodded. "Why do you think I want the angels? One just like them brought five hundred dollars last week on eBay. Think what we could get at the auction."

"Well, all I can say is it's about damned time she died. I could have used a trip to Bermuda last year."

Definitely Helena's family.

As the two hens finished their business and moved away from the window, Maryse leaned forward in her chair, straining to hear what the nun was saying. Sure enough, she was here for the will reading. This was getting stranger by the minute. Maryse picked up a couple of magazines and was trying to decide between *Law*

Review and *Law Today* when the door opened again and Harold walked in…followed by a fuming Helena.

Maryse scrunched down low in her chair, hoping Helena wouldn't notice her, but the ghost crossed the room and sat on the chair next to her. Harold checked in, gave Maryse a suspicious look, then took a seat across from her.

Helena glared at Harold. "Asshole," she said. "Do you know he had the nerve to drive over here in my new Cadillac with one of those floozies he was seeing?"

Maryse stared at her, a bit surprised. "What floozies?"

"Did you say something?" Harold asked, frowning.

"No," Maryse said quickly, "Just clearing my throat." She leaned to the side and held the magazine up in front of her face. "What floozies?"

Helena didn't bother to lean or whisper, but then she didn't really have to. "Damn man was always getting a piece of something or other on the side. Started almost as soon as we were married, although I didn't really know about it until after Hank was born. Cut him off right quick, I did. Not about to catch something from one of Harold's floozies. Probably rot my crotch out."

Maryse considered briefly the type of woman that would sleep with Harold Henry and decided Helena had probably made a wise decision. "So why didn't you divorce him?"

"No way! Oh, granted, Harold couldn't get half of my holdings—everything was inherited, so even the income drawn off it was solely mine. But when we were married, we had a prenup that gave Harold a boatload of money if I ever asked for a divorce."

Maryse lowered the magazine and realized that everyone in the lobby was staring at her. She gave them a smile and pulled her cell phone from her purse. "Sorry, I just remembered a call I need to make." She pretended to push in some buttons, gave a fake greeting to the nonentity on the other end of the line, then turned sideways in her seat and leaned in toward Helena. "So what would have happened if he left you?"

"He wouldn't have gotten a dime. It had to be my decision or he got nothing. Why do you think he's hung around all these years, cavorting with floozies, hoping I'd divorce him?"

Maryse cringed, with little doubt in her mind that Harold had probably paid dearly for his indiscretions. Good God, was a free ride and a luxury sedan really worth living with an angry, embittered Helena every day?

"And the payoff is for what exactly?" Maryse asked. Rich people were very confusing.

"Hmmpf. Apparently for being so useless he couldn't work and wouldn't be able to support himself. You have to understand. I married Harold when I was nineteen. I didn't get control of the trust until I was twenty-one. Since no one thought our marriage would last, the lawyers insisted on something to protect my inheritance. Then Harold insisted on something to protect himself, since he was about to deploy to Vietnam and figured that would give everyone too much free time to change my mind."

Maryse absorbed all this. "So how much money are we talking about?"

Helena stared at Harold in obvious disgust. "Upwards of half a million. So I figured no way. I had ultimate control of the estate upon death, so I decided Harold would just have to suffer living with me if he wanted to maintain his lifestyle."

Maryse leaned closer and whispered. "So what exactly did you leave Harold then?" After all, he was at the attorney's office with the rest of them, so that had to mean she'd left him something, despite her griping and complaining.

Helena smiled. "You'll see. You'll all see. Especially Harold."

Oh hell. This couldn't be good. And here she was wearing high heels and a dress and sporting a headache set to turn into a migraine at a moment's notice. Running was definitely going to be out of the question.

She was just about to push Helena for more information when a tall, thin man stepped into the reception area from the back office. He had not a hair on his head but seemed as though he was trying to make up for it with a long, flowing gray beard. His posture was as stiff as his suit, which had probably been purchased somewhere around the time he started growing the beard.

"If you will follow me, please," he said, and Maryse immediately recognized the pompous voice as the attorney who had phoned her. "We're ready to begin."

Maryse tossed her cell phone back into her purse as everyone in the waiting area rose and followed Father Time down the hall and into a small office at the back of the building. The others had already taken their seats, so Maryse perched on the edge of a particularly hideous gold lamée–covered chair, positioned right between Harold and the nun. The two hens were on the couch directly behind them. Everyone stared at the attorney, Wheeler, like they were waiting for him to pull a rabbit out of a hat. Or in her case, Hank Henry. *Where the hell was Hank?*

Wheeler took a seat behind a cherry-wood desk that occupied half of the room and gave them a sickly smile. "Thank you for coming. There were several people or agencies named in Helena's will, but this group represents those she wanted to be present for a reading. The remainder will receive notification by certified mail."

Maryse frowned, smelling a setup. She glared at Helena, but it did no good. She was too busy trying to strangle Harold from behind, but her fingers kept passing through his neck.

"What about Hank?" Maryse asked, unable to help herself. Damn it, that man was not going to get away with being married to her forever. If he didn't turn up soon, she was definitely going to pursue having him declared legally dead—again. And if she ever got her hands on him, it wasn't going to just be a declaration.

Wheeler reached over to the phone and pressed the speaker button. "Hank," he said, and frowned, "is joining us by phone. He felt his presence here wouldn't be prudent."

"Prudent, my ass!" Maryse jumped up from her seat, glaring at the phone. "You listen to me, you sorry piece of—"

"Uhmm," Wheeler cleared his throat and gave her a clear look of disapproval. "I'm sure that Mr. Henry would be more than happy to arrange a meeting with your attorney to discuss your unfinished business. However, your personal life has no place here."

Maryse glared at Wheeler, then at the phone, then at Harold and Helena for producing that pile of pond scum. She also made note that the pond scum had not uttered a word during the entire exchange. "Fine, then let's get on with it. Obviously, I have some business to do with my own attorney and the sheriff's department. I can't hang around here all day."

Wheeler nodded, and Maryse took her seat. He picked up an expensively bound stack of paper from the top of his desk and said, "All the words I read from this document are Mrs. Henry's. They have not been edited or altered by this office or any of my agents."

Here we go. If Wheeler was already claiming absolution and hadn't even read the first sentence, this was going to be a doozy.

The attorney cleared his throat and began, "I, Helena Henry, being of sound mind and bad attitude, do hereby make the following bequeaths upon my death..."

Harold leaned forward in his chair eagerly. Helena moved to stand behind Wheeler, looking like an excited five-year-old. Maryse slouched back in her chair and waited for the insults to fly.

"All of my real estate holdings in New Orleans, Baton Rouge, and Lafayette, as well as the income they produce, I leave to the St. John's Orphanage in New Orleans. I also deed to them free and clear the building they occupy, which is mine to give."

The nun gasped and from the shade of white that washed over her face, Maryse thought she was going to pass out. Maryse grabbed a notepad from Wheeler's desk and fanned the woman. Helena owned an orphanage? And she was giving them real estate?

Maryse glanced sideways at Harold, but he looked as confused as she was and more than a little annoyed. Maryse guessed the real estate was worth a lot.

The nun finally waved at her and managed to squeak out a "Thank you." Maryse put the notepad back on the desk and looked expectantly at Wheeler. God help her, this was starting to get interesting.

"My home and all the furnishings within, I leave to the Mudbug Historical Society, upon the condition that it be maintained as a historical tourist site, with a limit of four rooms available for rental as a bed and breakfast. All rental profits will go toward the maintenance of the property. In addition, I also leave the historical society my real estate holdings in downtown Mudbug. The rental income on those properties should more than offset any occasional shortfall in the maintenance of my home. Any remaining profits from the rentals are to be remitted to the Mudbug School District."

Looked like Harold better start packing. Maryse looked over at Helena, who gave her a huge smile.

Wheeler flipped the first page over and continued to read. "To my son, Hank Henry, I leave the sum of one million dollars in trust, upon the condition that he obtain respectable employment and remain clean, sober, and gambling-free for a term of five years—"

"Ha!" Maryse shouted at the speakerphone, where muffled cursing emitted. "Hank can't remain clean, sober, and gambling-free for five minutes."

"That will be enough, Ms. Robicheaux," Wheeler said and shot her a disapproving look. "Actual fulfillment of the terms will be determined by Randolph Wheeler, or his succeeding associate."

Good thinking on Helena's part putting in that succeeding associate clause. Wheeler would probably be dead in five years. Heck, if he had to spend his time checking up on Hank, Maryse only gave him a couple of weeks.

She glanced over at Harold, but he just shook his head at the entire exchange. He looked a bit disappointed but not really surprised.

"To my cousins, Sarah and Rose," Wheeler read, and Maryse heard the two behind her shifting on their couch, "I leave the remainder of my silver and china. You've been stealing it on holidays for years, so this way it will become a matched set again."

There was a sharp intake of breath from the nun, and the movement behind them ceased completely. "By the way," Wheeler continued, "none of the china is real. It's all a very clever reproduction."

Maryse winced and tried not to laugh as she glanced back at the two putrid faces behind her. *Rough one.*

"To my husband, Harold, I leave the Lower Bayou Motel. You've spent so many nights there with other women that I felt you should call the place home. It's been operating in the red for the last eight years, owes back taxes since 1986, and is covered with deadly asbestos. Nothing but the best for you, dear."

Maryse smiled as the nun gave Harold a disapproving stare. She probably hadn't been closed up in a room with this many sinners since Lent. The look on Harold's face was absolutely priceless. Even Wheeler had smirked when he delivered the last sentence.

Harold glared at everyone, then waved at Wheeler. "Get on with it. Get to the good stuff."

"Of course, Mr. Henry," Wheeler said, obviously holding back a smile. "My final asset of this distribution, the property secured by state lease known as the Mudbug Game Preserve and Wildlife Center, as well as the annual fees paid by the government for said lease, I leave to my daughter-in-law, Maryse Robicheaux Henry."

"That's bullshit!" Harold jumped from his chair, reached across the desk, and grabbed Wheeler by his throat. The two cousins squeezed onto one side of the couch, and the nun made the sign of the cross. Maryse scanned the desk for a sharp implement to defend herself with but didn't see a thing. Good God Almighty, Helena *owned* the game preserve? Maryse stared at the ghost in shock, but Helena only smiled and clapped, obviously enjoying the show.

"What the hell do you think you're doing?" Harold continued to yell. "Helena can only leave that land to family. Those are the rules of the trust, and Hank is her only son!"

Wheeler pried Harold's hands off his throat and smoothed his collar back down. "That may be the case, Mr. Henry, but Hank is not her only relative. Helena is perfectly within her rights to leave the land to her daughter-in-law, as long as the marriage lasted a minimum of two years."

"She can't cut me and Hank out of everything," Harold argued, "and you know it."

"Actually, sir," Wheeler said, "she *can* cut you and Hank out of everything and *you* know it."

Harold stared at Wheeler for a moment, then whirled around and narrowed his eyes at Maryse. "I don't know what you and Helena cooked up, but I won't stand for it. Hank is the rightful heir to that property. You're just the dumb piece of ass he made the mistake of marrying."

Maryse felt the blood rush to her face and her pulse begin to race. "You forgot dumb, *landowner* piece of ass. And believe me, the mistake was all mine."

A bright red flush crept up Harold's neck and onto his face. He clenched his fists, and for a moment, Maryse thought he was going to hit her. Harold glared for what seemed like forever and finally spit out, "I wouldn't start spending the money just yet. And I'd watch my back if I were you." With that, he stalked out of the office.

Helena winked at Maryse and hurried behind him, probably wanting a ringside seat when Harold told his floozies about his "big" inheritance. "I'll see you later, Maryse," Helena shouted over her shoulder as she left the office.

Maryse frowned. *Not if I see you first.* She turned back to Wheeler. "Some show, huh?"

"I'm sorry about that," Wheeler apologized to everyone. He handed the nun an envelope. "There are additional instructions concerning your inheritance inside of the envelopes. It will take a couple of days to push everything through probate, then you can collect your bequeaths."

The cousins glared at Wheeler and left the office, not bothering to take their envelopes. The nun thanked Wheeler and headed out wearing a dazed expression. It was no wonder. Her orphanage had just inherited the bank, and she'd probably heard more cussing in the past half hour than she had in the past forty years.

Wheeler watched as the nun closed the door behind her, then blew out a breath and slumped into his chair. "There are requirements of your inheritance that we need to discuss, Ms. Robicheaux, but I hope you don't mind if we go through them tomorrow. This entire exchange has exhausted me, and I have another appointment after this one."

"I understand. I'm feeling kind of tired myself."

Wheeler reached behind his desk and brought up a huge document bound in expensive leather. "This is all the instructions and restrictions that accompany the land inheritance. This land has been in Helena's family for well over a hundred years, so a lot of the old rules were established long before my time and yours. You need to review this document in its entirety as soon as possible."

He pushed the document across the desk to Maryse, and she lifted it, momentarily surprised by the weight.

"If you have no objection, I can meet you in Mudbug first thing tomorrow so we can go over the most relevant points. I'll give you a call this evening to arrange a place to meet. In the meantime, the only thing you need to know is that you can't leave town."

Maryse stared at him. "What do you mean I can't leave town?"

"It's one of the restrictions of the original estate. You must remain in Mudbug for a probationary period of one week. That's why I'm going to meet you there tomorrow. Once the probationary period is over, you're free to go anywhere, of course." He reached into his desk and handed Maryse an envelope. "There's a set of documents inside that detail Helena's agreement with the state for the lease of the preserve. The annual payment from the state is due next week, which means you'll be receiving a check for fifty thousand dollars."

Fifty thousand dollars a year! Maryse sucked in a breath and stared at Wheeler in surprise. "You're kidding me."

Wheeler smiled. "Not in the least, Ms. Robicheaux. Helena left you her most prized possession. It wasn't an easy decision for her. You should feel honored."

Maryse shook her head, the strangeness of the past two days washing over her. "But why?"

"One day, the land will be worth quite a bit of money…to developers and others. Helena was afraid that if it fell into the wrong hands, it would be immediately leased out to a chemical company or the like and the town she grew up in and loved would cease to exist. She held firm on the belief that you wouldn't allow that to happen, regardless of the money involved."

Maryse began to understand. If a chemical company leased the land, they'd close off the bayou, inserting sludge ponds for their runoff and new manufacturing facilities for their products where there was once marsh. The tides would shift, and with the tides, the shrimp, fish, and all other bayou commodities that Mudbug residents made a living off of would disappear. If those commodities ceased to exist, so would Mudbug.

Helena had given her a great gift, but how could she have been so sure that Maryse wouldn't sell out? Had Helena really had that much faith in her integrity, or was the only other choice so bad that she gambled on the second?

Maryse thanked Wheeler, lugged the giant leather book onto one hip, and made her way out of the building. As she stepped outside, she scanned the parking area for her truck before remembering it was sinking in the middle of the bayou.

Great. She yanked her cell phone from her pocket and pressed in 411. She was just about to hit the Talk button when Wheeler's receptionist rushed outside and let out a breath of relief.

"Oh, thank goodness, you're still here," the receptionist said. "I completely forgot to give you this." She handed Maryse a rental car agreement and a set of keys. "A very nice young man dropped these off while you were in the reading. He said to tell you not to worry about your truck. He arranged to have it towed to a friend at the dealership."

"He what?" Maryse asked, no doubt in her mind who the nice young man was.

The receptionist smiled at Maryse. "You're so lucky to have such a gentleman looking out for you. It's the red Honda Accord parked across the street." She gave Maryse a wave and walked back into the office.

"Gentleman my ass," Maryse said, even though no one was around to hear. She had no idea what kind of game Luc LeJeune was playing, but it was about to come to an end.

Chapter Four

Maryse raced back to her office, eager for two things: first, to confront the sneaky, bossy Luc and second, to study her lab supply book cover to cover to figure out exactly what she could buy with her lease money. This money could make a huge difference in her success, and it couldn't have come at a better time. She was starting to doubt her personal quest for a medical breakthrough altogether. Better lab equipment would aid in her research and her morale.

If only Blooming Flower had told her what plant she'd used in her medicine before she died. But the Native woman had been tight-lipped about revealing any of her secrets. With a little more time, Maryse knew she could have won the woman over, but time ran out. As it always seemed to where Maryse was concerned.

Maryse sighed. Despite her misgivings about anything associated with Helena, it was hard not to be excited about what she could do with the money. Just knowing that the alternative could have meant the end of Mudbug made her heart catch in her throat. But things had turned out for the better.

At least she thought it was for the better.

She tried to focus on the highway in front of her, but her temples were pounding in time with her heartbeat. Maryse was beginning to suspect that the bossy Luc was right and she needed to see a doctor. The aspirin she'd taken only thirty minutes ago hadn't done a thing. In fact, her headache was worse.

Yet another delay was annoying, but she refused to be one of those stubborn people who ignored all the signs until it was too late. Like her dad had. With a sigh, she pulled off the highway at the far end of Mudbug and headed for the hospital.

The emergency room was fairly quiet, and a nurse told her that a doctor should be able to see her almost immediately. She followed the nurse down the hall to a lab where a man in a green lab coat took an X-ray of the lump on her head. Then the nurse escorted her to an available room and said the doctor would be in shortly.

Maryse sat on the end of the hospital bed, the paper runner crinkling beneath her, and tried not to worry, especially since worrying tended to make the lump pound harder. It was just a bit of a goose egg. No worse than the ones she got as a kid playing around the bayou. Still, why did they always ask you to sit on those uncomfortable beds? Why couldn't you just sit on the chair in the corner like a normal person?

She was just contemplating a move to the corner chair when the door opened and Dr. Breaux walked in, followed closely by a much younger, cuter man who was smiling directly at her.

"Hello, Maryse," Dr. Breaux said. "This is Doctor Warren."

Maryse tried not to ogle.

"Doctor Warren transferred here from New Orleans last week. He'll be taking over some patients for me as I move into semi-retirement, so I want to introduce him to as many people in Mudbug as I can."

Dr. Hottie stuck out his hand, and Maryse shook it, the ache in her head suddenly not quite so painful. "Nice to meet you," she said warmly.

Dr. Warren cocked his head to one side and laughed. "You don't remember me, do you?" He still held her hand in his. "Advanced Chemistry, Mrs. Thibodeaux... *Christopher* Warren."

Maryse studied the man again, mentally running through the entire seating chart of high school chemistry. "Holy crap! Christopher?" She stared in surprise, the image of the thin, dorky, pimply-faced adolescent rushing back to her in a flash. "I would never have recognized you."

Christopher smiled. "Late bloomer."

Maryse laughed. "Better than not blooming at all, I guess."

"Uhmm," Dr. Breaux cleared his throat. "All class reunion business aside, we have three other patients waiting."

Christopher immediately snapped back to professional demeanor. "Of course, Doctor Breaux." He gently brushed the bangs away from Maryse's head and took a look at the offensive lump. "Got a doozy of a goose egg there."

"Is that your official medical opinion?" Maryse joked.

Christopher smiled. "Absolutely. Are you saying you're already unsatisfied with my services?"

Maryse struggled to maintain her composure. Was he flirting? Surely not. Two men in one week was so far beyond her average it wasn't even in the ballpark. Realizing she'd never answered, Maryse said hurriedly, "Oh no, that's not what I meant. I never thought it was that bad, but everyone kept insisting I have it checked out so..."

Christopher nodded. "That's always a good idea with a head injury, no matter how slight it seems."

He stuck the X-rays on a machine and flipped on the light. Dr. Breaux stepped over, and they analyzed the gray blobs and mumbled to each other. As Christopher studied the X-rays, Maryse studied him. Okay, so he wasn't exactly her type. Christopher was too pretty, too turned out, too *GQ*. Maryse liked her men a little more rugged. Five-star restaurants weren't exactly her usual fare—just give her a guy who could drive a bass boat and shoot a gun. Christopher looked too refined for shooting anything but photos with his phone.

But he's a doctor.

Maryse couldn't help but think of all the possibilities a successful relationship with a doctor might bring. There was so much she didn't know about the body's chemical reaction to medication, so much she needed to learn but only so many hours in the day. And far more importantly, a man like Christopher was probably a much safer bet than a ladies' man like Luc. God knows, she'd already made that mistake once and wasn't interested in being a two-time loser.

She took a look at his perfectly manicured hands, then glanced at her own chewed nails. She remembered Christopher from high school, the quiet, brilliant kid who hid in the back of the classroom trying not to draw any attention to himself. That was probably the only reason Maryse had noticed him...because she was busy doing the same thing but without the benefit of being brilliant.

He had helped her with her homework a couple of times, never actually looking her in the eye, his neck flushed with red the entire time. Christopher Warren had been a nice kid and had probably become a nice man. And maybe, just maybe, if she had another man around, she wouldn't spend so much time thinking about Luc.

Her mind made up, she flashed Christopher her best smile as he turned around to look at her. "Am I going to live?" she asked.

He returned her smile and nodded. "I'm afraid so, but with one whopper of a headache for a couple of days. I can prescribe you something stronger than aspirin for that, but otherwise, I just want you to take it easy until the swelling goes down. Try not to jostle your head and it will heal a little faster. If it lasts more than a week, I'll need to see you back here." He looked over at Dr. Breaux for confirmation.

"Doctor Warren is correct," Dr. Breaux said. "The X-ray doesn't show anything to cause alarm, but you should watch the lump over the next couple of days and come back in if it gets worse." He patted Maryse on the shoulder and nodded to Christopher. "I'll leave you to the prescription writing. That way I don't have to pull out my glasses again." He smiled at both of them and left the room.

"Alone at last," Christopher said, and smiled at Maryse.

Okay, he's probably flirting.

Christopher pulled a prescription pad from his pocket and began to write, then handed her the slip of paper.

She took it without looking and asked, "Can I get this filled at the hospital pharmacy?"

He flashed her a broad grin. "I rather doubt it. That's my phone number."

Definitely flirting.

"If your head isn't killing you in a couple of days," Christopher continued, "I'd love to take you to dinner. We can catch up on the post–high school life events, and I'd love to hear about the work you're doing here. Botany, right?"

Maryse nodded.

"Besides," Christopher continued, "any woman who wears a cocktail dress for an emergency room visit has got to be an interesting date. Call me whenever you feel up to it." He handed her a second slip of paper. "This is for your headache, and yes, the pharmacy should have them in stock."

Maryse held in a groan when he mentioned the cocktail dress. She hadn't even thought about how strange she must look. Heck, the whole day had already been so strange that now the dress seemed such a small matter. But hey, if it got her date offers from cute doctors, then maybe she'd have to reconsider Sabine's shopping suggestion. She took the second sheet of paper, and Christopher lingered a bit, making sure his fingers brushed against hers. She waited for a spark, for her skin to tingle, but had to admit that aside from wondering what brand of lotion he used to keep his hands so soft, she really didn't get much out of it at all.

"I'll give you a call," she promised, and stuck the slips in her purse.

He gave her arm a squeeze and walked out of the room. Maryse leaned over slightly to study his behind as he walked away. *Not as good-looking as Luc's.* With a sigh, she hopped off the table and made her way down the hall to the pharmacy. It didn't mean a thing. Most men in the world didn't have a butt as nice as Luc LeJeune's. Besides, butts weren't everything. One day she'd be too old to see it, and her arthritis too bad to squeeze it, right?

She was insane—there was no doubt in her mind. Apparently, she was more attracted to men who wouldn't stick around long enough to leave a scent on the sheets than men who would probably not only leave a scent but help with the laundering. Christopher was good-looking, successful, and seemed to be just as nice now as he had been in high school.

But even as she ran through Christopher's list of attributes, a mental picture of Luc flashed through her mind—leaned back in her office chair, looking at her with that slow, sexy smile, his jeans rippling in all the right places. Stopping in the middle of the hall, she closed her eyes, silently willing the scene to go away. Then she pulled the slip of paper with Christopher's number from her purse. No more playboys, regardless of how sexy their butts were. She was going to learn to walk on the safe side.

For once in her life, she was going to do the boring, responsible thing.

Maryse was relieved that Luc's Jeep was nowhere in sight when she pulled her rental up at the office. She was simply out of energy for confrontations. Ten or so a day was probably a national limit or something. She let herself into the office and went straight to her lab, unlocking the deadbolt with a key from her personal set. Then she pushed open the lab door and went straight for her catalog on the desk in the far corner.

She was two hours and at least thirty flagged items into her catalog when she glanced down at her watch and realized the time. Tapping her pen on the desk, she thought about her options—head home or into town for an early dinner with Sabine. She had just settled on early dinner when the office phone rang.

She checked the display and felt her heart speed up when she recognized the number for the lab manager at the university in New Orleans. "Aaron," she answered, "I didn't expect to hear from you so soon. I don't suppose you have any good news for me?" She waited expectantly, wondering if he was about to give her a way to spend some of her newfound riches.

"As a matter of fact," he began, and Maryse could feel him smiling over the phone, "I have excellent news. You know that one batch you threw in for the hell of it—Trial 206?"

"Yes."

"Well, it passed tests one and two with flying colors. I'm moving to test three this afternoon and possibly four tomorrow. Can you get me more? I might not have enough to carry through the remaining trials."

Maryse let out the breath with a whoosh and held in a shout. "That's fantastic! Let me check that number." She unlocked her desk drawer and pulled her notebook from inside, then flipped the pages past failure after failure until she reached the possible success, Trial 206.

Then she groaned.

"Is something wrong?" Aaron asked.

"No," Maryse hedged, "not exactly. But thanks to a couple of drunken fishermen and an out-of-control barge, Trial 206 might not be as easy to obtain as it was before. Those idiots took out the entire group of plants. I'll have to find another location. I know I've seen them somewhere else, but offhand, I can't recall where exactly."

"Don't sweat it, Maryse," Aaron said. "You're way ahead of the game. Even if you have to propagate your own plants, it would only take a few more months, right? Maybe you should check on seeds just in case."

Maryse tapped her fingers on her desk. "You're right. I'll get out my seed catalog and see what I can work out. In the meantime, I'll try to remember where I saw that other batch. Let me know how far you get with what you have. I'll also contact every nursery I can find and see if they happen to have a full-grown bloom."

"Sounds like a plan," Aaron said. "Chin up, Maryse. This is only a momentary delay, and this is the best run yet."

Maryse thanked him and hung up the phone, excited and frustrated all at the same time. She'd only thrown that specimen into testing for the hell of it. At the time, she hadn't been paying too much attention to whether that particular batch was a hybrid, like so many others in the bayou were. Without another look at it, she couldn't know for sure. And now she didn't even know where to find another. Her "momentary delay" was suddenly looking pretty major.

"Wow," Luc said, striding into her lab. "This is some setup for a botanist." He walked over to her desk and picked up her notebook, scanning the pages. "What are you doing in here, exactly?"

Maryse grabbed the notebook from his hands and shoved it in a drawer, locking it afterwards. "What I do in here is none of your business. I rent this space from the state, so it's off limits to anyone I haven't personally invited in. That list starts with you."

Luc gave her a lazy smile. "Aww, c'mon, Maryse. I thought we had come to some sort of working arrangement."

Maryse narrowed her eyes at him. "You mean an arrangement like you towing my truck and sending me a rental without asking? The kind of arrangement where the big, strong man takes over because the helpless female couldn't possibly handle things?"

Luc stared at her for a moment, and if she hadn't been so aggravated, his confusion might have been amusing. "I was only trying to help. My buddy works at the dealership, so I called in a favor. He's not charging you for the tow."

Maryse stared back at him, feeling just a tiny bit guilty but not about to admit it. "Look, Luc. I'm not trying to be a bitch, but I'm used to doing things for myself. I don't like people making decisions for me."

Luc shrugged. "Whatever. But maybe if you let other people make decisions for you, your life wouldn't be such a mess. Exactly how many people told you not to marry Hank Henry?"

Maryse felt the blood rush to her face. "That is none of your business, and you're not furthering your cause by insulting my intelligence. There were a lot of reasons I married Hank, none of which I need to discuss with you." She shook her head. "I simply don't understand what you get out of being in this backwoods place harassing me. Isn't there a more lucrative assignment calling you in this great state? Not that I've actually seen you out working on anything."

Luc gave her a smug smile. "I'm the nephew of the district operations supervisor, so I've got family at the top of the food chain. I pretty much get to do whatever I want."

"Then why on Earth would you want to be here?"

"It was either this or some forgotten forest in the middle of nowhere north Louisiana. This is close to my apartment in the city and the retirement home my grandparents live in now. Don't even try to get me pulled from this assignment. It would take a hurricane to remove me from this marsh."

Maryse gave him a matching smile. "Yeah, well, say hello to Hurricane Maryse. As of this morning, you're standing on my property, so your food chain just became extinct."

He gave her a puzzled look, but Maryse couldn't really blame him. It was a strange statement. "What do you mean, 'your property'?"

"Apparently, all of this land belonged to Helena Henry. The entire preserve. She leased it to the state for their studies and to keep it protected, but it was hers to own and hers to give. And this morning, it was willed to me."

Luc stared at her in obvious shock. "Helena Henry owned this land? And she willed it to you?"

"Yep. Which makes this my office that I'm leasing to the state that I'm leasing part of back to myself." Maryse paused for a moment, the absurdity of that business transaction just hitting her.

"So you're leasing from yourself," Luc said, "and you'd like me to respect your privacy. Is that about right?"

Maryse blinked, surprised Luc had caught on to everything that fast. "Yes."

Luc nodded. "I have no problem with that. Sorry, I never meant to make you uncomfortable. I guess I'm just used to dealing with a different kind of woman." He extended his hand. "Truce?"

Maryse hesitated for a moment, then rose from her seat and placed her hand in his, trying to ignore her body's response to his strong hand clasped around hers. She released his hand and stuck her own in her jeans pocket, silently willing the tingling to stop.

Luc smiled and exited her lab, closing the door behind him.

Maryse stared at the closed door for a moment, then sat on her desk. What was it with that man? No matter how hard she tried to stay angry at him, he always managed to diffuse the situation and leave her wondering how he would look naked. Luc LeJeune was definitely a walking hazard to her mental and emotional health. Just when she thought he was a complete and utter cad, he managed to turn the tables on her by saying something unexpected, and an apology had been the absolute last thing she had expected.

I'm used to dealing with a different kind of woman.

Yeah, Maryse would just bet he was. The sexy, self-confident kind of woman that Maryse would like to be but didn't have a clue where to start. And given her current situation, it didn't look like she was going to find time to research it anytime soon.

In addition to everything else she had on her mind, Luc's comment about his uncle had left her a bit unsettled. If his uncle was really as highly placed with the state as he claimed, Luc might still be able to make trouble for her if he thought she wasn't doing her job.

She'd just have to be careful—make sure she didn't let her personal research and the small matter of Helena Henry get in the way of her job any more than it already had, at least during work hours. Which meant the first item on her list was figuring out a way to avoid the ghost during working hours anyway. If the will reading had been any indication, anything involving Helena was bound to be trouble.

Maryse shook her head as her mind roamed back over the events of the morning. What a fiasco. Then, with a start, she remembered where she'd seen that other group of plants and groaned.

Directly across the bayou from Helena Henry's house.

Luc heard the lab door slam behind him and turned in his chair. Instead of the aggravation he'd expected, Maryse had that look of intent concentration mixed with excitement that you get when you have a great idea but are still trying to work out the details. She didn't even acknowledge him as she pulled on her rubber boots and hustled out of the office without so much as a wave or a backwards glance.

Luc sighed. So much for his powers of sexual attraction. He'd gotten women in bed with less than a handshake and an apology before, but Maryse Robicheaux was a force to be reckoned with.

Of course, with the day she'd had, Luc couldn't blame her too much for being distracted. She'd gone from a wrecked truck to inheriting a game preserve, and, technically, it wasn't even quitting time.

Still, he'd thought they'd moved beyond suspicious. But if the scene in her lab was any indication, Maryse's defense system was back in full force. But why? Was it really because he'd had her truck towed, or was it something else entirely? Granted, he sometimes had trouble remembering all that women's independence stuff. Not that he didn't like strong women—hell, he'd been raised by the strongest of women, his grandmother. But he was also Choctaw, and it was ingrained into them from a young age to take care of their responsibilities—especially to their women.

She's not your woman.

Okay, so he knew it was true, at least in the real sense of the sentiment. But until the DEQ was satisfied that his work in Mudbug was done, Luc felt responsible for Maryse, and if she was in some kind of trouble, then he felt obligated to help. In fact, if Maryse was the informant he sought, then it was his job to help. All kinds of trouble could be headed her way if the chemical company got wind that someone was airing dirty secrets to the DEQ.

He studied the locked lab door. That notebook...he hadn't gotten a good look at the page, but he'd seen enough to know that it wasn't filled with regular writing. Those symbols were chemicals equations, but high school chemistry was such a distant memory he'd never be able to scratch the surface of what exactly she had written, not even with all day to consider it. But he'd be willing to bet his department had someone who could decipher whatever Maryse had been so quick to hide.

He rose from his chair and studied the lock for a moment. It was one of the best, but not completely unbeatable. Reaching into his jeans pocket, he pulled out his cell phone and hit a speed dial.

"Wilson," his boss answered on the first ring.

"It's LeJeune. I need a set of B&E tools down here. Something that can get past a pretty high-tech padlock."

"What's wrong, LeJeune—the woman wearing a chastity belt?"

Luc counted to three, then replied. "Hilarious. She's renting office space from the state that she's turned into some sort of chemistry lab. I need to get in there and see what she's working on."

"She's running lab experiments?"

"That's what it looks like to me. Place is full of really high-tech equipment. We're talking a lot more than just a microscope and some test tubes."

"Why would a botanist need a chemistry lab? There's nothing in her job description to require it. From what I've read, she's supposed to just collect the samples and then they're analyzed someplace else. You think she's the informant?"

Luc studied the locked door for a moment. "Maybe, but it doesn't feel right. It's sort of an elaborate and expensive setup to turn someone in for polluting the water."

"Then maybe she's working with them. Did you ever think of that? Maybe she's testing for them, hoping the water gets back to an acceptable place before someone discovers their dumping sites."

Luc turned from the door and stared out the big front window at the bayou. "At this point, I guess anything is possible, although, I have to say, she doesn't really fit the profile of a criminal. And there was another incident today that might cause us some trouble."

"What kind of incident?"

"Apparently, that mother-in-law of hers owned this preserve and leased it to the state. Well, you'll never guess who she left it to."

"Good grief, LeJeune, and you think this botanist is pure as the driven snow? How the hell did the mother-in-law die?"

Luc rubbed his jaw with one hand. "I don't know exactly."

"Well, you best be finding out. This all smacks of a cover-up, and your unassuming botanist may be the biggest ringleader of all. You're letting a nice set of T&.A cloud your judgment."

"You know better, boss. I'm checking out everything."

"Hmm. I'm certain you are. LeJeune, do you have any idea how uncomfortable it is to have the whole damned EPA up your ass? Because that's what I have right now, and according to my wife, I've never had much ass, so it's getting crowded down there and I'm more than a little uncomfortable. You don't want me uncomfortable, do you?"

Luc closed his eyes for a moment, not even wanting to think about another man's ass. "No, we wouldn't want that."

"Good!" Wilson disconnected, and Luc pressed the End button on his phone. What a friggin' mess. The call had brought up a possibility Luc hadn't even thought of, and it didn't please him in the least. Was his boss right? Was his attraction to Maryse coloring his judgment? What if she was protecting whoever was making illegal dumps in the bayou? Then again, maybe his initial read was right, and she wasn't involved at all.

He took another look at the locked door and sighed. No matter what, Maryse Robicheaux was up to something, and the way she shot out of the office led him to believe that she was off to do something important and personal. After all, she had taken the day off work. Glancing at his watch, he realized it had been ten minutes since Maryse had fled the office. He flipped his cell phone open again and punched some buttons.

A map of the Mudbug area filled the display, and Luc watched as a small blinking dot came into view, moving rapidly across the bayou that stretched alongside downtown. So whatever couldn't wait had taken her into the bayou, and he'd be willing to bet everything he owned that whatever she was doing didn't have anything to do with her job as a state botanist.

But he was about to find out.

Maryse pushed down the throttle of her bass boat and zoomed across the bayou. Even though she'd been awake for hours, there was still that tiny thought lingering in the back of her mind that she'd wake up any moment and find the whole thing had been one big dream—parts of it a nightmare.

Of course, that theory already had two strikes against it. The first being that she completely lacked the imagination to even dream something this weird, and the second being that even if she had dreamed up a haunting, the last person she would have put in the starring role was Helena. And now, against her better judgment, she was headed down the bayou to a stretch of bank within easy view of Helena Henry's house. Not that Maryse knew where Helena hung out, exactly, but her house seemed to make the most sense. And the last thing Maryse needed today was another dose of Helena.

In fact, the more she thought about it, the more avoiding Helena seemed like the best plan. Maryse spent most of her days in the bayou, and even though Helena claimed she could walk on water, and quite possibly run, she probably couldn't keep up with a boat—not in ghostly high heels, anyway.

Of course, her cabin posed a bit of a problem. Helena had already "dropped by," so that wasn't safe at all. There was always the Mudbug Hotel, but it probably wouldn't take Helena long to get around to that one either, given that the hotel owner, Mildred, had essentially raised Maryse after her mother died.

She turned the steering wheel and guided her boat into a large offshoot of the bayou that ran parallel to downtown Mudbug. The bayou was lined with cypress trees on one side and historical homes on the other, Helena's estate being the largest, of course. Maryse could see the white, imposing monstrosity as soon as she made the turn. She wondered for about the millionth time what God could possibly be thinking by sending a scientist a ghost.

She'd always figured He had a sense of humor, but this was ridiculous.

Cutting her boat over toward the cypress trees, she let off the throttle and tried to find the tiny shoots of greenery she needed for the trials. They'd been here just last week, she could have sworn it, but no matter how hard she looked, the plant in question seemed to evade her. She had just leaned over the side of the boat to finger something that looked reasonably close to the plant in question when she heard shouting behind her.

Maryse groaned, afraid to look. She turned around and confirmed this world was definitely going to hell in a hand-basket.

Helena Henry was walking on water.

Chapter Five

The bayou tide was moving in a slow roll out toward the Gulf. But Helena Henry was a force of her own, inexorably making her way against the current. Every move forward put her a little farther downstream, and then every five steps or so, she'd jog a bit upstream, huffing like she was about to keel over.

If she hadn't already been dead, that is.

Maryse stared at Helena and frowned, not certain whether to be more worried about another visit with the ghost or the fact that her physical fitness level apparently wouldn't get any better in death. Perhaps she should start eating better and working out more. Or at least working out more—giving up beer was out of the question.

It took another couple of minutes for Helena to make it across the bayou and climb over the side of Maryse's boat. She slumped onto the bench, dragging huge breaths in and out.

"Are you all right?" Maryse asked.

"Of course not." Helena shot her a dirty look. "I'm dead."

"Damn it, I know that. I just thought...I didn't know...never mind." The whole situation was simply too mind-boggling for thought.

"Sort of an ass-ripper, huh?" Helena said. "You'd think you'd get a better body if you're destined to roam the Earth as a spirit."

Maryse shook her head. "You don't know any such thing about your destiny. Maybe the line's too long at the Pearly Gates—maybe there was a thunderstorm on Cloud Nine and all the flights are delayed." *Maybe Hell's full and they're waiting for an opening.*

"Maybe I'm stuck here until I figure out who killed me," Helena said.

Maryse sat back on her seat with a sigh. "We've already had this discussion, Helena. I'm not an investigator and don't want to be. In fact, I don't want to be involved in this at all. You've already got Harold gunning for me—not that I'm complaining about the inheritance—but my point is my plate is not just full, it's overflowing. I'm not about to get myself deeper in the hole by doing whatever you had in mind."

Helena grinned. "I was thinking we'd start with a little B&E."

"Oh, no." Maryse shook her head. "I am not breaking into anything. I know you might find this hard to believe, but you're not worth going to jail for, game preserve or no."

"Oh, c'mon, Maryse. You never want to have any fun. Besides, technically, I own the house we'd be breaking into."

"Not anymore you don't. The historical society does."

"But no one's there. I've already checked. It won't take ten minutes at the most."

Maryse shook her head again, her jaw set. "No way."

Helena studied her for a moment. "If you just do this one little break-in, I promise to go away for at least a day."

Damn. Helena was playing dirty. A whole day ghost free was very tempting. But would she keep her word?

"It's too much of a risk," Maryse said finally. "What if someone sees me? There's no way I could explain being inside your house when you're dead. Everyone would think I was stealing or something."

Helena laughed. "You...Ms. Goodie Two-Shoes...stealing? Not likely." She narrowed her eyes at Maryse. "I might have a cell phone number for Hank somewhere inside and perhaps even a last known address."

Maryse was instantly angry. "You told me you didn't know where Hank was. I always knew you were a royal bitch, Helena, but keeping me from getting a divorce after the way Hank treated me is low, even for you."

"Now, don't get your panties in a knot." Helena put up a hand in protest. "I didn't know where Hank was until today. He called a few hours ago, and Harold wrote down his information on a tablet next to the kitchen phone." She shrugged and looked away. "I guess he's still trying to figure out how to get some money and clear his worthless butt with the locals."

Maryse stared at her for a moment, but Helena wouldn't meet her eyes. Was that actually remorse…sadness she saw in Helena's expression when she talked about Hank and her money? Was it possible that Helena had been hurt by Hank's disappearing act, too?

Letting out a sigh, she pulled up her anchor, not even glancing at Helena. She looked both ways up the bayou to make sure it was clear, then started her boat and crossed the bayou to Helena's dock.

"Dock on the left side," Helena instructed. "That way the boathouse covers you from one direction and the cattails will hide you on the other." She gave Maryse a gleeful smile and clapped her hands like a five-year-old.

Oh goodie. All they needed were party hats and a cake.

Maryse edged the boat in between the dock and an enormous growth of cattails, then checked the bayou again. Still clear. And Helena had been right about the docking spot. The boat was almost completely hidden.

Of course, that in no way solved the problem of walking up the pier and across the backyard to the house, but hey, who was she to complain? She'd never even had a traffic ticket, but she was about to commit a crime with a woman who couldn't testify on her behalf and certainly couldn't be thrown in the clink along with her.

Helena hopped out of the boat, skipped across the remaining water of the bayou to the shore, then turned around and waved for Maryse to follow. Casting one final glance around, Maryse pulled off her rubber boots, stepped onto the dock, and hurried down the pier and across the yard behind Helena.

She expected Helena to go to the back door, but instead, the ghost trailed off to the side and ducked around behind a row of azalea bushes. Maryse pushed aside a bit of the dense foliage and followed her. There was a small path, about a foot wide, between the bushes and the house. When they reached a narrow window, Helena stopped and pointed.

"You're small. You should be able to fit through that."

"Excuse me? You want me to climb in a window like a thief? Why don't you have a key hidden outside somewhere?"

"Because I didn't want anyone to break in, silly. C'mon, the window is low enough for you to climb in, and the latch on this one has been broken for months."

The window was about four feet from the ground. God knew she wasn't an acrobat, but she could probably make it work. At this point, she'd stick her head in a lion's mouth for information on Hank. She reached up and pushed on the window, sliding it up until it wouldn't go any farther.

She placed both of her hands on the window ledge and looked over at Helena. "I am so leaving this house through a doorway. Got it?"

Helena nodded. "Whatever you want to do. Just hop on in there and open the side door for me.

Maryse stared at her. "Let me get this straight. I have to do circus moves through a window, but you get to stroll in through the door. Why don't you walk through a wall or something?"

"Oh, sure." Helena pouted. "Go picking on my weaknesses when I'm at a low point."

"You can't walk through walls?"

"Not exactly. Well, I did once, but I haven't perfected it yet. Last time I tried I almost knocked myself out. If you hadn't left your patio door open yesterday, I wouldn't have gotten into your cabin."

Maryse shook her head. "There is something incredibly wrong with all of this, but I don't have time to sort it out now." Before she could change her mind, she pulled herself up to the window and shoved her head and shoulders through. She lost her momentum about midway through, and she kicked her legs trying to edge through the narrow opening. Finally, she crossed the balancing threshold and tumbled through the window headfirst into a stack of dirty laundry.

"Yuck." She pulled herself up from the floor and brushed a really tacky pair of boxers from her shoulder. "You owe me huge, Helena," she yelled out the window.

"Yeah, yeah, just open the damned door."

Maryse picked her way through the dirty laundry, careful not to step on anything. Tennis shoes didn't protect you from being grossed out, and Maryse knew if any of Harold's boxers had touched her bare skin, she wouldn't be able to look at a Calvin Klein ad for a long time.

The side door had a single deadbolt that Maryse slid back before she pushed the door open. Helena strolled inside like this was all completely normal and jumped over the stack of laundry and into the kitchen. "This way, and hurry. Harold should be home anytime now. He'll be needing to pack."

Maryse crept down the hall and into the kitchen, catching a glimpse of Helena as she disappeared around a corner. "You kind of left out that part about Harold coming home, Helena!" She rounded the corner and saw Helena at the top of a humongous circular stairway, beckoning to her from the second floor.

"It's in my bedroom."

Maryse glanced out the front window at the driveway. Clear. She blew out a breath and followed Helena up the stairs, wondering what exactly "it" was and why it was in the bedroom.

At the top of the stairs, Helena pointed to a closed door. "That's my bedroom. I need to look in my safe."

"Your safe? I'm risking an arrest over your pearls or something?"

"No, no! Just please get in there and open the safe. I'm afraid things aren't going the way I'd planned."

"Sort of an understatement considering you're dead, huh?" Maryse pushed the door open and stepped inside. "Where's the safe?"

Helena pointed to an oil painting on the wall across from the bed. It was an original of Hank, probably around age three and long before he'd become a burden on society. That incredible smile was already in place, even on such a small child, and Maryse felt a tingle all over again as she looked at the man she'd married.

Holding in a sigh, she lifted the painting from the wall, exposing the safe behind it. She glanced at the combination lock, then looked at Helena. "Well, do you have dynamite or are you going to give me the combination?"

"Fourteen, three, forty."

Maryse twirled the dial and heard a click when she stopped on the last number. She looked over at Helena, who nodded, then pulled the lever to open the safe. She'd barely gotten the door open before Helena was standing almost on top of her, trying to peer inside.

"Damn it!" Helena ranted. "That son of a bitch didn't even wait until my body was cold before he took the cash."

"What did you expect? You didn't leave him anything from your estate. He's probably out pawning your silver right now."

Helena sighed. "You're right, but that's not what I'm worried about. Pull out that stack of papers in the back."

Maryse reached inside, removed a stack of envelopes, then looked at Helena.

"Flip through them," Helena instructed. "I'm looking for one from Able & Able."

Maryse shuffled through the envelopes one at a time, studying the return addresses. When she reached the end of the stack, she looked over at Helena. "There's nothing here with that name on it."

"Double damn!" Helena paced the bedroom up one way and down the other. "I knew it. There's no telling how long that worthless husband of mine has been pilfering from my safe."

Maryse studied Helena, a bad feeling washing over her. Should ghosts really be this worried about things they couldn't control? "What exactly was in that letter, Helena?"

Helena stopped pacing and looked at her for a moment, her expression wavering as if on the verge of saying something important. Finally, she shook her head and looked away. "Nothing to concern yourself with. At least not yet. If it becomes an issue, I'll let you know."

"You'll let me know? I have news for you, Helena. All of this is an issue for me. I don't believe in ghosts. I don't believe in breaking and entering, and furthermore—"

Before she could complete the sentence, a tiny red light in a small box on the backside of the bedroom door started to blink. Had that been there before? She didn't remember seeing a blinking light when she'd entered the room. Surely she would have remembered.

"Uh, Helena," Maryse said and pointed to the box. "What exactly is that red light?"

Helena whirled around to look at the light, then spun back around, a panicked look on her face. "It's the alarm. Harold must have set it when he left. It's on a delay, but we don't have much time left before it goes off."

Maryse tossed the stack of envelopes back into the safe, slammed the safe door and whirled the dial, then hung the picture on the wall as quickly as she could. She'd stepped one foot outside the bedroom door when the sirens went off. The shrill shriek of the alarm deafened her for a moment, and Maryse froze.

"Run!" Helena cried and ran down the staircase.

Maryse took the steps two at a time, passing Helena on the way, and almost fell as she hit the foyer floor. The scream of police sirens was far too close for comfort, and Maryse struggled to pick up the pace. Skidding on the polished wood, she dashed around the corner and onto the textured tile in the kitchen, where her shoes had a much better grip and she picked up some speed. She ran into the laundry room, shoving down the window where she'd entered the house. Then she rushed out the side door, locking it before she slammed it behind her.

She made for the huge hedge of bushes that separated Helena's yard from her neighbor's and ran as fast as she could to the dock. She jumped in the boat from shore, banging her knee against the metal bench, and stifled a yell. Limping over to the controls, she started the boat, threw it into reverse and shoved down the throttle.

The boat shot out from between the dock and the cattails, and she changed it to drive and forced the throttle all the way down again, causing the boat to leap out of the water and slam back down onto the bayou, jolting her so hard her teeth hurt. She looked back at Helena's house and blew out a breath of relief when she didn't see police or any curious neighbors observing her departure.

Her knee was throbbing now, and Maryse could feel a tiny trickle of blood down the front of her leg. Her aching head would probably never be the same. As soon as she rounded the bayou out of view of Helena's house, she'd stop and assess the damage. She slowed a bit, so as not to look suspicious, and twisted on the bench to look back at Helena's house. The police were just pulling into the driveway, and she breathed a sigh of relief that she'd be well out of their line of sight before they got out of their cars.

She turned back around and almost panicked when she realized she was headed directly toward an anchored boat.

She threw the throttle in reverse and the engine whined in protest. The boat jerked one direction, then another, and as every muscle in her body strained to hold her inside the bouncing vehicle, Maryse knew she was going to pay for this tomorrow.

Miraculously, the boat stopped just inches from the other vessel. Maryse sank down on the bench, trying to catch her breath.

"Quite a stop you made there," a voice sounded from the other boat. "Do you do everything as fast as you drive a boat?"

That voice was too familiar and wasn't one she wanted to hear. She raised her head a tiny bit and saw the smiling face of Luc LeJeune. Just what she needed—an opportunity for Luc to file a reckless endangerment charge against her with his uncle. This day just kept getting better.

"Hi, Luc." She tried to force her voice to normal. "I was having a bit of engine trouble. I thought I might have a little trash collected down there. Figured I'd blow it out."

Luc looked at her, still smiling, not believing a word of it. "Uh huh. Hey, what's that noise around the bayou? It sounds like an alarm? Cop cars have been racing along the highway to get here."

Maryse looked behind her even though she knew she couldn't see around the bend of the bayou to Helena's house. It bought her a moment, and in that moment, she was hoping to come up with a better answer than "I didn't hear anything."

"I don't know," she said. "I didn't hear anything." So much for the moment.

Luc studied her, a curious expression on his face. "Really? That's odd, because the sirens and everything are pretty loud. Of course, if you were working on your engine, you might not have heard it over the motor." He gave her another smile that clearly said, "you're full of shit and up to something and I know it." "What happened to your knee?"

Maryse looked down at her leg, just realizing that she'd been massaging the top of her kneecap. A patch of red was seeping through her jeans, and given that it was growing in size, she probably couldn't pass it off as an old stain.

"I banged it on the bench when I was working on the engine. I didn't even notice it was bleeding. Must have a sharp edge somewhere. I'll get the metal grinder after it tomorrow."

"After the bench or your knee?" Luc asked, clearly amused.

Maryse sighed. "The bench. Look, I need to get going. I have a lot of things to do tonight."

Luc waved one hand across the bayou, as if to say "What's stopping you?"

"I'll see you at the office tomorrow," he said as she backed her boat away from his.

Managing a weak smile, she turned the boat and headed down the bayou toward the station. She was halfway there when she realized she'd locked Helena inside her own house, and she hadn't gotten the promised information on Hank.

Damn it! Things were out of control, and she had to get a grip on them fast or she was going to end up costing herself everything.

Breaking and entering? What had she been thinking? All that drama for a fractured kneecap and a reinjury to her throbbing head, and she still hadn't gotten what she'd gone in for, which was information on Hank.

She'd hoped after the will reading that the situation with Helena would resolve itself and she could go back to her regular life, minus Helena Henry, of course. But it looked like things were far more dire than she'd initially thought, and her options were limited.

What she needed was professional advice, and the only two people she could think of to give it were her priest and Sabine. One of them had to know of a way to help Helena pass or cross or whatever it was that she needed to do.

And if anyone would know how to make that happen, it would probably be Sabine.

Luc watched as Maryse headed up the bayou in her boat, wondering what in the world was going on with that woman. He'd stepped right in the middle of something strange and for the life of him couldn't figure out what.

He'd followed after she left the office, the GPS he'd installed on her boat made finding her among the hundreds of bayous an easy task. But when he'd initially arrived at the location the equipment had specified, he wondered if there had been a malfunction. Her boat was nowhere in sight, even though the tiny gray monitor clearly showed a blinking red light not fifty yards in front of him.

Then the alarm sirens had gone off, and seconds later, he'd spotted Maryse running along a group of dense hedges, away from the house with the sounding alarm. He glanced down at the bank and saw a tiny tip of her boat peeking out from the cattails, suddenly realizing why she'd shown on the equipment but not to the bare eye.

She'd made a leap into her boat from the bank that Indiana Jones would have been proud of, and it probably explained the injury to her knee, but it didn't explain why a seemingly rational woman would break into a house in broad daylight. Before she could catch him spying, he'd hustled around the corner and anchored directly in her flight path.

He pulled his cell phone from his pocket and pressed in a number. His buddy and fellow agent answered almost immediately.

"LeJeune here. Brian, I need you to check on something for me."

"Go ahead," Brian said.

"There's a house in downtown Mudbug along the bayou where an alarm just went off. The police responded, so I know the alarm system is linked to an outside provider. I need to know who owns that house."

Luc heard tapping and knew Brian was working his magic on the computer. It took less than a minute to get the answer.

"The house belongs to a Helena Henry," Brian said. "You want me to pursue anything further?"

"No," Luc said. "That's it for now. Thanks." He flipped the phone shut and shoved it in his pocket.

Maryse had just broken into her dead mother-in-law's house. He was certain. And even though it probably had nothing to do with his case, he couldn't help wondering what the woman had gotten into. The information on Maryse from the DEQ research department didn't allude to anything remotely dangerous or illegal. Truth be told, on paper she was probably the most boring human being he'd ever read about. In person, well, in person obviously things were a bit different.

Luc smiled. He couldn't wait to find out why.

Fifteen minutes after she'd risked a criminal record, Maryse docked her boat and left the office before Luc could show up and start in with any more embarrassing questions. It was fast approaching supper time, and since she'd completely forgotten lunch, Maryse was on the verge of starving. She had thirty minutes to snag a clean pair of jeans and make the drive into Mudbug. Sabine would just be closing up shop for the day, so the two of them could grab some burgers, and Maryse could fill Sabine in on her ridiculous day.

She made the drive in twenty minutes flat, which was fast even for her. But then, being haunted tended to create a sense of urgency. As she parked her rental in front of one of the restored historical buildings along Main Street, she spotted Sabine through the plate-glass window of her shop, Read 'em and Reap. She was dressed to the hilt in her psychic getup—a floor-length, midnight-blue robe with stars and moons on it and a matching head wrap with a huge fake sapphire in the center. Her long earrings and dozens of bracelets glinted in the sunlight. With her jet black hair—dyed, of course—and black nails and lipstick, the picture was complete. And completely frightening.

Maryse smiled for a moment, unable to help herself. From the outside, two more different people had never been made than she and Sabine, and she was certain that more than a few Mudbug residents wondered how in the world they had ever become such close friends. But then people in Mudbug could sometimes be a little obtuse.

Those two poor little girls with no mothers. Maryse could still remember overhearing her first-grade teacher saying that to the principal their first day of school. They were different from the other kids and knew it. And Sabine didn't even have a father, just an aging aunt who had taken her in but couldn't tell her much if anything about her parents.

Now they were both short two parents. Sabine's parents from a car accident when Sabine was still a baby, and Maryse's parents lost to cancer.

Maryse frowned and tapped her fingers on the steering wheel. She hated being pitied and had felt the difference in the attitudes of the teachers and other kids even then. As much as Maryse missed her parents, and Sabine wanted to know something about her own, neither of them wanted the pity of people who would never understand. Pity was for those who couldn't do anything about it. She and Sabine had spent their lives trying to fill those gaps, and damn it, one day the holes their parents left were going to be filled.

Sabine's tarot cards were fanned out before a distraught, middle-aged, overweight woman with more jewelry than Sabine and hair that was entirely too big. There was a shiny-new, white Cadillac Deville parked in front of Sabine's building, so Maryse figured she better wait a minute until Sabine delivered the happy news to whatever rich idiot was currently seeking her "professional" advice.

Immediately, Maryse chastised herself for judging others and their beliefs. She'd always been the typical scientist, not believing in anything she couldn't put her hands on, and now she had a ghost stalking her. It had taken her years to buy into the unnatural ability of Raissa, Sabine's mentor, but the other psychic had been right about so many things that even Maryse had to admit Raissa had talents that couldn't be explained. God had been the only exception to her self-imposed rule of proof, and she still wondered whether if she hadn't been raised in the church she would have questioned His existence as well.

And despite all that, here she was—smack in the middle of a paranormal nightmare. She was about to tell her best friend, who believed in the existence of damned near anything, that Helena Henry was haunting her. For Sabine, who'd been trying to convince her of the supernatural since the first grade, this moment would be beyond value—just like one of those stupid commercials.

One lost tarot reading for closing the shop early—$15.

Three glasses of wine and a burger at Johnny's—$20.

Hearing your best friend, aka The Disbeliever, say she's being haunted by a ghost—Priceless.

She shook her head and sighed, feeling so far out of her element it wasn't even funny. About that time, Cadillac Woman broke into smiles, and Maryse figured Sabine had wrapped up the good news. She hopped out of her rental and started across the street before she could change her mind.

Chapter Six

As Maryse stepped inside Read 'em and Reap, Sabine looked up in obvious surprise.

"Maryse, is everything all right? What in the world happened to your head?" Sabine jumped up from her chair and rushed over to inspect Maryse's forehead.

"I wrecked my truck this morning." She held up a hand to stop the barrage that was about to ensue. "I've already been to the doctor, and I'm fine. It's just a bump and a hellacious headache. A couple of uneventful days and I should be good as new." Of course, she had a ghost of a chance at stringing together a couple of uneventful days. Literally.

Sabine stared at her for a moment, then narrowed her eyes. "Something's wrong."

"Of course something's wrong. This whole day was wrong."

Sabine shook her head. "I know that look."

"What look?" Maryse was already having second thoughts about telling Sabine about Helena. What if Sabine thought she was crazy? What if she was crazy?

"That 'I don't want to discuss it' look that you always get when you need help and don't want to ask." Sabine paused for a moment. "I'm almost afraid to ask, but did Hank show up for the reading?"

Maryse sighed. "I should have known I couldn't hide anything from you. But I don't want to talk here. I can't drink taking the pain medication, but I was thinking a burger and a painkiller might loosen me up enough for the subject I need to cover."

Sabine nodded. "Let me lock up and shed the robes. I'll meet you at Johnny's in a few." She grabbed a set of keys off her desk. "Get the corner table."

"Sure." Maryse headed out of the shop and into the hot, humid Louisiana evening. The sun was still beating down on the concrete, heat vapors rising from the street. The smell of boiled crawfish from Carolyn's Cajun Kitchen down the block filled the air and made her remember that it had been forever since breakfast.

She hesitated for a moment as she crossed the street to Johnny's bar, wondering again if she was making the right decision. If she told Sabine about Helena's ghost, she was leaving herself wide open for lectures on all kinds of unexplained phenomena—Bigfoot, the Loch Ness Monster, UFOs. She wasn't sure she was ready for a lifetime of hassle.

She bit her lower lip and cast a nervous glance back at Read 'em and Reap. On the flip side, there was the one huge advantage of letting her friend in on it—Sabine knew darn near everything about the supernatural, and anything she didn't know, she could find out. If anyone could make Helena go away, it would be Sabine. And getting rid of Helena was the number one priority, even if it meant going to near-death-experience meetings or looking at those blurred photos of God-knows-what that Sabine was always trying to push off on her as real.

Seeing no better alternative, she pushed open the door and entered the bar. A couple of fishermen sat at the old driftwood bar and waved a hand in acknowledgment when she walked in. Other than that, the place was empty. She made her way to the table in a dim corner, far from the bar, and took a seat. The owner and chief bartender, appropriately named Johnny, shuffled over to her a minute or so later.

"Sorry to hear about your mother-in-law," he said, brushing aside a stray strand of thinning, silver hair from his forehead.

"Really?" Maryse stared at him.

Johnny fidgeted for a moment, then gave her a grin. "Well, hell no, actually, but 'sorry' sounds a lot more polite. Did Hank show up for the funeral?"

"Not a chance. I figure he won't come around until he gets the money to pay off the local law enforcement."

Johnny nodded. "Sounds about right. I swear to God, that has got to be the most useless human being ever produced." He gave her an apologetic look. "Sorry, I know you married him and all."

She waved one hand in dismissal. "You haven't offended me. I was young and stupid. I don't blame myself for being taken in by Hank Henry. I'm certainly not the only one who was."

"That's for sure. I think he owed damned near everyone in town before he skipped out."

No shit. "Yeah, that's what I hear." It was all she could say about the situation without exploding.

"Well, what're you drinkin'?" Fortunately, Johnny saved her from dwelling on all Hank's debts.

"Could I get a club soda and a glass of white zin for Sabine? She'll be here in a minute."

Johnny nodded and clasped her shoulder with one hand. "You let me know if you need anything, okay? I promised your daddy I'd look after you, and I intend to keep that promise." He gave her a grin. "Can't have the old bastard coming back to haunt me, can I?"

Maryse gave him a weak smile. "Guess not," she managed as Johnny shuffled back to the bar to get the drinks.

Given a choice between Helena Henry and her dad, she'd have taken the "old bastard" any day. He'd been as hard as every other commercial fisherman in Mudbug and hadn't given an inch on anything, but at least he'd been honest and fair.

It couldn't have been easy on him, raising a girl on his own after her mother died, but he'd done the best he could, and she didn't think she'd turned out too bad. Except for the major slip of marrying Hank, she had a pretty good track record. And let's face it, if her dad hadn't come back from the dead to stop that wedding, she was pretty sure he wasn't ever returning.

Clenching her fists in frustration, she mentally cursed Hank Henry for about the hundredth time that day. If he hadn't got a hold of her at the absolute lowest point in her life—just after her dad had passed—would she have fallen for his act?

She liked to believe the answer was no, but the reality was that Hank Henry had charmed the pants off darn near every girl in town at some time or another. But none of them had been stupid enough to marry him. She frowned at her shortsightedness and shook her head as Sabine slid into the chair across from her, the bracelets on her arm clinking together like wind chimes.

"Did you order drinks already?" Sabine asked and brushed the bangs from her eyes.

"Yeah, I got you a glass of wine."

Sabine gave her a grateful look. "Thanks. It's been one of those weeks."

Maryse smiled. *Oh yeah, honey. Wait until you hear about my week. Yours has to look better after that.* "I haven't had the best week myself. In fact, that's what I wanted to talk with you about."

"I was worried when I didn't hear from you this afternoon," Sabine said, "but then I didn't really know how long the will-reading would take. Is that the problem...something to do with Helena's will?"

"Sorta." Maryse inclined her head toward Johnny, who was on his way across the bar with a tray of drinks, and Sabine nodded in understanding. She waited until Johnny had delivered the drinks, did his old-man flirting routine with Sabine, and shuffled back behind the bar before she got down to business.

"Hank didn't show, but the reading was very interesting," Maryse said and proceeded to tell Sabine all the events of the morning, from her truck wreck to the list of equipment she was going to buy with her lease money.

Sabine hung on every word, laughing at some points and gasping at others. "Good Lord!" Sabine said when Maryse finished her tale. "What a day. Makes my entire life look simple and boring."

"And that's not all. In fact, as screwed up as all that is, that's not even what's really worrying me."

Sabine stared. "You're kidding me. There's more?"

Maryse took a deep breath and pushed forward. "This is going to sound ridiculous, but I have to ask you a question. And I need you to answer me in all seriousness."

"Wow. This must be heavy. You know I'd never hedge things with you, Maryse. Ask me whatever you need to. I'll give you an honest answer."

Maryse studied her friend for a moment. Finally, she took a deep breath and said, "I need to know why a ghost would appear to someone when other people can't see it."

Sabine stared at her for a moment, then slowly blinked.

"Well, based on everything I've ever read or heard about, unless you're a conduit, a ghost will appear if you have something to do with them."

"A conduit—you mean like that kid in *The Sixth Sense*?"

"Exactly. Conduits are able to see a lot of ghosts, even if they've never met them before."

"Okay. So if someone sees a ghost and they're not a conduit, why would the ghost appear to them?"

Sabine scrunched her brow and gave her a hard look. Maryse gave her friend points for not reaching across the table to take her temperature. This had to be the very last thing Sabine would have expected from her.

Finally, Sabine cleared her throat and continued. "The commonly accepted theory on hauntings is that unless the ghost is stuck in a certain place, like a house or something, it's out walking about because of unfinished business or because it doesn't know it's dead."

"Unfinished business—like a murder?"

Sabine's eyes widened. "Certainly being murdered might cause someone's essence to stick around this world. Justice is a very powerful emotion. It sometimes overrides even death."

Maryse nodded and considered everything for a moment. "So how does the ghost pick who it will appear to?"

Sabine shook her head, a puzzled expression on her face. "I don't think the ghost has any say. I think it's visible to someone who's supposed to help and that's it. If the ghost got to pick, then it would just appear to whoever killed it and slowly drive the murderer off the deep end. It couldn't be much fun being hounded by a ghost."

Maryse nodded. *You think?*

Sabine reached across the table and placed her hand on Maryse's. "Where is all this going, exactly? This kind of stuff is so far beyond your usual fare that you're really starting to worry me. I mean, first you want to attend that horrible woman's funeral, then that weird inheritance, and now this?"

Before she could change her mind, Maryse leaned forward and looked Sabine straight in the eyes. "What would you say if I told you that I've seen Helena Henry—walking, talking, and still very dead?"

Sabine stared at her for a moment, obviously waiting for the punch line. When one never came, she removed her hand from Maryse's, completely drained her wineglass and sat it back on the table, her hands shaking slightly. "Helena Henry appeared to you?"

Maryse nodded and told her all about her first sighting of Helena at the funeral and her subsequent visit to her cabin, then the disastrous will reading. She left off the breaking and entering part of her day. Sabine already had enough to absorb.

"Murdered?" Sabine sat up straight as she finished her tall tale.

"That's what she says."

Sabine inclined her head and tapped a long, black nail on the table. "Well, if she says it's so, it probably is. I mean, what would be the point of lying now? Besides, if she's still hanging around, then there's obviously a problem."

"That's great to know and all, and very unfortunate for Helena, but why do I have to be involved in this? Why me?"

Sabine gave her a small smile. "Hardly seems fair, right? The most horrible human being you've encountered in your entire life, and now she shows up after death. What are the odds?"

"I don't even want to know. I just want to get rid of her."

Sabine turned her palms up and shrugged. "I don't think you can get rid of her until you figure out who killed her. It sounds like that's the problem."

"But I don't *care* who killed her."

Sabine shook her head and gave her a sad look. "That's not true, and you know it. You're the fairest person I know. Don't tell me it doesn't bother you that Helena was murdered. I'm not buying it."

"Unbelievable. I barely tolerate the living and now I have to be associated with the dead?" Maryse sighed and slumped back in her chair. "Okay, so maybe the fact that she was murdered bothers me…a little. But what am I supposed to do about it? I'm not the police. I'm a botanist. Studying plants does not exactly equip one to solve a murder."

"I don't think you were selected because of your crime-solving skills," Sabine said, her expression thoughtful.

"Then why would the forces of the universe select me at all?"

"I don't know. But you must be tied into everything. Maybe it's something to do with the game preserve."

Maryse groaned. "Are you sure?" This just kept sounding worse.

"I don't see any other explanation. Maybe the next time you see Helena, you ought to ask her."

"Yeah, right, like she's been forthcoming so far," Maryse said. "Besides, Helena was as shocked as I was that I could see her. I'm sure of that. So if she's visible to me for a reason, why didn't she say so?"

Sabine narrowed her eyes. "Helena may not have expected your ability to see her, but she knows good and well what she's gotten you into. There's something she's not telling you, and you can bet if it involves Helena Henry, it's not going to be pretty."

Maryse woke up the next morning in the Mudbug Hotel with a headache to beat the band. It had been late by the time she had finished explaining the entire Helena disaster to Sabine, and even longer before Sabine had managed to absorb it all. Once her friend had been able to breathe normally again, she'd given Maryse tons of good advice both for Helena and how to get rid of Helena. It was around midnight when they'd left Johnny's, and the late hour coupled with the fact that Helena might be at her cabin waiting had sent Maryse straight to the hotel for the night.

Maryse pulled on her clothes, trying to figure out how to leave the hotel without running into Mildred again. Exhausted as she'd been, she hadn't gotten to bed without sharing the saga of her wild day—well, everything except Helena. That was a bit too wild even for Mildred. And right now she didn't really feel up for any more lectures or discussion.

Her hopes were dashed when she found Mildred in the lobby instead of her office. The hotel owner was standing in the front lobby peering between the front window blinds. Her gray hair pointed in fifty different directions, and her long red nails made a sharp contrast with the bright white blinds.

"What's so interesting?" Maryse asked, and Mildred jumped, then cast a guilty look back.

"Nothing."

"You were concentrating pretty hard on nothing." Maryse stepped over to the window and lifted a slat to look outside. Downtown wasn't exactly bustling yet; it was still too early, but it was easy to see what had caught Mildred's attention. Luc LeJeune was bending over the newspaper machine outside of the café, and the hotel offered the perfect rear shot angle.

Maryse looked back at Mildred. "You really ought to take another look. He's bending over now."

"Really?" Mildred yanked the cord on the blinds, and they flipped open, allowing both of them a full view of the street. The hotel owner looked across the street just as Luc stood and turned, allowing her a full front view. She clutched one hand over her heart. "Lord have mercy. That has got to be the best-looking man I have ever seen in person."

Maryse held in a sigh. Like she needed any more reminders of just how attractive Luc was. "Mildred, I'm surprised at you."

Mildred turned to stare at her. "Are you kidding me? Only a woman with no pulse or the taste for women could look at that man and not wish to be younger, hotter, and in *really* good shape." She looked back out the window as Luc walked toward the café door. "The things I could do with that."

Now Maryse did sigh. She didn't want to think about doing things to "that" and damned sure couldn't afford to think about Luc doing things to her.

Mildred turned from the window and stared at Maryse with a critical eye. "It's official then—you died two years ago when that stupid Hank left, and you've been a walking corpse ever since." Mildred shook her head. "I know you've got a lot going on. Hell, you babbled for an hour after you staggered in here at midnight high on pain killers. The will, the money, your missing husband. Things are really weird, and I get that, but Maryse, when a woman fails to appreciate a man like that, well, she might as well hang up her bra."

"It's not that I failed to notice him. It's more like I already know him, and his type, so the new has worn off the butt-looking festival."

Mildred's eyebrows rose. "You know him?"

Maryse shrugged. "Yeah. He's a zoologist for the state, and he's set up shop in my office. Apparently we're going to be sharing space for a while."

Mildred reached into her shirt pocket, pulled out her inhaler, and took a quick puff. "You're sharing an office with Adonis? No wonder you're exhausted."

"It's not like that. It's work, and he's a total playboy and sorta annoying. Besides, I'm still married, remember?"

"Hmmpf. Some marriage. I'm thinking God would probably give you a pass on finding someone else since He hasn't bothered to produce Hank in the past two years. Maybe since you never manage to leave the bayou, God just brought a man to you."

Maryse rubbed her temple, thinking this conversation was way worse than the one she'd originally been trying to avoid and the biggest reason she preferred not to leave the bayou. "I'm sure that's it, Mildred. God sent me a man. Anyway, I really need to get going. I've got a ton of work to do today, so if I could just get some coffee and some aspirin, I can get on my way."

"The aspirin are in the cabinet, same as usual, but my coffeepot broke yesterday, and I haven't had time to get a new one." Mildred paused for a second, then smiled. "Hey, I've got an idea. We could step across the street to the café and have coffee and a muffin. I haven't had more than a ten-minute phone call from you in months. You can grace me with a half hour of your presence."

Bullshit. Maryse knew good and well why Mildred wanted to have breakfast at the café, and it had nothing to do with Maryse's less-than-stellar visitation record. Not that Maryse could really remember the last time she'd spent any quality time with Mildred, but that wasn't the point. Even though Mildred was trying to be sneaky and deceitful and conniving, Maryse couldn't say no to the woman who had dated her dad for over twenty years and practically raised her.

Maybe Luc would be so engrossed in his newspaper and his breakfast that she could slip in and out without a huge production. "Fine," Maryse said finally. "But we have to make it fast. I really do have a ton of stuff to do today."

Mildred practically ran to her office to grab her purse and some aspirin for Maryse, then rushed them both out the door. They had barely stepped inside the café when Maryse heard Luc call her name. So much for slipping in and out.

Mildred paused for a millisecond, but when it was clear that Maryse wasn't going to move, the hotel owner turned and headed straight toward the smiling zoologist. She stopped at Luc's table, Maryse in tow like a petulant teenager. "You must be Luc, the new zoologist," Mildred said. "I'm Mildred, and I own the hotel across the street. Maryse has been telling me all about you."

Maryse felt a flush run up her neck, and she fought the desperate urge to flee from the café as if on fire. Luc looked over at her and smiled. "All about me, huh? I didn't think you'd noticed."

Maryse waved a hand in dismissal and tried to sound nonchalant. "She's exaggerating. I barely know anything to tell, much less all."

Mildred slid into the chair next to Luc and motioned for Maryse to sit across from them. "Well," Mildred said, "we've got some time. You can tell us all about yourself over breakfast." Mildred waved at the waitress for coffee, then turned back to Luc. "So, are you married?"

Maryse downed the aspirin with a huge gulp of water and willed herself to disappear.

"No," Luc said.

"Girlfriend?" Mildred pressed.

"Not even close." Luc grinned.

Mildred narrowed her eyes at him. "You're not gay, are you?"

"Hell, no!"

"Thank God," Mildred said under her breath, but Maryse was certain Luc heard every word by the way his lips quivered with a smile. Maryse searched her mind for a way to stop the freight train of humiliation when Mildred rose from the table. "I just remembered I need to finish the books from last night," the hotel owner said.

Maryse stared. "You close the books every night at nine."

Mildred waved a hand in dismissal but didn't meet Maryse's eyes. "I went to bed early last night. There was a special on Lifetime I wanted to catch." She gave Luc a broad smile. "It was a pleasure meeting you. I'm sure Maryse will enjoy working with you." Then before Maryse could say a word in protest, Mildred spun around faster than a large woman ought to be able to and hustled out of the café, the door banging shut behind her.

Maryse counted to five, then looked over at Luc. "I'm really sorry about that. Mildred is...well...Mildred."

"I like her, although her subtlety could use a little work."

Maryse sighed. "That was subtle."

Luc laughed. "So I guess the Lifetime story doesn't hold?"

"Not even close. Unless it's forensics, cop shows, or a hockey game, you won't catch Mildred anywhere near a television. She likes her entertainment a bit violent."

Luc shook his head. "Wow. With friends like that..."

Maryse reached for the cup of coffee as the waitress slid it across the table and dumped a ton of sugar in it. "She's more than a friend. Mildred dated my dad after my mom died. She pretty much raised me."

"How old were you when she died?"

"Four."

Luc gave her a sympathetic look. "That's tough."

Maryse shrugged and stirred her coffee. "I had Dad and Mildred, so it was okay."

"Yeah, but it's not the same. My dad died when I was eight. I had tons of uncles and my grandfather, and my mom was super, but there's always that feeling that it's incomplete."

Maryse stopped stirring and looked at Luc. "Incomplete. That's the perfect word."

"Yeah, well." Luc shrugged and picked up his knife and the butter.

Maryse watched him as he buttered his toast, his eyes not meeting hers. It wasn't fair. No man should be this sexy and be in touch with his emotions. And no man should be able to touch her heart in the way he just had.

"So do your dad and Mildred still date?" Luc asked.

"No," Maryse said, her voice catching in her throat. "He died of cancer a little over two years ago."

Luc stared at her for a moment. "I'm sorry. I can't imagine burying both parents so young."

"I really should be going," Maryse said, and rose from the table. "I've got a ton of things to catch up on this morning."

Luc looked up at her and nodded. "I won't be in the office till later. I've got to run some errands in the city."

Maryse felt a momentary surge of disappointment but quickly squelched it. "Okay, then. Guess I'll see you later." She turned and walked out of the café, cursing Mildred for engineering her exposure to yet another facet of Luc LeJeune. Like she needed to find anything else about him attractive.

She shook her head as she crossed the street, mentally tabulating her list for the day. All she had to do was check on her truck, talk to the insurance company, meet Wheeler about the inheritance, get in eight hours of work for the state, avoid a ghost, locate a plant that she had absolutely no idea where to find, and figure out a way to wash Luc LeJeune from her mind.

Piece of cake.

Luc stood in the dealership garage in New Orleans, staring at the heap of mess that used to be Maryse's truck. He knew what he was about to hear from the Service Manager—had been thinking about it pretty much since the accident, but for the life of him couldn't make the facts add up. Someone had tried to hurt Maryse and used her truck to do it, but he didn't know why.

He was still having trouble believing Maryse could be his informant. It just didn't fit what he knew about her, although some of her actions were a bit suspect. But if it wasn't the chemical company trying to shut her up, then who was? If that ridiculous will reading had been before the accident, he'd say someone was out for the inheritance. Most likely Harold or Hank.

So his next guess was it had something to do with what she was working on in that lab of hers. All he had to do was get the proper tools, find a window of opportunity to break into the lab without being discovered, steal that notebook, make copies, and find someone to decipher it before things got any worse.

Piece of cake.

"You occupy space here much longer," a voice broke into Luc's thoughts, "I'll get you a set of coveralls and put you to work."

Luc looked over at his high school buddy, Jim, the Service Manager, as he walked across the garage to stand beside him. "Damn shame," Jim said and pointed to Maryse's vehicle. "The truck's got high miles, but the lady that owned it has taken care of it nice. It was in great shape before that crash."

Luc nodded. "You checked into the scheduled maintenance?"

"Yeah, pulled it off the computer first thing. Lady had that truck in here just a week ago for regular maintenance and everything checked out fine. I talked to the tech that worked on it, personally, and he said everything was in top shape."

"So why did a well-maintained, reasonably new vehicle lose its brakes?"

Jim pulled his hat off with one hand and rubbed his temple with the other. "You ain't gonna like the answer."

Luc looked at him, the inevitability of his friend's words already weighing heavy in his mind. "Someone cut the lines."

Jim nodded. "Yep. Almost clean through. They left enough so that the brakes would work for a couple of miles, then they would go to nothing almost immediately."

"So they fixed it so she'd think everything was working fine and hopefully build up enough speed before noticing anything was wrong, which is exactly what happened." He gave the truck one more look, then nodded to his friend. "Thanks, Jim. And if you don't mind, can we keep this between us for now? And remember, I'm a zoologist. No one can know what I'm really up to."

"Hell, I don't know what you're really up to, but I get what you're saying." Jim looked at the truck again and scratched his head. "What do you want me to tell the insurance company—or the lady?"

"Make something up that they'll both buy." He clapped his friend on the shoulder. "Something that doesn't have anything to do with attempted homicide."

Jim swallowed and looked at Luc, his expression grave. "You're gonna protect her, right? I don't really know her, but every time she's been in, she's always been so nice and friendly. This is a nasty piece of business, and I just can't imagine something a girl like that would be mixed up in that could get her killed."

Luc gave the truck one more look and shook his head. "She may not know herself."

Chapter Seven

Maryse made a mad run to her cabin, hoping to get in and out before anyone could discover her—namely Helena. She'd showered and changed the Band-Aids on her scrapes the night before at the hotel, so all she really needed was a fresh set of clothes. But her hopes were dashed as soon as she opened the door. A very irritated Helena Henry sat on her couch, staring at the wall in front of her.

"Where the hell were you last night?" Helena started bitching before she could even get the door closed. "I had to crawl through an open window to get in here, and the damned thing closed after me. I've been stuck in here all night with no way to get out. Do you have any idea how boring it is when you can't read a book or turn on the television? I spent hours reading the labels on cleaning supplies that happened to be turned in the right direction."

Maryse's head began to pound, and she walked into the kitchen to get a glass of water and one of Dr. Christopher's little pills. Mildred's aspirin weren't going to do the trick at all.

Helena rose from the couch and trotted after her. "And why in the world does your kitchen look like the cabinets spit up their contents?" She waved one arm over the counters, cluttered with utensils, pantry items, and cleaners. "Your housekeeping is an atrocity."

Maryse tossed one of the pills in her mouth and took a huge gulp of water, wishing she had the nerve and the time to take two of them and just go to sleep right where she stood. "We don't all have the luxury of ten thousand square feet of space to store our stuff, Helena, and I'm not even going to get into the cost of hiring a maid. It so happens that I'm installing some extra shelves in the cabinets and building a pantry in the corner, which is why all my stuff is on the counters. If I'd have realized I was going to have uninvited guests, I would have worked quicker. I'm sorry to offend your delicate sensibilities with my less-than-stellar housekeeping."

"Hmmpf. Got a mouth on you this morning, don't you? Who pissed in your corn flakes?"

Maryse stared at her. "*You. You* pissed in my corn flakes. You almost got me arrested yesterday, Helena, and Lord only knows what Harold's plotting to do to me now that I inherited the land."

Helena waved a hand in dismissal. "You weren't even close to being arrested. And Harold's too big of a pansy to do anything to you. He's all talk and no action—believe me, I ought to know." Helena looked over the contents of the counters again. "Shelves, huh? Well, at least that explains the power tools on the counter. I was really starting to wonder what you ate in here. Still, place like this out in the middle of nowhere, you ought to at least leave a radio or the television or something turned on when you're gone."

Maryse considered Helena's night dilemma and smiled. After all, Helena had bored everyone to tears for years in Mudbug running her yap. It seemed only fair that she be the one bored for a change. "It may surprise you to know, Helena, that I'm an adult and sometimes I don't sleep at home. Since I have nothing of value to steal, my cat spends his nights prowling the bayou, and the mosquitoes aren't as picky about their entertainment as you, I really see no reason to leave appliances running while I'm gone."

Helena glared but didn't bother to ask where Maryse had spent the night. "Well, since you've decided to show up today, we need to have a talk. Things might be a bit worse than I originally thought, and I need you to check up on something for me at the library."

Maryse shook her head. "I don't have time for any of your shenanigans today. I'm two days behind at my job, I have a meeting with Wheeler this morning to discuss the 'rules' that come with this land inheritance, and I have a whole list of personal things to take care of on top of everything else." Maryse walked into her bedroom and yanked some clean clothes out of the closet, Helena trailing behind her.

"You know how to use a computer, right?" Helena asked. "One of those women down at the beauty salon said you can find the answers to anything on the Internet. I figured we could find out about all this ghost stuff. You know, I'd really be a lot more help if I could touch things."

"God forbid," Maryse said and pulled on a clean T-shirt and jeans. "You've been too much help already. What I need is for you to ascend or rise or whatever and let me deal with the fallout by myself."

"But this is important," Helena griped. "You can think up new names for stinkweed some other time."

Maryse grabbed her keys and left the cabin, Helena close behind. "Sorry, Helena," she said as she walked to the dock and stepped into her boat. "I know my job may seem like nothing to you, but it's important to me, and I'd like to keep it. Besides, since naming stinkweed is what has paid your son's debts all these years, you don't really have any room to complain."

Helena stepped into the boat before Maryse could shove away from the pier and plopped down on the bench up front. "Fine, I'll just wait until this evening."

Maryse shook her head, wondering where in the world she was going to hide this evening. It had just become a top priority.

At the dock, Helena took one look at the rental car and looked back at Maryse. "What's with the car?"

Maryse opened the car door and started to get in, but Helena rushed in before her, crawling over the center console like a child. Maryse stared at the big pink butt glaring at her from the center of the car and sighed. Not a sight you ever wanted to see in life, much less this early in the morning and with a head injury.

There was a moment of concern, when Maryse thought Helena wasn't actually going to make it all the way to the other side, but finally the ghost twisted around and plopped into the passenger seat. Maryse slid into the driver's seat and tore out of the parking lot.

"Did you sell your truck?" Helena asked.

"No. I didn't sell my truck. I had a wreck yesterday."

Helena sat upright and turned in her seat to stare at Maryse. "What happened?"

Maryse shrugged. "I don't know. The brakes just failed for some reason, and I took a dip in the bayou. The truck's probably totaled."

Helena's eyes grew wider and looked Maryse up and down. "Are you all right?"

"I'm fine. Just banged up a little and pissed off that I'll have to buy a new vehicle when the other one was still in great shape." She studied Helena for a moment. "Why this concern all of a sudden?"

Helena sat back in her seat. "Have you read the instructions for the land inheritance yet?"

Maryse stared at Helena as if she'd lost her mind. "Are you kidding me? I just got it yesterday. Do you really think even if I had absolutely nothing else to do at all that I would rush home, break open a bottle of bubbly, and read the Encyclopedia Inherita? Jeez, Helena, I appreciate you leaving me the land and all, more than you'll ever know, but it's not the only thing I have going on."

Helena pursed her lips and stared silently at the dashboard. "I know you've had a lot thrown at you here lately, and you're not going to want to hear this, but I think it's really important that you understand all the rules. It's been so long since I've gone over them, but I keep thinking there's something I ought to remember."

"And that's why I'm on my way to meet with Wheeler. He should know everything about your inheritance, right?"

Helena shook her head, deep in thought. "Maybe. I hope so."

Maryse pulled in front of the café and parked the car. "Well, he better, because I bet that book is longer than the Bible and just as hard to interpret. I'm not trying to slack off on my responsibilities, Helena. I want to make sure I maintain control of the preserve, but there's no way I can finish something like that and even hope to understand it without some serious time and probably a translator."

Helena sighed. "You're probably right. That document is as old as the land and so is the language it was written in."

"Finally, we agree," Maryse said and hopped out of the car. "I'll get the basics from Wheeler and fill in the blanks as time and brainpower allow." She pushed the car door shut and walked a good five steps down the sidewalk when she heard Helena yelling.

"Damn it, Maryse," the ghost shouted from inside the car. "You know I can't open the door. I could suffocate in here."

Maryse walked back to the car and opened the passenger door to allow the angry specter out. She wasn't even in the mood to argue the suffocation comment and that whole "you're already dead" thing. She shook her head as Helena climbed out of the car. "You have got to learn how to walk through walls, Helena. I am not going to squire a ghost around town. Do you have any idea how weird this would look if someone was watching?"

"About as weird as you talking to a car door," Helena shot back, then huffed up the sidewalk to stand next to the café door.

Maryse steeled herself for her appointment, now complete with a ghost, and let them both into the café.

Wheeler was already there, perched in a booth in the corner and looking as out of place as a Coors Light distributor at a Southern Baptist convention. Maryse crossed the café, signaling to the waitress for a cup of coffee, and took a seat across from Wheeler, intentionally sitting too close to the edge to allow Helena to sit next to her. Helena glared, then took a seat next to Wheeler, who shivered for a moment, then looked across the café.

"Must be a draft in here," Wheeler said.

"Probably," Maryse agreed as the waitress slid a cup of steaming coffee in front of her for the second time that day. "I'm not trying to rush you or anything, Mr. Wheeler, and I really appreciate you coming all the way down here to talk to me, but if you don't mind, could we go ahead and get started? I have a very busy day and not enough daylight to get everything done."

Wheeler nodded. "Absolutely. This shouldn't take too much time. The basics for the land ownership are very straightforward."

"Really? Then why the enormous book?"

"The book is as old as dirt and written in circles. Plus, there are a lot of rules that simply don't apply anymore. Things to do with rice farming and possible exceptions for owning herds of cattle. Things you would never consider in the first place."

"Okay. Then give me the skinny."

Wheeler looked at her for a moment, probably not having a clue what "the skinny" was exactly, but finally decided she must mean the rules. "Well, the first item is one I covered briefly yesterday—you can't leave Mudbug for a period of one week, starting yesterday. If you take even a step outside the city limits and anyone has proof, the land will revert to the secondary heir."

"And who is that?"

"Hank. There is really no other option."

Maryse nodded, not really surprised. "And why this rule at all? I have to tell you, Wheeler, it sounds kinda weird."

Wheeler cleared his throat. "I agree that it probably sounds a little strange in this day and age, but back when the rules were written, health care wasn't what it is today and the country was at war. If a son inherited the land and was called off to war before he could decide on an heir and draw up the paperwork, his death might leave the estate in limbo indefinitely. And the state wasn't exactly diligent in ensuring the proper family maintained their estates. A lot of property was simply stolen by the state or passed on to political supporters."

"I see. So the one-week period is supposed to give me time to select an heir and have the paperwork drawn up so that the land can't hang in limbo with the state deciding how to settle it."

"Exactly. Selecting an heir is one of the first things I need you to address. Since you don't have children, you're not limited by the trust in any way as to who you chose, except that it has to be an individual and not a corporation." Wheeler paused for a moment. "You know, now that I think about it, you're the first person outside of the bloodline to inherit the land. Amazing it was held that way for so long."

"That is rather odd," Maryse agreed. "Why hasn't anyone sold it before now? Surely there have been offers, and I'm willing to bet that in a hundred years someone needed the money, even if Helena didn't."

"The land is held by the trust, not really the individual. The person who inherits gets limited control of the land and is the beneficiary of any income received off the land."

"And the trust doesn't allow for the sale of the land." Maryse felt the light bulb come on. "So then why would it matter who inherited at all?"

"Well, the original trust documents were prepared long before anyone considered the possibility that companies and individuals might enter into long-term leases, essentially giving the same benefits to the lessee as buying. Helena felt you wouldn't entertain those sort of offers, so she selected you."

"Lucky me," Maryse said, and smiled. "So you need me to select an heir, and it can be anyone I want, unless I have kids at some point and then things have to change. Is that the gist of it?"

"That's correct. If you have no objection, I'll be happy to draw up that paperwork for you as soon as you give me a name."

Maryse pulled a pen from her pocket and proceeded to write Sabine's name on a napkin. She pushed the napkin across the table to Wheeler. "I know it's not very official, but I figure you just need the name, right?"

Wheeler folded the napkin and placed it in his suit pocket. "That will do. I'll draw the papers up and make sure to get them signed and filed before the end of the one-week period. From that point forward, if anything were to happen to you, the land will be safe and secure in the hands you've selected."

Maryse straightened in her seat and stared at Wheeler. "From that point forward?" She narrowed her eyes. "So God forbid, something happens to me in the next week, what happens to the land?"

"It passes to the next heir—Hank."

"That's it," Helena shouted and jumped up from her booth. "That's the part I couldn't remember that I thought was important."

Maryse stared at Wheeler in dismay. "You're telling me I have to outlive Helena by a week or the land goes to Hank, no questions asked?"

Wheeler nodded.

"Unbelievable. And it never occurred to anyone that this rule might leave the first to inherit with a much shorter life span than originally intended?"

Wheeler shook his head. "I don't think they were thinking in those terms. It was simply a different world back then. And while I understand your concern, I really don't think you have a lot to worry about. Certainly, it's possible the land could be worth a good bit of money to developers at some point, but that's not the case at the moment. The state is the only interested party as things stand right now. Ten, twenty years down the road, things could change, especially if New Orleans continues to push its boundaries, but what you're suggesting is an awfully big risk for a payoff that might not even happen in a person's lifetime."

"But you said the land was Helena's most valuable asset."

Wheeler nodded. "Sentimentally, it was, and as I said, long-term the land will probably be worth more than any of us can imagine."

"I guess you're right," Maryse said, but one look at the pensive Helena, and Maryse wondered if there was something that Wheeler didn't know. Something that Maryse didn't want to know. "Is there anything else?"

Wheeler pulled some documents from a folder on the table. "I need some signatures for the paperwork for the state to ensure they make the check out to you rather than Helena, and there's a couple other documents needing signature…mostly just legal posturing, but required nonetheless."

Maryse pulled the stack of paperwork over toward her and spent the next fifteen minutes signing her name as Wheeler pointed out the correct spots. Finally, she passed the last document back to

Wheeler, who placed them all neatly back in his folder. "Well," Maryse said, "if that's everything, I guess I'll be on my way."

Wheeler nodded and rose from the booth. As Maryse rose, he extended his hand. "Thank you for meeting me this morning, Ms. Robicheaux. I'll call as soon as I have those papers ready for your signature. I can meet you here again if that's convenient."

"That's fine," Maryse said, and shook Wheeler's hand. "Just let me know." She turned from the booth and left the cafe, Helena trailing behind her. Maryse loitered a bit on the sidewalk, waiting for Wheeler to leave. She needed to talk to Helena and wasn't about to give the ghost a ride again. Hanging out with Helena all day simply wasn't on her list of things to do. Finally, Wheeler made it to his ancient Cadillac and pulled away.

Maryse glanced inside the café to make sure no one was looking and turned her back to the huge picture glass. "Okay, Helena, spill it," she said. "You've got this pained look on your face, and I have the bad feeling that you're about to say something else I'm not going to like."

Helena lowered her eyes and shuffled her feet. "I'm just concerned about the one-week clause. That's all."

Maryse stared at her. "Why? You heard Wheeler. It'd be too risky for Hank or Harold to try anything when the land isn't really worth much right now."

Helena bit her lower lip and raised her head to Maryse. "You remember that envelope I had you look for in my safe? The one that was missing?"

Maryse nodded. "How could I forget?"

"Well, it had some documents from a survey of the land."

Maryse closed her eyes in frustration. "So what did it say, Helena? Where are you going with this?"

Helena clenched her hands together and stared at Maryse. "It might have said that the preserve was full of oil."

"What!" Maryse cried, then glanced around making sure no one had seen her yelling into empty space. "Oil? Exactly how much oil might that letter have said was in the preserve?"

"It might have said there was billions of dollars worth..."

Maryse stared at Helena, horrified. "Billions, as in I don't even know how many zeros, billions?" Maryse felt a flush rise to her face. "Jesus Christ, Helena! You heard Harold threaten me at Wheeler's office. He probably took that letter before the will reading. He expected Hank to inherit the land. That's why he's so mad."

"Now, let's not get excited."

"Excited? Are you crazy? You've made me a moving target. One without a lot of places to hide given that I can't leave Mudbug. Do you really think Harold wouldn't take a shot at me over billions of dollars? He may be lazy, but he's not that lazy."

Helena took in a deep breath, and Maryse could tell that despite her protests, Helena was worried. Great. Just great.

"It's only six days counting today," Helena said. "We can come up with a plan."

"What kind of plan? Maybe locking me in a Kevlar box for a week? Even the bayou has a limited number of hiding places."

Helena shook her head. "I don't want you camping in the bayou. In fact, if you could not go into the bayou at all for a while that would probably be better. As long as you're surrounded by people, it will be much harder to get to you. And you do have a secret weapon."

Maryse narrowed her eyes. "What secret weapon?"

Helena pointed to herself. "Me. Think about it, Maryse. I can look out for you without anyone suspecting. I can warn you if anything is out of the ordinary."

Maryse stared at her. "Yeah, because everything else that's happened this week has been normal. You're not a weapon, Helena. You're the angel of death, and I don't want you anywhere near me. You've done quite enough."

Maryse jumped into her rental and tore out of the parking lot before Helena could fling herself on the trunk or anything else ridiculous the ghost may come up with. Six days. Unbelievable. Not quite a week, and it seemed ages. Suddenly, still being married to Hank seemed like such a simple problem.

She turned onto the gravel road and headed toward the office. She had to get her head on straight. Had to come up with a plan. Maybe she'd just have a heart attack right here and now and save Harold the trouble. A second later, she slammed on the brakes and brought the car to a stop in the middle of the road. The thought that had hit her was so horrible, so awful that she couldn't even breathe.

If Harold killed her, she might be stuck in limbo like Helena. Even worse, she might be stuck in limbo with Helena.

For all eternity.

Six days was looking shorter by the minute.

Luc eased the thin tool into the deadbolt on the door to Maryse's lab. Since he'd hacked her e-mail and found out about her appointment with Helena's attorney, he knew she would be late coming in. Unfortunately, the guy bringing him the tools got stuck in a traffic jam in downtown New Orleans, so he was getting started a good hour later than he'd planned.

He leaned in close to the door, listening for the tell-tale click that would let him know he was successful. It took a couple more seconds before he felt the tool give and heard the barely audible sound of the locking mechanism turning. He slipped the tool in his pocket to use inside on the locked drawer where the notebook was stashed, and grabbed a second tiny rod from the black carrying case that housed his breaking and entering tools. He'd need that one to relock the drawer and the door once he was done.

He closed the case and crossed the room to slip it inside his gym bag. If Maryse came back sooner than expected, the last thing he needed was for her to see the tool set and start asking questions. It wouldn't take a genius to figure out what the thin blades were for, and Maryse was no dummy. The case secure, he slipped into the lab and worked his magic on the drawer. A minute later, he pulled the notebook from inside and headed out of the lab and straight for the office copy machine.

He flipped page after page, copying as fast as the antiquated machine allowed. The front office window gave him a clear view of the road and the dock, which was good since he was never quite sure what mode of transportation Maryse might use. Either way, he should see her in enough time to get everything back to where it belonged. He hoped.

Ten more pages or so, he thought as he turned the notebook over and over again and prayed that the copier would hold out. He was only a couple of pages from the end when the copier whined to a stop. What now? He studied the copier display screen and groaned. The thing was jammed, and if that display was any indication, it was jammed all over.

He put the notebook on the table behind him and opened the feeder tray. As he pulled a sheet of paper lodged halfway in the feeder, he looked out the window. Shit, shit, shit! There was no mistaking the red rental car turning the corner. And it was coming fast.

Chapter Eight

Luc grabbed the notebook and ran into the lab. He shut the notebook in the drawer, then poked his tool in the lock, hoping it worked its magic. The lock clicked almost immediately and he rushed to the door, repeating the process on the deadbolt. He hurried over to the copier and pulled the documents off the tray and shoved them into his gym bag.

His pulse racing, he glanced out the window just as Maryse pulled to a stop in front of the office. Yanking open the panels of the copier, he prayed that he got the paper removed before she could offer to help. If any of the jammed pieces were partially copied, he was busted, pure and simple. There was no logical way to explain what he was doing with her personal property—or how he had broken into her lab to get it.

He flipped open drawers and panels and yanked the lodged paper from inside, cramming it into his pockets as he went. He was down to the last tray when he heard the office door open. He glanced into the tray at the offending paper and held in a stream of cursing. The paper was jammed in the rollers, crinkled like a Japanese fan, but if you flattened out the folded rows, Maryse's handwriting still showed on the document clear as day.

"Problems?" Maryse asked as she tossed her keys onto her desk.

Luc rose from the copier and shook his head. "Nothing out of the ordinary for a machine this old. Just a paper jam."

Maryse nodded. "It does that all the time. Let me take a look. I've gotten to be a real pro at fixing that piece of junk."

Luc waved one hand, desperate to fend her off. "No, that's all right. I'll get it."

Maryse stared at him a moment. "What's your problem, LeJeune? Would my fixing the copier somehow be an affront to your manhood?" She walked over to the machine and gave him a shove. "Move out of the way. I don't want to listen to you banging and cussing over here for the next thirty minutes. There's a trick to getting paper out of this spot."

Luc clenched his fists in a panic, searching for something, anything that would stop her from reaching into that panel, but he came up with absolutely nothing. His only hope was that she wouldn't take a close look at the paper while removing it and he could somehow get it away from her immediately following removal.

Maryse squatted down in front of the copier and looked at the offending paper. "You got it jammed in good. Usually you've got to unscrew this top piece to get the paper out, but after I went through that process for about the hundredth time, I got smart and installed a pin to hold it in place. See?" She pointed to a long, thin, metal pin slotted through the panel and into the roller.

Luc glanced at the pin and nodded, certain he hadn't taken a breath since she'd walked in the door.

"So all I have to do is pull the pin out," Maryse said and proceeded to remove the pin while holding her hand under the top panel. "And, voila, the tray drops and the paper is easily removed." She gently worked the paper out from between the roller and the panel and held it up in front of him, the tell-tale text facing her direction and just below eye level.

All he could think about was keeping her from looking at that paper, and the only way he knew to throw someone like Maryse off track was to give her something bigger to focus on. Before he could change his mind he yanked the sheet of paper from her hand, ignoring the surprised look on her face, and stepped so close to her that he could feel the heat coming off her body.

"Mechanically inclined women really turn me on," he said and leaned in to kiss her before she knew it was coming and could formulate a retreat.

As his lips touched hers, a spark hit him deep in his center, and the panic he felt began to subside. When she didn't pull away, he kept his mouth on hers, gently parting her lips for his tongue to enter. He involuntarily pressed into her, his arousal firm against her leg.

The instant other parts of him made contact, Maryse jumped back and stared at him, her face full of surprise and confusion. "What the hell is wrong with you, LeJeune? Are you bucking for a hostile work environment complaint?"

She stared at him, obviously waiting for an answer, but he couldn't come up with a single excuse that would fly. "I'm sorry," he finally said. "I just got carried away."

She gave him a wary look as she backed away and grabbed her keys from the desk. "Well, don't let it happen again." Without so much as a backward glance, she walked out of the office, slamming the door behind her.

Luc watched as she jumped in her boat and tore down the bayou. As the boat rounded a bend and disappeared, he slumped back against the wall next to the copier. What the hell had he been thinking? Maryse's threat was very real—behavior like that could get him a legal complaint and completely blow his cover.

He looked down at the piece of paper, still clenched in his hand. At least he'd gotten the paper without her seeing it, and that had been the whole point, right? But as he shoved the papers in a file and headed out of the office to take them to a scientist in New Orleans, he couldn't help but think he'd gotten way more than he bargained for.

Maryse pushed down the throttle on her boat and grimaced every time the bow beat against the choppy surface of the bayou. At the rate the boat was moving, she could probably have run faster, even with her injuries.

And running is just what you're doing.

That thought brought her up short, and she eased up on the gas and gritted her teeth as the boat bounced to a slower, less-jarring crawl. She'd gone to the office with the intention of actually getting some work done. Then Luc had pulled his playboy routine, and she'd panicked like a schoolgirl.

Jesus, you'd think she'd never been kissed. She was a married woman, for Christ's sake. Well, not really married, but married enough that she shouldn't have been so disturbed by a kiss.

But she was. And that really, really stuck in her craw.

Professional ladies' men like Luc LeJeune had no business putting the moves on women like her, especially when she wasn't exactly in her best fighting shape. She cut the gas on the boat and coasted to a stop. Sinking down on her driver's seat, she looked out over the bayou and took a deep breath, trying to clear her mind of the fog of Luc's kiss, but her evil brain brought it all back to her in amazing Technicolor.

Luc's lips, masculine and soft all at the same time, pressed against her own. All she could think of was how those lips would feel other places. When he'd slipped his tongue in her mouth, she'd almost melted on the spot. She couldn't allow herself thoughts about that tongue going other places. There were just some lines you didn't cross because you knew there was no returning afterward.

Her skin was still hot from his touch, so she stripped down to her sports bra, hoping the bayou breeze would cool her overstimulated skin. It was unnerving to be as old as she was and have this much loss of self-control. Even Hank hadn't stirred her up this way, and he'd been a pretty good playboy himself.

Luc LeJeune had all the makings of trouble. More trouble than Hank. More trouble than she needed in this lifetime and certainly more trouble than she needed right now.

Before she could change her mind, she yanked her cell phone from her pocket and pulled out the small slip of paper tucked inside the case. She pressed in the numbers and waited while the phone rang over and over, finally rolling to voice mail.

"Christopher, this is Maryse Robicheaux," she said when she heard the beep. "If you're still interested, I'd love to take you up on that offer for dinner. Just give me a call."

She flipped the phone shut, shoved it in her pocket, and eased her boat up the bayou. She was going to put Luc LeJeune out of her mind, even if she had to throw herself at another man to accomplish it.

Maryse docked her boat at her cabin early that evening in somewhat of a mild panic. Her workday had gone well for the state—she'd finally found that elusive Lady Slipper hybrid they were looking for, but she hadn't located the plant she needed for her trials. She'd just about been ready to try yet another area of the bayou when Christopher had returned her call. Not only did he want to take her to dinner, but he wanted to take her to dinner that night. At Beau Chené, a first-class restaurant just on the edge of Mudbug.

As she yanked open her closet doors, she tried not to think that this was the second time in less than a week that she probably didn't have anything nice to wear. After all, Christopher had already seen her one and only cocktail dress when she'd gone to the emergency room.

She pushed the clothes from one side to another, frowning the entire time. There had to be something that would work. Anything. She paused for a moment, and her brow crinkled in unpleasant memory. There was an outfit that Sabine had made her buy one year for a Christmas party. It was clingy and sparkly and she'd hated it at the time, but if she could find it, it would work perfectly for Beau Chené.

After going through every inch of her closet and each drawer of her dresser, it looked as though a hurricane had blown right through her tiny bedroom. She plopped onto her bed with a sigh. The tiny crunch of plastic when she flounced her entire body weight on her mattress brought her mind into focus, and she reached beneath the bed to tug out a plastic storage container.

She pulled off the lid and heaved a sigh of relief as the offensive garment, complete with way-too-high and incredibly uncomfortable heels, lay resting inside.

Her problem of something to wear was solved. Her problem of something to say was still in the hopper.

Twenty minutes later, she stepped out of the shower and saw Helena perched on her toilet. Maryse bit back a scream and quickly wrapped a towel around her chest as she shook the water from her hair. "Damn it, Helena, I know you can't knock, but you could at least yell or something. One of these days, you're going to give me a heart attack. Then where would that leave us?"

Helena glared, the showgirl makeup still as thick and dark as it was the day she was buried. In fact, everything about her was exactly as it was in the casket. Bummer. If Helena found out who gave the funeral home that outfit and figured out how to move things, someone was in a boatload of trouble. Maryse almost felt sorry for them.

Then she took another look at the putrid pink polyester. Well, maybe not sorry.

Helena huffed. "You're one to talk about leaving us in a bad situation. Based on the way you took off today, I figure you don't give a damn anyway, so why should I?"

"Because it would be a pleasant change?" Maryse started to brush out her damp hair. "You know, you caring about something besides yourself? Who knows, you might have centuries to figure it out." Maryse gave her a fake smile, fully expecting Helena to fly off the handle—or in this case, off the toilet—but Helena only looked at her with a sad expression on her face.

"I do care about other people…or did care…or hell, I don't know how to explain it now that I'm dead. It feels like I still care, but I don't know if that's possible. Is my soul still here?"

Maryse studied her for a moment, not sure how to answer, but Helena looked so troubled she couldn't stand holding out on her any longer. It was time to let the ghost in on her paranormal connection. "I told Sabine about you."

Helena stared at her in obvious confusion. "That nut at the psychic place?"

"She's not a nut...well, not exactly...She's just not like other people."

Helena raised her eyebrows.

"Okay. So she's a bit of a nut, but no one I know can tell you more about the paranormal, and that includes ghosts. You ought to be thankful I'm checking on things for you. And you shouldn't judge those who want to help."

Helena looked surprised. "She wants to help?"

"Sure, she wants to help." Wants *to help me get rid of you, anyway.* "Got all weepy when I told her about the situation." *Or maybe that was the six glasses of wine.* "Anyway, she thinks that you still have your soul and that's why you're still here. You can't transcend, or whatever, until your soul is put to rest. In your case, she feels that's by figuring out who murdered you."

Helena considered this for a moment, then nodded. "Kind of what we already figured except for the soul part, right? Hey, she didn't mention anything about how I would be able to touch things, did she?"

"As a matter of fact, she did. I asked specifically since it's a hell of a lot more useful for you to be able to move things than me. I'm not pulling a repeat of that stunt at your house."

"And what did she say?" Helena asked eagerly. "How do I do it?"

Maryse shook her head. "Sabine doesn't really know how to tell you to do it. She's never actually been dead or talked to a ghost. But her best guess was you had to will it to happen and assume it would. You couldn't go into it thinking it wouldn't work."

Helena frowned. "Will it to happen? That's it? If it was that damned easy, don't you think I'd have already done it?"

"You're doing it right now. You're sitting on my toilet. Why didn't you fall through if you couldn't come into contact with solids? And last time I checked, regular people did *not* walk on water."

Helena stared down at the toilet and scrunched her brow. "Why, I never thought of that. So it's a matter of faith, then?"

Maryse shrugged. "Guess so. You just have to figure out a way to think of touching things as naturally as you do sitting or walking on them."

Helena sighed. "Faith…that's a low blow. I was the most cynical person on the face of the Earth." She gave Maryse a small smile. "Guess I still am."

Maryse shook her head and picked up her blow dryer, directing the hot air toward her short waves. "Well, you're going to have to find a way to believe, because I'm not breaking and entering again, no matter how long you have to wander around here."

Helena waved one hand in dismissal. "Yeah, yeah, Miss Goodie Two-Shoes, so I'll practice tomorrow. Tonight, I have important business to discuss with you."

"Tonight, I have a date with Dr. Christopher Warren." She plunked the dryer down and pointed a finger at Helena. "And you will not interfere." Maryse walked into the bedroom and began to dress.

"But it's important," Helena whined, and flopped onto the bed, jettisoning throw pillows onto the floor when her weight connected with the springy mattress. Maryse glanced at the pillows and shook her head. Helena was never going to get it.

"Look," Maryse said as she wriggled into the tight, short black skirt, "I don't doubt in the least that what you have to say is important, to you anyway. And I know there are things we need to do, but the problem is I'm still trying to have a life. And while it may not seem like a great one to you, it's the only one I've got. I'd like to get some enjoyment out of it, if that's even possible."

Helena started to respond, but Maryse held up a hand to stop her. "Which means two things: One, I have to take care of my job, and it is a full-time venture. Two, I will not cancel a date with the most eligible bachelor in town."

"Bachelor is right. That cad's already dated half the women in New Orleans and probably bedded the other half without the prospect of dinner."

Maryse gave Helena a withering stare. "Oh, but your son was the pinnacle of honesty and ethics. Give me a break."

Helena frowned. "No. Hank was as useless as his father. I tried really hard with him but some things just can't be changed. Guess Harold's DNA won out."

"That's funny," Maryse said as she slipped the sparkly, low-cut blue top over her head and adjusted her bra. "I always got the impression you thought Hank was wonderful. If not, why did you defend him all those years? Why pay his bills every time he got in trouble? And most of all—why in the world did you make me pay you back for Hank's debts if you already knew how worthless he was? It's not like they were my fault." She walked over to her dresser and picked up a black eyeliner pencil.

Helena put her chin up in defiance. "I needed to test you."

Maryse dropped the mascara in the makeup tray and stared at her in disbelief. "Test me? What in the world for? To see how much I could take before I drowned myself in the bayou? Or were you itching for death then and thought I'd eventually strangle you?" The thought had crossed her mind more than once.

Helena shook her head and said in all seriousness, "I needed to test your character so I could decide what to do with the land. I couldn't just mess that up, you know."

Maryse turned from the dresser and frowned. "Okay, Helena, I can get that you had a big decision to make and not a lot of choices given your son's proclivity for uselessness, but you made my life miserable for two years. My life to some extent is on hold unless Hank shows up and does the right thing. You have to know that land or no land, I'm not happy to be in this position, and I'm certainly not happy to have you hanging around as a spirit. You were easier to avoid when you were alive."

Helena started to respond, but the phone rang. Maryse glanced at the display with a groan and flipped open the phone.

"Is anything wrong, Maryse?" Christopher asked. "You were supposed to be at the dock ten minutes ago."

Darn Helena. Now she was late for her date with the hottest catch in town. "I'm running a bit behind is all," Maryse said, not even going to answer the very loaded question about what was wrong. "I'll be there in two minutes." She flipped the phone shut, finished her makeup, grabbed her purse, and rushed out of the cabin, Helena in tow.

"You can't go out with him tonight," Helena begged. "There are too many important things we need to discuss and he's really, really wrong for you. I know."

"You don't even know him." Maryse tossed her bow line in her boat and eased down inside, one hand clutching her stilettos. "And like you're an expert at picking men. I'm not doing this tonight, Helena." She started the boat and threw the accelerator down as far as it would go. Giant sheets of water rose behind the boat and showered the land a good ten feet behind the dock, including the piece Helena stood on. Maryse looked back, hoping to see her doused, but the water passed completely through her and she stood perfectly still, staring forlornly at the boat.

Maryse prayed that whatever problem Helena had now wasn't worth skipping her date. Given her week, there was a lot to be said for anything remotely normal. Not that dating doctors was exactly the norm for Maryse, or dating at all for that matter, but damn if she wasn't going to give it a whirl.

At the dock, Maryse took one look at Christopher Warren and decided right then and there that she had made the right decision. He was definitely hot. His black slacks and black silk shirt were designer quality, and he wore them well, the clothes doing nothing to disguise a tight butt and perfectly toned chest and arms. His light brown hair glistened with natural blonde highlights and his pale green eyes focused on her as she made her way up from the dock.

Focus on your future. She paused for a moment to consider what smart children they would have and smiled. Christopher smiled back and leaned in to kiss her on the cheek. Maryse couldn't even think about enjoying it because at that moment she caught a movement out of the corner of her eye. Helena was walking across the bayou straight toward them, a determined look on her face.

Holy hell. Maryse took Christopher's hand and tugged him toward his shiny new Lexus. "We don't want to be late," she said in response to the somewhat puzzled look on his face. "And I don't want my hair to frizz in this humidity."

"Sure." He chuckled in understanding, vanity apparently a very good excuse for rudely rushing people. He opened the car door, and Maryse jumped inside, slamming the door before he could even reach the handle. He stared at her for a moment but finally turned and headed back to his side of the car and climbed inside.

He took his time getting the car started, then burned at least a minute inspecting his hair in the rearview mirror. Maryse kept a wary eye on Helena's approach the entire time. If he didn't get them the heck out of there, this was going to get ugly. Helena might not be able to open the car door, but she wouldn't hesitate to plop herself right on the hood.

"I'm starving," Maryse said, trying to hurry him along. "What time is our reservation?"

Christopher took the hint and put the car in gear, pulling slowly out of the parking lot just as Helena stepped onto the dock. Maryse half expected her to break into a run as they pulled away, but she guessed even ghosts had their limits. Or maybe it was too hard to run in pointy-toe heels and a polyester suit. Either way, Maryse held in a sigh of relief as she saw Helena fading in the mirror.

"We don't exactly have a reservation," Christopher said, "but I called in a favor. They'll fit us in whenever we arrive."

Maryse's eyes widened. "Really?" The restaurant was usually booked weeks in advance. "That must have been some favor." She sank back into the soft leather seat with a smile. Beau Chené was the stuff dinner date dreams were made of. It was fabulously exclusive, ridiculously expensive, and had more class than the entire state of Louisiana. The fact that it rested just inside the Mudbug city limits was a mystery within itself, but who was she to complain?

The only other time she'd graced that establishment was a dinner with Hank, Helena, and Harold. Not exactly a pleasurable evening for such an impressive place. But this time was different. This time she was dining with an attractive, intelligent doctor. She was going to have a good time, even if it killed her.

She caught Christopher looking over at her and gave him a sexy smile. This was going to be a night to remember.

A night to remember turned out to be a gross understatement. The look on Maryse's face when Helena walked into Beau Chené and took a seat at their table was probably one Christopher would never forget. In any event, it was bad enough to cause him to jump up from his chair and rush to her side, as she grabbed her glass of ridiculously expensive champagne and tossed the entire contents back in one gulp.

"You're white as a sheet," Christopher said and placed one hand on her forehead. "What's wrong? You look like you've seen a ghost."

Helena hooted, and Maryse choked on the last bit of champagne, spraying it across the table. She was afraid Christopher was about to start the Heimlich maneuver so she waved one hand to ward him off. Taking a deep breath, she tried to calm down, but with Helena laughing like a hyena, it was damn near impossible. Finally, she gained control of her breathing, although her blood pressure was questionable, and apologized profusely to Christopher for alarming him.

"I don't know what came over me," she said, trying to come up with a believable excuse fast. "I've had a pretty stressful week, and I guess it just all caught up to me in one moment."

Christopher nodded and took his seat again, gently caressing her hand. "Probably an anxiety attack. I heard a little around town about your mother-in-law and the situation with your ex, or sorta ex. That along with your wreck would be enough to send anyone in a spiral, but this sort of problem rarely continues once the issues causing them are settled. In a week or so, you ought to be back to normal."

"Gee," Helena said, "I could have made that diagnosis."

Before she could stop herself, Maryse frowned. Christopher noticed her expression and squeezed her hand, trying to reassure her. "I promise it will go away," he said. "There's nothing really wrong. At least nothing a great dinner won't help. If you're still up to it, that is." He removed his hand from hers and began to pour more champagne in her glass.

"Please," Helena said, and smirked. "This guy couldn't cure a cold sore. What the hell does he know about anxiety? Besides, hooking up with an asshole like this is enough to cause high blood pressure."

"That's enough," Maryse said, and shot Helena a dirty look.

Christopher stared at her, a confused expression on his face, but stopped pouring the champagne at half a glass. Great. Not only had Helena ruined a great dinner, Maryse wasn't even going to be able to drink enough to forget her misery.

"Would you like to order an appetizer?" Christopher asked and placed the half-empty champagne glass in front of her. "I hear the rum-soaked shrimp are delicious."

Before she could answer, Helena jumped in. "Ha! He's just trying to get you into bed and thinks now is a great time because you're vulnerable. Look how desperate he is to get alcohol into you—first the champagne, now the shrimp. What a louse."

Maryse finally reached the boiling point and she knew she was about to lose it. Helena's return from the dead, her wreck, that awful will reading, breaking and entering, Sabine's warning about Helena, and her unwanted and unprecedented attraction to Luc LeJeune swam violently in her mind like angry piranha. "Did you ever stop to think that someone might like me for some other reason than sex?"

The diners at the tables surrounding them grew silent, and it occurred to Maryse that not only had she not whispered as she'd originally intended, but speaking out loud to a ghost that no one else could see did not bode well for her date that everyone could see. Christopher stared at her in shock, his face beginning to flush.

"For the record," he said, keeping his voice low and controlled, "I wasn't thinking of sleeping with you at all. I mean, I thought about it, but that's not what this dinner is about." He shook his head and looked closely at her. "Maybe we ought to head home. You're obviously not feeling up to this yet."

Maryse clenched her hands and held in tears of embarrassment and anger, afraid to even look at Helena lest she do something even more foolish, like try to stab her to death with the butter knife or choke her with the two hundred-dollar champagne she'd barely gotten a taste of. "Maybe that's a good idea," Maryse agreed, since the only other alternative was dinner with Helena—something she obviously couldn't manage with any decorum or taste.

Feeling guilty, Maryse reached across the table to place one hand on Christopher's arm. "I'm really sorry about this, and I swear, I didn't think your intentions were anything but honorable. I just don't know what's come over me."

"That's all right," he said, giving her a curt nod, and Maryse knew he was miffed. "We'll call this one a night and try again some other time when you're feeling more up to it."

Meekly agreeing, Maryse plucked her purse off the chair, rose from her seat, and attempted to follow Christopher out of the restaurant without making eye contact with any of the curious patrons. Aside from marrying Hank, this had to be the single most mortifying moment of her life.

As she jumped into the car, hoping to erase the night from her memory and start all over, Helena walked through the car door and sat in the back seat. "Cool, huh?" the ghost said. "I figured out that walking-through-walls thing when I got to the restaurant."

Great. Just fucking great.

Maryse looked out the car window and watched Christopher tip the valet. "You had to follow me to the car, too?" she hissed. "Haven't you caused me enough trouble already?"

"Oh, please," Helena said, and gave Christopher a disgusted look. "I was only trying to stop you from making the biggest mistake of your life."

"The biggest mistake of my life was marrying your son."

Helena stared at her for a moment, then shrugged. "Okay, then the second biggest mistake of your life."

Maryse turned around in her seat and glared at Helena. "And why in the world would taking up with a good-looking, successful doctor be a mistake? Can you tell me that? I've known Christopher since we were kids, and all I ever wanted was a healthy relationship with a man. I got cheated the first time around."

Helena snorted. "Healthy relationship? You're barking up the wrong tree, honey. You might have known him as a kid, but one of you has changed. And it's not you. First of all, that doctor does not have 'relationships.' He has conquests. How do you think I knew where you were eating? I used to eat here several times a week, and your perfect doctor was always here with a different woman."

"I don't believe you," Maryse said. "Besides, what's wrong with dating other women? He didn't come back to Mudbug until a week or so ago. I could hardly ask for anything exclusive before we even reconnected."

Helena rolled her eyes. "You weren't interested in anything exclusive. You just wanted to get laid. You're not even wearing underwear."

Maryse felt her blood boil. "I never wear underwear!" she shouted, at the exact same moment Christopher opened the car door.

Maryse whipped around in her seat, trying not to groan. She could feel Christopher staring at her, but he didn't move. Finally, he sank into the driver's seat and started the car. As he pulled out of the parking lot, he leaned over and whispered, "Good to know."

Maryse just nodded and tried to smile, although she was certain it came out more like a grimace. She turned slightly and glanced at the backseat, hoping at least for the opportunity to give Helena the finger behind the headrest, but the backseat was empty.

What should have been the perfect date with the perfect man was ruined. Even worse, instead of fantasizing about her night with Christopher, the only thing she could think of was Luc LeJeune's kiss. It was all his fault she'd gotten into this mess to begin with. Maryse sank back in her seat with a sigh, feeling sexually frustrated for the first time in, well, forever.

And there wasn't a single battery-operated device in her nightstand to handle the job.

Chapter Nine

Unless Helena learned to fly, Maryse figured it would take her at least an hour to get to Maryse's cabin. Relieved to be rid of the ghost and frustrated that her date with an eligible doctor had ended with her thinking of Luc LeJeune, Maryse reached for the tequila bottle and poured herself a shot. She gritted her teeth as the bitter liquid burned her throat. She was a lousy drinker. A cold beer was one thing, hard liquor was another.

She poured another shot but couldn't get it past her lips. Disgusted with herself, Helena, and her night, she walked into the kitchen and began to make a peanut butter sandwich.

She didn't even care whether Christopher called her again. Which was good, because despite the intriguing underwear comment, he probably wasn't interested in being embarrassed in a fancy restaurant again anytime in this life. She took a bite of the sandwich and pulled a beer from the refrigerator.

She went back into the living room and plopped down on the couch, trying to ignore the fact that the reason Dr. Christopher held no appeal to her was because Luc LeJeune held entirely too much. Damn that man! Why did he have to go and kiss her? She was doing a fine job of pretending she didn't find him sexy as hell, and then he crossed that line. And once you crossed that line, there was no going back. Oh, she could pretend it didn't affect her, but she wasn't going to fool anyone—especially not Luc.

And all of this thrown at her when she really, really needed to be concentrating on finding that plant for the trials. Whatever Blooming Flower had brewed up for Maryse's dad had been working. The cancer was moving toward remission, and he hadn't experienced a single side effect—something that could rarely be said for the radiation treatment he'd refused. Then Blooming Flower had died without revealing her secret. The secret Maryse was still searching for. She took a long swallow of beer and flipped the remote to some boring talk show.

It was over an hour before Helena showed up. Maryse was about to go to bed when the ghost popped into the living room, walking straight through the wall and the television. For a moment, Maryse thought she was having a hallucination that someone had stepped out of the television set, but then her vision cleared a bit, and the pink polyester seemed to glow in the dim living room light.

"What took you so long?" she asked. "Couldn't catch a ride?"

"You know good and well no normal person's coming out into a swamp in the middle of the night."

Maryse glanced up at the clock on the wall. "It's only eleven. Hardly the middle of the night."

"When you're my age, eight o'clock is the middle of the night."

Maryse shook her head. Something else in life to look forward to. "Look, Helena, I'm a little drunk, and I'm tired. I'm in no mood to deal with you, especially after that stunt you pulled tonight. I know you might find this hard to believe, but I don't want to live alone on the bayou with only a cat for company the rest of my life. I'm an introvert, not a hermit. Snagging a doctor isn't exactly the worst way to go, regardless of whether you think I could have landed him or not."

"Hmm. You live like a hermit. When's the last time you got out of the bayou for anything…dinner, a movie, a night on the town? Maybe if you spent some time in the general population, you could meet a nice man. Something the doctor is not. He uses women."

Maryse waved one hand in the air. "I am not going to discuss this with you. It's simply none of your business. You never liked me anyway, so let me take my chances. What the hell difference does it make to you if I end up a two-time loser?"

Helena studied her for a moment, seeming to contemplate her next words. Finally, she sighed and said, "I never said I didn't like you. And besides, none of that matters now. We have bigger fish to fry, and I can't have a decent conversation with you if you're in such a snit."

"Well, then you're out of luck tonight." Maryse rose from the couch. "I'm going to bed. Are you staying?"

Helena sat on the couch and glared at the television remote. "Don't have much choice do I, if I want to talk to you. As long as I'm stuck here, will you at least change the channel?"

Maryse considered refusing for a moment. Hell, she considered turning the whole damned thing off and making Helena sit in the dark, but she just didn't have the energy to listen to the griping. "You know, you could have saved us both the hassle and stayed at the hotel. I'm sure there are at least twenty televisions on there with all kinds of things to watch."

Helena gave her a horrified look. "Oh, no—I already tried that one. Do you have any idea what those salesmen turn on when they are away from their wives? I can't believe Mildred allows that crap in her hotel. Good God, the things I've seen."

Some of the things Helena had seen were probably the same things Maryse could have been doing herself if her mother-in-law hadn't cheated her of the opportunity. But she thought it wise not to point that out. "Fine. What do you want to watch?"

"I heard down at the beauty shop that channel six is doing an all-night marathon of real hauntings," Helena replied, looking animated for the first time that evening. "That will be interesting. Maybe I could learn how to move things."

Oh goody. "Yeah, sure, and if things don't work out here with that little business concerning your soul, at least you'll know where to find friends."

Maryse awakened the next morning to the ringing of her telephone. She groaned and covered her pounding head with her pillow, trying to block out the shrill sound.

"Aren't you going to answer that?" Helena asked.

"No," Maryse replied without even looking out from under the pillow. "Go away."

"Sounds like someone needs coffee."

The phone finally stopped, and the answering machine kicked on. "Ms. Robicheaux," a polite voice began, "this is Mrs. Baker down at the insurance company. I just wanted to let you know that we finished processing the claim on your truck, and unfortunately, it is totaled. We'll be preparing two checks, one for the last payment due on your loan and the other for the balance due to you. If you don't receive that within ten days, please contact me at the office and let me know. Thanks and have a nice day."

Maryse pulled the pillow back and looked at the answering machine. Last payment? What the hell were they talking about? She owed another two years on that truck. Knowing she couldn't sleep until she sorted things out, she pushed herself off the bed and grabbed the phone off the nightstand to call her bank, happy to see that Helena had at least vacated the room.

When the branch manager picked up, Maryse explained what had happened and that she needed to verify the amount needed to pay off the loan on her truck.

"I hope you weren't injured in your accident, Ms. Robicheaux."

"I'll be fine. Just a little bumped around."

"Well, that's good to hear. Just one more second...ah, yes, you owe just a tad bit more than one payment on your truck. I can print the exact amount and fax it to you if you'd like."

Maryse rubbed her forehead, not sure she could stand all the confusion without at least taking an aspirin or fifty. "How can that be? I have two more years left on that loan."

"We've been splitting those extra checks every month and applying the money to your house and truck payments." The manager sounded confused. "Those were your instructions. I hope we didn't misunderstand."

"What extra checks?"

"Are you sure you're all right, Ms. Robicheaux?"

"I'm fine," Maryse replied, beginning to get a little irritated. "I'm just having trouble remembering everything. The doc says it will all come back in time."

"Okay," the manager said, but didn't sound completely convinced. "The first cashier's check was received in this office almost two years ago with instructions to apply it to your house. When you bought the truck, we received instructions to change application to half of the check on each of the loans. We've been doing that every month since."

"You've been receiving cashier's checks every month for almost two years?" A sneaky suspicion began forming in Maryse's mind—one she didn't understand in the least and wasn't even sure she wanted to. "Exactly how much are these cashier's checks for?"

"Five hundred twenty-five dollars. Are you sure you're all right, Ms. Robicheaux? This conversation is really starting to concern me."

"I have a doctor's appointment today," she managed to mumble. "Thanks." She hung up the phone and stared out the window over the bayou. She'd never sent the bank checks for five hundred twenty-five dollars, but she'd paid someone else that exact same amount every month for almost two years. "Helena!"

She stalked into the living room, but the ghost was nowhere in sight. It didn't take long to check every nook and cranny of a one-bedroom cabin, so it was only minutes before Maryse was certain the ghost had fled. And she'd bet it was during that phone call.

Maryse smelled a two-year-old rat. And she'd bet her truck payoff check that rat's name was Helena Henry.

Luc made it into the office a little early, but not for any reason except he just hadn't slept well. God knows, he wasn't attempting another break-in of Maryse's lab unless he did so in the dead of night. And given the woman's strange behavior, probably even that wasn't safe. Besides, he'd delivered the notebook to his buddy back at the agency. If anyone could get to the bottom of what Maryse was up to, it would be Brian.

He flipped his cell phone open just in case he'd missed a call but was once again disappointed by the blank display. Frustrated, he sat back in the chair and propped his feet on the desk. What the hell was he supposed to do now? Maryse was certainly easy on the eyes, so following her had been no hardship but had definitely been a study in bizarre. Still, it hadn't gotten him anywhere. From where he sat, the only thing Maryse was mixed up in was something to do with her in-laws and her missing husband, and he was no closer to finding the informant than he had been the first day here. If only the DEQ would let him branch out a bit and investigate some of the other residents, but his orders were clear—he was a zoologist and was to do nothing to make people think otherwise.

He rose from the desk and headed to the coffeepot on a corner table. At least making coffee was doing something productive. He dished the grounds up and was just about to fill the pot with water when his cell phone rang.

He reached into his pocket and, recognizing the agency's main number, he pressed the Talk button. "LeJeune."

"Luc, it's Brian. I got that information on the notebook."

Luc felt his hand tighten on the coffee pot handle. "And?"

"It was definitely chemical formulas—you were right about that."

"Okay, but for what?"

There was a slight pause on the other end. "We don't know exactly."

"Damn," Luc muttered. "Well, what *do* you know?"

"She's mixing up different plants, it looks like. Each combination is clearly identified by species and anything other than plants used to make the sample. They're all labeled with trial numbers, the way a big lab would do things."

"Okay, so she's trying to create something. Do we have any idea what?"

"Hell, it could be anything...weight-loss pills, hair products, a cure for insomnia...there's just no way of knowing unless we can see what she's testing this stuff on. You said there's no animals or anything like that in her lab, right? No refrigerators with little dishes with some of the mixture in it?"

Luc cast his mind back to his lab tour. "No, nothing like that. It's a tiny room. All that's there really is a couple of tables with the test tubes, burners, that sort of thing. I didn't see any evidence of testing on anything."

"Well, she's testing somewhere. All that effort is not for nothing. Have you gotten the trace on her phones yet? Maybe that will give you an idea where to head next, although I got to tell you, Luc, it doesn't look like this has anything to do with our case, and if the boss-man finds out, he's probably going to pull the plug on you."

"There's something going on with her," Luc argued. "Someone intentionally cut the brake lines on her truck."

"Unless it has something to do with our case, it's not your problem. Don't get involved, LeJeune. It always turns out bad."

Luc flipped his phone shut without answering. *Don't get involved.* Like it was that easy. He didn't understand his attraction to Maryse at all. Sure he'd dated plenty of women, but never for any reason other than a good time for a short time. Maryse pulled at him in a different way, and that made him very uncomfortable.

Usually women just hit him below the belt, and that was an easy fix, but Maryse challenged him on an intellectual level, and not just with his investigation. She was a complex woman, something he usually avoided like the plague. But for the first time in his life, he found himself wanting to figure her out rather than run for the hills.

No matter his discomfort, he wasn't about to leave her unprotected if someone was trying to hurt her. She may not be part of his case, but that didn't mean she shouldn't have some help.

He finished filling the coffeepot with water and turned it on. Glancing at his watch, he realized Maryse should be at the office any minute, assuming she wasn't off on one of her many mysterious adventures. He turned on the computer and bypassed Maryse's sign-on screen using a hacker tip he'd picked up from Brian the day before. As soon as the operating system loaded, he double-clicked the internet icon and logged into his e-mail. Surely the phone trace was back by now—at least the last couple of days' worth.

He scanned the e-mail files, sorting through the usual spam that not even the government could manage to screen…improve sexual performance, new stock alert, penis enlargement…ah ha, phone tap results. He glanced out the window as he printed the file, happy to see the road was still clear of Maryse's rental.

This is it? One page for two phones? No matter how busy Maryse appeared, apparently it didn't involve much in the way of phone calling. He scanned the list, looking for something that stood out—the state office, the attorney in New Orleans, her friend in Mudbug, her insurance company—and, wait a minute, a laboratory at a university in New Orleans.

Jackpot.

That lab must be running the tests on whatever it was Maryse was cooking up. Another glance out the window let him know he was still in the clear, so he opened his cell and punched in Brian's number. "Brian, it's LeJeune. I need you to hack something for me."

"Okay," Brian said, "what's the case file number?"

Luc hesitated. "This one is off the record. At least for the time being."

"Oh, man, not your botanist in distress again? Do you know how much hell I caught over that stripper in New Orleans?"

"She wasn't a stripper, she was a performer, and you helped get her daughter back from the molester ex-husband who'd made off with the kid. Surely that was worth an ass-chewing."

"I guess. But one of these days, LeJeune, you might want to think about settling down with one woman instead of rescuing every one you come in contact with. And if you want my help with your Sir Lancelot routine, you're going to have to come up with something besides doing a good deed to convince me to risk that ass-chewing again. After all, I'm not privy to the same perks you're getting out of these deals."

Luc sighed, not about to admit that he was yet to receive a single perk from Maryse Robicheaux. In fact, it was exactly the opposite. The woman seemed to frustrate him on all levels. Something he wasn't exactly used to. "How about two tickets to this week's game?"

"How are the seats?"

"The best—they're mine."

"Throw in the use of your Corvette for the night and it's a deal."

"Absolutely not." Even Luc didn't remove his black, 1963 split-window dream machine from the garage unless it was a special occasion. "You know I only drive the Corvette when it's important."

"And you haven't seen the woman I plan on asking to the game."

Luc clenched his jaw. "Fine, but if you get so much as a scratch on her, I'll kill you, and you know I know how."

"Sounds reasonable. What do you need?"

"I need you to get some information for me. There's a lab at Tulane University in New Orleans where Maryse is sending her stuff for testing. I need to know what she's testing and why."

"Jesus, LeJeune! Do you really think the university is just going to hand over that kind of information just because I ask nicely? Her tests are protected information, especially if she's working on something she can patent."

"So get a warrant."

"Based on what, exactly? Hell, you won't even tell me why you want the information or give me a case number to support it. How am I supposed to convince a judge to go along with this plan of yours?"

Luc frowned. "Don't you have a friend, a contact, someone who could get you a line on the information?"

Brian sighed. "I've got a buddy who works in the science department. He might be willing to ask around. But he's going to need some time to do it with any finesse or it will look suspicious. Then someone might tip off your botanist."

"Yeah, okay. If that's the best we can do."

"And I mean real time, LeJeune, not an hour or two. This could take days, maybe even a week."

Luc looked out the window as the Maryse's boat raced up to the dock. He reached over to shut down the computer. "Just do your best. Make it as fast as you can, but tell your friend not to draw any attention to himself. I can't afford exposure."

"No problem. I'll call when I've got something."

Luc flipped his phone shut and watched as Maryse docked. Even from a distance, Luc could see her mouth set in a straight line, her upper body tensed. What now?

She entered the office without even a glance over, then poured a cup of coffee and stood staring at the wall while she drank. Luc stared at her back, then dropped his gaze to her behind, nicely tucked in a pair of old, tight-fitting jeans. "Do I dare even ask?"

"What?" Maryse spun around and looked at him as if realizing for the first time that he was in the room. "Oh, sorry. Good morning."

Luc raised his eyebrows and stared. Okay, it was even worse than he thought. She was being polite. "Good morning. Is everything all right with you? You seem a little...distracted."

"I'm just a little pissed and more than a little confused." She refilled her coffee, then dropped into her office chair with a sigh. "My life used to be so simple, you know? I did my job, had my side interests, one friend, one surrogate mother...no drama, no issues."

"Except for Hank," Luc pointed out.

Maryse nodded. "That's a given."

"And now you have other issues?"

"Jeez, LeJeune, haven't you been paying attention the last couple of days? My mother-in-law is dead, and Hank has yet to show up so I can serve him. The worse part is that's the least of my worries at the moment."

Intrigued, Luc leaned forward in his chair. "So what's the worst?"

"The worst is wondering what the hell Helena Henry has been up to all these years. I mean, the woman was the Antichrist of

Mudbug. Even you had heard of her, and then she goes and leaves me the game preserve."

"Okay. But that's a good thing, right? I mean, if she'd have left it to Hank, he would have sold it off right away."

"Leased it," Maryse corrected. "The trust prevents an outright sale, but that's not the point." She picked up a pencil from the desk and started tapping it on the desktop.

Luc leaned back in his chair, giving her his full attention. "What else is there?"

Maryse looked over at him, her face full of uncertainty. "When Hank ran off, he owed money to a lot of the wrong kind of people. I had to borrow from Helena to pay them off." Then she told him about the payments she'd been making to Helena that had most likely been used to pay down her loans.

Luc sat back in his chair and stared at Maryse, now crystal clear on her confusion. "What the hell?"

Maryse shrugged. "I don't know. I mean, I have no frig-gin' idea. And it just makes me wonder how much manipulation has gone on behind my back. I get the feeling I was used, but I can't put my finger on how or for what purpose. There is no way Helena Henry paid that money on my loans to be nice. Helena doesn't know nice. Without an ulterior motive, she had no reason to get up in the morning."

"I agree. It sounds really strange, and given the source, I guess it would make me sort of nervous, too." He shook his head. "Too bad you didn't find out about the payments before the old bat died. You could have asked her yourself."

Maryse frowned and stared down at the floor. "Yeah, that is a shame."

Luc studied her for a moment. It was obvious from the way her eyes dropped to the floor that she was hiding something. But what? Given the weird situation she was in, it could be anything. In fact, Luc was surprised she'd even told him as much as she had. Obviously Maryse was in some mild level of shock if she was carrying on a personal conversation with him. Especially after that stunt he'd pulled yesterday, kissing her over the copy machine.

"I wish I had some advice," Luc finally said, "but I have to admit, I'm as stumped as you are. The whole thing is just too bizarre."

"Well, I'm not going to figure it out sitting around here." She gave Luc a small smile as she rose from her seat. "Thanks for listening. I know I haven't been the most pleasant person to be around, but I swear, I'm not usually this bad."

Luc shrugged. "You've got a lot going on, and I'm not the easiest person to be around, either."

Maryse laughed. "Yeah, you got that right. Anyway, I've got to get some work done today, whether my mind's in it or not." She pulled open a drawer in her desk and swore. "Crap, the map I need is at my cabin. I completely forgot I brought it home last week."

She pulled her sunglasses from her pocket. "Guess I'll be taking a detour before I work, huh? I'll see you later, LeJeune." She gave him a backwards wave and walked out of the office and down to the dock.

Luc watched as she threw the tie line into her boat and stepped down inside, pushing the boat from the dock as she went. What the hell was going on? Maryse was right—according to everything he'd ever heard, Helena Henry didn't do nice. And why charge her that outrageous interest, then pay her debts? Luc had no idea what Helena had been up to, but he had a feeling it wasn't much good. And he wondered just how much of a mess Helena's shenanigans had left Maryse in.

Something didn't feel right. And although he didn't like to talk about his feelings much, they were something Luc didn't ignore. He was much more intuitive than most—it's what made him so good at his job—and right now his senses were on high alert. Maryse Robicheaux was smack in the middle of something bad...he was certain.

And he was even more certain that she had no clue what it was.

He pulled his boat keys from his pocket and headed out of the office. If anything happened to Maryse, he'd feel guilty the rest of his life. She might not like him lurking around, but he saw no other way to figure out what was going on and offer her some protection. He'd just have to figure out a way to either watch her without being seen or come up with a reason for hanging around.

He had a five-minute boat ride to figure it all out.

Chapter Ten

All Maryse wanted to do was get the map and get into the bayou. With any luck, she'd be able to get some work done for the state and locate the plant she needed for the trials. But when she pulled her boat up to her cabin dock, Helena Henry was there, looking more upset than Maryse have ever thought possible.

"You can't go in there," Helena said, her face tense.

"Try to stop me. You still have some things to answer for, Helena, and don't think I forgot them just because you pulled a disappearing act this morning." Maryse stepped onto the dock and strode toward her cabin.

"No! Wait!" Helena hurried after her. "I think there's something wrong with your cabin."

Maryse stopped short. "What do you mean, something's wrong?"

"Your truck wreck got me to thinking. What if it wasn't an accident at all? So I've been watching your place as much as possible, figuring if the truck didn't work, then they might do something here. I made a quick trip to my house this morning after your phone call and hightailed it back here as soon as possible, but I was too late. I saw a man leaving as I walked across from the dock. He was carrying a duffle bag and got in a boat that was parked in that cove behind the cabin. Then he tore out of here something fierce."

"It was probably just kids. You know how teenagers traipse around the bayou."

Helena shook her head. "It wasn't a kid. This guy moved like an adult, his frame was mature—medium height and a ball cap."

Maryse stared at her. "Then who was it? C'mon, Helena, you know everyone in this town, same as me."

Helena shook her head again, the panic starting to show on her face. "I didn't see his face. And I couldn't catch up to the boat in time to read a license tag or anything. But he was up to no good. I know it. Why else would he dock in that cove and wade through the marsh to get up here when there's a perfectly good pier out front?"

Maryse glanced over at her cabin and bit her lower lip. Unfortunately, Helena was right—it didn't sound good. Suddenly, entering her cabin for a map didn't appear as easy as she'd originally thought. She looked once more at the cabin, then back at Helena. "So why don't you pop through a wall and take a look?"

Helena gave her a withering stare. "Don't you think I've already done that? I still can't move things. If he hid something in a cabinet or a drawer, I'd never see it. Not like I know what I'm looking for in the first place."

A sudden thought struck Maryse and she felt a chill rush over her. "Jasper was in the cabin this morning."

"Who the hell's Jasper?"

"My cat. I can't let anything happen to him."

Helena stared at her. "You mean that ragtag old tomcat missing an ear? That's what you're worried about?"

"I rescued that ragtag old tomcat from a fight with an alligator, and yes, I'm worried about him. He's family, whether you get that or not."

Helena shrugged. "You have strange ideas about family, Maryse, but it doesn't matter either way. The cat took off out the kitchen window as soon as I walked into the cabin." She frowned and pursed her lips. "Maybe it's true what they say about cats seeing ghosts. He shot out of the room the first time I visited you, too."

As interesting as Helena's observation may have been some other time, Maryse just couldn't care about it at the moment. "You're sure he's not in there?"

"Positive," Helena said, and nodded. "He was halfway across the marsh when I looked out the window, but I'll pop in and take another look." She strolled up the path and through the wall of the cabin, then reappeared a couple of minutes later. "He's not there. I checked every nook and cranny."

"Okay. So what do you think I should do?"

"I don't know, but I don't want you going in that cabin. What if they left the gas on or something?"

Maryse considered her words and weighed her options. "You think he could have rigged something…like an explosion, maybe?" She ran one hand through her hair and tried to think. "Okay, if he rigged something to explode, then it would probably happen when I opened the front door, right? I mean, one look at my kitchen and anyone could see I don't cook, and besides, I had my gas turned off when I started construction on the cabinets."

Helena shook her head, clearly miserable. "I guess. I just don't know."

"Well, hell, that's the way it happens in the movies." She blew out a breath in frustration. "How should I know? We didn't exactly cover this sort of thing in college."

"Well, it wasn't covered in the society pages, either, so I don't know why you're getting all pissy with me. I'm trying to save your skinny ass from whatever that man cooked up."

Maryse clenched her jaw, not about to launch into why she was pissy with Helena. If not for Helena and her games, Maryse's skinny ass would be nice and safe. She took another look at the cabin. Mind made up, she drew her keys from her pocket and began walking toward the front door. Helena started to protest, but Maryse beat her to the punch. "I'm not going inside. I'm only going to unlock the door."

She crept up the path, feeling like a fool for sneaking up on her own home, and stopped at her front door, easing the key into the lock. It slid in silently, and she heard the barely audible click of chambers rolling inside the door as she turned the key to the left.

Then she backed away from the cabin as quickly as possible and stopped at the dock next to Helena.

"What now?" Helena asked.

Maryse jumped into her boat and lifted the back seat to get into the storage box. "The latch on the front door is so old it doesn't hold anymore. Unless it's locked, even a good wind will blow it open."

"No wind today. Figures."

"No matter." Maryse reached into the box and pulled out a shotgun and a box of shells.

"What the hell are you doing?"

"Rubber bullets," Maryse explained. "I have to have them for the job. Not supposed to kill the critters, you know. They won't tear anything up, but it will be more than enough punch to open that door." Maryse grabbed the tie line for her boat and pulled it along the edge of the bank until it rested behind an overhang. "Better stand back," Maryse said as she loaded the gun. "I know nothing can touch you, but this might be scary if you're right about that guy."

Helena hesitated for a millisecond, then hopped into the boat next to Maryse. They stood on one side and peered over the edge of the bank. Satisfied with their position, Maryse lifted the shotgun over the bank and aimed it at the front door.

"You ready?" she asked Helena.

Helena covered her ears with both hands and nodded.

"Here goes," Maryse said, and pulled the trigger.

The shot seemed to happen in slow motion, although it couldn't have taken more than a second for the bullet to hit the door. The instant they heard the smack of the rubber on the wood, the door flung open, giving them a clear view of the inside of the cabin. Maryse was certain neither of them moved, or breathed, or even blinked, but as the seconds passed, only dead silence remained.

Maryse was just about to give the entire thing up as Helena's overactive imagination when the cabin exploded.

Maryse ducked behind the ledge and flattened herself against the dirt wall as flat as possible. If she hadn't been so frightened, she might have been amused to see Helena crouched there next to her as pieces of glass and wood flew everywhere—some hitting Maryse on her hands which covered her head, and some landing in the bayou behind them.

It took only seconds for the rain of glass and wood to stop, but it felt like forever. When the last piece of debris plopped into the water, Maryse waited another five seconds, then peeked over the bank and sucked in a breath at what she saw.

The cabin was completely leveled. Not a single wall remained, and even the bathtub was nowhere to be seen. That had her wondering for a moment since it was an old cast iron tub and had to weigh a ridiculous amount. She stared in stunned silence at the degree of damage, unable to make out anything, not even a wall. Absolutely everything had been torn apart by the blast.

Maryse swallowed the lump in her throat and tried to hold back tears when she caught a glimpse of something shiny hanging from one of the cypress trees. She strained her eyes to make out the object and realized with a jolt that it was a picture frame. Even with the metal twisted and black, she knew exactly what picture had hung in that frame.

Suddenly, Maryse's sadness and loss shifted to anger. Two years worth of anger, all bubbling forth at this exact moment. She screamed at the top of her lungs and pounded the embankment with her fists. Helena stepped back in surprise and fell off the back of the boat and onto the bayou where she rested on top of the water, rising and falling with the waves.

"This is all your fault!" Maryse shouted at Helena. "Like producing that sorry excuse for a human being you call a son wasn't enough—you had to rise from the dead, visible only to me, the person who probably despises you most, and then have the nerve to make me a moving target by leaving me some piece of land I was much better off without!"

Helena stared at her a moment, then looked down at the bayou, not saying a word.

"Look at this," Maryse cried, and waved an arm over the embankment at the disaster that used to be her home. "I have nothing left because of you. Everything I owned was in that house. And don't even talk to me about insurance because I don't want to hear it. How is insurance going to replace my mom and dad's wedding photo? How is insurance going to replace the Dr. Seuss books my mom read to me when I was a baby?"

Maryse bit her lip, trying to hold back the tears of anger that threatened to fall. "The only memory I have of her is reading those books. You've taken everything from me and given me nothing but trouble in return. I never thought I could hate you more than I did when I was paying Hank's debts, but I was wrong." She stared at Helena, but the ghost wouldn't even meet her eyes.

Disgusted, she started her boat and pulled away from the embankment, leaving Helena sitting on top of the bayou. Maryse's life was ruined. She had nothing left, not even the photos of her parents. She felt as if they were being erased from existence, all proof of her and her world being swept away. And even worse, obviously someone wanted her swept away with her memories.

Unless you beat the odds.

The thought ran through her head with a jolt. All of her anger at Helena and the situation with the will, at Hank for running out on her, at her mom for dying too soon, and her dad for following behind her mother with his stubbornness, came together in one instant, and she felt a sudden clarity run through her. There was one way to fix this. One way to make everything right.

Stay alive and keep that damned land.

Her resolution made, she shoved the throttle down on her boat and it leapt out of the water. Whoever had tried to kill her had made a fatal mistake in not getting the job done the first time, because now she was mad.

A mad scientist.

Luc had just pulled away from the dock when the explosion burst into the sky. "What the hell!" He raced down the bayou toward

Maryse's cabin. *Stupid, stupid, stupid. You should have followed her more closely.*

He made the last turn and stared in shock. Her home was gone, completely leveled. It looked like something you saw in war footage. He scanned the patch of land for any sign of life, or a body, but couldn't make out a thing. As he zoomed closer to the bank, all hope disappeared. There was simply no way anyone could have survived that blast. No way.

He was reaching for his cell phone when Maryse's boat came around from the back side of the island. He held his breath as he stared at the driver and was relieved and surprised to see Maryse driving the boat. He cut his throttle and yelled at her and she guided her boat over to his. As she drew closer, he could see tiny cuts on her arms and a couple of nicks on her neck.

She came to a stop next to him and he reached over for her arm. "Are you all right? What happened?"

She looked at him, the anger on her face clear as day, but Luc knew that even though she was moving, driving a boat, she had to be in shock. He glanced over at the leveled cabin. No damn wonder. "Maryse," he said, and gently shook her, "are you all right? Are you hurt?"

Maryse blinked and seemed to recover a bit of herself. "What? No, I don't think so. I mean, I don't feel hurt." She gave him a frightened look. "Unless you see something I don't. I'm in shock, right? I might not feel anything."

Luc gave her a quick once-over. "I don't see anything life threatening, although you should definitely be checked out. What happened? Do you know?"

Maryse looked back at her cabin, her face flushed, her jaw tight. "It just exploded. I was pulling up to the dock and it exploded."

She was lying. Luc knew it, but whether it was about something important or something stupid, he could only imagine. "Did you see anyone near the island?"

Maryse shook her head, but Luc could tell she was holding back again.

"There wasn't anyone but me," she said.

Luc flipped open his cell phone and dialed the police. "The first thing we're going to do is call the police. They need to get someone to look at this. Then we're getting you to a hospital, just to be sure." He held his hand out to Maryse. "Why don't you step over into my boat? I can tow yours back to the office."

Maryse hesitated for a moment, but he was relieved when she took his hand with no argument and stepped over into his boat. She kept looking back at the island—not at the demolished cabin, but scanning the entire area. What in the world was she looking for? Had there been another person there?

Luc got Maryse seated, then secured her boat behind his with a tie line. He was just about to pull away when Maryse yelled.

"Jasper!" Maryse pointed to the island at something moving around a clump of cypress trees. She spun around and looked at Luc. "That's my cat, Jasper. I was afraid he was in the cabin. We have to go get him."

Luc looked over at the small speck of yellow and smiled. "Of course we do." He slowly turned the boat and crept towards the bank. "I'm going slow so I don't spook him," he said. "The poor thing is probably already stressed enough."

Maryse nodded. "Thanks."

It took them a minute to get to the bank, and before he could even assist, Maryse scrambled up the side and called the cat. Luc looked over the embankment in time to see the old tom wrap himself around Maryse's legs and allow her to pick him up. She smiled and kissed the top of his head, then headed back to the boat, passing Luc the cat so she could get in.

Luc reached for the cat, who didn't even protest at being in a stranger's arms. Then again, animals usually had an instinct about when people were trying to help them. He rubbed the cat behind his one ear and passed the animal to Maryse after she took her seat. "He's a little rough around the edges, huh?"

Maryse nodded. "Yeah. He's definitely a fighter. I think that's why I like him so much."

Luc smiled. "Well, let's get back to the office and drop Jasper off there. Then we can take a trip to the hospital. I want to make sure that head injury from your car wreck wasn't aggravated by being so close to the blast."

Maryse shrugged. "Whatever you think."

Luc looked over at her as he pulled away from the island. She clutched the cat to her chest and stared straight ahead. Her face was drawn, her neck stilled flushed with red. Luc had absolutely no idea what the hell had just happened, but he'd bet his last dollar that Maryse knew something. Something she wasn't about to tell.

And from where Luc stood, that something was going to get her killed.

It took them about forty-five minutes to dock, secure the cat, and make the drive to the hospital. Maryse called Sabine on the way—one, because she knew Sabine and Mildred were bound to hear about her cabin soon and she didn't want them panicking, and two, because she was going to need a place to stay and something to wear if she planned on showering again. She figured Mildred would give her a room at the hotel and Sabine would come up with something temporary for her clothes-wise.

After reassuring her friend that she was unhurt, Maryse flipped her cell phone shut and leaned her head back against the seat, closing her eyes. She was doing her best to hold everything in, but she was still so angry with Helena that she knew Luc was suspicious about what was going on. Like she could tell him even if she wanted to. *Hey, Luc, it's no big deal. I'm just being haunted by my dead mother-in-law who left me a bunch of land full of oil that now apparently people are trying to kill me for.* Yeah, that would work. That was believable.

She held in a sigh as they walked into the emergency room, hoping this was Christopher's day off. The last thing she needed was to be embarrassed on top of depressed and angry. There just wasn't room in her head for another emotion. The admitting nurse took one look at her and motioned her toward the double doors to the side of reception. Maryse asked Luc to wait in the lobby, then followed the nurse down the hall.

Either they weren't busy at all or Maryse looked much worse than she thought. But as they passed a couple of empty rooms, Maryse decided it was the first. Obviously she'd picked a great time to have an emergency. They had passed three empty rooms when the nurse's pager went off. She glanced down at the pager, then shook her head.

"The second room on the left," the nurse said, and pointed down the hall. "If you don't mind taking a seat in there, I'll send the doctor right in."

The nurse muttered something under her breath as she turned, and although it wasn't clear, Maryse could swear she'd said "as soon as I find him." How exactly did one lose a doctor in a hospital? Didn't they have pagers too? She glanced back at the nurse who strode down the hall with obvious purpose and shook her head.

Turning back around, Maryse studied the doors in front of her. Second room on the right or left? Hell, she couldn't remember. Maybe she *did* have a head injury. Oh well, what was the worst that could happen—she opened the wrong door and saw someone naked or something? God knows she'd seen worse, especially lately.

She took a couple of steps forward and pulled open the door on the right. It was immediately obvious that this was not the right room. In fact, it wasn't a room at all—it was a storage closet, but the most interesting thing was it was already occupied.

By Dr. Christopher and a candy-striper.

Christopher apparently had a bit of a sweet tooth, because he'd taken the "candy-striper" title to heart. His mouth was all over the girl, and if the volunteer coordinators saw what was going on under that uniform, Maryse was fairly sure they'd have had heart attacks right on the spot.

They jumped apart as the light flooded in, but it was too late. Maryse had already seen enough. "What the hell are you doing?" she yelled, and took a good look at the rumpled candy-striper, who was grabbing for the thin strip of lace wrapped around her ankle and trying to shove it back up her butt where it belonged. "That girl isn't even eighteen. Are you crazy?"

Christopher jumped up and ran over to her. "Now, Maryse, this isn't what it looks like. I was just helping Emily with her anatomy class, and she didn't want anyone to see. She's a bit shy about presentation."

Maryse stared at him in disbelief and disgust. Why in the world had she thought this guy was a great catch? "Do you think I'm that stupid?" she asked, and Christopher inched toward her, his hands out.

Maryse stepped back. "Don't step one foot closer to me. I'm warning you."

"But, Maryse, honey, I swear I can explain."

Honey? Honey! She glared at Christopher as he made the fatal error of touching her arm. To hell with it. She clenched her hand and punched him as hard as she could in the jaw, causing him to cry out in surprise. Staggering backwards in shock, he fell over a towel rack, knocking Emily, who was still trying to reassemble her clothing, down on the ground in a heap. The sound of material ripping seemed to echo in the tiny closet. Maryse looked down to see the lacy thong now hanging in two pieces around one of Emily's skinny white thighs.

The commotion brought the admitting nurse and two orderlies rushing down the hall where they all screeched to a halt and stared at the spectacle in front of them. "Dr. Warren," the admitting nurse said, her lips pursed in disapproval. "I thought Director Stone was very clear about this the last time. I'm afraid I have no choice but to report you. And I'd start packing my things if I were you." The nurse looked at the candy-striper and frowned. "And shame on you, Emily. When your mother hears what I have to say…" She shook her head in obvious disgust and stomped down the hall, apparently in search of the director.

"Now see what you've done?" Christopher accused, struggling to rise from the floor.

Maryse laughed. "What I've done? Have you lost your mind? I wasn't the one in a compromising position with a minor."

Christopher rose from the floor and glowered at Maryse, his face bright red with embarrassment and anger. Emily, now reasonably covered and clutching what was left of her almost nonexistent underwear, scurried past and fled down the hall, probably trying to figure out how to avoid going home until she was sixty.

"Like you weren't seeing other people," Christopher accused. "We've only had one date anyway, and it was horrible. Hardly grounds for a commitment."

"You think I want a commitment with you?" Maryse stared. "You *have* lost your mind. At least I don't date children. You need serious help, Christopher, and if I were that girl's dad, I'd shoot you." Maryse paused for a moment, a vision of the rumpled Emily flashing through her mind. Why was she familiar?

Then it hit her—a video replay of her meeting with one of Hank's "lenders," who had insisted on receiving payment during his daughter's soccer game. "Oh my God," Maryse said. "You've been fooling around with the underage daughter of the biggest loan shark in Mudbug." Maryse began to laugh. "That nurse was right—you better pack, and right away. If Lou Marcel catches you, there won't even be anything left for the nutria."

Christopher blinked and stared at her, wide-eyed. "Lou Marcel is Emily's father?"

Maryse nodded and gave him a big smile. The orderlies chuckled beside her.

"Oh shit!" The color drained from Christopher's face, and he glanced down both corridors. "I've got to get out of here." With that, he spun around and sprinted down the hall. At the end, he made a sharp turn and slid on the waxed floor of the hall until he had to place one hand down to maintain his balance. The orderlies dashed after him, either wanting to see more of the show or to ensure he didn't leave the hospital before the director got a hold of him.

Maryse stared after them, shaking her head. What the hell had she been thinking? For once, she should have listened to Helena, and that was just wrong on so many levels.

First Hank, then Dr. Deviant. What a track record.

Maryse heard laughter behind her and spun around, afraid she recognized that voice. She did. Helena Henry stood in the hall, her shoulders shaking. Her guffaws would have carried to the next state if anyone could have heard her besides Maryse. "Oh my God," Helena said as she tried to regain control of herself. "That was the funniest thing I've ever seen. I wish I would have caught it from the beginning."

Maryse glared. "I am not in the mood for you, Helena. I left you back at the cabin for a reason. Why did you follow me here?" Maryse stalked across the hall toward the lobby. She needed the correct room, and apparently a new doctor. "My blood pressure is going to be through the roof when they take it, no thanks to you. I'll end up hospitalized for sure."

Helena looked contrite as she struggled to keep up with Maryse's pace down the hall. "I know you're mad, and I can't say that I blame you, but I had to make sure you were all right. I checked at your office, but when I saw your boat docked and Luc's Jeep gone, I hoped he took you to the hospital."

Maryse stopped short and gave Helena a hard look. "We need to talk, and we will, but not right now. You have a lot to answer for."

Maryse pushed the door to the lobby open and stalked through. Luc jumped up from his chair, looking somewhat surprised. "What's wrong?" he asked.

"Bachelor number two," Helena said and hooted.

Maryse shot her a dirty look and mumbled, "Don't even start." She waved one hand at Luc. "Nothing's wrong. I just need to find out if I'm actually going to see a doctor today."

Luc raised his eyebrows and looked from Maryse to the admitting nurse, who was standing behind the admissions desk frowning at both of them. "I saw that doctor take out of here like he'd been shot," Luc said, and gave Maryse a questioning look.

"Ha!" Helena said. "He hasn't been shot yet." She looked over at Maryse and shook her head. "I still can't believe you went out with him."

Maryse tried to block Helena from her mind and walked over to the nurse. "Can you please find someone else to take a look at me? I really need to get on with my day, and I've had quite enough of this hospital. I'm sure you can appreciate that."

The nurse gave her a curt nod and pointed back to the doors. "Take a seat in room two. The first one on the right. I'll have Dr. Breaux right in. But Ms. Robicheaux, the hospital director will want to speak with you about this situation with Emily."

Maryse sighed. "If he can't make it down before the exam is over, he can reach me at the Mudbug Hotel. Leave a message with Mildred." Maryse turned from the desk and stalked off to room two. She had just perched her hiney on the cold, hard table when Helena entered the room, followed closely by Luc.

Luc sat in a chair in the corner and looked over at Maryse. "So am I getting this right? Those orderlies said you caught that doctor in a storage closet with a loan shark's underage daughter?"

"Yeah," Maryse replied. "That's pretty much it."

Luc whistled. "Boy, I don't give him ten minutes to hide after her dad hears."

"Serves him right."

Luc gave her a curious look. "And you went out with this guy?"

Maryse stared at him. "How in the world did you know that?"

Luc smiled and pointed at Helena. "The ghost said so."

Chapter Eleven

Maryse froze at Luc's words and knew that she had stopped breathing altogether. After a couple of seconds of complete immobility, she cast an anxious glance at Helena, who was standing stock still, staring at Luc in obvious shock.

Maryse realized he was looking straight at Helena. "You can see her?" she managed to squeak out.

Luc nodded. "Plain as day. Absolutely horrid pink suit."

Maryse gasped and struggled to maintain her cool.

Helena stared at him in disbelief. "But how is that possible?" she asked.

Luc shrugged, not the least bit bothered by the situation. "I don't know. Family tradition, I suppose."

Maryse stared. "You hear her, too?"

Luc grimaced. "Unfortunately. Why do you think I looked behind you when you entered the lobby? I heard two voices approaching clear as day, but then you were the only one who came through the door. Helena walked through the wall a couple of seconds later." He looked from Maryse to Helena. "How long has she been hanging out with you?"

"Since the funeral, much to my dismay," Maryse said.

Luc looked at Helena, then back at Maryse and smiled. "No wonder you've been so bitchy. What the hell did you do to earn being haunted by your dead mother-in-law?"

Maryse bristled at his words. "First of all, I didn't do anything to make her show up. She just did, and now my life is pure misery.

Second of all, I've always been bitchy to rude, pushy people. Helena has nothing to do with that."

"Man, that's bad karma in a way I've never seen before."

Maryse shot him a dirty look, and Luc wisely decided to lead off from that line of conversation. "So the storage closet story?" he asked.

Helena hooted and dissolved in laughter, sinking down the wall and onto the floor in a heap. "I tried to tell her that doctor was a loser and a cad, but would she listen? No way."

"And you would know a cad, right?" Maryse shot back. "Especially since you married one and had the nerve to continue that genetic defect into the next generation. You should have at least done the world a favor and had Hank neutered when he hit puberty. That way we'd be sure the scourge on humanity couldn't continue."

Helena clamped her mouth shut and looked a bit sheepish.

Luc laughed and gave Helena a once over. "So what's with the pink suit?"

"Do you think it was mine?" Helena shouted, an indignant look on her face. "Last I checked, the morgue didn't ask the dead to pick out their wardrobe."

"Maybe it was one of Harold's floozies," Maryse suggested and took a good look at Helena. Something was different. It took her a second to realize that instead of the uncomfortable twenty-year-old pumps she used to wear, Helena's feet were now decked out in a brand new pair of Nike running shoes. Maryse stared at the shoes in amazement. "Helena, how did you change your shoes?"

Helena huffed. "Don't you think if I knew, I would have changed the whole outfit? Damn it, I was walking to the hospital and thinking a pair of running shoes would really come in handy. Next thing I knew, that's what I was wearing. As soon as I figure out how I did it, this pink monstrosity is gone."

Before Maryse could reply, Dr. Breaux entered the room, giving Luc a curious look.

Figuring that was his cue, Luc nodded to the doctor and said to Maryse, "I'll wait for you in the lobby." Then he left the room with Helena trailing behind him, yapping away as only Helena could yap. Maryse let out a sigh of relief. Maybe Helena would start hounding Luc and give her a break.

Thirty minutes later, Dr. Breaux pronounced her fit for anything that didn't encompass fast movement, eye strain, stress, or aggravation. Given her life at the moment, Maryse figured the only way to avoid that was death. Which would apparently fit right in with someone's plan.

At the front desk, she signed the papers for yet another insurance claim and turned to find Luc standing alone in the lobby. She glanced around but didn't see hide nor hair of Helena. She studied Luc for a moment. If he'd figured out a way to get rid of Helena, he might be worth keeping around. The lesser of two evils. Luc motioned to the front door, and she followed him out of the hospital with a clear view of the back end of his Levi's. Definitely the better looking of the two.

Maryse figured Luc would drive her straight to the hotel, but instead he parked in front of Johnny's Bar.

"You need to eat something," he said. "You have to take pain meds and probably haven't eaten today, have you?"

Maryse thought back to the odd phone call from the bank that had started her day. Good God, was that really only *this* morning? If every day was as long as this one, staying alive for another four days was going to age her a hundred years. She was definitely going to have to get a better moisturizer.

Luc was staring at her, and it took Maryse a moment to realize she had worked through everything in her own mind but hadn't answered his question. "Sorry. I had to think about it for a minute, but you're right, I haven't eaten yet today."

Luc gave her a sympathetic nod. "Then let's get some food in you. Besides, you and I have to talk." And after delivering that cryptic phrase, Luc headed into the bar before Maryse could even formulate a question.

They sat at the table in the corner—the private one that Maryse and Sabine preferred. They'd barely gotten seated before Johnny appeared at their table, wiping old grease off his hands with a dirty dishcloth, the worry on his face clear as day.

"Maryse!" He studied the cuts on her head and arms. "Are you all right? I was cleaning the grease traps and heard that blast all the way back in the kitchen. I thought for sure you were a goner until Mildred called and said you were on your way to the hospital." He scanned her again, an anxious look on his face. "So, you're okay? Nothing serious?"

Maryse smiled up at her father's friend. "I'm fine, Johnny. Just a raging headache and some cuts, but nothing life threatening."

Johnny looked a little apprehensive but nodded. "What happened?"

Maryse shook her head. "I have no idea. I was just pulling up to the cabin when it exploded. Good thing I wasn't any closer."

"Jesus, Maryse." Johnny tugged his blue jeans back up around his waist and took in a deep breath. "I saw the fire department head that way. Are they going to investigate?"

Maryse nodded. "Oh, yeah. The fire department, the police department, and who knows who else. Not that there's much left to look at."

"Doesn't matter," Luc said. "If the fire department suspects foul play, they'll call in specialists. There's very little that gets by an investigator trained for this sort of thing."

Johnny paled a bit and looked at Luc, his eyes wide. "Foul play?" He looked back at Maryse. "I never thought...you're sure?"

"The entire place was leveled," Luc said. "What are the chances that's accidental?"

Johnny stared down at Maryse and hesitated a few seconds before speaking. "Maryse, I heard a little about the will reading. Maybe you should take an extended vacation or something. Get the hell out of here until it's safe."

"And when will that be, Johnny? No one has any way of knowing, and I'm not leaving here with this whole inheritance mess hanging over my head." She clamped her mouth shut, not about to reveal the real reason she couldn't leave.

Johnny nodded but didn't look pleased. "Harold was in here raising hell last night about him and Hank being cut out of the will." He frowned. "You know, he'd be just crazy enough to try something like this."

Maryse nodded. "He's already threatened me, and believe me, that will be the first name I give to the police."

Luc shook his head. "I could be wrong, but I think whoever set that blast knew what they were doing. Someone with experience." He looked up at Johnny. "You got any ex-military in Mudbug?"

Johnny let out a single laugh. "Are you kidding? Hell, practically every man in this town over the age of forty was military. The economy back then didn't offer as many opportunities for young men as it does now."

Luc sighed. "I was afraid of that."

Johnny scrunched his brow in obvious thought. "Harold was military. He's always in here bragging about it."

"What did he do?" Luc asked.

Johnny shrugged. "No way of my knowing for sure, but he's always claimed he was special forces."

"Thanks, I'll look into that." Luc studied Johnny for a moment. "What about you?"

"Me?" Johnny laughed. "Oh, hell, I was a mess cook. Why do you think I opened this place? Toss some food on the grill, pour some beers. Just like being back in the service."

Maryse smiled. "You might need to throw a burger or two on the grill for yourself, Johnny. You've dropped a few pounds."

Johnny looked a bit embarrassed. "Wouldn't hurt me to lose a couple more." He placed a hand on Maryse's shoulder. "You let me know if you need anything. I'll send Jeff over to get your order." Johnny nodded to Luc, then walked back to the kitchen.

"Well," Luc said, "looks like the first thing we need to do is find out exactly what Harold did during his time in the military."

"And how are we going to do that?"

Luc grimaced. "We should probably start with asking Helena."

"Great," Maryse mumbled. She stared out the window for a moment, trying to roll everything that had happened to her in the past couple of days into some kind of sense, but it was so extraordinary that she couldn't even start. Giving it up as futile, she looked back at Luc. "What family tradition?"

"Huh?"

"Back at the hospital, you said you could see Helena because of family tradition. What does that mean?"

"Oh, well, it's simple really. People in my family have been seeing the dead for as many generations as there are stories about it. My great-great grandmother claimed to have seen over sixty ghosts in her lifetime. But then, she lived to be a hundred and five."

Maryse gasped. "Sixty ghosts!" She was completely unable to grasp the idea of seeing, and more importantly *hearing*, sixty Helenas. "How in the world did she live past a hundred with all those ghosts around? I'm ready to kill myself over one."

Luc laughed. "They weren't all around at the same time. Hell, that would give anyone a heart attack. In fact, I think the most she ever had speaking at once was two and they were twins, so I guess it sorta figured."

Maryse shook her head in disbelief. "And none of this bothers you? Because I have to tell you, I'm creeped out every time I see her, even if only for a millisecond."

"Hell yeah, it bothers me," Luc said. "Why do you think I left a small town and hightailed it to the city? There may be more ghosts roaming around, but it's a lot harder for them to figure out you can see them if they're among so many people. I've managed to fly below the radar for ten years. Until now. Damn small towns."

Luc glanced around the room and leaned across the table toward Maryse. "You know someone's trying to kill you."

Maryse was a bit taken aback at the directness. "Wow. I know the explosion couldn't have been an accident, so that's really the only explanation, but when you put it that blunt, it makes it even scarier than before."

Luc nodded. "It's not the first time, either."

Maryse stared at him and narrowed her eyes. "What do you mean?"

"My buddy at the dealership said someone cut your brake lines on your truck. Your wreck was no accident."

"And you're just now telling me about this? Don't you think that was information I needed before now?"

Luc had the decency to look embarrassed. "I'm sorry, Maryse, but I was a bit confused at first since your wreck happened before the reading of the will, so it didn't add up. Then after I heard about the whole inheritance thing, I figured Harold or someone else found out ahead of time and took a snipe at you. Cutting brake lines is not exactly a clear-cut route to death. In fact, it's probably not a good route at all."

Maryse slowly nodded, understanding his point. "But an explosion is a whole different story."

"Bet your ass it is," Luc said and narrowed his eyes at Maryse. "So are you going to tell me what you're involved in that's going to get you killed?"

Maryse nodded. "It's got to be the land. There's a clause in the inheritance."

"What clause?"

"The land inheritance has clauses tied to it that have to be fulfilled over the next week in order for the title to pass to me. One of the clauses is that I have to outlive Helena for seven days following her burial."

"Jesus Christ!" Luc stared at her for a moment, then lowered his voice again. "Then Johnny's right—you've got to get out of town for a while. I have family in places no one would ever find you. They can keep you protected for a week, easy."

Maryse shook her head. "I can't leave Mudbug. That's another one of the clauses. If I leave, everything passes to Hank, and he'd lease the land as fast as possible."

"He'd have to find a taker first," Luc said. "Maybe in ten years or so development would be pushing this way, but right now? Even the chemical company couldn't put together an expansion plan quickly. It would take years."

"Yeah, but didn't I tell you? Helena's only just bothered to mention that the preserve is full of oil."

Luc stared. "Good Lord, the woman's practically signed your death warrant."

"I don't think that was her intention, but it's certainly starting to look that way."

Luc looked out the window for a moment, then shook his head and looked back at Maryse. "Well, this problem is way too big to be solved over lunch, but I guess the first thing we need to do is get you somewhere safe. You think the hotel is okay?"

Maryse shrugged. "Heck if I know. Mildred lives there, and the hotel is usually at least half-filled with salesmen and such for the chemical company. I should be okay there, but I hate putting Mildred in the middle of this mess."

"I don't like it either, but you have to stay somewhere that's easy to watch, and the hotel is your best option in Mudbug. Are you going to tell Mildred what's going on?"

"What other choice do I have? My house exploded. She's going to wonder what happened, and Mildred's too sharp for me to pass off some bullshit explanation."

"And what about the Helena returning from the dead part?"

"Oh, no! I don't need Mildred worried about my sanity, too. She doesn't believe in this sort of thing and isn't likely to start regardless of what I say. No, Helena has to remain mine, yours, and Sabine's little secret."

"Sabine?" Luc asked.

"My best friend. She owns the psychic shop in downtown."

Luc's face cleared in understanding. "Ah, psychic, huh? So I guess she has no trouble taking on a haunting."

"Oh, she has plenty of trouble, especially with exactly who's doing the haunting, but she's doing some research to try and help us figure out some things—mainly how Helena can ascend or depart or whatever."

"You might want to put a hold on that."

"Why?"

"I would imagine that Helena knows plenty she still hasn't told you. Not to mention she's a much better choice for eavesdropping on suspects than either of us." Luc sighed. "Unfortunately, until we figure out exactly what's going on here, Helena is worth more to us dead."

The fear on Mildred's face was clear as day when Luc came hauling Maryse into the hotel. The hotel owner ran across the lobby, as only large women can run, and started to gather her up in a hug. Apparently, she remembered Maryse's injuries and placed a hand on her arm instead. "Oh, my God, child, are you all right?"

"I'm fine, Mildred. Just a few cuts and my head's pounding a bit again, but nothing to be concerned with."

Mildred stared at Maryse as if she'd lost her mind, then looked over at Luc, whose expression apparently didn't do anything to convince her to the contrary. She looked back at Maryse. "Nothing to be concerned with? Are you kidding me? That explosion at your cabin carried all the way to downtown. Why, when I heard it was your place, Johnny had to stop me from swiping his boat and heading over there myself. I swear I would have swam if I had to."

Maryse smiled. "I know you would have. I'm surprised Johnny won the fight over his boat."

Mildred flushed a bit. "Well, I couldn't get the damned thing started or I would have gotten away with it. Then I came back into the hotel and was just about to grab my keys and head to the dock when Sabine called and told me to hold tight and prepare a room for you." She gave Maryse a hard look. "What the hell is going on, Maryse?" She looked over at Luc. "And what is he doing taxiing you around?"

"It's sort of a long story. Why don't you put on a pot of coffee, and I'll take a shower. Luc will fill you in on the high points in the meantime."

Mildred pursed her lips, obviously wanting an answer right away but not about to argue the fact that Maryse could obviously use a shower. "Okay," Mildred said finally. "I've got a new caramel blend I can put on and some butter cookies I just baked yesterday. You go on with your shower. Sabine brought some clothes by earlier to tide you over until you can buy some more." She pointed a finger at Luc. "*You* can follow me to the kitchen and start explaining exactly what the hell happened and how you got in the middle of it."

Maryse smiled at the look of dismay on Luc's face. She knew he was probably itching to make phone calls or revisit the blast site or something that proved his cleverness or masculinity. Instead, he was stuck answering to Mildred over caramel coffee and butter cookies.

"Go ahead and tell her everything," Maryse instructed.

Luc nodded and headed through the double doors that Mildred had indicated. The hotel owner pulled back her shoulders and followed him. Maryse took one final look at Luc's retreating figure and sighed. Like she needed to feel any more attraction to Luc LeJeune. She'd spent the last couple of days trying desperately to ignore the sparks between them, and now here he was, looking out for her and seeing her ghost.

The first time she'd met him, Maryse had thought he was just another playboy with a roving eye, but apparently there was another side to Luc that he obviously didn't let out for just everyone.

He'd shown Maryse that other side, but for the life of her, she had no idea why.

Luc watched the hotel from across the street and saw Maryse close the blinds to her hotel room window. Good. She should stay put for a while, and if she got any foolish ideas about leaving the hotel before he returned, Mildred had promised to handcuff her to the stair railing. She'd even showed him the handcuffs, which had given him a moment of pause.

He looked across the parking lot, half-expecting to see Helena strolling around like she hadn't done anything wrong, but apparently the ghost had decided to lay low for a bit. He shook his head and walked toward his Jeep. He wasn't happy about seeing Helena, but it did explain why Maryse had been acting so strangely. In fact, given everything she had going on, he was somewhat surprised she'd held things together as well as she had.

He took one final look at the hotel, satisfied that Maryse was in capable hands, and pulled his cell phone out of his pocket as he climbed in his Jeep. He'd already had one text message today from his boss, and with everything that had happened, he hadn't had an opportunity to call in without blowing his cover. But he couldn't put off calling the office any longer. Wilson rarely called Luc when he was in the field. If he felt the need to leave a message, something must be up.

He dialed his office and his boss picked up on the first ring.

"Damn it, LeJeune!" Wilson shouted. "Where the hell have you been all day?"

Luc moved the phone a couple of inches from his ear until he was sure the yelling was over. "There was a situation with my suspect."

"Spill it, LeJeune. I don't have all day like you do."

"Someone tried to kill her."

"Are you positive?"

"Her house exploded."

There was a couple of seconds pause, and Luc knew Wilson was rolling this piece of information around in his mind. "Well, I guess that might be hard to construe any other way. So I take it she wasn't in the house?"

"On her way up to it when it blew. We just got back from the hospital."

Wilson groaned. "Do not tell me you're white knighting this woman around to doctor's appointments and to have her hair done. Are you trying to look suspicious? As far as she's concerned, you barely know her, LeJeune. Act like the stranger you're supposed to be before someone makes you."

"I'm not going to hair appointments, and I just happened to be in the vicinity when her cabin exploded so I took her to the emergency room. Any decent person would have done that—stranger or no."

"Maybe, but be careful. Remember, I never wanted you on the assignment in the first place. Your grandparents lived entirely too close to Mudbug for my comfort. There's still the possibility of you being recognized."

"My grandparents moved almost five years ago," Luc argued, "and I haven't been there to visit since I was in high school. They preferred to come to the city to see me."

"Family visiting preferences aside, you better stay low on this one or I'm going to yank you out."

"I understand, but I'm wondering if all this is related to our case. There's no way this was an amateur job. There's not a single piece of that cabin left over two feet long."

Wilson sighed. "Well, keep an eye on her for now, but I have to tell you, it's looking more and more like the informant is that accountant that Agent Duhon is on. I'm expecting a break anytime. And when I get it..."

"I understand," Luc said, and closed his phone. His time was running out. As soon as they had the informant, his business with Maryse was over and he would be expected back in New Orleans. And that left Maryse with no one to protect her but a fake psychic, a hotel owner with a pair of fuzzy handcuffs, and a ghost wearing bad polyester.

Luc gave her ten, fifteen minutes tops.

Maryse awoke the next morning with another pounding headache and immediately decided that head injury headaches were much, much worse than the drinking kind. Her poor body had seen more abuse in the last couple of days than it usually did in years. She groaned as she got out of bed and turned a tired eye to the alarm clock on the nightstand. Only six A.M. Habit, she knew, but if ever there was a day she'd have liked to sleep in, this would have been it.

The day before had been long and intense, first Luc filling Mildred in on the basics, with Sabine joining them for most of the conversation. Then Maryse had made her appearance, and it was all she could do to keep Mildred and Sabine from bundling her up and hauling her out of town, regardless of land, oil, inheritance, or anything else. She'd finally convinced them to leave it alone for the night at least, but she could tell that no one was happy going to bed with no plan of action.

She shuffled into the bathroom to survey the damage and groaned. It wasn't a pretty sight and definitely wasn't going to help her "stay in Mudbug" argument. Even Jasper, who was drinking out of the toilet despite a perfectly good bowl of water in the bedroom, paused for a moment and stared.

The bruises on her arms and legs from the truck wreck were purple with that nasty-looking yellow around the edges. The cuts were not deep and wouldn't scar, but they dotted her hands like bright red freckles. Fortunately, in all of this, she'd remembered to protect her face, but the stress and lack of sleep were showing there. The bags under her eyes were so dark they looked like she was ready to play a quarter in the NFL, and to top it all off, they were puffy, probably from all the yelling she did yesterday mixed with the intermittent tears last night.

She looked like a hybrid raccoon strung out on acid.

Although she knew her appearance should be the least of her concerns at the moment, Maryse also knew that unless she managed to pull off a semblance of control, she'd never convince Mildred and Sabine she should stay in Mudbug. Or if she did, they'd never want her to leave the hotel, and that just wasn't an option since it put Mildred at risk.

And then there was Luc.

A whole other problem and definitely an enigma. She knew he was more than a little troubled, especially with Helena in the mix, but if he had any thoughts or opinions on the situation, he'd held them in last night, instead choosing to listen for a change. Which made Maryse more than a little nervous. What was going on in that head of his? His revelation about seeing Helena had thrown her for a loop but also made her feel closer to him, something she'd definitely been trying to avoid.

Realizing she wasn't going to solve all her problems or get a decent cup of coffee standing in front of the bathroom mirror, she shrugged off the T-shirt Mildred had loaned her to sleep in and made a quick pass through the shower. Sabine, in her infinite wisdom, had started off Maryse's replacement wardrobe with loose-fitting sweats and T-shirts from Wal-Mart.

Given the bruises and the overall soreness, Maryse was happy with Sabine's choices. The sweats were a light, thin fabric and wouldn't be hot at all, and they were much less restrictive than the jeans Maryse usually wore. Probably wouldn't stand up very well to a day in the bayou, but at the moment, it appeared her days in the bayou were coming to a screeching halt. She fluffed her damp hair, pulled on her tennis shoes, then headed to Mildred's office, hoping the woman had taken mercy on her and picked up some donuts.

Mildred was in her office, but she wasn't alone. Sabine sat across the desk from her, and surprisingly enough, Luc occupied the other chair. Conversation ceased the moment Maryse entered the room, and she immediately knew that the three had been plotting some way to "take care" of her. She looked from face to face, but no one met her gaze. It seemed that the floor was far more interesting.

"It's a little early for a booster club meeting, isn't it?" Maryse asked. "And don't even bother making excuses. Sabine hasn't been out of bed before eight o'clock since high school."

Apparently, they hadn't prepared for her to wake so early, and no one had a ready excuse for their treason. Mildred cast a guilty look at Sabine, and Sabine and Luc stared at the wall past Mildred's shoulder. Maryse raised her eyebrows and stared at them one at a time, waiting for a response. "Cat got your tongues?" she finally asked.

"Now, Maryse," Mildred said, obviously going to take a shot at the peacemaker role. "We're just worried about you is all. This whole situation has gotten out of hand. And don't tell me you can handle it yourself. It's just too big for one person."

Maryse turned her back to them and poured a cup of coffee, making note that the coffeepot was the old one that Mildred had claimed was broken. Not that it surprised her.

She stalled for another couple of seconds, not yet ready reply. The truth was Mildred was right. This situation was too big for her to handle alone. But the last thing she wanted to do was involve people she cared about in her mess—people she considered family. Which left only Luc, and Maryse was too scared to have the sexy zoologist that close to her. She didn't need her attraction to him confusing things even more.

She stirred some sugar in her coffee and turned back to them with a sigh, easing herself into a chair next to Mildred's desk. "Look, I appreciate what y'all are trying to do, really, I do. But don't you see that I can't risk anyone else being involved? I've already lost too much. I can't afford to lose anything else. Surely you understand that."

They all looked at her for a moment, but no one said a word. Finally, Sabine blurted out, "I've lost a lot, too. You're the only family I have left, Maryse. Don't ask me to leave you alone, or you're going to piss me off." Sabine stared defiantly at Maryse, and Maryse knew it was hopeless. This was one of those areas where she and Sabine were cut from the same cloth.

Hurt one, you hurt the other.

And Maryse was forced to admit that if the situation were reversed, it would take her own death to peel her off protecting her friend. She shook her head at the impossibility of the situation, not having a clue how to proceed. "Well, did you geniuses come up with any way to get me out of this?"

They all shook their heads. Finally, Luc cleared his throat and spoke, his voice barely disguising his anger. "This entire situation is ridiculous. What the hell was that woman thinking? It's no wonder everyone hated her."

"Got that one right," Mildred agreed, and gave Luc a nod.

Maryse sighed. "I don't know what Helena was thinking." *Even though I talk to her on a semi-regular basis.* "Probably she just thought that the land would remain in the care of the state. And as long as I owned it, Mudbug wouldn't become one big oil field."

Mildred wasn't convinced. "Helena or her attorney should have known that worthless son and husband of hers wouldn't let you keep something so valuable."

Maryse stared at the wall for a moment, casting her mind back to the will reading. "I got the impression that all the 'rules' of the inheritance weren't exactly in the forefront of Wheeler's mind. He even said he needed to review everything again before we talked because it had been so long since he'd read everything over. Probably Helena forgot too, since she inherited everything as a child."

Luc shook his head. "Well, Helena should have reread the rules before she handed you a death sentence."

"There's nothing that can be done about this clause?" Mildred asked. "Can't you just give the land back?"

Maryse shrugged. "I honestly don't know. I've never asked."

Mildred looked at the others and gave them a nod. "Then I say your first order of business is getting in touch with that attorney of Helena's and finding out what your options are. He's got to be able to do something to protect you."

"Maybe," Maryse said. It was a thought, anyway, and better than anything Maryse had come up with so far. "I'll call him as soon as his office opens."

Sabine nodded to Mildred, then looked over at Maryse. "And what do you plan on doing today? We don't think you should be alone. One of us should be with you at all times, and we don't think you should be in the bayou at all."

Maryse stared at them. "You've got to be kidding me. You can't spend your entire day following me around. Mildred, you have a hotel to run. Sabine, you have a business, and Luc..." What the hell *did* Luc do exactly? "Luc has to do whatever it is he does for the state. Besides, I'd like to know what any of you could have done to protect me from that explosion. More likely, you'd have been hurt as much or more than I was."

"I can stick with you," Luc said. "I have a ton of vacation accrued. Long overdue, as a matter of fact. I can take a couple of days until the attorney can figure something else out."

Maryse stared at Luc in disbelief. "You actually want me to spend every waking hour of my day with you? Take you everywhere I go? We don't get along all that great in the few minutes a day we're in contact at the office. How the heck do you think we can manage an entire day?"

Luc shrugged. "I get along just fine. You're the one with the problem."

Maryse felt her pulse quicken. Luc was right. She was the one with the problem. The main problem being that even a small amount of time around Luc LeJeune led to thoughts that she had no business thinking. How in the world was she supposed to manage an entire day? "I am not going clothes shopping with him," Maryse said finally, "and that's my first order of business for today."

"Oh, c'mon, Maryse," Sabine pleaded. "What's the big deal? It's not like he's going to follow you into the dressing room."

Luc perked up a bit and smiled, and Maryse felt a flush start at the base of her neck and slowly creep up her face. She shot him a dirty look that should have cut him to his knees, but it only made him smile more. "I am not selecting undergarments with a man."

Sabine laughed. "You don't even wear underwear, Maryse."

"I do on Sundays," Maryse grumbled, feeling her independence slipping away even as she made her futile arguments.

"It's only Friday," Luc said, and grinned. "You've still got time to change your mind."

Chapter Twelve

Shopping with Luc wasn't quite as bad as Maryse had originally imagined and probably not near as sexual as Luc had hoped. But given her slightly rough condition and the fact that her job didn't exactly involve tailored dress-wear, Maryse saw absolutely no reason to shop for anything cute or nice at the moment. Even if she was back in the bayou sometime soon, alligators and nutria didn't appreciate fashion.

So a trip to Wal-Mart was as much shopping as Luc was going to see.

Maryse walked right into the women's athletic section and pulled shorts, sweats, and T-shirts off the racks and shoved them into the cart she'd conned Luc into pushing. That was it. No tube tops, no spandex, no sexy lingerie—no dressing rooms. Then it was off to find some sports bras.

Luc stared wistfully at the rows of lacy, multi-colored underwear and reached up to finger a pair in girly pink. Maryse hid a grin. He was barking up the wrong tree with her. Not only was underwear purely optional, but Luc LeJeune was the last person she wanted getting a view of anything she might wear in that area. There were some temptations you just avoided altogether.

Apparently deciding Maryse wasn't going to contemplate anything even remotely sexy, Luc gave up and yanked out his cell phone. Maryse ignored him and continued looking over her selection of active wear. She had just narrowed her choice down to two different crossed-back sports bras when Luc snapped the phone shut and gave her a curious look.

"There was a message on the office phone from someone named Aaron. He said that the mice cruised through the trial and he was moving on but he's going to need more of the sample before he can go any further after that. What does that mean? What is he testing?"

Maryse tried to appear completely normal, even though she wanted to jump and shout, head injury not withstanding. "It's nothing," she said, and waved a hand in dismissal. *Nothing but a successful Trial 3, which you've never made it through before now.* "Just some different stuff I'm trying out—you know, herbal remedies and such."

Luc narrowed his eyes. "What kind of remedies?"

Maryse turned away from him and concentrated on the bras. "Nothing that would interest you. Although two weeks ago, I found a natural cure for gas." She looked back at him with a broad smile.

Luc shook his head and shot her a disbelieving look, but thankfully he dropped the subject and took up position at the edge of the department where he could scan the magazines. *A successful Trial 3.* It was all she could do to keep from dancing in the aisles. She was close to the answer, she could just feel it. And for now, at least, that thrill totally overrode all the bad things going on.

Maryse picked a couple of sports bras from the rack and tossed them in the basket, then pushed her cart down the aisle, whistling as she went. She was just about to leave the section altogether when the pink, lacy underwear that Luc had been studying earlier caught her eye. She glanced down the aisle at Luc, who had a magazine open and was concentrating intently on whatever he was reading. Looking back at the underwear, she bit her lip, knowing that even looking at the underwear was trouble. Buying them was even worse. It was the equivalent of purchasing a ticket to the "Sleep With Luc" concert.

But then there was that whole death thing to consider, and that was the clincher.

If she died today, the last man she would have slept with was Hank. Hell, the *only* man she'd slept with was Hank, and on so many levels, that was just wrong. She glanced over at Luc once more. Before she could change her mind, she snatched the underwear off the rack, tugged them off the hanger, yanked off the tag, and stuffed them in her pocket. No way was she letting Luc see her buy those panties. That was just asking for it. At least this way, she was still in control. Unless of course, she was arrested for shoplifting before she could get through checkout and use the underwear tag to pay for her secret bounty.

She tried to act normal as she walked to the end of the aisle and called out to Luc. "I'm going to head over to checkout. Take your time. I'll meet you at the end of the register."

Luc nodded, and she could feel his gaze on her as she entered the only available check-out line, which was a mere six feet away from the magazine stand. She began placing her items on the belt, and when she finished, stepped close to the register, slipping the underwear tag to the clerk. "I liked these so much, I decided to wear them," she said, her voice low.

The clerk stared at her for a moment, obviously trying to decide if she was a loon or a thief. Loon must have won out, because the clerk took the tag from her, scanned it, and tossed it in the bag with her bras. "That will be one hundred eight dollars and thirty-two cents." She gave Maryse a shrewd look. "Unless you're wearing anything else."

Maryse shook her head and swiped her debit card, certain her face was beet red. She looked over at Luc, who plopped the magazine back on the shelf and turned toward the check-out lane. Catching her eye, he smiled and walked over to her.

"Ready?" he asked.

Maryse felt a slow burn in her center as she stared at the smiling Luc. Her hand moved involuntarily to her pocket and closed around the lacy underwear. "You have no idea," she said.

"Then let's do it."

Oh God. Maryse felt her knees weaken. There was no way out, she was certain. If someone didn't kill her first, she was going to sleep with Luc LeJeune.

As they exited Wal-Mart, Luc scanned the parking lot for possible threats but finally decided that the only threat to Maryse at the moment was him. He glanced over at her and held in a sigh. It simply made no sense at all. Maryse was so unlike the women he normally went for. His past conquests had all been girly and clingy and had the helpless woman routine down pat, whether helpless or not. They were fluff, eye candy…the kind of woman who made you look like a stud at the company Christmas party but not the kind you'd ever introduce to your family.

Especially not his family. Women like his mother and grandmother did not suffer weakness or fools.

Maryse, with her fierce and sometimes frustrating independence, was a breath of fresh air. And the fact that she didn't fall at his feet and overload him with compliments only made him more interested rather than less. He glanced down at the shopping bags he carried and shook his head. Her wardrobe definitely needed work, but for whatever reason, the faded jeans and rubber boots she'd worn into the bayou had never been a turnoff. In fact, it was exactly the opposite, which was uncharted territory for him.

He'd been with women who'd worn their stiletto heels to bed, and he had to admit, it was a huge turn-on. But on the occasion when his guard slipped and he allowed himself the luxury of that one-second vision of Maryse in his bed, damned if she wasn't completely nude except for those rubber boots. He felt his pulse quicken every time that picture flashed through his mind and knew that he would have to be very careful with Maryse Robicheaux.

Women who caused high blood pressure by wearing rubber boots were not to be taken lightly. If he made a genuine move in that direction, he knew there would be no going back. Maryse Robicheaux was no good-time girl or one-night stand. Maryse Robicheaux was the kind of woman who inspired men to make long-term plans.

They climbed into Luc's Jeep, packages in tow, and Luc pulled out of the parking space. As he exited the parking lot, Maryse pulled out her cell phone and punched in a number. Luc felt his pulse quicken for a moment, wondering who she was calling, but relaxed when she asked to speak to the attorney, Wheeler.

Clutching the steering wheel, he stared down the highway. What the hell was wrong with him? He was acting like a jealous husband, worried that his wife might be talking to another man. He needed to get a grip and get a grip fast. He wasn't going to be any help to Maryse if he spent all his time mentally undressing her rather than protecting her.

As Maryse finished her conversation and snapped the phone shut, he erased the rubber boot scene from his mind and looked over at her. "Wheeler meeting you this afternoon?" he asked.

Maryse nodded. "Yeah. I'm pretty sure he thinks I'm losing my mind with the questions I asked, but I didn't want to get into everything over the phone."

"Probably best to spring a house exploding on him in person," Luc agreed.

"He's meeting me at the café at two, hopefully with answers to all the questions that I asked." She sighed. "You know, somehow having this discussion over a cup of coffee and blueberry pancakes just seems wrong."

"Probably more of a shot of rot-gut whiskey sort of moment."

"Or battery acid," she said, and frowned.

Luc studied her for a moment, the questions she'd asked Wheeler rolling through his mind. "Are you really thinking about signing the land over to Hank?"

Maryse shook her head. "No. But if everyone thought that I could, and had, that would take the pressure off of me if the whole point of this mess was someone thinking Hank was going to inherit in the first place."

Luc studied Maryse for a moment, then frowned. She'd processed things quicker than he thought she would, so the thoughts rolling through her mind must be overwhelming. "You realize what you're saying?" he asked, just to be sure they were on the same page. "You think someone wanted that land so bad that they killed Helena Henry thinking Hank would inherit and make a deal. And when you inherited instead, they shifted to killing you."

He paused for a moment, carefully deciding on his next words. "It would take someone very desperate to attempt that in the first place. And it would take someone who knew enough about the land, and you and Helena, to know the score."

"I know what I'm saying," Maryse said, and stared out the car window. "Someone I know, possibly someone I consider a friend, is trying to kill me."

Maryse's two o'clock meeting with Wheeler started off a bit rocky. First off, both Luc and Sabine insisted on attending. Apparently they had decided that if Maryse couldn't come up with a better idea for protecting herself, they were going to wring one out of the attorney. Wheeler entered the café, took one look at Maryse, and gasped.

"Oh, my word," he said as he slid onto the chair across from her. "What happened to you?"

"A couple of things you should be aware of," Maryse said, and told him about the truck wreck and the explosion at her cabin.

Wheeler looked at Maryse, then over at Sabine and Luc, apparently hoping this was all a joke and they were the hidden-camera crew. When no one said a word, Wheeler looked back at Maryse, cleared his throat, and finally said, "Are you implying that someone is trying to remove you from the inheritance line?"

"Jesus, Wheeler," Maryse said, her exasperation with the situation overcoming any subtlety she might have otherwise had. "Where did you learn to talk that way?" She supposed his highbrow, cultured existence didn't allow him to say or think of such sordid things as murder, but damn it, they had no time to pussyfoot around reality. "I'm saying someone is trying to kill me. Are you with me now?"

Wheeler paled and used his table napkin to wipe his brow. "You're sure?" he asked, but as soon as the words left his mouth, he shook his head and looked contrite. "I'm sorry. Of course you're sure or you wouldn't be here talking to me. I guess it's just so startling because I can't imagine anyone running the risk of an arrest for something that may be worth considerable money someday but isn't really worth all that much right now."

"If only that were true, Wheeler," Maryse said, "but your client neglected to inform you of the billions of dollars in oil that are in the marsh. Seems she neglected to tell everyone that little bit of information, but apparently someone out there knows."

Wheeler stared at her for a moment, then drained half his glass of water. "Billions? I can see where that might be a problem. So what can I do?"

"I need to know what my options are. That's why I gave you that list of questions to research earlier."

Wheeler nodded and pulled a tablet from his briefcase. "I have all the answers here. Where would you like to start?"

Maryse took a deep breath and looked over at Luc, who nodded. "Can I give the land back to the estate?" Maryse asked.

Sabine stared at Maryse in shock. "If the land goes back to the estate, won't Hank inherit? I'm not saying you shouldn't do it, Maryse, but I thought you were dead set against that idea."

Maryse put one hand up. "I'm not saying that's what I want to do, but I need to know all my options and how they would work."

Maryse looked expectantly at Wheeler, but he shook his head. "I couldn't find any provision that would allow you to forgo your inheritance."

"Except being dead, of course," Luc threw in, his expression dark.

Wheeler paled and tugged at his tie. "Well, yes, of course there is that."

Maryse shook her head. "That's the kind of option I was looking to avoid." She drummed her fingers on the table and thought about her next move. "And the will you're drawing up for me won't be legal until the week has passed, right?"

Wheeler nodded. "That's correct. The land isn't yours to give until after the probationary period has passed. The only way you could create a document legally leaving the land to another party before the week was up is if there were no other direct heirs in line to inherit, but since there's Hank..."

Sabine straightened in her chair and glared at Wheeler, her normal good manners shot to hell. "This is bullshit! You're telling me she's inherited this land whether it gets her killed or not, and she has no choice but to sit around and wait for someone to fire the shot?"

Wheeler blotted his forehead with the napkin again. "I'm afraid that's the long and short of it, and I am truly sorry. I never would have let Helena put you in this position if I'd had any idea it would come to this. I just never imagined..." the attorney trailed off, obviously not even able to put what he couldn't imagine into words.

Maryse sank back into her seat and considered the information. "So you're telling me there's no way to back out of this except to take a short ride in a long hearse. And if something happens to me, you have no choice but to pass the land to Hank, a direct heir, who will most certainly lease it to the oil companies before my body's even cold. There's no option to preserve this marsh other than me remaining alive for another three days?"

Wheeler gave her an apologetic look. "You could kill Hank."

Sabine glared at him. "Do not give her any ideas."

Maryse patted her friend on the arm. "Don't worry, Sabine. As satisfying as that may sound, particularly at this moment, I'd still have to find him first." She leaned in closer to Wheeler and scanned the café, just to make sure no one could overhear. "Okay, Wheeler, so we agree there's no legal way for me to get out of this inheritance except dying, which sorta isn't a good option for me, so what if we drew up a fake document that said I was giving up all rights to the land inheritance and shifting the title to Hank?"

Wheeler stared at her in obvious confusion. "But such a document wouldn't be legally binding. That's what we just discussed."

Maryse nodded. "I know that, and you know that, but would anyone else?"

Wheeler's face cleared in understanding. "Normally, I would never be party to such an act, and I'm not real clear on the legality of my drawing up such a document, even just for talk, but given the situation, I agree that this might be the only way to buy you the time you need."

"Then let's do it," Maryse said. "Who knows. I might get really lucky and bring Hank out of hiding long enough to serve him divorce papers. I'd really like a divorce before I die and not the other way around."

Wheeler cleared his throat and looked at her, obviously uncomfortable. "Of course, this plan will only work if whoever is after you intended Hank to inherit in the first place."

Maryse nodded and stared down at the table. She'd already rolled that one around in her mind, but really, what other choice did they have? Surely whoever murdered Helena thought Hank would inherit. If even Wheeler had to look up the complete restrictions of the land inheritance, could anyone else possibly know all the mundane details?

Then there was the other thought, the thought still nagging at her from her earlier conversation with Luc. Maybe whoever wanted her dead hadn't planned on Hank making it through the week either. What if by pretending to shift the inheritance to Hank, she made him the next target?

"How long would it take you to draw up the fakes?" Maryse asked.

"I can probably have something by this afternoon," Wheeler said, "and there's nothing stopping me from notifying all concerned parties now about the documents in the works if I knew where to find them. That would buy you some safety. I'll give you my home number in case you locate Harold over the weekend."

"I don't think locating Harold will be a huge problem, and I'd bet anything he's in touch with Hank," Maryse said. "I'll tell Mildred to spread the word during her manicure at the beauty shop, and the whole town of Mudbug will know within a couple of hours." Maryse said. "So if you have the fake ready this afternoon, then the fraud just has to hold for three days."

"That's correct," Wheeler replied.

Maryse bit her lip. "Do it. I'll track down Harold so you can let him know." Maryse took a deep breath and stared out the café window, trying to assuage her guilt by thinking of everything rationally.

After all, if she was wrong about everything, Hank would probably only have to worry about staying alive for twenty-four hours or so. Way better odds than her three and a half days.

Luc insisted on taking Maryse back to the hotel after the meeting with Wheeler and Sabine seconded the motion, leaving her with no choice but to comply. Not that it mattered. She was sore and tired, and a nap probably wouldn't be the worst thing that could come out of the day, especially since she had a loosely formed plan rolling around her mind. A plan that involved a nightly escapade.

Maryse protested when Luc insisted on accompanying her to her room, but he refused to let her inside without checking the room first. Not wanting to waste valuable energy on an argument that she was going to lose anyway, she waved him inside. A minute later, he popped back in the hall and declared everything clear.

Which would have been accurate if Helena hadn't walked through the wall from the room next door, sending Jasper scurrying under the bed.

"Oh, no," Luc said, and pointed a finger at Helena. "You have caused quite enough trouble already. Maryse needs to rest, no thanks to you, and you need to start working on how to fix this mess you made instead of just popping through walls and aggravating people."

Helena looked a bit repentant, but it passed so quickly that if you hadn't been looking closely, you would have missed it. "I *am* here trying to fix this mess. Do you think I meant for any of this to happen? I might have been a bitch...might still be...but I never wanted to get anyone killed. And I certainly didn't want to roam the earth in cheap polyester."

Maryse waved a hand at Helena. "Don't you two start. There's no use getting your feathers all ruffled—or your polyester. Besides, I have something you might find interesting."

Luc narrowed his eyes at her, wondering what she had up her sleeve and why she hadn't mentioned it before now. Helena looked expectant, like an eight-year-old opening birthday presents. "What is it?" Helena asked.

Maryse reached into her pocket and pulled out a small ring of keys. "Christopher dropped these when he was scrambling in the storage closet. I figure one of them ought to open the door to medical records, right?" She dangled the keys in the air, jiggling them in front of Helena.

Helena's eyes widened, and she smiled. "Holy shit! Jackpot."

"Wait a minute." Luc cut in. "You're not thinking of breaking into the hospital, are you? That is just plain foolish."

Maryse turned to face him. "Oh yeah, and what would be less foolish? Letting Helena walk the Earth every day annoying the ever-living hell out of me until we find her murderer? Or maybe we should just let him get me first, then I can be stuck in limbo with her." She narrowed her eyes at him. "Of course, you'd be able to see and hear us both, right?"

Luc's jaw twitched at Maryse's words, and Maryse could tell she'd struck a nerve. "So can I ask exactly what you think you can gain by reading medical records?" he asked.

Maryse nodded. "I'm hoping that if I can figure out what someone put in the brandy snifter that killed Helena, it might tell us who did it, or at least narrow down the list of who I need to avoid for the next three and a half days. There can't be that many people in this town who know poisons *and* explosives."

Luc crossed his arms in front of him, silent for a moment and clearly not convinced. "Do you have any idea what could happen to you if you get caught? I don't even want to know what kind of charges you'd be up on. Medical information has gotten to be such a big deal lately that the authorities could probably find a way to make it a federal case if they wanted."

"Doesn't matter," Maryse said. "It would be a hell of a lot harder to kill me if I was locked up in a jail cell somewhere, right? So what's the downside?"

Luc placed his hand on her arm and squeezed. "You are not safer in jail. That I know for sure. Anyone in jail, including the guards, can be paid to get to you."

Maryse shrugged and pulled her arm away from his grasp. "So what do you suggest? That I sit around Mudbug and wait to die? Maybe I should spend every day standing in the middle of Main Street just to make it easier on everyone. At least that way, Mildred and Sabine would have a body to bury and would be less likely to be caught in the crossfire."

Luc crossed his arms in front of him again. "You put things in motion with Wheeler to cover you."

"Yeah, but can you guarantee that whoever is behind this will be fooled? They seem to know a lot about the inheritance rules. What if they don't buy the fake?"

"What fake?" Helena asked. "What have you done with Wheeler?"

Maryse looked over at Helena. "I asked him to draw up a fake document to transfer the land to Hank. I was hoping it might throw the bad guys off my trail long enough for the title to pass."

Helena stared at her for a moment. "Hmm. That's not bad, really."

"It's not a bad idea," Maryse agreed, "but it's hardly foolproof. Whoever is behind this was making their moves before the will reading ever happened, so there's always the chance they'll know the transfer document isn't legal."

Luc started to argue but apparently didn't have a good enough comeback. "Hell, I guess I don't like you taking chances, but you're right—sitting still isn't going to solve this problem either, no matter how much I hate admitting it."

"It has to be done, Luc," Maryse said, "and probably a lot of other things that border on illegal and go beyond unethical. But I'm simply out of options and running out of time. Whoever is after me has made it very clear what he's willing to do to get what he wants, and I'm not going to depend on a legal document to keep him from completing what he's already begun."

"She's right," Helena said. "I'm dead proof of it. This land has caused a mess of trouble that I swear I didn't even consider. I guess I really was beyond my prime if I didn't see this coming." She sank down onto the bed with a sigh. "All I was trying to do was avoid leaving the land to Hank. I couldn't trust him to do the right thing—with the land, or with the cash he'd get from making a deal with the oil companies."

Luc frowned at Helena. "I know you think you were doing some great service for this town, but I have to ask—what made you so certain that Maryse wouldn't sell out? How could you possibly know that she wouldn't be swayed by billions of dollars?"

He looked over at Maryse. "In fact, why the hell aren't you swayed by that much money? Jesus, you could afford to relocate the entire town if what Helena says about the oil is true. So why bother to keep this place as is?"

Helena looked over at Maryse, but when she never answered, Helena turned to Luc and said, "Maryse won't give up this land until she finds the cure for cancer that native woman made for her father. She knows it's out there, and she won't allow one single sprig of green to be cleared out, paved, or removed from that marsh until she's found her magic mixture."

Maryse spun around and stared at Helena. "How did you know?"

Helena shrugged. "I give a lot of money to the university you're using for the tests. It wasn't hard to find out from them what kind of tests you were running."

Maryse let this information sink in without replying.

"Cancer?" Luc said and looked a bit surprised. "Is that what you're doing in that lab?"

Maryse glared at Helena for letting out her secret and finally nodded. "Yes, but the subject is private and not open for discussion. Not now, not ever." She nodded toward the door. "Now, if you two could please leave me alone. I've got to plan a breaking and entering, and I'm probably going to need some rest."

Luc nodded and pointed a finger at Helena. "*You* are to meet me in the parking lot. I have some questions about your worthless husband and his military service."

"Okey dokey," Helena said, and flashed Maryse a grin. "I'll be back tonight." She waved goodbye and dashed through the wall, looking more excited than Maryse thought the situation warranted.

Luc walked over to stand directly in front of Maryse. "If you're going to go through with this crazy plan, at least let me drive you. You might need backup, or to leave in a hurry."

Maryse was surprised at his change in tune, but then she saw the compassion and admiration in his eyes. He got it. Maryse could tell. It probably hadn't taken more than a phone call to his grandparents to find out how Maryse's parents had died, and she knew with certainty that Luc understood why her research was so important, without her even saying a word.

"Okay, you can drive," she said, "but no more trying to talk me out of it."

Luc shook his head and stepped so close to her that she could feel the heat coming off his body. Her breath caught in her throat, and the overwhelming desire to have Luc LeJeune touch her crashed through every nerve ending in her body. When he placed his hand on her cheek and lowered his lips to hers, she felt her knees go weak.

His lips gently pressed hers, and she was surprised by the tenderness in his kiss. Then he ran his tongue across her lips, and the room began to spin. Her mouth parted, and she groaned as he wrapped his arms around her and deepened the kiss. His tongue swirled with hers in an erotic dance, and he pressed his hips into hers, his body lean and hard in all the right places.

She was just about to do something foolish, like rip off his clothes, or her own, when he ended the kiss, brushing his lips once more across hers. He released her and stepped back with a smile. "Just in case things go wrong," he whispered. "I didn't want to live with never having kissed you again." He ran one finger down her cheek, then walked out of the room.

Maryse shut the door and leaned back against it, not sure whether to head straight to a cold shower or fling herself out the window.

In case things go wrong.

Bastard. He'd just given her more to lose.

Chapter Thirteen

It was close to midnight when Maryse, Luc, and Helena pulled into the hospital parking lot in Maryse's rental. There were only a few cars parked in front of the administrative building, which was a good sign. That meant staff was light and could probably be worked around. Plus, Maryse had the added advantage of the invisible scout, Helena. It took a little convincing, but Luc had finally agreed to remain in the car, ready to start the engine and haul ass at a moment's notice, not to mention keep an eye on the outside just in case a sudden influx of staff should appear.

Maryse looked at the building once more, took a deep breath, and stepped out into the dim light of the parking lot. Helena stepped through the back door of the car and Maryse did a double take. "You changed clothes. But what in the world are you wearing?"

Helena looked like a Michael Jackson video combined with a Saturday morning streetwalker. The cat suit was solid black from neck to feet and had leopard patches across the boobs and each cheek of her butt, which amounted to a whole lotta leopard. Not to mention Maryse couldn't help but think there should be a legal weight limit on who got to wear spandex. Lumps abounded in all directions, mostly in places that lumps weren't supposed to be, and to top it off, she wore a black nylon mask that completely covered her head with only her eyes left showing.

"You like it?" Helena asked. "I thought I'd surprise you with my new ability. This is my covert operation outfit. Kind of a combination of James Bond and Catwoman."

Maryse frowned. That wasn't exactly the combination she'd come up with. "You can't run around wearing that, Helena."

"Why not?" The ghost put her hands on her hips and glared. "It's not like anyone else can see me, so I can hardly attract attention."

Unable to hold it in any longer, Maryse started to laugh, then clamped her hand over her mouth to muffle the noise. Luc stepped out of the car to see what the holdup was and his expression, a mixture of horror and confusion, was enough to put Maryse in tears.

"That is not necessary," Helena huffed.

Maryse peeked over at the ghost and saw she'd changed into black slacks, a black turtleneck, and black loafers. Thank God. There was simply no way Maryse could have followed that large leopard butt through the hospital without losing it.

Helena glared. "Now that I'm dressed as boring as you, can we get on with this?"

Maryse got control of herself and nodded. Luc took one final look at Helena and climbed back into the car, shaking his head. Maryse glanced around the parking lot, ensuring no one had witnessed her lapse in self-control, and was relieved to find the parking lot still clear. She gave Helena one final look, just to make sure she hadn't thrown in anything on the sly, like buttless slacks or a tear-off top with pasties, then started creeping toward the hospital.

"You know, it would have done us a lot more good if you'd learned how to touch things instead of change clothes. Then you could have gotten the file yourself," Maryse whispered as they snuck down the side of the building toward the employee entrance. "And I do not dress boring."

"Sure you do," Helena said. "I saw two decent outfits the whole time I've been hanging around and only one pair of spiffy shoes. According to the *Fashion Today* show I caught when I was hanging out at the beauty shop, you should be wearing those spiky heels everywhere, even to bed."

Maryse shook her head. "Do you really think I can tromp through the marsh in a pair of stilettos? The state would check me into the nearest mental institution if they caught me in something that stupid. Not to mention that outrunning an alligator might be a little difficult with those spiked heels in bayou mud."

Helena shrugged. "Okay, so maybe you can't wear them all the time, but you could when you're not working. If I could balance on the damned things, I'd wear them myself. I saw a real spiffy pair with a titanium heel advertised last night. You ought to get those. Very sexy."

Maryse stopped at the employee entrance and stared at Helena. "And just who do I need to look sexy for? My eligible doctor turned out to be a closet pedophile, literally on the closet part. Besides, I'm still married to your son, the disappearing idiot. And someone is trying to kill me. Lots of men would have a problem with all that, you know."

Helena gave her a smug smile. "Doesn't look like it bothers Luc."

Maryse stiffened. "Luc and I are friends. Sorta. That's it."

"Hmmpf. Didn't look like friends the way he kissed you back at the hotel. I could feel the heat off you two from twenty feet away."

Damn. She'd thought Helena was long gone before Luc had kissed her senseless. Maryse pulled the keys from her pocket and turned to the door. "You imagined it."

"Keep telling yourself that. You might start to believe it, but no one else is going to."

Maryse found the right key and eased open the side door designated for employees. "I am not listening to you, Helena," she hissed. "I have enough on my plate right now, and God knows, a man has never been the answer to my problems. They've usually been the cause. After all, I wouldn't be saddled with you if I hadn't married Hank."

Helena didn't look convinced but finally gave up her argument and followed Maryse down a dim hallway to the main corridor. "Where's the records room?" Maryse asked as they crept down the hallway.

"We turn left at the end of the main hall, and it's the last room on the left." Helena looked behind her, then ahead toward the corridor. "You know, this is sort of ironic. Walking down this hallway has the look of one of those near-death experiences you always hear about. Long white hallway, light at the end."

Maryse smiled wryly. "Did you see anything like this when you died?"

Helena frowned. "No. Not a thing. When I woke in that casket, I thought someone was playing a horribly cruel joke. It never occurred to me that I was dead, even after I yelled at everyone in the church and they didn't respond. Well, except you. But you passed out, so that wasn't exactly a help."

Maryse considered for a moment what kind of shock that must have been. "So what did you do after that?"

"I walked downtown, hoping someone would see me, say something to me, but everyone passed right by as if I wasn't there. I stopped in front of that big plate-glass window at the café and stood there, trying to see my reflection in the glass, but all that showed was the pickup truck behind me." She sighed. "It took me an hour to walk to your place. I cried the whole way. Not much else to do."

Maryse took a minute to absorb this and couldn't help but feel bad. What a nightmare. She couldn't possibly imagine how awful it must have been, but Maryse was certain of one thing—an hour of crying wouldn't have been enough for her. She'd probably still be wailing.

"Well," Maryse said finally, "let's get this over with and maybe we can see about getting you on to where you belong."

Helena nodded and stepped out into the lighted corridor. "It looks clear, but let me check at the end to make sure, then I'll yell for you. No use you sticking your head out or anything. You should be able to hear me yell from the end of the hall."

"That shouldn't be a problem," Maryse agreed. She could probably hear Helena yelling from the next building.

Helena disappeared around the corner, and Maryse leaned against the wall and waited for the yell to come. Her hands were sweating like mad between her anxiety over what she was about to do and the latex gloves that Luc had insisted she wear. It was a minute or so later when she heard Helena yell.

"All's clear!"

Maryse took a deep breath, stepped around the corner, and set off down the hall. Helena stood at the end of the hall next to a door with the words *Medical Records* stenciled on it in clear black letters. Maryse flipped to the first key on the ring, making sure she held the others tight to avoid any noise, and tried it in the latch.

No luck.

Maryse looked over at Helena, and Helena nodded, assuring her the hallway was still clear. She flipped to the second key and slipped it in the lock.

Bingo. They were in.

Maryse nodded to Helena and eased the door open. There was a loud squeak as she pushed, and she stopped for a moment, listening to see if anyone was coming to investigate. Helena checked both hallways and shook her head, so Maryse pushed the door open the remainder of the way and crept inside.

The room was pitch black, and she fumbled around for a moment, trying to find something solid to hold on to. Instead, she ran face first into a bookcase. "Damn it. That hurt." She rubbed her nose and grimaced, not even wanting to think about yet another bruise on her already battered body.

"Why don't you make more noise?" Helena asked. "I don't think everyone heard you."

"Don't give me any shit, Helena. Not all of us can walk through furniture."

"Then turn on your flashlight."

"I don't want anyone to see."

"Including yourself? Oh hell, I'll go back out into the hall and stand guard. Then will you turn on some damned light and stop running into everything imaginable?"

"Yes," Maryse hissed. "Just leave."

Maryse waited a minute in the inky darkness until she heard Helena call out to light things up. She pulled the small flashlight from her pocket and directed it at the bookshelf in front of her. The label at the top read "Current." Probably not the place she needed to look. She crept carefully down the row of bookcases, using her flashlight to scan the labels, and watched carefully for a change. *Current, Current, Current. Where the heck is Past?*

She turned the corner at the end of the row and shined her flashlight at the top of the next row of bookcases. "Dead Records," it read in large letters. *Dead Records?* Wasn't that a bit politically incorrect for a hospital? Maryse shook her head and ran her light across the folders jam packed on the shelves until she came to the H's.

"Find anything?" Helena's voice sounded next to her, and it was all Maryse could do not to scream. She glared at the ghost, but wasn't sure how effective it was because she wasn't positive Helena could see in the dark either. "Are you trying to ruin this? And why aren't you outside?"

"I saw the light go out and came to investigate, but it was just because you moved around to this side of the bookcases. You can't see the light now through the door."

Maryse swung her light toward the sound of Helena's voice and lit her up, standing right in front of the next set of shelves. "Yeah, well, that's great, but I can't see through you, so would you move over to the side a bit so I can read these files?"

Helena complied, and Maryse scanned the first row of files. *Harris, Hartman, Hector...aha...Henry !* Maryse ran her flashlight over the row of files until she reached Helena then stopped the light on the shiny label on the side. "Got it," she said, and reached for the file.

Helena reached at the same time and her hand passed right through Maryse's, sending a chill straight through her body. "Cut it out. You know I hate that cold, and besides, you haven't figured out how to pick up things anyway."

Helena yanked her hand back in a huff. "I keep practicing. I figured, of all things, I'd be desperate enough to want that file that I'd be able to touch it." She sighed. "Guess not."

"Now is not the time for you to practice ghost games," Maryse hissed. She yanked the file from the shelf, dropped quickly to the floor, and opened it, directing her flashlight onto the papers inside. The coroner's report was right on top, listing the death as *natural causes.* She scanned the page and found out that when Helena had been brought in, the attending physician was a doctor from New Orleans who had been filling in for Dr. Breaux, who was out of town that weekend for a medical convention.

But the attending physician had gotten in touch with Dr. Breaux right away and was given all the particulars of Helena's asthma problems and her subsequent failure to take his advice seriously. That was it. That statement alone had sealed Helena's fate as far as an autopsy was concerned, and without any other evidence to support foul play, Helena Henry had been buried without an argument.

But she'd come back to correct the mistake.

"What does it say?" Helena asked, hunching over Maryse and trying to make out the tiny print.

"It says you're dead," Maryse replied, trying to brush her off so she could make out the medications at the bottom of the page. "I really need a copy of all this, but I don't want to risk running the copy machine." Maryse rose from the floor and carried the file over to an available desk in the corner. Helena trailed behind her.

"I'm going to write down the names of these medications and a couple of notes," Maryse said, and grabbed a pad of paper and a pen off the desktop. "Anything you were taking on a regular basis would change your reaction to certain poisons. I need to narrow down the options as much as possible if we're going to get anywhere."

Helena nodded, and Maryse began to makes notes from Helena's file. She finished quickly, snapped the file shut, and was just about to suggest they get the hell out of there when a familiar name caught her eye.

She shined her flashlight at a file on top of the desk and drew in a breath. *Sabine LaVeche.* Why would Sabine's file be out on this desk? She hadn't been sick that Maryse was aware of. Not even a cold.

"What's wrong?" Helena asked. "Why aren't you leaving?"

Maryse pointed to the file, and Helena stared. "You shouldn't look at it. I know how you feel about Sabine, but it's her place to tell you if something's wrong."

Maryse glared at Helena, angry that she'd clued right in on her current ethical problem. "Oh, yeah. And just when do you think she should have taken the time to tell me about any crisis in her life—after my truck wreck or after my cabin exploded? Maybe she doesn't want to cause me any more worry than I've already got."

"Exactly. All the more reason not to look at it now."

Maryse looked back at the file and tapped her fingers on the desk. Surely Sabine would tell her if it was something serious, right? Even if things were a little weird right now. But there was that niggling doubt in the back of her mind. What if she didn't? What if something was seriously wrong and Sabine didn't want to tell her at all? In fact, if it wasn't serious, why hadn't she mentioned anything?

Maryse sucked in a breath as the one thing that Sabine would withhold from her came to the forefront of her mind. She grabbed the file up from the desk, yanked the cover open, and stared at the contents. Holding in a cry, she stared at the pristine white paper with those horrible words that confirmed her worse fear.

Sabine was being tested for cancer.

Maryse ignored the icy fear in her stomach and tried to slam down the cover on the file before Helena could see the horrible word on the test sheets. But she wasn't fast enough. Helena sucked in a breath and looked at her, her eyes wide.

"Oh my God," Helena said finally, her voice barely a whisper. "I thought maybe an unexpected pregnancy or some other nonsense that your generation is usually up to. I never thought for a minute..."

Maryse opened the file again and began to scan every page. The pages were all crisp, clean, and neat—so passive resting there, totally belying the information they contained.

"Are the results there?" Helena asked.

Maryse finished looking through the file and closed it. "No, only the request for the tests. But that wasn't the first one. There have been four others, all over the last three years."

Helena gave her a shrewd look. "But the others turned out okay, right? That's probably why Sabine never told you anything. She probably figured this one would be the same as the others."

Maryse looked over at Helena, her mind racing with the awful thought of a life without her best friend. "But what if she's wrong? What if this time is the one? More than once a year is an awful lot of times to think someone might have cancer. Doctors don't usually jump to that conclusion. And why now, right when I feel like I'm so close to discovering the secret and can't even get into the bayou to work?" She gave Helena a determined look. "This changes everything. My life isn't the only one at stake anymore."

Helena gave her a solemn look. "I promise, Maryse, I will do everything within my power to see that this turns out all right for everyone."

Maryse nodded, not even wanting to think about Helena's meager power. If only she could make Helena visible to the bad guys, maybe she could distract them with her wild wardrobe changes.

Maryse sighed. The earnest look on Helena's face let her know right away that she was sincere in her promise, if not entirely adequate to do the job, and Maryse didn't have the heart to point out her shortcomings. Not at that moment, anyway. "Let's get out of here," Maryse said. "We've already pushed our luck far enough."

Maryse had just replaced Helena's file when she heard a jangle of keys outside the record's room door. "Holy shit," she hissed, and Helena stared at her in alarm. "Don't just stand there," Maryse said, waving her arms at Helena. "Figure out a way to stop them from coming in here."

"How?" Helena's eyes were wide with fright.

"I don't know," Maryse said, and dove under the desk. "But you need to come up with something in a hurry."

Maryse peered through a narrow crack in one side of the desk, watching Helena hustle toward the door just as it swung open and someone entered. A second later, the lights came on and Maryse squinted, trying to focus in the bright glare. As her eyes adjusted, Maryse made out a nurse walking across the room toward the desk.

Helena vainly tried to knock items over in her path and finally resorted to jumping in front of her, but the nurse passed right through her continuing on her task. And it looked like that task was taking her, straight to Maryse's hiding place. When the nurse was a foot or so from the desk, Helena really turned up the volume. Only problem was, no one could hear her but Maryse.

Wailing like a banshee, Helena pummeled the nurse with invisible fists and feet that never connected with their mark. Oh, but she'd managed another costume change and was now wearing long, bright purple boxing shorts with a neon green muscle shirt and swinging at the nurse with a pair of black boxing gloves. Apparently, something had gone wrong in the change, however, and instead of the new Nikes, she was back in the old pink pumps.

Maryse shook her head and almost hoped she'd get caught. Jail had to be better than this. Just as she thought the nurse would swing around the desk and discover her hiding spot, the woman turned and walked down a row of the shelves. Maryse let out a breath and sucked it back in again until the nurse returned from the row and made her way back out of the room, securing the door behind her.

"Are you still breathing?" Helena leaned down to look underneath the desk.

"I'm not sure," Maryse said as she crawled out from her hiding spot. "Ask me again in a minute." Maryse brushed some dust off her pants legs and looked back at Helena, who was still wearing the boxing outfit. "What's up with the shoes?"

Helena threw up her gloves in exasperation. "Hell if I know. I hope this isn't going to happen often. I'd hate to see a mixed combination of everything I've worn since my death each time I try to change clothes."

"Well, at least take off those gloves. You look ridiculous."

Helena glared, then focused on her hands, a wrinkle of concentration forming across her forehead.

Nothing.

She relaxed for a moment, took a deep breath and focused again.

Nothing.

Maryse groaned. "Forget it. You can figure it out later. Let's just get the hell out of here before the nurse comes back."

Helena stomped through the wall of the record's room, then stuck her head back inside. "It's clear. We can make a run for it."

Maryse nodded. "Good." She eased open the door and stepped into the hall, locking the door behind her. She had just started down the hallway toward the employee exit when Helena yelled, "She's coming back. Run!"

Run? How was she supposed to do that without making any noise? She yanked off her shoes and ran as fast as possible down the hall, slipping her way across the cold, hard tile. She could hear the clacking of heels behind her and knew Helena wasn't far behind. She rounded the corner to the employee exit and stopped for a moment to peer back around, using a medical cart that was positioned at the corner to hide her face.

Helena was huffing down the hall as fast as her heels would allow, which wasn't exactly setting speed records compared to the nurse about twenty feet behind her wearing those white tennis-looking shoes that they all wear. Maryse spun away from the corner and dashed toward the employee exit. Helena could fend for herself. It wasn't like anyone could see her anyway.

Maryse had just unlocked the exit door and was about to edge through when Helena rounded the corner and hit the medical cart, sending all of the contents flying down the hall. Maryse let the door close with a bang and ran across the parking lot, waving her sneakers like an idiot and hoping like hell Luc was paying attention.

Apparently, he was on high alert, because the car started immediately, then raced across the parking lot, headlights off. He screeched to a stop beside her and she jumped in and yelled, "Let's go!"

Luc tore out of the parking lot without question, and Maryse turned around, kneeling over the front seat, her eyes fixed on the employee exit door. Sure enough, the nurse burst out of it as soon as they hit the parking lot exit. Helena came barreling behind the nurse and knocked her clear to the ground as she ran out the door.

"What about Helena?" Luc asked, watching the fiasco in the rearview mirror.

"We'll wait for her at the gas station down the road. There's no way I'm taking a chance on getting caught here. After all, no one can see her."

Maryse turned around and slid down into the passenger seat. "We can stop at the Texaco at the end of the street. I need a cold beer anyway."

Luc frowned. "You shouldn't drink while you're taking pain medication."

Maryse waved a hand in the air in dismissal. "I'm not taking those pills, and besides, there's not a painkiller strong enough to cover what I've been through tonight."

Luc looked in the rearview mirror once more. "That bad, huh?"

Maryse slumped in her seat, her entire body aching from all the running. "I don't think a beer is going to cover it, either."

Luc smiled. "Jack Daniels with a shot of cyanide?"

"Only if you make it a double."

Maryse had downed one beer and was seriously contemplating a second when Helena rounded the corner at the gas station. She was still wearing the gloves and apparently hadn't had any success in the shoes department, either. The only switch was her top, which had reverted back to the polyester suit jacket, but it was layered on top of the neon green muscle shirt. Put together with the purple shorts, it was a nightmare of monumental proportions.

Luc took one look at her and spit his soda on the ground, his face contorted in agony, and Maryse knew he'd taken as much soda up the nose as he'd put onto the pavement.

"What the heck happened?" Luc finally managed.

"Apparently, Helena is having a bit of a wardrobe malfunction," Maryse replied. "Don't even ask how she got that way. She can't tell you." Maryse turned to Helena and glared. "And why did you have to pick running out of the hospital as the time to figure out how to touch things? Are you trying to get us caught?"

"Do you think I was trying to turn that damned cart over? If I wanted for it to happen, it never would have. Then that nurse with an ass as wide as a barn had to get in front of me on my way out the door and it happened again. But can I get these things off?" She shook the gloves again. "No, that would be far too convenient."

The throbbing in Maryse's head began to amplify. "Let's just get back to the hotel," she told Luc. "I have some research to do on Mildred's computer."

Safely back at the hotel, Luc tried to insist that Maryse go straight to bed. Maryse had worked to hide the fact that her head was killing her, but she figured it showed on her face plain as day. Luc finally convinced her to take half of a pain pill, and after fifteen minutes or so, she started to feel a bit more human.

Normally, she would have thought that anyone taking Vicodin after drinking beer probably wasn't in the best condition to research the chemical makeup of prescriptions drugs, but Maryse didn't feel the least bit out of it. Maybe all the stress had worn off any chance of a buzz. It figured. The only good side effect was that the issues with her head had completely distracted her from her carnal thoughts of Luc.

She glanced over at his perfectly formed butt, tightly clad in faded jeans.

Well, almost completely.

She tore her gaze away from the Adonis of asses and plopped down into Mildred's office chair. Then she pointed at the door. "I can't work with you two underfoot."

Luc frowned but didn't say a word. After checking every window in the office and securing the latches—again—he perched outside the door and sent Helena outside to patrol the perimeter of the hotel. She didn't look particularly pleased with her assignment, especially as she was still wearing the pumps, but couldn't exactly argue since Luc strolling around the hotel at two A.M. would have looked a bit suspicious.

When her self-imposed bodyguards left the room, Maryse logged onto the Internet and began her research. She started with the chemical makeup of the medications Helena was taking and did a quick map of the areas of the body affected by them. Then she did a search of agents that would cause a respiratory collapse in spite of the medications taken, but without causing so much of an attack that it brought on suspicion. Last was the really fun part—figuring out how someone could have gotten their hands on one of those agents. It took a little over two hours to complete her work, and she had narrowed it down to a liquid contained in nuclear reactors and two different plants, one of which grew across almost every square inch of the preserve.

Which narrowed her suspects down to everyone in Mudbug. Again.

Chapter Fourteen

Morning came far too soon for Maryse, and she groaned as she pressed the buzzer on the alarm. She forced herself to a sitting position and looked at Jasper, who was curled up at the foot of the bed, giving her a hard stare. She reached over to rub his head. "I know you don't like being cooped up here, Jasper, but I swear it's only temporary and it's for your own good." She sighed and rose from the bed, hoping a shower would help her clear her mind and focus on the day ahead.

The shower refreshed her far more than she'd thought possible, and Maryse decided that staying alive for another day probably had a great effect on her mood. She dumped one of her Wal-Mart bags out on the bed and pulled a pair of gray yoga pants and a pink T-shirt out of the pile. The pink and white sports bra would do nicely, so she pulled that on first. She was just putting her first leg in the yoga pants when she saw the pink panties peeking out of the pocket of her sweats.

Damn. She'd forgotten about those undies. She bit her lower lip and stared at the tiny bit of string and lace. *It's not Sunday.* She tore her gaze away from the sexy panties and stuck her other foot in the yoga pants. *But they match.* She looked at the undies again. *You have no business dividing your attention right now.* She closed her eyes, trying to block the pink lace from her mind. *What if someone kills you and you're not wearing underwear? They'll talk about you forever.*

That did it.

Before she could change her mind, she stepped out of the yoga pants and grabbed the panties. The barely-there scrap of fabric clung to her curves, revealing more than they covered. The shade of pink was perfect against both the tanned and non-tanned parts of her body, and since a lot of both was showing, that was a good thing. Maryse turned to face the mirror and was surprised at the woman that looked back at her. She was almost...well...sexy.

She lifted one hand to her hair and fluffed her bangs a little. Okay, so she needed a cut, and a few highlights wouldn't hurt, and the combination of too much stress and not enough sleep had left bags under her eyes that her tinted sunscreen wouldn't put a dent in, but the rest of her wasn't all that bad. Which surprised her. How long had it been since she'd taken a real interest in her looks—months, years? She couldn't even remember.

And now Luc LeJuene had her longing for highlights and a better brand of makeup. Like she didn't have more important things to worry about. But even the thought of sudden death didn't stop her from pulling out the sunscreen, teasing her bangs just a bit to get that fluff she wanted, and positioning her breasts in the sports bra for the best display possible. By God, if she was going to croak, at least she was going to look good in the coffin.

With all her vacillating over underwear and makeup and eye bags, she was twenty minutes late for the morning meeting and still racking her brains trying to come up with assignments. Her goal was to make everyone feel useful while cleverly keeping them from harm's way without them figuring out what she was doing. A bit of a challenge to say the least.

"Good morning, everyone," Maryse said, and tried to sound cheery as she entered Mildred's office. She poured a cup of coffee and glanced around at the sober group. Luc still looked as frustrated as he had the night before when she'd delivered the bad news about the plant used to kill Helena. Sabine and Mildred both wore grim expressions, and she figured Luc had spent the last twenty minutes filling them in on the hospital escapades and subsequent lack of information they'd gained.

"Try and look a little more festive, people," Maryse said. "As far as I'm concerned, every day I can stay alive is cause for celebration."

They looked a bit guilty, and Maryse could feel some of the tension lift.

"Sorry, Maryse," Sabine said. "You're right. We should approach this with a positive attitude."

Like you approached your testing? Maryse wanted so badly to ask her friend that question, but now was definitely not the time. She looked closely at Sabine but couldn't find a single item different than it had been for years. Her skin looked fine, her hair was as thick and lustrous as ever, and although she seemed a bit less perky than usual, it was not quite seven-thirty in the morning and a good two hours before she usually awoke.

Maryse was just about to start in with her plans for the day when Helena entered the room through an exterior wall. Maryse did a double take. The gloves were gone, thank God, and so was the boxing/pink suit outfit. It was replaced, however, with blue jeans, the Nikes, and a T-shirt that read "I See Dead People."

Maryse tried to contain herself over the T-shirt but made the mistake of looking over at Luc, who had his face buried in his coffee mug, obviously straining not to laugh. She shot Helena a frown and cleared her throat to begin the meeting. "I suppose Luc filled you in on last night's hospital raid?"

Sabine and Mildred nodded, not saying a word, but Maryse noticed that Mildred's lips were pursed. Oh, boy. Maryse knew that as soon as Mildred got her alone, she was in for it. And since Mildred didn't know about Helena's rising from the dead, it was going to be hard to convince the hotel owner that last night was a necessary risk.

Maryse held in a sigh. It seemed that at almost every turn, she was pissing people off. Except Helena, who spent all of her time pissing *Maryse* off. "Okay," Maryse said finally, "so you know that we're back at square one with trying to figure out who might be trying to kill me. I have assignments for everyone so that we can cover more ground."

Maryse looked around the group, waiting for dissenters, but no one said a word. "Mildred, I need you to check in with your friends at the beauty parlor and find out where Harold's living and what he's been up to. I need to give Wheeler a way to reach him, and his cell phone's been disconnected."

Mildred nodded. "I think I know some people to get in touch with about that."

"Good. Luc, I need you to contact your uncle with the state and see if he can get a line on any of the oil companies who've shown serious interest in the Mudbug preserve. I know a corporation is a lot of ground to cover, but if we know who's interested, we might be able to find out who's been talking to them about the land."

Luc looked thoughtful for a moment, then said, "I'll call him as soon as the office opens this morning. He should have some ideas."

"Good. Were you able to find out anything about Harold's military service yesterday?"

Luc glanced at Helena again and frowned. "My sources seem to think we're on the wrong track there. Regardless of what Harold bragged about in Johnny's, they don't think there's any way the man had the skills for anything beyond cleaning toilets—and that's a direct quote."

"Got that shit right," Helena said. "Not that he actually ever cleaned a toilet."

Maryse shook her head and sighed, careful not to even glance in Helena's direction. "I'm inclined to agree with your source. So we'll leave that one alone for now unless more information comes to surface."

"What can I do?" Sabine asked.

Maryse glanced around at the group, not knowing at all how her next statement would go over with them. Finally, she looked back at Sabine. "I need you to make a trip to New Orleans and talk to Raissa."

Sabine gasped and her mouth formed a small *o*. But the reaction was only temporary. Apparently, her memory of Helena following Maryse around kicked in and the request no longer sounded strange.

Mildred cleared her throat and gave Maryse the ole lifted eyebrows look, and Maryse knew she wasn't buying one word of it. Given that Mildred didn't know about Helena, Maryse figured the hotel owner thought she was assigning Sabine something trivial to get her out of town and to safety, and she wasn't entirely wrong. But there was also the flipside. Now that Maryse had been forced into believing in the "spirit world," she figured she'd tap all sources. Raissa had made some interesting revelations in the past—all of which turned out to be true. Maybe she could do it again.

At this point, Maryse would take any edge she could get.

"What are you going to do?" Sabine asked.

"First, I'm going to check with the police and see if they have any information on my cabin exploding, and then I've got a couple of things to check at the office," Maryse replied. "Luc can drive me, so you don't have to worry about that." She looked over at Luc for confirmation. "That okay by you?"

Luc nodded, casting a sideways glance at Helena. "Fine by me."

"Okay, then, it's settled, and everyone knows the plan."

Mildred started to speak when the bells at the hotel entrance jangled. She jumped up from her desk and hustled out front to deal with her customers. Sabine waited until Mildred had closed the office door behind her before giving Maryse a shrewd look. "Helena's here, isn't she?"

"Oh, yeah. Sitting right next to you on the couch, as a matter of fact. How did you know?"

Sabine looked at the space on the couch next her, then back at Maryse. "You got that look on your face."

"What look?"

"Well, for lack of a nicer description, a look like you had really bad gas. Then Luc almost spit up his coffee, and I knew he could see her, too." She turned to look at Luc. "You can see her, can't you?"

"Every bit of her," Luc agreed, "which is sometimes very unfortunate." He gave Maryse a grin.

"I don't have to take this grief," Helena said.

"Yes, you do," Maryse said, and translated the conversation for Sabine.

Sabine shook her head in dismay. "This is so unfair. Why do you two get to see her and I can't? All those séances and midnight cemetery ceremonies trying to call my parents, and nothing. I've spent my entire life studying the paranormal to get the answers I need about my family, and I'm the only one in the room who can't see a ghost."

Luc shrugged. "It's not really all it's cracked up to be, Sabine. And believe me, you should be grateful you can't see and mostly *hear* Helena. She's no Casper."

Sabine tried to continue her pout but couldn't stop the giggle that finally erupted from her. "I guess you're right. Helena certainly isn't my first choice of the dead person I'd like to speak to."

Helena crossed her arms in front of her and glared. "You people should have more important things to do than rag on me. Why don't you get on with them?"

Maryse narrowed her eyes at Helena and smiled. "Funny you should bring up everything that needs to be done, because something I need done involves you directly. I just couldn't say anything in front of Mildred."

Helena gave her a wary look. "Okay, so what am I supposed to do?"

"Find Hank."

There was one beat of silence before everyone started in on her at once.

"I don't like it," Luc began.

Sabine jumped at the same time. "For Christ's sake, Maryse, what if he's the one trying to kill you?"

"Calm down, people. I didn't say *I* was going to confront Hank. I just want to know what he's up to. It's the only way to figure out whether he *is* the one trying to kill me. Do you think I just want to sit around waiting for it?"

Helena pursed her lips. "All of this is irrelevant because I have absolutely no idea where Hank is. I checked that pad of paper at my house. It was a motel room on the outskirts of town, but he's not there anymore. I checked."

"If we play this right," Maryse said, "we may be able to get him to come to us."

"How's that?" Helena asked.

"I'd bet my boat that Harold's still talking to Hank. As soon as Mildred finds out where Harold is staying, you can sit tight with him until he talks to Hank or leads you to where he is."

"Absolutely not," Helena said, and shook her head. "I am not spending my day watching over that man and whatever whore he's taken up with. No way."

Maryse leaned over, her face just inches from Helena's. "You'll do it all right."

"Or what?"

Maryse pointed at Sabine. "Or she'll start the proceedings for an exorcism."

Helena looked back and forth between Maryse and Sabine, not entirely convinced Maryse was serious but afraid of the alternative. And since Helena knew as much about ghosts as Maryse, even though she was one, she had no way of knowing whether or not an exorcism would do something harmful to her.

Which is what Maryse was counting on to keep her in line.

"You'd do that?" Helena asked, looking at Sabine and Maryse made the translation.

Sabine gave the couch a solemn nod. "In a heartbeat."

"Well," Helena said, and huffed. "Fine lot you are, ganging up on a defenseless ghost."

Luc snorted. "You're about as defenseless as a rattlesnake, Helena."

Sabine smiled and rose from her seat. "Means to an end, Helena. I'm going to get out of here. I need to put a closed sign on the shop and head to New Orleans to catch Raissa before she gets too busy." She leaned over to give Maryse a hug, then gave Luc a stern look. "Don't let anything happen to her."

Luc raised one hand as if giving his oath. "I promise."

As Sabine left the office, Helena turned to Maryse. "So what am I supposed to do until Mildred finds Harold—plot ways to kill him, write my memoirs, bikini wax…?"

Maryse grimaced. "Sit tight at the hotel and keep a watch for anyone who might attempt to blow it up. When Mildred gets the info, Luc and I will pick you up and take you wherever." She looked over at Luc, who nodded in agreement.

"Stay at the hotel?" Helena pouted. "This has got to be one of the most boring places on Earth."

Maryse grinned. "There's a whole group of traveling salesmen on the second floor. I bet they're on the pay-per-view movie log."

"Yuck," Helena said as she rose from the couch and disappeared through the wall.

Luc raised his eyebrows, and Maryse smiled. "Old joke."

Luc shook his head and put one arm around her shoulder, giving a light squeeze. "Let's go take care of things at the office."

Maryse nodded and started toward the door, not wanting to think about how nice Luc's arm felt draped across her shoulder. Not wanting to remember how her hair raised on her arm when he'd kissed her the night before. But that thin strip of lace beneath her yoga pants gave her away. She may be fooling Luc for now, but she wasn't fooling herself.

It took a five-minute phone call to confirm that the local cops didn't know any more now than they did the day before. Then Maryse and Luc headed out for the office. When they pulled into the office parking lot, Maryse was momentarily surprised to see cameras mounted on each corner of the building. She looked over at Luc who hurried to explain. "I had a buddy of mine who does security put up a couple of things. Just in case."

Maryse absorbed this for a moment, not sure how to feel about her every move being watched or recorded, but she couldn't argue with the advantage the cameras provided. "Thanks," she said, even though the thought of starring in her own movie made her more than a little self-conscious. "I really appreciate this, Luc." She squeezed his arm and pulled out her keys, wondering why Luc had gone to so much trouble for someone he barely knew.

After all, he was just another low-paid governmental scientist. He could study rat droppings in any set of mud and water across the state of Louisiana. There was no reason for him to stay here, especially with the danger that was very, very real.

Unless his reasons are personal.

She shook that thought off and unlocked the door. Luc insisted on entering first and did a quick inspection of all the rooms. When he was satisfied everything was clear, Maryse took a seat at her desk and checked phone messages. The first three were from Aaron, and he sounded excited. The fourth trial had worked and the mice hadn't gotten sick yet—something most cancer treatments couldn't offer at all.

Ecstatic, Maryse made a hasty call to Aaron, explaining that she was temporarily staying at the Mudbug hotel, just in case he needed to reach her after hours and couldn't get her on her cell. Aaron asked what was up with the hotel, but Maryse figured her house exploding would be information overload, so she played it off as repair work being done. She didn't want Aaron's focus to be on anything but the trials. After getting a few more details on the tests, she hung up the phone, jumped up from her desk, and danced a jig.

Luc looked over at her and smiled, her excitement obviously infectious. "Good news, I take it?"

"The best! Aaron said the mice came through the fourth trial with flying colors and haven't even had to take a sick day."

Luc frowned, and she felt her spirits drop a bit. What could possibly be wrong with that news? "What's the matter?" she asked.

"What?" Luc's eyes took on focus, and he appeared to jerk himself back into the present. "No, nothing's the matter. In fact, that's great news."

"Then what was the frown for?"

He gave her a direct look and asked, "Is this Aaron another Christopher?"

It took Maryse a second to figure out what he was trying to ask in an indirect way. Then she let out a laugh. "No way. Aaron's been in a relationship with the same person for eight years now."

Luc narrowed his eyes at her. "That doesn't make a difference to some people."

"With a man."

Luc blinked once and looked a bit startled. "Oh, well I guess that does make a difference." He gave her a curious look. "What exactly are you using for the test, and where did you find it?"

Maryse shook her head and gave him a smile. "If you're really nice, one day I might show it all to you, but for now, I'd like to keep it on the down-low. At least until I know I'm really onto something." *And I can find it again.*

"Oh, I can be nice."

He smiled and stepped directly in front of her, his body so close she could feel the heat radiating off him. The hair on her arms immediately stood on end, and her heart beat so loudly, she was certain he could hear it. This time, Maryse knew there was no way in hell she was holding herself back. She had the underwear to prove it.

He lifted one hand and gently touched the side of her face. "But research is not exactly what I'm really interested in seeing at the moment," he said.

Before she could reply, or protest, or breathe, he lowered his lips to hers. Even though he'd kissed her twice before, she was still unprepared for her body's instant response as his lips connected with hers. Every inch of her skin tingled.

She moved closer to him as the kiss deepened, aligning her body with his. She pressed her hips into him. He stiffened immediately, and she reached around and placed her hands on the butt that she'd been longing to squeeze for days. Luc's hands dropped to cup her breasts.

He stroked the sensitive nipples through her shirt as his tongue mingled with hers, first slow and sexy, then increasing in intensity. Maryse could feel the warmth of his hand and groaned as his fingers stroked her engorged nipples and wished there wasn't so much fabric between them. She was just about to tear off her own clothes, then launch for Luc's when he slid his hands down to her waist and pulled her T-shirt and sports bra over her head.

Her breasts stood at full attention as the cool air of the room blew over them, but Luc immediately set to warming them back up, cupping her breast in his hand, stroking the nipple with his thumb, while trailing kisses down her neck. When he put his lips on her other breast she felt her knees weaken. Luc paused for a moment and gave her a sexy smile, knowing with certainty what he was doing to her untrained flesh.

"Don't stop," she whispered. "I want you to touch every square inch of me."

Luc laughed and lifted her onto the desk. "Oh, I have absolutely no intention of stopping. I was only repositioning you for what I had in mind next." He lowered his head to her breast again and took it in his mouth, swirling his tongue around and around until she thought she would beg for more. As his mouth worked its magic, he reached down and slid her yoga pants off and let them fall into a heap on the floor. His hand went back to her waist, but when he came to the lacy underwear, he paused. He pulled back ever so slightly and looked down at the thin strip of pink that barely covered her. He placed one finger inside the fabric at her hip and started to slide it toward her center. "My God, Maryse. Do you have any idea what you do to me?"

Maryse sucked in a breath as his hand moved slowly downward to the place she desperately wanted it to be. "I was hoping you'd show me," she said.

Luc lowered his head to her neck once more and trailed kisses all the way down to her breasts, all while slowly inching his finger toward her core, building a sweet anticipation that she thought might send her over the edge before they got any further. Maryse bit her lip to keep from encouraging him to hurry. Finally, he rubbed his finger across her sensitive nub, and pleasure flashed through her, making her groan.

He stroked her slowly, gently, as his mouth continued its assault on her breasts, and just when she thought she was going to lose it, he stopped and started trailing kisses down her stomach as he worked the bit of lace off her body. As he inched closer and closer to her throbbing sex, she eased back until she was lying on the desk, certain that any moment she would melt into a puddle on the floor.

When his warm tongue made contact with her, it felt like a jolt of electricity burning from her center and spiking through the top of her head. Her vision blurred, and the room moved in waves. Up and down, he continued his assault, then switched to a gentle swirl. Maryse wished like hell she had something to grip... comforter, bedsheets...anything. Luc increased his speed, and her legs began to quiver, her breathing stopped altogether, and she clutched his hair in both her hands. Then the orgasm hit her like an atomic bomb, and she cried out as wave after wave of intense pleasure rushed over her body.

Her hips began to buck and thrash around, but Luc held them in place, obviously not yet done with her. He slowed his pace, and Maryse panted, trying to get her breath back, and before she knew it, the heat at her center was building again. Just when she thought he would send her over the edge again, Luc stopped his assault and rose up. It was only then that Maryse realized he'd pushed down his jeans and she could see every perfect square inch of him.

Luc rolled on a condom, gathered her in his arms, then kissed her deeply. Holding her face in his hands, he entered her. She gasped as he filled her and gently bit the soft flesh of his neck. Luc groaned and increased his stroke both in speed and length. She dug her nails into his back, clinging to him like a drowning woman, as he entered her over and over, each stroke better than the last, until she felt the fire building to an inferno.

"Oh God, Luc," she started, then couldn't continue.

Luc held her tighter and drove deeper. As her body clutched around him, they moved together again and again until she climaxed, pushing him over the edge with her.

They clung to each other for a while, neither of them wanting to move. Then Luc moved back enough to lower his lips to her again. "You are the most incredible woman," he whispered and kissed her again.

Maryse smiled as he finished the kiss. "I'd have to say that incredible thing works both ways. I don't think I can move my legs."

Luc laughed and drew her close to him again. "Then I guess we'll just have to stay here until you can."

Maryse lay her head on his shoulder and tried to concentrate on breathing. She was beginning to think she might actually recover when the alarm went off, shrieking with a high-pitched whine. Maryse jumped off the desk in a panic, scanning out the windows for movement, and certain that any minute, she was going to have a heart attack. But hey, at least it removed the necessity of finding something to say during that uncomfortable period following post-coital recovery.

Luc yanked on his pants, ran to his desk, and pulled a 9mm out of his top drawer. "Get down and stay down," he ordered, then left the office through the back door.

Maryse sank down onto the floor and slid around behind the desk, dragging her clothes with her as she went. She wiggled around on the cold, hard tile to pull on her yoga pants and T-shirt, then peeked around the desk and snagged her tennis shoes. These days she never knew when running might be called for.

Ready for action, she peeked over the top of the desk looking for a weapon, but the two best options were a stapler and a letter opener. Both required a proximity to the killer that she wasn't really interested in achieving, but unless she wanted to scotch tape the killer's hands together and mark the event on the calendar, the stapler and letter opener were her best options. She grabbed the two items and slid back down behind the desk.

She listened intently for any sound of Luc, but the alarm was so loud it drowned out everything. What had tripped it? And more importantly, what did they have planned for her?

And what was Luc doing toting around a gun, especially something like a 9mm?

Sure, most people that worked on the bayou carried some form of protection. Maryse had a 12-gauge and the pistol with the rubber bullets, but a 9mm? There wasn't anything in the bayou requiring that kind of rapid fire to stop. Even an alligator would back off a gunshot in a heartbeat.

Her mind flashed back to Luc's actions when the alarm went off—the way he crept down the hall, pressed flat against the wall. And when he'd left out the back door, it had been weapon first, just like in the movies. Except she got the feeling Luc wasn't imitating a movie when he'd left. It appeared to be a natural reaction from someone who had been through that same routine over and over again. Which made no sense at all for a zoologist.

But made all the sense in the world for a cop.

Chapter Fifteen

It was probably only five minutes before Maryse heard the back door creak open, but it felt like hours. She peered between the cracks of the desk and tried to see who had entered the office. She clutched her weapons and made the hasty decision that if the bad guy found her hiding place, she would stab him in the crotch with the letter opener, then staple his eyes. It was the best she could come up with.

When she heard Luc's voice yelling from down the hall, she let out a huge sigh of relief. She crawled out from under the desk and had just achieved a standing position when Luc ran into the office.

"Are you all right?" he asked and did a hurried check of the room, gun still firmly gripped in his right hand.

"Was anyone out there?"

Luc frowned. "No. But they could have gotten away before I made it outside."

Maryse nodded. "So what do you think happened?"

"I'm not sure, but I'm going to find out." He pulled out his cell phone and pushed in a number.

Whoever was on the other end of the call must have been sitting with the phone already at hand because Luc spoke as soon as he finished dialing. "Did you get anything?" he asked.

Maryse stared at him for a moment. She'd assumed he was calling the police, but that question didn't sound like anything you'd start with when calling 911.

Luc was quiet for a couple of seconds, then clenched his jaw. "I see," he said, and flipped the phone shut.

"Who was that?" Maryse asked, almost afraid to know the answer.

Luc picked his gun up off the desk and shoved it in the waistband of his jeans, then strode to the front office window and peered between the blinds. "We've got to get out of here," he said, ignoring her question.

"Why? Who did you call? What did they say? What's going on, Luc?"

"Later," Luc said, and opened the storage closet. On the top shelf sat computer and a monitor, flashing alternating pictures of each side of the outside of the office. Luc pulled a flash drive from the CPU and slid it into his jeans pocket.

Maryse stared at him in disbelief. "You had that recording? And couldn't someone just steal the flash drive?"

"Wouldn't do any good. There's a satellite on the roof. It's sending a feed to my buddy in New Orleans. That's who I called. The flash drive only covers part of the building."

Satellite feed? Monitored footage by remote in New Orleans? Maryse's head started to spin. Something was very, very wrong here. That was an awful lot of energy and time, not to mention the cost, to spend on a woman Luc hadn't even known the week before. "Luc, has someone broken in here before?"

Luc barely glanced at her and nodded, then looked out the window again. "The back door was unlocked the day after your truck wreck. I thought maybe you'd just forgotten to lock it, but then I clearly remembered checking it the night before. After your cabin blew up, I figured it couldn't be a coincidence."

Maryse blinked, trying to absorb everything, but it was like trying to take in *The Godfather* trilogy in a single sitting. "So what exactly did your buddy in New Orleans see when the alarm went off?"

Luc turned to face her, his expression grim, his jaw set in a hard line. "The suspect was behind the office. He was wearing a backpack and holding what looked like a spool of wire."

"And he probably wasn't hiking." Maryse studied Luc's face, certain there was more he wasn't telling her—like maybe why a zoologist was using words like "suspect."

Luc shook his head. "Not likely. He was probably about to rig another device like the one used on your cabin. Regardless, we need to get out of here and stay out until the week is over. This place is too remote. Not nearly enough escape routes."

Maryse narrowed her gaze and stared Luc straight in the eyes. "And exactly how many escape options does a zoologist need?"

Luc's expression went completely blank, and he looked away. "There's something we need to talk about," he finally said, "but it needs to wait. It wouldn't take much to launch a fire bomb in here."

Fire bomb? Launch? Hell, her stapler wasn't going to cover that one at all. "Fine. We're leaving now, but as soon as we're out of the parking lot, you're going to start talking."

Luc nodded and pulled the 9mm from his waistband. "Wait here a minute." He opened the front door and peered out with the gun clutched up near his shoulders, ready to take aim and fire. Then he edged out the door. A couple of seconds passed before he stuck his head back in and motioned her beside him.

Given that Maryse was certain she wasn't going to like whatever Luc was about to tell her in the car, the last place she wanted to be was close to him, but it was a better option than running with her stapler. Barely. She slipped outside and waited while he locked the door, then crept behind him, practically glued to his hip. Luc was on high alert, scanning all directions for a sign of movement.

Or bomb setters.

Maryse tried to maintain her cool, but with every step she grew more and more anxious to get away from this isolated stretch of bayou. This was all Helena's fault—her and her damned money. If this is what you got for mingling with "society," when it was all over, Maryse was burying herself deep, deep in the bayou where only the mosquitoes could find her.

They were almost to the car when a nutria scurried out of the underbrush directly in front of them. Before her mind could even register the small, beaver-like creature, Maryse dropped the stapler and hauled ass to the car, beating Luc's strides by a mile. She grabbed the door handle and yanked, thankful she didn't have long nails to break, jumped inside, and scrunched down as far as possible on the floorboard. Luc jumped in a second later, started the car, and tore out of the parking lot like they were on fire.

Which lately could be a real possibility.

When the rattle from the floorboard went away, Maryse knew they'd reached the highway. She inched up from her fetal position and onto the seat, albeit somewhat slouched, but at least in a semi-sitting position.

"You all right?" Luc asked, the concern evident in his voice.

"Oh, just peachy. I'm getting so used to people trying to bump me off that tomorrow I probably won't even run. In fact, I was just thinking I ought to wear my best dress every day to save the undertaker the time later on."

Luc gave her a small smile. "You're doing great, Maryse. Most people wouldn't have made it this long without having a nervous breakdown."

Maryse glared. "And what makes you think I haven't? Do I seem remotely normal to you?"

"You're completely out of your element. You've had a ton of physical and mental stress put on you in a very short time—not withstanding your new paranormal abilities."

A gross understatement. "Yeah, out of my element. Sorta like a zoologist toting a nine like a character from *Law & Order*?"

A light flush crept up Luc's face, and Maryse knew she was in for some very bad information. Luc stared out the windshield a few seconds before speaking. "I got involved with you because it was my job."

"And that job is...and let's just stop pretending the answer is zoology."

"I'm a special agent for the DEQ."

Maryse straightened up in her seat. This was definitely not the answer she'd expected. "You're kidding me."

Luc pulled his ID out of his pocket and passed it to Maryse. Son of a bitch. Special Agent Luc LeJeune. Maryse's hands dropped into her lap seemingly of their own volition, like the badge was too heavy. "What in the world would the DEQ want with me? I'm the most boring person on Earth—or used to be anyway. What could I possibly be doing so wrong that it would bring a state investigation down on me?"

Luc shook his head. "It's not you. At least it didn't start out being you."

"What the hell are you talking about?" Maryse felt beads of sweat begin to form on her brow, frustration and confusion overwhelming her.

"The agency got a tip that a chemical company was dumping waste into the bayou. The informant claimed to be a resident of Mudbug, and on the surface, the information seemed to check out. Then the intel stopped—no more letters, no phone calls, and all attempts to locate this person failed. I was sent down here to find the informant and verify his claims. We're under a bit of pressure from the EPA."

"Oh my God! Is it toxic? Where is it?"

"We don't even know for sure that the dumping is going on, much less what the waste is or where it is. There's no reason to get excited just yet. If the dumping is going on, the site could be anywhere in the surrounding area, not necessarily in Mudbug."

Maryse took a minute to process this information. "So you think someone is dumping toxic waste into the bayou somewhere, and you're undercover to find the guy who tipped you off. Then why are you hooked up with me?"

Luc stared out the window again. "At first it was business. Then it got personal. I thought you'd figured that out."

Personal? As in he liked her so he was trying to protect her? And business—what business? She wasn't in any danger when Luc first arrived. "So you came down here to locate a mole and instead, you end up seeing ghosts and playing protector for me. Does that cover it?"

Luc nodded. "I guess so. I care about you, Maryse, and you don't have the training or ability to deal with something like this. I was afraid something bad would happen if I didn't help—am still afraid."

He cared about her? He *was* spending an awful lot of time putting himself in danger. But the fact remained that he didn't care enough to tell her the truth. Not until he was left with no other choice. "And what does your agency think of your extra-curricular activities?"

Luc frowned. "They're not happy. They think I've drawn too much attention to myself and they're afraid it will blow my cover."

Maryse narrowed her eyes, certain that something in his story didn't ring true—not exactly. How was Luc supposed to discover the informant when he'd been shut up in an office with her? "But you're still here."

"I couldn't leave you this way."

Bullshit. "Why not? You could lie to me this way." Then a thought came to mind—a memory of Luc trying to read her notebook that day in her lab. "You thought I was the informant."

"That was one possibility, yes."

"And the other possibility?"

Luc looked out the window down the highway, a slight flush creeping up his neck. Maryse stared at him for a moment, then it hit her. "Oh, my God. You thought I was covering for the chemical company. Somehow hiding the evidence of the pollution."

Luc jerked his head around to look at her. "No, I never thought that, even when the agency suggested it. I looked into your research because I thought you'd come across the source. I didn't know what you were working on until Helena let the cat out of the bag." He sighed. "I'm sorry, Maryse. I didn't want to lie to you, but I couldn't tell you the truth. Don't you understand that?"

Maryse looked directly in his eyes. "All I understand is that every man I've been with has used me in one form or fashion, and you've turned out to be no different."

He put one hand on her arm, but she brushed it off. "Don't even bother. In fact, you can drop me off at the hotel and return to your high security office in the bayou. I won't be needing your services any longer, *Agent* LeJeune."

Maryse didn't say a word as Luc drove the rest of the way back to the hotel, and Luc was obviously smart enough to know he wasn't going to talk his way out of this one. But the longer she sat in silence, the angrier she became. What the hell had she been thinking? Not only had she allowed herself to be used by another lying asshole, she'd actually welcomed him with open arms—and legs. What was it about her that she couldn't find an honest man to save her life?

Which was sort of an ironic question since apparently a *dishonest* man had done just that.

She stared out the window and held in the tears that threatened to fall. Damn it. Why did she always have to cry when she was mad? Just when she'd thought her life couldn't get more screwed up than it already was, she had to go add insult to injury by sleeping with Luc.

And even worse—she'd enjoyed it.

No more men, she vowed, as Luc swung the car onto Main Street. Society might as well give her a wimple and start calling her "sister."

They pulled into the hotel parking lot, and before Luc brought the car to a complete stop, Maryse jumped out, slamming the door behind her, and stalked into the hotel. She could hear the car idling behind her but forced herself to look straight ahead and never hesitate in her stride. When she reached the door to the hotel, she heard the engine rev as the car screeched out of the parking lot. She glanced down the street as she stepped into the hotel and saw the car round the corner to the highway.

Probably going to see his "buddy" in New Orleans. Another DEQ agent, she had to assume at this point. Maybe they were going to review the tapes and see if Luc recognized the man outside the office. And then a terrible, horrible thought hit her. Her eyes blurred, and she walked headfirst into the corner of the door.

Video tape! Satellite feed!

And she'd been having sex with Luc right there on the desk in the middle of the office.

Sex on her desk wasn't exactly the way she'd always pictured herself on film. No, for her first foray onto camera, she'd had something a bit more dignified in mind, and something requiring a lot more clothes. Something like accepting the Nobel Prize for Medicine.

Her one foolish dream.

"Something wrong with you?" Mildred asked as she entered the hotel office, completely cutting into her thoughts of a royal romp.

Maryse frowned. A shorter list would probably be what wasn't wrong. "Nothing more than the usual." *And a videotaped orgasm with a lying DEQ agent.*

Mildred stared, not looking in the least bit convinced. Time for a distraction.

"Any luck locating Harold?" Maryse asked.

"Yep. Sara Belle down at the salon says she's almost positive she saw Harold unloading a suitcase at that fleabag motel on the outskirts of town."

Maryse groaned and slapped her forehead. "Helena left him that motel. Why didn't I think of that?" And even more, why didn't Helena think of that? Did she have to do all the work here?

Mildred narrowed her eyes at Maryse. "You're not thinking of tailing Harold, are you? 'Cause I don't have enough savings to post bail for murder. I don't want you anywhere near Hank Henry unless the police are involved. With guns. And Mace. Lots of Mace. And maybe one of those electric rods that makes you stupid senseless when it touches you."

"A stun gun," Maryse provided, although it was pointless information. Hank was already stupid senseless. Being jolted with fifty thousand or so volts of electricity might even make for an improvement. And if not, it would certainly make for a good show. "I'm not going to tail Harold," Maryse assured her. "I'll have someone else do it. Someone less conspicuous than me."

Mildred nodded. "Good. Probably needs to be Luc then. You know I love Sabine, but she's not exactly the sharpest tool in the box. You don't have to know where you came from to decide where you're going. If only she'd get her head out of the damned clouds and down here on Earth, that girl could probably make a lot of herself."

"Sabine's fine, and lately, she's backed off a lot on the whole parental search thing." Maryse waved a hand in dismissal. "I know you think the whole paranormal thing is complete bunk, but at least she's making money. There are probably worse things."

Mildred stared at her for a moment. "*I* think the whole paranormal thing is bunk? Last time I checked, you weren't exactly jumping on that bandwagon either. Did you hit your head too hard in one of those mishaps of yours?"

Oops. Momentary lapse of consciousness. And definitely all Luc's fault. She gave Mildred a sheepish smile. "Of course, I don't buy into that stuff. I've just given up trying to convince Sabine otherwise. As long as her business is successful, I guess I just decided who cares."

Mildred narrowed her eyes, and Maryse knew the hotel owner suspected something was up. Something Maryse wasn't telling her. In ten billion years she'd never come up with the ghost of Helena Henry, so Maryse figured she was in the clear as long as she didn't spout off something stupid again.

"Well, why don't you try to rest," Mildred said finally. "I'll be right here if you need me." She pointed to the front of the hotel. "And no standing in front of the plate-glass window."

Maryse nodded and left the office. There was no way possible she could rest. Between ghosts, attempted murder, and videotaped sex, she was about to have that nervous breakdown she'd been putting off. And avoiding Mildred until she had control of her racing emotions probably wasn't a bad idea. If she stayed in the office with Mildred's hawk eye on her, she knew she'd end up confessing her sins of the flesh. And she wasn't ready to discuss her romp with Luc the Liar, especially given her track record with questionable men.

She snuck in a call to Sabine but got her voice mail. She left her a brief message with instructions to come directly to the hotel when she got back from visiting Raissa, then closed her phone, shoved it in her pocket, and sighed. Finally deciding she couldn't stand around in the hallway until Sabine showed up, she grabbed a bottle of Pledge and a rag from the storage closet and began to polish the spindles on the stairwell. She finished that chore in about thirty minutes, and then Sabine walked in, saving her from doing something really strange, like vacuuming the lobby. Sabine stared at her for a moment, then sniffed the air. Since the entire stairwell smelled lemony fresh, there was really no hiding what she'd been up to.

Sabine raised one eyebrow. "You want to tell me why you're avoiding Mildred?"

Maryse glared. "I thought you weren't psychic."

Sabine laughed. "It doesn't take a genius to see that something's wrong if the woman who hates cleaning more than root canals starts breaking out the Pledge on a building that's not even hers."

Maryse shrugged. "I'm stressed."

"Bullshit. You drink when you're stressed. You clean when you're avoiding."

"Well, Mildred hasn't figured it out, so I guess it doesn't matter."

Sabine shook her head. "Mildred knows damned good and well why you're cleaning. She also knows that you won't breathe a word to her about whatever secret you're keeping until there's no other choice."

"Got that right," Maryse mumbled.

"She also knows that you'll tell me if it's important, and I'll tell her."

Maryse stared at her so-called best friend in dismay. "Is this what the two of you do when I'm not around? Plot ways to analyze my life and then share things I've told you in confidence?"

Sabine had the good sense to look guilty. "It's not like that. It's just that Mildred and I both worry about you, and you don't make it easy on people by secluding yourself so much on the bayou. I've seen you more since Helena died than I have in the past six months."

Maryse sank onto the stairs. "You know you're welcome at my place anytime, or at least you were when I had a place. And Mildred too. I know I didn't come to town often, but it just wasn't necessary. I had everything there that I needed."

Sabine sat beside her on the stairwell and gave her a sad smile. "But don't you see, Maryse? You didn't have everything you needed. You're losing sight of people, how they operate, what motivates them. If you were more social, you would have seen Christopher coming a mile away." She paused for a moment, then took a breath before continuing. "And I hope this doesn't make you mad, but I don't have to be psychic to see what's going on between you and Luc. Right now, I'd bet anything that's what drove you to dusting."

Maryse felt her back tense at the mention of Luc's name. Was she really that easy to read? "Are you saying I have to become the life of the party or I'm always going to get screwed? If so, then I'm in trouble. I just don't have what it takes to conquer the world."

"Raissa's worried about you. She has the feeling that you're overlooking something important because it's too close to you. She's going to do another reading tonight and call me." Sabine placed her hand on Maryse's and squeezed. "You don't have to conquer the world, Maryse, but you can't hide from it either."

She wasn't hiding, Maryse wanted to yell. But somehow the words hung in her throat. She wasn't hiding. Was she? Her laboratory work was the most important thing in her life, and it required an enormous amount of time, but surely no one was going to blame her for spending her time in the lab.

But as soon as that thought crossed her mind, she got flashes of long Saturdays where she'd finished up everything at the lab by noon and spent the rest of the day reading medical journals or cruising the bayou looking for hybrid plants that she might not have used for testing before. If she wasn't working on her research, then she was tearing apart her kitchen to put in shelves or some other household chore that wasn't really necessary. She hadn't even picked up a novel or turned on the television in longer than she could remember.

Was her motivation to find a cure really as selfless as she'd thought? Or had the strain of watching her father waste away provided her with a convenient excuse to lock herself away from life?

"Maryse." Sabine gently shook her arm. "Are you all right? I wasn't trying to hurt your feelings."

"I know," Maryse said. Sabine hadn't hurt her feelings, but she'd unknowingly unlocked a floodgate that made it frighteningly clear that Maryse had been living away from the world far too long.

Chapter Sixteen

Before Maryse could mull over her newfound revelation and figure out what the hell it meant for her future—if there was one—Helena walked through the hotel wall and ruined the entire moment.

"Helena's here," Sabine said.

Maryse stared at Sabine.

"It's that look on your face…remember, like you have gas," Sabine explained.

Helena shot Sabine a dirty look, then asked, "Did Mildred find Harold?"

"Yeah," Maryse said, "he's at that motel where you left him. Are you ready to do this?"

Helena sighed. "I'm as ready as I'll ever be to see Harold again, or Hank, for that matter. But I guess I sorta owe you given that this whole mess is my fault."

A bit of an understatement.

"Okay," Maryse said. "I'll check out with Mildred and tell her Sabine and I are going to the store to pick up some stuff I forgot yesterday." She turned to Sabine. "That's assuming, of course, that you'll drive, since Luc sorta left in my car."

Sabine wrinkled her brow, obviously wanting to delve into the topic of Luc but not wanting to do it now. "Sure, as long as you're not carrying any kind of weapon in case we run into Hank. I don't have enough money for bail."

Maryse sighed. "Now you're starting to sound like Mildred."

There was a bit of a scuffle in the parking lot while Sabine and Helena argued, with Maryse as the translator, over who would ride shotgun. Sabine thought Maryse should ride shotgun and Helena thought she deserved the seat as she would be doing all the legwork once they got there.

Maryse looked at Helena and pointed to the backseat. "You can't sit in the front, Helena. Sabine is not going to drive around town with me in the back like she's chauffeuring. The key to investigating is to avoid attention, not attract it."

Maryse guessed the image of two adults and a ghost in a car flitted through Helena's mind, because she got into the back seat and stopped grumbling. Sabine made the drive to the Lower Mudbug Motel in under twenty minutes and parked across the street in a lot for an all-night diner. Maryse scanned the seedy area with a critical eye and hoped they wouldn't get jacked for Sabine's 1992 Nissan Sentra while sitting there, but the only other choices were an X-rated video store or a tattoo parlor.

Helena frowned when Maryse pointed to the motel, but she didn't say a word as she left the car and walked through the lobby into the dilapidated old building. She returned a couple of minutes later to report that the asshole was indeed inside with one of his floozies, and not even the same one he'd left in the car at the reading of the will. Maryse's mind flickered for a moment onto exactly what kind of woman, much less two, took up with someone like Harold Henry, but she didn't have the time to ponder it now and probably didn't have the requisite intelligence, or lack thereof, to understand it all.

Their mark established, she pulled out her cell phone and gave Wheeler a call, instructing him to give her five minutes, then make the call to Harold at the motel. She closed the phone and looked at Helena. "You're on. Maybe this time you'll get lucky and Harold will be naked."

Helena glared at her, got out of the car, and stomped all the way to the motel and through the wall. Sabine shook her head and looked over at Maryse. "You know, you really shouldn't bait her that way. It just frustrates you more."

"I know, but the woman is impossible. I'm fairly certain that if it turns out either Hank or Harold killed her, a Mud-bug jury would not only let them off, but probably give them a medal."

Sabine smiled. "I know what you're saying, I really do, but I'm starting to think that maybe Helena isn't all that bad. After all, she made sure the town was protected by giving you the land, and she used the money you paid her to pay down your debts."

"Which, now that you mention it," Maryse interrupted, "she still hasn't really explained."

"And she gave all that stuff to an orphanage," Sabine continued, ignoring her outburst. "I guess I'm starting to wonder if there wasn't a purpose behind Helena being a bitch all these years."

Maryse stared out the windshield at the Lower Mudbug Motel. "Well, if there was, I'm not getting it."

It seemed to take forever for Helena to return, but it couldn't have been more than ten minutes before Maryse saw her leap from the second floor and hit the ground with one of those military rolls. She was wearing green camouflage and looked like a rolling bush except for the black smudges glistening under her eyes, which made her resemble a linebacker given her rather dense frame. When her body finally lost all momentum, Helena lay completely still, sprawled on the weedy lawn of the cheap motel, and for a moment, Maryse wondered if it was possible to die twice.

A few seconds later, Harold came hurrying out of the hotel entrance. Maryse and Sabine ducked down in the car, trying to peer over the dashboard. Helena burst into the backseat seconds later, still huffing and puffing from her Rambo acrobatics.

"Where's he going in such a hurry?" Maryse asked Helena.

"He called Hank as soon as he got off the phone with Wheeler," Helena replied. "He's going to meet him now."

Maryse repeated the information to Sabine, who had already started the car and was inching toward the parking lot exit as

Harold left the motel in a late model, rust-covered sedan. "Hang back a little," Maryse instructed. "I don't want him to see us."

"I'm trying," Sabine said as she pressed down on the accelerator, "but he's driving like an idiot."

"He is an idiot," Helena said.

"Hell," Maryse said as she peered over the dashboard and watched as Harold pushed the upper limits of the rusty sedan. "We should have had Helena ride with Harold."

Sabine's hands were clenched on the steering wheel as she inched her car faster down the highway. Maryse was pretty sure her friend had almost reached her limit of speed and fear when suddenly Harold's car jerked over to the side of the road and disappeared into the brush. Sabine cut her speed and eased onto the shoulder, then slowly pulled up to the spot where they'd last seen Harold.

A rutted trail overgrown with grass and weeds led into the bayou. Maryse cursed under her breath. "We can't follow him down there. He'd see us coming for sure, and we have no idea what we'd be running into."

"We don't have to follow him," Helena said. "I know where he's going."

Maryse yanked around in her seat to look at Helena. "Where?"

"My family had a camp off this trail," Helena said. "Harold told me years ago that it had fallen in such disrepair that it wasn't habitable."

"And you never checked?"

Helena looked at Maryse as if she'd lost her mind. "Tromp around in the bayou? No thanks. Not all of us have your higher aspirations, Maryse. And I damned sure don't cotton to running into snakes or alligators or even bugs."

"The only snake down that trail is Harold," Maryse shot back, "and probably Hank."

Helena shrugged. "Probably. Harold only started staying at the motel a couple of years ago, so he was taking his bit of snatch somewhere before that. Most likely it was the camp, but I never thought of it."

Just like Helena to forget something important. Maryse pointed to the trail. "Well, now's your chance to get caught up on things happening behind your back."

Helena crossed her arms in front of her and shook her head. "Absolutely not. I am not wading into the marsh."

Maryse threw her hands in the air. "What do you think is going to happen to you? You're already dead!"

Helena glared. "You don't have to keep reminding me of that, you know. It's rude."

"Maybe it's hard to take you seriously when your face looks like a linebacker for the Saints."

"Well, crap," Helena grumbled and waved her hands in front of her face like a magician. If she pulled a rabbit out of her ear, Maryse swore she was going to kill her.

"What about this?" Helena asked a couple of seconds later. "Is the black gone?"

Maryse took one look at Helena, then closed her eyes and counted to ten. The black was gone, but she had managed to replace it with a vibrant, traffic-stopping orange. "Yeah, it's gone, and just in case it's deer season, you've got that covered too."

"Well, it will just have to stay that way," Helena said as she drifted through the car door and tromped off into the marsh.

As soon as she was gone, Maryse repeated the conversation to Sabine. "So now we just have to decide what to do next," Maryse said.

Sabine shook her head. "No, we don't. You're going to call your attorney and have Hank served. That's it."

Maryse cast a wistful glance down the trail. Oh, but for the chance to throttle the life out of Hank Henry. "But don't you think—"

Sabine cut her off with a hand. "No, I don't think, and you don't either. You promised."

Maryse turned in her seat and looked Sabine straight in the eyes. "Just like we promised to never keep secrets from each other?"

Sabine averted her eyes. "I don't know what you're talking about."

Maryse wanted to be angry with her friend for keeping something so important from her, but her fear was so evident that Maryse's heart broke in two. She clasped her hand gently over Sabine's. "I know about the tests."

Luc leaned over Brian and studied the monitor, then banged one fist on the desk, unable to hold in his frustration any longer. "Damn it! There's no clear shot of his face."

Brian looked up at him and let out a breath. "I tried everything, Luc. I know what you were hoping for, but this guy just didn't give us the right view. Man, I'm sorry."

Luc scanned the blurry image one last time and clapped Brian on the shoulder. "It's not your fault. This guy knew what he was doing."

Brian nodded. "Yeah, with the collar on that jacket turned up, the sunglasses, and his cap pulled down so low, one might think he was trying not to be recognized."

"One might," Luc agreed. "So what were you able to get?"

Brian pulled a sheet of paper off the printer and handed it to Luc. "I figured you'd want a copy of the analysis, but basically, this is what we have: the guy is about six feet tall, large frame, and looks like he was built at some time but his body's lost its tone. His body movement puts him roughly in the fifty to sixty age range, assuming no debilitating injuries on a younger man, and he's white. That's about all I can give you."

Luc sighed. "Great—an old, flabby, white male. You've just described half of the men in Mudbug."

"I know it's not much, but this along with the info you got on the explosion at the cabin makes me think you were right on your military assumption. Whoever this is, they had rigged explosives before, and based on the switches, they're either former military or learned from someone who was."

Luc nodded. "Once again, half the men in Mudbug. And what about the petroleum company info I called you about on the way here?"

Brian nodded and pulled up another file on his computer. "I cross-referenced all the companies licensed to drill in Louisiana with current operating locations. I figured companies with a base already established near the area would be the most likely to know about the land and want to acquire it."

"Good thinking." Luc leaned toward the monitor and studied the page as it opened. "Three companies, huh? You think it's good information?"

"I think it's as close as we're getting to start. But don't ask me what you're supposed to do with the info from here."

"I have an idea about that," Luc said.

Brian groaned. "Man, I hate it when you get ideas."

"Don't worry. This one is easy and completely legal."

"Well, that's a change. Lay it on me."

"I need to know if any residents of Mudbug own a significant amount of stock in any of the companies. I can't imagine a board of directors would vote to bump someone off in the hopes that they can acquire some oil-filled land. There's plenty of it to be had in Louisiana and other people willing to lease. So it's got to be someone outside the company but with a vested interest in the company's success."

"Already ahead of you." Brian clicked to open a spreadsheet and pointed to a list of names. "These are the eight Mudbug residents who own stock in any of the three petroleum companies. Most have small investments. Nothing worth acting crazy for sure. But this one..." Brian pointed to a name on the spreadsheet. "He has a 5 percent share and a brother on the board of directors."

Luc read the name. "Thomas Breaux." He looked at Brian. "The doctor? Shit. That would explain everything."

"How do you figure?"

"We have to figure that Maryse wasn't the first target. Her mother-in-law had to be first, and Breaux was her doctor. If anyone would know how to bump off Helena Henry and get her buried without an autopsy, it would be her doctor."

"I don't suppose I have to tell you how he paid for medical school, right?"

"The military. Jesus, Brian," Luc said, and shook his head. "How do I get myself mixed up in this shit?"

Brian looked up at him and cocked his head to the side. "You know, I would say it's the white-knight syndrome—that whole damsel-in-distress thing, but this time it's different."

Luc shoved his hands in his pockets and avoided his buddy's gaze. "I don't know what you're talking about. This is hardly the first woman I've helped out of a tough spot."

"Yeah, but it's the first one you've fallen for." Brian smiled. "Unbelievable, LeJeune. I never thought I'd see the day. This botanist must be something else to have you so wound up."

Disappearing husband, exploding cabin, killer inheritance, a dead mother-in-law who hadn't quite left this world, and let's not forget trying to save the world from one of the worst diseases known to man. "Yes, she's something else all right," Luc agreed.

Brian grinned and opened his mouth, probably to rib Luc some more, but the door to the lab flew open and the boss strode in. "Damn it, LeJeune," he ranted. "You don't check your messages, you don't return calls, and now you're standing in the office and haven't checked in with me. I yanked you off the Mudbug assignment yesterday. Why weren't you in the office this morning?"

Luc looked at Wilson but didn't meet the other man's eyes. "I have a couple of things I need to wrap up down there."

"The hell you do! We've got our informant."

Shit. "Who is it?"

"That accountant that Duhon was following. Seems the profit margin increased a little too much for his taste, and he decided he was James Bond or something. Fucker isn't five foot two and scared of his own shadow, but he went poking his nose into things and found all the big shot's secret files. Then he made the phone call to the DEQ, got scared they'd kill him or something, and has been trying to find a new job ever since. Dumbass."

"Sounds like it," Luc said, stalling until he could figure out some reason to convince Wilson to let him stay in Mudbug another couple of days.

"Anyway, I need you to work with our scared shitless Sherlock and the other agents to gather enough evidence to prosecute. We have enough information to pin down the dumping sites, so your days of dallying with that botanist are over."

"There's some other things I'm looking into. Just a couple of days, boss, that's all I need."

"No way, LeJeune. You better be in this office at ten tomorrow morning for debriefing. Otherwise, don't bother coming in at all." Wilson spun around and strode out of the office, slamming the door behind him.

Brian whistled. "I haven't seen him this worked up since the Superbowl."

Luc nodded. "Football can be very emotional." He stared out the window for a moment, then looked back at Brian, the vaguest notion of an idea forming in his mind. "Hey, have you started mapping out the spots that informant said the dumping occurred?"

"Yeah, we've drawn samples from three so far."

"Can you get me the info on the exact locations and the results of your testing?"

"Not a problem. I'll e-mail everything as soon as I scan it all in."

"Okay," Luc said. "Do me another favor. E-mail me the phone number of the lab guy here who researched Maryse's work."

Brian narrowed his eyes. "I'll do it, but, dude, you are gonna be in some serious shit if you don't let this botanist thing go."

Luc stared at the shadowy figure on the monitor. "I can't. Not just yet."

Sabine stared at Maryse in shock. "How did you find out? Everything was supposed to be confidential."

"Your file was on the medical records desk when Helena and I broke into the hospital," Maryse said. "I'm sorry, Sabine, but I had to look. You understand, right?"

Sabine sniffed and rubbed her nose with her free hand. "I guess so. I probably would have done the same thing. But, Maryse, you have to know that everything is going to be fine. This one is no different than the others. I'm sure of it."

More than anything in the world, Maryse wanted to believe Sabine, wanted the faith of her friend's conviction, but the scientist in her knew the reality. And the girl who'd lost both her mother and father to the same disease was scared to death. "How can you be sure? Maybe you need to see a specialist. I know a doctor in New Orleans."

Sabine shook her head. "I'm nowhere near needing a specialist now or in the future. I've asked Raissa about this. She thinks I'm going to be fine."

"She thinks?" Maryse squeezed Sabine's hand. "That's just not good enough, Sabine. Please, please promise me that as soon as this is over, you'll let me take you to New Orleans and see that doctor I know. For me."

The tears that had been hanging on the rim of Sabine's eyelids finally spilled over, and she nodded. "Okay. I promise." She leaned over and clutched Maryse in a hug. "If you promise to be around to take me, I'll promise to go."

Maryse sniffled and tried in vain to hold back her own tears. "That sounds fair."

"Who died?" Helena's voice cut into their moment. "Oh wait, that would be me." The ghost grinned.

Maryse frowned at Helena and instructed Sabine to drive. "We don't want Harold catching us parked on the side of the road or we're busted."

Sabine edged off the shoulder and onto the highway, then made a quick U-turn and stomped on the accelerator. Maryse waited until they were out of sight of the trail, then turned in her seat to face Helena. "Well, are you going to fill me in?"

"Hank was there," Helena said, and frowned.

"And?"

"And what? The moron was there with his even more moronic father."

Maryse counted to five. "What did they say, Helena?"

Helena sighed. "Harold yelled at Hank for being so useless that I didn't leave him the land. Hank said it wasn't his fault and he didn't know anything about my will before the reading, which is true."

Maryse stared at Helena, but the ghost wouldn't meet her gaze. "What are you not telling me?"

Helena looked at Maryse, her sadness evident in her expression. "Harold said Hank wouldn't have to worry because it looked like he'd scared you into giving up the land."

"So it was Harold who tried to kill me." Maryse slumped back in her seat, not sure whether to be happy the mystery was solved or alarmed that Harold still walked the streets. God forbid he caught on to the fake land transfer before the week was up.

"I guess it must have been Harold," Helena said finally, "but I still can't believe it. Luc said those explosives were rigged by a professional. Harold was military, but I married the man, and I can tell you for certain, no one would ever let him work with explosives. Hell, he couldn't even grill chicken without burning himself, and the television remote—forget it."

"But according to Mildred, Harold was always bragging at Johnny's about his special forces tour," Maryse argued.

Helena shook her head. "I never went to Johnny's so I can't say, but if Mildred says so, then I guess it's so. All I know is Harold used to tell me after he came home from a bender that it was amazing how the world 'evened things out' over time."

Maryse stared at Helena. "What the heck is that supposed to mean?"

Helena shrugged. "I don't know, but I always took it as some remark about his military service."

"What's going on?" Sabine asked.

Maryse felt instantly guilty. "I'm sorry, Sabine. I keep forgetting you can't hear her." She filled in the blanks of her conversation with Helena.

"I don't like it," Sabine said when she finished.

"Maybe Harold had help from someone else. After all, if he's in cahoots with the oil companies, couldn't he find someone to pay for that kind of service—especially with the amount of money on the line?"

"It's possible," Sabine said, "but somehow it just doesn't feel right. Maybe we've been looking in the wrong place. Maybe it isn't Harold at all."

Maryse yanked her cell phone from her pocket and pressed in the speed dial for her attorney. "But what else is there?"

Thirty minutes later, a new stun gun in hand, Maryse took one look at Mildred's hotel, knowing she should probably go inside. As Sabine had pointed out before, they couldn't be certain Harold was the one gunning for Maryse, and it was much smarter for her to lie as low as possible until they were certain no one else had a hidden agenda. But the very thought of closing herself up in that tiny room, or even worse, sitting in Mildred's office and enduring the older woman's scrutiny, made her feel claustrophobic. And what difference did it really make in the big scheme of things? She could be inside in an interior room, hidden in a closet, and covered in Kevlar with a stun gun pointed at the door, and a bomb would still kill her.

"Maryse Robicheaux," Mildred's voice broke into her thoughts. "Get your skinny butt into this hotel." Mildred stood in the doorway of the hotel, hands on her hips and a disapproving look on her face. "Why don't you just stand in the middle of the street wearing a target on your back next time?"

As Maryse stepped onto the sidewalk, she heard the zing of something small and fast passing right by her head, then a crack of glass. She took the remaining two steps to the plate-glass window on the front of the hotel and looked eye level at a tiny hole that had pierced clean through the glass. A hole the size of a bullet.

Maryse jumped back from the window in horror as a second shot hit the brick building just above her head. In the split second she was trying to decide which way to run, someone slammed into her, half-shoving, half-carrying her into the entrance of the hotel. They landed on the hardwood floor of the hotel foyer, and Maryse struggled with the weight of the person on top of her, pummeling the attacker as much as she could given the restraint. She screamed for Mildred to call the police, when the weight lifted and she was yanked to her feet.

"Hank!" Maryse stared at him in disbelief. "What the hell are you doing?"

Her wayward husband grimaced and touched a growing red spot on his shirt, just below the chest. "I'm getting shot and beat to a pulp, that's what."

"Holy shit! We have to get you to the hospital."

Before she could move, Hank grabbed her arm. "Are you stupid? Someone is shooting at you."

Maryse's jaw dropped, and she stared at her husband, then laughed. Hank calling her stupid was a real eye-opener.

"Don't worry about it," Mildred said. "I've already called 911." She shot Hank a dirty look. "And the coroner, just in case I get lucky." She motioned them to the office. "Get off my rug before you bleed on it," she said, then stalked into her office and began yanking first-aid supplies out of a storage cabinet.

Maryse had to hand it to her—for someone who had professed the burning desire to saw Hank Henry's balls off with a dull butter knife, Mildred showed a remarkable amount of restraint and concern. Grabbing a clean towel from the cabinet, she instructed Hank to lie on the couch. Kneeling beside him, she gently pulled his shirt away from his chest. Hank moaned in agony. Mildred placed the towel against his side to soak up the excess blood, then lifted it to assess the damage.

Maryse leaned over, almost afraid to look when Mildred sighed with obvious relief. “It’s only a surface wound,” Maryse said.

“Only?” Hank stared at them in disbelief. “Well, it hurts like death.”

Mildred folded the towel over to a clean side and pressed it back against the wound. “It’s going to hurt,” she said. “That’s a tender part of the body, and it bleeds a lot.”

“Try to calm down,” Maryse instructed. “Deep breaths. It will help slow the blood flow.”

Hank looked up at her, still not convinced he wasn’t going to die right there on the couch, but he nodded and took a couple of deep breaths. A minute later, the paramedics and the cops came storming into the hotel. The paramedics carted Hank off to the hospital, one officer riding along, and the rest of the Mudbug police department took a stance in Mildred’s office and began firing questions like a semi-automatic weapon.

When they were done, Maryse ran some water in the sink and placed the stained towel in there to soak. She didn’t know why. The towel was most certainly ruined, but the activity kept her from thinking about Hank and about how she felt finally coming face to face with him. She thought she’d hate him. She thought the sight of him would either disgust her to the point of illness or madden her to the point of homicide.

And then he’d gone and taken a bullet that was meant for her.

Shit.

Chapter Seventeen

It was almost two hours later before one of the cops could provide Maryse with an armed escort to the hospital. Mildred had voted against it, but Sabine, who had run into the hotel shortly after the police, understood why she needed to go. Or maybe not why, exactly, but just that it was something Maryse had to do. Besides, a bullet wound and restraint in a hospital bed might be the only way she could have a face to face with Hank Henry.

As Maryse walked down the hospital corridor toward Hank's room, she wondered for the millionth time what she was going to say. She'd had two years to rehearse this moment, and now that it was here, she couldn't think of a damn thing to say to the man who'd saved her life.

Her husband.

That last thought stopped her dead in her tracks. She leaned against the wall outside Hank's door and caught her breath. What in the world could convey the range of emotions that Hank brought out in her? She didn't think words existed to describe what she felt, even if she was certain of what that was.

She had just built the courage to enter the room when Helena stepped into the hall and put one finger to her lips. "Not now," she whispered, and Maryse wondered what possibly could have made Helena Henry go quiet. She motioned to Maryse's pocket where she kept her cell phone. "Does that thing have a recorder?"

Maryse pulled her cell phone from her pocket and nodded.

"Then turn it on. We might be able to use this."

Maryse had no idea what Helena was up to, but she pressed a button and hoped it was the record. Otherwise, she'd just taken a picture of her own crotch. She leaned in closer to the door, and placed her phone as close as she could to the opening.

And that's when she was able to make out Harold's voice. A very unhappy Harold.

"What the hell were you thinking?" Harold raged. "You could have been killed and that damned land would have reverted back to that worthless piece of ass you married!"

Maryse clenched her jaw. Harold Henry had the nerve to call her worthless?

"Maryse is not worthless," Hank said.

Maryse frowned. Now Hank was defending her? Things were definitely weird.

"Besides," Hank continued, "that attorney said she drew up papers to transfer the land, right?"

"Oh, yeah," Harold said. "As long as she stays of that mindset for the next couple of days, there's no problem at all. But it's not like her death would exactly be a bad thing. At least then we'd know she couldn't change her mind."

"You're the one who tried to kill her," Hank accused.

"I already told you I didn't shoot at anyone." Harold's voice grew louder. "I would never risk shooting someone in broad daylight, and why the hell would I shoot you?"

"Well, someone shot at her," Hank argued. "I have the proof under these bandages."

"Which is why you should damned well stay away from that slut. I don't know what kind of crap she's into that has people shooting at her, and I really don't give a damn, but you need to stay away from her. I put my ass on the line over that piece of marsh, and I will not see it fall into the hands of some pseudo-hippy scientist."

"How exactly did you put your ass on the line?" Hank asked.

"Stop pretending you don't know," Harold said. "Left to nature, Helena would have outlived me by a good fifty years just to spite me."

There was complete silence for a moment. Then Hank said, "Are you telling me you killed my mother?" His voice registered his disbelief, and once again, Maryse wondered just how dumb Hank really was. She glanced over at Helena, but the ghost stood stock still, her expression completely blank.

"You killed my mother?" Hank repeated.

"Oh, good God, Hank. Grow up." The disgust was evident in Harold's voice. "Your mother was a royal pain in both our asses. She thrived off being hateful, and no one is sorry to see her go, least of all me. So I slipped some rat poison into her coffee, so what?"

Maryse frowned. Helena had said she'd died after drinking brandy, not coffee.

"What the hell is wrong with you?" Harold continued to complain. "The woman cast you out of her life years ago. Why would you give a shit what I did?"

"She didn't cast me out," Hank said. "She paid me to leave. She's been paying me to stay gone. A monthly transfer to a bank account in New Orleans."

Maryse's jaw dropped, and she stared at Helena.

"Uh-oh," Helena said, and bolted through an exterior wall, making following her an impossibility.

Coward. But Maryse would deal with Helena later. Right now, she needed all the damaging evidence she could get on Harold.

"What do you mean she paid you to stay away?" Harold asked.

"She said I wasn't going to ruin Maryse's life, and as long as I kept out of town and didn't contact her, she'd keep making the payments."

"Well, why didn't you divorce her before you left, or in absentia, or something?"

"I'm no attorney. I figured Maryse could get a divorce even if I was gone. I had no idea we were still married. Mom said to leave right then and never contact Maryse or anyone else in Mudbug again. And I kept that promise until I saw Mom's obituary and called you."

"Moron! It never occurred to you that if Helena kept you married to Maryse, she intended even then to leave that land to her? There is no way you're my son. You're too stupid for words."

"I think this conversation is over," Hank said. "Get out of my room."

"Oh, this is far from over," Harold threatened.

"Yes, it is. The land will transfer to me in a couple of days. I'll lease it out and give you a cut of the money, but you have to get out of my sight. I would never have been part of any of this. And if anything happens to Maryse, I will disappear and leave you with nothing."

"I've already told you I had nothing to do with shooting at that tramp," Harold raged.

"And her cabin exploding," Hank pointed out. "Rumor has it the device was military issue, and we all know who was special forces."

"Oh, for Christ's sake, I lied. I was a mess cook. I've never even shot a gun after basic training. Are you happy now?" "If Maryse is alive in two days, I will be. Are we clear?"

Maryse looked for a place to hide. Either Harold was going to stomp out of the hospital and figure out how to shoot a gun again or throttle Hank right there in his hospital bed. Either way, she didn't want to get caught eavesdropping in the hallway.

There was an empty room across the hall, so Maryse slipped inside, leaving the door cracked a tiny bit so that she could see Hank's room. A couple of seconds later, Harold stormed out of the room, his face beet red.

Unbelievable. Hank Henry had finally grown a set of balls. If she didn't have it on tape, she wouldn't believe it herself. She waited until Harold had rounded the corner before easing out into the hall and slipping into Hank's room. He looked up in surprise as she entered. Then a guilty look crossed his face.

"You heard everything, didn't you?" he asked.

"Yeah."

He sighed and stared at the ceiling. "I'm really sorry, Maryse. Sorry for everything. Me being a shitty husband and leaving you high and dry. My dad causing you all this trouble, and my mom putting you in this position to begin with. If I hadn't married you, none of this would be happening."

Maryse felt her heart begin to pound in her chest. She wanted to yell at him or maybe throw something large and heavy, but as she studied his face, she realized that for the first time since she'd known him, Hank Henry was actually being sincere. Before she could think better of it, she crossed the room and sat on the edge of his bed.

"Why did you marry me, Hank? Was it all some big joke or some ploy to make your mother think you'd grown up? And why me? I'd never done anything to you."

Hank shook his head, his expression sad. "I never meant to hurt you, and I swear I didn't marry you because of Mom. I married you because you are the best person I've ever known." His gaze locked on hers. "I figured if I was going to change for anyone, it would be you."

Maryse bit her lower lip, not sure what to say. Hank Henry respected her? That was news. But in the back of her mind lurked the question that had burned inside of her for two long years. "Did you love me?" Maryse finally asked.

Hank nodded. "I loved you as much as I could love anyone. I'm just not sure I understand what love really is, or if I'll ever be able to do it right." He took her hand and squeezed. "You deserved better than me, Maryse. So much better."

"Then why didn't you contact me? You left me hanging for two years, Hank. Your mom's money aside, you could have at least called or wrote a letter or something."

"You're right, and I'm sorry. It was a shitty thing to do, and I'm ashamed of it." Hank dropped his gaze. "When I first left, Mom arranged for me to be in rehab. She hoped I'd get straight and make my marriage to you work. But I wasn't ready to change, so it was a futile effort."

Hank looked back at Maryse, unmistakable regret in his eyes. "I was selfish, and I was immature. I convinced myself that you were better off without me, and that wasn't exactly a lie. So I took the easy way out and disappeared. Hell, I didn't know you wouldn't be able to divorce me. Mom never said anything, and I guess now we know why."

Hank reached over and took Maryse's hand in his. "I am so sorry for everything, Maryse. Can you ever forgive me?"

Maryse sniffed, trying to keep her unbidden tears at bay.

"Hey," Hank said. "You're going to be fine. You know that. And I don't want that damned land, okay? This whole mess makes me sick."

"What about Harold?"

Hank's jaw set in a hard line. "My murdering father will get his eventually." He gave her an apologetic look. "But I'm afraid I can't sit around and wait on it. I don't think I'd come out too good with the cops. Dad will make sure everyone believes I was in on it from the beginning."

Maryse shook her head and held up her phone. "That's not a problem. I have the entire conversation recorded."

Hank looked stunned for a moment. Then his face broke out in a broad smile. "You're really something. Holy shit, that's something." He laughed, then clutched his side and groaned.

Maryse handed him a cup of water and watched him grimace as he took a sip. "You have to be tired," she said, realizing his injury hurt more than he was letting on. "I should get out of here and let you rest. And don't worry about a thing. I'll turn this over to the police and everything will be fine. You'll see."

Hank gave her a sad smile. "Thanks, Maryse, for everything."

Maryse removed her hand from Hank's and eased out of the room as Hank's eyes closed. When she reached the hall, the dam burst, and the tears she'd been holding in for two long years came pouring out. Tears of sadness and joy and relief, all at the same time.

Hank had actually cared about her, and that made her feel so much better about herself and her marriage. But more importantly, she had realized that her marrying Hank hadn't been the stupid action of a grieving daughter. The truth was she'd loved Hank then. She just didn't love him now.

But admitting that at one time her feelings had been true and real had allowed her to let it all go.

Luc was in the hospital lobby arguing with the nurse behind the desk and growing more aggravated by the moment. "I need you to listen to me! The police said they brought her here—check again. Maryse Robicheaux. Do you need me to spell it?"

The frustrated nurse stood and put her hands on her hips. "Look, Mr. LeJeune. I've lived here all my life, and I know how to spell Robicheaux. No one by that name has been checked in today. Someone is mistaken."

Luc held his tongue and stalked away from the desk. Maryse was somewhere in this hospital, possibly under the care of his primary suspect, and no one could tell him a thing. He yanked his cell phone from his pocket, determined not to leave the hospital until he had seen Maryse with his own eyes. Hell, maybe even checked her pulse. He had just pressed in the number for the Mudbug police when Maryse walked into the hospital lobby, a dazed expression on her face.

It was all Luc could do to stop himself from grabbing her in an embrace and never ever letting her go, but based on their last conversation, he figured that wouldn't be a good idea. Instead, he settled for squeezing her arm. "Are you all right? The police said someone had been shot and they'd taken you to the hospital. I thought..."

Maryse came out of her stupor and shook her head. "No, I'm fine. It was Hank who got shot."

"Hank? Are you kidding me? How?"

"He pushed me out of the way and took a bullet in the process." Maryse looked at him. "He saved my life."

Luc felt his heart drop. He should have been the one to save Maryse—be her hero. "Then there are miracles in this world," he said, trying to sound normal. "How bad is he hurt?"

"It's only a surface wound. Hurts like the dickens, and he was bleeding like a stuck hog, but he's going to be all right."

"Good, that's good," Luc said, trying to sound like he meant it. "And you? Are you all right?"

Maryse nodded. "I'm going to be just fine."

Luc wondered a bit at the way she'd phrased her words but was too afraid of the answer to ask. Maryse and Hank had obviously come to some sort of common ground, and Hank was still her husband. "Can I take you back to the hotel?"

Maryse pointed to the hospital entrance just as a police cruiser pulled up. "I have an armed escort. Mildred and Sabine insisted."

"Good," Luc said, and nodded, hoping his disappointment didn't show.

"So," Maryse said, and smiled, "I guess I'll see you around."

Luc heard the unspoken question in her voice, but he heard the uncertainty behind it, too, and he knew that if Maryse and Hank were reconsidering their relationship, the last thing she needed was another complication in her life. "Actually, my assignment here is over. I'm supposed to report back to New Orleans tomorrow."

"Oh."

Her smile dropped, and Luc mentally cursed himself for being the bastard Maryse had accused him of being.

Maryse shrugged. "Well, then, thanks for everything, and good luck." She walked out of the hospital entrance without so much as a backward glance, climbed into the waiting police cruiser, and rode away.

Out of Luc's life. Back to her own.

It was long after midnight before Maryse finished explaining her cell phone recording to the police and returned to the hotel. She struggled to keep her emotions under control as she talked to Mildred and Sabine, assuring them that the police were handling everything with the recording, that she was fine, Hank was fine, and she was suffering no lingering effects from almost dying—again.

She begged off any further conversation, claiming exhaustion. She managed to make it to her room and into the shower before the tears started to fall.

Tears for her marriage that never really was and a promising relationship that was never going to be. What was it about her that she only attracted men with ulterior motives and no staying ability?

By the time she'd finished her shower and her crying jag, the exhaustion she had claimed earlier was no longer merely an excuse. But as she stepped out of the bathroom, a very contrite Helena Henry was perched on the edge of her bed. Maryse held in a sigh, knowing that it was high time she and Helena had that heart to heart Helena had kept promising her. Maryse just didn't have a clue where she was supposed to get the energy to do it.

"How did it go with the police?" Helena asked.

Maryse pulled some clothes out of the chest of drawers and began to dress. "If you're so interested, why didn't you stick around? Afraid I might figure out a way to strangle you?"

Helena stared at the floor, a guilty expression on her face. "I know what I did was wrong, but I swear, I never imagined any of this happening. I had my reasons, and at the time I thought they were good ones."

Maryse turned her hands palm up. "Then I think it's high time I hear them. Everything, Helena. No more secrets."

Helena raised her gaze back to Maryse and nodded. "You deserve the truth. You deserve a lot more than that, actually, but before I tell you everything, you have to know that I never, ever intended to put you in any danger. Quite the opposite, actually."

"Okay. Then go ahead. Let me have it."

Helena took a deep breath and gazed around the room, as if deciding where to begin. "I guess I'll start with your mother," she said finally.

Maryse stood straight up and stared at Helena. Her mother had been the last thing in the world she'd expected Helena to talk about. "My mother?"

Helena smiled. "Your mother was the kindest, gentlest person I've ever met. She volunteered at the orphanage, teaching the older kids math and reading stories and playing games with the younger ones. They all loved her very much, and she was so great with them."

Maryse sank onto the edge of the bed next to Helena. "I never knew she volunteered there. No one ever told me."

Helena gave her a sad smile. "She quit before you were born. In fact, she quit right after finding out she was pregnant with you. She'd seen so much sadness, so much heartache in those children that she wanted to make sure her own never suffered a moment's pain, never shed a tear thinking her parents didn't love her."

Maryse nodded, the lump in her throat making speech impossible.

"The doctors had told her she wouldn't be able to carry a child to term," Helena continued, "so you were a real miracle for her."

Maryse felt the tears well up again. "I wish I could remember," she said, the sadness of her loss sweeping over her.

"I do, too," Helena said, her voice barely a whisper. "When your mom was first diagnosed, she thought she'd beat it. But she got worse and worse and knew things weren't going to get any better. Before she passed, your mother asked me to make sure you were taken care of. She knew your dad was a good man, but she was afraid he might not be able to see to all the things you would need."

Maryse stared at her. "My mother asked you to look after me? Did she know you at all?"

Helena laughed. "I know it's hard to believe, especially from where you sit, but your mother...well, your mother knew the real me. So the first year or so, I did my best to see that you had the woman's input you needed, although your dad did nothing to make it easy on me. We never much got along, even though I always respected him, and I know for a fact that he loved you more than anything."

"And after the first year?"

Helena waved one hand in dismissal. "Oh well, then your dad started seeing Mildred, and I could tell straight off how much she loved you. Almost as if you were her own. So I bowed out, knowing you were in great hands."

Maryse stared at Helena, certain the woman was leaving something out of her story—again. "And you had nothing to do with me after that?"

"Well, not directly," Helena hedged. She waited for a couple of seconds, obviously hoping Maryse was going to go off on another subject, but finally realized that wasn't going to happen. "Fine. I left you to your dad and Mildred until it was time for college. Then I saw to it that you got the education your mother would have wanted you to have."

Maryse's eyes widened in surprise. "You were the source of my scholarships? Good God, Helena, that must have cost you a fortune."

Helena shrugged. "I had more than enough money, and besides, you were a damned good investment."

Maryse took a deep breath and tried to absorb everything Helena had said, finding it hard to wrap her mind around her mother and Helena Henry plotting over her care and nurturing. "So what the hell happened with Hank? I'm pretty sure my mom wouldn't have approved of that arrangement at all. In fact, she's probably turned over a time or two since then."

Helena looked embarrassed. "I didn't find out about you and Hank until it was too late. I tried to get him to have the marriage annulled, but he was hell bent on keeping you." She shook her head. "I knew my son would never do right by you, so I decided to do both of us a favor and send him packing."

"He told me you sent him to rehab."

"Yeah. Well, the people you paid for Hank's debts weren't exactly the only people looking for him. I knew if he stuck around that not only would he be in danger until I could sort the whole thing out, but you would be too."

Maryse considered this for a moment. "I didn't know."

"I know that, and I got it all handled in a couple of months' time. I guess I figured rehab was the last place that sort would go looking for a guy like Hank. And I was hoping he'd straighten out...grow up and become a good man and a good husband. I was just fooling myself. Hank is just like his father."

Maryse shook her head, remembering her conversation with Hank. "He's not just like him, Helena. There's some good in Hank. It's just buried under that bullshit front. He didn't know what Harold did, and he's upset about it."

Helena looked at her, a hopeful expression on her face, and in that instant, Maryse realized that regardless of his transgressions, Helena Henry loved her son.

"You really think so?" Helena asked.

Maryse nodded. "And if I ever get my phone back from the police, you can hear it yourself."

"Well, that's something," Helena said. "I guess I didn't give him enough credit, then or now. Maybe you two could have made it work. Now, I don't know. All I knew then was that I'd promised my good friend that I'd make sure her daughter was taken care of, and I didn't see that happening as long as Hank was around."

"I get that, Helena, in a demented, completely screwed up sort of way. But why in the world didn't you arrange for us to divorce? Why keep me hanging all these years?"

Helena sighed. "Because of the land. After Hank left, I had that survey done and found out about the oil, and I always suspected Harold was digging through my safe. That missing letter proves it. I knew if I left the land to Hank that Mudbug would become one big refinery and the town would cease to exist. This was my home. I couldn't let that happen, so I used you, and for that I am sorry."

"And the bills? Why make me pay Hank's debt, then turn around and pay off *my* debt?"

Helena looked down at the floor. "I was worried that you might not be a good choice either, and if that was the case, then I might as well produce Hank and let you two divorce. I didn't really know what kind of adult you'd turned out to be, and marrying Hank wasn't exactly points in your favor."

"So you were testing my character? Is that your ridiculous defense?"

Helena shrugged. "I guess so, and putting it that way does kinda point out how stupid and cruel it was. I figured that out when you made the payments without fail or complaint. That's why I started using the money to pay off your debt. I was too proud to just tell you to stop."

Maryse stared at Helena and shook her head. "Unbelievable."

She looked at Maryse, her eyes pleading for her to understand. "This whole mess is about that damned land. I thought I was saving the town and giving you a great asset at the same time. I swear, Maryse, if I'd had any indication from you that you had started a new relationship or that being married to Hank was preventing you from doing something you wanted, I would have taken care of it...regardless of what happened with the land."

"But I just disappeared to my cabin in the marsh and stayed quiet all these years."

Helena nodded. "I didn't figure still being married to Hank made a difference to the way you were living. It never occurred to me that still be married might keep you from trying to have a life again. I've stolen two years from you, Maryse, and there's nothing I can do to fix it now. You have no idea how sorry I am. For everything."

Maryse rose from the bed. "I believe you're sorry, Helena, but what you did was wrong."

"Can you ever forgive me?"

"I forgive you, but I'm not happy with you. I hope you can understand that."

Helena nodded and rose from the bed. "I'm not happy with me, either." She gave Maryse a sad smile and walked through the bedroom wall into the hallway.

Maryse lay on the bed and hugged one of the bed pillows. She had enough to think about for the next ten years.

It was well after two A.M. when Maryse heard Helena's voice right beside her bed. Jasper took off like a shot, and Maryse opened one eye and looked at the agitated ghost, then the alarm clock. "It's the middle of the night, Helena. Go away."

"Ssssshhhhh." Helena put a finger to her lips. "There's someone outside your window. You've got to get out of here." Maryse bolted upright and stared at the window, trying to make out anything in the inky darkness. A second later, she heard the faint sound of scraping outside, which couldn't possibly be good since her room was on the second floor. She rolled out of bed and onto the floor, then crawled over to the door and eased it open. The squeak of the hinges seemed to blast through the night air, and as Maryse slipped into the hall, she heard glass breaking behind her.

"Run!" Helena shouted, and Maryse stumbled to her feet, dashed down the hall, and then took the stairs two at a time. When she hit the landing on the first floor, she panicked for a moment, not having a single idea which way to go. The only options were out of the hotel or toward Mildred's room, essentially putting the other woman in danger. The pounding of footsteps on the stairs prompted her into action, and she pushed open the back door to the hotel and ran outside.

The shriek of the hotel alarm made her heart stop beating for a moment as she realized she'd just alerted the killer to her exact location. But as she ran down the alley, she realized that it might work to her advantage if the cops responded to the alarm before the killer found her. She felt the sting of glass under her bare feet but didn't care as she dashed around the corner of the hotel, praying that the gate was open. She came to a stop in front of the ten-foot iron gate, securely fastened by a padlock and chain. Shit! Frantic, she scanned the fence for a way over and, finding none, switched to looking for a place to hide but also came up with nothing.

Police sirens screamed in the distance, and she felt her hopes rise. She only had to hold out for another minute or so. Just sixty more seconds and help should arrive. Surely the killer would bail when the police arrived. But as she heard the hotel door slam, she knew she didn't have even twenty seconds before she would be looking at the killer face to face. She backed up a couple of steps, then ran toward the fence and leaped as high as possible, clutching desperately at the top rail.

Adjusting her grip, she pulled herself up the fence, her arms straining with the effort, and for a moment, she didn't think she was going to make it. Then a bullet whizzed by her head and struck the building to the side of her and a burst of adrenaline hit her, propelling her over the fence and onto the other side. She landed, slamming into the concrete with such force she was afraid she'd broken something in the process. As she jumped to her feet, a second bullet grazed her shoulder and hit the Dumpster in front of her. Realizing there was no possible way to exit the alley without leaving herself wide open, Maryse dove behind the Dumpster and curled into a ball, hoping like hell the police arrived before the killer got through the gate.

She heard the blast of a bullet hitting metal, then the rattling of a chain and felt her heart drop. She shut her eyes and prayed harder than she'd ever prayed before. Nothing but a miracle was going to save her now. Seconds later she heard his breathing clear as day and knew he was standing right in front of her. She clenched her eyes harder, her life racing before her in Technicolor, and wondered what she had done so wrong in life for it to end this way.

Chapter Eighteen

"I never wanted things to go this way, Maryse," the killer said.

Maryse's eyes popped open, and she raised her head in disbelief. "Johnny?" she said as she stared at her father's best friend. "But why?"

Johnny shook his head.

"If I'm going to die, shouldn't I at least know why?"

"Because you had to go poking your nose in where it didn't belong. Why couldn't you leave things alone?"

Maryse's mind raced with questions but not a single answer. "I don't know what you're talking about. What did I do?"

Johnny sneered. "Don't play stupid with me. I know all about those tubes you send to New Orleans for testing. You knew the chemical company was dumping waste in the bayou, and you figured that's what killed your dad, so you were going to get even. All that crap about trying to find a cure for cancer. You weren't looking for a cure—you were looking for the cause."

Maryse's head began to spin. "You're telling me you knew the chemical company was dumping toxic waste in the bayou? You knew that's what killed my dad and you never said a word?" She stared at the man in front of her. "I thought you were his friend."

"I was his friend, and I watched him waste away from that disease, and all I could think was that's not going to happen to me. No way."

A wave of nausea washed over Maryse. The thinning hair, the weight loss. She'd thought it was diet or age, but she couldn't have been more wrong. "You have cancer."

Johnny nodded. "And no insurance. As long as I keep the chemical company's secret safe, they'll keep paying for my treatments."

"But other people could die because you haven't told."

"I was going to report them as soon as I was in remission, but then you had to get in the way, and I couldn't afford to have them busted just yet. I've got another year, at least, of chemo to go." He leveled the gun straight at Maryse's head. "I'm sorry it has to be this way, Maryse. Sorrier than you'll ever know. But I promise you won't feel a thing. Not after the first few seconds, anyway."

Maryse felt her blood run cold as she watched Johnny's finger whiten on the trigger. This was it. The end of the line. An entire life devoted to one cause and her work left unfinished. What had been the point? She clenched her eyes shut and waited for the shot to enter her body, waited for her life to fade away, and when the shot came, she almost passed out from fear.

It wasn't until she heard Luc shouting that she opened her eyes. Johnny lay splayed in front of her, his vacant eyes staring up at the night sky, a single bullet hole through his temple. Luc crouched in front of her and pulled her up from the ground, his eyes searching every square inch of her body.

"Am I dead?" Maryse asked.

Luc let out a strangled cry. "No!"

Maryse started to cry, and Luc pulled her close to him, wrapping his arms around her and kissing her forehead. "I wasn't sure," she said between sobs. "I mean, with you being able to see dead people. I just wasn't sure."

Luc let out a single laugh and held her even tighter. "I didn't even think about that." He pulled back a little and placed his hands on each side of her face. "You are very much alive, Maryse Robicheaux, and you're going to stay that way to a ripe old age."

Maryse rested her head on Luc's chest and relaxed as his arms tightened around her. For that moment, she would choose to believe him.

It seemed Maryse had barely gotten her breath before the backup arrived in the form of cops, an ambulance, and the coroner. She felt the thrill of victory pass through her as she realized the morgue could just as easily have been there for her if not for Luc's shooting accuracy. She still didn't know how he'd found her, or why he was even looking, but at the moment, she didn't care.

The paramedics whisked her off to the ambulance to assess the damage, and Luc joined a group of cops over to one side, probably giving his statement of the events. One paramedic was bandaging her shoulder while another tended to her cut feet when Mildred came rushing up. The hotel owner took one look at Maryse sitting in the ambulance and Johnny lying dead in the alley and began to sway.

She sucked in air like a drowning woman, and a paramedic shoved an oxygen mask over her face until her breathing became regular again. Maryse waited until she had taken a few normal breaths before explaining what had happened, leaving out, of course, the part that Helena had played in everything. Which brought Maryse up short. Where was Helena, anyway?

Mildred listened to Maryse's story, her eyes growing wider and wider with each sentence until finally she'd finished her tale of horror. Mildred gasped as Maryse finished, and the paramedic hovered, oxygen mask in hand. She waved one hand in dismissal and told Maryse her own version of the night's events.

She'd jumped up as soon as the alarm sounded and ran straight to Maryse's room. When she found the door standing wide open, the window broken, and the empty bed, she'd run back downstairs to call the police, expecting the worst but hoping for the best. Maryse kept waiting for Mildred to blast her for running out of the hotel rather than to her for help but was relieved when it seemed that her substitute mother was going to let it go. Or was reserving it for a later date when she needed a good guilt trip to use.

Family was a wonderful thing.

Since Maryse's injuries were minor, the paramedics released her to Mildred, and they headed back to the hotel with instructions from the police to await questioning within the next thirty minutes. Maryse looked around for Luc, anxious to speak to him, to fill in the missing pieces of the story, but she didn't see him anywhere.

Disappointed, she followed Mildred into the hotel lobby, wondering why Luc had left so abruptly. In the alley, it had seemed like he'd really cared. Was that all just part of his job? She was just about to march outside and insist on seeing him when Sabine burst through the doorway in a panic.

As soon as she locked her gaze on Maryse, she ran across the lobby and grabbed her in a hug. "I'm fine," Maryse said as Sabine squeezed harder. "Okay, well maybe now I have a broken rib, but other than that, I'm fine."

Sabine released Maryse and brushed the tears from her face. "Don't you dare joke about this, Maryse Robicheaux. I could have lost you." She hugged her again, and Maryse felt the tears well up in her eyes once more.

"It's all over now," Maryse said through her tears. "It's all over."

Sabine released her once more and gave her a smile as Mildred hustled into the room with a glass of water and some aspirin. "You sit right down on that couch," Mildred directed, "and I don't want one bit of lip. All these goings on, it's a damned wonder you haven't had a heart attack—or given me one. You're going to relax for a minute if I have to sit on you."

Maryse grinned at Sabine, not caring in the least that Mildred was being bossy and pushy. Being bossy was simply her way of assuming control of the situation, her way of finding relief. Maryse relaxed on the couch and propped her sore feet on the coffee table, then took the water and aspirin from Mildred and downed them both.

The hotel door opened, and Luc walked in with a man he introduced as Agent Stephens. Maryse worried for a moment that this man might have seen her in fewer clothes and a much more compromising position, but she wasn't about to go there now.

"More agents," Maryse finally asked. "Is something wrong?"

Agent Stephens smiled. "Not at all, Ms. Robicheaux. And please, call me Brian. Everything is actually great."

Maryse looked from Brian to Luc, hoping for confirmation and an explanation. "Really?"

Luc nodded. "The local police picked up Harold at the motel where he was staying. He's in a small dingy cell, and he won't be leaving for a long time. We're betting the DA goes for the death penalty."

Maryse shook her head. "He can't."

Luc looked confused. "Harold confessed to murdering his wife. That rates the death penalty in Louisiana."

"Except that Harold didn't kill Helena."

All movement in the hotel ceased, and everyone stared at Maryse.

"How can you know that?" Sabine asked.

"Simple," Maryse said. "Harold said he slipped rat poison in her coffee, but Helena's medical file didn't indicate any of the symptoms from rat poisoning at all. He may have tried to kill her—and me—but he didn't succeed in either case."

"Shit!" Luc said. "Not exactly the outcome I was looking for."

Maryse nodded. "I understand, but Harold's confession should be enough to get a court order to exhume Helena's body, right? With a proper autopsy, looking specifically for foul play, we might get some answers."

Luc looked over at Brian, who nodded. "Should be easy enough for the local DA to get," Brian said.

"And what about Hank?" Maryse asked. "Did the police get a statement from him?"

Brian glanced over at Luc, clearly unsure how to answer. Luc looked at Maryse and shook his head. "Hank's gone. His hospital bed was empty when the locals went to question him, and the nurse confirmed he never checked out through proper channels."

"Gone?" Maryse tried to hide her disappointment. Why had Hank left? At this point, he couldn't be found guilty of anything except being stupid, and that wasn't a crime or half the people she'd ever met would be in jail.

Luc handed her an envelope. "He left this in the room."

She took the envelope and opened it, pulling the papers from inside. It was a signed divorce decree. No note. Only Hank's signature, putting an end to the marriage that never really was. She supposed he figured it was the least he could do for her. Maryse passed the papers to Mildred, who gave an exalted cry and waved them in the air at Sabine, who cheered.

Brian Stephens smiled. "Well, I guess if you guys don't need anything else from me, I need to report back to New Orleans and fill them in on this latest angle in our case against the chemical company. Luc can explain the rest." He gave everyone a wave and exited the room.

Maryse looked over at Luc. "The rest of what? I mean, I guess with the killer being Johnny—" Maryse choked a bit and had to clear her throat before continuing. "He said it was all because of the illegal dumping, so I guess that's relevant to your case, right? But I still don't understand why he thought I was getting evidence against the chemical company."

Luc looked at her and sighed. "I think I do."

Maryse stared at him in surprise. "How can you know?"

"I can't know for sure, but I have a damn good idea what happened. One of those plants you sent for testing was selected from a contaminated area. When the head honchos at the chemical company realized that you pulled a plant from contaminated water and shipped it off to a lab in New Orleans, they assumed you were on to them and put pressure on Johnny to fix the situation."

Luc stared down at his feet for a moment. "I'm really sorry, Maryse, that it was Johnny. I know you thought he was your friend. If it makes you feel any better, I don't think he was in his right mind any longer. The desperation that goes along with a terminal illness can break people. Obviously he wasn't strong enough to do the right thing."

Maryse sniffled. "I know. I keep trying to tell myself it wasn't personal, and it certainly wasn't about my dad, but it's hard, you know? I mean, Johnny claimed this dumping is what gave my dad cancer in the first place, and he never spoke up. What kind of man does that?"

Mildred stepped over to Maryse and put one hand on her shoulder. "No *man* does that, honey. When it comes down to it, there's just no excuse good enough, and we're all going to have to live with that."

Maryse shook her head. "I guess that explains Harold's comments about the irony of life. He wasn't special forces—Johnny was. Harold was the mess cook."

Luc nodded. "I'm sure you're right."

Maryse took a deep breath. "Then I guess it's just a matter of going through my notes to find the contaminated area. I documented every location that I got plants from. It has to be one of the more recent ones or they wouldn't have panicked, right?"

Luc stared her straight in the eyes but didn't respond, and his hesitation made her nervous. "What?" Maryse asked. "What are you not telling me?"

"We've already found the contaminated area," Luc said.

"But how?"

"The agency found the informant, and he gave us some of the dumping spots. I sorta broke into your lab and copied your notebook back when I first got here. Then things got weird with your inheritance and everything else, and for awhile I totally missed the clues that were right in front of me. But when I started thinking about everything, it made sense. The illegal dumping, your cancer tests, and the recent success that Aaron reported...well, I checked your notes and compared it to the information we'd gotten through our informant."

Maryse didn't know whether to be happy that the contaminated area was already identified and could be cleaned up, scared to death that she'd been hanging out in it, or mad at Luc for stealing her data. And despite all that information, she still couldn't help feeling that there was something missing from his explanation. Before she could question what, Luc sat on the couch next to her and took her hand in his.

"I hate to be the one to tell you this, Maryse, but your trials were a sort of false positive."

Maryse stared at him. "What do you mean?"

"You didn't discover a plant that cured cancer. What you discovered was a plant loaded with radiation from the illegal dumping."

Maryse's head began to spin. It couldn't be true. She was right there, right on the verge of the solution. "No," she whispered.

Luc looked at her with sad eyes and squeezed her hand. "I'm sorry, Maryse. So very sorry."

Maryse stared at him, unable to think, unable to breath. Blooming Flower had never had a magical cure. She'd simply given her dad the radiation treatment he'd refused, courtesy of a contaminated plant. Maryse's entire career, her whole adult life, had been a farce. There was no cure, at least not one in Mudbug Bayou, and she was no closer to saving lives that she had been before her advanced degrees and thousands of hours of extra work. And even worse, she'd unknowingly endangered everyone else in the process of trying to find a cure that didn't even exist.

She rose from the couch, unable to face the people in the lobby, her friends, her family who had unconditionally believed in her. Believed the lie. "If you guys don't mind," she said, "I'd like to be alone for a while." She hurried out of the lobby without waiting for a response, not wanting to see the disappointment, the pity, that would probably line every face in the room. All she wanted was to lock herself away in her room until the disappointment was gone.

And the fear.

All this time, Maryse had thought she was right on the verge of success. It's the only reason she hadn't launched into panic over Sabine's test. She thought she'd be able to help her friend if things turned out for the worse.

But it had all been a lie.

Maryse stared at the ceiling in the hotel room...but it hadn't changed, not once in the last two hours of her looking at the same spot the painters had missed next to the fan. She sat up in bed, feeling claustrophobic and restless. She needed to get out of the hotel, away from the town and the people and out into her bayou where she felt at home. Where things made sense. But the only way out of the hotel was down the stairs and through the lobby, since setting off the alarm with the back door probably wouldn't be a good idea given the situation.

She got out of bed and opened the window, hoping for a breeze or something to make her feel less like a caged animal, and noticed the drain pipe just outside the ledge to her room. She leaned further out the window and reached one hand over to test the strength of the pipe when Helena's voice boomed next to her.

"What the hell are you doing? Don't tell me you were gonna jump. After all we've been through, you want to end it now? And from the second floor? You'd probably only break your foot." Maryse slid back inside the window and stared at Helena before sinking onto the bed in a huff. "I was not going to jump. And where were you? I kept expecting to see you around, and then finally I wondered if everything had finally, well, you know..."

"Made me disappear," Helena finished. "Afraid not." She sat on the bed and frowned. "I just figured you had enough to deal with without me hanging around the room and only you and Luc seeing me, so I sat behind the front desk and took it all in."

"Then you heard everything?"

Helena nodded. "I heard everything." She gave Maryse a shrewd look. "And I know what you're thinking."

Maryse shook her head. "You couldn't possibly."

"You're thinking everything you've done in life was a waste because the cure wasn't real and the only relationship you had wasn't exactly a success." She stared at Maryse for a moment, but Maryse wasn't about to give her the satisfaction of knowing she was right.

"The worst part is," Helena continued, "there's a grain of truth to all of that."

Maryse sat bolt upright on the bed and glared at Helena. "You've got a lot of nerve saying something like that to me. You of all people."

Helena held one hand up before she could continue her barrage. "I didn't mean that the way it sounded. Well, not exactly. Oh, hell, I never could get things out right. Might have made life a lot easier if I'd ever learned some tact."

"It's apparently not too late."

Helena grinned. "Why start now when the only people it would benefit are you and Luc?"

"Why indeed?" Maryse sighed. "Please just go away, Helena. I've got enough to think about without you mucking things up more."

"Not until I have my say."

"You've had your say for years, and it's been nothing but aggravation and trouble. You've got five more minutes of my life, Helena, then I *will* pitch myself out that window."

"Fair enough." Helena took a deep breath. "The reason I implied that some of your life has been a waste wasn't because the cure turned out to be a fake, and it certainly wasn't because you married my useless son—that one is totally on Hank."

"Then why..."

Helena gave her a sad smile. "It's because in looking for the cure, you shut yourself away from the very society you purported to want to save. How do you even know people are worth saving anymore if you don't get out of that swamp and meet any?"

Maryse started to fling back a retort but clamped her mouth shut, remembering that Sabine had said the same thing. "I meet people," she said finally.

Helena snorted. "Yeah, that Dr. Do-Kiddies being one of them. You've locked yourself away from the world, Maryse, and I know you think you had a good reason to do so, but I'll be the first to tell you that if you don't change, you'll regret it. I do."

Maryse stared at her. "You regret your life? But you had everything...well, maybe not in the husband and kid department, but the money, the respect of the town."

Helena waved one hand in dismissal. "Respect? Oh, please, I was *tolerated* by this town, and that was all my own fault. For all intents and purposes, I was the biggest bitch on the face of the Earth. Oh, I might have done a couple of good things with my money, but I never really lived myself. I even chose to marry Harold because I knew I'd never really love him so I wasn't in danger of being hurt."

"I don't understand. Why would marriage have to hurt?"

Helena sighed. "That's my own hang-up. My childhood was miserable. My father was a tyrant who barely tolerated girls and remained angry with my mother until the day he passed for producing a daughter rather than a son, then having the nerve to die while giving birth."

Maryse stared at Helena in disbelief, unable to comprehend that degree of spite. Unable to imagine a childhood spent with a man who blamed his only child for the gender she'd been born with.

"He died when I was eight," Helena continued, "and all I can remember is being relieved. Then guilty because I was relieved, you know?"

Maryse nodded. "I can see that."

"I stayed fairly locked away from the world with a guardian, a tutor, and a live-in nanny. But when I turned twenty-one and gained control of my inheritance, that's when the circus started. People who'd never spoken a word to me in my life practically lined up at the gate of my house with their hand out. I couldn't even walk into town without someone hitting me up for money—business loans, medical bills, scholarships, it never seemed to end."

Suddenly, Maryse understood. "So you became the biggest bitch in Mudbug because all anyone wanted from you was your money. And you funded the orphanage because you could relate to children that didn't have anyone looking out for them."

Helena nodded. "That was what I told myself—convinced myself was a good reason. But I was wrong, Maryse. Dead wrong."

"How so?"

"There are good people in this town, people who wouldn't have wanted a thing from me. People like your mother, and you, and Mildred." She smiled. "And even your nutty best friend. By shutting myself off, I denied myself the pleasure of friendship, of knowing what it felt like to have someone care for you that wasn't being paid to do it."

She gave Maryse a hard stare. "My life could have been so much more, and it took dying to realize that. Don't make the same mistakes I did, Maryse. This world would be a much better place with you in it."

Maryse looked at Helena, decked out in blue jeans, the "dead people" T-shirt, and neon blue Nikes. A far cry from the unrelieved black she'd always worn. But it was too late to share her newfound style with anyone. Too late to leave a different mark on this Earth. Because for everyone but Maryse and Luc, Helena was already gone, and Maryse had stopped living so long ago that she'd been dead longer than Helena.

Maryse didn't even try to hold in the tears as they rolled out of her eyes. She cried for Helena, the little lost girl and the older lost woman. She cried for herself—the life she'd never bothered to live and had almost lost—and the realization that she still had an opportunity to change it all before it was too late.

She looked up as Helena rose from the bed. "Where are you going?"

"My five minutes are up," Helena said. "And I've probably given you enough to think about." She walked to the door, then looked back. "There is one last thing."

Maryse looked up at her. "What's that?"

"When Johnny broke into your room, I ran out of the hotel desperate to find a way to help. Luc was sitting in a car across the street from the hotel, and if I had to guess, he'd been there for a while and wasn't planning on moving."

"He was watching the hotel," Maryse said. "You sent him to save me. That's how he knew."

Helena nodded. “Luc LeJeune is no Harold or Hank Henry, Maryse. And I think I overheard him say he needed to pick up some stuff at the office first thing in the morning before he cleared out of town.” And with that, she disappeared through the wall.

Maryse rose from the bed and pulled on her shoes, knowing with a certainty she’d never felt before exactly what she needed to do. But first, there was someone else who needed to hear Helena’s speech.

Chapter Nineteen

Despite the fact that it was darn near sunrise and nobody had really slept the night before, Maryse figured she'd find Sabine in her shop. Peering through the window of Read 'em and Reap, she saw Sabine sitting at her table in the center of the room, eyes closed and her hands covering a crystal ball. She was wearing her purple robe, one she brought out for only two reasons—stress or trying to contact her parents.

Maryse sighed. All the drama with Maryse and the land and Sabine's own medical worries had probably driven her to the edge. But none of that was going to prevent her from what she needed to do. She took the last couple of steps to the shop entrance and pushed the door open.

Sabine looked up in surprise when the bells over the door jangled, then realizing it was Maryse, her expression changed to worry. She jumped up from her chair and hurried over. "Are you all right?" she asked. "Is everything okay?"

"Actually, I'm not all right." Maryse smiled. "I'm fantastic. I just had an interesting conversation with Helena."

Sabine studied her for a moment. "Are you high? Did the paramedics give you some drugs or something?"

Maryse's smile faltered a bit. Okay, so obviously telling people to take their lives back wasn't her strong suit. How in the world was it that Helena, of all people, did this so much better? Maryse took a deep breath and repeated Helena's story from the beginning. Sabine listened in rapt attention, her eyes growing wider until

Maryse wrapped it up with Helena's ultimatum on living life and regrets.

"Wow," Sabine said when Maryse finished. "Helena didn't pull any punches."

"No." Maryse took a deep breath and pushed forward. "And neither do I." She placed her hand on Sabine's arm. "You're not living either, Sabine. Your obsession with your parents has kept you so grounded in the past that you have no future."

Sabine stared at her in surprise, then pulled away her arm. "How can you say that? You know what it's like not to have a parent. How can you blame me for wanting to know something, anything, about mine?"

Shit. This wasn't going so well. "That's not what I meant. Look, Sabine, I'm just excited by my new outlook on life. I want you there with me...like you always have been."

Sabine's angry expression softened, but before she could speak, a glow of bright light appeared a couple of feet from the table, and they both stared in disbelief. "What the hell?" Maryse asked as the light swirled round and round, something slowly taking shape in the center. *Please, God, no more ghosts.* She didn't think her heart could take the strain.

As the shape took form, Maryse realized they were looking at a young couple, smiling over at them. The man was tall and thin, the woman petite and slender. Their haircuts and clothes betrayed the era of their existence, and Maryse knew they had been gone from this world for some time. The woman looked directly at Sabine and extended one hand. A flash of silver at the woman's neck caught Maryse's eye and she cried out. "Her necklace. Sabine, look at her necklace."

Sabine looked at the woman, and her hand flew to her throat, clutching the matching locket she wore. The only thing she had of her mothers. "It's them," she whispered.

Maryse nodded, unable to speak.

"They're beautiful," Sabine said, and started to cry. "My parents. I finally know my parents." Sabine took a hesitant step toward the light, but as she moved, the light began to dim and the couple faded away into blackness. With a final blink, they were gone.

"No!" Sabine ran to the spot where the light had been, but there was nothing left to see. She sank onto the floor, tears streaming down her face.

Maryse rushed over to her friend. "Please don't cry," she begged as she sat on the floor and hugged Sabine. "I don't want you to be sad. I don't want anyone I love to be sad, not one more moment of their lives. It's too short."

Sabine choked a bit and laughed. "You ninny. I'm not crying because I'm sad." She pulled back from the hug, and Maryse could see that even through the tears, there was a smile on her face. "I'm happy," Sabine said. "I'm thrilled. I finally got that sliver of closure that I've always prayed for." Sabine grabbed Maryse's shoulders with both hands and shook her. "I saw my parents, Maryse. Do you know what that means?"

Maryse wiped at the tears lurking in the corners of her eyes, wondering that she had a single ounce of fluid in her left to cry after the night she'd had. "It means the world is getting two new members?" Maryse smiled. "I hope it's ready."

Maryse gave Sabine another quick hug, then rose from the floor. "I'd love to stay and make plans for our takeover of humanity, but I have some unfinished business with a fake zoologist."

Sabine smiled. "Let the takeover begin."

Maryse left the shop with a spring in her step. If everything could turn out so good for Sabine, why couldn't it turn out that good for her? But the apparition just outside the shop door brought her up short. Maryse took one look at the guilty expression on Helena Henry's face and knew something was up, and in a flash, she knew exactly what it was.

"You did that," Maryse accused. "You created the image of Sabine's parents."

Helena shrugged and shuffled her feet. "Well, you weren't exactly getting anywhere with that lame speech of yours, and I didn't need you sinking back in to your former existence just because Sabine was stuck in hers." Helena grinned. "Besides, I kinda like the nutbag, and I wanted her to be happy. Is that so bad?"

"I guess not. But making up visions of dead parents to fool a daughter is sort of low, even for trying to make someone happy. You've got to stop manipulating people, Helena. Even if you think it's for their own good."

Helena glared at her. "What do you take me for, a charlatan? I admit, I created the image, but the people were really Sabine's parents, or the likeness at least."

"But how do you know what they looked like?"

Helena shrugged. "I took a look on the other side, and there they were. I think they're always close to her."

Maryse stared. "You can look on the other side? Then why can't you go there?"

Helena gave her a sad smile. "I tried, but they told me it's not my time yet. Apparently, I still have some work to do here."

Maryse smiled and shook her head. "You know, I never thought I'd hear myself say this, but I'm sorta glad you're not going yet, Helena. I would have missed you."

Helena nodded. "Of course you would. Not many have been graced with my stellar personality transformation like you have."

Maryse groaned and pointed a finger at her as they walked down the sidewalk to Maryse's rental car. "That is *not* an invitation to show up unannounced or to harass me over the television channel. Well...as soon as I actually have a television, and a house to put it in."

Helena raised her hand as if taking an oath. "I promise I will not intrude without making an appointment. Although, I've already seen you naked, so I don't know what else there is."

"Because I plan on being naked with someone else. That is, if things work out."

Helena grinned. "You know, I always did think Luc had a fantastic butt. I wouldn't mind seeing it just once."

"Helena!" Maryse cried, but the wily ghost walked through the wall of the not-yet-open beauty shop, making following her an impossibility.

Maryse headed to the parking lot and jumped in her rental car. She pulled out onto Main Street and drove through town, then merged onto the gravel road and sped toward the office, her mind whirling like a tornado. What if Luc's interest in her had only been because of his job? What if he had only cared about her enough to not want her dead? Or even worse, what if the sex was so bad that he'd changed his mind?

Good God, the possibilities were endless.

She rounded the corner down from the office and saw Luc's Jeep parked outside. *There's still time to change your mind.* She eased her foot off the accelerator. *You're not even divorced from the first man who made you look like a fool. Do you really want to run that risk again?*

The car rolled to a stop, and she stared at the Jeep once more, biting her lower lip. Was love really worth the risk? But then she remembered Luc's face when he'd lifted her in the alley, his fear that she was hurt, then the utter relief when he realized she was okay. She remembered exactly how warm his arms felt wrapped around her and how the soft touch of his lips grazed her face. And she remembered her body's response to him.

She pressed down the accelerator, and the car leapt forward. Definitely worth it.

Luc looked up in surprise when she walked in the office. "I thought you'd still be in bed," he said.

"Or hiding in a closet?" she joked.

Luc smiled. "No, not you. Although that might have made things easier." He studied her for a moment. "How are you doing?"

Maryse nodded. "I'm fine. I mean, overwhelmed on some things and still disappointed on others, but it will all pass in time. At least that's what I'm telling myself."

"Probably an accurate statement."

Maryse pointed to the box of video cameras Luc was packing. "So I guess you're clearing out, huh?"

"Yeah. I figured you wouldn't need the security equipment anymore, and I sorta appropriated it without permission."

Maryse smiled. "I bet. So how much trouble are you in?"

Luc shrugged. "More than I'd like and less than the boss-man would, I'm sure."

Now or never. Maryse stepped closer to him. "And was it worth it?"

Luc locked his eyes on hers. "Definitely."

Maryse took another step towards him, her body so close she could feel the heat coming off of him. "If you'd like to prove that statement, there's still about ten minutes before the office is supposed to open."

Luc's eyes widened. "Are you sure?"

"I've never been more sure."

Luc smiled and ran his finger across her lips. "You know, that statement lacks punch coming from someone with so much uncertainty in her everyday life."

"Sure, point out my flaws when I'm standing here pouring out my heart."

Luc leaned over and kissed her gently on the lips. "I love you, Maryse Robicheaux. God help me, I'm head over heels for you."

Maryse felt her heart pound in her chest. "Are you sure?"

"I've never been more sure."

"Says the guy who sees ghosts. Like that's not uncertain."

Luc wrapped his arms around Maryse and pulled her close to him. This time his kiss wasn't gentle but sensual, and Maryse felt her legs grow weak. "I love you, too, Luc LeJeune," she said. "God help us both."

Luc laughed. "We're a mixed pair, Maryse. Me with a one-bedroom studio in the city and you living in a hotel. What are we supposed to do about that?"

"Actually, I've been thinking about that...about everything that's happened over the last week. I know what I thought was a cure wasn't really, but the thing that made it different is that the mice didn't get sick. I think it's something worth pursuing. If I found a way to alleviate illness during radiation, that wouldn't be a cure, but it'd be a hell of a lot better than the way it is now."

"That's a great idea, Maryse."

"So I was thinking that since your job and the university lab are in New Orleans, maybe keeping your apartment there isn't such a bad idea."

"And what about Mudbug?"

"I've got the insurance money from my cabin and the land lease money coming soon. I was thinking about building again, somewhere on the bayou, just on the outskirts of town. Nothing fancy."

"No more hiding out in boat-access-only living quarters?"

Maryse smiled. "I've missed out on things for too long. I'm not going to make that mistake again. So do you think you can handle living in a small town again...part time at least?"

Luc planted small kisses down the side of her neck. "I think I'm going to love it."

"You know," Maryse said as she reached around to squeeze Luc's butt. "I've never made it with an undercover agent before. At least, not that I was aware of."

"Really? So you're telling me there are no other men in your life?"

Maryse grinned. "Well, there was this zoologist, but his exit strategy needed work."

Luc drew her lips to his again, the promise of everything to come in his kiss. "Who says I'm going anywhere?"

Helena Henry stepped out of the beauty shop that evening and crossed Main Street. Maryse and Luc had just pulled up in front of the hotel, and from the rumpled looks of their hair and clothes, Helena had serious doubts they'd been doing any botany back at the office.

She smiled as Mildred and Sabine walked out of the hotel to greet them. Luc took Maryse's hand in his and spoke directly to the two other women. From the ecstatic looks on their faces, Helena had no doubt what news Luc was delivering. He was still talking when Mildred grabbed him in a hug, probably crushing every rib in his body. Even from her place across the street, Helena could see the tears in the hotel owner's eyes.

Helena felt her own eyes mist a bit, both with joy and regret. Pretty soon Maryse would have a whole new mother-in-law to deal with. She could only hope the next one didn't cause Maryse the trouble Helena had.

But all that was behind them now. Maryse was safe, and the land was protected. Luc had put things in motion, and Helena had no doubt that her exhumation was just around the corner. Maybe then she'd get the answers she needed to leave this Earth.

The foursome finished their hugs and walked into the hotel, and Helena had no doubt Mildred would be breaking out a bottle from her champagne stash. Helena looked around at the quaint little town and sighed. It was all so peaceful, so normal.

But for now, someone in Mudbug had still gotten away with murder.

The End

Read Mischief in Mudbug for Sabine's story.

Mischief in Mudbug

Chapter One

Sabine LeVeche placed her hands over her crystal ball and looked across the table at Thelma Jenkins. It didn't take psychic ability to know that Thelma's problem was her husband, Earl, same as always, which was a good thing, since Sabine didn't have an ounce of paranormal gift in her body. But today, she would have given anything for the ability to know where Earl had squirreled away his secret stash, if the money even existed.

"Can you see the money?" Thelma asked.

Sabine held in a sigh. On any other day, she would have pretended to see the money in a suitcase or a box or under a bush, something that would send Thelma off happily on a witch hunt to buy Sabine two weeks of peace and quiet. After all, Thelma didn't need the money. She just couldn't stand the idea of Earl keeping something from her and was convinced he'd been skimming off their gas station profits all fifty years of their marriage.

At least that's how Thelma presented it.

The reality was, Alzheimer's was fast taking Earl away from this earth, and Thelma was desperately looking for something to distract her and fill her time. Looking for the mythical treasure of Earl fit the bill nicely.

Sabine focused on the crystal ball and tried to remember all the tales she'd told Thelma before and come up with something different. "I see the money...no, wait, he's taking the money into a jewelry store. He's exchanging it for diamonds...a bag of uncut diamonds."

Thelma sucked in a breath, the prospect of hunting for diamonds obviously even more exciting than a box of dirty money. "When did he do that?"

Sabine shook her head. "I can't tell for sure, but he placed the diamonds in a red shoe box and put it in the attic." She squinted at the ball. "The image is fading." She held her hands over the ball another couple of seconds, then looked up at Thelma. "It's gone."

Thelma stared at her, her brow wrinkled in concentration. "The attic, huh? Was it the attic in our house?"

"I couldn't tell for sure, and remember, Thelma, there's no way of knowing if the diamonds are still there. Earl could have moved the diamonds or even sold them sometime after the vision I saw. But my guess is he hid them where he had easy access, so that would limit it to your house." God forbid Thelma got arrested for breaking into every house in Mudbug, Louisiana, and digging through their attics.

"What a load of bullshit!" The voice came from out of nowhere, and Sabine felt her spine stiffen. She stared at Thelma, but the blue-haired woman just stared back at her.

"Did you hear that?" Sabine asked as she glanced around her shop, Read 'em and Reap, hoping that someone was hiding behind one of the many shelves of candles, tarot cards, and other paranormal paraphernalia. But as she peered in between the shelves, she didn't see a thing.

"Hear what?" Thelma asked, glancing around the shop. "There wasn't anyone here when I came in, and no one's come in since."

Sabine nodded. That's what she'd thought, but then where had that voice come from? Her imagination was great, but it usually didn't talk out loud.

"You didn't leave the back door open, did you?" Thelma asked.

"No. In fact, it's broken. I keep calling the landlord about getting it fixed, but he says everything has to go through the owner's estate attorney, and he never hurries. Right now, I couldn't open it without a crowbar."

Thelma reached across the table and patted her hand. "You've been under a lot of stress lately, dear, what with people trying to kill Maryse and all. You probably need a vacation."

"You're probably right," Sabine agreed.

"Give it a rest." The voice sounded again and Sabine jumped up from her chair. "That asshole Earl has been teasing Thelma for years over that money."

"Who's there?" Sabine looked frantically around her shop.

Thelma stared, her eyes wide with shock. "I didn't hear anything," she whispered. "Do you think it's the spirits?"

No, Sabine didn't think it was spirits. Obviously someone was having a bit of fun with her. The voice sounded familiar but made Sabine's nose crinkle like she'd encountered something unpleasant.

"So tell me where the money is," Sabine said loudly, figuring if she played along with the charade, she'd eventually expose the trickster. "You seem to know more about it than I do."

"She doesn't need the damn money," the voice answered. "She already has more money than Bill Gates and still won't pay for a decent hairdo. Why give her more?"

Sabine sucked in a breath. She looked over at Thelma, whose eyes were wide with either fear or excitement. "Is the spirit still talking?" Thelma whispered.

"Oh, yeah," Sabine said, wondering momentarily if Thelma was going deaf. How could she not hear that? Sabine walked across the room to look between the shelves. Finding them empty, she strode to the front of the store and peered behind the counter. Empty. "They're still talking. They said you don't need the money and you have a bad hairdo."

Thelma gasped and put one hand on her puffy blue hair. "Why, that's just downright rude. I didn't think spirits were rude once they crossed over."

"You'd be surprised," Sabine muttered, thinking about Helena Henry. Her best friend, Maryse, had gotten more than a handful when her dead mother-in-law turned up as a ghost even harder to get along with than Helena had been as a living, breathing human.

"Oh, for Christ's sake," the voice boomed again. "Tell her the money is in her mattress. She's been sleeping on it for years."

Sabine sucked in a breath. No, it couldn't be. God wouldn't play that unfair. "The money's in your mattress," Sabine said as she rushed over to the table and pulled Thelma out of her chair.

"My mattress?" Thelma repeated as she allowed herself to be hustled to the door. "No wonder Earl never wanted to get rid of that lumpy piece of crap."

Sabine nodded and opened the front door to the shop, pushing a confused but excited Thelma out the door. "I'm sorry, Thelma," Sabine said, "but something's come up that I have to take care of. I'll call you tomorrow."

Thelma shook her head. "You young people are always rushing around to something. Slow down, Sabine, all you've got in this world is time and when it's done, it's done."

Sabine slammed the door shut, locked it, and flipped the "Closed" sign around in the window. When it's done, it's done. Like hell. Her heart pounding, she turned slowly around and faced her empty shop.

"I know you're there, Helena," Sabine said, then felt a wave of nausea sweep over her at her own words.

"Well, I'll be damned! You did hear me," Helena said. "For a minute there, I thought you'd actually gone psychic."

Sabine's gaze swept from side to side, casing every square inch of her tiny store. "I can hear you, but I can't see you. Where are you exactly?"

"I'm standing next to your table. See?"

Sabine looked at her table but didn't see anything out of the ordinary—until her crystal ball began to rise from its stand and hover a good two feet above the table. "I see the ball, but I can't see you."

"Hmm. That's weird, right? I mean, is that supposed to happen?"

"How am I supposed to know? You're the ghost."

"Sure, sure, always trying to make me responsible for everything. Hell, all this paranormal stuff is your bag. I didn't ask to stick around after I died, and no one handed me an instruction manual when I crawled out of my coffin."

Sabine yanked her cell phone from her pocket, punched in a text message, then slipped her phone back into her pocket. She stared at the ball, still suspended in midair, not even sure what to say, what to do. Aside from drinking, nothing else really came to mind. She was saved from reaching for the bottle by a knock on the door.

Sabine hurried to unlock the door and allowed Maryse to enter. "That was fast," Sabine said. Thank God.

"Luc and I were having a late breakfast across the street at the café," her friend said, the worry on her face clear as day. "What's wrong? Your text message seemed a bit panicked."

Sabine pointed to the hovering ball. "I sorta have an issue here."

Maryse looked over at the table and frowned. "Helena, what in the world are you trying to do—give people heart attacks? That's not funny."

"Oh, admit it, Maryse, it's a little funny," Helena said. "You shoulda seen the look on Sabine's face."

Maryse shook her head. "I don't need to see that look. I've worn it for weeks now. Would you stop freaking people out and find something to do?" Maryse turned to Sabine. "Please tell me she did not do that in front of a customer."

Sabine shook her head, squinting at the area surrounding the hovering ball, trying to make out a body or form or outline or anything, but she saw absolutely nothing.

"I have plenty to do," Helena argued, "and I was doing some of it. I was helping that fool Thelma find Earl's money. She's been bitching about that money for forty years. Everyone down at the beauty shop is tired of hearing about it."

Maryse sighed. "And how were you planning on helping—hitting Thelma on the head with that ball? It's not like you could whisper it in her ear. No one can hear you but me."

Helena laughed and Sabine cleared her throat. "Actually, Maryse," Sabine said, "that's the issue. I can hear her. I just can't see her."

Maryse stared at Sabine, her jaw slightly open. "You can hear her?"

Sabine nodded. "Loud and clear, unfortunately."

"Oh my God," Maryse said and sank into a chair. "That can't possibly be good."

"Hey," Helena said, "no use being rude about it. I'm not doing anything to Sabine."

Maryse glared at the ghost. "Yeah, you weren't doing anything to me either, but not long after you appeared, people started trying to kill me."

Sabine sucked in a breath and stared at Maryse. "Oh my God! You don't think…I mean…"

Maryse cast a worried look from the hovering ball to Sabine. "There's no way of knowing for sure, and God knows, this is one of those times I wish I was a decent liar. But it's like you told me before, if it involves Helena, it couldn't possibly be good."

Sabine sank into the chair next to Maryse, her head beginning to swim. If Helena was appearing now…or doing a voice-over, however you wanted to look at it, Sabine knew it couldn't possibly be a coincidence. She rubbed her fingers on her temples and silently willed her head to stop throbbing.

Maryse laid her hand on Sabine's arm. "What is it? What are you not telling me?"

Sabine stared at her friend, hoping her voice wouldn't sound as shaky as she felt. "I have an appointment with Dr. Breaux in an hour to discuss my biopsy results."

Maryse reached for Sabine's hand and gave it a squeeze. Sabine closed her eyes and focused on breathing. Any moment, Dr. Breaux would walk through his office door, sit down at the desk across from them, and give her the news. After Helena's appearance at her shop, Sabine hoped she was ready for what Dr. Breaux would say.

When the abnormalities had appeared four times before, Dr. Breaux had always called her with the good news. The fact that he'd asked her to see him in person coupled with her new ability to hear Helena Henry had the acid in her stomach working overtime. If more people could see or hear the shameless specter, antacid company profits—or alcohol sales, depending on preference—would shoot through the roof.

Sabine hadn't even thought about Helena being the Angel of Death, until Maryse had pointed out the timing of Helena's appearance and Maryse's run for her life. Even though Sabine had always wanted to have a paranormal experience, if Helena Henry was the only option, she'd just pass altogether. A nice, boring job at the bank posting deposits and counting pennies would be preferable.

"It's going to be fine," Maryse said, and Sabine knew her friend was trying as hard to convince herself as she was Sabine.

"Uh huh." Sabine opened her eyes and took a deep breath, not at all convinced. "And what about the Helena factor?"

"It's just a coincidence...a fluke. Luc hasn't been able to see or hear her since that night she sent him to save me."

"Really? I didn't know that."

"We didn't know it, either, until she showed up at the café this morning while we were having breakfast and Luc never noticed her, not even when I pointed her out. Probably you'll never hear her again, much less ever see her."

"And if I do?"

Maryse sighed. "I'll pray for you. I mean really pray...down on my knees, begging for mercy sort of praying. I'll even do it in church and wear a dress."

Sabine smiled. She would almost pay to see the very skeptical and comfort-loving Maryse begging God for relief, wearing a dress and heels—if it didn't require Helena Henry appearing to prompt the action.

"Let's hope it doesn't come to that," Sabine said.

Maryse was about to reply when Dr. Breaux walked into the office. He gave both of them a nod and took a seat behind his desk. "I wanted this meeting with you to discuss the results of your latest tests." He looked at Maryse, then back at Sabine. "I'm afraid the news is not good."

Sabine sucked in a breath, unable to ask the question that raced through her mind.

"I'm so sorry to tell you, Sabine...you have acute myeloid leukemia. Now, as far as leukemia goes, this is the best one to have. Seventy percent or more of patients go into remission after treatment, and unless the leukemia returns, they go on to have long, productive lives."

Sabine blew out the breath she'd been holding, and her eyes blurred as she was overcome with dizziness. This can't be happening. She leaned all the way forward, trying to breathe, as the room began to spin. She felt Maryse's hand on her back, but somehow the touch seemed surreal, as if in a dream. It's astral projection. I don't have a paranormal ounce of blood in my veins and yet today I've heard a ghost and projected my spirit out of my body. She dragged in a deep breath and tried to focus. You're losing it, Sabine.

"Sabine," Maryse's voice cut into her labored breathing. "Do you need me to get you something...a cup of water...?"

Sabine lifted back up to a reasonable position, her head still spinning. "No, I'll be fine. At least, I think I will."

"Of course you will!" Maryse's hand tightened on hers and her friend leaned forward in her chair, an intent look on her face. "Do we know what caused this?"

Dr. Breaux shook his head. "I don't have any way of knowing for sure. It could be a result of the chemical dumping you discovered going on in the bayou, or it could be completely unrelated."

Unbelievable. Sabine wanted to scream with the injustice of it all. All her life, she'd been so careful—no coffee, no substitute sweeteners, no diet sodas, no smoking...all the things that might cause cancer. Aside from her occasional glass of wine, she didn't have any vices to speak of. And now there was a chance she'd contracted the horrible disease from picking flowers on the bayou.

Sabine looked over at Maryse and saw the fright on her friend's face, plain as day. Oh, she was trying to hide it, but Sabine knew better. Inside, Maryse was on the verge of a heart attack. Sabine drew in a deep breath and looked at Dr. Breaux. "And the treatment?"

Dr. Breaux sat back in his chair and sighed. "Begins with chemotherapy. If we don't achieve the desired effect, we add radiation therapy to prevent the disease from moving into the brain and central nervous system."

"That sounds harsh," Sabine said.

"You're only twenty-eight and in good health. I'm not saying the treatments will be easy, but you are in the best of possible shape to handle them."

Sabine swallowed. "And if that doesn't work?"

"A bone marrow transplant is always an option," Dr. Breaux said and gave them a pained look. "Unfortunately, the most successful match for a treatment like this is a close relative."

Sabine clutched the arms of her chair until her fingers ached. A relative? Could this situation get any worse? Sabine's parents had died in a car accident when she was just an infant. A distant great-aunt on her mother's side of the family had raised her, but no amount of searching, either through earthly channels or paranormal, had yielded any information at all about Sabine's father or any other relatives of Sabine's mother. She might as well be searching for the fountain of youth.

Dr. Breaux cleared his throat. "I know your great aunt is dead, Sabine, but I looked into things, hoping to find another relative—at least on your mom's side."

Sabine shook her head. "I've already looked, Dr. Breaux. You know I've exhausted every channel."

Dr. Breaux nodded. "I know you've exhausted all of your available channels, but sometimes if one is, um, creative, one might find information by matching medical records."

Sabine stared at Dr. Breaux. "So did you find someone?"

"Yes," Dr. Breaux said. "Your aunt had a nephew."

Sabine straightened in her chair. "A nephew? How is that possible? I asked, over and over again, and she always denied having any family at all."

Dr. Breaux looked down at his desk for a moment, then back up at Sabine. "My guess is she didn't want people to know."

"Who is it?" Sabine asked, almost afraid to hear the answer.

Dr. Breaux sighed. "Harold Henry."

"Jesus H. Christ!" Maryse jumped up from her chair. "Harold Henry? Are you kidding me?"

"I'm afraid not," Dr. Breaux replied.

"I'm related to Harold Henry?" Sabine asked in dismay.

Maryse slumped back into her chair. "Not that it matters. Harold won't work. Even if he wasn't in jail and he agreed to do it—which would never happen—he's old and has fifty million things wrong with him. High blood pressure, heart problems, and God knows what else."

"I agree," Dr. Breaux said. "Harold wouldn't be a very good choice, even if he was a match." He hesitated for a moment, obviously not wanting to say the next thing on his mind. "But Hank might be. You're the same blood type, anyway, so that's a start."

Maryse groaned and covered her head with her hands. Harold and Helena's son, Hank Henry, her ex-and always-disappearing husband, made professional illusionists look like amateurs with his ability to vanish into thin air.

"And there's no other way?" Sabine asked, starting to feel more than a little desperate. "Can't we look for another match, outside of my family?"

"Of course we can look," Dr. Breaux said. "I've already started the process, but I don't have to tell you the odds of finding a perfect match outside of a family member or the odds of success with anything less than a perfect match. I want the best possible odds."

Sabine nodded. "I understand. So what do we need to do now?"

Dr. Breaux picked up her file. "We'll start the chemo right away. There's an opening next week if you can arrange it. If there's any chance you can locate another family member…just in case…"

Sabine sighed. "I've been searching for my family since I was old enough to read, Dr. Breaux. Unless there's a miracle, I don't see it happening now when it hasn't all these years."

Dr. Breaux gave her a sad nod. "I understand, Sabine."

"But we'll be happy to try again," Maryse said. "Hank can't hide forever, and maybe it's time to try less traditional methods." Maryse stared at Sabine, obviously trying to communicate more than her words. "Who knows, something might appear now that didn't before."

Helena! Well, it was certainly a less than traditional route, and God help them both—it was the best idea Sabine had heard in years.

Chapter Two

Raissa Bordeaux stared across the table at Maryse and Sabine, an uncertain look on her normally focused face. "So let me get this straight," Raissa began, "Maryse started seeing her dead mother-in-law weeks ago, and now you see her, Sabine?"

Sabine glanced over at Maryse, looking for permission to tell Raissa everything. Maryse nodded, and Sabine began her explanation. "No. I can only hear her. We're not sure why I can't see her, but Maryse still can." Sabine hoped her mentor—a real psychic—might have some answers.

Raissa's bright green eyes glowed with interest. "Okay. So both of you can hear her, and Maryse can see her, so what exactly do you need from me?"

"Does that sound normal to you?"

Raissa laughed. "Hell, no. It's probably the most bizarre thing I've ever heard."

Sabine sighed and tried to control her disappointment. "Darn. We were really hoping you would know what was going on with the audio/video display."

"This one is a first for me," Raissa said.

"Okay," Sabine replied, "then this is our next problem. You know I've been trying to locate my family."

Raissa nodded.

"Helena once created an image of my parents for me to see. She said she looked on the 'other side' and asked for them, and they appeared. Unfortunately, she can call them and see them, but they don't answer when she talks to them." Sabine frowned at the thought of being so close, yet so far away from an answer. "We thought that if Helena could create the image again, you could draw it, and it might give us more to go on. I've never even had a photo of them, so this could be a huge breakthrough."

"You want me to draw a portrait of your parents from a dead woman's image?"

Maryse laughed. "You know, Raissa, for a psychic, you seem to be having an awful lot of trouble with this."

"I get visions, not apparitions." Raissa shook her head. "Sabine, I thought you'd finally put this behind you. Why are you starting it all up again now?"

Sabine swallowed. "I need to find a family member."

Raissa's face cleared in immediate understanding, then sympathy. "You have cancer, don't you?"

Sabine nodded, struggling to maintain composure.

"Oh, Sabine," Raissa said, "I am so, so sorry. How are you planning to use the drawing?"

"I don't know yet, exactly," Sabine admitted. "Show it around? Maybe run an ad in the newspaper?"

Raissa was silent for a moment, then looked at Sabine. "Several years ago, a client mentioned a private investigator here in New Orleans who specializes in missing persons. I think he's usually working on more recent cases—consulting with the police, that sort of thing. But if you'd like, I could contact him and see if he's available to help you. I remember his rate being quite reasonable."

Sabine nodded. "If you can recommend someone, that would be great. I started saving to buy a house, but this is a little more important."

"I can help, too," Maryse added. "Since I've got the grant with the medical research company in New Orleans, I don't need my own lab equipment anymore. I still have a lot of the money from my inheritance."

Raissa nodded. "If you need any more, I've got a bit stuck back myself. And let me know if you need someone to cover at your shop. I can always shift my clients around."

Sabine felt tears gather in her eyes and she sniffed. "Thank you both so much. I don't know what I'd do without you."

Raissa smiled. "That's what friends are for, right?" She looked over at Maryse. "Well, if you two think this ghost can produce the image, I'm game to try it. Hell, it would probably be the most interesting thing I've ever done. Is the ghost here now?"

Maryse rose from her chair and opened the front door of Raissa's New Orleans' shop, then motioned to someone on the sidewalk.

"What the hell were you thinking?" Sabine could hear Helena the Horrific Ghost bitching before she ever entered the shop. "Leaving me standing out on the sidewalk like some vagrant. That's not respect, I tell you."

Maryse waited for Helena to enter the shop, then closed the door behind her.

Raissa looked over at her. "What? Is she not here?"

Sabine shook her head. "Oh, no, she's here, believe me. I might not be able to see her, but I could hear her bitching from three parishes over."

Maryse nodded her head in agreement. "That's why we left her outside. Trying to have a conversation with Helena around is like trying to watch a movie with a two-year-old."

"I see how it is," Helena ranted. "You expect me to do you favors, but you want to insult me. And what the hell are we doing here anyway…talking to another nutbag?"

Sabine closed her eyes and sighed. "Raissa is an artist, Helena. I want you to reproduce that image of my parents so Raissa can draw it."

"Hmm. A new approach to your lifetime of futility. Why don't you let this go, Sabine?"

"I have my reasons, Helena." Sabine and Maryse had already agreed that the less Helena knew, the better. The ghost would be certain to want to "help." And Helena's help was something they were hoping to do without, except on a very selective and clearly instructed basis. "Can you produce the image or not?"

"Of course I can produce it. Tell the nutbag to break out her charcoal."

Sabine looked over at Raissa and nodded. "She's ready whenever you are."

Raissa pulled a drawing pad and pencil from a table behind her and flipped to a blank sheet. "Ready."

"Go ahead, Helena," Sabine instructed.

There were several seconds of dead silence, and for a moment, Sabine was afraid that Helena wasn't going to be able to pull it off. Then a small orb of light began to glow just to the side of the table. Raissa gave a small start when the orb appeared and watched in fascination as it grew in size and detail, ultimately depicting a man and woman standing in the center of the light.

Raissa stared at the image, her eyes wide, then finally asked, "How long can she hold that?"

"We're not sure," Sabine said.

Raissa laughed, her expression still mingled with excitement and disbelief. "Then I best get to drawing."

Raissa closed the door to her shop a little early that evening. She didn't have any late appointments scheduled, and walk-ins would just have to wait until the next day. Maryse and Sabine had left, happy as clams, a couple of hours before with a fistful of photocopies of Raissa's drawing. The original and a couple of spare copies, Raissa had locked away in her filing cabinet for safekeeping. Her door secure, Raissa closed the blinds, emptied the cash and receipts from the register, and carried it upstairs with her to her studio apartment above the store.

The apartment was cool in contrast to the store, where the door admitted summer heat and humidity along with the customers. She shrugged off her black robe, a necessity for her customers even though what she wore made no difference as to how she did her job, and pulled on shorts and a T-shirt. There was a nice chilled bottle of Pinot Grigio in her refrigerator and she was tempted to pour herself a glass, or two, and pile up on the couch with a good book, but she knew her mind was whirling too much to relax even if she drank the whole bottle.

She settled for a bottled water and sat at her tiny kitchen table. God knows she'd seen things that any twenty people would never run across in their lifetimes...and that was a good thing. But nothing had prepared her for what she'd witnessed today. She'd drawn a sketch of two dead people from a hologram created by a ghost. That and a plane ticket would get her a spot on Jerry Springer.

Or an even smaller apartment with padded walls.

She reached across the tiny table for her laptop and connected to the internet. There was something about the man in that drawing that looked familiar, but for the life of her, she couldn't figure out what.

She did a quick search for private detectives around the area. She clicked on the first link and studied the list of names and numbers. Atwater, Baker, Cooke...none of them was right. Deacon, Farris, Howard, Lawther...no, further down. Villeneuve—that was it. Raissa reached for the cordless phone on the cabinet behind her and dialed the number on the listing. The detective answered on the first ring.

"Villeneuve," he said, his voice strong and crisp.

"Hello, Mr. Villeneuve. My name is Raissa Bordeaux, and I'm interested in hiring you to locate some family members."

"Are the family members missing, Ms. Bordeaux, or are you performing a historical search?"

"More of a historical search, I suppose, but my goal is to find living relatives."

"What do you have to go on?"

Raissa sighed. "Not much, I have to admit. A couple of surnames and a drawing of two family members."

"I assume this is your family?"

"Actually, no. It's a friend of mine who's looking. I'd love to help her, but I simply don't have the knowledge or connections to research something like this. I understand you're an expert at this sort of thing, and I think you being from the area is an advantage. I've already exhausted all the resources I have."

"And what sort of resources would those be, Ms. Bordeaux?"

"I'm a psychic. I talked to dead people."

Beau Villeneuve walked into a café in Mudbug, Louisiana wondering why he'd ever agreed to this job. He didn't need the money and never would thanks to a reclusive grandfather who hoarded every penny he'd ever made.

So the job was never about the money, which allowed him to be selective...pick only the cases that interested him. The harder the better. And that was the crux of it, really. Boredom. Some days he wished he'd never left the FBI, but that was another thought for another day. Maybe another year.

And there weren't too many cases more challenging than missing-family searches. He had yet to take on one that turned out well. When people disappeared without a trace, there was usually a reason, and it was rarely a pleasant one. Plus, people who had gotten away with disappearing for ten, twenty, thirty years were never happy to be "found." He'd discovered that firsthand.

Still, Beau had recognized the determination in Raissa Bordeaux's voice. If he didn't take the job, she'd just move on to the next detective who would. A detective who most likely wouldn't have the experience and skill at working these family situations. A detective who most likely would open a rash of shit for the searcher and have no idea how to deal with it. And Beau just didn't want that to happen. Raissa seemed genuinely concerned for her friend and really wanted to help.

He grabbed a local newspaper from the rack next to the door and took a seat at a table in the corner of the café with a clear view of the door. Raissa had laid out the case the night before at a local pub. He wasn't sure what he'd expected when he'd met with the psychic, but she hadn't looked or talked like a nut. In fact, he'd admired the way she'd presented the facts, minimal as they were, in such logical order. The only question she wouldn't give him a straight answer to was where she got the image for the drawing.

She'd claimed she'd had a vision, but Beau wasn't buying it. Regardless of any so-called psychic ability, she was one hell of an artist. The drawing was highly detailed and ought to give him something to work from. He'd studied it for over an hour the night before, thinking about the job. Thinking about the people depicted. Like Raissa, he had the nagging feeling in the back of his mind that he'd seen the man somewhere, but knew that was probably unlikely as the man in the photo had died more than twenty years before.

Assuming Raissa had her facts—and her visions—straight.

He was two cups of coffee down and halfway into a story about an alleged UFO sighting when the door to the café opened and a young woman walked in. Raissa's description hadn't done the woman justice.

Certainly she was tall and thin with long black hair, but Raissa hadn't mentioned the perfect skin with a beautiful tanned glow, or the grace with which she walked, almost like watching a dancer. Get a grip, Beau. Women are not part of the equation. Not then, not now, not ever. You don't need the money. You should turn down the job.

Against his better judgment, he raised a hand as she scanned the café. The vision nodded and headed toward his table. Beau felt his heart rate increase with every one of her choreographed steps. Maybe she isn't near as impressive up close. Maybe she has buck teeth and a speech impediment. But when she reached the table, she gave him a shy smile, her pale blue eyes not quite meeting his own.

"I'm Sabine LeVeche," she said, the words rolling off her tongue like music.

And that's when Beau knew he was in serious trouble.

Sabine slid into the booth across from the detective, her heart racing because of the task at hand and the appearance of the man who was going to perform it. He was so young, so rugged, so manly. Sabine had no idea what she'd been expecting, maybe some gray-haired man wearing a Sherlock Holmes hat...but that was ridiculous. Still, she'd only worked with a private detective once before and the chain-smoking, mid-fifties burnout hadn't even remotely resembled the gorgeous man across from her.

She took a deep breath, hoping to slow her racing pulse, and pushed a folder across the table, praying that her hands didn't shake. "Mr. Villeneuve, I know Raissa gave you some information about my family, but this is everything I have. Twenty years of research."

He reached for the folder and flipped through the sparse set of papers Sabine had given him. "Not a lot to show for twenty years." He looked over at her. "That must be very disappointing."

"You have no idea."

Beau studied her for a moment, a contemplative expression on his face. Then his expression shifted back to business mode, and whatever it was that Sabine had thought he was going to say was apparently pushed back. "So tell me what you do know," he said. "I like to hear the story firsthand if I can. It gives me a better feel for the situation and sometimes opens up avenues of investigation that might not have been explored."

Sabine laughed. "If you can find an avenue I haven't explored, then you're the best detective in the world, Mr. Villeneuve."

"Call me Beau."

"Okay, Beau. I guess I'll start at the beginning, what I was told of it anyway. I was only six months old when my parents had a fatal car accident."

"You weren't in the car?" Beau asked.

"I was in the car. Some folks around here called it a miracle, and I suppose it was, but apparently they were riding with the windows down and I was thrown clean when the car rolled. The fireman who worked the scene probably wouldn't have found me at all, except they'd brought their dog with them. He set up a howl, and they found me perched in a clump of marsh weeds, not a scratch on me."

"Wow! That's incredible."

Sabine nodded. "The police did a search to locate the closest relative, trying to find someone to care for me until the state could decide what to do. They came up blank on my father. His name didn't appear in records anywhere except for a driver's license that had been issued a little over six months before. They finally got lucky with my mother and came up with my great aunt in Mudbug."

"And she took you in?"

"Yes. Aunt Margaret was a nurse. She never married and, to hear the talk, never even dated much. All I know is she took me in. Gave me a home, food, clothes…took care of me."

Beau nodded. "And your mother? What did your aunt have to say about her?"

Sabine frowned. "Not much. She didn't really know my mother or her parents that well. Apparently they were from the dirt-poor branch of the family that lived deep in the bayou—in huts, really. All Aunt Meg knew was that my mother's parents had died young, probably when she was a teenager, and she didn't know of any other children at all."

"Was there any other family?"

"Not that Aunt Meg was aware of." Sabine frowned, recalling her recent conversation in Dr. Breaux's office.

"What's wrong?"

"Well, my whole life Aunt Meg always said she had no other living relatives, but I just found out this week that was a lie."

Beau leaned forward and stared at her. "Why would she lie?"

Sabine shrugged. "Since my aunt passed away years ago, I can only guess it's because the relative she failed to mention was her nephew, a loser of monumental proportions. Harold is in jail right now for an assortment of charges, attempted murder being two of them, and who knows what else the cops will find now that they're looking."

"Then it's just as well you weren't obligated to exchange Christmas cards or anything."

Sabine smiled.

"I need to tell you up front that I journal all my cases from start to finish, but I promise any documentation I acquire or create will always remain confidential. Writing things down helps me reach logical conclusions, and I tend to remember things more easily if I write them longhand."

"Do most detectives work like that?" Sabine asked.

"I can't speak for other detectives, really. I started keeping journals when I was a kid. The habit just stuck, I guess." He looked down at the table and fiddled with a packet of sugar.

Sabine, sensing he was somewhat embarrassed, continued. "Well, that's basically it in a nutshell." She reached for the gold heart-shaped locket that was always around her neck. "This locket belonged to my mother. That information in that folder and this piece of jewelry are all I really know about them."

Beau looked back up at her. "And a drawing from beyond."

Sabine nodded. "Raissa's very talented. I'm fortunate to know her."

Beau narrowed his eyes at her. "Do you really buy into all that psychic stuff?"

Sabine laughed. "She didn't tell you?"

"Tell me what?"

"Raissa's my mentor. I own the psychic shop across the street."

Beau hopped into his vehicle and stared at Sabine as she unlocked the front door of her shop. Read 'em and Reap. Good God Almighty! He'd stepped into the middle of a nut parade. And the worst part was, against his own better judgment, he'd picked up a banner and agreed to march. No doubt about it—he was going to make a colossal fool of himself over a beautiful woman who walked like a ballet dancer. Maybe he needed to reconsider his vow of bachelorhood and settle down with a nice accountant or something. Women like Sabine LeVeche could only get him into trouble.

Sabine turned before entering the shop and gave him a wave and a smile. Beau waved back and started his truck, hoping the drive back to the city would clear his head and help him make sense of the mess he'd just gotten himself into. Not one psychic but two. And he had actually agreed to embark on a search for dead people with his biggest lead supposedly coming from the dead people themselves. For a man who was more than a skeptic, it was an irony he wasn't quite ready to fathom.

As he drove out of town and onto the highway to New Orleans, he pulled Raissa's drawing out of the envelope and took another look. He knew he'd seen that face somewhere before, but not exactly that face and not in person. For the life of him, that's all he could remember. Given the sheer number of photos he'd viewed when he was an FBI agent, God only knew when he'd seen a picture that resembled the man in the drawing. Hell, there was nothing to say he'd even seen it while working at the FBI. Raissa had claimed she thought the man looked familiar, too, so for all he knew it could have been a likeness in a local newspaper.

But for some reason, that didn't feel right.

He took another glance at the drawing and frowned. Somewhere buried in the depths of his mind was the answer. He slipped the drawing back into the folder and concentrated on the road ahead of him. As soon as he got back to his apartment, he would pull out his journals from his FBI years. Maybe something in them would spark his memory. Beyond the basics of background searching, the drawing was his best lead for now.

Unless, of course, Raissa or Sabine could call up more spirits to give them an address.

Sabine opened the tiny window in the corner of the attic of her store's building and stuck her head out, hoping for a breeze. She coughed once, wheezed a couple more times, then pulled her head back inside and stared at Maryse, who was already tugging on boxes tucked in the far corners of the room.

"I can't believe you haven't looked at any of this stuff since last time," Maryse said.

"Please, you act like my aunt stored the secrets of the world in those boxes. We've been through this before and didn't find a thing."

"We were eighteen. What might be important now is something we might not have noticed or understood then."

Sabine sneezed and tugged another box from its hiding spot. "I guess so. But if all I end up with is a cold, you're making me soup every day."

Maryse waved a hand in dismissal. "You live across the street from every restaurant in town and they all deliver. Besides, I burned the toast this morning. Luc won't even let me use the microwave."

Sabine laughed. "Smart man." Her scientific-minded friend gave a whole new meaning to the term "nondomestic."

"I don't have to take this abuse from both of you. And if I find an anti-aging formula in here or a Farmer's Almanac for 2015, or something equally as cool, I'm not letting you in on it."

"Who the hell reads the Farmer's Almanac?" Helena's voice boomed from the doorway.

"Farmers," Sabine shot back. "What do you want, Helena?"

"I saw the 'Closed' sign for the shop and thought I'd come see what you were up to."

"We're cleaning out the attic," Sabine said.

"Hmmmpf," Helena grunted. "Looks like this shit's been here for a hundred years. You're not much of a housekeeper, are you, Sabine?"

Sabine stared at the empty doorway. "I guess your attic was spotless?"

"Of course. I paid people to clean it twice a year."

"Never mind." Sabine rolled her eyes, and Maryse grinned. Sabine turned around and opened a box of ancient clothes. She pulled out the first couple of garments, then waved one in the air. "Hey, Maryse, you think one of the playhouses in New Orleans would be interested in these?"

Maryse looked up from an old steamer trunk that she was struggling to pull into the middle of the room. "Cool! I think they'd be thrilled."

"Some of this material is fantastic, and so well-preserved. I might keep a couple myself and make something of them."

Maryse nodded. "If anyone can make it wearable, you can. That pink would look good on you." She pointed to a pretty calico dress.

Sabine held up the dress and studied the color. "I don't know. This is the same color as that T-shirt I wore to that breast cancer walk in New Orleans last month. A picture of me, Mildred, and a couple others ended up in the newspaper and the shirt made me look all washed out."

"None of you look good in the newspaper," Helena said. "Look at that shot of Maryse the local paper had. Maryse looked like the running year of bad weather."

"Well," Maryse said, "the next time a ghost wakes you up in the dead of night because a man is crawling through your bedroom window to kill you, and you have to run down the street in your pajamas and bare feet, and you just miss dying by a half a second, then you can tell me how bad I look."

"She's got a point." Sabine glanced over at the doorway, an idea forming in her mind. "Helena, are you planning on sticking around for a while?"

"Yeah, although the beauty shop is a hell of a lot more interesting than the two of you. Now, if Maryse would let me in her house when Luc was there...that would probably be something to see."

"Not on your life," Maryse said and glanced over at Sabine, who was holding up a large lime green dress with ruffles from top to bottom. "What's with the gigantic ruffle thing?"

Sabine grinned. "I was thinking that Helena ought to wear it. Then I could see her. Or her clothes anyway."

"Oh no," Helena said. "I'll wear a hat or something or a wristband, or even one of those cone bras like Madonna wore in that video, but I'm not wearing that monstrosity. No one over the age of four should ever wear ruffles, especially across their butt. And green? Jesus, I'd look like moving shrubbery."

"I hate to admit it," Maryse said and laughed, "but she's right."

"Probably so," Sabine agreed, "but I'd still like to see it."

"No way," Helena said.

"You know," Sabine said, "I could still work in that exorcism Maryse and I discussed before. You wouldn't want me to sic the power of God on you, would you, Helena?" Sabine knew an exorcism wouldn't do a thing to the ghost, but Helena still wasn't sure.

"Fine," Helena huffed. "Throw that damned thing toward the door."

Sabine tossed the ruffled nightmare toward the doorway and grinned at Maryse as Helena grunted and complained while tugging.

"Are you happy now?" Helena asked.

Sabine took one look at the doorway, now totally eclipsed in a sea of jiggling green, and howled in laughter.

Maryse shook her head. "That is just wrong."

Sabine wiped at her eyes, tears of laughter blurring her vision. "You ought to see it without Helena in it. Oh my God, that is just the funniest thing I have seen in forever."

"That's it," Helena said. "I'm taking this thing off."

And that's when the sound of glass breaking downstairs made them all freeze.

Chapter Three

Sabine froze, straining to hear any further noise from downstairs. She eased up beside Maryse, who was standing stock-still, her eyes as wide as an owl's.

"What the hell," Maryse whispered. "I thought the shop was locked."

"It is," Sabine said. "Do you have your cell phone? Mine's downstairs."

Maryse shook her head, her eyes wide. "I forgot it at home. Shit."

"Oh hell," Helena said. "I'll go check it out. Not like anything can happen to me." And with that, the green blob floated out the door and down the narrow attic staircase. Sabine peered after her, still not taking a breath.

There was dead silence for several seconds, but it felt like an eternity. Great. Just when Helena flapping her jaws would have been appreciated, she had to go silent. Sabine couldn't take just standing there for another moment. She looked over at Maryse, who nodded. As quietly as possible, they began to creep down the stairs but didn't make it two steps before the ancient staircase creaked, the noise seemingly amplified in the dead silence of the building.

They stopped short, but it was too late. A crash came from the storage room at the back of the shop and then a terrifying scream. Sabine rushed down the remainder of the stairs and rounded the corner in her upstairs apartment, grabbing a butcher knife from the kitchen counter as she took the next set of stairs down into the shop. She skidded to a stop at the back door, and Maryse stumbled into her from behind, sending them both sprawling.

Sabine hit the wood floor hands and knees first and felt a piercing pain in her palms. She jumped back up, looked at her hands, and saw tiny shards of glass embedded in her skin. Someone had broken the window in the door. Helena was nowhere in sight. Neither was the screaming intruder.

"It's ten o'clock in the morning," Maryse said, staring at the door. "It's broad daylight, Sabine. I mean, I know this is the back of the building, but what kind of person would risk trying to break in right now?"

"I was just wondering the same thing." Sabine peered out the broken window and looked up and down the alley. "And where in the world is Helena?"

Maryse's eyes widened. "At this point, God only knows." Maryse reached over to open the door, but it didn't budge. "The landlord still hasn't fixed this?"

"No. And I guess it's a good thing. That's why they couldn't get inside." Sabine looked over at Maryse, who stared at the door, a worried look on her face. "What's that look?"

Maryse sighed. "I was just wondering how much of this has to do with you hearing Helena, like she's some bad-luck curse or something."

"She can't control the universe, Maryse. I know her appearance or rising or whatever it was brought you nothing but trouble, but that's no reason to think she's responsible for this."

Maryse didn't look convinced. "Maybe not, but in all the time you've lived here you've never had a problem."

Sabine nodded. "Yeah. I guess I need to call the police, right?"

"It won't do any good, given the caliber of our law enforcement, but you should still get something on record." Maryse glanced around the room at the broken glass. "I guess I can't clean up the glass until after the police taken a look, but I'll move those boxes of inventory over in case it starts to rain. Once the cops are done, we can figure out something to do about the window until your useless landlord bothers to fix it."

Maryse had just shifted the first box away from the door when a huge shaking mass of green fabric burst through the wall. Sabine jumped back in surprise, then realized what she was seeing. "Helena, you scared the crap out of me!"

"Sorry." The ruffled horror slumped onto a box against the wall, and the cardboard sagged under her weight. "Can't breathe."

Sabine stared at the wheezing pile of green. "You're dead, Helena. Why do you need to breathe?"

"You know," Helena said between pants, "I'm well aware of that without you and Maryse constantly reminding me. And don't ask me why I need to breathe. You're the one who's into all this paranormal crap. You tell me."

Sabine sighed. "Did you see anything?"

"Of course I saw something. You think I went running down the alley in this dress for nothing?" Helena coughed, then wheezed out more air, sounding like a leaky air compressor. "There was someone out back. They broke the window in the door."

"Who was it?"

"I don't know," Helena said. "Whoever it was wore a turtleneck, a ball cap pulled down real low, and black sunglasses."

"A turtleneck?" Maryse asked. "In Mudbug in the summer?"

"I'm just telling you what I saw," Helena said. "He was a little taller than you, Sabine, and moved fast. I couldn't even come close to catching him."

Which meant absolutely nothing, as two-year-olds and eighty-year-old invalids were also known to move faster than Helena. "Was that you who screamed?" Sabine asked.

"No. It was him, but I have no idea why. I ran downstairs and when I saw the arm reaching in through the broken window, I hauled ass through the wall to get a better look. Then he screamed and took off running. Must have cut his hand or something."

Sabine looked over at Maryse, her lips already quivering. One look at her friend, collapsed against a storeroom shelf, and Sabine lost it. Laughter resounded in the storeroom and Sabine clutched her side. "Don't you see…oh my God…now I can't breathe…the dress, Helena…you ran through the wall wearing the dress."

"It's like one of those B horror movies," Maryse said. "Revenge of the Bridesmaid's Dress."

There was dead silence for a couple of seconds, and then Helena started to laugh. "I didn't even think about it. I'd completely forgotten about the dress, even though the damned thing was impossible to run in. What a sight that must have been."

"I would have definitely screamed," Maryse said.

"Me too," Sabine agreed. "So how far did you chase the man? Did you see a car or anything that I could tell the police?"

"He ran to the far end of the street and into the park. When I got to the end of the trail, he was already gone. I saw a white pickup truck hauling ass out of the park. That must have been him. But he was too far away for me to see a plate or anything."

"Well, then I guess I better call the cops and tell them I chased an intruder into the park."

"Sure," Maryse said, "and the first thing you can explain is just how you chased an intruder through a door that's been wedged in place since the Civil War."

"Crap," Sabine said.

Maryse nodded. "Been there, done that crap."

"Hey," Helena interrupted, "while you two dream up some bullshit story for the cops, why don't one of you help me out of this damned dress? I think it's stuck."

Sabine reached over with one hand, grabbed the dress, and pulled, but the dress didn't budge.

"I swear when this is off of me," Helena griped, "I am going back to my MTV eras of fashion."

Sabine took a firm hold on the dress, right at the zipper, and yanked as hard as she could, ripping the dress in two. "As long as your fashion quest doesn't include this dress, I think we'll be okay. I don't think I ever want to see this again." She tossed the dress in a box of rags next to the back door, and the light in the room dimmed. She took another look at the broken window. "Oh, no. Here comes the rain, and we left the window open upstairs."

"You go get the window," Maryse said. "I'll get the rest of the boxes out of the line of fire."

Sabine hurried up the stairs and into the already darkening attic. She felt the wall for the light switch, certain they'd left the light on when they'd gone after Helena. She found the switch and flipped it up and down. Nothing. Great. "Maryse," she yelled down the stairwell. "Can you bring me the flashlight from the storeroom, please?"

"No problem. Be there in a minute," Maryse yelled back.

Sabine inched into the room and started shuffling toward the tiny stream of light coming in the open window. She'd made it halfway across the room when lightning flashed across the sky and through the open window, striking a metal rack against the wall. Sparks flew from the rack as the sound of thunder exploded around her. Sabine lurched backward and tumbled over something big. The large object rolled with her and they both crashed to the floor, Sabine's head banging against the hardwood planks.

Sabine had no idea how long she'd been out when she felt heat on her face. Opening one watery eye just a bit, she saw a single beam of light that seemed to stretch out infinitely in front of her. Oh my God. I'm dead. She clenched her eyes, squeezing the tears out, then opened the lids again.

And saw Helena Henry leaning over her, encased in the beam of light.

"I am dead!" Sabine cried.

"Oh, give it a rest," Helena said. "You're just as alive and strange as you were ten minutes ago."

Sabine struggled to rise from the floor and felt a hand on her arm.

"Don't move yet," Maryse said. "You must have banged your head good. You were out completely."

Sabine stared into the darkness behind the beam of light. It sounded like Maryse, but that couldn't be if she was dead. Suddenly the attic light flickered on and a dim glow filled the room. Sabine blinked twice and looked up at Maryse's worried face. Relief washed over her and she laid her head back down, hoping the dizziness would pass soon.

"I thought I was dead," Sabine said. "The flashlight looked like a hallway…you know like those stories you hear from those people who died, then returned. And then I saw Helena. Jeez, I must have banged my head hard."

Maryse peered down at Sabine and bit her lip. "You saw Helena?"

"Yeah, but I must have imagined it, right?"

Maryse motioned behind her and a couple of seconds later, Helena Henry stood right next to Maryse, peering down at her.

"Oh, no," Sabine said. "It wasn't my imagination. I see her… but what the heck is she wearing?" The hair was the same, all poufy and gray, and the streetwalker makeup looked just as it had in the coffin. Unfortunately, Helena's outfit matched the makeup. The leather bodysuit, complete with cone bra, stretched in directions it wasn't intended to, straining to hold in all of Helena. It was a partial success.

Maryse grimaced. "Helena's going through an unfortunate rebellious phase in her fashion journey through the ages."

Sabine blinked again and stared at the ghost. "What year did we all dress like hookers?"

"Oh for Christ's sake!" Helena bitched. "I am not dressed like a hooker. Didn't you people ever watch MTV? I'm wearing a Madonna outfit."

"From the nineties, maybe, but that's questionable," Sabine said and rose to a sitting position.

"I'm working my way through the generations." Helena crossed her arms and glared.

Sabine looked over at Maryse. "Thank God I missed hair bands of the eighties."

"The seventies weren't any better." Maryse leaned in a bit and whispered, "Cher."

Sabine rubbed her temples and groaned.

Maryse placed her hand on Sabine's arm. "Do you think you can get up? We still need to call the police, and I'll bet you'd like an aspirin about now."

Sabine moved her head from side to side. "I think so. I don't feel dizzy, anyway."

Maryse offered her hand and helped pull Sabine into a standing position. She felt a rush of blood into her head and pressed at her temples. "An aspirin is sounding better and better." She looked over at Helena and blinked. The cone bra was starting to blur. She stared harder but the ghost began to slowly fade away, until nothing was left at all.

"She's gone," Sabine said.

"Who's gone?" Maryse asked. "Helena's standing right here."

Sabine clenched her eyes shut for a moment, then looked again. Nothing. "I can't see her anymore. What does that mean?"

Maryse slowly shook her head. "I don't know, but I don't like it. Let's get out of here."

Sabine stepped forward and looked down at the trunk that had caused her fall. It was flipped over backward, the contents spilled out onto the floor. "Guess that was one way to get that thing opened."

"Yeah," Maryse agreed, "but not exactly what I was shooting for. Don't worry about the mess. I'll pick it up later."

Sabine started to move, but then something within the scattered hats and ancient purses caught her eye. She leaned over a bit, straining to focus in the dim light.

"What is it?" Maryse asked.

"There's something in the bottom of the trunk." Sabine knelt and reached inside the trunk for the object. It felt like paper wedged into the bottom of the trunk. Sabine gently worked the paper from side to side, careful not to tear it. Finally, it came loose and she pulled it out.

Maryse leaned over to see. "It's a diary page. See the date at the top? She's talking about the crop prices dropping."

"A diary? My aunt didn't keep a diary."

"That you know of," Helena pointed out. "It's a generational thing. Lots of women kept diaries during the Vietnam conflict. All the men going off and us left here to manage. Some took comfort in writing it all down."

"Did you keep a diary?" Sabine asked.

"Hell, no," Helena said. "Put all your feelings down on paper just so someone can get a hold of it later and pass judgment? I don't think so. I was damned happy when Harold went off to serve…not so happy that he came back. How would that look to people if I'd written all that down?"

"If they knew Harold, it would look really smart," Sabine pointed out.

Maryse leaned over and peered into the trunk. "Is there more? I mean there can't be only one sheet. And how did it get wedged in the bottom? I thought it was solid."

"Good question," Sabine said. She stuck her hand into the trunk and slid one long fingernail into a gap between the bottom and the side. "There's a false bottom. It must have come loose when I fell. Let me see if I can work it out." She stuck another fingernail in the gap and gently pulled on the bottom. It held firm for a moment, then broke loose from the sides of the trunk. A stack of journals fell out on top of it.

"Holy crap!" Maryse said.

Sabine stared at the books. "I can't believe it. All those years and I never knew she kept a diary. But why would she hide them like this? Why not tell me before she died?"

Maryse shook her head. "I don't know. But I think we ought to take them all downstairs and find out." She picked up one of the journals and flipped through the hundreds of pages of handwritten text. "It may be, Sabine, that your aunt knew more about your family than she admitted."

Sabine nodded and started to gather up the journals. She'd already had the same thought. It was the next thought that worried her. If her aunt knew something about Sabine's family, why had she hidden it from her all these years?

Late that night, Sabine grabbed a bottled water and two more aspirin from the kitchen, then crawled into bed with the book she'd been trying to finish for two weeks. It had been a long and exhausting day, what with the break-in, the absolutely useless time spent with the local police, and then the trip to the hospital that Maryse had insisted on to check out her head. She'd tried to nap that afternoon with limited success and had instead spent a good portion of the time scanning through some of her aunt's journals. Unfortunately, she hadn't found anything of relevance, but the logical, systematic way her aunt had documented such a volatile time in history made Sabine think that had her aunt been born in a different era, she would have made a great scientist, or maybe even a detective.

She propped herself up with a stack of fluffy pillows and snuggled into the pale pink sheets and comforter, figuring she had twenty minutes tops before sleep caught up with her. She opened the book and started at the marked spot. The hero had just saved the heroine from a killer and his arms were still wrapped around her. A fleeting image of Beau Villeneuve clutching Sabine and moving in for a kiss flashed through her mind. Where the hell had that come from? She lifted her water and took a sip. Like she needed a roadmap to answer that question. Beau Villeneuve was quite frankly the best-looking man she'd come into contact with in...well...forever.

And she couldn't have met him at a worse time.

Sabine was pretty sure he didn't buy into the psychic connection, but she might have still made a run at him had her situation been less complicated. She set her book on the nightstand and sighed. Who are you kidding? You've never made a slow stroll at a man, much less a run. Twenty-eight years in Mudbug, Louisiana, and she'd spent most of her time trying to talk to dead people instead of the living. And then when she finally got the opportunity to talk to the dead, she was saddled with Helena Henry. Not exactly what she'd had in mind.

Beau Villeneuve was just another piece to the puzzle that wasn't going to ever form a clear picture. Sitting across from him in the café, she'd felt a tug that she'd never felt before...a desire to know this man, inside and out. But with her life hanging in the balance, the last thing Sabine was going to do was complicate an already impossible situation by developing feelings for a man she might not be around to see grow old. It wasn't fair...not to her and especially not to him. She turned off the lamp and lay down, hoping she dreamed about anything besides death, ghosts, family, and the good-looking man who would never know she was interested.

It felt like she'd barely fallen asleep when Sabine bolted upright in her bed, her pulse racing. There was noise downstairs in her shop. She glanced at the alarm clock and saw it was just after midnight. Much, much too late for anyone to need anything legitimate. And with the attempted break-in that morning, she wasn't about to take any chances. She eased out of bed and pulled open her nightstand drawer. Within easy reach and already loaded rested the nine millimeter she'd purchased years before.

Mudbug might be a small town, but Sabine was a single woman living alone. Residents of Mudbug may call her crazy, but no one was going to call her stupid. She lifted the pistol from the drawer and crept out of the bedroom. The stairwell door creaked just a bit as she eased it open, and she froze. The only sound she could hear was the ticking of the old clock in her living room.

Then she heard rustling downstairs and knew whoever it was hadn't fled. Which wasn't good. When faced with the possibility of a homeowner in a small town in Louisiana, most thieves would flee—unless they were on drugs. But then, most thieves didn't try to break into buildings in broad daylight, either, even if it was the back door.

Unless theft wasn't their primary objective.

Clutching the pistol, she crept down the stairs, hoping they didn't creak under her weight. She reached the bottom without incident and peered around the corner into the shop. A silhouette stood silently by the cash register. She squinted in the dark, trying to make out the figure, and as her vision shifted just a bit, she realized the person wasn't trying to break into the register, as she'd originally thought, but was instead writing something on the pad of paper she usually kept under the counter.

Now or never. Please God, don't let him have a gun, too.

She took a deep breath and tightened her grip on the pistol. Her heart pounded in her chest, making the silence seem ever more sinister, more empty. With a silent prayer, she flipped on the shop lights and stepped around the corner, her gun aimed directly at the figure. It took a moment for her to focus and realize that the man standing at her counter was someone she knew.

"Jesus, Hank! You scared the shit out of me. What in the world are you doing in my shop in the middle of the night? For that matter, what are you doing in Mudbug at all?"

Hank Henry, disappearing husband extraordinaire, remained frozen in surprise and fright, his hands in the air. Finally, he found his voice. "You're not going to shoot me, are you?"

"No...well, probably not." Sabine looked closely at him, trying to figure out what he was up to, but all she saw was the good-looking guy Maryse had been unfortunate enough to fall for and marry.

He stared a moment more, then apparently deciding she probably wouldn't shoot him, he lowered his hands and sucked in a breath. "Jesus yourself, Sabine. I already got shot once in the last month. I'd really like to avoid it again if I could."

Sabine tried to hold in a smile but only partially managed to. Hank, in an unusual fit of heroism, had taken a bullet that wasn't meant for him. It had definitely improved his rating with Maryse and Sabine, but Hank was far from out of the woods. There was still that two-year disappearance, and Sabine wasn't yet ready to forgive Hank completely for all the trouble he'd brought to her friend...bullet or no.

"Well, if you stop putting yourself in situations to get shot, you might have a better chance at keeping your innards intact," Sabine said. "You darn near bought it."

Hank swallowed. "Yeah, I can see that. Damn, Sabine, what are you doing with a nine? That's a helluva gun for a chick."

"I'm a helluva chick, Hank. You still haven't answered my question—what are you doing in my shop and how did you get in?"

"I still have a key from back when I was with Maryse." He pulled it from his pocket and slid it across the table to Sabine, a sheepish look on his face. "I need to talk to you, but couldn't risk being caught by the Mudbug cops. I haven't exactly got all my past transgressions worked out. Although, the way things look now, I would probably have been safer with ole Leroy."

Sabine had to laugh. Deputy Leroy Theriot was more likely to shoot himself in the foot than actually apprehend a criminal. "You ever thought of using a phone?"

"Yeah, but this was sorta important and I felt kinda funny doing it over the phone. Please, Sabine, I need to use your restroom first, but then I really need to talk to you."

Sabine sighed. "Restroom's on the far right wall. The break room is through the door behind the counter. Meet me in there when you're done. I'll make some tea."

Hank relaxed a little and headed off. Sabine stepped into the break room and pulled a box of decaffeinated tea from the cabinet. It was far too early for coffee and if she could hear whatever Hank had to say and get rid of him soon, there was still a chance of sleeping again. She nuked two cups of water in the microwave and dipped the tea bags in them until the water turned a deep, rich brown. Sabine took in the sweet smell of cinnamon and spice and smiled.

She had just set the cups and sugar on a tiny table when Hank entered the room. She motioned to the other chair and he took a seat, reaching for the cup of tea and the sugar spoon almost immediately.

"Thanks for the tea, Sabine. And I'm really sorry I scared you. That's not what I was trying to do. I thought I'd make it here before you went to bed, but I got held up. So then I thought I'd just leave you a note and hide out somewhere around town until you woke up and could meet me."

"And what is so important that you risked the Mudbug police department and a nine millimeter bullet?"

Hank looked down at his cup. "I heard about the cancer."

Sabine froze. "How? No one is supposed to know."

"I was in that attorney's office, Wheeler, when Maryse called trying to hunt me down."

Sabine stared at Hank. "Maryse told you about my cancer?"

Hank looked stricken. "Oh, crap, you didn't know. She probably didn't want to get your hopes up in case she couldn't find me or something. Shit. I can't seem to do anything without causing trouble." He sighed. "Maryse didn't tell me. She told Wheeler to explain why she needed to find me. I guess he thought I wouldn't do the right thing if I didn't have all the facts."

Sabine rolled this over in her mind, trying to bunch all the facts together into something that made sense, and all at an hour she should have been curled up in her bed not thinking at all. "So Wheeler told you everything, and then you came here. Why, exactly?"

Hank grinned. "Well, cousin, I thought if we were a match, I would give you some bone marrow."

Sabine sat back in her chair, stunned. She stared at Hank Henry, the most selfish, most irresponsible person in the world, and tried to come up with any reason whatsoever for this charade. Hank just stared back, the grin still in place, his expression completely sincere. Well, that tore it all.

She felt the tears well up in her eyes and reached for a napkin. "I can't believe you'd do that for me, Hank."

Hank looked a bit embarrassed. "Oh, hell, it's nothing but a test for now. We don't even know if I'm a match or if you'll ever need me. You're a really good person, Sabine. You've always looked after Maryse, and I know neither of you believe me, but I do care about her."

Sabine sniffed. "Just not enough to be her husband."

Hank sighed. "I'm not in any shape to be anyone's husband. I've got too many issues, Sabine. All I could do is bring her down.

And the reality is, I care about Maryse a lot, but I don't love her like that DEQ agent does."

"How do you know about Luc?"

"I've seen them together out on the bayou, but they didn't see me." Hank smiled. "They look good together, Sabine. Right. Like two pieces that fit perfectly together. And after everything I put her through, I'm really glad she's happy."

Sabine sniffed again. "Me, too."

"So...I wanted to let you know that I saw a doctor in New Orleans this morning to do the tests. Wheeler called in a favor, so it's all sorta anonymous...you know, given my situation. The doctor will send Wheeler the results and he will contact you. If that's all right, that is."

Sabine smiled. "That's fine, Hank."

Hank rose from his chair. "Then I guess I best be clearing out of here before anyone sees me."

Sabine rose and followed him to the shop entrance. Hank opened the door just a crack, but before he could slip through, Sabine grabbed his arm. "Thank you, Hank."

Hank stared at her for a moment, then leaned over to kiss her forehead. "You're going to be fine, cousin. I can feel it." He smiled and slipped out the door and into the night.

"Thirty damn years," Helena's voice boomed, and Sabine spun around. "Thirty years for him to grow a conscience, and technically, I'm not even around to see it."

Sabine sighed. "Where are you, Helena?"

"At the counter."

Sabine saw her stapler hovering a foot above the counter. Great. "Exactly how much did you hear?"

"Well, since I saw Hank sneaking into your shop and followed him in, everything. Nice pistol, by the way."

Sabine groaned and leaned against the shop wall. "I could have shot him, Helena! Why didn't you yell or something?"

"If you'd have gotten to the actual shooting part, I would have said something. Maybe. Probably."

"He's your son, Helena, and he did take a bullet that wasn't intended for him. Can't you cut him a little slack?"

"I'm not ready to move on yet. Seem to be having that problem everywhere." Helena began to laugh.

"If you're done enjoying the show, I'm going back to bed."

"So," Helena said, "I guess now I know why you dragged me to New Orleans and had that nutbag draw your parents. You're looking for a match, right?"

Damn it. The very conversation she'd been hoping to avoid. Sabine sighed. "Yes."

"Well, why the hell didn't you say so? I'm sure I can help."

Sabine rubbed her temples with her fingers, trying to stop the rush of blood into her head. "That's sorta what I was afraid of."

Chapter Four

Beau slammed the journal shut and tossed it onto the floor with the rest of the pile. Nothing. Eight hours of reading his own scribbles and he wasn't any closer to identifying the man in the drawing now than he had been when he started. At this point, he'd welcome a spiritual intervention. Hell, right now it might be the only way to locate the man.

Her father was the key to it all, Beau was certain. There was little information on Sabine's mother. It seemed she'd never held a job and didn't drive, but her name was accurate and he'd traced her back to high school photos. No secrets there. Mom was who she said she was, and Sabine's aunt had been correct in thinking the Sabine's mother was the last of her family line.

But her father had no past to speak of except a license that wasn't even a year old. Skinny amount of data for an American, even for that day and age. After hours of searching boxes full of handwritten payroll records, Beau had tracked him to a warehouse job on the docks in New Orleans and had located the ancient building in a seedy part of downtown that used to house the apartments where her parents had lived. It had been condemned for years, so there was no information to be gained on that avenue.

The social security number he'd used for the application hadn't matched the name on the license. In fact, the number belonged to a man who had died some ten years before Sabine's father took that job. Beau had already figured the name on the license wasn't the man's birth name, but he had yet to discover why it had been changed. If he could discover anything at all. Even more interesting was the fact that no one had put out a missing person's report for a man of his description at the time.

True, the father could have been from another state. Communication between police departments wasn't anything like it was today, but still, surely someone knew that this man, his wife, and his infant child were in New Orleans and set off alarms. But according to Sabine's research, no one had. Not in Louisiana anyway.

Beau rose from the couch, walked into the kitchen, and pulled a beer from the refrigerator. It was two a.m. and long past reasonable drinking time for most people, but then the great thing about being self-employed and independently wealthy was that you didn't have to live like most people. Beau was a night owl, pure and simple. Even during his time at the FBI, he'd always requested and always received night surveillance on takedowns. Ten years and not even once had someone tried to slide into the vampire role with him.

And then the thought of vampires led him right back to Sabine LeVeche and her strange way of living. What exactly caused a seemingly normal woman to launch off into believing in tarot cards and ghosts and rubbing rocks together for luck? Beau understood the overwhelming desire to know where you came from, understood it personally, but talking to dead people was one avenue he'd never even thought for one second to explore. He walked back into the living room.

What was Sabine doing right now, he wondered? Was she eating catfish and throwing back beers? Was she sitting in her apartment pouring over the limited information she had on her parents for the millionth time? He shook his head. More likely she was sleeping. Which sent him off on a whole other line of thought.

The mental picture of Sabine lying on a giant canopy bed draped in white gauze flashed across his mind. Her tanned body in crisp clarity against the bright white background, a giant ruby in the center of a silver headband the only vivid color in the image. The headband was also the only clothing she was wearing. Well, except for all those dangly bracelets like she'd had on at the café.

He shook his head and grabbed the television remote, frustrated he'd allowed his imagination to run away with him. Undressing a client was a line Beau had never crossed, not even in his fantasies. Then a horrible thought crossed his mind. If there was any truth at all to this psychic mumbo jumbo, could Sabine see his thoughts if they were about her? Shit.

He flipped channels, looking for something worth watching. This was the huge downside of being a night owl—there was rarely anything good on TV. He was just about to give it up as a loss and log on to the internet when a History Channel special on war criminals caught his eye. The commentator narrated the background of the people pictured in the photos on screen, going into great detail about their many crimes against the American people. He started to feel a tickle at the back of his neck.

He stood stock still in the middle of the living room, staring at the television, but the picture was no longer clear. The photos on the screen began to blend together in a kaleidoscopic blur. The commentator's words ran together into a single noise. And then, in a flash, it hit him...exactly where he'd seen the man in the photo.

In the FBI's most wanted files for war criminals.

He dropped onto the couch and took a huge gulp of his entire beer. Jesus, his memory was a pain in the ass; sometimes it was on, sometimes off. But when it was on, it was usually a hundred percent. He'd known when he took this job that it was probably going to end badly. Innocent people normally didn't make themselves disappear. But the guilty made a career of it. Granted, there was no way the man in the drawing could be the criminal he remembered. The age was all wrong. But he would bet anything they were blood relatives. He set his beer on the coffee table, the desire for it completely gone.

He glanced at his watch. One other person would still be up about now. Someone who had access to the FBI database and probably wouldn't mind giving him a little help on this. He reached for his cell phone and pressed in a number.

"Turner," the man answered on the first ring.

"Hey, it's Villeneuve."

"Villeneuve! How the hell are you?"

"Doing good, man. How 'bout yourself?"

"Can't complain, and wouldn't waste the time on it if I could."

Beau laughed. "I hear ya."

"So what the hell are you calling me in the middle of the night for? I know it's not to discuss football, politics, or religion."

"I wish. This case I'm on just took a turn that makes politics and religion look like better options for discussion."

Turner whistled. "Doesn't sound like much fun. What can I help with?"

"I need access to some files…FBI files. Nothing that will raise any eyebrows. All old shit—back during Vietnam."

"Sounds okay to me, man. Hey, if you're coming now, do you think you could pick me up a burger and another six pack?"

"I think I could manage." He closed his phone, grabbed his keys and the case folder, and headed out of his apartment. Maybe I'm wrong. Maybe my memory is totally off and the guy in the drawing has nothing to do with a wanted criminal from a long since dead war.

Then the vivid recall of the young man in uniform flashed across his mind, imprinted there as if he'd seen it just seconds ago. Everything in perfect clarity, right down to the three freckles on the bridge of his nose.

That perfectly matched the three he'd seen on Sabine.

Sabine clenched the steering wheel of her car, well aware that it was far too early in the day to be up and moving, much less driving around downtown New Orleans with Helena Henry.

"By the hotdog stand is good," Helena said, directing Sabine to a corner about a block away.

For the life of her, Sabine couldn't figure out exactly what Helena wanted to do here. "What are you up to, Helena? You wake me up first thing this morning, even though you know I didn't get hardly any sleep last night. Then you insist I drive you to New Orleans—"

"First thing! Are you kidding me? It was eight o'clock already."

"I have a head injury, and I'm not a morning person. Besides, I was busy almost having to shoot intruders last night, remember?"

"No shit. Well, while you were busy playing Cops and getting your beauty rest, I was formulating a plan of action."

Sabine groaned and pulled up to the curb. "Why does that worry me so much?"

"Jesus, for such an artsy-fartsy liberal sort, you're just as uptight as Maryse. I'd think a so-called psychic would have a broader mind."

"Well, it might help if I knew what I was supposed to be broadening my mind to."

"You'll see. Just circle the block. If I'm not here when you come back, circle again."

Sabine stared at the empty but very vocal passenger seat. "And how the heck am I supposed to know if you're here?"

Helena laughed. "Oh, you'll know. But just in case I need to give you some getaway instructions, you might want to roll your windows down. Okay, I'm outta here."

There wasn't so much as a stir of the air as Helena left the car, but a minute later, a floating hotdog that appeared to be eating itself gave her away. Dead people could eat? Good God. Sabine pulled on her sunglasses and slid down in her seat. What the hell was she thinking? Hooking up with Helena? Letting Helena help? Helena's brand of help had almost gotten Maryse killed.

You're desperate.

Sabine pulled away from the corner and hoped that whatever Helena had gotten her into wasn't illegal. But she didn't hold out a whole lot of hope. Helena had never believed the "rules" applied to her when she was alive. Death had given her an entirely new avenue on life...one that could get her living, breathing accomplices in a whole boatload of trouble.

Sabine circled the block and approached the hotdog stand again, keeping an eye out for any stray floating hotdogs. Nothing.

She pressed the gas and circled once more, hoping no one had noticed her circling and called the police. She was almost to the end of the block when she saw a group of policemen rush out of a building a block away. "Police Substation," the sign on the building read. Great. Just what she needed was the police only a block away with Helena breaking God knows how many laws just down the street.

They could start with stealing hotdogs.

She stopped at the corner and watched as the cops came to a halt in the middle of the street, looking both directions, confused expressions on their faces. A bad feeling washed over Sabine. Something wasn't right. What in the world were they all doing standing in the street? What were they looking for?

A horn sounded behind her and she jumped. She lifted one hand to wave at the angry motorist and started to make the turn, and that's when she saw the hotdog stand hurtling down the sidewalk toward her car. Which might not have been so odd in itself, but the fact that there was minimal slope to the road and no wind at all made the situation far from normal. Not to mention the small matter of the cart owner running ten yards behind and yelling at the top of his lungs.

The horn behind her sounded again and Sabine panicked, torn between pulling over for the other motorist to pass and hauling ass back to Mudbug as fast as her old Sentra would manage. Abandoning the last semblance of common sense, she jerked the wheel to the right and stopped the car at the curb, waving as the honking motorist drove around her and gave her the finger.

"Prepare to haul ass!" Helena's voice sounded above the fray.

Sabine whirled around in her seat just as the hotdog stand launched off the sidewalk behind her and landed in the street, sending hotdogs flying in all directions. The police had locked in on the commotion and were running toward the stand, closing in on her parking space by the second. To heck with this. Sabine put the car in gear, but before she could stomp on the gas, a mailbag flew through the open passenger's side window and landed on the floorboard.

"What the hell are you waiting for?" Helena yelled, her voice booming right next to Sabine.

Sabine floored the car and squealed away from the curb. She glanced in her rearview mirror just in time to see the cops chasing the hotdog stand onto the other side of the street. Barely slowing, she rounded the corner and accelerated onto the highway from the service road. She'd driven at least a mile down the road before she took a breath and looked over at the passenger seat.

A hotdog hovered just inches from her face. "Want one?" Helena asked.

Sabine pushed the hotdog away. "No, I don't want one. What the hell is the matter with you? You stole something from that police station, didn't you? All those cops were looking for you… but I don't understand why or how."

A chunk of the hotdog disappeared and Helena said, "Me eifer."

"Don't talk with your mouth full. Jesus, I would think someone of your upbringing would have some manners."

"What's the point? No one to see them but you and Maryse."

Sabine lowered her window a bit, grabbed the remainder of the hotdog and tossed it out onto the highway.

"Hey! What did you do that for?" Helena yelled.

"Two can play at the no manners game. And why in the world are you eating? You're—"

"Don't say it. I know I'm dead. I'm eating for the normal reason—I'm hungry."

"How can you be hungry?" Sabine shook her head. "Never mind. I don't even want to know. You've completely negated an entire lifetime of studying ghosts. Cone bras, eating hotdogs. It's simply too weird for me to process."

"If it's too weird for you, then I must be the anomaly of ghosts. Not for nothing, Sabine, but you're not exactly running with the normal crowd."

Sabine sighed, not even wanting to think about the irony of that statement at this very moment. "Start answering questions, Helena. Why were all those cops trying to find you and what's in that bag?"

"Just a police file that I thought might come in handy."

"You stole a file from that police station? Oh God. No wonder they were looking for you."

"I know. I guess maybe that barcode strip thingie set off the alarm."

"Are you crazy?" Sabine asked. "No. Never mind. You don't need to answer that."

"I don't know why you're getting all huffy. This would have been a lot harder before when I couldn't touch things. Remember, Maryse had to break into the hospital for those medical records herself."

Sabine rubbed her forehead with one hand, not even wanting to recall Maryse's foray into breaking and entering into the hospital's medical records room. It was one of those things Sabine still couldn't quite believe her straitlaced scientist friend had gotten roped into. Until now. She stared at the highway, a flashback of the runaway hotdog cart still vivid in her mind. At the moment, Maryse's actions didn't seem near as strange since Sabine was currently making a getaway with stolen police records and pilfered hotdogs.

Sabine stared at the bag once more but couldn't hold the question in any longer. "What file did you steal, Helena?"

The bag on the floor rustled a bit and a manila folder appeared to float out of it. The file spun in midair so that Sabine could see the typed words on the side. She took one look at the lettering and groaned. "You stole the police file from my parents' wreck? What were you thinking? As soon as they figure out what file is missing, they're coming straight to my door."

Helena laughed. The mailbag flipped upside down, dumping a stack of manila folders and two more hotdogs onto the floorboard. "They'd have to figure out exactly which one I was after first."

Chapter Five

Sabine gave Maryse a smile as she slid into the booth across from Sabine at Carolyn's Catfish Kitchen. "You're late...but why is that not a surprise?"

"Hey," Maryse protested. "You're the one that's always late, not me."

"Not since you've got a hunky DEA agent in your bed. You've ceased to be the morning person you used to be and it's almost noon. In fact, you're not much of a night person anymore either."

A light blush crept over Maryse's face. "Luc's next assignment is going to take him out of town, probably for a month or better. I'm making sure he doesn't forget what he's got waiting back home."

Sabine laughed. "Okay, I would sorta get that except that it's so obvious that Luc is over the top in love with you. I don't think he's going to forget a single square inch of you." She reached across the table and placed her hand on Maryse's. "I am so happy for you, Maryse. Seeing you and Luc together makes me believe there's hope for me, too. If I make it that long, that is."

Maryse squeezed Sabine's hand. "Do not think that way. There is no way in hell I'm letting you leave me here alone with Helena. And besides, as my best friend, you owe it to me to wear some tacky pink taffeta dress for my wedding."

"Pink?"

Maryse grinned. "Fuchsia. Glowing so bright you could see it from space. Maybe with a lime green bow."

"Yuck!"

Maryse sobered. "Seriously, I don't want to hear any talk like that, okay? You start the chemo soon and that will probably be the end of it. With any luck, I'll be able to help you out on that part of things."

"You're right. I'm sure within no time at all I'll be back to my exciting life."

Maryse cocked her head to one side and stared at her friend. "You sound like that's a bad thing. I thought you were happy with your life."

Sabine sighed. "I am. I was. Oh, I don't know. I guess my life seemed fine before I found out it might end prematurely. Then I guess I started thinking about it and well…there's a whole lot I haven't done."

"Okay, like what?"

Sabine frowned, not exactly ready with an itemized list. "Oh, I don't know—see a live play, scuba dive, leave this state, have an entire day at the spa…"

"Sounds easy enough. "

"You're kidding me."

"Not at all. Today, I want you to get a notebook and start jotting down all the things you want to do. Anything you can think of. Then we'll start tackling them. I can't guarantee we can do them all, depending on what you come up with, but I'm game to try." Maryse cast her friend a nervous look. "Unless you're still wanting to be abducted by aliens. That's sorta not on my list of things to do ever."

Sabine laughed. "I was ten years old when I said that. And believe me, Helena has been enough of a journey into the unexplained to last me a lifetime. I was actually thinking about giving up the shop and becoming a bank teller or something."

"Helena tends to have that effect on people."

"You have no idea," Sabine muttered and lowered her eyes to the table.

"Oh, no. I know that look. I wore it too many times over the last month. What have you let Helena talk you into?"

"Well, she said it was just an errand in New Orleans, and technically all I did was drive..."

Maryse groaned. "What did she do?"

"She stole the police file on my parents' wreck and a bunch of others from the station. The barcodes tripped the alarm, and half the cops in downtown came running out after her."

"Oh, God. Why didn't you call me for bail?"

"Oh, we didn't get caught. Helena caused a runaway hotdog stand accident and used the diversion to hop in the car with the stolen files and at least five hotdogs. I'm never going to get that smell out of my car."

"Helena is enjoying death way too much. It's really not fair at all." Maryse shook her head. "Okay, so I get the police file thing... in a Helena thinking sort of way, but what's up with the hotdogs?"

"Apparently, Helena is hungry. Don't even ask. I have no idea."

Maryse raised her eyebrows and stared at Sabine for a couple of seconds. "Alrighty then. So what did you do with the files?"

"I made a copy of my parents' file—wearing gloves, of course—then mailed them all back to the police. Then I called that detective Raissa found to let him know about the file."

"Bet that went over well. How did you explain having a copy?"

"I just said a well-meaning friend thought she'd help me out. And since she'd already broken the law, I figured he might as well take a look at the spoils." Sabine felt a blush creep up her face as she recalled her earlier conversation with Beau.

Maryse studied her for a moment. "So you never actually told me about this detective. What's he like?"

Sabine felt her face heat up even more. "He's nice. Seems very competent."

"Uh huh."

Sabine looked down at her coffee, concentrating on stirring the already mixed sugar. "He's got experience in this sort of detective work."

"Uh huh."

"And he seems nice."

"You already said that."

Sabine sighed and looked up at her grinning friend. "So what do you want me to say—that he's hot? Well, he is. The hottest guy I've ever seen in person, okay? Are you satisfied?"

"Not yet. But I'm getting there. And what do you propose to do with this hot detective?"

"I don't propose to do anything with him, except give him information to help me. Jeez, just because I find some guy hot doesn't mean I should jump on him like some floozy."

Maryse laughed. "You are the furthest thing from a floozy that I could locate in Mudbug. You know, for all your fussing at me to get out of the bayou and into society, you're not exactly the pinnacle of the social scene, either. When was the last time you got any?"

"Maryse! What a question."

"That long, huh? Well, I can't really bitch at you as I was on a two-year draught myself after Hank left, and Mudbug doesn't exactly have the best to pick from. But you've had some dates off and on. Nothing came of those?"

"No. A couple were buttheads. A couple were nice, but there just wasn't any spark."

"I get you. And this Beau...there's a spark there?"

"More like a volcano waiting to erupt."

Maryse whistled. "I know that feeling. Do yourself a favor and don't put it off. That eruption is something out of your wildest imagination."

Sabine shook her head. "I can't go there."

"Why not? Why are you so afraid of letting go?"

"It's not the eruption that scares me. It's the cooling off. How can I start something with a man, knowing good and well I may not be here to finish it?" She brushed at her eyes with her fingers. "I heard from Wheeler just before lunch. Hank's not a match."

Maryse sobered. "I'm really sorry. I had hoped there was an easy answer to all this. And I understand your apprehension about moving forward when you don't know if you're going to hit the wall, truly I do. But you don't know what the future holds...none of us do. Disease is not the only thing that can take us away from this world—you saw that with me over the last month. But putting your life on hold waiting for a death that might not come for another fifty years is like already dying."

Sabine felt the tears begin to form in her eyes. "I hate it when you're right."

"So if this detective is interested, you're not going to turn him down, right?"

Sabine shrugged. "I'll add it to my list, but it's not at the top."

"Really? Because I was hoping to get at least one thing crossed off the list today. Please tell me the spa day is at the top of the list. I could sooooooo use a massage."

"Not exactly."

Maryse stared at Sabine, her hesitation clear as day. "Why do I get the feeling I'm going to regret this?"

Sabine gave Maryse an evil grin, unable to resist teasing her friend since she'd just shoved reality down Sabine's throat. "I was thinking bungee jumping."

Maryse shut her eyes and clenched her hands. "That made me dizzy just thinking about it. You know I'm afraid of heights."

"And you know I'm afraid of relationships."

Maryse put her head face down on the table and covered it with her arms. "What time are we going?"

"I think before supper would be best."

"Yeah, I'd hate to waste a good meal on plummeting out of control toward the ground wearing a rubber band on my ankles." Maryse lifted her head and looked back at Sabine. "Fine. I'll do it as long as you promise not to turn down anything the detective offers."

"Oh, no. I'm not locking into that agreement. What if he sells insurance on the side, or even worse…Tupperware?"

Maryse laughed. "Okay, but if he's peddling anything but expensive plastic or disability insurance, it's a go." She studied Sabine for a moment. "You know, I've never seen you this riled up over a guy. Not since Johnny Arceneaux put that frog in your lunchbox in first grade."

Sabine smiled. "Well, you know how much I love frogs." The door to the café opened and Sabine glanced over, then froze as she saw who was standing there.

"What's wrong?" Maryse asked. "It's not Helena, is it?"

"No," Sabine whispered. "He's early."

"Who's early?"

"The detective. I was supposed to meet him here in a half hour. He's early."

"Great! Now I can see what all the fuss is about."

"Don't you dare."

Maryse grinned and turned all the way around in her seat. She held for a couple of seconds, then spun back around to face Sabine, her eyes wide. "Holy shit! You are in big trouble."

The instant he walked into the restaurant, Beau zoned in on Sabine like he had preset radar. She was sitting in a corner booth with another woman, who had turned around when he walked in and given him a comprehensive up and down before turning back to Sabine. He briefly wondered if he'd passed the friend's test, then got agitated at himself for caring…or wondering…or whatever he was doing.

No strings, Villeneuve.

His entire adult existence centered on keeping things simple, uncomplicated. He'd learned that one the hard way. He carried his own baggage, and he wasn't interested in carrying anyone else's. It had always been his experience that women were the most complicated people on earth. And their baggage usually came in matched sets. Hell, if the line he had on locating Sabine's family turned out to be accurate, she would soon be faced with more baggage than a freight train.

Unless you can talk her out of wanting to know.

Sabine waved at him and he smiled. Quickly catching himself, he put on his game face and crossed the restaurant, resolved to talk Sabine out of this quest of hers. It couldn't possibly bring her anything but misery. And if there was any way at all, he intended to spare her the disappointment he'd suffered.

As he stepped up to the table, the other woman sitting with Sabine rose and extended her hand. "I'm Maryse Robicheaux, Sabine's best friend. It's nice to meet you." She looked over at Sabine and grinned. "Sabine has been telling me everything about you."

A light blush crept up Sabine's face and she glared at Maryse. Beau shook Maryse's hand. "Beau Villeneuve."

"Well, this has been fun," Maryse said, "but I have to run."

"Oh, no you don't," Sabine argued. "You said you had another thirty minutes."

Maryse smiled. "But that was before you made plans for us tonight. Now, I need to see my attorney and remove you from my will." She winked at Beau and hurried out of the restaurant.

Beau slid into the booth across from Sabine, wondering how in the world she made jeans and a plain blue polo shirt look so elegant. Maybe it was her hair, twisted in a complicated knot, with shiny black locks framing her face. Or maybe it was the silver earrings shaped like a teardrop.

Maybe you should get your head out of the clouds and focus on business.

"Should I even ask what your plans are for tonight?" Beau asked.

"No. I was trying to play a joke on Maryse, but apparently it backfired. She always gets the last word. I don't know why I bother."

"I like her," Beau said, trying to block out the sweet smell of Sabine's perfume. "She doesn't dance around things, does she?"

"No. Finesse was never Maryse's strong point. I think she sees it as a waste of good creative energy and time."

Beau nodded. "She's probably right."

"Really? Then maybe you should try taking her shopping with you. We've been officially banned from two boutiques and a pet store."

"A pet store?"

Sabine waved a hand in dismissal, at least twenty bracelets jangling on her arm. "It's a long story and doesn't end so well for the turtle." She pulled a manila folder from a bright pink shoulder bag and slid it across the table. "This is the file I mentioned when I called."

"The file your friend 'appropriated'?" Beau scanned the police records inside.

Sabine sighed. "Yeah, that's the one."

"This friend wouldn't have been Maryse, would it?"

"Oh, God no! Maryse can be painfully direct and sarcastically entertaining but would never break the law. Well, almost never... okay, definitely not this time."

Beau smiled. "Convinced yourself yet?"

"Not completely. Was it that obvious?"

"Well, let's just say I didn't have to be psychic to get it."

Sabine laughed. "Good. Raissa and I already have the spirit world covered. It's the real world I can't seem to make any headway in."

Beau sobered. "That's another thing I'd like to talk to you about. I've got a lead on your family."

Sabine's eyes widened. "You're kidding. So soon? I can't believe it!"

"Don't get excited just yet. It might turn out to be nothing."

"Still, a lead in a matter of days when I've come up with nothing for over twenty years is definitely something."

It's now or never, Villeneuve. Beau took a breath and pushed forward. "I guess what I wanted to say is, before I get too far, I just want to make sure you really want this."

Sabine stared at him. "Why wouldn't I?"

"Lots of reasons, and probably things you never thought of."

"Like?"

"Well, what happens if your family doesn't turn out to be the kind of people you hoped they would be?"

"You mean they might be conservatives?"

Beau smiled. "That's possible, of course, but what I had in mind was something a little worse."

"Fundamentalists? Yikes." Sabine's expression grew serious. "I understand what you're insinuating. My family could turn out to be people who don't share the same value system—and while I know on the exterior I may look a little questionable, I assure you I'm really a law-abiding bore."

Beau nodded. "And your family could be the kind of people that HBO makes movies of the week about."

"Like the weirdo that tried to break into my building in broad daylight...and with three—two—people right upstairs?"

Beau's senses went immediately on high alert. "Someone tried to break into your building? When?"

"Yesterday midmorning." Sabine gave him a rundown of the attempted break-in.

"Did you get a good look at him?"

Sabine shook her head and described the intruder's outfit. "The Mudbug police dusted for prints, but they only found mine and Maryse's."

"What did the police say? Has there been a problem with random break-ins lately?"

"I've never had a problem, and the only other breakin the police know about was at the hospital last week. The whole thing is very weird."

"Do you keep much cash around?"

"No way! I take everything but a hundred dollars of change for the register to the bank every day right before closing. Everyone in town knows that, and even someone who didn't only had to watch me for a couple of days to figure it out."

"Could be junkies. They're not always smart with their targets. And that would explain the break-in at the hospital, too," Beau said, but his mind was whirling with possibilities. He didn't believe in coincidences—especially not this kind. What if something Sabine had done had made someone nervous? It could be her search for her family or something else entirely, but either way, Beau wasn't about to dismiss the timing of the attempted break-in. It might turn out to be nothing, but it would be foolish to ignore. "This is exactly the sort of thing I was worried about. And things could get far worse the closer we get to the truth. What if these people you're looking for simply don't want to be found?"

"You're thinking what I don't know can't hurt me."

"Exactly."

Sabine studied him for several seconds, then sighed. "I understand what you're saying, and I appreciate that you're trying to protect me from what might be an ugly situation. The fact that you're having this conversation with me after informing me you have a lead tells me you're not happy with the direction the lead is taking you."

"No. I'm not."

"I wish I could tell you I didn't care and just let the whole thing drop, but that's just not possible. I know you're trying to protect me and that's very sweet, but the reality is, not finding my family could be far more detrimental to me than anything you come up with." She reached across the table and placed her hand on his. "Thank you for caring. Most people wouldn't even have given it a second thought."

The skin on Beau's hand tingled under Sabine's gentle touch, and he fought the urge to pull his hand out from under hers before he did or said something he'd regret. "I've had nothing but second thoughts since the moment I met you," Beau muttered, then sucked in a breath. "Oh hell, I said that out loud, didn't I?"

Sabine stared at him, her eyes wide. "I've thought of you, too."

Beau felt a queasiness in his stomach. Back out while there's still room. "So what are we going to do about it?" Shit.

The color rushed from Sabine's face. She pulled her hand away from Beau's and jumped up from the booth. "We're going to pretend this conversation never happened. Thank you for the update, Mr. Villeneuve. I hope the file helps." She spun around and hurried out of the café without ever looking back.

What the hell? Beau watched the door shut behind her, then slumped back in the booth, replaying the conversation and Sabine's response over and over in his mind. Unbelievable. All those years of carefully guarding himself from crossing that line with a woman and the one time his resistance was too low, he'd run into the only person in the world more scared of relationships than he was.

Chapter Six

Sabine rushed out of the restaurant and crossed the street to her shop. She let herself inside and hurried upstairs without turning the sign out front to "Open." She didn't have any appointments that afternoon and anyone important had her cell phone number. In her tiny kitchen, she pulled a bottled water from the refrigerator and twisted off the top. Her hands shook as she lifted the bottle to her lips and took a drink.

"It's official," she said to the empty room, "you are a nutbag."

She dropped into a chair at her kitchen table and set the water down. Beau Villeneuve was the best-looking man she'd ever met in real life, and he was nice. He'd actually tried to talk her out of locating her family because he was afraid she'd get hurt. Even worse, most improbably, he was interested in her. Helena's rise from the dead had surprised her far less.

And you ran. Idiot.

She propped her elbows on the table, covered her face with her hands and groaned. A twenty-year search for her family she could handle. Helena Henry rising from the dead she could handle. Heck, she'd been teasing Maryse when she suggested bungee jumping, but even that she could have handled. But apparently a date was out of the question. Maryse was right—she was already dead.

She reached for the water and knocked a stack of her aunt's journals onto the floor. With a sigh, she reached over to pick them up. A sentence in one of the open books caught her eye. She lifted the journal and started to read.

September 2, 1963

A peculiar thing happened at work today. A woman and her husband came into the hospital with an infant who had an ear infection. I did my normal check on the baby, a beautiful little boy, while asking the mother our standard questions. When I asked her about breast-feeding, she got flustered, then looked at her husband. I'm not for certain as I could only see him out of the corner of my eye, but I swear he shook his head.

Although she'd been chatty before, the woman immediately clammed up and simply said no, she wasn't breast-feeding, with no further explanation. She answered the remainder of the questions with clipped responses, her gaze darting back and forth between me and her husband.

Dr. Breaux came in to do his exam and gave the woman a prescription and some written instructions. As he was writing out the instructions, an orderly came by and told the husband that he'd left the windows down on his car and it was starting to rain. It was obvious the husband didn't want to leave his wife alone, but with both Dr. Breaux and I standing there, it would have appeared odder for him not to.

Dr. Breaux finished shortly after the husband left and as I was wrapping up the baby in his blanket, I tried to chat with the wife, asking her some questions about her recovery after the delivery. She hesitated with her responses, and based on her answers, I am suspicious that she never gave birth.

Before I could pry any further, the husband returned and hustled the wife and the baby out of the room. The tension coming off of them both was so strong I could feel it, but for the life of me I don't understand what the problem was. If the baby is not their biological child, why all the secrecy?

If they weren't honest about the child's parentage with a doctor, what in the world were they telling people who knew she hadn't been pregnant? Perhaps the child belonged to an unmarried relative and they were protecting the woman's reputation. I hope that is the case since the only other alternative I could come up with for all the lying is that the baby was bought on the black market.

The scene in the exam room played in my mind over and over the rest of the day.

Sabine sat back in her chair and stared out the kitchen window. Black marketing babies. What a horrible thought, the level of desperation it would take to go such a route to have a family. She shook her head. And Sabine thought locating her family was hard. Imagine a black-market child ever finding their biological family. It was a sobering thought, especially given Sabine's current medical crisis.

Wondering if her aunt had ever come in contact with the woman again, Sabine lifted the journal and skimmed the pages, looking for any mention of babies. It was a couple of months later before she found another entry.

November 4, 1963

Sissy and her husband, friends of mine from high school, came in today with their baby. She's about three months old and has a face like a cherub. Sissy could hardly contain herself. She had rheumatic fever when she was a child and knew that it would be unlikely she'd ever have a baby. They'd put their name on the adoption list the year before and her dream had come true. I was a bit surprised, as healthy white babies are in high demand and not so easy to get through the proper channels.

When her husband left the room to speak with Dr. Breaux, I made a comment to Sissy about their good fortune, and she confided in me that the adoption had been private. The woman had been poor and unable to care for the baby. Apparently the father had been killed in Vietnam. The woman had asked the priest at their church to find a good home for the little girl. I asked whether they had any personal information on the mother or the father, in particular their medical history. Sissy told me the priest had only said that the mother was a devout Catholic.

In less than two months, I've seen two healthy white babies being raised by women who didn't give birth to them and live in the same small town. I have a bad feeling about it, but I don't know what can be done. I worry that those mothers didn't give up their babies voluntarily. Or even worse, maybe the mothers are dead.

Something's not right about any of this. I am going to check the obituaries for the past year and see if I find any military widows who had recently given birth. Hopefully, I am wrong in my suspicions. All I can do for now is pray for those babies and their mothers.

Sabine flipped through the rest of the journal and three more after that but didn't find another reference to the women or the babies. Frustrated, she placed the last journal on the table. There had to be an answer. Aunt Meg wasn't given to flights of fancy. If she'd thought something was wrong, then something had been.

Sabine tapped her finger on the stack of journals, but a good answer didn't magically appear. She glanced down at her watch and shook her head. No wonder. Before figuring anything out, she'd need some lunch. She was deliberating between a grilled cheese or ham sandwich when the chair across from her slid back from the table. It took her a second to register the indentation on the chair cushion and process exactly what that meant. "Helena, jeez, you scared me."

"You sure are jumpy lately."

"Two break-ins in one week are a little beyond my lifetime limit," Sabine said. "I'm allowed to be a little on edge if someone just strolls into my apartment and I can't even see them."

"I guess."

"Is something wrong, Helena?" The ghost's voice didn't sound right, and for the first time since that horrible cone bra sighting, Sabine wished she could see her.

"Today's the exhumation."

Sabine sucked in a breath. "I'm sorry. I'd completely forgotten." Maryse's week-long adventure in trying to remain alive had produced a whole lot of surprises, one of them being the exhumation of Helena's body. They were looking for evidence of murder, something the police and the coroner hadn't considered the first time around.

"Well, you've got other things on your mind," Helena said. "I know that. But Maryse is off at the lab in New Orleans still trying to save the world with one of her concoctions, so I didn't really have anyone else to talk to."

"Are you worried they won't find anything?"

"No. Yes." Helena sighed. "That's just it. I feel funny, but I'm not sure why. You know that feeling that you get before you go to the dentist or something?"

"Yes, I know that feeling well." And ran out of a restaurant because of it. "I think it's fear, Helena, even though you can't put your finger on what it is exactly that you're afraid of."

"Fear. Hmmmm. Maybe you're right."

"I think I am. This is a huge event for you. You're sure you were murdered, but what if the medical examiner doesn't find any evidence of that…where does that leave you? Not to mention that even if they prove you were murdered, that doesn't tell us who did it. And there's just the overall ickiness of knowing your body is going to be lying on a table somewhere. That would definitely make my stomach flutter."

"Yeah. I think no matter what, it's the 'where does that leave me' question that haunts me the most. What if I never leave here? What if this is it—death's cruel joke for the lifetime of bullshit I put people through?"

Sabine considered this for a moment. "I don't think you're being punished for being a bitch, if that's what you're asking. I honestly believe that you're still around because no one has solved your murder. Apparently the world is just not in balance until that happens, so you're stuck in the transition."

"But what if we never know? What if the man who killed me dies without ever being caught and I'm doomed to roam here like this forever? I mean, right now I have you and Maryse, but what about a hundred years from now or two hundred? Once you guys are gone no one will even know about me, much less care."

"You can't think that way. I'm sure this will all work out all right."

"You mean like your life is working out? Face it, life sucks and the earth barely tolerates our existence. Thanks for listening, Sabine. I'll see you later."

"Wait!" Sabine cried, but there was no answer and the depression in the cushion was gone. "Damn." She picked up the journal and opened it to the first entry she'd read. What if someone had killed those women for their babies? What if they were roaming the earth like Helena, still waiting for someone to set them free? What if everyone had forgotten?

And now Sabine was the only one who knew anything about them at all.

If ever there was a time that Sabine wished she didn't have a conscience, it would be now. She already had enough on her plate: Helena's murder, her missing family, her cancer, and now her completely unexpected and unwanted attraction to Beau Villeneuve. She probably wouldn't sleep for a year at this rate.

But what if others were stuck in between?

Sabine slumped back in her chair with a sigh. Even though she didn't have a psychic bone in her body, that didn't mean she didn't believe in the afterlife and spirits and, well, pretty much darn near everything. And even if she hadn't before, Helena was a pretty convincing argument. Sabine couldn't bear the thought of someone else's soul in limbo. She could at least spend a couple of hours looking into it.

She rose from the table and grabbed her purse. She'd start at the library. They had microfiche for the Mudbug newspaper for as many years back as there had been one. The obituaries would be a good place to start. Her aunt hadn't made another note about the women in her journals, so Sabine had to assume she'd either let the whole thing drop, hadn't found out anything in her own search, or hadn't been able to prove anything if she had. She picked up the journal from the table and slid it into her purse. At least she had a decent idea of the dates to start looking.

From his booth at Carolyn's, Beau had a clear view of Sabine's building. She'd left the restaurant almost an hour ago but still hadn't changed her shop sign to "Open," which meant she either didn't have any appointments for the rest of the day or she'd cancelled them because he had absolutely no skill at asking a woman for a date. And why should he? He'd shot more people in the line of duty than he'd asked on dates. Which, now that he thought about it, must say something about him, but he had absolutely no idea what.

He took one last bite of an absolutely heavenly banana pudding and rose from the booth. That attempted break-in at Sabine's still weighed on him. The hospital break-in didn't really concern him, as that was a choice spot for a drug user to try to get a fix if they couldn't find any other way. But there was nothing about Sabine or her business to suggest it was worth breaking into her building, especially in broad daylight. Even if the burglar had thought no one was inside, it was a huge risk, even from the back door. Again, the desperation of junkies came to mind but he didn't want to force that to fit. Not just yet. Nothing about Sabine had made him think she used illegal drugs, and she'd been vehement in her denial of keeping anything but a minimal amount of cash on hand.

Beau pulled some bills out of his wallet and set them on the table. He mulled over the possibilities, limited as they were, as he paid the bill. The timing of the attempted break-in coupled with his search for Sabine's family troubled him, but for the life of him he couldn't see where the two could have intersected. Sabine had never come up with anything remotely close to the angle he was working now, and all his activity so far had been restricted to FBI files and news articles. The family had no way of knowing that he was researching them. Not yet. So they had no way of knowing about Sabine.

Which meant her trouble was coming from something else. But what? And who would try a break-in in the middle of the morning, in broad daylight, and with occupants inside the building? It was damned odd, but if Sabine couldn't even handle Beau admitting his attraction, she sure as hell wasn't going to start unloading her secrets on him. And then there was always the chance that Sabine had no idea what had set this into motion. So many times in his work with the FBI, he'd seen cases of normal people thrust into the middle of something sordid without ever intending to step in shit. Certainly none of them realized it until it was too late.

Beau stuffed his change in his wallet and turned to the exit. He looked across the street just in time to see Sabine lock the front door on her shop, hurry to her car, and drive away. What now? He exited the restaurant and paused outside on the sidewalk, making a quick assessment of the town. The entire downtown wasn't any bigger than a city block, but with the wooded areas and the bayou surrounding every side of the tiny town, there were too many possibilities for an unobserved approach to make Beau happy with Sabine's safety.

The hotel was the tallest building on the street. If he could manage a front room, he'd have a clear view of Sabine's building—the front of it anyway. He hoped she'd taken the necessary precautions with the back door after the last attempt. It was something he'd ask her about as soon as he had an opportunity. If she'd let him see the door and secure it, even better. Mind made up, he walked down the street to the hotel and stepped inside. A large woman with silver hair sticking up in all directions looked up from the counter as he entered.

"Hi," she said. "Are you here for the sales convention?"

For a fleeting moment, Beau considered lying, but quickly changed his mind. The town was simply too small and once his cover was blown he'd have an even harder time convincing Sabine to trust him than before. "No. I'm here doing a little work and need a room."

"Welcome. My name's Mildred and this is my hotel. 'Bout how many nights you need to stay?"

Beau considered this for a minute. "I'm not really sure. Are you full, or can I negotiate something for a day at a time?"

Mildred shrugged. "Fine by me. But the hotel's completely booked a week from now. Think you'll be done with your work by then?"

Beau nodded. "I hope to be." He pulled his license and a credit card from his wallet and handed them to Mildred. It was only Tuesday and with any luck, he would either figure out what was going on or reassure himself that it was an isolated incident and be satisfied Sabine was safe.

Mildred ran his credit card and pushed the receipt across the counter along with a pen. "What kind of work do you do, Mr. Villeneuve?" she asked as she glanced down at his license.

"Research, mostly."

"Sounds fascinating. Medical?"

"No." Beau pushed the completed registration card back across the counter. "Family history stuff mostly. Is there a room available in the front of the hotel?"

Mildred pulled a key from the pegboard behind her and handed it to Beau. "Third floor." She studied him for a moment. "Anyone I might know?"

"It really wouldn't be appropriate for me to say without permission."

Mildred gave him a shrewd look. "Not for nothing, Mr. Villeneuve, but I've most often found that opening up family business long since dead is like stepping on a land mine."

"I couldn't agree more." Beau took the key and started toward the stairwell.

Sabine shoved the copies she'd made from the library microfiche into her shoulder bag and waved at old Mrs. Hebert, the librarian, as she exited the building. Three possibilities to fill two possible slots—Amelia Watson, Sandra Franks, and Ruth Moore, all living in nearby bayou towns. No cause of death was listed, or surviving family. But at least she had a starting point.

She'd gone through the microfiche index for ten years preceding their deaths but had found no mention of any of the women. She'd ask Mildred and Helena if they knew any of the names, even though both would have been teenagers at the time of the women's deaths. Beyond that, Sabine felt she'd spent enough time chasing a "bad feeling." If Mildred or Helena had never heard of the women, then Sabine had already decided she would let it go without regret. Well, with almost no regret. Who was she kidding? She'd probably feel like crap but what other choice did she have? Maybe when things were more settled in her own life she'd pick it up again.

She glanced at her watch and realized it was getting toward suppertime and she still hadn't eaten lunch. No wonder she was starving. She briefly considered the limited options in her apartment. She really had to get to the grocery store. And since Maryse had known good and well that Sabine had been joking about the bungee jumping and Luc had left that afternoon for his undercover assignment, Sabine knew her friend would remain at the lab in New Orleans until all hours of the night. Which put her out of the running as a dinner date.

Sabine looked over at the hotel. There was always Mildred. Sabine hated the thought of sitting across a table from Mildred knowing that she was hiding her cancer from her, but if she didn't see her soon, Mildred would wonder and besides, she could go ahead and ask her about the three women and get that out of the way. The hotel owner had raised Maryse after her mother died, and ran herd over Maryse and Sabine from childhood to their early twenties, doing her best to keep them from doing something foolish. She was moderately successful except for their teenage years and Maryse's disastrous marriage to Hank.

Mind made up, Sabine started across the street for the hotel. She found Mildred behind the counter, wrapping up her daily accounting. The hotel owner looked up and smiled as Sabine entered the lobby.

"I haven't seen you in days." She gave Sabine a critical look. "How are you?"

Sabine took one look at Mildred and sighed. "Maryse told you."

Mildred walked around the counter and gave Sabine a hug. "Oh, honey," she said as she pulled back. "You know Maryse never could tell me a lie—not that I didn't know about, anyway. And not telling me something like this is the same as lying in my book. What I don't understand is why you didn't tell me yourself."

"It wasn't that I was trying to keep it from you, exactly. It's just that…well…I didn't want you worrying about me. We haven't even really gotten past everything that happened to Maryse, and I didn't want to throw something else on you this soon. And I know how you feel about my looking for my family. I knew you wouldn't be happy with me starting it up all over again, much less in full force."

Mildred sighed. "I guess I figure little good ever comes from digging up the past. I don't want you hurt, Sabine, and it just might be that finding them hurts more than never knowing them. I've always believed family is about sharing your life, not your blood, but I understand why this is different. I just wish there was another way."

"I love you, Mildred, you know that? But let's not put the cart ahead of the horse. We don't know what's in store for me, so there's no use worrying about a bunch of things that may or may not happen. Believe me, I spend enough time worrying for everyone."

Mildred gave her a sympathetic look. "I understand you trying to protect me, Sabine, but you know good and well that I'm no shrinking violet. If you or Maryse need me, I want to know about it and be right in the middle of everything, raising Cain and getting things done. That's what friends do."

Sabine brushed an unshed tear away from her eye. "No, that's what mothers do. Maryse and I are so lucky to have you."

Mildred smiled. "Yes, you are. So I assume that means you're taking me to dinner. I could sure use a mess of catfish and a glass of wine."

Sabine laughed. "As a matter of fact, I'd love to."

Mildred reached behind the counter and grabbed her purse. "Ready?"

Sabine nodded. "Can you leave? There's no one to cover the desk."

Mildred waved a hand in dismissal. "Julia should be here any minute. That girl is always five minutes late. Besides, we'll just be across the street so it should be fine."

They stepped outside, and Mildred pulled the lobby door closed behind her. "Now," Mildred said and gave her a shrewd look, "are you going to tell me what you really wanted to talk about?"

Beau eased down the remainder of the stairwell as the door closed behind the hotel owner and Sabine. He stared through the lobby window after them. He'd known from the beginning that Sabine was keeping something from him...most clients did. The trick was deciding whether it was something important to the investigation or merely something private and perhaps embarrassing to the client. Beau hadn't really gotten the impression that Sabine was holding back anything concerning her family, so that must mean it was personal.

And apparently something so dire she'd also kept it from the woman she considered a surrogate mother.

Which was very interesting when considered with all the other facts that Beau had. Like the fact that Raissa had just recently had the "vision" of Sabine's parents, but had been friends with her and known of her situation for years, or that a "friend" had stolen a police file of her parent's car wreck just this week but no one had ever done this before. And even though he knew she'd hired an investigator in the past, she'd claimed it had been years before and he had no reason to think she was lying.

So why the big push now?

Was Sabine's secret related to her search for her family? And if so, how? And was the break-in at her shop tied in to all of it, some of it, or none of it?

He crossed the lobby and looked across the street. Sabine and Mildred were entering the catfish restaurant. They were both smiling as if nothing was wrong, but from their earlier conversation, Beau doubted that was the case. More likely they were making small talk now and would have the bigger discussion once they were left to themselves. He deliberated for a moment walking across the street and getting a bite himself, but there was no way to do that without alerting Sabine that he was staying in town. The last thing he needed was Sabine to be suspicious of him or he'd never be able to help her.

His FBI buddy had gotten him all the information on the guy he'd remembered, and based on Beau's subsequent research, a picture of Sabine's family had started to take shape. He had nearly completed his investigation, more and more convinced that he'd not only identified her father but also located a whole host of living relatives. The kind that came with baggage. He'd dragged his feet on putting the final touches on the file, hoping to convince her to give up the search, but even if the earlier restaurant performance hadn't convinced him, he now knew for sure that Sabine had an ulterior motive for starting her search all over again and with such enthusiasm.

Whatever was up with Sabine LeVeche was serious business. He felt it in his bones. And even though he knew he shouldn't care, he wasn't even going to bother trying to pretend he didn't.

Chapter Seven

Sabine gave Mildred a hug and crossed the street to her building. They'd sat in the restaurant for hours, starting with catfish and ending with far too many cups of coffee. Now it was getting late and the hour coupled with the storm that was moving in had brought darkness to the dimly lit downtown area. Out of the corner of her eye, she saw a shadow move off to her left. She whirled around and stared into the inky darkness, trying to make out where the movement had come from. Two buildings down was a stack of crates outside of the general store on the corner. The owner's car was parked in front of the crates parallel to the sidewalk, even though the lines clearly were painted perpendicular. No matter, since there was so little activity this late in the evening.

She took a couple of steps closer to the end of the street and peered closely at the stack of crates. Was there something moving behind it? She shot a look back at the restaurant and bit her lip. There were only a few patrons inside and with the music playing and the general buzz of talking and serving, it would be unlikely anyone inside would hear her if she called for help.

Go back to your apartment, lock yourself inside, and call the police.

And tell them what? That you're spooked over some creepy diary entry from forty years ago? Yeah, they'd love to hear that, especially after her phone call today, asking for an update on their nonexistent investigation on her break-in. Sabine got the impression that if Leroy and company never heard from her or Maryse again as long as they lived, it would be too soon. The Mudbug police were well-equipped to deal with drunk and disorderlies, or poaching, or off-season hunting, but breaking and entering and murder went a bit beyond their scope.

Then another thought crossed her mind—what if it was Hank? He wasn't exactly square with the local law, so hiding behind a bunch of crates waiting to talk to her wouldn't be a stretch. "Hank? Is that you?" Silence.

She bit her lower lip, then pulled her cell phone from her pocket. She pressed in 9-1-1 and slipped her phone into her palm, her thumb hovering over the Talk button. At least she could scream. They wouldn't have any idea where she was making the call from, but the police station was at the far end of town and surely someone would come running outside if she made the call. Surely.

She took a deep breath and headed toward the crates. One, two, three, four, five, she counted each step as she went, like knowing the number somehow made a difference. The crates were only twenty feet or so away and she stood stock still, trying to make out any shift in the shadows cast out into the street, straining to hear anything besides the wind blowing between the buildings.

Nothing.

She let out her breath and shook her head. You're imagining things, Sabine, and the only thing you're accomplishing is scaring yourself. What was the point? If she wanted to lay wide-eyed in her bed all night, there was a twenty-four-hour run of horror movies on one of the local channels. At least that way she could have dry, non-blinking eyes and a pounding heart in the comfort of her pajamas and her bed. Not to mention a glass of wine to thin the blood and a double-fudge chocolate brownie to top off the sugar coma.

Then something moved again, just beyond the crates.

If she hadn't been looking directly at the shadows cast far out into the street, she would have missed the tiny sliver of movement, but she was certain she hadn't imagined it. Something was behind those crates. The shadow had seemed too long for an animal, so that left only one other option. And the only reason to lurk in the shadows was if you were up to no good.

She tightened her grip on her phone and leaned over to the side, trying to peer beneath the car. "Hank, is that you? If it is, come out. You're giving me the creeps."

And that's when he rammed her, his shoulder catching her right in the collar bone.

She'd grossly miscalculated, Sabine thought as she slammed down onto the sidewalk. He hadn't been behind the crates. He'd been hiding in the shadows on the side of the car, not five feet from where she'd stopped to listen. She screamed as she hit the ground, pain shooting through her shoulder as it took the brunt of the fall. She struggled to press the Talk button on her cell phone, but the fall had jostled it in her hand, and Sabine was certain the call didn't make it through.

She rolled over and jumped up as fast as possible, knowing that a standing opponent was in a much better position to defend themselves than one lying down, but she was no sooner standing than the ski-masked figure shoved her, trying to knock her to the ground again. Sabine struggled to maintain her balance, and for a moment, she didn't think she was going to manage. But at the last moment, she managed to spin around and clock the masked figure in the shoulder with her heel.

The attacker stumbled backward. Through the slits in his mask, Sabine could see his eyes widen with surprise. He paused only a second to stare at her, then turned and ran into the woods at the edge of downtown. Sabine stared after him, sending up thanks for the seven years that she'd spent the time and money driving to New Orleans for martial arts lessons. Finally deciding that he wasn't going to try for a repeat performance, she picked up her cell phone from the sidewalk and hurried down the sidewalk to the police station.

No use sending up the alarm...especially not with Mildred right across the street and already worried about her. Her attacker was long gone and short of an Olympic sprinter or a bloodhound, there was going to be no catching him. Not tonight anyway. She paused for a moment before opening the door to the police station. This was really a waste of time, and she knew it, but regardless of their ability, it was still their problem. Maybe if odd things continued to happen around town, the city council might just figure out that an inept ex-fisherman and his otherwise unemployable nephew might not be the best choices to keep the city safe. She sighed as she pulled the door open.

Getting a competent police force was as likely as the town banning beer and losing religion.

Sabine exited the police station after what was probably the most frustrating thirty minutes of her life. Oh, there was a whole lot of writing—longhand—on legal pads, and the constant nodding and glances between Leroy and his idiot nephew, but it all amounted to nothing. The reality was, the business with Maryse had shocked the town but absolutely no one was willing to believe it was anything but an isolated incident—the ravings of a madman. And now that the madman was gone, there couldn't possibly be anything more than the normal redneck offenses going on in Mudbug.

At least that's what they wanted to believe.

There was noise across the street and she looked up in time to see the last of the patrons leaving the restaurant and the owner locking the door behind them. She glanced down at her watch and sighed. It was past time for her to be in pajamas, and she was going to regret every minute of her Kill Bill routine the next morning when her alarm went off.

"Is everything all right?" The voice sounded close to her and caused her to jump. Beau was standing next to his truck.

"Oh," she said, flustered. "I didn't see you there."

"Sorry. I didn't mean to startle you."

"No, it's not, I mean…I just didn't expect to see you here."

"I needed to talk to a few people around the area. The conversations went a bit longer than I thought they would, and I was hungry." He shrugged. "I decided to have dinner before I started the drive back. So…is everything all right?"

Sabine shook her head. "No. I don't think so, but I can't put my finger on it."

Beau stepped onto the sidewalk and looked closely at her. "What happened?"

"I saw someone lurking in the shadows on the corner when I left the restaurant." She let out a single laugh. "Listen to me—lurking in the shadows. I sound like a B horror movie." She looked at Beau, expecting to see him smiling, but his expression was serious and he didn't look happy.

"Lurking where, exactly?"

Sabine pointed to the end of the street. "The corner, just in front of the general store. I know I should have just minded my own business and gone home, but after the attempted break-in at my shop, I thought maybe someone was trying to break into the store."

"And you thought you'd apprehend a thief? Why in the world would you put yourself at risk like that? You've got a police station just down the block."

Sabine smirked. "Yes, and the state of our policemen is why I thought I was a better choice for the job. I might look fragile, but I assure you I can take care of myself."

"Really…you packing?"

"No. I mean, not on me. I do have a pistol if that's what you're asking."

"Not going to do you a bit of good in your sock drawer."

Sabine sighed. "Look. I appreciate your concern, really I do, but I'm trained in martial arts—seven years of training to be exact."

"So you learned that new how-to-stop-a-bullet karate move. Is that what you're saying?"

"Oh, good Lord! Are you always this aggravating? So maybe I shouldn't have gone looking for trouble, although I hardly equate walking down Main Street with entering a war zone. Besides, I didn't get anything but a little dirt on my pants, but the guy sneaking around is going to feel the throbbing in his shoulder for a couple of days."

Beau studied her for a moment, then smiled. "Martial arts, huh? I assume you kicked him?"

"Yeah, I was off-balance so I used it to my advantage."

"I'm impressed. That's an advanced reaction. Well, at least let me walk you home. I know you don't need an armed guard, but you'll damage my chivalrous male ego if you turn me down."

Sabine stared at him, aggravated that she hadn't insulted his manhood, aggravated that he was impressed, aggravated most of all because she liked the fact that he was impressed. "Fine. If we run into trouble between here and the thirty steps to my doorway, you are free to take control."

Beau grinned. "I'll keep that in mind."

He fell in step with Sabine and they walked up the sidewalk to her building. For just a moment, Sabine thought he was going to take her hand in his and found herself disappointed when he didn't. What the heck are you thinking? If he touches you, it's all over. Get your mind off the guy and onto bigger problems.

They were halfway to her building, but the walk already felt like it had taken hours. She had to find something to take her mind off the gorgeous man next to her. Something to keep her from committing the ultimate sin—inviting him inside. She scanned the businesses on Main Street looking for inspiration. Catfish, banks, dirty car, special on canned goods, massage—crap! She blinked once and looked past the Mudbug Hair Salon & Spa. Rubbing naked bodies wasn't likely to make her forget anything—in fact in the split second it had crossed her mind, she'd added two or three more things to the list of what she'd like to do with Beau Villeneuve.

"Something else on your mind?" Beau asked.

"No." Sabine held in a groan, certain her face was flaming red. Thank God for a cheap town and dim street lights. "I mean, no more than any other day."

"You've got a lot going on. Maybe you ought to take a break."

"And do what? Even if I had unlimited funds and someone to take over my business for a while, geography isn't going to stop my mind from whirling."

Beau sighed. "No, it's not."

Sabine stopped in front of her shop and looked at him. "You say that like someone who tried it."

"Tried it and failed miserably." He looked down at the sidewalk.

Sabine bit her lip, knowing she should let this conversation end and go inside, but her curiosity had already gotten the better of her. "So how far did you travel to not forget?"

Beau looked back up at her. "In miles—who knows? Three continents, eleven countries, God knows how many cities, and a couple of islands that aren't even on the maps."

"Wow. You weren't kidding. I've never even been out of Louisiana."

Beau stared. "Wow. You're kidding."

Sabine held up two fingers. "Scout's honor. Unless you count the Gulf of Mexico for an offshore fishing trip."

Beau laughed. "Not exactly a world tour."

"No big deal, I guess. And the way things have been lately, there's plenty of excitement in Mudbug."

Beau's expression sobered. "A personal tour of the Australian outback is exciting. What's been going on in Mudbug lately is criminal, and that's just dangerous." He looked up and down the front of the shop building, then twisted the front door handle. "You sure you don't want me to take a look around? Everything looks okay, but…"

Sabine shook her head. "I'll be fine, but I appreciate the offer and the walk. Besides, you have a bit of a drive back to New Orleans."

Beau stared at her for a moment, as if he was contemplating saying something, or God forbid, doing something, but finally he nodded. "All right then. Goodnight, Sabine." He headed back down the sidewalk to his truck and Sabine let herself into the shop and made sure the new lock was turned all the way. She peeked out between the blinds and saw Beau sitting in his truck, looking at her shop. He waited a couple of seconds more before starting his truck and pulling away.

Sabine sighed. The triple threat—sexy, intelligent, and kind. Beau Villeneuve was the kind of distraction she just didn't need, but damned if she didn't want him anyway.

It was almost lunchtime, and Beau paced the microfiche room in the New Orleans library for at least the tenth time, holding his cell phone but not wanting to make the call. He'd verified everything he could and then spoken with the family's attorney. He was almost positive that he'd found Sabine LeVeche's family. After recognizing the man from Raissa's drawing in the Vietnam war criminal files, he'd dreaded the outcome. On the upside, the war criminal was an identical twin and hadn't been seen since the war. With any luck, the remaining brother was Sabine's grandfather, but Beau still didn't feel right about any of it.

The family's attorney had been short and dismissive when he'd first contacted the man the day before. Not that Beau blamed him. Based on his research, the family was quite wealthy and probably always had their share of nuts trying to get a piece of their money. Beau expected he'd have to contact the man again, but first thing that morning the attorney called asking for a photo of Sabine and the particulars of her upbringing. Less than an hour later, he'd called again, the incredulity in his voice apparent, stating that the family would like to meet Sabine at her earliest convenience.

No request for DNA testing, birth records, or any of the other hoops Beau had expected them to ask Sabine to jump through. Which bothered him even more. They knew something they weren't telling. No wealthy family accepted a long-lost granddaughter without some proof. It had to be something about Sabine's father. Aside from his driver's license, which didn't reflect his real name, no other form of ID was ever found in his car or in the apartment the couple was renting in New Orleans.

Supposedly, he was the oldest son of one of the wealthiest families in the parish. Yet he lived like a pauper with no past? People who abandoned their inheritance without looking back were running from the people who controlled the money. But why? What had those people done that was so horrible that an eighteen-year-old left the comfort of his family's estate and took a job working on the docks for minimum wage with a wife and infant daughter to support?

It couldn't possibly be anything good.

Shit. He'd been putting off the call to Sabine for hours. He couldn't put it off forever. Now that the family was aware of her existence, there was nothing to stop them from contacting her directly if they felt he wasn't moving fast enough for them. He started to press her number into the cell phone, then changed his mind. He scrolled through his call list and found the number he was looking for. He pressed the Talk button and waited for the woman to answer.

"Raissa? This is Beau Villeneuve. I need to talk to you about the research you hired me for. Can you meet me this afternoon?"

Thirty minutes later, Beau slid into a booth in a bar across the street from Raissa's shop. He gave the psychic a nod. "I really appreciate you meeting me." He gave Raissa the basics of his search and explained his current dilemma of how to approach meeting the family.

Raissa listened intently and when he was finished said, "I'm glad you called. I can see why you're not comfortable with this."

"I'm sorry to put you in the middle, but I didn't know who else to talk to. I mean, I've met Maryse, but she and Sabine seemed a little close for Maryse to be objective and, well..."

"And you didn't want to panic Maryse given the recent events in her own life." Raissa smiled. "Don't look so surprised, Mr. Villeneuve. You're a detective—former FBI. You'd be remiss if you didn't check the background of everyone Sabine is close to."

Beau nodded. "Please call me Beau. And you're right, of course."

"Well, Beau, I further deduce that once you started reading up on Maryse you were probably far too interested to stop at the surface level. She's had an amazing past month."

"Amazing is one way of putting it—so is frightening, overwhelming, and beyond statistically fortunate."

"It's certainly no secret that Maryse is lucky to be alive. The things that happened to her were fantastic but some of them could have been prevented. That entire situation still vexes me. I should have been more on top of it from the beginning. I knew something wasn't right—beyond the obvious. I could feel it in my bones."

Beau studied Raissa for a moment. "In your bones? No visions, no ghostly warnings?"

"The phenomenon doesn't work that way. It's usually very obscure, unplanned, and certainly not scheduled. To make matters worse, the dead are often confused and even when trying to help they can give mixed signals or the wrong information entirely. It's not an exact science."

"Some would argue that it's not a science at all."

Raissa inclined her head and studied him. "Some would also argue that the Holocaust didn't happen and that we never landed on the moon."

"Touché."

"Regardless of its fantastic nature, I still feel I should have picked up on something before things got that out of control for Maryse."

"How? Who would have thought those kind of things were going on in such a quiet little place? Who would ever have believed that such hideous secrets were hidden in a small town? Easier to hide in a crowded city where everyone isn't constantly in your business."

Raissa nodded. "There is some truth to that, of course. And people often migrate to large cities to 'disappear,' but in a small town, if you've very good, you can disappear in plain sight."

"What do you mean?"

"In the small town I grew up in, there was a drunk. He was upper forties to early fifties and everyone called him Walker because he was usually so drunk he couldn't even find his car keys, much less operate his car, so he walked everywhere he went. His house was at the end of an otherwise tidy little street of bungalows. But Walker's house was rundown—the roof sagging on one end, paint peeling from every square inch of wood. He didn't do much—picked up odd construction jobs from time to time, when he was sober enough. Then he usually went on a bender after that. Left town for a couple of days and came back snookered as ever."

Beau shrugged. "Okay, so almost every town has a drunk like Walker. Nothing special about that."

Raissa smiled. "No one in the town thought so either, until the day he disappeared."

"Disappeared?"

"His mail started piling up and people began to realize that no one had seen him for a while, although no one could put their finger on exactly when. A group of people went to his house and knocked on the doors and windows, but he never answered. His car was in the driveway, so he wasn't off on a bender. Finally, they called the fire department and had them break down the door, afraid he was dead."

"But he wasn't?"

"Not even close. The house inside was neat as a pin, although a layer of dust had settled over everything. There was no sign of Walker anywhere, and even more interesting, there was no sign of a bottle. The house was completely empty of booze. In fact, he didn't even own a shot glass, a bottle opener, or a corkscrew. When they went to leave, one of the men tripped over the kitchen rug and discovered a door in the floor beneath it. You'll never guess what they found in that makeshift basement."

Beau leaned toward Raissa, fascinated. "Bodies?"

Raissa laughed. "Nothing so evil. No, they found a printing press. Walker had been counterfeiting money. It took a while for the local police to sort it all out, but finally the truth emerged. No one knew exactly how long Walker had been manufacturing money, but a couple of people remembered when the 'benders' began."

"And they weren't benders?"

"Not at all. Walker waited until he had a good bit of the fake money ready, then took a trip to Las Vegas to launder it through the casinos. The police finally tracked down banking records where he'd transferred large sums of money from a bank in Las Vegas to the Cayman Islands. By the time Walker had disappeared, those transfers amounted to over three million dollars."

"Holy shit! What a story."

Raissa nodded. "All anyone in town saw was a drunk, and they didn't look any further."

"Hiding in plain sight," Beau said, his mind whirling. "It's brilliant."

"And simple. If Walker had been a recluse who rarely spoke and didn't get out among town, people would have gone poking around."

"Instead, he invented a personality that was loud enough for people to stop looking any further. They took it at face value and left it at that."

"Which is exactly what happened in Mudbug," Raissa pointed out. "And if I had to guess, might be what's happening with your search for Sabine's family."

Beau stared at Raissa for a couple of seconds. "You 'guess'?" He leaned in and lowered his voice. "Exactly how does that psychic thing work? I'm not saying I buy into it, but I'm not so hardheaded as to think I have all the answers, either."

Raissa studied him for a moment, then smiled. "You're attracted to Sabine, and you're worried about this less-than-normal way of life she has."

Beau sat back and put on his game face. "I didn't say anything like that."

"You didn't have to. And before you think the spirits are telling your secrets, I'll let you in on one aspect of my ability—a lot of it is simply the talent of reading people extraordinarily well, then putting everything together in one neat little package. Logic, deduction, an innate flair for understanding the psychology of human behavior. Not all is paranormal, Beau. A lot of what I do is no different than your FBI profilers would accomplish with the same information. It's just that sometimes, I have a little advantage."

"Okay, so maybe I find her interesting, and yeah, she's definitely not hard on the eyes…something you failed to mention, I might add."

"I wasn't aware that was part of your job-considering criteria."

"It's not. It shouldn't be. Oh, hell, I didn't ask to be attracted to her and don't want to be, if the truth's told. But it's too late to undo what's been done and that includes finding her family."

Raissa, who'd obviously been enjoying his flustering, sobered when he mentioned Sabine's family. "You're afraid they're hiding something."

"Barely legal teens don't usually run away from millions in inheritance to live in squalor."

Raissa sighed. "And people who have millions to leave in inheritance should have been able to find a missing teenager with relative ease—especially as he was less than a hundred miles from his hometown."

Beau nodded. "There's something else. It's Sabine. She's hiding something."

Raissa waved a hand in dismissal. "We're all hiding something."

"You know what it is, don't you?"

"Yes, I know some of Sabine's secrets. Do I know the particular one you've picked up on? I have no idea."

"And if these secrets are relevant to the case?"

"Then I would have already told you what I knew. I'm not a fool. I'd break a confidence if I thought Sabine was at risk from the things I knew."

Beau clenched his jaw, then released. He didn't like it but knew he wasn't going to get anything out of Raissa. "Okay. You know what's at stake. Knowing Sabine, how do you think I ought to proceed?"

"There's no going back now. Everything's already been set in motion."

"I know. That's the problem."

Raissa lifted her wine glass and swirled the red liquid around inside. She gazed at it as if in a trance, or looking for some magical sign. Hell, for all Beau knew, she might have been doing just that. Finally she frowned, sat the glass down, then looked him straight in the eyes. "Then I guess, unwanted attraction or no, you're going to have to keep an eye on Sabine for a while. You and Maryse are the only people they wouldn't question being part of the family reunion process, and you're much better equipped to handle what is likely to come than Maryse."

Beau narrowed his eyes at Raissa. "Exactly what did you see in that wine glass?"

"Nothing in particular. It's just that it suddenly struck me how much the color resembled recently spilled blood."

Beau walked from the pub to the parking lot, still uneasy from his conversation with Raissa. Everything the woman had said made sense, yet he was still hesitating over doing the one thing he knew had to be done. He passed the parking lot and kept walking, circling once around the block, his mind whirling with all the possibilities, most of them not good.

Finally, unable to come up with a good reason to delay any further, he pulled his cell phone from his pocket and pressed in Sabine's number. Maybe she wouldn't answer. Maybe she'd be watching a movie or painting her toenails and this entire conversation could wait until he was ready. Like maybe 2056.

But she answered on the second ring.

"Sabine," he said, "it's Beau."

"Hi, Beau," she said. "How are you today?"

"Er, fine. I'm fine. Um, Sabine, I have some news for you."

"Oh." Her previously pleasant voice took on a somewhat fearful tone. "What is it?"

"I think I've found your family," he pressed forward before he could change his mind.

He heard the sharp intake of breath and waited for her response.

"Oh my God," she said finally. "So fast? I mean, I'm glad, but I can't believe it. I guess I never really thought you'd find anything...after all these years, you know?"

"I understand. Sometimes you just need a fresh eye and a stroke of luck," he said, mentally cursing the television special on war criminals.

"I guess so. So what now? I mean, what am I supposed to do? Do I write to them, call them? I know I can't show up on someone's doorstep and expect them to be happy about it."

"That's all been taken care of for you," Beau explained. "The family is quite wealthy, and I was certain they'd want all contact made through their attorney. I've spoken to him already and provided him with the information I had. He's spoken to the family and apprised them of the situation."

"So what do I do now?"

"They want to meet you. If you'd like, I can set up the meeting and go with you if that would make you more comfortable. I know this is very scary, and awkward, so please let me know how I can best help you."

"Yes...I, um, yes, that would be fine. I mean, set up the meeting and let me know what they say."

Beau felt his jaw clench involuntarily. "All right then. I'll call you as soon as I know something." He flipped the phone shut and shoved it in his pocket, trying to convince himself that everything had already been set in motion before his phone call. That call hadn't changed anything.

At least that's what he was going to keep telling himself.

Chapter Eight

Beau looked over to the passenger's seat and studied Sabine. "Are you sure you're ready for this?"

Sabine stared at the enormous iron gate and swallowed. Somewhere on the other side of the ten-foot stone fence was an estate, just forty-five minutes from Mudbug, where her family lived. Living, breathing relatives. Her dad's people. It all seemed like a blur. Twenty-odd years of searching with absolutely no results and now she had an entire family...grandparents, aunts, uncles, cousins, maybe even a dog. It was more than overwhelming. It was like waking up into a whole new existence.

She realized she hadn't answered and looked over at Beau. "I think so. I don't know. Maybe not?" She covered her face with both hands. "I'm sorry. You must wish you were anywhere but here with me."

Beau gently pulled her hands down and placed his hand on top of hers. "There's nowhere else I need to be. That's all that matters."

Sabine looked up at him. "I can't tell you how much I appreciate you doing this. I should have waited until Maryse could come."

"But that would have been another two days, right?"

Sabine nodded. "Yes. She would have cancelled her plans, but the man she is speaking with is a scientist and could have information leading to the break she's been looking for in her own research. He's only going to be in the country a couple more days, and going to Houston was the only opportunity Maryse had to talk to him."

Beau didn't look completely convinced that the reason was good enough to dump her best friend on the eve of discovering her long-lost family, but Sabine couldn't help that. What she couldn't say was that Maryse's research had led her to a medication that could possibly eliminate the side effects of radiation treatment.

A medication Sabine herself would most likely benefit from in the very near future.

The truth was, Maryse had begged Sabine to put off this meeting until she could be there, but Sabine had already waited for so many years that even another two days felt like a lifetime. Besides, she had the rest of her life to introduce Maryse to her family. However long that turned out to be.

"They know I'm coming?" Sabine asked.

"Yes."

"And they know why?"

"I told their attorney everything," Beau assured her. "He spoke with the family and they asked him to arrange this meeting. There shouldn't be any surprises. At least not on their end."

Sabine caught the tone of his voice as he delivered the last sentence. It had been a sticking point between them, but other than the bare minimum, Sabine had insisted that Beau hold off giving her any detailed information about her family. She wanted to get a clear impression of them without the bias of any information Beau had uncovered during his investigation.

No surprises. Yeah right. She took in a deep breath. "Okay. Let's do it."

"You're sure?"

Sabine nodded. "I'm sure."

Beau squeezed her hand, then lowered the truck window and pressed a button on a speaker mounted in front of the gate. A man's voice sounded over the speaker, asking his name. Beau gave the man the information and a couple of seconds later, the gate began to open. Beau put the truck in gear and pulled through the gate and into an enormous courtyard. Acre after acre of sculpted hedges, row after row of beautiful flowers—a palette of color set against a lush lawn.

Beau guided the truck around a bend in the drive and the house came into view. Sabine gasped. It looked like something out of Gone with the Wind. A front porch complete with white columns reaching from the ground to the roof spanned the width of the main house. Wings stretched out from both sides of the main structure, making the entire thing at least the length of a football field.

Sabine finally found her voice. "Oh, my God. I know you told me the family was wealthy, but I had no idea…"

Beau stared in awe. "I had no idea either. I mean, there's wealth and then there's this. I haven't ever come in direct contact with this before."

Sabine swallowed. "Me either. Not even close." She said a silent prayer of thanks that she'd forgone her normal eclectic dress and decided on her navy pantsuit, a splurge at a designer shop having a good sale.

Beau circled a twenty-foot fountain and parked in front of the house. A middle-aged man wearing a brown suit came out to meet them. "I'm Martin Alford, the Fortescues' attorney."

"Beau Villeneuve," Beau said and shook the man's hand, "and this is Sabine LeVeche."

The man turned to Sabine and studied her for a moment. "Ms. LeVeche. It's a pleasure to meet you. I was very surprised when I got Mr. Villeneuve's phone call. We'd given up hope of ever hearing anything about Adam."

Adam Fortescue. Her father, although that wasn't the name that had been on the driver's license he carried in his wallet the day of the accident. It had been two days since Beau had given her the news that he'd located her father's family and she still couldn't wrap her mind around it.

"I'd given up myself," Sabine said.

The attorney nodded. "I can imagine this has been a shock for you as well…to find your family has been so close all these years."

"A huge one," Sabine agreed.

"Well," the attorney said, "are you ready to meet them?"

Sabine took a deep breath and looked over at Beau, who nodded. "I'm ready."

The attorney smiled. "This way, then. They're anxious, too, if it makes you feel any better." He turned and motioned them toward the house.

Beau stepped close to Sabine and took her hand in his, giving it a squeeze. She looked over at him, grateful for the strength his presence gave her. She took the first step following the attorney. Then another. And before she knew it they entered the mansion through a set of hand-carved doors.

Sabine tried not to gawk as they stepped inside, but the interior of the home was even more impressive than its exterior. She didn't know much about art and antiques, but one look at the paintings hanging in perfectly placed picture frame molding and the decorative tables nestled in front of them with beautiful ornate vases and crystal bowls screamed rare and expensive. The ceiling in this front room was vaulted all the way to the second floor and had an enormous crystal chandelier hanging in the center. Huge staircases spiraled on each side of the room, forming a balcony on the far wall.

"They're in the library," the attorney said and motioned to the hallway on the left.

Sabine followed slowly, trying to clear her mind, focus on the event she'd been wanting for over twenty years. She felt like she was in a dream and any minute she'd wake up back in her apartment, just as frustrated and alone as she'd always been. Her feet connected with the wood floor, her heels resounding on the handscraped wood, but she didn't feel the connection at all. It was almost as if she were gliding, floating in a forward motion. Surreal, that was the word for it.

The attorney opened a door at the end of the hallway and motioned for her to enter. She felt Beau give her hand one last squeeze. Then she took a deep breath and stepped through the doorway and looked at her family for the first time. A regal woman with silver hair stood next to the fireplace, holding a glass of wine. Her cream linen suit was obviously custom tailored and the diamonds surrounding her neck sparkled in the bright light. A man in a gray smoking jacket and black slacks stood beside her and Sabine stared, her breath catching in her throat. He was a perfectly aged re-creation of the image Helena had produced. Any shred of doubt she had that maybe Beau had made a mistake, that this wasn't her family, disappeared in an instant.

A woman sitting at the long table in the center of the room gasped. She had the same eyes and bone structure of the silver-haired woman, but that was where the similarities ended. The woman was probably in her fifties but the lines on her face belied the opulence surrounding them. Maybe living in such a state of presumed grace wasn't everything it was cut out to be. The woman rose from her chair and walked over to stand in front of Sabine. She reached up with one hand and touched Sabine's face, an amazed and somewhat fearful look on her face. The flat gray of her suit made her skin seem sallow. Her eyes were dull and lifeless.

"You look just like him," she whispered. "I didn't want to believe, but it's true."

Sabine froze, not certain what to do. The woman stared at her without blinking and somewhere deep in her gaze, Sabine saw something that didn't look right...didn't look stable.

The older woman stepped over to them and gently removed the younger woman. "You have to excuse Frances. She's a bit overwhelmed with all of this. She was very close to Adam when they were children, as twins often are."

Sabine snapped her attention to the older woman she presumed was her grandmother. "They were twins?" Surely that wasn't right. Sabine's father was only eighteen when he died. That would make him forty-six now. Frances looked at least ten years older than that.

"Yes," the older woman said. "A difficult birth but a blessed one as I got a boy and girl in one shot. Twins run in the family. It's something to keep in mind when you decide to start a family yourself." She smiled at Sabine. "I'm your grandmother, Catherine."

Sabine smiled back, but it felt weak. This was all so much more overwhelming than she'd ever imagined. Her vision blurred and she saw a distorted Catherine staring at her.

"Sit," Catherine said and guided her into a chair. "Hand me that glass of water," she directed Alford.

"Sabine?" She could hear Beau's voice next to her but couldn't force herself to turn and look.

"Poor dear," Catherine said, "this has all been a shock to you, too, hasn't it?" She placed a glass in Sabine's hands and helped guide it to her lips.

Sabine took a sip, then a deep breath in and out. Her vision sharpened and she looked over at Catherine and nodded. "I guess it has been a shock. I didn't realize..."

"I should have," Beau said and squeezed her arm. "Do you want to finish this another time?"

"No," Sabine said. "I'll be fine." She looked at Catherine, her grandmother. "I'm sorry about that. I promise to behave myself from now on." She smiled.

Catherine smiled back. "Well, since you're not going to hit the deck on us, I'd like you to meet your grandfather, William." She motioned to the silver-haired man who had been hovering at the end of the table. He stepped forward, and Sabine rose to greet him.

He studied her for a minute, almost making her uncomfortable with his scrutiny, then extended his hand. "You're the spitting image of your father." He smiled. "A bit prettier, though."

Sabine took his hand in hers and smiled back. "Thank you." Sabine looked over at the attorney. "And Mr. Alford? Is he family, too?"

"Not officially," Catherine said, "but he's here so often that it was either make him an honorary member or catalog him with the furniture." She smiled at her joke. Alford didn't look nearly as amused.

Sabine turned and gestured to Beau. "This is Beau Villeneuve. He's the private detective who solved the mystery."

William shook hands with Beau. "Guess we owe you a huge thanks. We never knew what happened to Adam and had no idea that he had a baby. We're sad to hear of his death, although after all these years we really didn't expect anything different. But Sabine is a surprise, and a good one at that."

"I'm glad I could help," Beau said.

"Why didn't you know?" Sabine asked, unable to hold back the question that had been stuck in her mind ever since Beau had told her that her family was in Louisiana and very well off. "Why did he leave? And why didn't you look for him?"

Catherine shot a look at William, then looked back at Sabine. "We didn't exactly approve of the relationship between him and your mother. Adam had plans to go to medical school. When we realized how much time he was spending with her, we were afraid he'd do something foolish and jeopardize his future. I'm afraid we forbade them to see each other, which looking back was foolish on our part, as it only made them more determined to be together."

"We did look," William said. "I don't want you to think we didn't, but it was if he'd vanished."

"And my mother's family?" Sabine asked.

Catherine shook her head. "She lived back in the bayou. We tried to locate her family, but no one back there would talk to us. We don't even know if she had any here."

William placed one hand on Catherine's arm. "It was a hard time," he said. "The police couldn't assist us, as Adam was an adult and had left on his own volition. We hired private detectives but with nothing to go on, we finally gave up after six months of futility. We honestly believed that he'd contact us again. And when he didn't, well, we were afraid the worst had happened."

Catherine nodded. "For years, every time the doorbell rang, my heart leapt in my throat with fear that the police were there to tell me he was gone." She sniffed and touched her nose with the back of her finger. "We didn't even know about you, Sabine. If we'd had any idea that your mother was pregnant when we forbid Adam to see her, we wouldn't have handled things that way. You're our granddaughter. We would have changed our plans to ensure you had a proper home and upbringing."

Sabine took all this in and nodded. "It must have been quite a shock when Mr. Alford told you about me."

"Oh, well, at first, certainly," Catherine said, "but then we were so excited, so happy that there was a piece of Adam in this world. We made a horrible mistake with our son, Sabine, and it cost us, him, you, and Mother. We're going to do everything we can to make up for that now. That is, if you'll allow us to."

Sabine studied Catherine's face, the anxiety, the sadness. "I'm certainly willing to try."

Catherine sniffed again, then nodded. "Well, now that the uncomfortable part is taken care of, what do you say we move into the living room and have coffee and some of Adelaide's great cookies? I happen to know she made a new batch this morning. We have so much to talk about and there's no point in being parched or uncomfortable while doing it."

Sabine and Beau rose and followed the family into a sprawling room filled with soft, plump leather furniture in beautifully blended earth tones. Sabine and Beau walked toward a chocolate-brown loveseat placed next to a beautiful stone fireplace, but before they could sit, an old Creole woman entered the room with a tray of cookies, a young Creole woman close behind her with coffee.

The old woman stopped short when she caught sight of Sabine, her mouth forming an "o." For a moment, Sabine was afraid she might dump the entire tray on what was most certainly a ridiculously expensive leather rug, but she steadied herself and placed the tray on a coffee table in front of the couch. She hurried over to Sabine and gathered her in a crushing hug.

Sabine was momentarily surprised at such an emotional response, especially since her family had been much more reserved, but she wrapped her arms around the woman and squeezed. When the woman pulled back, Sabine could see unshed tears in her eyes.

"Child," the woman said, "You are so beautiful. It's an omen that you come now. I feel it in my bones. Good's gonna come from this."

"Oh, Adelaide," Catherine said, waving a hand in dismissal. "Don't start with that voodoo nonsense of yours. I'm sure Sabine doesn't believe it any more than the rest of us." Catherine frowned at Adelaide, and then her expression shifted once more to her standard regal, bored look. "Adelaide has been with the family for all of her seventy-eight years. Her mother worked for my great-grandmother." Catherine gave the woman an indulgent but somewhat frustrated look. "You have to excuse her. She still holds to the old beliefs of her family."

"I have no problem with those beliefs," Sabine said and gave Adelaide a smile. "And I certainly hope this is a good omen. Thank you."

Catherine narrowed her eyes at Sabine. "You don't believe in that sort of thing, do you?"

Sabine shrugged. "I believe there are far more things in this world that can't be explained than can."

Frances gasped. "But surely you're a Christian. You do believe in God, don't you?"

"Yes," Sabine said, "but I don't limit His creations to only those I can understand."

Frances relaxed a bit but still seemed far more stressed than the comment deserved. "Well, I suppose you could have a point."

Adelaide laughed. "Oh child, it's gonna be so good having you home."

Sabine smiled back, comfortable that at least one person was truly happy to meet her and hopefully lacked a hidden agenda. "Well, it's not exactly my home. I already have a home in Mudbug… and a business, for that matter. But I hope to visit."

"You own a business?" Catherine asked and shot the attorney a questioning look "What kind of business is it?"

Sabine groaned inwardly. Apparently Alford had judiciously elected to leave out any information about her profession, not that she was surprised. After her exchange with Frances, she was afraid the answer to that question might push the family into scheduling a full-fledged exorcism. "It's a retail shop of sorts," she said, hoping that would distract them for a couple of days.

Catherine perked up a bit. "Clothing? I couldn't help but notice your shoes. They're very...interesting. I thought maybe one of those shops that carries old, unique items."

Sabine looked down at her pumps. They were white with different varieties of multi-colored flowers covering them. The five-inch heel was dark redwood. Interesting? Unique? Catherine uttered those words like she was wearing fuzzy, bunny house slippers. "Actually, I got these at Macy's."

Catherine glanced down at the shoes again and frowned. "Really? I've never seen anything like them before."

Sabine stared at Catherine, starting to feel a little irritated at their stiff-minded beliefs. Might as well lay it all out now. "I love the unique. I'm a psychic, and I own a paranormal shop in downtown Mudbug. I sell different magical items, herbs for spells, candles, that sort of thing. And I do tarot readings as well as channel dead relatives for those who are interested in talking to the other side."

The room went completely silent. Everyone was staring at her, with the exception of the lawyer, who looked irritated with the entire mess. The expressions ranged everywhere from confused (Catherine), to excited (Adelaide), and horrified (Frances).

Frances removed the hand that was covering her mouth. "You sell pagan items for profit?"

Sabine nodded. "I haven't ever heard it put quite that way, but yeah, I guess I do."

Frances stared at her, her eyes wide with fear, "You don't...I mean...I've heard that some people sacrifice chickens."

Catherine frowned. "You've been reading the newspaper again, Frances." She shot a look at Adelaide, who looked down at the floor. "You know reading the paper gets you upset."

"That's okay," Sabine said. "It's a common enough question." From fools. "I don't do anything like that in my shop. It's really more about fun than anything else."

Adelaide started to laugh. "Just what this family needed—something to shake the foundations."

William frowned at Adelaide. "Our foundations are fine, Adelaide. Don't you have something to take care of in the kitchen?"

"Certainly, Mr. Fortescue," Adelaide said. "I'll just leave you folks to sort out the rest of Sabine's life for her." She gave Sabine a wink and headed to the kitchen.

"Well," Catherine said, "this is certainly unexpected but nothing so dire as can't be fixed. You're a Fortescue now. I'd be more than happy to give you the money to start another enterprise... perhaps clothing, as we talked about before?"

"But I—"

Catherine gestured to Sabine to take a seat. "We have plenty of time to talk business. Now, it's time to talk family. Frances helped me pull all the photo albums from when she and Adam were children. I thought you might like to see those first."

Sabine sat on the couch and looked over at Beau. He was trying to appear nonchalant, but Sabine felt the tension coming off him. He looked around the room, barely glancing at the people, and for some inexplicable reason, she knew he got more in that glance than most would in a bio. He was sizing them up, reading them like he would a newspaper, then systematically calculating the inherent risks and consequences.

Sabine took in a deep breath and tried to concentrate on the album Catherine had placed on the table in front of her. Tried to squelch the bad feeling that she had just stepped into the eye of a hurricane.

It was long after dinnertime when Sabine and Beau drove through the giant iron gates on their way back to Mudbug. Sabine had been silent during the long drive down the winding road back to the highway, and Beau fought the urge to ask for her thoughts. But eventually he couldn't stand the silence any longer. "So…that was something."

Sabine looked over at him and smirked. "Don't you mean it was 'interesting'?"

Beau laughed. "Good Lord, woman. Remind me to never, ever comment on your shoes unless I think they're fabulous."

"It wasn't just the shoes, although the general holier-and-better-than-thou attitude got on my nerves." She frowned. "It was something else…just a feeling, but, oh heck, I don't know."

"A feeling like everyone in the room was performing a dance and you were the only one who didn't have the choreography?"

Sabine stared at him. "Wow. That's it exactly. You have an excellent way of describing things."

Beau shrugged. "I've seen that dance a time or two before."

"With the FBI?"

"With the FBI, in my private work, and unfortunately, in my own family."

Sabine studied him and Beau knew she wanted to ask about the reference to his family, but she apparently decided it was either rude or not the time. "So was that what you were expecting, given what you already knew about them?"

Beau considered this a minute. "You never know exactly what to expect from people, no matter how much you read about them on paper. But to some extent, it was what I was expecting."

"What part?"

"Everyone lies, Sabine. What you have to figure out is whether the lies are important."

Sabine stared out the windshield, her expression thoughtful. "Everyone lies. You really believe that?"

"Yeah. I do."

"I guess I do, too," Sabine said. "Although some are little white lies and some are told to keep someone from being hurt and others are told to avoid embarrassment."

"That's where the 'important' part comes in."

"I lied to you," she confessed. "Well, not exactly a lie, but I didn't tell you the entire truth."

Beau's hands tightened on the steering wheel, certain Sabine was about to tell him the secret. The one she'd kept even from Mildred. "The truth about what?"

"I'm not psychic. Not even a little. In college, I majored in business but had no idea what I was going to do when I graduated. Then one day I walked into a tarot shop in New Orleans as a last resort to find out anything about my family and met Raissa. Her shop was amazing. All those cool candles and powders and books. And the people who came in were so happy to see her." She sighed. "I guess I thought if I could recreate that for myself, I might find the answers I was looking for. Stupid, huh?"

Beau knew Sabine would be hurt if he showed her an honest reaction, but he couldn't stop the wave of relief that washed over him. Sabine was normal, kinda. At least far more normal that he'd thought she was just minutes before. But there was no way this was what she'd been keeping from Mildred. The hotel owner would have known that from the beginning.

Sabine shifted in her seat and Beau realized he had never said anything about her revelation. The anxious look on her face said it all. "It's not stupid," he said. "Creative, inventive, perhaps a shade of desperate, but not stupid at all."

Sabine smiled. "Thanks."

"No problem. So…Raissa, is she just in it for the pretty candles, too?"

"Oh, no! Raissa is the real deal. Her predictions are scary accurate. Makes Nostradamus look like he was smoking weed."

Beau laughed. "So you believe in it, but you can't do it?"

"Pretty much."

"Well, being open-minded rarely leads to surprises. At least, that's my opinion. So have you ever seen anything supernatural?"

Sabine smiled. "Once, I saw a ghost."

"Were you scared?"

"I was horrified, but that was because of her outfit."

"Ah, then maybe those people are your family."

Sabine grinned. "Touché."

"The drawing that Raissa did…was it really from a vision?"

Sabine's expression grew serious. "Yes."

Beau felt his curiosity rise. He hadn't believed for a moment that the psychic had gotten a drawing that accurate from a vision, but for the life of him, he hadn't been able to locate anything in Raissa's life that could have connected her with the Fortescues any way other than through Sabine. "But how did she see it? In a dream?"

"No. A ghost channeled it so that she could draw it for me."

Beau looked over at Sabine. "And you believe that?"

"I have to believe it. I saw it."

Beau immediately felt it—that twinge that Sabine wasn't exactly telling him the whole truth, but about what, he had no idea. Especially as she seemed completely sincere and adamant about the ghostly vision part of her story. "Well, now that you've met your family, there are some things I need to tell you about them and I don't think we should put it off very long."

Sabine nodded. "I know. I appreciate you respecting my wishes to meet them unbiased by the facts. But now that I've met them, I want to know what you found out."

"Of course. When do you want to do this?"

"I'm free tonight." Sabine looked over at him. "That is, unless you have plans already."

"No plans except taking care of my client."

A light flush crept up Sabine's neck and she lowered her eyes. "You're sure…I mean, it's not exactly a short drive back into New Orleans and I don't want to put you out, especially if you have things to do tomorrow."

"Not a thing but dirty laundry, and I'm pretty sure it won't care if I sleep in." Beau felt his jaw flex with the lie, but he didn't want Sabine to know he was staying across the street in the hotel. Not yet. Not until he had a damned good reason, and a gut feeling usually didn't qualify as a damned good reason for spying on a woman. Not to the woman, anyway.

"Well, I have leftover pot roast, chips, and sugar cookies. I can offer you a great sandwich and we won't have to worry about being overheard. Is that all right by you?"

Beau felt his pulse quicken. Alone with Sabine in her apartment. That was far more than all right. "That's fine," he said, hoping his voice sounded normal.

Chapter Nine

Sabine took a second bite out of her sandwich and tried to chew, but the roast beef that had been so juicy and filled with flavor the night before now tasted like cardboard. What the hell had she been thinking? Inviting Beau into her apartment? Feeding him roast beef? She should have suggested the restaurant. It was usually loud, and there would have been little chance of being overheard. No, instead she had to play happy hostess, serving home-cooked food just mere feet from the bedroom in her tiny apartment.

Like she didn't have enough trouble already. She should have told Beau no when he'd asked if she'd like him to accompany her to meet her family, although his offer had sounded more like an order now that she thought about it. Regardless, she couldn't afford to keep putting herself in this position. She was already horribly attracted to him, and spending time in such close proximity to wine and beds and the sexy lingerie in her dresser drawer wasn't the smartest thing to do.

But he's open-minded.

She held in a sigh. The men she'd dated in the past couldn't be bothered to hear anything about her job, her shop, her beliefs. They liked her but didn't buy into anything they couldn't prove. Which shouldn't have bothered her since, technically, Maryse had never believed either until Helena showed up. But Maryse had never had that smirk on her face when Sabine talked about the paranormal. Her friend had always respected her beliefs even if she hadn't been able to match them with her own.

And now this super sexy, kind, intelligent, single former FBI agent had actually listened to what she had to say about supernatural occurrences and considered the facts as seriously as he would have a fingerprint or a smoking gun. Sabine wasn't going to fool herself with thinking he believed everything she'd said, but he hadn't discounted it either. Which meant he was a rare individual.

"I hope I haven't scared you with all this," Beau said.

Sabine snapped back to the present. "Not exactly, although I must admit it's a little strange." Beau had been telling her dirty family secrets over the sandwiches and now she struggled to make some sense of it all.

She pulled a pad of paper over in front of her and began to write. After a minute, she pushed the pad over to Beau. "Is that right?"

"Looks good to me."

Sabine looked at the family tree for a minute. "So the long and short of it is that my grandfather had a twin brother, Lloyd, who disappeared during Vietnam and was wanted for treason. The family is filthy rich and has spent almost a hundred years answering to essentially no one."

Beau nodded. "The FBI questioned them repeatedly about Lloyd and had them under surveillance for several years, but no one has seen hide nor hair of him since the Vietnam War."

"Any chance the family helped him hide?"

Beau shrugged. "Anything's possible, but the government tracked their funds for a long time. No money left their bank accounts that wasn't reasonable and explainable. And nothing was transferred to other countries."

"So most likely he died in Vietnam and his body was never recovered."

"Most likely."

"Well," Sabine said finally, "I'm glad you were so thorough. I would hate to start asking questions about the family twin legacy. Those people are so uptight, they'd probably have me removed from the property and banned for life."

"It does seem they're a little touchy about appearance," Beau agreed. "Based on the local gossip, at one time the family was a huge force in local charities, politics, and church, but ever since Vietnam they've become more reserved. Catherine still hosts several charitable events for the church during the year, but otherwise, she rarely interacts with the locals, and Frances is almost never seen out of the house except for church."

"Small wonder there," Sabine said. "I thought her head was going to spin around when she thought I killed chickens for a living."

Beau laughed. "I'd say Aunt Frances is definitely missing a step or two upstairs."

Sabine shook her head. "Hiding yourself away is counterproductive, really. Then people only assume you have something to hide, and let's face it, you probably do."

"Probably."

Sabine sighed. "I guess you're right. A family that old is bound to have secrets. What about William?"

"William seems to be the biggest disappointment locally. Apparently, before he left for the war he was always involved in a bunch of community service. He worked with underprivileged children at the local library, teaching them to read. He co-chaired several fundraisers to buy medical equipment for the clinic in town and was key in the development of a senior network that provided drop-in care for limited mobility seniors living alone, and all of that while he was still in high school."

"Wow, he sounds great."

"Past tense, I'm afraid. The William who came back from Vietnam isn't the same man as before. The only charity he attends to now is the local bar, and from what I hear, he's a big contributor."

Sabine shook her head. "Post-traumatic stress?"

Beau shrugged. "There's really no telling. Lots of men come back from war changed forever."

Sabine's mind went back to the scene in the living room when she'd described her business. "So what's the story on crazy Aunt Frances?"

Beau crinkled his brow. "You know, that's one thing I was never able to get much of a line on. Both kids attended the private Catholic school in town, but some of the older residents seemed to remember your father. He did some volunteer work down at the clinic, most particularly for a Dr. Grey, but the doctor died several years ago so I wasn't able to get any more than that."

"Makes sense with the family saying he was going to be a doctor."

"Yeah. Even wealthy families usually don't frown upon working for a living if you're a doctor."

"But the locals didn't really know Frances?"

"Not really. She attended private school until she was seventeen and was homeschooled after that with a private tutor from another parish. He's dead now, so that led nowhere. Other than that, she's never seen outside of the house, except attending church, always at her mother's hip and never speaking a word to anyone."

"Agoraphobic?"

Beau shrugged. "I don't know, and I seriously doubt you'll ever get them to admit it if that's the case. Whatever those people are hiding, they've been doing it successfully for a long time. That's why I thought you needed what little facts I had before you had any more interaction with them...assuming you want to, of course."

Sabine looked out the window and across Main Street. At the moment, she would honestly have to admit she didn't want any further interaction with them. The entire meeting had been like the tiny pop of a firecracker when she'd been setting up for a dynamite experience all these years. But then what choice did she have? "I...guess I do. I mean, I don't really know them yet and they don't know me. I suppose things could get better."

"I suppose."

Sabine smiled and looked over at Beau. "This is what you were warning me about, wasn't it? You and Maryse are cut from the same cloth in certain ways."

"Really? How's that?"

"Oh, Maryse has always supported my search for my family, even though I believe that for the most part, she's thought it was a waste of time. She thinks the relationships you choose to make are far more important than the ones that are forced on you. She's always saying 'you have to love your family, but you don't have to like them, or want to spend time with them.' "

Beau grinned. "You're right. We are cut from the same cloth. So what's up with Maryse's family that she doesn't have to like them?"

"Oh, nothing at all with her blood family. Her mom and dad are both dead and there's no other siblings. I think she's referring to her ex-husband and his mother when she makes that statement."

"That bad, huh?"

Sabine grimaced. "You have no idea. Helena Henry as a mother-in-law is enough to drive a girl to the convent."

"I read about Helena's death in the paper, then all the excitement that followed. That wasn't that long ago."

"Yeah, the funeral was last month."

"Well, then it looks like Maryse is free and clear again." He smiled at Sabine.

Sabine tried to smile but wasn't sure she managed it convincingly. "Seems like she should be," she hedged.

Beau glanced down at his watch and rose from the table. "It's late. I need to take off and let you get some rest. I'm sure you're exhausted."

Sabine rose from the table and walked with Beau to the door. "I am a little tired. I think I'm going to take a long, hot bath, then climb directly into bed."

Beau froze when she mentioned a bath and bed, and she stepped far too close to him for her own comfort, and probably his. He studied her for a moment, the desire in his eyes apparent. Even though she knew she should step away, open the door, and send him on his way, she didn't. No, she inched even closer…and tilted her head toward his.

His breath caught. She knew he was waiting for her to turn tail and run like she had at the café. When she held her ground, he lowered his head, his lips barely brushing hers. Her lips started to tingle and the tiny shock of pleasure radiated all the way down to her toes. He paused for just a second, but then moved in for a deeper kiss, his lips locked on hers.

She leaned into the kiss, her body perfectly molding into his. He wrapped his arms around her, and she felt the hard lines of his chest press into her. She parted her mouth, and he deepened the kiss before pulling away from her lips and trailing kisses down her neck. She sighed with pleasure, her skin jumping alive with every touch of his lips. She opened her eyes just a tiny bit, wanting to see his face, the desire that she knew would be there—and saw something move in the kitchen.

Somehow, she managed to keep herself in check, but as she opened her eyes completely, it was clear that they weren't alone. The refrigerator door stood wide open and a huge hunk of rapidly disappearing roast beef dangled just outside of the door. Instantly, Sabine's mind jerked back into reality. What the hell was she doing?

She broke away from Beau, her quick retreat leaving him with a confused expression. "I-I'm sorry…I can't…" She stepped to the side, praying he didn't turn his head or Beau Villeneuve was going to get a crash course in the "I want to believe" games.

Beau's expression hardened. "That's all right. I understand. You won't have to remind me again." He opened the door and stepped through it.

"Wait," Sabine called after him, but he hurried down the stairs, never once looking back.

Sabine waited until the door slammed shut, then trudged downstairs to lock the door. She peeked out the front window, but Beau's truck was already gone. Frustrated with herself, she went back up to her apartment.

The roast beef was still floating, but now a jar of mayonnaise was suspended along with it, the roast beef seeming to dip itself in the jar then disappear in pieces. "I don't care if you're dead—this is still breaking and entering, not to mention theft. And at the very least, it's just plain rude, even for you."

The sandwich stopped moving and hung in midair. "Oh, please," Helena said, "You were so wrapped up in that detective, I could have slaughtered a cow and started a barbeque right on your kitchen table and you wouldn't have noticed."

"Oh really? So why is it that I sent him packing as soon as I saw you?"

"Hmmmm, guess I didn't exactly put that together."

"How could you? You were too busy robbing me of my leftovers."

"Next time I'll be less obvious."

"Ha!" Sabine laughed. "You're about as unobtrusive as a freight train running through here. Besides, I don't want you sneaking, either."

"I can see why, if you're going to act like a hooker at your front door. Although, there's a huge advantage to you not being able to see me. That Beau is damned good looking…almost as good looking as Maryse's man, but she always catches me. With you, I have a really good shot at seeing some prime male behind before I leave this earth."

An image of making love with Beau flashed through Sabine's mind. Helena was right—his behind was grade-A prime beef. And the image would have been perfect, except for the floating buffet at the end of the bed. Sabine shuddered. No way. "From now on, you will announce yourself before you walk through the walls, do you understand me, Helena? I can still do that exorcism."

"Yeah, yeah. Jeez, you and Maryse are such bores. It's a wonder men are interested in you at all."

Sabine thought about the look Beau had flashed her just before he practically ran out of her apartment. "I don't think that's something I have to consider any longer."

"Oh, I wouldn't write him off just yet…not with the way I've seen him look at you." The roast beef began its journey into the mayonnaise again. "Damn! This is some of the best roast beef I've ever eaten. If you gave him some of this, he'll definitely be back."

Sabine sighed and sank into a chair at the kitchen table. "What if I don't want him to come back?"

The sandwich stopped moving again and just hung there. Finally, it moved forward along with the mayonnaise jar and then they both came to rest on the kitchen table. The chair across from her slid backwards and the cushion flattened.

"You're afraid," Helena said. "You're afraid of letting him close to you because of the cancer."

"Maybe. Yes. Well, wouldn't you be?"

"Probably. The question is, are you scared for him or yourself?"

Sabine buried her head in her hands, her heartbeat pounding in her temples. "I wish I knew."

"I know my opinion probably doesn't count for anything, but I'm going to tell you like I told Maryse. Don't make the same mistakes I did. I lived a pretty damned long life of nothing, hiding myself from people, afraid to make connections because I might get hurt. I married a man I knew I could never love, had a child that I never could connect with, and died without a single friend to my name."

Sabine looked across the table at the empty space, wishing she could actually see the woman who was speaking. "You think the risk is worth it? To admit your feelings for someone who might not feel the same way? To share your darkest secret knowing it could be the one thing that drives them away? Or even worse, to have them stay and love you and in the end, lose it all to a dreadful disease?"

"But you'll never ask yourself what if."

Tears began to form in Sabine's eyes. "I hate it when you're right." She wiped at her eyes with the back of her hand, silently willing the unshed tears to disappear. "I met my family today."

Her comment was met with dead silence and for a moment, Sabine wondered if Helena had left, but the seat cushion was still flattened. Finally, Helena spoke. "I didn't realize. So what happened? I mean, if you feel like telling me that is…wow, I can't even imagine…almost thirty years of not knowing, right?"

"Just about. They're…different, I guess would be the polite way to describe them. Wealthy. Hey, maybe you could help me understand things along that line. I know people with money have a different set of rules, but I'm having trouble getting a handle on it. The meeting today was, well, I guess the best word is 'weird.' "

"Wealth often comes with conditions. Most people don't realize it because the wealthy keep everything hidden. But family structure is paramount. Keeping appearances is the second priority, right after keeping the money. It's definitely a different world. And not often a pleasant one for children."

"Yeah, I'm kinda getting that."

"So who is the family? Anyone I would know of?"

"Maybe. They're not that far from here. The family name is Fortescue."

"Holy shit! The Fortescues? Jesus, no wonder you said they were weird. Hell, weird is polite. Nuts is a better description."

Sabine felt her pulse quicken. "You know them?"

"As well as one half-ass recluse can know another. I never had much interaction with the whole family, but I did deal with Catherine before she married William. The family pretty much dropped out of sight during Vietnam and never really emerged again except church events, and I always tried to avoid church events. My hypocrisy only extended to writing checks, not actually attending. The rumor mill was always running on about them though."

"Really? About what, exactly?"

"Some said Frances went crazy, and that's why they didn't come out, but that never made sense to me. Frances was only a baby during Vietnam and attended the Catholic school in town for some time. Some said Catherine was the crazy one and she made Frances that way, since she dropped out of school her senior year. Some said William was never right after the war. No matter, most everyone assumed someone—or everyone—in the family was crazy. Then the son disappeared when he was a teenager—hey, that must have been your father. Damn, this is getting interesting. And seeing as how William's brother had disappeared years before, everyone wondered what religion exactly was being practiced in that house. Last I checked, Christians didn't make people disappear, but that family had more than their share of missing relatives and no answers for it, according to the local police."

"So what did people think happened?"

"There was speculation that the family was hiding the wanted brother, Lloyd, during and after Vietnam, which is why they pulled back so much from society. But I figure there was probably all sorts of government agencies just itching to find Lloyd, so there was little chance they could have hidden him all those years, even in that monstrous house of theirs. More likely he died in Vietnam and was never recovered."

Sabine nodded. "That seems to be the most likely. And my father? Did you know anything of him besides his disappearance?"

"Seems the townspeople knew your father pretty well. Apparently he didn't stick to the rest of his family's rules about associating with the lower class. There was always rumors that he'd taken up with someone the family didn't or wouldn't approve of. Most thought he'd simply run away with the girl, even though he was giving up a fortune in inheritance to do it."

"And when no one saw him again?"

"I don't know. People speculated for a while, but I think they finally decided that the family must have given him some money to keep their secrets and stay away. After a while, no one spoke of him at all."

Sabine considered this for a moment. "But if anyone knew anything, or even thought they knew anything, they might be willing to tell me now, right?"

"Possibly, but I wouldn't swear to it. Some think the past is better left buried. Some just don't want to get involved in other people's business…not the serious kind anyway. General gossip over extramarital affairs and plastic surgery is one thing, speculating about the possibilities of bribery and murder is entirely different. And with Catherine and William still alive, it might not be the smartest thing to go speculating on."

"But it's possible someone would be willing to?"

Helena sighed. "You're not going to let this go, are you? I suppose I could come up with a name or two for you to start with, but you have to promise me to be careful. Hell, Maryse got caught up in all that mess just by doing her job. You asking questions about things people might want to keep buried is a lot more risky."

"I want the truth, Helena, but you're right. I promise to be careful, and if it starts to look dangerous at all, I'll stop. Okay?"

"It's already dangerous. The wealthy don't like their secrets in the public eye, even if everyone else wouldn't blink twice at them. Everything's a possible embarrassment to them. Everything's a possible slur to the family name. Whole lot of bullshit if you ask me, but then, I didn't exactly play by the rules of money. Probably why I never got invited to those fancy parties. Ha."

"If I didn't know any better, I'd guess that part was intentional."

"You've been hanging around me too long."

"That is an overstatement." Sabine rose from the table. "I'm going to take a hot bath and crawl in bed with a glass of wine."

"Hmmmm, wine sounds good. Hey, I wonder if I can get drunk. What do you think?"

"I think we're not going to try. Good night, Helena."

"Wait a minute. If you have a phone book, I can probably jot down a couple of names for you. My memory's not what it used to be, but the phone book should bring it back."

Sabine pulled a thin local phone book from her kitchen drawer. She placed the directory, a pad of paper, and a pen on the table in front of Helena's chair, then headed off to start her bath.

Twenty minutes later, she emerged from the steamy water feeling much more relaxed. Especially for someone whose life was falling apart at every end. She pulled on her pink cotton pajamas and headed into the kitchen to see what Helena had found. The ghost hadn't made a noise the entire time Sabine was in the bath, which meant she was either engrossed in her studies or all that food had put her in carb overload and she was asleep on the kitchen table.

"I came up with three names," Helena said as Sabine entered the kitchen, "but I think one of them died a couple of years ago, so maybe only two. Hell, to be quite honest, the other two might be dead by now, too. These women were closer to my mom's age than mine."

Sabine leaned over and took a look at the list, but the names weren't familiar to her. "Do they live in Mudbug?"

"No. The dead one was from Rabbit Island and the other two were up around Bayou Thibodeaux."

"That's close to my family, right?"

"Yeah, a couple of miles up the bayou from town, but they could be anywhere now. Still, if anyone's going to know the local gossip, it would be these two. If they're still alive."

Sabine nodded. "I'll check tomorrow." She stepped into the kitchen, pulled a brand-new bottle of wine from her refrigerator, removed the cork, and poured herself a generous glass. Then she took a couple of sugar cookies from the cookie tin, since apparently Helena had helped herself to the ones on the table, and headed to the bedroom. "I'm off to bed, Helena. Turn off the kitchen light when you're done, all right?"

"No problem," Helena replied.

Sabine placed the glass of wine and cookies on her nightstand next to the latest thriller she was reading and climbed into bed. Between the hot bath, the wine, the sugar, and the book, she ought to be out like a light in no time. She took a nice, slow sip of the wine, a huge bite of a cookie, and opened the book to her marker. She'd barely read the first two sentences when she realized something was wrong.

Her breathing constricted, like a whooping asthma attack, and she could feel her heart beating double-time in her chest. She tried to sit up straight, hoping to expand her lungs a bit, but she seemed rooted in place, her limbs not responding at all. She tried to yell, but it came out not much more than a whisper. "Helena. Helena, help."

She strained to hear something…anything moving in her apartment, but only the ticking of the kitchen clock met her ears. This is it. I'm going to die. Frantic, she struggled with her lifeless body, but couldn't move her hand more than an inch. "Help. Helena, help."

"What the hell are you whispering for?" Helena's voice boomed next to her. "Speak up if you want something."

Sabine opened her mouth, at least she thought she did, but no sound emerged. She looked at the side of the bed where she'd heard Helena's voice, frightened beyond belief. Helena was her only chance. If the ghost couldn't figure out what was going on, she was going to die right here in her bed.

"Holy shit!" Helena said, apparently realizing something was very wrong. "Just hang in there. I'll dial 911."

Sabine saw the cordless phone rise from her dresser and heard the numbers being depressed. Then the phone glided across the room and stopped with the mouthpiece at her lips. The operator answered and Sabine struggled to get out a word. "Help." Her voice was so faint, she didn't know if the operator had heard her at all. "Help," she said again and slipped into unconsciousness.

Chapter Ten

Beau tossed Sabine's file on the dresser with his gun and wallet and plopped back onto the worn-out recliner with a sigh. Another hour of reading over the same information and still he had nothing. He reached for the remote and turned on the television. He needed a distraction—one that didn't have coal-black hair and a body that was an art form. He shook his head. Stupid. That woman is nothing but trouble, yet you insist on humiliating yourself over her. Real smart, Villeneuve. He jumped up from the chair and paced the length of the room, all three steps of it, then turned and paced it again. The job is officially over, and it's not your business to play bodyguard. Get back to New Orleans and forget your ever met Sabine LeVeche.

He sat on the end of the bed with a sigh. If only it was that easy.

It should have been easy. It should have been a piece of cake. It wasn't like Sabine was the first woman he had ever been attracted to. But this woman…this woman with strange beliefs and a huge can of worms for a family had stopped him cold in his tracks.

It just didn't make sense.

Sabine LeVeche was everything he didn't want in his life. Her beliefs defied logic and science. She was smack in the middle of a huge family drama, and her family was a nightmare of old-school beliefs and even older money. God only knew what they had been hiding behind those stone walls for all these years, and Beau didn't want to know. But Sabine would, and that's where his dilemma came in. Sabine LeVeche would look for answers until there were no questions left.

Beau knew all too well that those questions just might unleash a nightmare.

The family had been polite enough and had seemed as if they were glad to learn of Sabine, but they were still guarded in the information they dispensed. He wasn't even going to launch into the weirdness factor. It went without saying. If Sabine veered off into the wrong line of questioning, they'd close ranks in a second, complete with the attorney to back them up. The attorney had hovered over the group the entire afternoon. Always standing and studying the room like he was getting ready for a major coup. If Beau had been a lesser man, he might have found it unnerving. Instead, he'd just found it annoying.

And none of it is your problem.

Mind made up, Beau leaned over to untie his tennis shoe. He was going to get a good night's sleep and first thing in the morning he was going to head back to New Orleans, send an itemized bill to Sabine, and try to forget everything he knew about this case. He couldn't afford to get involved on a personal level. Already the dreams were starting to return. It had taken him years to get a good night's sleep again. He wasn't about to jeopardize that for a stranger who'd repeatedly made it clear she had no interest in getting to know him better.

He pulled one shoe off and had just started on the second when he heard the sirens. His heart leapt to his throat and the completely irrational feeling that something bad had happened to Sabine washed over him like rain. He jumped up from the bed and peered out the hotel window. The ambulance exited the highway and raced into town, sirens screaming. He hadn't taken a breath since he'd leapt off the bed, but when the ambulance screeched to a stop in front of Sabine's store, the air all came out in a whoosh. He didn't even stop to grab his other shoe before he tore out of the hotel, almost knocking down the hotel owner as he ran across the street.

The paramedics had already burst in through the front door of the shop and Beau ran past the policeman standing at the door without bothering to identify himself. He dashed up the stairs, the policeman close behind him, yelling for him to stop. He ran into the apartment and, finding the front rooms empty, dashed into the bedroom. What he saw brought him up short.

The paramedics wheeled Sabine out on a gurney, an oxygen mask strapped to her pale face. She looked unconscious. "What's wrong with her? What happened? Damn it, someone answer me!"

"We don't know. You have to move, sir!" one of the paramedics yelled as they rushed past him with the gurney.

"Where are you taking her?" he called after them.

"Mudbug General," the paramedic called back as they hurried down the stairs as fast as they could go.

Beau started to follow, but the policeman who had chased him upstairs hitched his pants up with one hand and put his other on Beau's chest. "Buddy, you ain't going nowhere until you tell me who the hell you are and how you know Sabine."

Mildred, who had followed close on the heels of the officer, rolled her eyes at Barney Fife, then fixed a hard stared on Beau. "I'd like an answer to that question myself."

Beau reached into his pocket, then remembered he'd dashed out of the hotel without one of his shoes, much less his wallet. This wasn't going to go near as quickly as he'd like. So far, he was as unimpressed with the Mudbug police as Sabine was, but he'd bet money that the hotel owner could take him down if he failed to satisfy the two of them. "I'm a private detective, former FBI. I was hired by Ms. LeVeche to find her family. I'm staying at the hotel across the street and ran over here when I saw the paramedics enter Sabine's building. My wallet is in my hotel room."

"I'll be needing to see that before you can leave town." The officer stared at him for a moment. "So I can assume that when Ms. LeVeche is able, she'll verify your story?"

"Of course. Jesus, I just had dinner with her here, in this apartment. I only left a little over an hour ago, max. What the hell happened? Why did the paramedics come?"

"There was a 911 call from the phone here, but no one spoke. When that happens, the rulebook says we have to assume a crime is happening or someone's croaking, so the police and the ambulance have to pay a visit."

"And since there was no sign of forced entry, you assumed a medical emergency and the paramedics entered," Beau said.

The officer narrowed his eyes. "I didn't have time to check for 'forced entry,' as you call it. Damned medics had broke the door down before I got here."

Mildred looked at the cop in disgust. "For Christ's sake, Leroy, you're a block away and the hospital is ten miles up the highway. If you'd stop wasting taxpayer money looking at internet porn, you might be able to do your job. Although I still have my doubts."

Beau's opinion of the hotel owner went up a notch.

"I'll check out your story, Mr. Villeneuve. And assuming Ms. Mildred will vouch for you staying at her hotel, I guess I'll let you drop by with that identification. In the meantime, I'd prefer it if you stuck around Mudbug. At least until Sabine can verify what you've said."

"I'm only going as far as the hospital, as soon as someone tells me where it is exactly," Beau assured the man, who gave him a brief nod and left.

"Good," Mildred said, giving Beau a shrewd look. "I'll give you directions and you can give me a ride. And since I'm 'vouching' for you, you can explain on the way why you're staying in my hotel and requested a room that faced Sabine's store. Sabine told me her family was located days ago, so why all this bull about having business with her now?"

Beau sighed and motioned Mildred down the stairs. "I'll tell you, but you're probably not going to believe me."

"Try me," Mildred said and headed down the stairs and out the door.

Beau made the fifteen-mile drive to Mudbug General in ten minutes flat, hoping like hell that the policeman was back at the station checking on his story or looking at some of that internet porn

Mildred had mentioned and not pulling over speeders headed out of town. Mildred had left a message for someone, probably Maryse, as soon as they got in the truck, then demanded he give her the details of his surveillance. He filled her in on the basic points of the situation and had just wrapped up when they reached the hospital. He tore into the parking lot and screeched to a halt in the closest parking space he could find to the emergency room. He jumped out of his truck and ran to the hospital. Mildred was hot on his heels, surprising him by how fast the large woman could move.

A nurse at the front desk gave them a dirty look when they burst into the lobby, but her expression shifted to concern when they asked for Sabine. "The doctors are working on her, but she's stabilized," the woman said. "I haven't heard any details yet, but Dr. Mitchell will be out as soon as there's something to tell." She gave Mildred a sympathetic look. "I'm sure we'll know more about your daughter soon. Is there anything I can get you while you wait?"

"No, thank you," Mildred said, "we'll just wait over here if that's okay." She pointed to a couple of chairs in the corner of the room with a clear view of the hallway to the emergency room.

"That's fine," the nurse said.

"Guess there's nothing left but the waiting." Mildred sat on the edge of one of the chairs, her hands clenched together in her lap.

Beau studied her for a moment. "You didn't correct the nurse when she assumed you were Sabine's mother."

"No cause to correct the facts, is there?"

"I thought her aunt raised her."

Mildred nodded. "She did, as best she could anyway. Margaret was no spring chicken when the state gave her custody of Sabine, and she didn't get any younger. Then Sabine met Maryse in elementary school and they were tied at the hip ever since. So you might say I got a double blessing."

Beau stared at Mildred in surprise. "You're Maryse's mother? I thought Sabine told me her parents were dead."

"They are. Her mother died shortly after Maryse's birth and her father a couple of years ago. I helped with the baby after her mother died, and eventually her father and I started seeing each other on a personal basis. Did right up until the day he died."

Beau nodded in understanding. "So you are their mother. In all the ways that count anyway."

Mildred sniffed and looked down at the floor. "I like to think so. Those girls mean the world to me. All that business with Maryse last month damned near gave me a heart attack, and now this. You told me on the way over here that you stayed in the hotel to look out for Sabine because you had a bad feeling but no evidence. What is going on with my girls, Beau? You gave me the facts, but that doesn't tell me anything. Tell me what you think—I don't care if you can prove it or not."

Beau took a deep breath and slowly blew it out. "I didn't know anything about Maryse's situation until Sabine mentioned it. Then I read up on it and I think it might have damned near given me a heart attack, too. She's very lucky to be alive. But the man who was after her is dead, right? Probate is over and the father-in-law is setting up residence in a New Orleans jail awaiting trial." He shook his head. "I can't see where that has anything to do with whatever is going on with Sabine."

"Just because we don't see it doesn't mean it's not there."

"You're right, of course. I'm just a little surprised to hear someone else try to make two and two equal five like I do."

Mildred waved a hand in dismissal. "Oh heck, I've been doing the hotel accounting long enough to know that two and two equals whatever you want it to be. It's simply a matter of perception and misdirection."

Beau smiled. "Okay. So let's say there's a common factor, but we don't know what it is. We also don't know if the common factor is the cause of the problem or not. It could be something as simple as them being friends, or Maryse inheriting money, or it could be nothing at all."

Mildred gave Beau a shrewd look. "Maryse isn't the only one set to come into money now, right?"

"Yeah...I started worrying about that all of about two seconds after I found out who Sabine's family was. Unless they're putting up an awful good front, the Fortescues have more money than any family I've ever met."

"I was gonna have breakfast with Sabine tomorrow morning and hear all about the meeting. Guess that might have to wait now. So did the Fortescues accept what you told them about her?"

"They seemed to take it all in stride. I'm sure when it comes down to the details, someone, most likely the attorney, will insist on a DNA test."

"But you have no doubts?"

Beau shook his head. "No. Sabine is the spitting image of her father, and the grandfather, for that matter. If you could have seen those pictures of when he was young…it was mighty convincing. By my estimate, Sabine is poised to inherit a fortune."

"You really think they'll just hand over a buttload of money to someone who is still essentially a stranger, DNA or no?"

Beau nodded. "Yeah, I do. Once word gets out that Adam had a daughter and she was found, the family will do everything they can to make up for lost time. Remember, appearances are the most important thing to the Fortescues. And what would people think if they didn't bring Sabine into the fold and treat her as the grandchild she is?"

"And you think that might make someone unhappy?"

"Maybe. There's only the aunt left in the house with the grandparents and they don't associate with any extended family, but assuming no aunt and no Sabine, there's any number of estranged cousins and such who would probably come into a tidy sum when the grandparents were gone. The aunt didn't strike me as all that healthy looking, so she probably isn't a huge concern. She seems emotionally unstable and it might be that she couldn't even withstand her parents' death."

"Which leaves Sabine."

"Exactly."

Mildred sighed. "Does it strike you that all these problems seem to center on money, even though Maryse's situation ultimately wasn't about the money, per se?"

"Oh, yeah. If there's one thing I learned in the FBI, it was that money is the greatest motivator of all. We had a saying there—'there's three things you don't mess with, a man's money, his wife, or his children—in that order.' "

Mildred gave him a knowing look. "Some days, it just pays to be poor, single, and childless."

Sabine awoke with a series of wires attached to various parts of her body. She blinked, trying to clear her blurry vision, then blinked again. Her eyes were still watery, but she could make out a small hospital room, like the equipment hadn't given that away. No separate bathroom, so she must be in the emergency room. Helena must have been able to make the call. Thank God. The last thing she remembered was calling to the ghost for help.

"Sabine, can you hear me?"

Sabine looked across the room but didn't see anyone. "Helena? Is that you?"

"Yeah. I'm standing next to your bed."

Sabine turned to the side, expecting to find nothing but air, and sucked in a breath when she saw Helena, clear as day, standing next to her bed. "Holy shit! I really am dead this time."

Helena peered down at her, her eyes hidden behind a pair of polarized sunglasses. "You can see me again?"

"Of course I can see you. For some god-awful reason, you're dressed like John Lennon. Why wouldn't I be able to see you? We're both dead and apparently stuck here."

"Uh, I hate to point out the obvious, but hospitals as a general rule do not attach heart monitors to dead people. And even if they did, I'm fairly certain dead people wouldn't have a pulse."

Sabine twisted around to get a good look at the monitor behind her and felt relief wash over her. Sure enough, her heart was beating. Albeit, it was probably beating a good bit faster now than it had before, but that was fixable. Dead wasn't.

"What happened?"

"I don't know, but I don't think you'll have to wait long for an answer. In a minute, they'll let Mildred and that hunky investigator in here."

"Hunky investigator? What's he still doing here?" She shook her head. "Never mind that. Have you been here the whole time? Have the doctors said anything?"

"Yeah, they've said plenty, but not a damn thing I understood. They're moving you to a room, though, so I guess that's good news. I'm really glad, Sabine. I know I am a real annoyance to you and Maryse, but I don't want to see anything bad happen to either of you." She sighed. "Sometimes, I wish—"

Before Helena could finish her sentence, the door burst open. Mildred went straight to Sabine's side, walking through Helena, and clutched Sabine's hand in her own. "My God, Sabine, you've scared the life right out of me." Beau was right behind her.

Sabine squeezed Mildred's hand and watched as Helena strolled through the hospital wall. "Looks like I came closer to scaring it out of myself. What happened? Have you talked to the doctor?"

Mildred shook her head. "They're coming in a minute, but I insisted on seeing you now."

Sabine smiled. "I bet you did. Maryse?"

"I got her voice mail, but I left a message."

"I thought you'd be halfway back to New Orleans by now," Sabine said to Beau.

"You didn't tell her you were staying in the hotel?" Mildred asked.

"You're staying at the hotel?" Sabine repeated. "Since when?"

Beau paused for a moment before answering. "I checked in three days ago."

Sabine frowned at Mildred. "You knew this and didn't tell me?"

Mildred raised her hands in protest. "I didn't know who he was until tonight. Darn near ran me over getting to your apartment when he heard the sirens. You know I wouldn't keep something like that from you, Sabine." Mildred shot a dirty look at Beau. "You didn't tell me you were lying to her."

"I wasn't lying, exactly." He stepped next to the bed and looked down at Sabine. "That break-in at your place worried me. I just didn't like the sound of it, but then I've been accused of being paranoid, so I didn't want to get you riled up in case it turned out to be nothing."

"So you thought you'd spy on me for a couple of days, then let me know if you thought I was in danger...something I might have needed to know before tonight. Where the hell is that doctor?" Sabine flashed an angry glance at the door to her room, agitated that they were keeping her waiting.

Beau ran one hand through his hair. "I swear, Sabine. If I'd thought...I didn't know..."

"Stop," Sabine said. "I'll decide how I feel about all this after I find out what happened to me. For all we know, this might be nothing."

"Nothing?" Mildred said. "You were unconscious. It's a miracle you dialed 911 before you passed out. That can't be nothing."

"She's right," a voice sounded from the doorway.

They all turned to look at the young doctor who had entered the room. "I'm Dr. Mitchell. I just started here last week. I would say it's a pleasure to meet you all, but I'm certain we'd all rather it be under different circumstances." He smiled at Sabine. "You are one lucky lady. The paramedics are amazed you managed to dial for help given the state you were in when they arrived. And since I'm assuming none of us would like a repeat performance, we're going to have to rethink your dinner choices."

Sabine stared at the doctor. "What are you talking about? I had a roast beef sandwich, same as yesterday."

The doctor studied her. "Any dessert? Cookies, perhaps? A brownie?"

"I took a glass of wine and some sugar cookies to bed."

"We had cookies at the Fortescues', too," Beau reminded her.

"You had cookies. I moved two of mine onto your plate so no one would think I was being rude when I didn't eat them."

Beau gave her a surprised look. "I didn't even notice."

Sabine rolled her eyes. "Some detective."

The doctor narrowed his eyes at her. "You're certain. You've had nothing else to eat or drink since lunch but your sugar cookies and wine?"

"Of course I'm certain. What is this about? You're starting to worry me."

"You had an allergic reaction," the doctor replied. "The kind of reaction that can kill people."

"Peanuts? You're saying peanuts caused this?" She shook her head. "I know I'm allergic to peanuts—have known forever and I promise you I avoid them like the plague. Why do you think I didn't eat the cookies when they were served? I don't take any chances. There is no way I ate a peanut, not even accidentally. I cooked the roast beef myself yesterday and have eaten three meals from it now. The bottle of wine was brand new. I opened it last night."

"And the cookies?" the doctor asked.

"I made them," Mildred said. "A couple of days ago, and I assure you they didn't contain peanut oil. I'm allergic to peanuts myself and I've been eating those cookies ever since I baked them."

Sabine stared at the doctor. "You must be mistaken."

"I was with her from mid-afternoon until last night through supper," Beau added. "She only had the roast beef and a bottled water for supper."

"And the wine," the doctor asked Beau. "Did you drink any as well?"

"No," Beau said and looked a little embarrassed. "I left before Ms. LeVeche retired for the night."

"Where did you get the wine, Ms. LeVeche, and is it a brand you drink regularly?"

"Yes, it's my favorite zinfandel, and Mildred gave it to me day before yesterday. Mildred, Maryse, and I like the same brand, but it's not sold here in Mudbug, so anyone who's going to New Orleans usually picks up a bottle or two when they're there."

The doctor turned to Mildred. "Do you remember where you bought the wine?"

Mildred nodded. "Sure. At Bayou Beverages just on the highway before you get to the city. Why? Is that important?"

"It could be if someone else reports a problem." The doctor made a note in his file. "Who else knows about your allergy?"

"Everyone," Sabine replied. "Everyone in Mudbug, anyway. The restaurants are very careful with my food preparation and no one ever brings me Christmas goodies with nuts. I figured keeping something like that a secret was bound to be trouble."

Dr. Mitchell nodded. "And usually it is, but I wonder if this time it didn't work against you."

Sabine felt a wave of cold wash over her. She wasn't sure what he was getting at, but she was certain she wasn't going to like it. "Surely, you're wrong, Dr. Mitchell," Sabine said, trying to clutch onto a reasonable explanation. "Maybe something else…a spider bite or something simple like an anxiety attack?"

The doctor shook his head. "I'm not mistaken. The symptoms are textbook and the tests showed peanut oil in your stomach." He looked at Beau and Mildred, then back at Sabine, obviously nervous. "Ms. LeVeche, I don't know how to say this any other way, but since you and your friend are certain of your dietary intake, I think you need to contact the police. They're going to want to search your apartment and test that bottle of wine and the food."

Sabine stared at the doctor in shock. "The police? Test my food?"

The doctor nodded. "There is a chance the wine was somehow tainted before the sale, but I honestly can't imagine peanut oil being any part of the process for wine-making, so it's a real long shot. And you need to start considering who might have the access and the desire to do something like this. Any new business associates, friends, a slighted customer…the police are going to want to know."

Sabine tried to answer, but her voice caught in her throat. The only new things in her life were Beau and her family. Surely Beau had no reason at all to harm her; in fact, he'd been trying to tell her that digging up the past might not be a good idea. But her family?

They barely knew her, so it was highly unlikely they knew about her allergies. Besides, she wasn't asking them for anything and didn't want anything, except to gain a better knowledge of her parents. Hell, Catherine had been the one suggesting the Fortescues fund a new business for Sabine that was apparently more "worthy" of the grand family name.

Sabine took a drink of water and tried to keep her hand from shaking. "I…I don't really know what to say."

"The doctor's right," Beau said. "If you ingested peanuts, it probably wasn't an accident. I'll call the police and get them over to your apartment and have them send someone here to get all the information from you. Tell them to talk to me afterward. I can provide all the details on the new people in your life."

Sabine shook her head. "I'm not about to let the police tromp around my apartment, digging through my drawers, taking inventory of my stuff. And not for nothing, but the Mudbug police still haven't come up with anything on the break-in or the lurker I kicked. I seriously doubt they'd have any idea what to do about a poisoning." Especially since the small matter of Helena Henry's poisoning had seemed to fly right past both the police and the doctors. Sabine's odds did not look good with the "experts" of Mudbug on the case.

"Now, Sabine," Mildred said, "I think you ought to listen to the doctor, and to Beau."

"Fine," Sabine said. "If the hospital will release me, I'll take care of everything with the police."

Dr. Mitchell shook his head. "I'm sorry, Ms. LeVeche, but I can't do that. We really need to monitor you overnight to ensure nothing else is wrong. I'm not trying to scare you, but you had a major attack. Quite frankly, you're lucky to be alive. If the paramedics had been just a couple of minutes later…"

"I'll contact the police and meet them at your apartment," Beau offered. "I'll oversee everything. Make sure they do a thorough job. I have connections in New Orleans. I'll make sure anything that needs to be tested is sent to a lab there."

Sabine sighed, feeling her independence slipping away.

Beau held one hand up. "I promise I won't go through your panty drawer."

Mildred shook her head. "She doesn't have a panty drawer. What her and Maryse have against covering their rear, I simply don't know."

Sabine groaned and pulled the sheet up over her head, but not before seeing the embarrassment on the doctor's face and the grin on Beau's. "Get out of here, all of you, before I just go ahead and die to escape it all." It was bad enough that all the medical personnel of Mudbug General already had a good idea of her feelings about undergarments.

She heard Beau laugh and Mildred said, "I'll go with Beau and let them into your apartment. I'll be back as soon as we're done with the police. Don't worry about a thing. You just work on getting better."

Sabine waited until she heard the door close, then pulled the sheet down and thought over everything that had happened that day. "What the hell is going on?" she asked out loud.

"I don't know," Helena answered, making her jump.

"Jesus," Sabine said, sucking in a breath. "I didn't know you were still here."

"Can you still see me?"

Sabine nodded. "The John Lennon thing still isn't working for me. Why did you come back?"

"I thought maybe someone ought to keep an eye on you and since the others all left..."

"What could possibly happen in the hospital?"

"Hmmmm, well, although I started to feel weird after I drank that brandy, technically, I was in the hospital when I died," Helena said.

Sabine stared at the wall. "Shit."

"But having an overnight stay here does give us all sorts of other possibilities."

"Like what?" Sabine didn't like the sound of that at all.

"Oh, I was thinking that taking a peek at the medical records of the Fortescues might be a good idea. Obviously someone's out of their damned mind because I can't think of anyone else who'd want to kill you. Maybe if we read their medical records, we can see if there's any history of mental illness."

"Oh, no. Maryse already did that breaking-and-entering medical-records search with you and it wasn't exactly an overwhelming success."

"Yeah, but this time there's no breaking or entering. That's over half the battle. Besides, don't tell me you're not just a little interested in getting a peek at those records. You're still looking for a match, right? You might just get two possible answers with one small, unobtrusive trip down the hall."

Sabine bit her lower lip. Any other time, she would never, ever agree with what Helena was saying, but the ghost did have a point. If someone had tried to poison her, the medical records might indeed give her the clue she needed to identify who it was. And it certainly wouldn't hurt to look for their blood types while she was at it. A matching blood type didn't mean a bone marrow match, but it was a good start.

Shit.

"Okay," she said before she could change her mind. "We'll do this tonight."

"If you don't want to risk it, I understand. I can get the files myself and bring them to you."

"Oh, no! I am not going to have a repeat of the New Orleans police department on my hands. There aren't any hotdog stands in the hospital to cover up your exit, and hospital carts do not move themselves down the hallways, especially on level ground."

"Fine, if you're going to get all picky and geographical on me. You're still going to need a key, though. The lock on that door is a deadbolt and doesn't open from the inside."

Sabine threw her hands in the air in frustration. "Then what are we even talking about this for? I don't have the keys and wouldn't know the first thing about picking a lock."

"Oh, I can get them."

Sabine groaned, knowing from the sound of her voice that Helena's offer would come with strings attached. "Out with it, Helena. What do you want?"

"Well, I just figured that while we were in the records room you might be able to get a copy of my autopsy report."

Sabine narrowed her eyes. "Is that all?"

"Scout's honor." Helena worked up her best sincere look.

Sabine frowned. It sounded so simple. Copy a couple of sheets of paper in exchange for a set of keys. Unfortunately, she already knew that anything involving Helena was never easy or without consequences.

Helena or the Mudbug police. Her two options for solving a crime.

Sabine sighed. "What time should we do this?"

Chapter Eleven

It was two more long hours and after three a.m. before Sabine was transferred to a private room. The entire time, Helena had been champing at the bit—and a bag of beef jerky from the vending machine. Watching the ghost inhale the dried meat, Sabine couldn't help thinking people should be very, very careful what they wished for.

All her life she'd wanted to see a ghost, and she'd gotten Helena.

All her life she'd wanted to find her family, and now it looked like it might have been better—and safer—if she hadn't.

All her life she'd wanted to find "the" guy. The guy who made her heart skip a beat, who made her skin tingle with the slightest touch, who made her palms sweat when he looked at her. And in he'd walked, just after she'd been given a potential death sentence by cancer, and a much more probable one by poisoning unless they got a grip, and fast, on what the hell was going on.

Sabine pushed herself out of the wheelchair and slid into her new hospital bed with a sigh. The nurse gave her a critical eye for a couple of seconds, then went about the business of checking her blood pressure for the hundredth time since she'd been brought to the hospital. She'd been too critical of Maryse, Sabine decided. She'd accused her friend of avoiding life, of avoiding relationships, especially when Luc had come on the scene. It wasn't like her accusations were untrue, but now that Sabine found herself in a frightening similar position—her world upside down, everything she'd known as fact now in question, her life in danger, and a veritable Adonis just waiting for the word—she regretted having ever pushed her friend.

The overload to her emotional and mental systems was staggering, and although she'd thought it was as high as possible, Sabine's respect for Maryse shot up even another notch. As soon as she saw her friend, she was going to give her a huge hug, a high five, and an apology. Then she was going to demand her secret. How the hell had she handled all this pressure without exploding?

The nurse removed the cuff and made some notes on her file. "I'll be back in a couple of hours. Try to get some sleep." She pulled the covers up on the bed, flipped out the lights, and left the room.

"Thanffkt Godfft," Helena said, her mouth full of jerky. She paused for a minute and swallowed. "I thought she'd never leave. Are you ready?"

"No, but that's totally irrelevant, isn't it? Do you have the key?"

Helena nodded. "Swiped it from the front desk." She tugged at the key ring wedged in the front pocket of her entirely too-tight blue jeans and finally managed to wrench it loose while pushing up the bottom of her spandex tank top by two inches and at least three stomach rolls. "I should probably change into something loose and comfortable for the mission, right?"

"You should probably change into something loose and comfortable because I can see you."

Helena glared at Sabine. "You skinny broads are all the same. You don't think fat people should dress fashionably."

"No. I don't think fat people should show their fat. There are plenty of fashionable tops that don't let your stomach hang out."

Helena stuck out her tongue, complete with partially-chewed jerky. "Anorexic."

"Glutton."

Helena grinned. "You got me there, but damn, do you realize I've eaten over six thousand calories a day for the past week and haven't gained a pound? How many people get that opportunity?"

"You could also jump off the roof of the hospital and not die, but I don't see you racing up the stairs to try that."

"Where the hell's the fun in that? I'm just doing things I would have liked to do while I was alive. I don't recall ever wanting to jump off a building, although I would have probably pushed a person or two." Helena frowned for a moment, and then her face brightened. "Hey, what do you think the odds are I could find a way to have sex? I didn't do hardly any of that while I was alive. And now I wouldn't have to worry about getting one of those CDs or anything."

Sabine closed her eyes and counted to five. "STDs, and no, I am not about to start an escort service for the dead. It would be fraught with misery and no profit at all." Sabine went to the door and peeked outside. "It's clear. Let's just get this over with."

She stepped out into the hall, and a second later Helena strolled through the wall to join her. Sabine took one look at the ghost's new wardrobe creation and almost choked. Helena glared and went off down the hall, the full nun's habit she wore giving her the appearance of gliding. Sabine stared after her in dismay. The fat rolls were covered, sure, but somewhere in the heavens, Jesus was surely crying.

Sabine made the sign of the cross and followed Helena down the hall.

Since Sabine had been placed on the second floor, they opted for the stairs over the elevator, figuring it was the safest option to avoid detection. At the end of the hall, Helena motioned for Sabine to stop while she stepped around. "It's clear," Helena said and waved her on. "The records room is at the end of this hall. I hope this time goes better than last."

Sabine's mind raced with arguments against what she was about to do, but her feet continued to move, one in front of the other, until finally she was at the end of the hall, standing behind the largest penguin she'd ever seen and watching her struggle with the ancient lock.

"Finally," Helena said when the lock turned at last. She pushed the door open and slipped inside, Sabine close behind. "The Dead records are on the last row. Guess that's sorta fitting. All the living assholes are on the first three. You start there and get some dirt on the Fortescues. I'm going to find my autopsy report."

Sabine cringed. Dead records. That was rude.

Sabine slipped to the front row and looked down the rows of shelves until she'd located the F's. Field…Fontaine…Fox. She looked beyond Fox but the Fu's had started. She looked more closely, pulled each file out a little from the shelf. At the spot where the Fortescues' files should have been, assuming there were any at this hospital, there was a single sheet of bright orange paper. Sabine pulled the paper from the shelf and saw that it contained a list of every member of the Fortescue family, alive and dead, and some she'd never heard of. Cousins, she supposed.

But where were the records? There must have been files at some time. Otherwise, why have a sheet of paper marking this spot? Sabine could understand medical personnel pulling a single file in order to treat a patient, but an entire family? That was just weird.

A sudden thought flashed through her mind and she moved to the next row. Landry…Lattimer…LeVeche. She pulled her file from the stack and opened it. She frowned at the results of her biopsy, but as she flipped through the file, everything seemed in order. Maybe the Fortescue files had been checked out for review.

She stepped over to the medical records manager's desk and went through the files stacked on top. Nothing. She was just about to give up when she saw a sliver of orange peeking out from under a stack of paper in the In box. Sabine pulled the orange paper from the box and began to read, her heart beating faster as she read. It was an inventory of files stolen during the hospital break-in. There were a bunch of names on the list, but the ones that stood out to Sabine all ended in Fortescue. Everyone in Mudbug had assumed it was junkies that had broken into the hospital; only Sabine didn't see any drugs on the list of missing items. Just medical records.

It wasn't possible. The hospital break-in happened before she knew about the Fortescues, before Beau knew, before he'd even been hired. Something was very, very wrong with all of this. It couldn't possibly be random.

"Hey." Helena's voice caused her to jump. "I need your help here." Helena shoved a file in Sabine's face. "The autopsy report is there, but I don't understand all that medical mumbo jumbo. Can you take a look and jot down the important things? That way if you don't understand it either, we'll have something to show to Maryse."

Sabine nodded, trying to get a grip on the situation. The last thing she wanted to do was let Helena in on more than she already knew. And Sabine needed to make some sense of everything before she could formulate an opinion, much less a plan. She took the file from Helena and sat down at the desk, pulling a legal pad and pen toward her.

She read the first line of the autopsy report and sucked in a breath.

"What's wrong?" Helena asked. "What does it say? I don't understand, Sabine. What killed me?"

Sabine continued to read down on the report, growing more surprised with every word. "I've got to write this down. Maryse will understand it better than I do."

Helena stared at her. "But you know something. I saw that look on your face. There's something in that file you didn't expect to see. Why won't you tell me what it is?"

Sabine shook her head and wrote furiously. "I can't be sure. I think I'm confusing my terminology and I don't want to tell you the wrong thing. Let's just get it all down and talk to Maryse. Okay?" Helena didn't look the least bit convinced, but she didn't argue either.

Sabine continued to write, word for word, everything in the report. Maybe by the time she talked to Maryse she'd have come up with a way to tell Helena that the autopsy had found no sign of foul play.

And that Helena had been dying of cancer.

Sabine stood at the hospital room window. The sun was just beginning to rise, casting an orange glow over the marsh. She'd barely slept, only managing ten-minute increments, and was positive she looked as bad as she felt. The nurse had already been in to check on her and promised to bring breakfast in directly. Sabine could hardly wait. Hospital food was so tasty. She'd just decided that a shower might not be a bad idea when Helena came huffing into the room, still wearing the habit, and threw a stack of files behind a recliner in the corner. Before Sabine could get a word out of her mouth, the nurse bustled in with Sabine's breakfast. Sabine glanced over at Helena, who'd collapsed in the recliner wheezing like she'd just run the New York marathon, and tried not to even think about what Helena had tossed behind the chair.

Sabine excused herself to the bathroom, hoping it would hurry the cheerful, chatty nurse along. It probably took all of a minute before she heard the door close, but it felt like hours. Sabine stepped out of the bathroom to find Helena sitting up in her bed, a half-eaten pancake dangling from the plastic fork.

"You know," Helena said as she shoved the other half of the pancake in her mouth. "Hospital food isn't near as bad as I remember." She stabbed a half-cooked sausage with the fork and wolfed it down.

"You have a serious problem. This is just so not normal."

Helena rolled her eyes and poked at the scrambled eggs. It lifted in one big blob. "The fake psychic is telling me this isn't normal. Hell, you think I hadn't already figured that out?"

"I don't mean this as in everything, I mean this"—she pointed to the empty plate—"is not normal. Dead people do not need to eat. Dead people shouldn't even want to eat. Ghosts should not develop addictions, Helena."

Helena gulped down the coffee, then belched. "Guess ghosts shouldn't lose their manners either, huh? But what the hell. You're the only one who can hear me."

Sabine closed her eyes and counted to ten, trying to keep herself from wishing that she or Maryse had strangled Helena when she was alive. At least then they could have said they deserved having Helena haunt them from beyond.

Sabine peeked behind the recliner. Just as she'd feared, there was a stack of files that look suspiciously like those she'd seen in the records room the night before. "What did you do, Helena?"

Helena, who had been licking residual syrup off the breakfast plate, placed the now spotless plastic dish on the table. "Just some files I thought we'd need." She swirled her finger around the inside of the coffee cup, then licked it.

Sabine felt her jaw clench involuntarily. "What files? Damn it, Helena! I wrote down everything we needed last night. Why would you take more? They'll send me to jail if they find those files in here. What were you thinking? And why aren't you saying anything?"

The ghost had gone strangely silent and it took a second for Sabine to realize that she was glancing at the doorway. Sabine whirled around, fully expecting to find the chatty nurse calling for a straitjacket and police backup, and let out a breath of relief when she saw Raissa standing in the doorway, a curious expression on her face.

"Raissa, thank God!" Sabine collapsed into the recliner, what little was remaining of her energy completely drained. "I thought for sure I was on my way to a padded room or jail, whichever one had available space. What are you doing here?"

Raissa stepped into the room and closed the door behind her. "Maryse called me. She got held up at the airport in Houston and thought you might need to hear a voice of reason since Mildred called yelling at her twice last night."

"Mildred yelled at Maryse?" Sabine stared at Raissa. "What in the world for?"

Raissa smiled. "Apparently this attempt on your life is all Maryse's fault because she went and tried to get killed first and you always want to do everything Maryse does."

Sabine groaned. "I wanted to do everything Maryse did in second grade. I haven't wanted to since. Well, except that one time I saw Luc walk out of the shower wearing nothing but a towel. I have to admit that Maryse definitely got that one right."

Raissa laughed. "I confess to a lingering bit of jealousy myself. Not only is the man hot, but he's so obviously over the moon for Maryse. Makes you want one of your own."

"Only for a moment. Once they put their clothes on, then there's bills to pay and work to do and in-laws to deal with, and we all know how that in-law thing worked out for Maryse the first time." Sabine glared at Helena.

Raissa followed Sabine's gaze and studied the hospital bed. "I take it the ghost is here? Either that or you are on some really good drugs and your bed is incredibly lumpy."

"Oh yeah," Sabine said. "She's here in all her glory—every should-be-expanding pound of her."

Helena jumped off the bed. "I don't have to take this abuse." She stalked out of the room.

Sabine gave a silent prayer of thanks and reported Helena's exit to Raissa.

"Well, since I'm pretty sure you're not going to be arrested for having someone else eat your hospital food, do you want to tell me what she stole?" Raissa said.

"Hospital records." Sabine pointed over her head and behind the recliner. "She threw them behind the chair when the nurse came in. I am going straight to jail if they catch me with these files in my room."

Helena stuck her head in through the wall. "Please," she said. "Like you wouldn't have been in trouble if we'd got caught in the records room last night. You weren't whining when it was about you."

"Breaking into the records room is not the same as stealing the records," Sabine shot back, but she seriously doubted her voice carried the same conviction as her words. "Don't you have a buffet to conquer?"

Helena gave her the finger and popped back out the wall.

"And take off that habit," Sabine yelled after her. "It's sacrilegious."

Raissa raised her eyebrows, and Sabine remembered the psychic could only hear one side of the conversation. "We sorta helped ourselves to the medical records room last night."

"And it required wearing habits?" Raissa shook her head. "Never mind. I don't think I want to know. What were you looking for exactly? Or is this answer going to be as bad as the habit one?"

"I wanted to check the files on my family."

"You were hoping to find one with a 'psychotic killer' notation on it?" Raissa asked.

"No. I mean, I was kinda hoping for some indication of instability or something. I thought that might narrow things down a bit."

"And you're certain your family is the problem?"

"Yes, no…I don't know. All I know is my family is the only thing new in my life, well, except Helena, so I figured it has to have something to do with them. And they'd have to be crazy to want to kill me, because I'm not asking for anything…yet, and even if I get around to it, it's not going to be money. I've already turned down a business loan from Catherine."

"Sounds reasonable—in the sort of reason you and Maryse have taken to since Helena appeared. So what did you find?"

Sabine frowned. "Nothing."

"No crazy people?"

"No. No records."

Raissa stared at her. "The only doctors in the town have their offices here, right? Are there any in the Fortescues' town?"

"Not anymore," Sabine said. "The last doctor retired years ago and has never been replaced."

"Then their records should have been transferred here. Unless you think they went all the way to New Orleans to see the doctor."

Sabine shook her head. "Their records were apparently here at one time. But on the shelf where all the Fortescue files should have been was this orange piece of paper with a list of their names."

"So someone checked them out?"

"That's what I thought at first, but when I shuffled through the manager's desk, I found a sheet of paper listing all the files that were stolen in the hospital break-in a couple of weeks ago." Sabine felt a chill run through her. "There were other people's names on the list, but they didn't appear related. Except for the

Fortescues. But Raissa, no one knew we were related then—not me, you, them—you hadn't even hired Beau when the break-in happened."

Raissa narrowed her eyes. "You're right. That's very strange."

"It can't be a coincidence. Not after this."

Raissa shook her head, her expression thoughtful. "No, I don't believe it's a coincidence, but I can't put the pieces together, either. I'll do a reading this afternoon and let you know if I come up with something."

"Thanks."

"So…if your family files were missing, what did Helena steal?"

Sabine groaned. "I don't even know. She ran into the room just ahead of the nurse. It's a miracle the nurse didn't see a floating file display. How in the world would I have explained that one?" Sabine rose from the chair and reached for the files.

Raissa smiled. "And just think—you're supposed to be equipped to deal with the dead."

"No one could be prepared for Helena," Sabine said as she stood back up, files in hand. "The Spartans couldn't have prepared for Helena. You know, I'm not really sure she didn't pass over. I'm starting to think Satan couldn't handle her either so he sent her back."

Raissa laughed. "Well, the next time you or Helena need to procure some illegal data, let me know and I'll loan you my scanner."

"Scanner?"

"Yeah, a scanner," Raissa said. "Mine is small—just big enough for a sheet of paper, and really thin and portable. You could scan all the documents Helena stole onto a USB, then review them at your leisure on your home computer. No hand cramps, floating file scares, or habits required."

"I never even thought about something like that. You constantly amaze me with your grip on technology."

"Hey, the spirits don't help with filing and I don't want to rent storage. Digital file cabinets are the way to go." Raissa walked over to Sabine and gave her a hug. "I'm going to clear out. I want to talk to Beau before I head back to New Orleans and open the shop. You let me know if you need anything. Promise?"

Sabine nodded. "Promise."

Raissa gave her a wave and left the room. Sabine looked down at the files, then frowned when she saw who the records belonged to—Helena's family. Why in the world would Helena want those? Her parents were long dead—they couldn't possibly have killed her.

Sabine shoved the files in her overnight bag and zipped it shut. Helena wouldn't be able to return them until nighttime. Which would give Sabine plenty of time to ask the ghost what the hell was going on.

Chapter Twelve

It was past sunrise before Beau finished up with the Mudbug police, locked up Sabine's apartment, and loaded the evidence bagged for testing in his truck. Logic told him that Sabine had to have been poisoned in her apartment and most likely by something she consumed that night, but for the life of him, Beau couldn't figure out how anyone had gotten inside. There was no sign of forced entry on any of the doors or windows, and since the property manager had gotten approval to replace the locks after the break-in on both the front and back doors, anyone who'd previously had a key was out of luck.

Someone could have jimmied the lock, but the new technology would have been extremely difficult for anyone but a professional. There was always the locksmith to consider, but the company the property manager used was based out of New Orleans and had been in business forever. Still, Beau supposed he would talk to someone there after he finished at the lab.

He was just climbing in the truck when he heard Mildred yelling from across the street. The hotel owner came running toward him, clutching a stack of white Styrofoam boxes. "I was hoping to catch you before you left for the hospital. Can you give me a ride?"

"Sure," Beau said and motioned her into the truck, "but I thought you were driving Sabine home after they released her."

"I was," Mildred said, her face flushed with the exertion. "Doggone battery on my car is dead again. It's happened four times now in the past two weeks, but I haven't had time to get another. I don't need the car that often, so I've been borrowing Sabine's, but in all the excitement, I've misplaced my spare key."

"Do you need some help?" Beau pointed to the stack of boxes, about to topple as Mildred struggled with the seat belt.

"What—oh, no, thank you." She clicked the belt into place and righted the boxes. "I got breakfast for all of us over at the café. I figured you haven't had time to get anything, same as me, and I know my Sabine. She's not going to eat any of that hospital food."

"I don't blame her," Beau said as he started down the highway to the hospital. "So do you need me to give the two of you a ride home?"

"No. You've got much more important business to take care of in New Orleans. I'll get Sabine's keys from her and have one of my friends give me a lift home. Then I'll come back for Sabine."

"You sure you have time? I can't imagine Sabine is going to sit in that hospital one minute longer than required, even if it means walking home."

Mildred laughed. "You got my girl pegged, all right. But not to worry. They won't release her before noon. Dr. Breaux doesn't make rounds as early as he used to and even though that Dr. Mitchell seemed sharp, Dr. Breaux's probably going to want to see Sabine himself."

"Dr. Breaux's the local?"

"Yes. In his seventies and still kicking." She shifted in her seat to stare at Beau. "So are you planning on taking care of my girl?"

Beau gave a start and glanced over at Mildred. "Depends on what you mean by taking care of. I'm going to find out who's trying to hurt her, and I'm going to do my damndest to see that whoever it is doesn't get another shot."

Mildred sighed. "Why do you young people make everything so difficult? I've seen the way you look at her. You darn near ran me over trying to get to her apartment last night, and the way you were shouting questions at those paramedics…all I'm saying is it looked like a lot more than concern for a client to me."

Beau groaned inwardly. Was his attraction to Sabine really that apparent, or was the hotel owner just fishing and hoping? Either way, Beau wasn't about to accommodate her. Sabine's rejection was embarrassing enough kept between the two of them. He wasn't about to share it with anyone else.

"I look at her like a cop does a potential victim. I was FBI, remember? And I'm not about to lose a client…not on my watch. I'm going to protect Sabine, but once I know what's going on here and the guilty party is in jail, then my job is done."

Mildred studied him for a moment. "Your job, huh? Okay then."

Beau glanced over at her as he pulled in to the hospital parking lot and knew he hadn't fooled her for a minute. But at least she'd stopped pressing the issue. For the moment.

Sabine was sitting cross-legged on the end of her hospital bed watching television when they walked into her room. Beau took one look at her and felt his heart leap. Never before had he wanted to gather someone in his arms and hide them away from the world to protect them. He'd known he was lying to Mildred when he'd told her that Sabine was another victim he was trying to protect, but he hadn't realized quite how much he was lying.

He swore the room got brighter when she smiled at them. He blinked once, certain he was seeing things, but reality was perched on the end of the bed, so obviously happy to see them. Beau managed a weak hello as Mildred dropped her breakfast box on the table and gathered Sabine for a hug. Beau placed the boxes on the tray next to the bed and tried to get a grip.

It simply wasn't fair, he decided. No one should look that good, ever. Much less after being poisoned, almost dying, and spending the night in a hospital, which contrary to what it should be was never restful. No makeup, a drab green hospital gown, her hair tied in some strange-looking knot on top of her head, and she was still gorgeous. Why couldn't Raissa have been friends with a sixty-year-old retired librarian or something?

Mildred finally released Sabine and pointed to an empty hospital food tray on a small table next to a recliner. "Don't tell me you ate that garbage?"

Sabine looked momentarily guilty. "Not a chance. I dumped it down the toilet. Didn't want the nurse to make a fuss. Besides, I knew you wouldn't let me starve."

"Darn straight," Mildred said and pulled a couple of sodas out of her handbag. "Pancakes and sausage for everyone. You two go ahead and start. I'm going to check with the nurse and see what time they'll be releasing you." She handed Beau a box and gave him a wink.

"Oh, and Sabine," Mildred said as she paused at the door. "I must have dislodged your gown when I hugged you. Your heinie is showing." She grinned and left the room.

It was an involuntary reaction, and God knows he should have figured out some way to stop it, but Beau couldn't help looking at Sabine's butt. Her face blushed ten shades of red as she grabbed the hospital gown and tugged it together in the back, but not before he saw the silky smooth curve of her bottom peeking out.

Sabine groaned. "She'll use this forever as a reason I should wear underwear."

Beau grinned. "Hard to argue with her at the moment. Not that I'm agreeing, mind you."

Sabine looked over at Beau and shook her head. "You know, normally I would have gone into hiding over something like this. The fact that flashing a man with my bare butt is the least of my problems is a real testament to just how screwed up my life is at the moment."

"A butt like that should never be hidden away. Statues should be erected in its honor."

Sabine's lips quivered with amusement. "Maybe I won't die of embarrassment today, then. So are you hungry?"

"Starved." He just wasn't saying for what.

She patted the bed. "You can sit on the bed with me if you'd like," Sabine suggested as she uncrossed her legs and turned to the side. "The table is long enough for both of us to use it."

Beau swallowed when Sabine said the word "bed" but took a seat next to her and pulled the table in front of them. "How are you feeling?"

"How do I look? I mean the rest of me, not just my butt."

He choked on his soda and set the can on the table. "Great. You look great."

"For an almost dead woman, you mean?"

To hell with it. Beau looked directly at Sabine. "You're beautiful. A little paler, perhaps, a little tired around the eyes, but otherwise just as beautiful as you were yesterday and the day before."

Sabine's eyes widened and for a couple of seconds said absolutely nothing. The room was so quiet that Beau could hear the ticking of his watch. Shit, shit, shit, shit...it seemed to echo in his mind.

Finally, she gave him a shy smile. "That's the nicest thing anyone has ever said to me. Thank you."

Beau shook his head. "I wasn't saying it to make you feel better. Damn it, Sabine, you're a beautiful, desirable woman, and any man who doesn't see that is stupid or blind. I'm neither."

"No," she agreed. "You're definitely not the stupid one in this equation." She sighed. "Before Mildred gets back and more importantly, before I say something I'll regret, I need to tell you about something I did last night."

Beau felt a momentary wave of disappointment, but it was quickly gone. As much as he would love to hear Sabine say something she'd regret, the fact that she'd apparently done something the night before that she didn't want the hotel owner to know about had him intrigued. "Okay. Shoot."

Sabine took a breath. "I snuck into the medical records room last night, hoping to get some background information on my family."

Of all the things she could have said, this wasn't even on the list. "You broke into the medical records room?"

"No, it was unlocked," Sabine said, but the look on her face immediately told him that she wasn't being completely honest.

"Okaaay," Beau said, deciding it was easier to let however she'd gained access to the room slide. "And did you find out anything?"

Sabine told him about the missing files and the corresponding list.

"Wow." Beau shook his head, trying to wrap his mind around the information Sabine had given him and the repercussions it had on his investigation. "I don't even know what to think."

"Me either."

"I don't like it." Beau turned to face Sabine. "You've been looking for your family for years. Even if someone has always known you're related to the Fortescues, why go after their medical records right before you hired me? I could understand if this had happened after I started poking around, but this makes no sense at all."

"I wish I knew, but I've run through every possible scenario and there's simply nothing I've done recently or in the past to warrant this kind of action. Unless it was a past life." She gave Beau a shaky smile.

"You're not safe in your apartment," Beau said. "Until we figure out what's going on, I don't think you should stay there."

"It's my home, Beau. I have to stay there."

Beau shook his head, ready to argue. "I couldn't find a single sign of forced entry. That means whoever got in had a key. Even if I installed deadbolts only on the inside of the doors, I still wouldn't think it was safe. Someone is too close…their access is far too free." He took in a breath and before he could change his mind said, "Let me stay with you. I can sleep on the couch."

Sabine instantly shook her head. "No way!"

"I promise I won't do anything to make you uncomfortable. I won't even tell you you're beautiful."

"I can't. I can't have you in my space that way. My apartment is tiny. There's no way I could feel comfortable staying there with you even if you were a mute. This isn't about you, Beau, it's about me. You scare me." She ran one hand across the top of her head. "Not like the someone trying to kill me scares me. The way you make me feel scares me. I'm afraid if I cross that line with you, there's no return, and a future between the two of us is filled with impossibilities, most of which you don't even know about."

"So explain them to me."

"No. There are certain things I can't talk to you about."

"Can't or won't?"

"Doesn't matter. You're going to have to take my word for it."

Beau struggled to hold in his frustration. Why was she making things so hard? She felt the same pull that he did. Why was she struggling so hard against it? And why are you pushing so hard for it? "Fine. Then at least consider staying at the hotel until this is settled. That way you can have your own private space, but Mildred and I are close by to keep watch."

Sabine was silent for a moment, then nodded. "I'd feel better knowing you and Mildred were close."

"Just not too close and only me."

Sabine looked down at the bed. "No," she said, her voice barely a whisper.

Beau rose from the bed. "Then I guess since we got all that decided, I'll take off. I've got to drop off the stuff for testing at a lab in New Orleans, and then there's a couple of other things I want to look into before I come back. I'll see you sometime this evening, okay?"

Sabine looked up at him and nodded. "Thanks, Beau. For everything."

"You're welcome," he said and left the room before he did something even more stupid than telling her how beautiful she was. Like kiss her.

Again.

It was after noon before Sabine was ensconced in a room at the hotel. It had been a relief to find that Beau had kept the Mudbug police's destruction of her apartment to a minimum, but it was still going to take hours to get everything back where she wanted it. Since she wouldn't be living there anyway for the time being, she supposed it shouldn't matter. She'd endured almost an hour of Mildred's puttering around the hotel room, bringing her some soup and crackers for lunch, fluffing her pillows, and generally treating her like an invalid, but Sabine understood that Mildred wouldn't feel good unless she thought she was doing something to help.

Finally, Mildred had gone downstairs to balance the books, and Sabine was left in the peace and quiet she'd been waiting for. She grabbed one of the four tote bags she'd packed and pulled out the hospital files that Helena had stolen. Raissa had gladly agreed to loan her the scanner and would meet Beau somewhere in New Orleans so that he could bring it back with him that afternoon or evening, whenever he managed to finish up and return to Mudbug. Sabine figured as long as the files were already stolen she might as well get a copy of everything. If nothing else, it would save the trouble of ever having to break into the hospital records room again.

Sabine already knew what Maryse was going to say. Maryse had warned her nine ways to Sunday about Helena and her shenanigans, and Sabine was just starting to get a clear view of the problem. Helena was definitely a pro. She came out with these outlandish requests when she knew you were at a personal low and somehow made them seem completely logical and necessary. Then when the dust had settled, you were left wondering how you'd gone temporarily insane.

Sabine opened Helena's folder and started to read the autopsy report again. She hadn't been mistaken—Helena definitely had cancer, and it was very advanced. In fact, Sabine doubted the woman would have had more than six months to live. She flipped past the autopsy report and through the other papers in Helena's file. This file only contained the last ten years, but it was a revealing ten years. Helena had asthma and her blood pressure was borderline, but otherwise, she'd been deemed healthy at every checkup. If she'd been sick with colds or the flu or the occasional virus, she hadn't been to the doctor for them.

And there was absolutely no other note about the cancer other than the autopsy.

Which made no sense. Helena should have had some symptoms—dizziness, lethargy, pain. If the cancer had been caught soon enough, she most likely would have been given a round of chemo, then progressed to the radiation treatments. If that didn't work, she would have been a candidate for a marrow transplant, like Sabine. But apparently, no one had known.

Sabine closed the file and bit her lower lip. Could Helena really have ignored the symptoms that easily? Or even stranger—could she have really lived with cancer advanced to the stage it had and had no symptoms at all? Was that possible? She was just about to open Hank's file when Maryse burst into the room.

"Are you all right? What did the doctor say? What did the police say? Where's that investigator and what the hell is he doing about all this?"

"Whoa," Sabine said and laughed. "One question at a time or my brain might explode."

Maryse grimaced and sat down on the end of the bed. "I know the feeling. Start talking, woman."

Sabine spent the next fifteen minutes filling Maryse in on everything that had transpired, including her newfound ability to see Helena and their break-in at the hospital. Maryse listened closely, occasionally interjecting an "oh no," "good Lord," or "shit."

When Sabine was finished, Maryse blew out a breath and stared at her for a moment. "You've got some nerve, Sabine LeVeche, trying to one-up me on this. Wasn't one attempted murder enough?"

Sabine smiled. "Raissa told me Mildred yelled at you."

"Yelling would have been polite. That woman scalded my eardrum over the phone. I snuck in the back door of the hotel to come see you. I'm not sure I can take another round."

Sabine laughed. "I think that was stress and temporary insanity on her part. Mildred knows you didn't have anything to do with this. If I hadn't insisted on finding my family, none of this would be happening. I should have let this go years ago."

"A week ago, I would have agreed. But things are different now. We need to find a donor and your family is the best possibility.

Besides, the break-in at your house and the hospital happened before you found your family. Maybe the two aren't related."

"Someone stole all of my family's medical records and you think that's not related?"

"Okay, so maybe it's related. But you still have no idea who did it or why. You say the Fortescues seemed surprised...what if there was a third party trying to connect the dots? A reporter or something. It will be a huge story. 'Missing daughter of heir to millions finally found.' I can just see the headline already."

"Maybe, but it's a stretch."

"I think you should ask Beau to check into it. He might have connections that can get information we can't. We can't even ask without admitting we know what was stolen."

"You're right. I should probably ask Beau." Sabine stared out the hotel window for a moment and sighed.

Maryse narrowed her eyes at Sabine. "You make that sound like such a chore."

"I don't want to talk about it."

"I do. I mean, I did before you protested, but now I'm dying to. C'mon, Sabine. Luc's been gone for days. Please tell me that one of us is getting some action."

"I am not getting any action. I'm surprised at you. You know I don't play fast and loose, and with everything else going on, the last thing on my mind is getting some action."

Maryse raised her eyebrows. "Methinks she doth protest too much. Granted you have a lot on your plate, but I still don't think sex is the last thing on your mind. Remember, I've seen the guy, and I know from experience that even attempted murder does not squelch the desire for a hot man—especially if the hot man is interested in you."

"You don't know he's interested in me." Sabine struggled to direct the conversation away from her. "He's just doing his job."

Maryse laughed. "I saw the way he looked at you in the café, and I've seen that look before. Thank God, I stayed alive long enough to see that look on a regular basis."

"He kissed me," Sabine blurted.

Maryse stared. "And..."

"And what? That's it. He kissed me and I asked him to leave." Sabine felt a flush start to creep up her neck.

"Oh boy!" Maryse bounced up and down on the bed like a child. "I remember the first time Luc kissed me. My whole body was on fire and I thought my head was going to pop off my shoulders and into outer space. I went stomping out of the office, mad, flattered, sexually charged, and scared to death."

Sabine felt all her resolve crumble. "God help me, Maryse. I am scared to death. I've never felt this way about someone. I mean, I hardly know him. How can he have this effect on me?"

Maryse reached over and took her friend's hand. "I don't have an answer for you, even now that I've lived it myself. You were always the one that believed everything had intent and purpose—bad and good. Maybe people are linked before this life and if they find each other again, that link overrides everything lived this lifetime."

"I don't know that I believe in past lives," Sabine said.

"Okay, so what if your souls were hanging out in the same office before they were assigned a mother? Whatever you want to believe. I just know that when I met Luc, I felt things I hadn't felt before, and I'm not just talking about the sexual attraction—although certainly that was part of it." She blew out a breath. "As a scientist, I want to think maybe it's pheromones or some other biological draw that happens to fit Luc and I together better than I'd fit with others. Maybe he's the first man I've met with the same biological imperative that matches mine."

Sabine studied her friend. "You don't believe that for a minute, do you?"

"No. I believe it's love."

Sabine squeezed Maryse's hand, so profoundly happy for her friend and yet scared to take the same gamble herself.

"There's no scientific explanation for love, Sabine, but we can't deny its existence."

"I barely know him," Sabine argued.

"Yet you're drawn to him."

"It might just be lust."

"What's the downside if it is?"

Sabine stared down at the bed. "What if I die?" she whispered.

Maryse hugged her. "What if you don't?"

Chapter Thirteen

Sabine shoved the medical files Helena stole into a backpack for Maryse and played lookout since her friend insisted on sneaking out the hotel's back way to avoid Mildred. Sabine had barely made it back to her room before her cell phone rang. It was a number she didn't recognize and she was surprised and pleased to hear Beau's voice when she answered.

"I'm at the lab in New Orleans. Raissa dropped the scanner off here, so I'm heading back that way in a few minutes, but something else has come up."

Sabine felt her pulse quicken. "With the tests?"

"No. It will be a while before we know something for certain on that end. I got a call from the Fortescues' attorney. He wants to talk to you at his office this afternoon. I started to say no because of everything that happened last night, but I didn't want to tip our hand on the poisoning. If he hears through the grapevine, that's one thing, but I thought we'd better keep it quiet as long as we can."

"Definitely. No, you did the right thing. So did you tell him I'd be there?"

"I told him I'd check with you. He got a little agitated and asked for your cell number, which I refused to give him."

"What do you think he wants?"

"I don't know, but my guess is the Fortescues are putting some pressure on him about something. I don't think he'll be put off forever. More likely if you don't show up there, he'll show up in Mudbug."

Sabine stepped to the window and looked out across Main Street at her shop. "You think I should go?"

"I think…oh hell, I don't know what I think. I'm in a bad position here, Sabine. Professionally, my mind is screaming for you to go because whatever he wants might give us some insight into all the other things going on. Personally, my mind is screaming at me to drag you to New Orleans and put you in a safe house."

Sabine thought about her upcoming radiation treatment. "That's not an option. I have something important to do next week."

"Something worth risking your life for?"

Sabine pressed her fingers to her temple. The irony was overwhelming. "In this case, yes."

"Care to tell me what it is?"

"No. There are certain aspects of my life that I intend to keep private. This has nothing to do with the other situation, I assure you."

"Fine." His voice was short and Sabine could tell he was frustrated with her.

"Do you have the attorney's number so that I can schedule the appointment?"

"I'll do it. Is four-thirty okay?"

Sabine glanced down at her watch. Two and a half hours from now. "I'm sure it will be fine. I just need to check with Maryse about driving me there. Mildred is hellbent on me not driving and won't give me back my car keys."

"Don't worry about it. I plan on going with you. I want to see what Mr. Alford has to say."

"That's not necessary."

"Yes, it is. I have a lot of experience at reading people and probably know more about the law than you do. I want to make sure this attorney isn't trying to pull something off for those nuts."

"Fine, but there's someone else I want to try to see while we're there, if she'll meet with me, that is."

"Who?"

"Someone who might have known the Fortescues back when my father was a kid. Unless you think it's a bad idea."

"No...no, I think it's a really good one as long as her memory is sound. I'll pick you up around three-thirty, okay?"

It was just shy of four-thirty when Beau and Sabine pulled up in front of Martin Alford's office. It was a beautiful antebellum home just off the main street in town. What was once most likely a carriage house had been converted into his place of business, a small, tasteful sign identifying his estate law practice. They walked up the beautifully landscaped path to the office entrance and Beau rang the buzzer at the side of the door. Sabine looked around nervously and plucked a New Orleans newspaper from the top of the bush beside the door. She twirled the loose end of the plastic wrapper around on her finger, every possible scenario imaginable running through her mind. The attorney opened the door a minute later and motioned them inside.

They took a seat in two overstuffed taupe leather chairs placed in front of an ornate redwood writing desk, and Sabine handed the attorney his newspaper. Alford thanked her and took a seat behind the desk, his expression almost one of embarrassment. "I'm so sorry to ask you here on such short notice, but we've had a situation arise."

Sabine sat up straight in her chair. "What kind of situation?"

"Catherine asked the domestic staff to keep your identity confidential, at least until all the particulars could be worked out, but apparently Adelaide has been talking at the grocery store, and news is starting to spread."

"Why would she deliberately disobey Catherine?"

Alford shrugged. "I don't think she was trying to cause trouble. Adelaide's mind simply isn't what it used to be. Dementia, Alzheimer's, or maybe just old age. Either way, her reliability isn't, well, reliable."

Sabine glanced over at Beau, wondering where this was going, but he looked as confused as she felt. "What does all this have to do with me, Mr. Alford?"

"I need to ask you to have a DNA test. I'm sorry to move straight to the legal aspects of this so soon after your reunion, but I'm left with little choice now."

Sabine suddenly understood. "The family wants to make sure I'm the real deal before Adelaide spreads any more tales."

Alford jumped up from his chair, an agitated expression on his face. "No, I'm sorry, that's not it at all. I don't mean to imply that the family doesn't trust you because nothing could be further from the truth. The family is certain you're Adam's daughter and so am I. You look exactly like him, and the dates and facts surrounding your birth coincide with the things we know from our end."

Sabine stared at him. "Mr. Alford, I have no issue with providing a sample for a DNA test. In fact, I fully expected to be asked to. I guess what I'm not understanding is why the urgency now if not for the family's protection?"

"It's not for the family's protection. It's for your own." The attorney sank back into his chair. "Over the years scam artists who found out about Adam showed up pretending to be a long-lost granddaughter or grandson. They've always proved to be frauds, but not before they've stolen from the house or managed to get money out of Frances—she's very gullible."

"The family is worried that everyone will think I'm another scam artist."

"Yes. They don't want this to cause any trouble for you, and the reality is, without medical proof of your claim, you will probably endure a certain level of animosity from the townsfolk."

"I see," Sabine said, although she didn't really buy his explanation for a moment. More likely the Fortescues didn't want to cause any more embarrassment for the family, but Sabine saw no benefit to pointing out the obvious to the one man who probably knew that to begin with.

He gave her an apologetic look. "I am so sorry about this, Ms. LeVeche. We were hoping to explain this situation and take care of these things over time. No one wanted to make you prove yourself as soon as you walked in the door. The Fortescues are a lot of things, but ill-mannered is certainly not one of them."

Sabine held in a smile. Only the most proper—and mentally imbalanced—of people would consider a DNA test rude when there were millions at stake. "Is there a facility I need to go to?"

Alford shook his head and pulled a bag from his desk drawer. "All I need is a hair sample and I can send this off. Again, I apologize for this, Ms. LeVeche. I also lost both my parents when I was very young. I know how important family is. The Fortescues wanted to give both sides time to get to know each other before making it public. No one wanted things to get out this way."

"There is no need to apologize, Mr. Alford. No harm has been done but a little tongue-wagging. I assure you, tongues have wagged about me a time or two in the past. I'm a psychic, remember?"

Alford looked relieved. "Yes, of course. I'm just so used to dealing with the family, and they're so...I guess particular is the best word." He gave Sabine a small smile. "I sometimes forget that the rest of society is not as stringent. The family has arranged for a rush on the tests. They should be notified with the results by tomorrow morning and will contact me immediately following. If you'll give me a way to reach you, I'll let you know as soon as I've spoken with the family."

"No problem," Sabine said and jotted her cell number down on the back of one of her business cards. "I also have a question for you, Mr. Alford. I wondered if I could get a copy of my father's medical records, after the DNA results are back, of course. I've had a couple of minor medical issues come up in the past, and that information would be nice to have."

"Certainly," the attorney said, but Sabine could tell the question has flustered him. Was the attorney aware that her father's records had been stolen, or was he just hesitant to agree to provide any personal information about the family?

When the DNA results were back, she had every intention of pressing him again.

Ruth Boudreaux's home was a spacious Victorian, just a couple of blocks from Alford's office. Sabine had called several times that afternoon but had been unable to get a hold of anyone. She asked Beau to stop by the house just in case Mrs. Boudreaux was home now and would agree to speak to her.

The woman who answered the door clearly wasn't Ruth Boudreaux. For one thing, she was at least forty years younger, and her accent was northern. "May I help you?" she asked politely.

"I hope so," Sabine said. "My name is Sabine LeVeche. I've been trying to get in touch with Mrs. Boudreaux. I've been doing some family research and I think she might know some of my relatives."

"My name is Anna. I'm Mrs. Boudreaux's nurse." She motioned them inside to a formal living room. "If you tried to reach her today, we were probably at church at the time. Mrs. Boudreaux insists on praying daily and lighting a candle for two of her brothers. She lost them in Vietnam."

"Do you think she will speak to me?"

"Oh, certainly. Mrs. Boudreaux enjoys having visitors. It's just that, well, her memory's not quite what it used to be."

"Alzheimer's?"

"Yes. Not horribly progressed yet, but there was an incident with the stove and the family felt it best if she had someone with her full time."

"Of course," Sabine said, trying to hide her disappointment. "Well, I suppose it can't hurt then. Anything she can remember is more than I know now, and there aren't so many alive any longer who were around at that time."

"Oh," the nurse brightened. "You want to ask her about the past? You might be in luck, then. On a good day, her memory of years past is very vivid. It's more recent events that she can't seem to recall." She motioned them down a hallway. "If you'll come with me. She's sitting in the sunroom. The light is good for her and she often spends evenings in there."

Feeling a bit more hopeful, Sabine followed the nurse down the hall and into a huge sunroom at the back of the house, Beau close behind. The room was on the west side of the house and the late afternoon sun cast a warm glow over the multitude of blooming plants, causing a burst of color throughout the room. A thin, silver-haired lady sat in a rocking chair at the far corner, gazing out the window at a group of birds playing in a fountain in the backyard. She looked up when they entered the room.

"Mrs. Boudreaux," the nurse said. "This lady is doing some research on her family and would like to speak to you about them."

Mrs. Boudreaux looked up at Sabine and squinted. "Do I know you, dear?"

"No, ma'am," Sabine replied. "I don't think we've ever met before. But I think you know my family."

"Who's your family?"

"The Fortescues."

Mrs. Boudreaux's face cleared and she smiled. "Why, of course. That's why you seemed so familiar. You're the spitting image of your father. Why don't you and your husband pull up a seat, and I'll see what I can do to help you."

Sabine momentarily cringed at the woman's assumption that Beau was her husband, but it wasn't worth correcting. She and Beau pulled two wicker chairs closer to Mrs. Boudreaux and took a seat. "So you knew my father?" Sabine asked.

"Of course I did. We attended twelve years of school together, and goodness knows how many times we shared a pew in church. Why, William was almost a brother to me."

Sabine immediately understood. Mrs. Boudreaux didn't remember Sabine's father, Adam. She remembered her grandfather. "That's nice, Mrs. Boudreaux."

The woman studied her for a couple of seconds. "Something I don't understand...why don't you just talk to William if you have questions?"

Sabine was prepared for this very question. "I've been estranged from the family for quite a while. We've just recently come together again and I don't want to say anything that might upset the relationship. I understand that people of certain social status don't like to be reminded of or discuss things that might cause embarrassment or sadness. I don't want to inadvertently upset someone if I can prevent it."

Mrs. Boudreaux looked pleased. "Very proper of you to remember the family status in your reconciliation. And I suppose since you are family and your purpose is honorable, God won't consider my talking to you gossip."

"I'm certain He wouldn't, Mrs. Boudreaux, or I wouldn't even have asked."

Mrs. Boudreaux gave her a single nod of approval. "Well, I can honestly say that the only scandal I'm aware of concerning the Fortescues would have been that business during the war concerning William's brother, Lloyd. He always was the disreputable one of the family. You would never have known those two boys were raised in the same household, much less born identical."

"So I take it their looks were where the similarities ended?"

"Heavens, yes. William was a true gentleman, as far back as I can remember. Even in grade school he was always protecting the smaller children from bullies or helping young ladies up the steps." She smiled. "Our skirts were much longer in those days, and sometimes a steady hand on your elbow helped when you were balancing books in one hand and clutching a large portion of your skirt in the other."

Sabine smiled at the image of her grandfather helping a young, and likely beautiful, Mrs. Boudreaux into the schoolhouse. "But Lloyd wasn't a gentleman?"

"Absolutely not. Lloyd was one of the bullies, always stealing lunch money from the younger children when William wasn't looking. He'd sooner push girls down the steps than help them up, and he was always playing pranks on the teachers, many of them cruel."

"I imagine once you were older, all the girls chased William."

Mrs. Boudreaux blushed. "Well, of course, we weren't so forward back then as children are now. Why sometimes I just cringe at the way they dress and behave in church, and it's even worse at the market. I have to wonder what kind of future this country has with them as adults. But yes, William had his share of admirers."

"Anyone special?"

"Not that I ever knew, but I always wondered. Sometimes there would be parties or other events in the school gymnasium. We were mostly chaperoned, but I'd see William sneak out sometimes and not see him again for hours."

"So where did you think he was going?"

Mrs. Boudreaux shrugged. "I always assumed he was seeing someone the family wouldn't have approved of. Once at church, I was certain I saw him slip a piece of paper to one of the girls in the back pews. The poorer families sat toward the back of the church then."

"Do you remember the girl's name?"

"Heavens, no. I'm not even certain I knew it then, but she was a good Catholic, always at Mass. Not that it would have mattered to his parents. William's inheritance depended on his making a good marital match. The Fortescues would have insisted. And besides, they'd already picked Catherine for William. The Fortescues had political aspirations for William, and Catherine's family had the right connections."

"And that's who he married, so I guess the family was happy."

"I suppose they were."

"You don't sound convinced."

Mrs. Boudreaux waved a hand in dismissal. "Oh, it's probably nothing. We were all children at the time, and I guess if one is going to be foolish, that's the time to do it."

"You did something foolish?"

"Not me, dear. Catherine. I had a silly fight with my best friend at a dance one night and decided to walk down the hall and regain my composure. At the end of the hall, I saw Catherine kissing someone in the stairwell. I thought it was William, but when he looked up and saw me, he winked, and I realized it wasn't William at all, but Lloyd."

Sabine considered this. "So Catherine fancied Lloyd, and William fancied someone unsuitable, but they still married."

"Well, yes, dear. Wealth comes with duty, and a marriage between Catherine and William merged two of the most powerful families in southern Louisiana. The elder Fortescues died in a car crash soon after William and Lloyd left to begin their military service. William was firstborn and the estate, its staff, and the largest portion of the family's assets became his responsibility upon his parents' death."

"So he did his duty and married Catherine."

"You make it sound like such a sacrifice. William and Catherine began seeing each other before he left for the war. All that other nonsense happened in high school, and besides, there were the children to consider."

"What children?"

"No one really spoke of such things back then, it wasn't proper, but everyone close to her knew Catherine was pregnant when she and William married. The brothers had been home on leave just a couple of months before, which made the timing possible."

She wrinkled her brow. "And then there was the wedding itself. A rushed affair. Just the minister in the Fortescues living room and hardly the event that a family of that status would normally have hosted. But then, William was given only a brief leave to make arrangements for his inheritance and attend his parents' funeral, and Lloyd was already missing in Vietnam and wanted by the military police and the FBI. With his parents' death, Catherine's pregnancy, and all the investigation surrounding Lloyd's disappearance, it's no wonder the family kept the wedding so private."

Sabine glanced over at Beau, who nodded. She pressed forward. "Then after his military service, William came home and he and Catherine raised the children. Did everything go well then?"

Mrs. Boudreaux smiled at Sabine. "You were such a beautiful little girl, Frances. Always so full of life and energy. And the questions you would ask. You wanted to know the answers to everything. Precocious is the word, I think. But then I'm not telling you anything you don't already know."

Thoughts raced through Sabine's mind. The elderly woman was obviously confused, but would it do any harm to pretend to be Frances? It took only a moment for her to make up her mind.

"Actually, Mrs. Boudreaux, I don't remember much from my childhood. I wasn't...well for some time."

Mrs. Boudreaux continued, "You were just beginning your senior year of high school when I started to notice the change. Before, you'd always been so sweet, so outgoing, but over time you became more and more withdrawn. You barely spoke to people in town and when you did your voice was clipped and filled with anger. Your teachers were at their wits' end. You were their best student, but your marks had slipped so low they were afraid you wouldn't even graduate. Then you got meningitis and after a prolonged recovery, Catherine insisted on private tutors for the rest of your education. Why, we hardly saw you again in town after that."

"And that's when my parents shut themselves away, also?"

"Well, Catherine was always busy with her church charities and such, but William was never the same after Vietnam." She frowned. "Such a shame what that kind of tragedy can do to a man. A real shame."

"Yes, it is," Sabine agreed.

Mrs. Boudreaux leaned forward in her rocker and patted Sabine's leg. "I'm so glad you got well, Frances. It's been so nice talking to you, but if you young people don't mind, I'm going to take a nap before dinner."

"Of course," Sabine said and rose from her chair. "Thank you so much for taking the time to talk to me, Mrs. Boudreaux. It's been a pleasure meeting you."

Mrs. Boudreaux nodded once, then dropped off to sleep. Sabine and Beau quietly left the room and let the nurse know they were leaving. They had no sooner turned onto the freeway when Sabine's cell phone rang.

"Maryse," Sabine said. "What's up?"

"Something went wrong with the car. Mildred's been in an accident," Maryse said, her voice shaky. "I'm at Mudbug General."

"I'll be there in thirty minutes," Sabine said. "Call me as soon as you hear anything." Sabine closed her phone and looked over at

Beau, panic already sweeping over her. "We have to get to Mudbug General. Mildred's been in a car accident."

"Don't start worrying until we know the score," Beau said. "I'm sure she's going to be fine. Maryse is with her, right?"

Sabine shook her head. "You don't understand."

"Understand what?"

"She was driving my car."

Chapter Fourteen

Beau tried to get control of his emotions as he raced into the hospital parking lot. Until he had more information, he needed to remain calm, objective. One thing he knew for certain, though: he'd paid far too many trips to the hospital in the last couple of days. They rushed into the emergency room and found Maryse waiting for them right inside the door.

"How is she?" Sabine asked.

"The doctors say she's going to be fine. Her foot is broken and there's some burns on her hands and arms, but they can't find anything else."

"Burns!" Sabine cried. "Oh my God. What happened?"

Maryse shook her head. "I'm still not quite sure. All I know is Mildred was on her way back from an errand in New Orleans and drove off the road and into the ditch. I don't know if the car caught on fire before or after she ran off the road. She was only half conscious when they brought her in and all I could make out was her saying 'Tell Sabine it was the car.' Then the doctors took her away and now she's out for the count."

Beau felt his jaw clench. Cars did not arbitrarily catch fire. "Do you know where they took the car?"

Maryse nodded and pulled a business card from her pocket. "One of the state troopers gave me his card. He wrote down a number on the back for the shop they towed the car to."

Beau took the card from Maryse and looked over at Sabine. "I'll need you to call the garage and give them permission to talk to me about the car."

Sabine nodded, her face pale. "You don't think it was an accident, do you?"

"No, and neither do you. You didn't from the moment Maryse called."

Beau pulled out his cell phone and stored the number to the garage, then gave the card to Sabine. "I'm going to the garage now, so give them a call before I get there. If you need to leave the hospital before I get back, do not go alone." He looked over at Maryse. "I want someone with her at all times."

Maryse nodded. "I know the drill."

Beau studied her for a moment. "Yeah, I guess you do. The safest place is the hotel, so if you leave before I get back, go straight there. Eat at the hospital, or get something here to go, but don't under any circumstances have anything delivered or eat any food Mildred or Sabine have on hand."

"No problem," Maryse agreed.

Sabine's eyes were full of fear. Fighting the overwhelming urge to pull her into his arms, he squeezed her arm instead. "I'll be back as soon as I can. We're going to get to the bottom of this. I promise you."

Sabine threw her arms around him in a crushing hug. Surprised, Beau circled his arms around her, trying not to dwell on how their bodies molded together in a perfect fit, or how his heart leapt at the warmth of her body. He buried his head in her neck, breathing in the sweet smell of her hair.

"Thank you," she whispered, giving him a final squeeze before she dropped her arms and took a step back.

"You're going to be fine," he promised her.

Maryse placed a hand on Sabine's shoulder. "Of course she is," Maryse said, then grinned at Beau.

Beau gave his new ally a wave and headed out of the hospital. Mudbug didn't have a shop large enough for the kind of damage he imagined was done to Sabine's car, so he figured it had been towed to New Orleans. A quick phone call verified his hunch and provided him with the location of the shop and the technician who was looking at her car.

He made the drive in just under an hour and hurried into the service garage. Sabine's car was in the first stall and what he saw brought him up short. The entire front of the car was scorched black, the remnants of the fire almost glowing against the pale silver of her car. The black extended past the front seat and halfway into the back.

Beau said a silent prayer of thanks that Mildred had made it out of this wreck with as few injuries as she had, then gave a second thanks that Maryse and Sabine hadn't seen the car. They would probably have had heart attacks. He was just about to step inside and ask the receptionist to locate the manager when he saw a stocky, middle-aged man walking his way.

"You must be Mr. Villeneuve," the man said and extended his hand. "I'm Russell Benoit, the manager here."

Beau shook the man's hand. "Please, call me Beau."

The manager nodded and pointed to the car. "Ms. LeVeche said you were a friend and I should tell you everything I knew about her car." He blew out a breath. "I gotta be honest with you… this is a matter for the police, not a friend. I called them about twenty minutes ago."

Beau nodded. "I figured as much. I'm also a private investigator, former FBI. Go ahead and tell me what you've found. You're not going to surprise me."

The manager's eyes widened. "Well, that makes this a bit easier, that's for sure." He motioned Beau over to the car and wrenched open the hood. Some of the engine had already been removed, probably as they looked for the cause of the fire, and the manager pointed to a hole on the right side. "Look down through there. You see that little piece of metal on the bottom that's a bit shinier than the rest, right there next to what's left of the fuel line?"

Beau peered through the hole and located the shiny piece of metal. "Yeah. It doesn't belong there, right?"

"Not even close."

Beau straightened. "So, what, someone shoved it in the fuel line?"

The manager shook his head, a concerned look on his face. "I don't think you understand. A cut fuel line can't cause a fire, not by itself."

Beau stared at the manager. "Okay, so then what caused the fire?"

The manager ran a hand through his hair. "A bomb."

It was a little over an hour before Sabine and Maryse were allowed to see Mildred. Sabine teared up at the sight of her "mother," hands and forearms bandaged and her foot in a cast. She felt Maryse's hand on hers and gave it a squeeze. Together they stepped close to the bed and looked down at the woman who had raised them. "She's going to be okay, right?" Maryse asked the nurse, even though they'd just spoken to the doctor in the waiting room.

"Yes," the nurse said, reassuring them. "It looks much worse than it is. She's a strong woman and I imagine she'll be up and around in no time."

Mildred opened her eyes and looked around the room. "Damned hospitals. I hate hospitals."

The nurse gave them a sympathetic nod. "She's receiving a bit of painkiller through her IV. You can visit for a few minutes, but I wouldn't expect her to make much sense."

Sabine thanked the nurse and she left the room. "Mildred," Sabine said and leaned over the bed. "Can you hear me?"

"Of course I can hear you, Mom," Mildred said. "I'm hurt, not deaf."

Sabine looked over at Maryse, who raised her eyebrows. Apparently there were some really good drugs in that IV. "Mildred, it's Sabine and Maryse."

Mildred blinked once and stared at them. "Well, of course it is. Who did you think you were?"

Maryse placed her hand over her mouth, but Sabine still heard the giggle. Not that she could blame her. It was kinda funny, in a someone-tried-to-kill-you-be-cause-they-thought-you-were-me kind of way. Mildred closed her eyes and let out a snore. Sabine was just about to suggest they leave and let Mildred rest when Helena Henry walked through the outside wall and into the room.

The ghost scrunched her brow in confusion. "What are you doing back here, Sabine? I've been looking for you everywhere. I was sure they released you hours ago."

"I was released hours ago," Sabine said and gestured to the bed. "Mildred had a car wreck."

Helena stepped between Sabine and Maryse and peered over at Mildred. "Oh, man, that looks bad. Is she going to be all right?"

"The doctor says she will be. She's got some burns and a broken foot, but otherwise, she's okay."

Helena shook her head. "Damn woman is too cheap. Don't tell me she doesn't make enough money at that hotel to buy a decent car."

"She wasn't driving her car," Sabine said. "She was driving mine."

Helena jerked around and looked directly at Sabine. "You don't think..."

"I don't know what to think yet. Beau's at the garage talking to the mechanic. But Maryse said when they brought her in that Mildred was saying something was wrong with the car."

"Shit." Helena looked back at Mildred, who was awake again and squinting at them.

"Sabine," Mildred said, "who's your friend?"

"That's Maryse, Mildred." Sabine whispered to Helena, "She's on drugs."

"Well, heck," Mildred said, "I know who Maryse is. I mean the one next to you."

Sabine felt her blood run cold. She heard a sharp intake of breath but couldn't be sure whether it had been Maryse or Helena. She's hallucinating. That's got to be it. Please God, let her be hallucinating. "I don't have another friend here, Mildred." It wasn't exactly a lie. Sabine hadn't yet gotten to the point of considering Helena a friend, and the jury was still out on if she ever would.

Mildred gave her an exasperated look and pointed directly at Helena. "Then who is the fat woman with the pompadour hairdo?"

Helena straightened up and glared at Mildred. "Who the hell is she calling fat? And that do of hers has looked like a hat helmet since the 1960s."

Sabine looked over at Maryse, but it was clear her friend was going to be no help. Her expression wavered between needing to pray and wanting to cry. Sabine took a deep breath. Calm down. Obviously she can't hear Helena or she would have made a comment back to her. That just means she can see her. Which meant... what? Sabine rubbed her fingers on her temples, certain that at any minute, her head was going to explode.

Before she could form a plan of action, or arrange for a mass burial, the nurse walked back in. "I'm sorry," the nurse said, "but I'm going to have to ask you to leave for the time being. We'll transfer Ms. Mildred to a room in a couple of hours. Dr. Breaux wants to keep her overnight for observation, but assuming everything goes well, she should be able to go home in a couple of days."

Sabine nodded at Maryse, then narrowed her eyes at Helena. Helena glared back but stomped out of the room after them. "Well, that was rude," Helena bitched as soon as they stepped into the hall and closed the door behind them.

"What was that?" Maryse asked, her eyes wide. "We've already had this discussion about what happens when someone sees Helena."

Helena looked at Maryse. "What happens? You never told me anything."

"Death, Helena," Sabine said. "Maryse has this theory that you're only visible to people who are close to death."

Helena shot Maryse a dirty look. "That's just as rude as Mildred calling me fat."

"And just as accurate," Sabine shot back. "Name me one person who's seen you whose life hasn't been in danger."

"Well, that's hardly fair since I'm mostly trapped in Mudbug. Maybe if I ventured out some, more people might see me and prove your theory wrong. Besides, Luc can see me."

"Could see you," Maryse corrected. "And you're not the first ghost he's seen."

Helena spun around to look at Maryse. "Luc can't see me anymore?"

"You didn't notice that when you sat down at breakfast and he never said a word?"

Helena shrugged. "I just thought he was ignoring me. So what does it mean that Mildred can see me? I mean I know she was in danger from the car wreck, but it was Sabine's car, so that doesn't add up at all."

Sabine shook her head. "I don't know. Maybe it has something to do with the drugs, and being in an altered state of consciousness. Maybe it allows people to see things they couldn't otherwise. Remember, the first time I saw you was when I'd given myself a concussion in the attic."

Maryse nodded, obviously happy to grasp any explanation that didn't involve death. "That makes sense. I mean, as much as any of this does."

"Maybe," Sabine said, but she still wasn't convinced. "Let's get out of here. I feel like locking myself in my hotel room and not coming out again for a week."

"I know the feeling," Maryse said and gave her a sympathetic look. "Do you want to grab something to eat before we head out?"

Sabine shook her head. "I really don't have much of an appetite. If I'm hungry later, I'll ask Beau to get me something. Unless you're hungry."

Maryse shook her head. "Not a chance. I can't eat when I'm stressed. I've lost twelve pounds over the last five weeks. And I didn't really have them to lose."

"I could eat something," Helena interjected.

"No," Sabine said. "I'm positive you won't starve."

"Fine," Helena pouted. "Will you at least give me a ride to Mudbug? I stashed some books in the hedges outside of my house.

I thought you might want to see them, Sabine. We can pick them up on the way to the hotel."

Sabine narrowed her eyes at Helena. "Please tell me you did not steal anything else."

"How the hell can I steal my own things? The books have pictures and newspaper clippings from years ago. They belong to me. I cut out the clippings. I pasted them in the books."

"You donated your house and everything in it to the Mudbug Historical Society," Sabine reminded her.

"I'm sure if they could understand any of this and take a vote, they'd all agree that you not being murdered is worth my borrowing my own books for a couple of days. You're going to have to stop being so uptight, Sabine. Killers don't play by the rules. If you want to get ahead of him, you're going to have to ignore them, too."

Sabine sighed and started down the hall and out of the hospital. She really, really hated it when Helena was right.

"Pull over here," Helena instructed and pointed to a huge hedge that stretched the length of her former residence. Maryse pulled over on the shoulder of the road in front of the stretch of bushes. Helena hopped out of the car and ran through the hedge.

Sabine shook her head. "Thank God she's a ghost. Otherwise those bushes wouldn't have survived."

Maryse nodded in agreement.

A couple of seconds later, Helena emerged from the hedge carrying a stack of albums that had managed to make it through the hedge-passing with only some scratches. She tossed the albums onto the backseat through the window, then slipped into the car. "Now, pull up in the next drive where that magnolia tree is," Helena instructed.

"Why?" Sabine asked. "We've got the books."

"I forgot something," Helena said. "What does it matter? Remember that whole 'rule' discussion we had?"

Sabine sighed and motioned for Maryse to pull into the drive. Maryse shook her head and muttered, "This feels way too familiar."

Helena rolled her eyes and jumped out of the car as soon as Maryse stopped. "Back in a minute," she said as she started off across the lawn to the huge home next to her own estate.

Sabine sat us straight in her seat. "Where's she going? That's not her house, or her garage, or her boat house."

"You think I don't know this?" Maryse shot back. "That's Lois Cormier's house."

"What could Helena possibly want there?"

"I don't know but I'm positive it's not going to be good."

Ten minutes later, Helena still hadn't emerged from the house. Sabine looked over at Maryse, who was alternating between looking at the house and checking her mirrors for visitors. "I think we should leave," Sabine said. "We have the books and Helena can find her own way to the hotel."

"You're right," Maryse agreed and started the car.

"Wait!" Sabine said before Maryse could put the car in gear. "I think the front door's opening."

"Oh, no," Maryse whispered. "I hope the alarm isn't on."

"Get out of here. Now!"

Maryse put the car in reverse just as the front door of the house flew open and Helena came running out dragging an enormous garbage bag, stuffed to the brim. "Hurry up!" Helena yelled. "That alarm is going to go off any second."

"Crap, crap, crap," Maryse said as she threw the car in drive and floored it. "I thought I was done with this nonsense."

"Just leave her," Sabine said as she scanned the neighborhood, hoping to God no one had seen them yet.

"That will only make things worse, trust me," Maryse said as she screeched to a stop next to Helena. The ghost yanked open the car door and lifted the bag just high enough to get it onto the floorboard before she jumped in herself, slammed the door, and collapsed on the backseat. Maryse floored the car and they were pulling out of the driveway before the alarm went off.

Sabine glanced over at Maryse, who was slumped as far down in the driver's seat as she could be and still see over the steering wheel. If dealing with Helena wasn't so aggravating, it might have been funny. Maryse had been driving the same rental car ever since she and her truck had taken an unexpected dip in the bayou weeks before. Everyone in Mudbug knew it was her just by seeing the car, so unless she was planning on reporting it stolen, hiding while driving wasn't really going to get her anywhere.

They pulled onto the highway and were a good mile down the road before a cop car came racing past in the opposite direction. Maryse let out a huge breath that she'd probably been holding for the last two miles and sat up a little straighter in her seat.

"Helena!" Sabine yelled at the ghost, who was laid out on the back seat like she was having a heart attack. "What in the world was so important that you risked getting us arrested? And it better be good."

"It's a surprise," Helena said, but the guilty look on her face gave her away.

Sabine reached over the seat and grabbed the trash bag, which was surprisingly heavy. She yanked the bag over the car seat, its contents clanking and rattling. "What did you steal? Their silver?" She opened the bag and looked inside, then groaned.

"I'm afraid to ask," Maryse said.

"It's food! She broke into someone's house to raid their pantry." Sabine looked back at Helena. "This is low, even for you. How could you justify stealing food when you don't even need to eat?"

Helena sat up in the seat. "Lois is on a cruise for the next two weeks. The food would have gone bad and been thrown away. What's the big deal?"

Sabine reached into the bag and pulled out a can of sweet potatoes. "This expires two years from now."

"Oh, sorry. I must have accidentally picked up that can."

"Bull, Helena. You went through that woman's pantry and took whatever you wanted. You have an eating disorder and need to get help." Sabine clutched her head with both hands. "Oh, God, I cannot believe I just said that to a dead person."

"I can," Maryse said. "I gave up on logic weeks ago."

Helena glared at Sabine. "Have you seen Lois Cormier's ass? Trust me, I'm doing her a favor."

Sabine threw her hands in the air and turned back around in her seat. "I give up. You know, I thought a time or two that if you weren't already dead, I would take on the job. Now, I'm just wondering if it's not safer and a heck of a lot more peaceful if whoever's trying to kill me is successful. Whatever afterlife there is has to be less aggravating than this."

Maryse shook her head. "I thought that, too, but then I was afraid if the killer was successful but didn't get caught, that I'd just be stuck in limbo with Helena."

Sabine shuddered. "Oh, God, you're right."

"Maybe you should just leave town," Maryse suggested.

"For how long?" Sabine shook her head. "We have no idea why someone is after me. Leaving will most likely only postpone the inevitable."

Maryse sighed. "You're right. I know you're right." She looked over at Sabine. "Well, look at the bright side—at least we've got plenty to snack on while we try to sort all this out."

"That's what I was thinking," Helena said. "And I figured while we were having a snack, Maryse could tell me what she figured out from my family's medical files. You've looked at them, right?"

Maryse looked at Sabine, waiting for a cue, and Sabine nodded. Now was as good a time as any to deliver the news. "Okay," Maryse said. "We'll talk as soon as we get back to the hotel."

Fifteen minutes later they were ensconced in Sabine's hotel room, Sabine perched on the dresser, Maryse pacing all five steps that was the length of the room, and Helena sitting on the end of the bed, stuffing her face with truffles and apparently completely oblivious to Maryse's discomfort.

"So shoot," Helena said. "Let me have it."

Maryse stopped pacing and looked down at Helena. "I don't know how to tell you this any other way, Helena, so I'm just going to put it all out there."

"Go for it."

"You had cancer, Helena, advanced. Even if someone hadn't murdered you, I don't think you could have made it a year."

Helena dropped her truffle and stared. "But...how...I didn't feel...I mean, I was a little more tired than usual, but I was getting old, so I thought...but that's not what killed me?"

"No," Maryse said, "but unfortunately, the autopsy didn't find anything, either."

"What?" Helena shook her head. "I'm not crazy. There's no way my death was natural. I was there...I ought to know."

"No one's giving up on this, Helena. Sabine and I want you to know that."

Helena sighed. "I know you are doing your best, and I appreciate it all. Cancer, huh? I guess that gives me something else to think on." Helena rose from the bed. "I'm going to take a walk and sort this out, okay, guys? I'll check in later."

"We understand," Sabine said and watched Helena leave through the wall. When she was certain the ghost was gone, she looked over at Maryse. "You left something out. I can tell by your face."

"I know, but she was already struggling with the other stuff. I guess I figured we should give her a little time to adjust before we hit her with the rest."

"What else is there?" Sabine asked.

Maryse looked at Sabine, a pained expression on her face. "Based on the medical files, there's no way Hank is Helena's son."

It was almost eight o'clock before Beau made it back to Mudbug. After his conversation with the garage manager, he'd called a buddy who knew something about explosives and had agreed to come immediately and take a look at the car. His friend verified the manager's assessment of the situation, but poking around the engine for a while and studying some of the pieces recovered from the blast, he concluded that whoever had constructed the bomb was no expert.

Damn internet.

All you needed was an ISP and Google and information of all sorts was at your fingertips. Beau parked in front of the hotel and rushed inside. He knew Maryse had been with Sabine the entire time, but ever since he'd found out about the bomb, he'd been counting the seconds until he could see Sabine with his own two eyes. The peanut oil had been clever and could have been deemed an accident, but strapping a bomb to someone's car was an act of desperation, and that wasn't a good sign at all.

Beau hurried up the stairs and knocked on Sabine's door. Maryse gave him a brief quiz, then unlocked the door and let him into the room. He paused for a moment as he stepped inside, not sure what to think of the display. There was food everywhere—canned goods, boxes of crackers, chips, a loaf of bread, peanut butter, three different varieties of cookies, and he couldn't even count how many pieces of chocolate candies.

Sabine sat cross-legged on the bed, a stack of photo albums and discarded chocolate candy wrappers in front of her. She looked up at him and smiled.

"Please tell me this did not come from either of your houses," he said.

"No," Sabine reassured him. "It was a, uh, well-meaning friend."

Beau glanced around at the grocery store display. "She kinda overdid it, huh?"

Sabine grimaced. "She tends to overdo everything."

"Did you find out anything about the car?" Maryse asked.

Beau paused, not wanting to tell them about the bomb until he knew more about the device used and who had the ability to design it. His buddy had promised him that information as soon as possible. "Something caused the fuel line to catch fire," he said finally, "but the manager's still looking into it. We should know more by tomorrow."

Maryse rose from the chair in the corner and picked up a stack of papers sitting on top of the scanner Raissa had loaned Sabine. "Looks like my shift is over." Sabine rose from the bed and Maryse gave her a hug. "I've got to go feed the cat, and I'll take a look at all of this tonight." She looked at Beau. "Unless you need me to stay here tonight."

"No," Beau said. "I moved to the room with the adjoining door. That way Sabine can still have her space and I can indulge my paranoid, overprotective tendencies."

Maryse grinned. "It's not paranoia if they're really out to get you." She stepped out of room and gave Sabine a wave. "Don't do anything I wouldn't do," she said and closed the door before Sabine could even formulate a reply.

"I should really get new friends," Sabine said.

Beau laughed. "I like her. The way she goes after life full speed, she probably doesn't have a lot of regrets."

"Ha. Before you start heralding all her living-life-with-gusto qualities, I'm going to inform you that prior to drawing the short end of the someone's-trying-to-murder-me stick, Maryse was one of the worst introverts ever."

"No way. Really?"

"She used to live in this two-room cabin on the bayou. You couldn't even get to it without a boat, unless you wanted to swim with the gators. If she ran out of food, she'd go fishing before she'd drive into town to the general store. It was nothing for me to go a month without seeing her, unless Mildred and I ganged up on her."

Beau stared at Sabine. "I never would have guessed any of that. What changed?"

"Well, someone trying to kill you tends to force you to take a closer look at your life, although I never really understood how much until now. And there was Luc."

"So the handsome hero clinched the deal." Beau reached over to the dresser and grabbed a bottle of water, looking for any distraction from the fact that he was in a hotel, with Sabine, alone.

Sabine smiled. "A storybook ending."

Beau nodded. "Not bad considering it was a horror story."

Sabine sobered. "Speaking of which, I know I'm working on a sequel, so why don't you go ahead and tell me what you didn't want to say in front of Maryse."

Beau struggled to maintain his composure. "What makes you think I'm hiding anything?"

Sabine shrugged. "I just know."

"So now you're psychic?"

"No," Sabine said and frowned. "I just know you weren't giving us the whole story. As much as I've been trying to avoid it, I'm drawn to you in a way I've never felt before and can't explain given the length of our relationship. It's like we're connected on some different level." She laughed. "I know that's probably all too woo-woo for you, but if I had a more scientific explanation, I'd give it to you."

Beau couldn't put his feelings into words, either. "I know exactly what you're talking about, and I don't have an explanation either, scientific or otherwise."

"So you're going to tell me about the car."

Seeing no other way around it, Beau nodded. "It was a bomb."

Sabine's eyes grew round and she sucked in a breath. "A bomb. Oh my God. I mean, I was expecting something, but a bomb is so... evil. I know that sounds melodramatic—"

"No," Beau cut her off. "It doesn't. I believe evil is alive and well and flourishing in a society that wants to excuse away abhorrent behaviors. I sometimes think some people are just born bad."

Sabine moved closer to Beau and placed her hand on his arm. "I'm glad you're here with me. There's an inner peace I have when I'm with you that I don't otherwise."

"You just feel safe."

"No. It's more than that. I can't explain it."

"Then don't." Beau leaned forward and brushed his lips against Sabine's. He waited for her to pull away, and when she didn't, he moved closer to her and pressed his lips to hers.

Chapter Fifteen

The touch of Beau's lips on hers sent Sabine's body into overdrive. Her skin tingled as if she'd never been touched before, and in a way, it was true. Certainly, she'd never been touched before like this. Beau was different, special, and even though she knew the last thing in the world she should be doing is kissing him back, that's exactly what she did. As their kiss deepened, he pulled her body close to his.

He was hard and ready, and Sabine moaned as he pressed his hips into hers. He broke off their kiss and began trailing kisses down her neck until he was at the sensitive flesh just at the vee of her blouse. Sabine sucked in a breath, then gasped as he pulled her blouse aside and lowered her lacy bra just enough to take one hardened nipple into his mouth. He slowly swirled his tongue, sending her into fits of pleasure.

Knowing there was no going back now, Sabine slid her hand across the front of Beau's jeans, stroking the long, hard length of him through the denim. He paused for a moment, his breathing irregular. Then with one swift motion, he lifted her off the floor and gently laid her on the bed. He unbuttoned her blouse and expertly removed her bra, then lowered himself to continue his erotic assault of her breasts. As his mouth worked its magic, he unbuttoned her pants and slid one hand inside.

For the first time in weeks, Sabine thanked God she didn't wear underwear.

He found her sensitive spot and swirled his fingers around it, matching the pace of his tongue on her nipple. Sabine felt the pleasure building in her until she was afraid she would explode. She placed her hand over his and gasped. "Wait. I want it to be together."

Beau nodded and leaned down to kiss her deeply, his tongue dancing with hers. Then he rose from the bed and shrugged off his clothes. Sabine sucked in a breath when she looked at him, so hard and hot and so totally male. She reached out with one hand and circled the length of him, then ran her hand up and down, squeezing slightly every time she approached the tip. Beau closed his eyes and groaned, and she increased the pace.

Mere seconds later, he moved her hand away and rolled on protection, then rose over her on the bed. He leaned down to kiss her, then entered her in a single stroke. Sabine gasped with pleasure and clutched his back, digging her nails into his skin. She thrust her hips up to match his strokes. As they found their natural rhythm, she felt the pressure building in her.

"Now, Beau," she whispered, "I can't hold it any longer."

"Yes," Beau said as he moved with increased intensity. Suddenly his body stiffened. "Now."

The orgasm crashed over her like a tidal wave, every nerve ending in her body responding. They cried out at the same time and Sabine clutched his back, pulling him deep inside her as the pleasure rolled over her again and again.

Beau leaned back in the bed against the stack of pillows and Sabine lay against him. He wrapped his arms around her, trying to control his warring emotions. He couldn't lose her and knew his only chance was to convince her to give up her newfound family and anything that went along with them.

"Sabine," he said quietly, "there's something I need to tell you."

Sabine shifted a bit so that she could look up at him. "What is it?"

Beau took a breath, trying to decide how to begin, how to end, how to explain the horror, the heartache, the devastation. Finally, he decided to start at the beginning. "I was raised by a foster family.

When I was two years old, my mother gave me to nuns at a church in New Orleans and left."

Sabine's eyes widened in surprise. "Why?"

"The nuns didn't know why. She'd only said she couldn't take care of me and asked them to give me to someone that could. Then she left. The nuns tried to locate her or my father, but she didn't give them any name. She didn't tell them where she was from or where she was going. She simply gave me to the nuns and disappeared."

"So the nuns raised you?"

"No, they gave me to a couple from the church who couldn't have children. They were thrilled to take me and were wonderful parents. I will always be grateful to them."

"But you wanted to know."

Beau nodded. "I had to know why a woman would raise a child for two years, then abandon him to strangers. Why she would never come back to get him. What kind of person could do that, and why? When I joined the FBI, I chose to specialize in missing persons. Every single day, I tried to find people who had vanished, and every night I applied my new skills to finding the answer to my own private mystery."

"And did you ever find them?"

"Yes. I won't go into all the details, except to say that it took six long years of digging before I caught a break. I'd found a man who might be my father." Beau ran one hand through his hair. "I was working in D.C. at the time, but I booked the first flight to New Orleans and drove a couple of hours to a small town north of the city. When the man opened his door, I knew at once that I'd found half of my answer. It was like looking into a mirror twenty years away."

Sabine shifted in the bed so that she could face him, her torso propped against his chest. "What did he say?"

"He didn't say anything for a while. Then finally he said, 'I guess your momma sent you.' I told him I didn't know my mother and that I'd been raised by a foster family. That I'd been looking for him and my mother for over six years. He invited me in and I thought that was it. I was about to get all the answers I'd been searching for. The puzzle would be complete."

"But you didn't?"

"No. He didn't know where my mother was. In fact, he hadn't seen her since that very day she'd left me with the nuns. She'd been going to visit her sister in Mississippi, or at least that's what she'd told him. He'd driven her to the bus station and bought her a ticket to Gulfport. Her sister called that night, wanting to know why we weren't on the bus. The ticket had been collected at the exchange in New Orleans and her luggage was on the bus when it reached Gulfport but there was no sign of my mother."

"So something happened to her between New Orleans and Gulfport."

"That's what everyone thought, which is why the police didn't even concentrate on New Orleans with their search. If there was an announcement on the news, the nuns wouldn't have seen it, and since my parents were poor, the only photos of me were as an infant and my mother from her high school yearbook. They didn't even have a wedding photo."

"So no one would have recognized you from the photos, even if they'd seen a news story."

"Not likely. The police searched every bus stop between New Orleans and Gulfport, but they never found a thing. She'd simply vanished. Finally, they assumed we'd been taken by a person or persons unknown and the file was shoved to the back of the cabinet in favor of others that had more evidence and might be possible to solve."

"So you had to give up?"

"No. I talked extensively to my father about my mother's behavior before that trip. Something could have happened to her, certainly, but her leaving me with the nuns was deliberate. My father spoke of her erratic behavior—drinking, paranoia, said she always felt like someone was watching her. It sounded like a mental breakdown to me. And I figured that's what she meant when she told the nuns she wasn't fit to take care of me. So I started looking at mental health facilities around Louisiana."

"Smart," Sabine said. "And the perfect explanation for why she never returned."

Beau nodded. "That's what I thought, too. It took another two weeks before I came up with anything, but finally, I found a nurse that had worked at a facility in Monroe. She remembered a woman who'd come to the home at around the time I was asking about. The woman couldn't remember her name and had no identification. A full medical exam had revealed that she'd given birth, but when they asked her about the baby, she became confused and always insisted that she didn't have a child. Finally, they decided that the baby must have been stillborn and that perhaps that was what had sent her over the edge."

"She didn't remember. That's so sad."

"I thought so, too. The woman stayed at the home for three years. She never regained her memory. Finally, the state issued her new identification and the home assisted her with finding a job and a new place to live, as she was otherwise quite competent to take care of herself. She went to work at a local library and, as far as the nurse knew, was still working there. Only you would understand my excitement, the thrill of knowing that the thirty-year-old mystery of who I was would finally be solved."

Sabine nodded. "I understand."

"I couldn't find a listing for her in the local phone book, so I called the library and found that the woman I was sure was my mother would be at work that afternoon. Four more hours and I would have all my answers. Then I called my father with the news and he was elated. I waited for her in the parking lot of the library, certain I'd recognize her, and I did. She was older, of course, and her hair was starting to gray, but I could still clearly see the woman from that high school photograph."

Sabine put her hand over her mouth. "Oh, Beau, what a moment in time."

Beau grimaced. "Yeah. It was a moment all right. I started walking toward her and she looked at me. I could tell by the look on her face that she knew exactly who I was. She shook her head and said 'Please leave. Leave and pretend you never saw me.' I knew then she'd been pretending amnesia all those years. I opened my mouth to ask why. I deserved a reason. That's when a car squealed into the parking lot. It was my father. She looked at the car and her face went completely white, filled with fear."

Sabine sat upright and stared at him. "Oh no!"

"I immediately knew why she'd left—why she'd given me away, and why she'd stayed hidden all that time. My father jumped out of the car and took her out with a single shot to the head, then he turned the gun on himself."

Tears ran down Sabine's face and she wrapped her arms around him. Beau hugged her tightly, choked with emotion. "I've never told anyone all of that, until now."

Sabine pulled back a bit and looked at him. "Why did you tell me, Beau?"

"Because I need you to understand how family can hurt you. Biology doesn't make people care. Please, Sabine, I'm begging you, let this thing with your family go. Stop all contact with them. Have an attorney draw up papers stating that you relinquish any part of the estate you might be entitled to."

Sabine pulled away from him. "I can't," she whispered.

Beau rose from the bed, his heart breaking in two. "What in the world could possibly be worth your life? Please explain to me why these people, these strangers, mean more to you than everyone who loves you?"

Sabine looked at the pain so clearly etched on Beau's face and her mind raced trying to find a way to erase it. Right now he must think her incredibly shallow, or greedy for the possible inheritance, because from his standpoint, there simply couldn't be a valid enough reason to keep oneself in such danger. She had to tell him the truth. Even if he was angrier at her than before. "My life," she began, "is worth so much to me that I'm willing to risk it in order to save it."

He stared at her for a moment. "That makes no sense."

Sabine sighed. "It does if you need a bone marrow transplant."

Beau's eyes widened in surprise, and Sabine knew that of all the things he'd expected she might say, that wasn't even on the list. He dropped back down on the bed next to her. "You have cancer?"

Sabine nodded. "Acute myeloid leukemia. I start treatment next week, but in the event that treatment isn't effective…"

"You'll need a bone marrow transplant," Beau finished. "And the best possible scenario is a blood relative." Beau wrapped his arms around her. "Oh, Jesus, Sabine, why didn't you tell me?"

Sabine's body responded instantly to the warmth of Beau's embrace, and her heart broke all over again for what she knew could never be. "I didn't even tell Mildred about it, Beau. If Maryse hadn't snitched, she still wouldn't know."

"And all that time Maryse spends in labs with scientists?"

Sabine nodded. "She's been looking for a cure for cancer for years, and all that stuff last month brought it to a head. She hasn't found a cure, but all the experts are fairly certain she's found a way to prevent ninety percent of the side effects from radiation treatment."

Beau's face cleared in understanding. "I thought it a bit strange that someone who obviously cared about you deeply was gone so often when important things were happening, but she's trying to push the test through to get you the drug."

"Actually," Sabine hedged, "she kinda already gave me a round of it. She's been prepping me for a couple of weeks before my first treatment. But she's pushing for the grants and the tests to make sure the formula is the best she can get. She lost her mother and father to cancer…it's pretty much been her lifelong pursuit to not lose anyone else."

"She must be frantic, and Mildred. She dated Maryse's dad forever, didn't she? That's why you didn't tell her."

"I didn't want Mildred to worry as much as I didn't want to drag you into my problems or guilt you into helping me do something you didn't think I should be doing."

Beau pushed back enough so that he could look at her. "But I helped you anyway."

Sabine nodded and brushed a tear from her cheek. "I know."

"So, in the beginning when you were pushing me away, was it that you really weren't interested or were you afraid to get involved because of the cancer?"

Sabine closed her eyes for a moment, trying to formulate the right response. The response that would let him know she cared without leading him on. "I still am afraid, Beau. I have feelings for you, and I'm not going to deny that, but I can't make you any promises when I don't know what the future holds for me. I'm not in a position to consider anyone else but myself right now, and it's not fair to you to keep you on hold."

Beau dropped his hands from her and stared at her for a moment. Finally, he sighed. "I think you're wrong, but I respect your wishes."

Sabine's relief warred with her guilt. She didn't deserve this man or his protection. She placed one hand on his arm. "I am so sorry that taking my case has opened wounds in you that were better off closed."

"It's probably time I put them to rest for good. But I've got to be honest with you. When this is over, I'm going to ask you to reconsider."

Sabine nodded, praying that when it was all over, she'd have any reason at all to gamble on a future with Beau. "I'll be waiting," she said.

Beau leaned over and brushed his lips gently against hers. "Let's get some rest. I know you're as exhausted as I am." He gathered her in his arms and they lay back on the bed. Minutes later, his breathing changed and Sabine knew he was asleep.

She lay there, enveloped in the warmth and caring of the most perfect man she'd ever met, and prayed that tonight wouldn't be the last time she ever felt this secure.

Sabine had no idea what time it was when she opened one eye and glanced at the dresser. The red light of her cell phone blinked off and on, seemingly magnified by the darkness. Beau was snoring beside her, so she eased out from under his arm and stepped over to the dresser to retrieve her cell phone. As she pressed the message button, she crossed the room and opened the drapes, surprised to see the sun already shining brightly. Maryse was going to kill her for sleeping so late with Mildred in the hospital. She was surprised her friend hadn't already stormed the hotel, but since Maryse was also hoping Sabine would get lucky, that probably explained everything. When she heard Martin Alford's voice, she stiffened, frozen in place as he gave her the results of the test.

It was official. Sabine was a Fortescue.

She sank down on the end of the bed and blew out a breath. This was it. It was exactly what she'd been looking for. Well, maybe not the weirdness and definitely not the threats on her life and Mildred getting caught in the crossfire, but she was one enormous step closer to finding a matching donor. Someone in the family might not want her around, but Sabine seriously doubted that every family member was conspiring to kill her.

If they could just find whoever was trying to kill her, everything could go back to some semblance of normal, and God willing, Sabine would have plenty of time left on this earth to enjoy the pure mundane. Beau stirred and looked up at her. The expression on her face must have worried him, because he immediately sat up.

"What's wrong?" he asked.

"Nothing. Alford called. I'm officially a Fortescue."

Beau ran one hand through his hair. "Well, that's a good thing, right? I mean, considering everything else. Jesus, I never thought I'd be glad for you to be related to those nuts."

Sabine smiled. "Perspective is a real bitch sometimes."

"Definitely." Beau looked over at the window and frowned. "I can't believe we slept that late."

"I'd like to believe I wore you out," Sabine said and grinned, "but I'm guessing the murder games were probably a bigger exhaustion factor."

"Well," he said and looked her up and down, "since we're already starting late, what's another half hour?"

Sabine's body immediately responded to his suggestion. Her nipples hardened and she felt an ache in her core. The same ache that Beau had quenched the night before. She hesitated for a moment, knowing this was a really, really bad idea, but then the memory of incredible pleasure overrode all common sense and she took one step toward him.

And that's when someone banged on the motel room door.

"Sabine, Beau!" Raissa's voice sounded outside the door. "Are you there?"

Sabine froze for an instant, then went into overdrive, tossing Beau his clothes and tugging on her own. The oddity of calm-and-collected Raissa banging on her hotel door at a time when she'd normally be opening her shop had sent Sabine into a bit of a panic. Fortunately, Beau sensed her urgency and was dressed, of sorts, before Sabine yanked open the door. Raissa burst into the room, holding a folder and looked relieved when she saw Beau there as well. "I've been trying to reach you since last night," Raissa said. "Don't you people answer your cell phones?"

Sabine felt the heat rise up her neck and shot Beau a sideways look. He didn't look any more comfortable. At least neither of them planned on volunteering exactly why they had ignored their phones. "I overslept and was just checking messages," Sabine said. "I'm sorry we worried you. Did you drive all the way over here for that?"

Raissa shook her head. "I've got some information for you, but I'm not sure what to make of it." She opened the folder and stepped between Beau and Sabine so that they could both see the stack of papers inside. "That whole issue with the missing medical records concerned me, so I called in a favor. A lot of hospitals have started making digital backups of all their files, so I did some poking around to find out if Mudbug General had joined the wave of the future."

Sabine stared down at the first sheet of paper. "Holy crap, Raissa. This is my dad's file."

Beau raised his eyebrows and looked at Raissa. "People owe you favors that include hacking a hospital's database? I don't suppose you're going to tell me what you did for them?"

Raissa looked a bit flustered but waved one hand in dismissal. "I don't suppose I am. I expect you to use the information and pretend you have no idea how you got it. And don't, for any reason, let anyone see it. My friend broke at least a hundred different laws to get this."

Beau smiled. "Given the type of friends you have, Raissa, I'm not really interested in becoming one of your enemies. So I assume there's something interesting in here and not just your usual run of the flu and athlete's foot?"

"Anyone insane?" Sabine asked.

"Well," Raissa said. "There's nothing on Frances until she was seventeen and she was hospitalized for meningitis, but after that the rest of her file reads like something out of a Stephen King novel. That woman has some serious issues."

"What's wrong with her?" Sabine asked.

"Paranoid schizophrenic, according to this. Apparently they keep her fairly well-medicated so there's minimal outbursts, but it says in her file that the last time they hospitalized her, she swore someone was coming out of the ground to get her. It's no small wonder she's been kept in the house and drugged to a stupor."

"God, that's awful," Sabine said.

"Another interesting thing," Raissa continued, "is that all the Fortescues are allergic to peanuts. It's in all their records, except Catherine, but she's a Fortescue by marriage."

"So any of them could have guessed I had the same allergy, given that it was that prevalent in the family."

"Unfortunately, yes," Raissa said, "but that leads me to the really interesting part."

Sabine stared at her. "There's more?"

"Oh, yeah, and it's a doozy." Raissa flipped through a couple of sheets and pulled one from the middle of the stack. "This is part of your father's file, except, well, take a look at the test."

Sabine and Beau leaned over to read the line Raissa was pointing to. Sabine gasped. "He was impotent." She read the next line out loud. " 'Impotency most likely as a result of scarlet fever as an infant.' But it's not possible."

Raissa stared at the paper, then looked at Sabine. "Maybe it's a huge coincidence that you favor them. Maybe you're a distant cousin—"

"No," Sabine interrupted. "Alford left a message this morning. The results of the DNA test were positive."

Beau and Raissa stared at her, then looked at each other, then back at her. No one seemed to have any idea what to say. "Maybe the test was wrong," Sabine suggested. "That can happen, right? I mean, men who have vasectomies sometimes still surprise their wives with a baby."

Raissa frowned. "I don't know that this is the same thing. Your father was working for a doctor at the time they ran these tests. It looks like he was taking part in some sort of medical trial, but the file doesn't state for what. I guess anything's possible..."

Beau shook his head. "But it's more likely that if you're really related, your father is a different Fortescue."

"My mother got pregnant by a different Fortescue?" Sabine sank onto the bed, her mind whirling with a million jumbled thoughts. "But even if that were the case, that wouldn't show up as a positive paternity, not if I were the child of some distant cousin, would it?"

"Not likely," Raissa said. "It would have to be an uncle, or a grandparent, I think, to register that closely."

Sabine covered her hand with her hands. "Oh, Lord, that's awful. My dad couldn't possibly have known, could he?"

"Don't go down that road just yet," Beau said. "There's always another explanation."

Sabine looked up at him. "Like what?"

"Well, the Fortecues could have lied about the results," Beau said.

"Why would they do that? What could they possibly have to gain by pretending I was Adam's daughter?"

Beau looked at Raissa, who frowned. "Maybe so you'd stop looking for your father," Raissa said.

Sabine stared at her for a moment. "Then that means they know the truth."

Raissa nodded. "I think they've always known."

Chapter Sixteen

The shrill ring of Sabine's cell phone cut into their conversation, and Sabine flipped it open, desperate for any possible distraction. Her mind was overloaded, her emotions overwhelmed. This was so much more confusing than she'd thought it would be. And so much more dangerous. She glanced at Beau and Raissa, who were studying her with matched looks of concern, and pressed the Talk button.

"Sabine?" Catherine Fortescue's voice was the absolute last one she expected to hear at the moment, and the last one she was prepared to speak to.

"Ye-yes." Sabine pointed to the phone and signaled to Beau and Raissa.

"Sabine, this is Catherine Fortescue. I hope I didn't call too early."

"No, Catherine," Sabine said, trying to keep her voice calm. "I've been up for a while."

"Good, then that means you've gotten the message from Mr. Alford about the test results. I can't tell you how pleased the family is to have Adam's child with us. I'm sorry we had to jump to legal proof so soon after our first meeting, but now all that unpleasantness is behind us."

"I understand," Sabine said, "and I told Mr. Alford that I'd expected to take the test. It wasn't an inconvenience, I assure you."

"Thank goodness. I was a little concerned. It's all so tacky, really. But the reason I called is that we'd like to meet with you to get to know you better and to start working on some of the more unfortunate legal work required to set up your trust fund."

"Oh no," Sabine protested, "I already told you I didn't want any money."

"The Fortescue estate is quite clear on the rules for heirs. You're the firstborn child of a firstborn child, and that comes with certain privileges, as well as obligations, I'm afraid. While I certainly have the utmost respect for your wishes, we really don't have much choice in the matter. Of course, you're free to do whatever you'd like with the money once the fund is established and transferred."

"Of course." No point arguing. She'd just deal with it later.

"If you're available, we'd love to have you over tonight for dinner."

Deciding the best possible decision at the moment was no decision, Sabine said finally, "I need to check my schedule at the shop first. If that's okay, can I give you a call in the next hour or so and let you know for sure?"

"That will be fine," Catherine replied. "And please feel free to bring your detective friend. Mr. Alford says he has a reputation for being quite a specialist at this sort of family dynamic. He might be able to lend some advice."

"Thank you. I'll let him know." Sabine said goodbye and closed the phone. Beau and Raissa were brimming with impatience. "Catherine wants me to go to dinner tonight to 'get to know me better and start the legal work for my trust fund.' " She looked at Beau. "You're invited."

Beau shook his head. "I don't like it."

"Nobody likes it," Raissa pointed out, "but it does present an opportunity for the two of you to get a closer look at the Fortescues in a somewhat manageable environment. The sooner you find out what they're hiding, the sooner Sabine's life might get back to normal."

Beau stared at Raissa as if she'd lost her mind. "How the hell is that manageable? Possibly confronting a killer on his own turf? Especially that turf—isolated doesn't even begin to describe the

Fortescue estate. That's the quickest way to ensure a call to the coroner in my experience."

Raissa shrugged. "So go about your normal business and wonder if today is the day, or if it's going to happen in Sabine's apartment, or her shop, or this hotel. Since Sabine's poisoning never got out and Sabine herself hasn't mentioned it to the family, whoever took that shot at her probably thinks the entire thing was dismissed as accidental. Same with Mildred's accident in Sabine's car."

"Great," Beau said. "So he's not on the defensive. Instead, he's looking for another opportunity to strike."

Raissa shook her head. "If it is a Fortescue behind this, do you really think he will take a shot at Sabine while she's on the family estate? Talk about bringing down the house of cards, unless of course he is insane, but then it's not going to matter where you are or what you're doing, he's going to keep trying. And most likely get more desperate. This dinner might be an opportunity to do a little spy work. Especially if one of you could get out of the Fortescues' sight long enough to do a little snooping."

Beau blew out a breath and looked at Sabine. "I still don't like it, but Raissa's right. We can't lock you up in this hotel room and wait for another bomb escapade. And at least I was included in the invitation so you don't have to make up some excuse to bring me along. Not to mention that I'm guessing they won't be put off forever."

Sabine nodded and glanced over at Raissa. The psychic mouthed the word "Helena," and all of a sudden Sabine understood exactly why Raissa was suggesting this was a great opportunity to snoop. And what could possibly be a better weapon than the spy no one could hear or see?

It was inching toward evening and Helena Henry sat propped up on the bed in Sabine's hotel room, eating her third moon pie since arriving ten minutes before. Sabine wasn't sure whether she should be amazed or disgusted. However, a critical review of Helena's current outfit—some leather/spandex, studded combination reminiscent of eighties hair bands—gave Sabine pause. Despite eating the gross national product in carbs, fat, and sugar, the ghost was right. She hadn't gained a single pound.

Maybe jealousy was a more appropriate emotion, although Sabine wasn't quite ready to trade in her life for a permanent, calorie-free binge. She looked over at her half-eaten lunch of plain turkey sandwich on the dresser. Yet.

"So are you clear on what I need, Helena?"

"Yepfft…marphmellows sticking…wait." She chewed a couple of seconds more, then swallowed twice and took a huge breath. "Man, that's good. I haven't eaten moon pies in forever."

Sabine narrowed her eyes at Helena. "Where exactly did you get…no, never mind. It's better if I don't know. Do you understand the plan?"

"I'm a bitch, not a moron. I hitch a ride with you and that sexy detective to the nutso house, then take a look around and see if I can find any skeletons in their closets." Helena straightened up. "Hey, do you think they really have a skeleton in the closet?"

"I hope not. But anything you find that looks suspect, you report immediately back to me. Just no yelling, and for God's sake, no eating while you're there."

Helena frowned. "No one said anything about not eating. Damn. Rich people always have fancy food when they have important company. What could be more important than a long-lost granddaughter? Maybe I could sneak a dessert or a dinner roll?" She gave Sabine an expectant look.

"Absolutely not! I am not going to play distract-people-from-the-floating-roll all evening. You will sneak and snoop and get dirt on these people as if you're searching for a bottomless pot of red beans and rice. I don't think I should have to remind you that this is a matter of life or death. And you of all people ought to know what an iffy thing death is."

Helena sighed. "Fine. You don't have to go all guilt trip on me. It's not like I want you stuck here with me. Now, that detective would be a whole other story." Helena's expression brightened. "Hey, I don't suppose there will be a little truck hanky-panky?"

"You don't suppose right," Sabine shot back, but the disappointed look on Helena's face was too comical for her to maintain her stern stance. Finally, she smiled. "But if you're really good, I might see what I can do about a big pot of gumbo when we get back."

Helena clapped her hands. "Whoohoo! Can we have beer, too?"

"I don't know. Can you get drunk?"

"I can try."

Sabine grimaced. "That's what I was afraid of." She was about to follow that up with the no alcohol rule when Beau knocked on the connecting door and poked his head in.

"Are you ready?" he asked. "I thought you were talking to someone on the phone."

Sabine forced a smile. "Just hung up. Give me a sec and I'll meet you in the lobby."

"Everything okay with Mildred?" Beau asked.

Sabine nodded. "It's all settled. Maryse is going to stay with her tonight, for which I will officially owe her a trip to New Orleans for a manicure and pedicure because she has to sleep in the stinky hospital in a lumpy recliner."

"Not exactly a bad deal. I thought you women loved a pedicure."

"I love pedicures, and if I wasn't having one with Maryse it would be a good deal, but she takes picky to a whole new level. There was this incident a couple of years ago with a bottle of Purple Passion polish and the local police..." Sabine shook her head. "No, I don't even have time to explain. I'll be downstairs in a minute."

Beau grinned and closed the door behind him.

Sabine gave Helena a stern look. "You will be quiet on the ride over there. I'm not going to give him any reason to think the insanity is hereditary." Helena nodded and pulled another moon pie from the box. Sabine snatched the pie and the box from her hand. "And no food. It's not invisible like you, remember?"

Helena climbed off the bed and cast a wistful glance at the moon pie box. "You're such a grouch, Sabine. What is it about you and Maryse?"

Sabine grabbed her purse and tucked her cell phone in a side pocket. "Gee, I don't know. There's that whole someone's-trying-to-kill-me thing, or the I-can't-live-a-normal-life-in-my-own-house and my-friends-are-getting-caught-in-the-fallout thing, and hey, we could always throw in getting-haunted-by-the-constantly-bitching-and-eating-ghost-of-the-nastiest-person-I-knew-in-real-life part of the equation."

"Well, if you put it that way," Helena grumbled and headed out the door and down the steps to the lobby.

Sabine followed, praying that this whole thing didn't blow up in her face. Praying that she'd even be around tomorrow to pray.

The drive to the Fortescues was painfully long and silent. Sabine was afraid to say anything lest she give Helena a reason to start sounding off and blow their cover. Beau was suspiciously silent and appeared to be in deep thought. Over what, she had no idea. At this point, it could be anything—her situation with the Fortescues, her earlier cancer announcement, the new information Raissa had provided, their lovemaking the night before, this fall's football lineup.

She sighed and rested her head back on the seat.

Beau looked over at her. "Anything wrong?"

"Aside from the obvious, no. I was just thinking that a full night's sleep last night might have been a good idea given what we're doing now. My mind's all fuzzy."

"Whoohoo!" Helena sounded from the back of the car. "Why weren't you sleeping? Details, woman, I want details. You can start with the bottom half and work your way up."

Sabine closed her eyes again and clenched her jaw. Do not respond. Do not even look at her.

"I know what you mean," Beau said. "This whole thing was bizarre to begin with and it just keeps throwing angles at us that I didn't see coming and can't seem to fit to anything else. I wish it would all clear up. I have this overwhelming feeling that we're missing something, but I'll be damned if I can figure out what."

Sabine straightened in her seat as they pulled through the massive iron gates of the Fortescue estate. "Well, you've got a couple of minutes to figure it all out. Otherwise we're back to Plan B."

"There's a Plan B?"

Sabine looked at the opposing structure and felt a cold shiver rush across her. "Yeah, stay alive."

Two hours later, Sabine was mentally and emotionally drained as she'd never been before. Catherine and her ideas about "proper" behavior for a Fortescue, Frances's interruptions with scripture that didn't apply to anything they were speaking of, William's uninterested silence, and Alford's mild annoyance had gotten on her last nerve. In fact, it was more likely the last nerve was gone, too, and now they were eating away at bone.

Dinner had been an elaborate affair, served by the enthusiastic Adelaide, and while Sabine had to admit the food was fantastic, the atmosphere was so...oppressed, she guessed was the best word... that it made it difficult to enjoy the meal. Finally, the last dish was cleared away and they left the stiff, formal dining hall for the relative comfort of the living room. Alford excused himself, claiming he had some documents to review for a client meeting the following morning. Sabine didn't think he was telling the truth for a minute, but since contemplating the fuzz in her navel would be more interesting than hearing Catherine drone on any longer, she could hardly blame him for escaping. After all, he had to deal with the family far more than she did and had probably heard Catherine's opinions every week for the last twenty or thirty years.

A couple of times Helena had popped her head into the room, but only long enough to shake her head at Sabine and pop back out again. Sabine was growing dreadfully afraid that she was enduring this insult to her entire life for nothing.

They had just settled in the living room with coffee and Catherine was droning on about the high-end, dresses-only clothing store that Sabine should open when Adelaide hurried into the room, interrupting Catherine's monologue on "proper fashion for heiresses."

"Mrs. Fortescue, a storm is moving in something fierce and there's a leak around one of the library windows. It came up so sudden-like, I'm afraid we didn't even know until quite a bit of the floor was soaked."

Catherine frowned and left the room. She returned a minute later, a grim look on her face. "Adelaide is right. I can't see an inch beyond the hallway window. The living room is so well insulated we couldn't hear a thing." She looked at the housekeeper, her agitation obvious and unusual for the normally ultra-composed woman. "Have you checked the news? Where is the storm coming from?"

Adelaide shook her head. "Can't get any signal on the television. As soon as we realized it was raining, we tried. I got an old radio up in my room. You want me to get it?"

"Yes," Catherine said. "That would be very helpful." She looked at Sabine and Beau. "I'm so sorry about all of this. The storm must have shifted at the last minute. If you'll excuse William and me, there are some things we should tend to in case we lose power." Catherine nodded at her husband and they left the room through opposite doors, the quickness in their step belying the calm presentation.

Sabine shot a look at Beau. No power meant no lights. Shut up in this house with a possible killer and no lights wasn't an option Sabine hadn't considered, and she didn't like considering it now. As soon as Catherine left, Sabine crossed the room and retrieved her purse from the table in the corner. She opened it and ensured that her pistol was still safely tucked inside, then walked back across the room, purse in tow, and pulled a cough drop from a pocket inside. She sat the purse on a table within easy reach and looked over at Frances, who was sitting ramrod stiff, her face filled with fear.

"Frances?" Sabine asked. "Are you all right?"

Frances twisted the edge of her sweater with both hands. "I don't like the storm. I put them in the garden, but they came back. It was the water."

Adelaide came into the room and patted Frances on the arm. "Now, Frances, you didn't plant any flowers this spring and besides, William fixed the drainage years ago. Those plants aren't going anywhere." Adelaide helped Frances up from her chair. "Why don't you let me get you settled in your room before the worst of this comes? I'll bring you a cup of hot chocolate as soon as you're tucked down deep in them covers."

Frances looked at Adelaide with a blank stare for a couple of seconds, then nodded. "Hot chocolate does sound nice."

"Of course it does," Adelaide soothed. She turned to Sabine and Beau. "Give me a minute to see to Frances, and then I'll get you two some flashlights from the kitchen. Just in case." She guided Frances out of the room and into the hallway.

"It's the 'just in case' that worries me the most," Sabine whispered. "What are we supposed to do now?"

Beau crossed the room and checked up and down the halls at both entrances. "I don't know, but that storm is starting to worry me."

"Maybe we should start home before it gets any worse."

"Too late for that," Martin Alford's voice sounded from the front entrance, causing Sabine to jump. "The bridge is already under water, and the river was still rising. It will take hours after the rain subsides before the river will be low enough to cross."

Sabine stared at him. "Surely there's another way. A way around?"

"Not to speak of," Alford said, as he wiped at his dripping wet face with a tissue. "A long ways back there was a road that ran north of here and circled the river, but when the Fortescues acquired the land containing the road about thirty years back, they closed off the road and it's since grown over so you wouldn't really know it was there unless you knew where to look."

"Oh, I don't know that I'd like living here knowing that every time it rained I was cut off from the rest of the world. What if they have an emergency?"

Alford brushed wet hair off his forehead and reached for a tissue to wipe his brow. "If there's a serious situation, there's plenty of room to land a helicopter, and those pilots can fly in just about anything. Of course, you'd have to take one of the horses to actually get into town as the phones usually go right along with the power, but it's rarely necessary. The bridge usually doesn't go all the way under. It just happens when it rains hard and fast, a real downpour."

"Where did this come from?" Sabine asked. "Everyone thought the storms were headed east of here."

Alford nodded. "They are, but not far enough east for us to avoid a bit of the lashing. It was clear as a bell when I left and not five minutes later the bottom dropped out of the sky. I thought I'd get past the bridge before it went under, but with all the rain we've had lately, the river was already running high and this storm is really pouring it out."

"So what do we do?" Sabine asked. "I mean, if Mr. Alford is right and we won't be able to get over the bridge until tomorrow—"

A huge clap of thunder boomed through the house, causing the walls to shake. The lights flickered once, then again, then went off completely, leaving the room pitch black.

"Holy shit!" Sabine passed her hand over the table until she found her purse, then lifted it up and pulled it on her shoulder.

"Just stay still," Beau advised and stepped closer to Sabine, finding her hand with his. "Adelaide said she'd be back with flashlights. She can't be much longer."

Sabine felt her pulse begin to increase and hoped Adelaide came before she was in cardiac arrest mode. She looked to the doorway that Adelaide had escorted Frances through and saw a faint flicker of light. She squinted, trying to make out the source, and as it grew closer, she realized it was an old-fashioned oil lantern. The lantern cast an eerie glow on Catherine's face as she walked into the room.

Catherine's gaze stopped on Alford. "Mr. Alford...I was afraid you might not make it out in time. I can only assume the bridge is underwater."

"Yes," Alford said. "I don't think it's going to be passable for quite a while after the storm stops."

"Then you'll all stay here," Catherine said and looked over at Sabine. "I'm so sorry about this inconvenience. If I'd had any idea the storm would hit here, we would have postponed dinner. Adelaide is finishing up with Frances. I'll have her make up three guest rooms on the same hall."

"Do you have any flashlights?" Beau asked. "Adelaide was going to bring some back with her."

"Yes," Catherine said. "We keep several in the kitchen for just this reason. I'll go get them. William is bringing in more lanterns from the garage, and there's the generator, of course, but it only produces enough power to light the kitchen. I'm afraid you're going to have to relive ancient history for a night—except for the indoor plumbing part, of course." She gave them a smile, then turned and walked toward the kitchen. Alford fell in step behind her.

"If you don't mind," he said, "I'd like to get one of those flashlights and check on my car. I think I left an interior light on."

"Of course," Catherine said and the two left the room through the entrance to the kitchen.

The light in the room faded with Catherine's lantern, and once again Sabine and Beau were cast into darkness. "I don't like it," Beau said, keeping his voice low. "It's not safe. I don't want you in that room alone. I'm staying with you."

"Catherine would never agree to that. It wouldn't be 'proper.' "

"Then I'll sneak in after she's gone."

"With all of us occupying the same hallway? If you use a light, Alford or Frances will see it and if you don't use a light, you'll take out one of the five thousand antiques they have lining every hall in this monstrosity."

"I'll take my chances."

Sabine opened her mouth to respond, but felt a jab in her side from Beau's elbow. She looked over at the entrance as Catherine walked back into the room, carrying two flashlights. A second look revealed Helena strolling behind her, a worried look on her face. Catherine handed them each a flashlight and said, "Adelaide has already started putting out the linens. It will only be a bit longer before the rooms are ready. I know it's a little early, but I figured it would be better to retire now than risk walking around with the lanterns. I worry about fire, especially in a house this old."

Sabine just nodded, trying not to look at Helena, but dying to know what the ghost had found out.

"I don't blame you," Beau said. "Just let us know when everything's ready. We're not going anywhere."

Catherine tried to smile at his attempt at a joke, but it came out more like a grimace. Whatever was bothering her seemed to intensify right along with the storm. She nodded and left the room.

Sabine watched as the light of the lantern faded away, then turned on her flashlight and faced Beau. "I know this wasn't in the plans and I'll admit this house and the people who live here give me the creeps, but this might also be the opportunity to get to the bottom of this."

Beau stared at her as if she'd lost her mind. "We are trapped in this mansion out of a horror novel and you think this is some sort of opportunity? An opportunity for what—a shallow grave?"

"An opportunity to catch the killer in the act."

"You're not exactly convincing me of anything here, Sabine."

"If I'm in a room alone, then the killer might take a shot at me."

Beau shook his head. "Which is exactly my problem with all of this. No way. I'm not letting you stay by yourself."

"But I have a plan—"

"Damn it, Sabine! You want me to sit in my room, and who knows how far away that is, and wait for someone to attack you? And what? Hope you can fight them off or yell loud enough for me to hear you and get there in time? That's a bullshit plan and you know it. And if you want to throw in the insanity angle then our number one suspect is Frances and her room is on the same hall."

"It's not like I'm unprotected, Beau—you've seen me shoot. I'll be fine. If they'd slipped anything into my food, I'd be laid out on the floor already, and I won't drink the hot chocolate. That way I can stay conscious."

"Really? And if the killer gets creative and pumps gas through a vent in your room—what then? You going to tell me you can shoot people in your sleep? Because if so, you should have warned me last night and I would have worn a bulletproof vest to bed."

"Whoohoo!" Helena hooted and danced a jig. "Sabine got lucky." Helena looked Beau up and down. "Really lucky. Damn."

Sabine felt her checks burning red and was glad the flashlight didn't give away her mortal embarrassment. Bad enough her roll with the sexy PI had been announced to Helena, but even worse, she'd had a vivid recall of just how good Beau Villeneuve looked in bed. She bit her lower lip, struggling with a way to let Beau in on her secret weapon, but there simply wasn't any way to lessen the blow. "You trust me, right?"

"This has nothing to do with me trusting you. It's about not trusting them."

"What if I told you I could ensure that even if something happened to me, you could be notified?"

Beau shook his head. "Our cell phones don't get a signal out this far. I've already checked. And even if they did normally, they wouldn't in this storm. Maybe if the rooms are right next to each other, but I seriously doubt prim and proper Catherine is going to go for that."

"What if I had a more elusive, albeit much more offensive, method of calling you for help?" She bit her lip, then pressed forward before she could change her mind. "I snuck someone into the estate with us."

"Where, in your handbag? Even if there wasn't a monsoon outside, there's no way into this fortress that isn't covered with iron bars or security cameras."

"She rode with us in the truck."

Beau blew out a breath of frustration. "I don't have time for games. We have to come up with a plan, and right now the best one I can think of involves walking out of here and swimming across that damned bayou of alligators. It's the safer of the two options."

"She's a ghost. Helena Henry's ghost, to be exact."

Beau stared. "What do you want from me, Sabine? Jesus, I've kept an open mind about everything, but telling me I taxied a ghost over here is way beyond my limit."

"Helena," Sabine said and pointed to a desk in the corner. "Get that pad of paper and pen and bring it over here so that you can answer some questions. And make it fast. We need to go from 'no way in hell' to 'I believe' in a minute or less."

Helena lifted the paper and pen from the desk and walked over to stand next to Beau. The look on his face was beyond comprehension, and Sabine could only imagine what thoughts must be racing through his mind. Helena began to write and Beau looked down at the paper in amazement.

I am Helena Henry. I was murdered and have been visible to Maryse since my death and more recently to Sabine. Sorry if this startles the shit out of you, but it's not a fucking picnic for me either. I've been here spying on these psychos for hours and haven't had a thing to eat. Deal with it and let's get this over with.

Chapter Seventeen

Sabine waited anxiously for Beau to react, worried that she'd thrown way too much at him at once, especially with everything else going on. He stared at the paper as if it were going to explode. Then he took one hand and slowly passed it through Helena. "It's colder. I swear, the air is colder where she's standing." He looked at Sabine. "I can't believe it, but it's real." His expression instantly shifted to one of immediate realization. "Holy mother of God, she's been following you around all this time. That's how you got into the medical records room."

Sabine nodded. "She's also the one who created the vision for Raissa to draw my parents from. Helena's been involved from the beginning, and she's going to see it to the end. I'm so sorry to spring it on you like this. I'd hoped you would never have to know."

"That might have been nice." He glanced at the paper once more then looked at Sabine, a pained expression on his face. "She wasn't in the room last night..."

"No! Maryse and I have a strict rule about unannounced visiting—especially bedroom visits."

The pen began moving again and Beau leaned over. A single word appeared.

Spoilsports.

Beau smiled. "She's kinda a handful, isn't she?"

"You have no idea. But she'll also do anything to help me. If anything happens to me while I'm alone in my room, Helena will alert you."

Beau stared at the wall for a couple of seconds, obviously lost in thought. Finally, he looked Sabine directly in the eyes. "It was Helena who called 911 that night in your apartment, wasn't it? That's why no one ever spoke. You were already passed out."

Sabine nodded.

Beau paced the length of the room twice, then stopped and looked at the pad of paper again. "You know this is insane, right?"

"Seems to be no shortage of crazy in this house. Why should we be any different?"

"I do have an idea. It's not very nice, but I think if you can pull it off it might get Adelaide's tongue loosened. I'd be willing to bet she knows everything that goes on in this house."

"What's the idea?"

Beau smiled. "Adelaide believes in spirits, the afterlife, right? Couldn't Helena create visions for her just like she did for Raissa? I figure if Adelaide is the one to settle you in your room, then you might have a chance to call up spirits via Helena, and get Adelaide to tell some family secrets."

Sabine frowned. "But if Adelaide's memory is going, like Alford said, is anything she says really dependable?"

"We only have Alford's word that Adelaide's mind is going, and he's getting that directly from the Fortescues. What better way to discount the ramblings of an old woman than to say she's losing her faculties?"

"You have a point." Sabine looked over at Helena. "Do you think you can help me spook the housekeeper?"

Helena shrugged. "I could probably manage a vision or two… for a piece of that chocolate cake I saw y'all eating."

Sabine sighed. "I'll see what I can do, but it's going to have to wait. Now, before Catherine gets back, tell me what you've found, Helena. You had a strange look on your face when you entered the room."

"The first place I checked was Catherine and William's room. Catherine had this box of clippings on William with parts of the text highlighted—everything he'd ever done, looks like, from birth to the war. But after the war, there was nothing. I assumed at first that after she got married and had the kids, she was just too busy to keep up with it any longer, but then I started reading the highlighted text and it didn't make sense at all."

"Why not?"

"Well, like the article about William receiving a medal of bravery for being shot in the leg trying to help another soldier. You'd think she would have highlighted his name and medal of bravery, right? But instead, she'd highlighted the text that mentioned the shot he took to the leg. They were all like that. I couldn't make any sense of the things she highlighted. I started to take them, but I figured it wasn't a good idea."

"No," Sabine agreed. "We don't want anyone to get suspicious. And be careful when you search and make sure you put everything back exactly as you found it, okay?"

"I'm being careful," Helena promised. "After that I took a trip to Frances's room and what a doozy that was. The woman has more crosses in that tiny space than the entire cathedral in Rome and a candle on every level surface. I figure either she's trying to repent for something major or believes in vampires. Then I found a newspaper stashed in between her mattresses."

Sabine nodded. "Catherine mentioned something about Frances reading the newspaper again. I got the impression they tried to keep it from her."

"Well, the odd part about this one is it was a month old. So I flipped through it and you'll never guess what I found—that photo of you at that breast cancer walk in New Orleans. Your picture was circled along with a comment in the article about you owning Read 'em and Reap."

Sabine sucked in a breath. "That's how she knew about me before Beau contacted Mr. Alford. She saw me in the paper and noticed my resemblance to her brother. Could it have been Frances who tried to break into my store?"

Helena nodded. "I wondered that myself, so I took off out of there and made my way through the garage and the carriage house.

Sure enough, in the carriage house there was the white truck that I saw in the park the day of the break-in."

"You're sure it was the same?"

"It was the same make and model. I'm pretty sure there's another one or two in the world like it but it's too big of a coincidence to ignore, don't you think?"

"Yes," Sabine agreed, "and with Catherine busy with church things and William throwing them back at the bar, Frances would have had plenty of opportunities to take the truck and pay me a visit. But for what?" Sabine frowned and repeated everything Helena had said so far to Beau.

Beau shook his head. "Maybe she was going to talk to you but when the shop was closed, she figured no one was there and she'd do some snooping. Lord only knows for what…a birth certificate, pictures? Either way, I don't think it's a coincidence that the truck is the same make and model as the one Helena saw."

Sabine frowned. "But what about the person I kicked that night outside of the general store? That couldn't have been Frances. A kick would have sent her sprawling."

"Not necessarily," Beau said. "Sometimes the insane can show remarkable strength if they're experiencing an adrenaline rush. It's documented all the time."

"And the poison…the bomb? Do you really think Frances is capable of those things?"

"No," Beau said, "but I think she's capable of getting someone else to do them, and I'm sure she's got the trust fund to back it up. But we also have to remember that anyone with access to the household could have used that truck. Frances might be winning the insanity wars, but we still don't know for sure it was her that tried to break into your store, or that attacked you on the street. And if it was, we don't know that she was alone."

"True. But who would help her commit a crime and why?"

"She'd do it for the inheritance," Helena chimed in. "If the Fortescues' estate was set up anything like my family's, then your father, as firstborn, would inherit the house and all its contents, along with his share of the estate. Since he's dead, his portion would pass to you as his firstborn."

"And skip Frances entirely?"

Helena nodded. "The house could, yes. And I'm guessing this place is worth a pretty penny."

Sabine repeated Helena's comments to Beau. "It reminds me of something Catherine said when she invited me to dinner. About being the 'firstborn child of a firstborn child.' "

"So quite possibly, a fortune at stake," Beau said, "and more importantly, her home. Maybe Frances was afraid she'd have to leave."

"I would never do that," Sabine protested.

"You and I know that," Beau said, "but Frances doesn't, and she's not exactly playing with a full deck. The more I hear, the less I like this idea of you playing bait, Sabine. I think—" He stopped talking as Adelaide walked into the room.

"If you are ready," Adelaide said, "I can take you to your rooms now."

Beau's mind raced with possibilities, none of them good. This situation had gone from bad, to horrible, to out of the fucking world in less than ten minutes time. If there was ever a situation where he needed to think quickly and clearly, it was now. But the overload of information, coupled with being stranded in Hell House—accompanied by a ghost, no less—had his mind racing out of control. Keeping Sabine safe, then getting her out of that house was his top priority and he needed a plan. Yesterday.

"That's fine, Adelaide. We're ready to go to our rooms now," Sabine said, and she took the lantern Adelaide held out to her.

"There's another in Mr. Villeneuve's room," Adelaide explained as they walked down the dark hallway and into the west wing of the house.

Beau committed every step of the hallway, every turn to memory. Knowing exactly where everything was located was key, especially if they needed to leave in a hurry. Adelaide stopped at the first room and motioned to Beau. "This one is yours, Mr. Villeneuve. There are some spare clothes on the bed, if you'd like to change. It's just a pair of shorts and a T-shirt, but it will likely be more comfortable than what you're wearing."

Beau smiled at the anxious housekeeper. "It's all fine, Adelaide, and I really appreciate all the trouble you've gone to."

"Oh, well," Adelaide said, apparently at a loss for not only being thanked but complimented as well. Even in the dim light, the flush on her face was evident.

"If you ladies don't mind," Beau said, "I'm going to follow Mr. Alford's example and check on my truck before I turn in." He looked at Sabine and inclined his head toward Adelaide, hoping she took the cue to try the Helena scam on the housekeeper once they were alone in her room.

"Mr. Villeneuve," Adelaide said before he could leave, "there's a big urn next to the front door that has some umbrellas in it. You help yourself."

"Thanks, Adelaide." He took the lantern off the dresser and headed down the hall, weaving his way toward the main entrance of the house.

He plucked a small umbrella from a large ceramic pot next to the door and stepped out into the hurricane. The wind and rain blew at an angle, making the umbrella more of a hindrance than a help, so he tossed it against the door and ran for his truck, holding one arm over his eyes to shield them from the worst of the pelting raindrops. Once in his truck, he tested his cell phone but wasn't surprised to find it had no signal.

He retrieved his spare revolver from the glove box and grabbed a backpack from the backseat. He pulled a pair of walkie-talkies from inside and checked the batteries. He didn't think the reception would be great, but the walkie-talkies might provide enough communication for him to stay in touch with Sabine. Despite Sabine's reassurances and Helena's dedication, Beau still wasn't convinced that the ghost was the best possible protection. But if she could shoot a gun, then his spare revolver might just come in handy.

He squinted in the darkness but couldn't make out the attorney's car anywhere in the front drive. Lucky bastard probably had an indoor parking spot. Although he didn't think it possible, the rain was coming down even harder now than before. He tucked the revolver in the waistband of his pants and slung the pack over his shoulder, then ran for the house, using the meager light of the lantern to help guide him.

He took a second to retrieve the umbrella and hurried inside, pausing only long enough to shake the water from his hair. He'd noticed earlier that the room Adelaide had prepared for him had an attached bathroom. Hopefully, the bathroom would have towels. After running in the monsoon, he was going to need one or two. Taking a right turn from the entrance, he stopped short at a door right at the edge of the hallway.

Figuring he could snoop as well as Helena, he peered both directions in the darkness. Deciding the coast was clear, he eased open the door and held his lantern close to the opening. A bevy of jackets and boots filled the tiny closet. He rifled through at least ten women's jackets, all too large for Frances, but then if you rarely left the house, Beau guessed you rarely needed a jacket. He searched the pockets for anything interesting, but Catherine Fortescue was apparently not the type of woman who carried miscellaneous items in her jacket pockets. It didn't really come as a surprise.

At the back of the closet, he found a men's navy blue raincoat, likely William's. Beau stuck his hand in the two outside pockets and came up with a key. It looked like a door key and fairly new, but there was no indication what door it was to. He placed the key back in the front pocket, then slipped his hand inside the interior pocket. He felt something round and plastic, but couldn't even guess what it might be. He pulled the object from the pocket and lifted the lantern to see his bounty.

His heart skipped a beat when he realized he was holding a bottle of peanut oil.

He reached back in the pocket again and drew out a syringe. Beau slipped the peanut oil and the syringe in his pocket and started to close the door when he remembered the key. He'd seen that key before. Reaching into the front pocket, he located the key and pulled it out again. He lifted the lantern so that he could get a good look at it and in a flash, it hit him—it was just like the key Sabine had used to open her shop—the locks that had just been replaced by the property manager who worked for the estate that owned the building, which just might be the Fortescue estate for all anyone knew. Why hadn't anyone considered that before?

With a clear idea of exactly how Sabine was poisoned despite drinking from an intact bottle of wine, Beau closed the closet door. As he walked silently back to his room, his mind worked to make sense of what he'd found. Unfortunately, the only part that made sense was how William Fortescue had managed to poison his granddaughter. But why? Something to do with the DNA test results? Someone in the Fortescue family knew the truth about Sabine's parents, maybe the whole family, and for whatever reason, they were determined to keep that truth a secret.

Even if it meant lying about her being family until they could kill her.

As he turned the corner for the hallway to his room, he caught a glimpse of something white moving at the far end of the hall. He turned his lantern down as low as it would go and crept to the end of the hallway, then peered around the corner. He could see a lantern across the room, but the light cast from it was too dim to make out the person carrying it. Suddenly, a flash of lightning lit the sky and filtered through the far wall of what must have been a sunroom since the wall was all glass. In the burst of light, he saw Frances opening a door to the gardens. She was wearing a long white dressing gown and carrying a shovel. Without so much as a backward glance, she walked out into the storm.

Sabine followed Adelaide into a room several doors down from Beau. He probably wasn't going to like the distance between them, but there was really little she could do. "It looks fine, Adelaide. Thank you."

"Would you like for me to get you some hot chocolate, Ms. Sabine? I figured we could all do with a little warm milk and chocolate."

"That sounds wonderful."

The housekeeper nodded and started to leave the room.

It's now or never. "Adelaide, wait!" Sabine grabbed the woman's arm and closed her eyes. "The spirits are talking. They said your name."

Sabine felt the woman stiffen and opened her eyes to see if she was up for the game. Adelaide stared back at her, eyes wide as saucers. "The spirits said my name?" Adelaide asked. "Why would they do that? I'm nobody."

Sabine shook her head. "You believe, Adelaide. The spirits are highly selective about who they speak to. It's an honor." Sabine waved one hand in the air, signaling Helena to get to work.

A dim glow began to form next to the bed and Adelaide grabbed Sabine's hand in hers and squeezed so hard Sabine was certain she'd broken something. "Look at that," Adelaide whispered. "You didn't say they'd show themselves, too."

Sabine shook her head. "They rarely materialize. I think it takes a lot of energy. This must be very important."

Adelaide nodded but never took her eyes off the expanding light. In the center of the light, two people began to come into shape, and Sabine had to hold herself back from giving Helena a high five. The ghost had chosen William's mother and father to create. Who better to get Adelaide to part with her secrets than the people she'd served the longest?

"Oh, my Lord," Adelaide said as the figures sharpened.

Sabine leaned toward Adelaide and whispered. "I think they want to ask you something."

"Anything," Adelaide said, "they can ask me anything. Aren't they beautiful? Just like in the picture over the fireplace."

"No shit," Helena grumbled and Sabine cut her eyes at the ghost. Helena huffed once and turned her concentration back to the apparition she was creating.

"I can hear her," Sabine said. "She's saying your name, Adelaide." Sabine closed her eyes for a couple of seconds, then looked at Adelaide. "She wants to know why."

"Why, what?" Adelaide asked.

Sabine shook her head. "I don't know. She's just saying 'why, Adelaide, why?' "

Adelaide dropped Sabine's hand and put her hand over her mouth. "Oh no! I'm so sorry, madam. I'm so sorry, but I swear I didn't know. Not until a long time had passed."

The possible scenarios raced through Sabine's mind, but she couldn't hit on one. She made the split-second decision to go vague again. "She wants to know why you didn't tell anyone when you found out."

"I wanted to," Adelaide cried. "Oh, I wanted to so bad, but Catherine told me that no one would believe me, and if I said anything, she'd just say I did it. That I hated you and wanted you gone. But I swear I had nothing to do with the car wreck." Adelaide let out an anguished cry. "Catherine said no one would take the word of a pagan housekeeper over the lady of the estate. And there was the babies. What would have happened to Frances and Adam? And my brother in that nursing home in New Orleans? Catherine was paying for it all. What would have happened to him? Oh, madam, please forgive me, I beg you."

Sabine's mind whirled with every statement Adelaide made. Surely she'd gotten it wrong. Adelaide couldn't possibly be saying that Catherine had killed William's parents. What was the point? William was going to inherit everything. She would never have wanted for anything. Sabine searched her mind for the next question to ask, but before she could formulate the words, the door to her room flew open and Beau hurried inside.

"Shit!" Helena griped as she lost concentration and the apparition vanished.

"No!" Adelaide cried. "Don't go, madam. I'm sorry. I'll make it right. I swear to you."

Beau barely glanced at the housekeeper. "Thank God you're all right," he said to Sabine. "When I was coming back from the car, I saw Frances leave the house. She was carrying a shovel."

"Oh, no," Adelaide said, her face filled with fear. "I have to stop her. Her mind is so fragile. I can't let her do it again." Adelaide rushed out of the room, and they could hear her footsteps pounding down the hall. Sabine glanced at Beau and they ran out of the room in pursuit of the housekeeper.

"This way," Beau yelled at Sabine when they reached the end of the hall. "This is where Frances went outside."

The door to the sunroom stood wide open, rain pouring inside. Adelaide was nowhere in sight. Beau held the lantern out in front of them and they ran out the door and into the storm. "Which way?" Sabine yelled, straining to make herself heard over the wind.

"I don't know," Beau said, turning from one direction to another. "There!" He pointed to a spot in the far end of the garden. Sabine could barely make out something white before Beau grabbed her hand and pulled her with him.

The rain felt like needles on her skin and almost blinded her. Beau slowed and Sabine knew he was having as much trouble maneuvering in the storm as she was. She pulled her hand from Beau's and held it over her eyes, hoping to get a better look ahead. Beau glanced back, then did the same, and they crept across the backyard until they were close enough to see what was happening.

Frances was digging like a madwoman around some old blackberry bushes, and Adelaide was frantically trying to get her to stop. So far, it looked like she'd gone at least two feet deep. No matter how hard Adelaide tugged, Frances kept lifting more mud from the hole she'd created. Frances's eyes were fixed on the ground, never blinking, never wavering, despite the torrent of rain hitting her face. She didn't seem to hear Adelaide or feel the housekeeper's hands on her arm.

Beau handed Sabine the lantern and went to assist Adelaide. He tried to take the shovel from Frances, and Sabine saw the shift in her face. Her eyes went black as night and anger coursed through her. She screamed and tried to attack Beau with the shovel, but his hold on it was strong and she couldn't break his grasp. She let go of the shovel and launched at his face with her hands.

Before Sabine could even take a step to help, Beau had grabbed one of Frances's arms and twisted it behind her, then wrapped his arms around her entire body. He lifted her completely off the ground and turned toward the house. Sabine took a step toward them and stepped into the completely forgotten hole. She cried out as her ankle twisted on impact and Beau stopped short and turned around to look at her.

"I'm fine," Sabine said as she moved her foot around, making sure she hadn't broken anything. And then she hit something solid. She leaned over with the lantern and put her hand down in the water-filled hole, trying to locate what her foot had hit. Finally, she felt something long and hard and worked her fingers around it.

"Sabine, c'mon," Beau yelled over the storm.

Sabine pulled her bounty from the water, and Frances screamed. Then Sabine took a good look at what she held: a human bone.

Sabine flung it to the ground and jumped out of the hole. Frances thrashed about, screaming like a banshee, and Beau struggled to maintain his grasp. Adelaide instantly dropped to her knees, praying to God Almighty to forgive her.

"Go!" Sabine yelled to Beau, and he started toward the house, struggling to maintain control of Frances. Sabine pulled Adelaide to her feet. "Pray later. You've got to help with Frances." Adelaide nodded and hurried toward the house. Sabine grit her teeth and bent over to pick up the bone. The smooth, hard surface shouldn't have caused so much emotion, but it was knowing what that surface was that made Sabine almost wretch.

She ran to the house and into the sunroom after Adelaide, then followed the housekeeper down the hall and into Frances's room, where Beau was trying to keep the woman restrained on her bed. She was soaking wet, and the white gown clung to her scrawny body. Her hair stuck to her face, the silver almost translucent in the lantern light. She turned toward Sabine and Adelaide as they entered the room, but she looked right through them, her eyes wild with fright.

Sabine hid the bone behind her back, certain that Frances would launch off again if she saw it. Adelaide rushed over to the bed and rubbed Frances's head as if petting a dog. "Now, now, child," Adelaide said, "you're going to be fine. It was just a scare is all. You don't like storms, remember? It's just the storm."

Frances seemed to calm a bit at Adelaide's words and slumped back on the bed. Adelaide picked up a cup of water that was sitting on the nightstand and lifted it to Frances's mouth. "You just need to drink a little water and relax, okay, child? You'll feel a lot better once you've had your water."

Beau released his hold on Frances and stepped back from the bed. They watched as Frances took one sip and then another, then quietly drifted off in what appeared to be a restful sleep. "Drugs?" Beau asked.

Adelaide nodded. "She'd had some of the water before she went outside, which is why it kicked in so fast now. But she was so worked up earlier that her body was still moving even though her mind was shutting down. Poor thing. She's always been afraid of storms."

Sabine held the bone out to Adelaide. "Maybe this has something to do with it."

Adelaide nodded. "I thought she'd forgotten, but many years ago it rained so hard and for so long that one of the bones washed up from the ground. Frances ran out in the storm in a fit and saw it. I dragged her away, but it was too late. Ever since then, she's always been afraid when it rains. That's why I drugged her as soon as I heard the storm moving in."

"Who is...was this?" Sabine asked. "And why are they buried in the backyard? Don't lie to me, Adelaide. I know this is human."

Adelaide nodded and looked at the floor, her face full of shame.

Sabine waited a couple of seconds for a response, but when none was forthcoming, she pressed again. "You as much as admitted to me earlier that Catherine had killed William's parents. There's no way they were buried in the backyard, so this is someone else. Who, Adelaide? Who else did Catherine kill?"

"Lloyd," Beau said. "It has to be. He came home, and the family couldn't risk hiding him so they took the easy way out."

Adelaide lifted her eyes to Beau's. "It weren't that simple. Catherine killing the elder Fortescues was all part of her plan."

"Her plan to what?" Beau asked.

Sabine stared at Adelaide, and suddenly it hit her. "Her plan to marry Lloyd and still inherit everything."

Chapter Eighteen

"Lloyd?" Beau repeated. "Oh my God, you're right. Everyone thought he'd changed because of the war, but it wasn't the war at all. He'd changed because he was an entirely different man." Beau looked at Adelaide. "It's William that's buried in the backyard. You knew all these years and never said anything?"

Adelaide wrung her hands together, tears streaming down her face. "I swear I didn't know what they'd done until years later. It was Catherine who got Lloyd back from Vietnam and hid him at her family's lake house until they'd finished setting it all up. I mean, I knew Lloyd was pretending to be William. I'd practically raised those boys. They could never have fooled me, but Lloyd told me William was killed in Vietnam and that he'd taken his dog tags so that the military police wouldn't arrest him.

"I didn't know they'd killed William until Frances dug up the bones in the garden. My poor Frances. Her mind was already gone when Adam found her that night. She'd uncovered the bones and started screaming. That's how he was able to get you away. Oh, my sweet, sweet Adam. He tried to do right."

Sabine's head began to spin. "What are you trying to say—that Frances was going to bury me alive in the backyard? Frances is my real mother?"

Adelaide nodded. "Please don't blame her, Ms. Sabine. It weren't her fault. My Frances was crazy from the disease."

"What disease?"

Adelaide blanched. "Lloyd brought it back from the war and gave it to Catherine. She never knew until Frances's mind started going. When Frances got meningitis, the doctors found it. She'd had it since she was born—passed from Catherine."

"Syphilis," Beau said, the disgust in his voice apparent. "Adam had scarlet fever when he was an infant. That's what his medical records said, remember? They would have given him penicillin. Catherine had the scarlet fever too, so neither of them carried the syphilis any further."

Sabine covered her mouth with her hand. "Oh, my God. But Frances didn't get the scarlet fever, so she never got the drug. That disease ate away at her for all those years. And my father? Who is my father, Adelaide?"

Adelaide shook her head and rubbed the unconscious Frances's arm. "I don't know, I swear. Someone hurt her. I found her in the bath scrubbing herself with steel wool. She'd already started to bleed in some places. I'm so sorry, Sabine. I would have told, I swear, but someone had to take care of Frances."

"Adam knew, didn't he?" Beau said. "He saw the bones and knew his mother and father had killed someone. That's why he took Sabine and ran."

"Yes, and since he worked with the doctor, I'm guessing he peeked at Frances's medical reports and knew she was losing her mind and why." Adelaide said. "I begged Catherine to let him go, let them be, but she couldn't risk it. She tracked Adam and his girlfriend down and messed with their car. She never thought you'd find the family, Sabine, or she would have hunted you down, too."

"Is that why she's trying to kill me now? So that I won't find out the truth?"

Adelaide started to answer but then froze. A horrified look came over her face. Sabine knew even before she turned around that Catherine was standing in the doorway. What she hadn't planned on was the pistol that Catherine held, pointed straight at her.

"Don't flatter yourself," Catherine said, "I had no reason to harm you. You thought Adam was your father and had no reason to think otherwise. I would have settled a nice trust fund on you and you would never have been the wiser. Killing you would only have served to draw attention to the family, and that's the last thing I wanted." She stepped into the room, and Lloyd stepped in behind her. "It's a shame you couldn't hold your tongue, Adelaide. I knew it was a mistake to keep you all these years, but you were the only one who could care for Frances. She's been a trial since birth."

"She's lying," Beau said. "I found the peanut oil and syringe in Lloyd's pocket. They did try to kill you."

Catherine spun around and looked at Lloyd, who shook his head. "No way. Catherine's right. Sabine wasn't a threat to us until now, and if I'd tried to kill her, she wouldn't be standing here."

"Well," Catherine said with a smile. "It won't be for much longer." She motioned Sabine and Beau toward the other side of the bed. "I really don't want to get blood on this suit. I'm trying to avoid complications in my story for the police."

Sabine inched over to Beau. His jaw was clenched, and Sabine knew he was calculating every risk, every percentage of success if he reached for his pistol. But as long as Catherine was pointing her gun straight at Sabine, she knew he wouldn't take the chance. And that was most likely going to get them killed.

"I think," Catherine said, "I'll take this golden opportunity to clear up all my problems. I mean, I'm going to claim that Frances went crazy and killed everyone. When she wakes up she won't know whether she did or not." With that, Catherine whirled toward the doorway and shot Lloyd twice in the chest.

Sabine covered her mouth as she screamed. It was as if time hung suspended. The shock registered on Lloyd's face as he looked down at the red stain growing on his white dress shirt. He touched it and held up his hands, staring unbelieving at the blood dripping from his fingertips. He looked at Catherine, bewildered. He took one step toward her and stumbled, then crashed to the floor in a heap.

"Finally," Catherine said, "I can live the life I wanted without hiding in this musty old estate. Lloyd never could manage to act like William in public, so I had no choice but to become a virtual recluse. It's been like living in a prison. Worthless husband, crazy daughter, meddling housekeeper. But that's all about to change."

In the doorway, something moved, and Sabine squinted in the dim light, trying to make out what was in the hallway. A second later, Helena walked into the room and right through Catherine to stand between the murdering matriarch and her next victims.

"What a fucking mess," she said. "I can probably knock that gun out of her hand. If you want me to do it, blink twice."

It was a long shot, depending on Helena to get her ghost skills right on demand, but it still wasn't as long as the possibility of Catherine shooting and missing them from a distance of ten feet. Sabine said a silent prayer for all of them and blinked twice. Helena nodded and her brow wrinkled in concentration as she turned to face Catherine. At the same time, Catherine lifted the gun and pointed it directly at Beau's chest.

"I think I'll start with lover boy here. Might as well clear the room of men. And after all, if not for him, we wouldn't be in this position to begin with, would we?" She smiled at Sabine and her finger whitened on the trigger.

And that's when Helena struck. She jumped across the room, faster than Sabine would have ever given her credit for, and hit Catherine's arm with a semblance of a karate chop. The chop probably wouldn't have been hard enough to make Catherine drop the gun under normal circumstances, but being assaulted by an invisible assailant was apparently enough of a shock for her to loosen her grip. Catherine cried out as the gun fell from her hand and skidded a couple of feet across the floor.

"It's the spirits!" Adelaide screamed and threw her arms around Frances.

Catherine instantly recovered and dove for the weapon, but Helena drove her into the hardwood floor in a body slam the WWF would have been proud of. Catherine hit the ground with a thud and started to move when Beau said, "I wouldn't do that if I were you."

Helena rose from the floor with Catherine's pistol, a huge grin on her face. "How was that for a save? You owe me big, Sabine."

Catherine's eyes widened at what looked to her like a floating gun. Adelaide started to pray again, and Sabine had little doubt that the Catholic church was getting a new member come Sunday.

"Now, Helena," Sabine said, looking uneasily at the gun. "Be careful with that. The safety's not on. It could go off."

Helena turned to face Sabine. "What, do you think I'm stupid? I know how a gun works, see?"

Before Sabine could stop her, Helena reached up with her other hand and tried to engage the safety. She must have pushed too hard because she lost her grip on the gun and it spun around on her finger that was placed in the trigger hole. "Shit!" Helena said and tried to catch the gun, but instead, she pulled the trigger.

Luckily for all the good guys, the gun was turned backwards and facing straight at Helena's chest when it went off. The bullet passed right through the perturbed ghost and hit Catherine in the thigh. The murdering bitch went down with a cry and wailed as if she were dying.

Sabine took a step forward and grabbed the gun out of Helena's hand. "Give me that before you kill someone." She shot a look back at Beau, who was shaking his head.

Beau motioned to Catherine. "Move over by the bed. Sit next to the post."

"I'm fucking shot, you asshole," Catherine shot back.

"Then crawl, bitch," Beau shot back, "unless you'd like me to give the gun back to the ghost and have her put a bullet in your other leg."

Catherine shot daggers at Beau and pulled herself across the floor to the bed. "You'll never prove any of this. Bunch of devil-worshippers, bringing demons into my house. I'll press charges against you, and the local police will never believe a word you say."

"Oh, that's rich," Helena complained. "The bitch killed half the local population but I'm a demon." She looked over at Sabine.

"Can I poke her in the leg, please? Or maybe pour alcohol in the wound?"

"No, Helena, as much as I would like you to, I can't allow you to pour alcohol into Catherine's bullet hole." She looked down at Catherine and smiled. "I wouldn't keep calling her a demon if I were you."

"You're all crazy," Catherine said.

"No, they're not," Adelaide said, breaking off prayer long enough to put in her ten cents. "And the police will believe them, because I'm going to tell everything. Like I should have done all those years ago."

Beau motioned to Sabine. "I brought a backpack in from my truck and dropped it somewhere in the hall when I saw Frances with her shovel. There's a set of handcuffs in the front pocket."

It only took Sabine a minute to retrieve the pack and less than that for Beau to secure Catherine to the bedpost. Sabine looked down at her, still amazed and appalled all at the same time at all the evil stemming from one central source. All those people murdered, and for what—money…a title…a house? Sabine would never understand.

But Catherine had denied any attempt on Sabine's life.

"The least you can do," Sabine said to the murderess, "is tell me why you were trying to kill me. It's all coming out anyway. I deserve to know."

Catherine gave her a dirty look. "I already told you I couldn't be bothered."

"Then what about the peanut oil and syringe that were in Lloyd's jacket pocket?" Beau said.

Catherine frowned. "The jacket in the hall closet?"

"Yes."

"I'll be damned," Catherine said, a thin smile on her face. "Lloyd's jacket is in our bedroom. The jacket in the hall must belong to Mr. Alford."

Sabine stared at Beau in horror.

"Damn it!" Beau cursed and ran from the room, his gun in the ready position. Sabine rushed out behind him.

At the end of the hall, Beau pushed open the bedroom door and stuck the lantern inside. An open briefcase sat on the bed and Sabine could see a glow coming from underneath the bathroom door. Beau eased the bathroom door open and peered inside as Sabine lifted a folder from the briefcase.

"No one's there," Beau said.

Sabine opened the folder and looked at the black-and-white photo on top. It wasn't recent, if the woman's hairstyle and clothes were any indication, but there was something about her face...She flipped the photo over and read the penciled words at the top corner. Mom, 1955. She flipped the photo back over and took a second look. Still nothing. She handed the photo to Beau for his inspection and looked at the next document. It was a death certificate for a Sandra Franks, identifying the cause of death as drowning. Sabine frowned.

Sandra Franks was one of the names she'd found when searching for the women from her aunt's journals. But what in the world was Alford doing with her death certificate? Mom, 1955.

Sabine stretched her mind to recall the conversation they'd had at Alford's office. He'd mentioned losing his parents at a young age. She flipped to the next sheet and found a copy of a journal page. Her pulse began to quicken:

I'm afraid for me and my children. I haven't heard from William in over four months, and even with him in Vietnam, that's a long time. He promised to put a stop to this charade his family is putting on about his engagement to Catherine. He swears I am the only one he will ever love, and I believe him. He's told Catherine he will never marry her, but I think she has her mind set on being a Fortescue. I'm afraid for my babies. If his family finds out, I'm not sure what they will do. Even worse, I'm not sure what Catherine will do.

She claims to love William and want a life with him, but I see the way she looks at Lloyd in church and I know the way the wind blows. There have been noises outside of my house three nights in a row, and now the dog is missing. I'm afraid someone has found out William is the father of my children, and that has put us all in danger.

I pray daily that I will hear from my love, but there is a stone deep in my stomach that tells me it is already too late, and I will never see my William again.

Sabine's heart pounded in her throat as she turned to the next page. A birth certificate.

Twins. A boy, Martin Samuel born at 10:10 a.m. and a girl, Mildred Grace born ten minutes before.

Sabine sucked in a breath as her whole world came crashing down around her. She yanked the photo from Beau, not wanting to see what she already knew was there, not wanting to believe that this was far from over. But it was right there staring her in the face. The curve of the smile, the wide-set eyes and upturned nose. Sandra Franks was Mildred's mother. The woman who had raised Sabine was adopted, and Mildred had never said a word.

Or maybe she hadn't known.

Panicked, Sabine shoved the folder at Beau. "It wasn't me!" she cried. "It wasn't me Alford was trying to kill."

Beau stared at her, wide-eyed. "Sabine, what are you talking about? Of course he was trying to kill you."

"No. Read the papers. Look at that picture. Catherine and Lloyd killed William's girlfriend in order to pull off their plan. But Sandra already had William's babies, so they gave them away. Twins. Martin and Mildred. My Mildred. She's been the target this whole time." Beau glanced down at the photo and his face instantly grew a shade lighter. "Holy shit! It was Alford who said the bridge was out."

Sabine grabbed Beau's arm. "We have to get to Mudbug! The phone lines are all down and the cells will never work, especially with the storm. We have to warn Mildred. He's probably on his way. Or already there."

They ran back into Frances's bedroom and Beau looked over at the stricken Adelaide. "Adelaide, I need you to watch Catherine for a bit. I'll send the police as soon as I can notify them, but in the meantime, I need you to stay here and keep watch. Can you do that?"

Adelaide nodded fearfully. "I think so. Do I have to use the gun?"

Beau shook his head. "Not unless you know how."

Adelaide blew out a breath. "I know how. And I'm a sight better than that ghost."

Helena huffed. "Look who's talking shit now. You were all frozen like a pack of steaks until I got here."

"Helena, we all know you saved the day," Sabine said, "now I need you to stay here with Adelaide and make sure nothing else happens. Can you do that?"

"Yeah, sure."

Sabine nodded to Beau and they hurried out of the room.

"But I'm getting a piece of that chocolate cake," Helena yelled after them.

Mildred sat in her hospital bed, staring at the static on the television and wondering if the worst of the storm was blowing over, or if this lessening was only a lull. She was worried about Sabine, about this dinner with her "family." Mildred was old-fashioned in a lot of ways, but family wasn't one of them. Blood didn't make someone love you. It didn't make someone treat you right. Not a single one of the people she considered family was related by blood, but when it came to family, Mildred considered herself the most blessed woman in Mudbug.

She had two beautiful daughters, who were fast becoming the women she always knew they'd be. They had integrity. They had respect for themselves. They cared about others and never even blinked at self-sacrifice for each other or for Mildred. They were her greatest joy, and when she was feeling a little vain, her greatest accomplishment.

She smiled as she thought of them, how they'd shown their character even in such trying times, and she knew without a doubt that no matter what happened, her two girls would survive and thrive. And that peace of mind was worth more to her than any amount of money in the bank.

"Lord have mercy!" Maryse burst into the room, both hands full and dripping water from every inch of her and the bags she carried. "It's a doozy out there."

Mildred glanced out the window and nodded. "I thought it was slacking off some."

Maryse dumped the bags on the floor and shook off her raincoat. "It is now, but when I left the hotel it was a torrential downpour. I deliberated between bringing your bags or just starting to build an ark right there in the middle of Main Street." She grinned at Mildred and tossed her raincoat onto the tile floor of the bathroom and grabbed a towel off a shelf next to the door.

Mildred laughed. "That would be a sight, wouldn't it? An ark in downtown Mudbug. And can you even imagine getting two of everything on board?"

"Yeah...two idiots, two fools, two rednecks...the hardest part would be narrowing it down to which two. And I don't care if they're God's creatures, I'm still not taking snakes."

"That's my girl," Mildred said. "I just wish Sabine were here instead of with those people."

Maryse lifted a duffle bag from the floor and wiped it with the towel, then handed the bag to Mildred. "Sorry about the wet part—couldn't be avoided. And I'm with you on the Sabine thing. I know the Fortescues are her family, but everything's been wrong since she found them. Well, and I guess even before."

Mildred nodded and waved one hand at the window. "Like the calm before the storm."

Maryse's eyes widened. "Shit. I didn't even think of it that way. And I hope your poetic expression isn't lining up with our atmospheric conditions."

"Have you heard from her?"

Maryse bit her lip. "No. Cell phone reception's been spotty though, with the weather. Even if she tried, I don't know if she could get through."

"I don't feel right. I don't want to trouble you, Maryse, but I'm worried. I feel like something big is about to happen. And not something good, but I can't put my finger on what."

"Or why, or who, or how." Maryse sat on the edge of her bed, a worried expression on her face. "I feel it, too. Been feeling it for a while, but the truth is, tonight it all seems intensified somehow. I thought maybe it was just the storm. You know, like some creepy horror movie."

"The 'dark and stormy night' introduction. Makes for a great gothic tale, but a nerve-racking reality."

She sighed. "You know, it was always so easy for me to dismiss Sabine's beliefs about things we couldn't see. Not that I ever dismissed her or thought any different of her for believing. I just couldn't make that leap myself."

Mildred nodded. "I know. I have the same hesitation, but the older I get, the less inclined I am to say 'never.' It tends to come back and bite you." She paused for a moment, thinking about her next words, the best way to say them. "I know something has been going on with you and Sabine lately. Something that is bothering you both and that you don't want to tell me about. Maybe when all this has settled down, you'll think about letting me know."

Maryse looked stricken, and Mildred knew she'd hit a nerve. "We're not trying to leave you out or make you feel unimportant, Mildred. I promise you." She laid her hand on Mildred's. "But you're right. There have been some things happening to us that, well, we didn't really think you'd take the right way...or take at all."

Mildred patted her hand. "I know exactly what you're saying, and you were right...then. You were right until I woke up in this hospital and saw Helena Henry standing next to my bed big as life and the two of you talking to her."

Maryse's eyes widened. "You really saw her? We hoped it was the drugs making you confused."

"I saw her all right. At first I thought maybe I'd imagined it, but it was too vivid, and you looked too frightened when I said something for me to think it was just me being high."

Maryse jumped up from the bed and paced the tiny room. "That's not good. I have this theory, you see, that when someone sees Helena, they're in danger. That seems to be the pattern. That's why Sabine and I were worried. And since you saw her after your car wreck, it makes me think it's not over for you."

Mildred took in a deep breath and let it out slowly. "But that would explain this feeling we have, wouldn't it? Something's coming, and maybe somehow Helena is connected to it all."

Maryse stopped pacing. "That's what I think, and you're right, the three of us need to have a long talk when this is over. Whatever 'this' is. But not now. Right now, it would be overload, and we need to keep our minds focused on looking for whatever it is that's coming. Being blindsided sucks."

Mildred nodded. "We're going to be fine, Maryse. We may not know what we're up against but we know something's there. That makes us more prepared than most in our situation. I know I've sent you running all over tonight, but if you don't mind, would you pop down to the cafeteria and pick us up a couple of large coffees? I'm thinking sleep isn't really the best idea at the moment."

"Of course," Maryse agreed and hurried out of the room.

Mildred unzipped the wet bag she'd just gotten. She'd been carrying it around in addition to her purse for a couple of days—had been compelled to for reasons she couldn't attest to, but then things hadn't been normal in Mudbug for quite a while. Oh, there was a spare set of clothes on top to hide the real reason for the bag, but the cold, hard reason for it was nestled in the bottom. She pulled the pistol from its holder and carefully loaded it. A blast of thunder echoed through the room, and she looked out the window at the raging storm. Maryse was right—that storm was setting her on edge even more than before. She tucked the gun under the edge of her covers right by her hip and hoped to God she was faster than whatever the winds were blowing her way.

Chapter Nineteen

Beau pressed the accelerator on his truck, pushing the vehicle as fast as he could down the muddy road. "The storm is slacking off some," he said, hoping to reassure Sabine, who sat rigid on the passenger's seat.

"What if the bridge is out now? What if we're too late? What if he gets to Mildred?"

"Stay calm, Sabine. Mildred is still in the hospital, and Maryse was going to be there with her. It's not like she's alone, by any stretch. And maybe we're wrong about all of this."

"Mildred was firstborn. That must be important or Catherine wouldn't have mentioned it to me. As their attorney, Martin would know just how important it was. I'd bet he's been stalking the family his entire life, waiting for a chance to claim his rights."

"So why wait? Catherine would have paid him plenty to go away."

"I think...I know it sounds strange, but I don't think it was just about the money. I think it was about being a Fortescue. And if we assume Martin didn't know William was actually Lloyd, then the only way that would happen is if William admitted to an affair before he married Catherine."

"And since Martin knew Catherine, he knew that would never happen," Beau finished. "So he was biding his time thinking that when they passed, he'd come in for the biggest piece of everything as firstborn. But somehow he found out about Mildred. How do you think that happened?"

"It had to be that newspaper article—the same one Frances had. Remember, when we were at Martin's house, I brought a New

Orleans paper inside. Mildred looks just like his mother. He would have seen the resemblance right away, and guessing that he had a sister out there somewhere wouldn't have been so big a leap to make."

Beau nodded, understanding Sabine's logic. "But that still doesn't explain poisoning you or the car bomb. That was your wine and your car, Sabine."

"That's just it," Sabine said, her voice growing more excited. "That bottle of wine was one Mildred picked up. I'd just gotten it from Mildred the day before. And since her car's been on the blink, she's been driving mine. If Martin came to Mudbug to spy on her—"

"He would have thought the car was hers," Beau finished, and his pulse began to race. "Shit, you're right. It makes total sense, as much as any of this does. And the break-in at your shop was probably Martin, too. It gave him a shiny new key to your building and access to anything you might have on Mildred."

"Oh no! I have a master key to the hotel. It's hanging on a rack in my kitchen with a label on it, plain as day. What a moron! I may as well have opened the door for him myself. And what do you want to bet that the whole dinner was Martin's idea. Being stuck at the Fortescue estate would have been the perfect alibi for him. If it hadn't been for Frances digging up dead people, we would never have known he was gone."

Beau nodded and felt his jaw tighten. It was very slick, very smooth. To have done all the things they imagined, Martin Alford couldn't be completely sane, but he wasn't all-out crazy like Frances. He was cunning and clever. Beau slowed as they approached the bridge, praying that Alford had lied and that the water hadn't risen since the attorney had made his escape. He blew out a breath of relief when he saw the water swirling just underneath the wooden structure.

"He lied," Sabine said. "Thank God, he lied. Now if we can get to Mildred in time..."

"We'll get there." Beau pressed the accelerator halfway to the floor and the truck launched over the bridge and onto the road beyond. "Check the phones. See if we've got a signal yet."

Sabine grabbed Beau's phone from the seat next to her and looked. "No, damn it." She pulled her own phone from her pocket and peered at the display. "One bar."

"Try it. Call 911."

Beau glanced over as Sabine punched in the numbers and was certain she was holding her breath. The relief on her face let him know right away that the connection had gone through. Sabine handed the phone to Beau. "You explain. I'm going to sound hysterical."

Beau took the phone and gave the local cops a brief description of the situation at the Fortescue mansion, then explained the situation with Mildred. The dispatcher was stunned, but he promised to get police to the Fortescue mansion and the Mudbug hospital as fast as humanly possible. Beau pressed End and handed the phone back to Sabine. "Call Maryse. Her phone might not pick up in the hospital, but it's worth a try."

Sabine took the phone and pressed in Maryse's number. A couple of seconds later, she shut the phone, the disappointment on her face clear as day. "It went straight to voice mail."

Beau turned the wheel hard to the right and the truck lurched onto the highway. "Don't worry about it. We'll be there in ten minutes." He prayed they weren't already too late.

Mildred was digging in her duffle bag for her mace when she felt the hair on her neck stand up straight. She looked up and sucked in a breath when she saw the man standing next to her bed holding a gun.

"Hello, Mildred," the man said, "or should I call you sister?"

Mildred studied the man, but didn't see anything familiar. "You're no one to me and I'm fine keeping it that way."

The man sighed. "I wish it could have stayed that way, but Sabine ruined it for everyone."

Mildred's mind raced, trying to make sense of what the man was saying. "What does Sabine have to do with any of this?"

"I was just waiting to stake my claim. I finally had the proof I needed after all these years to prove I was William's rightful heir. I could have left you alone, and you would never have known. But then Sabine turned up—questioning them about the family and the past, convincing them she was related. It was only a matter of time before they met you, and Catherine saw the truth."

Mildred's head swam in confusion. "There was a DNA test. Sabine told me."

The man shifted the gun in his hand, obviously agitated. "Adam was sterile. I read his medical records. There's no way he fathered a child. Why the Fortescues lied about the results, I don't know. But they'll pay—they'll all pay for what they did. I should have been firstborn. But that's something I can fix."

He leveled the gun at her head and pulled a syringe from his shirt pocket. "You're going to take a nap, little sister. One you won't wake up from, I'm afraid." He stepped closer to the bed, needle poised for injection.

Mildred's heart pounded so hard she thought it would burst. There was no way she could reach her gun. He'd won, even though she'd tried to prepare. She closed her eyes and began to pray.

A whistling noise echoed through the silence, and her entire body went stiff. She wondered for a moment when the pain would come, but suddenly a heavy weight fell across her. Opening her eyes, she saw the man who claimed to be her brother slumped across her, a single bullet hole through his temple. Raissa stood in the doorway, her gun still drawn, the silencer explaining the whistling.

"Who was he?" Mildred asked.

"Martin Alford," Raissa said as she stepped over to the bed and checked the man's neck for a pulse. "The Fortescues' attorney."

"Was he my brother?"

"Maybe."

Mildred slumped back on the bed, her pulse still racing. "How did you know? How did you know to come here?"

"I guessed."

Mildred stared at Raissa for a moment, then let out a single laugh. "That's one heck of a guess, Raissa."

Raissa removed her hand from Alford's neck and sighed. "I was really hoping I was wrong."

Mildred pulled her gun out from the covers and sat it on the tray next to the bed. "I'm glad you weren't wrong. It's over, and we're all still alive, and that's the most important thing."

Raissa glanced at Mildred's gun and raised her eyebrows. "You knew someone was after you?"

Mildred shook her head. "I guessed."

Raissa smiled. "That's one heck of a guess."

"Make that two of us who hoped we were wrong."

"Well, being as we were both right, I guess we need to call the police and get this process started before the nurse comes in to take your temperature and has a heart attack."

Mildred pulled her legs out from under the covers and climbed out of bed. She stuck her hand out toward Raissa. "Give me your gun."

Raissa stared at her. "What? Why?"

"Honey, I know what hiding looks like and you've been at it a long, long time. Are you going to tell me you want the police poking around into your background?"

Raissa's eyes widened and Mildred placed one hand on her arm. "I don't know what you're running from, and I don't care. I've known you for a long time, and you're a good woman. I know you have good reasons. You and I both know the police won't even think twice about my shooting a man who came here to kill me. It will all go away in a matter of weeks."

"I don't know...what if they guess...how are you going to explain..."

"I won't explain much of anything. I'm in a hospital, worried for my life, and on drugs—as far as they know. Give me your gun, Raissa. I figure it's not registered to you, right? I can always claim I got it from Maryse's dad years ago. No one will think any different. Bayou men buy and sell this stuff all the time."

Raissa glanced at Alford then back at Mildred, obviously torn. Finally, she placed her gun in Mildred's hand. Mildred handed Raissa her own firearm. "I don't want you without protection, and I figure me toting two guns around might raise some eyebrows. If you wouldn't mind taking that with you."

Raissa took the pistol and slipped it in her purse. "Thank you, Mildred. I'll get this back to you as soon as I replace my old one."

Mildred waved one hand in dismissal. "Keep it. Mine's not registered either." She gave Raissa a wink and the other woman smiled. Mildred lifted the phone, dialed 911, and gave a brief description of the problem. Somehow it didn't surprise her to find out that Beau Villeneuve had already called the police and they were in route. She hung up the phone with a smile.

"What?" Raissa asked, and Mildred explained to her to Beau had already sent the police.

Raissa smiled and squeezed Mildred's hand with her own. "The house of cards is crumbling."

Mildred grinned. "We better get your prints off that gun, get mine on it, and call for the nurse. Tell her someone died in here and it damned sure wasn't me." Mildred reached for the phone as Maryse strolled into the room, wrestling with a cardboard coffee tray.

"Sorry it took so long," Maryse said, still looking down at the tray. "There was an incredible line down there and—" She looked up and saw Mildred standing next to the bed, pistol still in her hand, and the dead man slumped over her hospital bed.

All the color washed out of Maryse's face and the tray of coffee crashed to the floor, Maryse following closely behind. Mildred looked down at her and shook her head. "Sure, someone tries to kill her and she runs out of the hotel barefoot and not wearing underwear. Sometimes tries to kill me and she's a shrinking violet."

Raissa grinned. "Well, maybe we should get 'Violet' off the floor before the police get here."

Sabine bit her lip as Beau tore into the hospital parking lot and screeched to a stop in front of the main entry. They both jumped out and ran past a startled nurse who yelled after them. It seemed by unspoken mutual decision they both decided the stairs were the best choice, because neither even slowed as they passed the elevator. Sabine skidded on the polished floor as they burst out of the stairwell and onto Mildred's floor, but there was barely a pause before she picked up speed again and dashed down the hallway after Beau.

She saw him pull his gun from his waistband, and she pulled her own pistol from her purse and dropped the bag in the hallway. They rounded the last corner and burst into Mildred's room, guns blazing and ready to do some serious damage.

"Good heavens!" Mildred looked at the doorway as they burst into the room.

It took less than a second for Sabine to take it all in—Martin, dead on Mildred's bed, and Raissa standing over a white-faced Maryse, fanning her with a bedpan. She paused only long enough to click on the safety on her pistol, then rushed over to Mildred and wrapped her arms around the woman who had raised her and crushed her in a hug.

Mildred squeezed her back and rubbed her hands up and down Sabine's back, just the way she used to do when Sabine was upset as a child. "It's fine, honey. Everything's going to be just fine."

Sabine felt the tears surface and didn't even bother to try holding them in as she released Mildred and looked her in the eyes. "This has been the single most horrifying and terrifying day of my entire life."

"Tell me about it," Maryse mumbled.

Sabine looked over at her best friend and smiled. "Should I even ask?"

Raissa shook her head. "No, but it's worth a year of bribes later on."

Mildred cocked her head to one side and studied Sabine for a moment. "When I called the police, they said you'd already dispatched them here. How did you know?"

Sabine blew out a breath. "I found a bunch of papers in Martin's briefcase. They tied everything together. You were the one in danger all along, although I'm sure he would've come after me next. He was insane and obsessed with his quest."

"Is he my brother?"

Sabine nodded. "I think so."

"And you? Why did that man say you weren't Adam's child?"

"Because I'm not. Frances was my mother. Adam and his wife took me to save me from the Fortescues and oh, hell, it's a long screwed-up story that I'd rather explain after a hot bath and at least ten hours of sleep."

Mildred nodded and gave her another hug. "Of course, dear. What a shame. Like either of us cared about the Fortescues or their money."

"You might have to start caring," Sabine said.

"I'll deal with that when William dies."

Sabine glanced over at Beau, then looked back at Mildred. "You're right. No use inviting trouble."

"You're one to talk." Mildred glanced over at Beau, then back at Sabine, a smile on her face. "If you could have just seen the two of you, busting in here like something out of a movie." She leaned close to Sabine and whispered, "The two of you together looked right."

Sabine brushed a single tear from her face with the back of her hand. "Well, you always told me not to contradict my elders..."

Three hours later, Sabine crawled into her bed at the hotel, certain she was going to sleep for a week. Mildred was tucked in her bed at the hotel, absolutely refusing to stay in the hospital another minute. The hospital staff didn't argue over the release, probably glad she was going and worried about being sued for letting killers have free access to the patients. Maryse was asleep on her couch, refusing to give up her patrol duties, especially after passing out on the job.

Mildred had given her statement to the Mudbug police and explained how Raissa walked in after the fact, but Sabine knew she was lying about that part. Once the dust had settled on all of this,

Sabine was going to get the truth out of her. She turned off the lamp and pulled up the covers. She was just about to doze off when she heard the connecting door open.

"Sabine?" Beau whispered. "Are you asleep?"

"About two seconds from being." She propped herself up on her elbow and looked over at him. "Did you get everything settled at the Big House of Horrors?" Beau had left for the Fortescue estate right after the police arrived at the hospital. Without a sane person in the mix, he was afraid the state police wouldn't have any idea what to do with a murdering socialite, a dead husband, an insane daughter, the terrified housekeeper, and the body in the backyard. Sabine only prayed that Helena hadn't decided to "help" while the police were there.

Beau walked over to the bed and sat next to her. "It's a real mess over there. Even the state police were blown away by all of it. Catherine's still tight-lipped, but Adelaide is singing like a bird. They had to sedate Frances again and cart her off to the hospital. I'm thinking she might need permanent care."

Sabine's mind flashed back to Frances, digging in the garden in the middle of a hurricane. The expression on her face was a mixture of so many things—fear, revulsion, horror, and not an ounce of sanity left. "After all that, it's no wonder."

Beau placed his hand on Sabine's. "I'm afraid you don't know everything. Hell, I'm starting to wonder if anyone does. That place was a regular house of horrors during Catherine's reign." He paused for a moment, the indecision on his face clear.

"What is it, Beau? There's nothing that could shock me now."

Beau nodded. "I know. And this isn't shocking as much as it makes sense but is incredibly sad." He took a deep breath and blew it out. "The police found another body in the backyard with William...an infant. I think Frances had twins."

Sabine's eyes clouded with tears. "Twins...yes, that would make sense, given the family history. I guess Adam couldn't save the other baby."

"I guess not. It's all so tragic. I mean, obviously Catherine deserves no sympathy. She's been evil from the beginning, but

Frances's mind eaten away by that horrible disease, William killed just because Catherine wanted more status and money than Lloyd would inherit, and Martin's mother murdered and her babies stolen. Then Adam taking you and hiding from his family because he knew it was the only chance for you to live." Beau squeezed Sabine's hand. "Adam must have been an incredible man."

Sabine brushed a tear from her cheek. "I think he was, and my mother...well, the woman I thought...oh, you know. I mean, she had to know what they were doing and she agreed to it to save me. They were still my parents in every sense of the word for as long as they lived."

Beau nodded. "They loved you enough to die for you. I'd say that definitely makes them mom and dad." Beau leaned down and wrapped his arms around Sabine. "I am so sorry, Sabine. I expected something bad when I took your case. That's why I wanted to stick around even after we found your family. I didn't want you working with someone inexperienced with these things."

Sabine gave a single laugh. "You mean inexperienced with an evil grandmother, a crazy aunt, and a gun-toting ghost?"

Beau released Sabine a bit and pulled back enough to smile down at her. "The ghost was more than anyone would want to take. I gave her a ride back into Mudbug. She was in my truck and passed me a note. I had to stop at the convenience store and buy her a dozen hotdogs and a whole box of moon pies. I didn't think the dead were supposed to be so expensive."

Sabine smiled. "Helena sorta operates by her own set of rules."

"Well, I never would have believed it if I hadn't seen it, and I like to think I'm fairly open-minded. All the same, I'm glad she's around."

"Me, too," Sabine said, "but don't you dare ever tell her that."

Beau laughed, and then his expression grew serious. "And what about me...have you given any more thought to having me around? I wouldn't bill you for it, of course."

Sabine sobered. "I don't know. I'm drawn to you like I never have been to anyone else. I care about you, and more importantly,

I respect and admire you, but I don't even know what my own future holds. How can I ask you to live that way?"

"You mean one day at a time with you?" Beau placed his hands on both sides of her face and lowered his head, brushing her lips gently with his. He pulled back a bit and looked at her. "I love you, Sabine LeVeche. I don't care if we have fifty years together or two weeks. What I do know is that I don't want to live one more minute of either of our lives without you."

Sabine's heart pounded in her chest and tears filled her eyes. Everything around her seemed to blur, but Beau remained clear. It was a huge risk, but she knew she had to start living. It might be her last chance to do so. "I love you, Beau. God help us both. I don't want to spend another minute without you in my life, either."

Beau pulled her close to him and hugged her as if he would never let go. And the wonderful thing is that Sabine knew he wouldn't.

"We're going to do everything possible for you, Sabine," Beau promised. "Even if it means extorting bone marrow from Frances."

Sabine leaned back a bit and looked at him, her eyes filled with tears but her heart full of the love for this man who had put everything on the line to protect her. "That won't be necessary. Mildred was tested last night in the hospital. She's a match."

Beau's eyes lit up with the hope and promise that Sabine felt for the first time in a long time. He lowered his lips to hers and she melted into his embrace, hoping she had a long, long time to feel as good as she did right now.

One week later

Sabine closed her shop and walked upstairs to her apartment. She could hear soft music playing inside before she even opened the door, but nothing prepared her for the gorgeous man standing in her kitchen, chopping vegetables and wearing nothing but an apron and a smile.

"I'm making you my famous spaghetti," he said.

She walked into the kitchen and pulled his apron to the side, laughing as he playfully slapped her hand away. "Tease," she said. "So does your secret recipe call for cooking in the nude?"

He pulled her into his arms and kissed her. "No. You call for me cooking in the nude. For some reason, when I'm around you I don't feel like wearing clothes." He eased back from her a bit and studied her face. "How are you feeling?"

Sabine smiled. "No side effects from the radiation at all. I think Maryse may be up for a Nobel Prize some day."

"And did the doctor call with your test results?"

"Just before I closed up. He said I'm responding well to treatment and everything looks great."

The relief on Beau's face was apparent. "Then I have a surprise for you."

"What kind of surprise?"

"The kind that involves you leaving this state for the first time. And it has a beach, and a private hut, and a minister waiting for a phone call from me. That is, if you're willing to marry a naked chef."

"Well, I don't know. You might want to put on clothes before we meet with the minister."

"Is that a yes?"

She leaned in and kissed him gently on the lips. "That's a definitely."

The End

Who killed Helena? – Find out in Showdown in Mudbug.

Showdown in Mudbug

Chapter One

Raissa Bourdeaux went through the uses of the different-colored candles for what had to be the hundredth time. She knew Mrs. Angelieu was more interested in gossiping than actually buying anything, so there was really nothing more to do but continue to point to items and wait her out. She glanced at her watch and was dismayed to find it was hours before closing. Monday had been a very long day.

"And then," Mrs. Angelieu said, her face animated, "I told Lucille that I just couldn't believe she'd bring that casserole dish to the church. Why, it belonged to her mother, and everyone knew what a harlot her mother was. It's a wonder God didn't send lightning down right there in the middle of her potato salad." She gave Raissa a single nod and waited for confirmation.

"Well," Raissa said, struggling for something that wasn't rude, "that certainly would have been a show. But God hasn't really been that obvious since the Old Testament. I mean, I haven't heard of a burning bush in a long time."

Mrs. Angelieu laughed. "You always know how to put things in perspective, Raissa. That's why I love talking to you. I consider it my weekly dose of reality."

"Oh, you don't have to come to me for that. Just turn on any news channel."

Mrs. Angelieu sobered. "It's just horrible about that missing child, isn't it? My Lord, I can't imagine what those parents are going through."

"What missing child?"

"Why, it's been all over the news today. That sweet little six-year-old girl who went missing from her bedroom last night. Just vanished."

Raissa frowned. "I haven't had the TV on all day, so I didn't know. That's very sad."

Mrs. Angelieu nodded. "Well, I'm going to take one of these pretty blue candles and get out of here. Maybe you can have a nice glass of wine and relax a little. I don't mean to offend you, Raissa, but you look a little tired."

"It's been busy lately," Raissa said as she rang up Mrs. Angelieu's purchase and wrapped the candle.

"Well, that's better than being bored, I suppose," Mrs. Angelieu said as she took her bag. "I'll see you next week." She waved to Raissa as she exited the shop.

Raissa locked the front door and put the closed sign in the window. She had no other appointments and simply wasn't in the mood to deal with another Mrs. Angelieu. The old woman couldn't have been more wrong about being bored. A couple of weeks before, Raissa's close friends had found themselves in a mess of trouble. After a harrowing week of bombs, poisonings, a disgruntled ghost, and too many lies to count, Raissa would have welcomed a day with nothing better to think about than whether God should send lightning into the potato salad of a former harlot bowl owner.

She turned off the lights for the shop and headed up the back staircase to her apartment above the store. It was small, but it suited her perfectly. Raissa had learned long ago to economize. At any given time, she might need to put everything important into her car and disappear. It had been a long time—more than nine years—since the last time she'd had to change everything in her life but the clothes on her back, but she knew that possibility was always there. Long-term plans were not part of her life.

She poured a glass of wine and turned on the television. The news had preempted local programming to feature more about the missing girl. As soon as the picture flashed on the screen along with the girl's name, Raissa clunked her wine down on the coffee table, the liquid sloshing onto the carved wood surface. Melissa Franco, the abducted child, had been in Raissa's store many times with her mother, Susannah. They didn't necessarily believe in the paranormal, but every month the little girl convinced her mother to stop in after their visit to the doctor across the street. The pretty candles and stones in the front display were apparently too much for the child to resist, and her mother always bought at least one more item for Melissa's growing collection of pink and purple.

The reporter suggested the girl had run away, but Raissa didn't buy that for a moment. Melissa was always happy and very inquisitive, asking Raissa endless questions about her shop, the candles, and ghosts. She was obviously doted on by her mother and didn't even cross the street without first grabbing her mother's hand. Not the kind of girl who would have run away from home. And certainly not the kind of girl with the street smarts to remain hidden in the midst of a citywide manhunt.

As the report began going over the details of the case, Raissa's pulse began to race. Melissa had been asleep in her bedroom the night before, and there was no sign of forced entry. She'd simply vanished. Raissa took a big gulp of her wine, her hand shaking as she sat the glass back on the table.

Not again. Not after all these years.

Her head began to pound and she pressed her fingertips to her temples. Everything flooded back to her in a rush. The unanswered questions about entry into the house—every case the same. The seemingly identical victims, although she could never make a connection between the families. The girls, returned a week later, but with absolutely no memory of the abduction or anything that had happened to them while they were missing. Two years of undercover work blown by her trying to solve those cases. The man she knew was guilty, but couldn't find evidence against.

The reason Raissa had fled protective custody nine years ago.

Detective Zach Blanchard stood in front of his captain's desk and waited for the ass-chewing that was most certainly coming. The captain had already gnawed off one side this morning, but apparently someone had noticed Blanchard still had a little ass left and thought he could do with losing the rest.

"What the hell were you thinking?" Captain Saucier's face was beet red. "You interrupted the mayor in the middle of a city-planning meeting to ask him to provide an alibi for his son, whose daughter is missing. It's official, Blanchard. You've lost your fucking mind!"

Zach took a deep breath and started to explain. "According to Mr. Franco, he was with his father at the time of Melissa's disappearance. I needed to have that corroboration, and that meeting was scheduled to run all day. I didn't want to waste any more time investigating someone I don't think is guilty while the real kidnapper gets away."

Captain Saucier stared. "Statistics have shown time and again that a parent is often involved in the disappearance of a child, yet somehow you know *this* father can't possibly be guilty. Fine. Problem is, you've now indicated that he's a suspect to the entire city commission."

Zach bit back a response, certain that the fact that he'd been on the receiving end of a gross miscommunication, which had led to the unfortunate city-planning meeting interruption, wasn't going to matter one bit to the captain. "You're right, sir. That was a miscalculation on my part, and I hope it hasn't caused the mayor or his family any inconvenience."

"Inconvenience...You mean like being called a suspected kiddie killer on the evening news? No, they're used to that kind of thing. After all, they're in the public eye." The captain slammed one hand down on the desk. "From now on you don't so much as shit without clearing it with me first. Do you understand me, Blanchard? I've got the entire city up my ass with a microscope. Do you have any idea how uncomfortable that is?"

"No, sir. I don't."

"Damned right you don't, and with that kind of police work, you never will." He pointed a finger at Zach. "You *will* do everything on this case by the book. No hunches, no running off on rabbit trails, no funny business."

"Yes, sir."

"I mean it. Screw this up, and you'll still be writing parking tickets when you're walking with a cane."

"Everything will be by the book. I promise." The captain didn't look convinced, but he didn't start yelling again, either. Zach figured that was his opportunity to give the captain a nod and clear the room before his boss found out Zach had questioned the mother again that afternoon and the woman had collapsed in a faint just before he left.

By the book.

Just hearing the captain say those words rubbed him all wrong. He always did things by the book—except for that one time—and apparently he was never going to live that down. It was the damned book that said he should interview and alibi every member of the household as close to the disappearance as possible. Panic, stress, and unfortunately in some cases, guilt, tended to set in quickly and sometimes clouded people's minds to information that could lead to a break in the case.

So the mayor's assistant hadn't exactly told him that the entire city council was in that conference room. Matter of fact, she hadn't told him it was the conference room he was barging into. If he'd known that, he might have figured out the mayor wasn't alone. He *was* a detective, after all.

He was concentrating so hard on being aggravated that he almost walked right past the woman seated in front of his desk.

"Can I help you?" he asked. She was a looker, without question.

The woman met his gaze, and he felt his breath catch in his throat. Her eyes were a bright green, like the color of well-cut emeralds. He'd never seen anything quite so gorgeous on someone's face. She rose from her chair and extended her hand. "Detective Blanchard? My name is Raissa Bordeaux. Detective Morrow said I should speak with you."

Zach shook her hand, momentarily surprised by the firmness of her grip, then glanced across the room at Detective Morrow, usually a first-rate asshole. Morrow smirked, then shot out of the building. Great. Zach slid into his chair across the desk from the woman, certain this was going to be a waste of time. "How can I help you, Ms. Bordeaux?"

"I have information on the kidnapping of the Franco child."

"Okay," Zach said, and picked up a pen. "What kind of information?"

"This isn't his first time. That child is one of many who have been taken."

Zach stared. "Melissa Franco is the first child abduction this city has seen in a while that wasn't a custodial issue. I think you're mistaken, Ms. Bordeaux."

"The others didn't live in New Orleans. There were girls in Baton Rouge, in Florida, Mississippi, and New York. Surely there's a way you can compare this case with other kidnappings."

The FBI keeps a database that we can use for such things, but what I'd like is a damned good reason why I should query that database. My boss isn't big on notifying the feds of anything going on in his precinct. He likes control."

"This is far bigger than your boss knows. If this is like the other cases, we're on a short clock. All of those other girls were returned a week later."

"With no memory of what happened, right? I've heard this tale before, Ms. Bordeaux, when I was a kid and my parents were trying to scare me into staying in the backyard."

Raissa raised one eyebrow. "Oh, they all remembered something, but probably not anything you'd want to hear. You have a narrow window of opportunity to catch this person, and I'm guessing, since the victim is the mayor's granddaughter, you don't want to mess this up."

Zach narrowed his eyes at the woman. "And how exactly do you know about these other kidnappings?"

She hesitated—rarely a good sign—then sighed. "I'm a psychic, Detective Blanchard. I saw the other girls in a vision."

Zach felt his jaw clench. "I see. Well, thank you for your information, Ms. Bordeaux. I'll be sure to add your name to the reward list in case of an arrest."

Raissa's face flushed with red and her eyes flashed with anger. "I debated a long time whether to come here, and it certainly wasn't because I care about extorting money from a frantic family. Do yourself a favor and check the database. Unless, of course, you're not interested in getting the best of your friend, the helpful Detective Morrow."

"I can't access that database without a direct order from my captain, which I'm not likely to get off the vision of a so-called psychic. There's a little girl missing out there and you're wasting our time."

Raissa leaned across the desk and lowered her voice. "The house had a security system that was armed, but the alarm never went off and it was still engaged the following morning. There is no trace evidence, and unlike most public kidnappings, you haven't received a ransom request."

Zach straightened in his chair. "We haven't released that information."

Raissa rose from her chair. "One of us is wasting time, Detective, but it's not me." That said, she walked out of the precinct without so much as a backward glance.

Zach leaned back in his chair and shook his head. A psychic. Yeah, right. No wonder Morrow had been so tickled to send her over to Zach. "By-the-book Blanchard" had limited-to-no patience for anything remotely screwy. Psychics were definitely screwy. Likely, Morrow had fed her the information about the security system and ransom note just to make the practical joke more believable.

He watched as she passed on the sidewalk in front of the big window at the front of the station, and couldn't help admiring her long lean legs, or the way she filled out a pair of jeans. What a shame. She was probably the best-looking woman he'd seen in forever.

Unfortunately, nut or no, the woman was right. He should run the case through the FBI database even though the captain hadn't quite gotten to that point. Time *was* of the essence, and the case had strange components that would send up an immediate red flag if there were others with the same MO. He sat up straight and logged on to his computer, hoping like hell that the mayor's granddaughter didn't fit the profile of the other missing girls. If that was the case, the captain might have a heart attack, and with the way things stood now, Morrow was next in line for his job.

Raissa stopped at the corner of the block, angry at herself. *You should have left it alone, but noooooo, you had to go taunting him with what you knew.* She punched the button for the crossing light and jammed her hands in her pockets, trying to control the urge to slug someone. *But it's a child, just like the others, and maybe this is the time he'll be caught.* She watched the screen on the other side of the street and tapped her foot. *It's not your problem anymore. You risked everything before and got less than nothing. Why risk it again?*

She heard running steps behind her, but before she could turn around, someone hit her from behind, launching her into the street—and directly into the path of an oncoming bus. Before she'd even tensed the muscles in her legs to move, an older woman yanked her by the arm, darn near pulling it from her shoulder, and she leaped up from the street just as the bus came to a screeching halt a good five feet beyond the spot where she'd been lying. Raissa clutched her shoulder with one hand and spun around.

But the street was empty.

She figured whoever had pushed her had kept running and was long gone by now, but where was the woman who had pulled her out of the street? The bus driver rushed off the bus, his face white as a sheet.

"Are you all right? I saw that guy push you, but I couldn't stop. I don't know how you managed to move that fast, but I'm glad of it."

"Did you see the guy who pushed me?"

"Yeah, but he was wearing one of those hooded shirts and sunglasses. Coulda been anyone."

"And the woman?"

The bus driver shook his head. "Didn't see no one but you."

Raissa motioned to the street. "You had to have seen her. The woman who pulled me out of the street."

The bus driver studied her for a moment. "Ma'am, I don't know how to tell you this, but there weren't no other woman anywhere on this street. I gotta have perfect vision to drive this bus, and that's what I got." He looked around the street, then back at Raissa. "Maybe you should pay a visit to the Lord's house sometime soon. That's the only explanation I got."

Raissa nodded. "Thank you, Mr..."

"Cormier. Been driving for going on thirty years and ain't killed no one yet. I'm glad that didn't change today. You going to be all right? I can call nine-one-one or something."

"No, thank you, Mr. Cormier. I'll be fine."

The bus driver nodded. "Well, if you need anything, you can find me through the bus company. Like I say, I didn't get a good look at that man or nothing, but I'd be happy to talk to the police, if they was asking."

"I appreciate it, Mr. Cormier, but at this point, I think there's little the police could do."

"You're probably right. You be careful, miss." He climbed back onto the bus and gave her a wave as he pulled away from the corner.

Raissa lifted a hand in response, then hurried across the street to her car. She slid into the driver's seat and looked over at her uninvited passenger. "I'm going to die, right?"

The ghost in her passenger seat frowned at Raissa. "Crap."

Raissa stared at Helena Henry, feeling her pulse race. Of course, she'd known the ghost was around. Maryse and Sabine could both see her and had told Raissa about her. But knowing her friends were telling the truth and seeing the truth in her car were two totally different things. Then there was that small matter of Maryse's theory on Helena's appearances.

"This isn't good, is it?" Raissa finally asked. "Maryse says every time you're visible to someone, their life is in danger."

Helena sighed. "I wish I could argue, but I'm afraid my track record speaks for itself."

"It was you who pulled me out of the street, wasn't it?"

Helena nodded.

"But why are you here? At the street corner? In my car?"

"Well, I was...I thought...you see...Oh, hell, I just had this feeling that you were in trouble, so I've been following you around."

"A feeling?"

Helena waved one hand in dismissal. "I know. Now I sound like all the rest of you nutbags with your spirits and tarot cards and psychic visions, but damn it, I don't know how else to explain it. You were on my mind for days and no matter what I did, I couldn't shake it, so finally I got Maryse to drop me off at your shop."

"Maryse knew about this and didn't tell me?"

"She didn't want to worry you. She said if you saw me, then we'd rally the troops. Otherwise, she was putting it down to my overactive imagination. Well, that and the fact that I started a diet last week."

Raissa's head began to spin. "This is too much to process right now. I'd love nothing better than to drive home and pour myself a glass of the strongest thing I have in my apartment and mull this over, but I've got something urgent to do."

Helena shrugged. "Unless you plan on drinking the Drano under your sink, I don't think you're going to figure it out today anyway. But I wouldn't mind a glass of wine, and maybe a slice of that cheesecake you bought today at lunch. Just don't tell Maryse. She's picking me up in an hour."

Raissa started the car and pulled out of the parking lot. "I thought you were on a diet."

"Hey, I just saved your life. Are you going to deny me a little piece of pie?"

"Helena, I'll buy you pies for the rest of your life if I manage to stay alive like the others."

"Cool!" Helena smiled. "That will show that skinny bitch Maryse. She keeps harping on me about my diet, but I think she's just jealous that I don't gain weight."

"Then why are you on a diet?"

"Maryse and Sabine refuse to keep feeding someone they can't take as a tax deduction, especially as I don't need to eat in the first place. And it's not like I can walk into a grocery store or diner and load up. It was getting a bit exhausting trying to steal when it has to be in my pockets or it's visible to everyone, and I feel guilty about the stealing part, unless it's someone I really don't like." Helena looked down the street at the police station, then back at Raissa. "Hey, you went to the police about that little girl that's missing, didn't you? Did you get a vision or something?"

"I got something."

Helena stared at her for a couple of seconds. "You're not really psychic, are you?"

Chapter Two

Raissa strolled into the Internet café across town, her laptop tucked under her arm. Her normally casual look had been replaced with a loud pink blouse, skintight black pants, and a wig with long red curls. As she waited in line for a latte, she pulled a mirror from her purse and studied the ceiling edge around the room while pretending to check her lipstick. She closed the mirror and tucked it back into a huge silver bag. She'd been right—no security cameras.

She placed her order and received a compliment from the clerk on her long turquoise nails with purple dolphins, then collected her coffee and took a table on the patio outside that offered her the best view of the street corner. Placing the laptop on the table, she gave the street the once-over, her eyes safely hidden behind the polarized lenses of her sunglasses. After a quick glance back inside the shop, she peeled the dolphin nails off her fingertips, satisfied that no one would ever think that the dolphin-nail-wearing woman and Raissa Bordeaux were the same person.

When her fingers were free of the long nails, she opened her laptop and started working. It took only minutes to get to the files she'd come for, even with the added time of diverting the FBI firewall security, but then she hadn't been known as the best hacker at the bureau for nothing. She inserted a flash drive and began the download of every case file she could think of that might be relevant, every possible angle she could come up with that might keep her alive. Her fingers flew across the keyboard, and the screen scrolled with page after page of downloading data. She looked at the time and checked the street again. A minute, maybe two, was all she had left before they closed in on her.

She opened the last log she wanted to check and scanned the list. The second-to-last entry was the one she expected to find. Mission completed, she pocketed the flash drive and deposited the laptop in the trash-can before she left the cafe. A block from the café, she slipped into the alley and pulled a large trash bag from her purse. She shoved the sunglasses, wig, and purse inside, along with the fake nails she'd removed earlier, then buried the bag in a Dumpster behind a Chinese restaurant. As she exited the alley, she peeled the wax off her fingertips, scattering the remains on the sidewalk as she went.

She had a moment of regret at the thought of the laptop crushed alongside latte remnants, but the reality was, it was marked. If she used it to access the Internet again, the trace would begin automatically. Still, it always killed her to sacrifice good computer equipment, which is why she always picked up old systems at garage sales and secondhand stores. With minimal tinkering she could upgrade them to suit her purposes.

She glanced at her watch as she hopped into her car. Despite his obvious disdain and disbelief of her profession and the "evidence" she'd given him, Detective Blanchard had run the case through the bureau—just ten minutes before. She knew it would take at least forty-five minutes for him to get clearance approval and for the information to queue. She figured that gave her about an hour to double-check that everything was in order at her shop before the surly detective paid her an "unofficial" visit.

That meant an hour to ensure that the outside of every door and window of her shop was free of fingerprints, just in case she'd properly read the serious and quick-thinking Detective Blanchard. Once he realized Raissa was right on all counts, the logical thing to do would be to scrutinize the source. And since the source in this case didn't want her fingerprints run through a national database, at least not until she'd had an opportunity to come up with plan B, an unscheduled date with Windex was in order. She smiled.

How unlucky for Detective Blanchard that Raissa had nine years of experience in remaining out of sight.

Zach scrolled down the screen, scanning the result of the FBI database search he'd done earlier. His pulse quickened as the screen scrolled, child after child. All six years old. All blonde with blue eyes. All missing from a locked house with frantic parents who had been cleared of any involvement. All had been returned a week later, and medical examinations had revealed no injury or abuse. None of the cases had ever yielded a decent set of clues, much less been solved.

And every single child had claimed she'd been abducted by aliens.

Shit.

He scrolled back to the top of the page and checked the cities—Tallahassee, Orlando, Gulfport, Jackson, Baton Rouge, Brooklyn. Son of a bitch. That psychic had nailed it.

Damn it! How in the world was he supposed to explain to his captain that a psychic had tipped him off? And that the chief suspect was apparently a character from *The X-Files*. He shook his head. The answer was simple—he didn't explain. They would have run the case through the FBI database eventually. Zach could just claim that the odd aspects of the crime made him decide to do it sooner rather than later. He wouldn't even mention the alien thing. The captain could just read that himself.

But there was also a whole other issue to deal with.

Zach didn't believe for one second that the woman he'd met was really psychic. Zach didn't believe in psychics at all. Which meant that Raissa Bordeaux had come about that information some other way than through spirits or tea leaves. And the only way that came to mind was that she knew who had kidnapped those girls.

Or had done it herself.

Zach combed the printouts of everything he could find on Raissa Bordeaux, which was next to nothing. A mere two pages. A ten-year-old would have a file bigger than this woman. Raissa—no middle name—Bordeaux had appeared in New Orleans nine years ago. She'd worked as a waitress at a bar downtown for about a year, and then she'd opened her little shop of paranormal tricks. Her driver's license was nine years old, and as far as he could tell, she hadn't been issued one prior to then. Her Social Security number showed only her waitress income and the business, and beyond that, Raissa Bordeaux didn't exist.

No arrests, no credit history, not even a parking ticket. It was as if the woman had appeared out of thin air nine years ago.

Zach frowned and tapped his pencil on the desk. Women who abducted children usually did so because they wanted their own, or they were involved in a baby-selling ring. But these missing girls had been too old to sell to couples wanting an infant. It was more likely Raissa Bordeaux knew so much because she was somehow involved with the man who had taken the girls. Zach wasn't buying that "vision" nonsense for a moment, but fronting for some guy running drugs, prostitution, kiddie porn, whatever—*that* he'd buy.

It was a shame that all the real lookers hooked up with piece-of-shit men. As long as he lived, Zach was certain he'd never understand the attraction. But there was really no other explanation. Either Raissa Bordeaux liked little girls and was playing a game with the police, or she knew a man who liked little girls and she wanted out of whatever she'd gotten herself into.

Zach was banking on the latter.

He rose from his chair and grabbed his keys off the desktop. It was time to pay Ms. Bordeaux a visit. And maybe try to pick up a random fingerprint while he was there. She might be able to change her driver's license and Social Security card, but fingerprints are forever.

When the buzzer to her apartment sounded, Raissa glanced at her watch and smiled. One hour, ten minutes. She walked over to the window and saw the unmarked police car parked at the curb across the street from her shop, just as she'd expected. She pressed the intercom button in her kitchen. "Can I help you?"

"Ms. Bordeaux?" Zach's voice boomed over the intercom. "It's Detective Blanchard. I need to talk to you."

Raissa smiled at the formal yet agitated tone of his voice. "Certainly. I'll be right down."

Detective Blanchard stood just outside the shop door, staring at the items in her display window, a look of consternation on his face. "You're working late, Detective," Raissa said.

"Yes, well, given the circumstances, we all are."

Raissa nodded and stared at him. He stared back for a moment, obviously waiting for a question or an invitation, but Raissa wasn't about to make it that easy. Keeping Detective Blanchard off balance was a must. She couldn't afford for him to figure out her angle. Better he decide she was a weirdo who tracked child-kidnapping cases than know the truth.

Finally, he cleared his throat. "I had a couple of questions for you, if you have the time."

"Sure. Like what?"

"I checked on similar cases, and you were right. In fact, you were too right. Every single city had a matching case file. I want to know how you got that information, Ms. Bordeaux."

"I already told you, Detective Blanchard. I'm psychic. It came to me in a vision."

Zach's jaw clenched. "We both know that's a load of horseshit. Now, you can either give me the answer I want here, or you can give it to me back at the station."

"I know nothing of the sort, and it's particularly bad manners, even for a police officer, to refer to someone else's livelihood as horseshit. Especially when that horseshit is most likely going to put you ahead of Detective Morrow on the captain's list, right?"

"This has nothing to do with Morrow or the captain." Zach's face began to redden. "This has to do with a child abductor that I'd damned well like to find."

Raissa nodded. "I'd like that, too, but I'm afraid there's nothing else I can tell you. I don't have any more information than what I've already given you."

"You're lying. Either you took those girls yourself, or you know who did." Zach blew out a breath. "Look, Ms. Bordeaux, it's obvious to me you're hiding from someone. There's no record of your existence before age twenty-four. I know you're not who you say you are, and if you push me, I'll dig into your background until I get what I'm looking for."

Raissa cocked her head to one side and studied him. "You know, I believe you would. The only problem with that is then you'd be spending all your time and energy on me, which will get you no closer to finding that little girl or her abductor. You're going to have to trust me on this, Detective. I don't kidnap children, and if I knew who did, I would give you that information."

"You're walking a thin line, Ms. Bordeaux."

"Aren't we all?"

"No. My past is an open book. I suggest that unless you want me to finger you for this kidnapping, you open up your own."

"I wish you'd concentrate on the facts you have and the things you can control. I'm not your problem, I assure you."

Zach shook his head. "You're a problem all right. And your assurance means nothing. I don't even know who you are. How am I supposed to trust anything you say?"

Raissa shrugged. "Then don't trust me. Waste time chasing rabbits, and he gets away with it again. I'm sure I don't have to tell you that none of those cases yielded any clues, except the extraterrestrial kind. Do you really want the mayor's grandchild on Channel Four saying she was abducted by ET?"

Zach's eyes narrowed. "How did you know they all claimed aliens took them?"

"Because I could read their thoughts at the time. How do you think I knew about them at all?" Raissa stepped inside the shop. "If we're done, I'd like to get ready for dinner."

"We're done for now, but don't get too comfortable with that. I'll be back."

"I look forward to it, Detective," Raissa said and closed the door behind her. She sneaked over to the far corner of the shop and waited a couple of seconds, then peeked through the blinds. Sure enough, the detective was trying to pull a fingerprint off the front door to her shop. What a shame she'd wiped that door handle clean just thirty minutes before.

She watched as he bent over and studied the handle. An even bigger shame was that such a nice butt was wasted on such an uptight man. She dropped the blinds slat and sighed. Not that she had any business admiring butts, anyway. Men were a luxury she couldn't afford. She'd tried the occasional fling, but too many times the man wanted to get serious, and Raissa couldn't go there. She had been safe for a lot of years. No man was worth risking her life for—not even if the sex was absolutely fabulous.

She grabbed her purse from behind the counter and slipped on a pair of lacy black gloves. The dead bolt on the door didn't so much as squeak, and she thanked God again for whoever had invented WD-40. In a flash, she twisted the doorknob and flung the front door open, practically yanking the handle out of Zach's hand.

He jumped back as if he'd been shot, and it was all Raissa could do not to laugh. His expression went from horrified to guilty to aggravated faster than a race car shifting gears. Raissa stepped outside and stared at him, her eyes wide with faked surprise. "Why Detective! I didn't know you were still here." She glanced at the handle, covered with fingerprint powder, then back at Zach, who slipped his hand with the brush behind his back.

"I appreciate the care of my door handle, but it only requires a good moisturizer. Powder really isn't necessary." She locked the door behind her and gave him a big smile, waving one gloved hand as she walked out into the hot summer evening.

It was almost eleven p.m. before Raissa finished her business and headed back to her apartment. The street from the parking lot to her shop was dimly lit, and Raissa stayed alert, knowing that anything was possible on a dark New Orleans street. Normally, she tried to limit her nightly excursions, but the people she needed to see didn't do daytime. Unfortunately, her investigative trip hadn't yielded her the information she'd hoped for.

She was certain she knew who had taken those girls but had never been able to prove it. She'd been close, so close, to the answer—or so she believed—when everything had fallen apart. She'd tried for years to shut those bright blue eyes from her mind, but in her dreams they still haunted her. Why were they taken, and what horrible things had happened to them that they couldn't remember?

But even though Melissa Franco's disappearance was exactly the same as the others, no one had seen the man she suspected. Not for at least six months, best she could figure, which troubled Raissa more than she wanted to admit. Granted, New Orleans wasn't his territory, but he had family here and was the lead man in Baton Rouge for Louisiana's most notorious mobster. Sonny Hebert valued trust above everything else. If no one had seen Monk in six months, then what did that mean? She could think of only one possibility, and it involved a trash bag, rocks, and the Mississippi River.

She was half a block from her shop when she saw a shadow move in front of the alley. She stopped for a moment and studied the street, looking for another sign of movement in the shadows, listening for a sound that might tell her whether it had been animal or human.

There was nothing but silence.

You're overly alert. But even thinking it didn't alleviate the uneasy feeling she had as she studied the alley. And since that uneasy feeling had saved her butt more times than she could count, she wasn't about to start ignoring it now.

She slipped her pistol from the holster on her ankle and edged closer to the building, silently creeping toward the alley. It seemed even her breathing echoed in the stale night air, and she paused just long enough to control her breaths. Five more steps.

She eased up to the corner and studied the shadows that stretched out onto the sidewalk in front of the opening. No movement. Then she focused all her attention on listening, trying to decipher any noise that might indicate the threat her body so clearly felt was there. She waited five seconds, six seconds, seven—and then she heard it. The tiny shuffle of feet on the cement. Barely a whisper. But unmistakable.

She gripped her pistol with both hands and lifted it to her shoulder. Taking one deep, silent breath, she whirled around the corner and came pistol to face with a man.

He threw his hands in the air as soon as he saw her gun, and the sheer terror on his face made Raissa wonder if she'd mistaken a simple bum for a professional killer. But a quick glance disqualified the bum theory. Blue jeans, T-shirt, and tennis shoes weren't exactly a tuxedo, but they were clean and the man's hair was short, his face completely shaven. This was no bum.

He stared at her, his eyes wide, and finally tried to speak. "Raissa? Raissa Bordeaux…right?"

She studied him for a moment. Something about him looked familiar, but she was certain she'd never met him before. She never forgot a face. "Who are you and how do you know my name?"

The man's eyes widened even more and he swallowed. "My name's Hank. Hank Henry."

And suddenly Raissa realized that she'd seen a picture of him in the Mudbug newspaper. Hank Henry—the disappearing ex-husband of her friend Maryse and son of the recently risen Helena Henry—was a legend in Mudbug. Mostly for being a coward and an idiot, not exactly the sort of legacy most people wanted to leave behind. Good-looking, smooth talking, and utterly useless was exactly how Maryse had described her ex, and taking a closer look at him, Raissa decided she'd probably agree with the "good-looking" assessment, but the smooth talking was nowhere in sight.

Apparently pistols pointed at his head gave Hank stage fright.

But then, given his propensity for activities that were not necessarily legal and his never-ending shortage of cash, Raissa wasn't convinced that his lurking in the alley was benign. After all, he'd been hiding out for years, and his mother's death had only profited charities and not her wayward son. Why show up now? "What do you want?"

"I need to talk to you. It's important. I...well, I...I think you might be in danger."

Raissa narrowed her eyes at him. "From who?"

Hank's gaze darted between the gun and Raissa. He swallowed again and looked at her. "Sonny Hebert," he whispered.

Raissa sucked in a breath, her heart pounding in her chest. She glanced behind her, then back at Hank. Whatever else Hank Henry might be, the one thing Raissa was certain about was that he wasn't a killer. "I think you better come with me." She tucked the gun in her waistband and motioned for Hank to follow. He gave her a nod and fell in behind her.

A couple of minutes later, Hank was seated at her tiny kitchen table, and she set two glasses of scotch on the table with the rest of the bottle between them. "I figured this wasn't the sort of conversation that called for coffee or tea."

Hank looked grateful but not the least bit relieved. Whatever had him hiding in a dark alley waiting to accost a woman he didn't really know must be heavy, which was worrisome at best. The Hank Henry she'd always heard about was usually in minor trouble, but nothing of the sort that had him stalking women and looking as jumpy as a cat. "How do you know Sonny Hebert?"

Hank froze for a second, then stared down at the table. "Look, I did some stupid things in the past. Really stupid. I had a gambling problem, and I owed the wrong people money."

"You borrowed money from the Hebert family to gamble? That's not a problem—that's a death wish."

"Don't you think I know that? But I swear, when I made the deal, I had no idea the Heberts were behind it. It was one of their cousins, different last name, and I didn't make the connection until it was too late."

"So all this hiding out you've been doing isn't from the Mudbug police."

"Heck, no. Spending some time in the Mudbug jail would be a relief compared to this, but I can't get caught staying anywhere too long, especially in places I can't walk out of. Know what I mean?"

Raissa nodded. Oh yeah, she knew exactly what Hank meant. Anyone could get caught—and in jail, you were a sitting duck.

"Another month and I'll have all my fines in Mudbug paid, so it won't be an issue." Hank leaned forward a bit in his chair and looked directly at Raissa. "Ms. Bordeaux, you don't have to believe a word I say, but I want you to know that I'm clean. Been clean for over a year. I did some time in rehab—different name, of course, and nowhere near New Orleans. I'm a changed man, and I want to live a different life, but I can't do that with the Heberts looking for me under every cypress tree in Louisiana."

"How much do you owe them?"

Hank raised both hands in the air. "Nothing! I swear I don't owe them a dime. We had a deal, and I worked off my debt. Working off that debt is what sent me to rehab. I'm not a great man, and I know my morals are lacking, but I don't have the stomach for the way those men live. I had to get clean. There wasn't any other choice."

Raissa frowned. "So if you don't owe them, what do they want?"

"They keep asking me to do stuff…jobs, you know? I've told 'em I'm straight and I don't want any trouble, but seems like whenever I go to one of my old haunts, there's always one of the family hanging around."

"There's plenty of people who'd be happy to do Hebert's bidding and take the paycheck. So why keep bothering you?"

Hank blew out a breath. "I think it's because they think I know something."

"Know what?"

"That's just it. I don't know. But they keep asking these strange questions about people in Mudbug and stuff."

Raissa mentally counted to five. "So they're asking you questions, trying to get you to admit to something they think you know, but you don't know what that something is?

Hank nodded. "Yeah. I mean, I guess I saw or heard something I wasn't supposed to, but hell, how am I supposed to know which thing it was? These people didn't do picnics and bowling league. It could be anything."

Raissa tapped one finger on the table and stared at the wall behind Hank. "No, it couldn't be anything. You were privy to the inner workings of a mob family for a while and, I'm sure, saw plenty. But whatever they're afraid you know, I'll bet it doesn't have anything to do with extortion, or loan-sharking, or even murder."

"What then?"

"Something worse, much worse."

Hank's eyes widened, and Raissa knew exactly what he was wondering—what's worse than murder? If only she had an answer.

"So," Raissa continued, "you said you thought I was in danger from the Heberts. What makes you think that?"

Hank lifted his glass and downed the rest of the contents. Hand shaking, he placed the glass back down on the table. "Because they asked me to kill you."

Chapter Three

Raissa slammed her scotch glass onto the table. "They asked you to kill me?"

Hank nodded, clearly frightened. "Not you by name, exactly, but they said that friend of my ex-wife's that was a psychic…but they were clear that it wasn't Sabine. I told 'em no, straight out. I ain't never killed no one, and I ain't about to start."

Raissa narrowed her eyes at Hank. "How did you find me?"

"I remembered Sabine saying your shop name before, so I looked it up." His eyes widened. "Oh, shit. I led them right to you, didn't I?" He jumped up from the table. "Jesus, I didn't even think—How could I be so stupid?"

Raissa rose from her chair and placed her hand on Hank's arm. "Don't worry about it. They know about your connection to me, so they already know how to find me, I'm sure."

Hank stared at her for a moment, still not quite buying it. Finally, he blew out a breath and sank back into the chair. "Then why come to me at all? If the Heberts want you gone, and they know who you are and where to find you, they could have already handled this. Why ask me when they already knew I wasn't going to do it?"

Raissa sat back down and thought for a minute. "I think, given my connection to Maryse, they figured you would warn me."

Hank still looked doubtful. "You're saying they're sending you a message? What message?"

Raissa's jaw involuntarily clenched. "That if I don't disappear on my own, they're going to help me."

Zach sat low in his car just down the road from Raissa's shop. He'd seen her coming down the block and wondered why she stopped before reaching her building. When she slipped the pistol from her ankle holster, he'd been ready to bolt from the car, but something had stopped him. The ankle holster for one. Sure, plenty of people carried in New Orleans, and a single woman living in a downtown apartment would be remiss not to have some form of protection, but an ankle holster was definitely not the most common place for a woman to carry a gun.

And it was the way she moved—as if she'd been trained for exactly what she was doing.

Against his better judgment, he'd waited as she entered the alley, giving her ten seconds before he hurried to assist. When the seconds had passed and she hadn't appeared, he cursed himself and his stupidity and eased out of the car and across the street. He crouched behind a mailbox and listened. For a moment, all he heard was the regular noises of the street—paper rustling on the sidewalk, the sound of car engines in the distance—but then it trickled down to him. The sound of voices.

So Raissa's instincts had been right. There had been someone in the alley, but apparently that someone was more interested in talking than in something more insidious. He was just about to move closer when Raissa and a man stepped out of the alley and hurried to her building. Her pistol was tucked in the waistband of her jeans, and she didn't seem the least bit concerned about protecting herself from the man who followed her.

She glanced his way as she unlocked the door to her shop, and he ducked behind the mailbox, hoping she hadn't seen him. A couple of seconds later, he heard the door click shut. He watched until he saw the light in the upstairs apartment come on. Deciding

Raissa was done with whatever she was up to that night, he crept back across the street and climbed into his car.

Zach hadn't recognized the man who had been hiding in the alley, but Raissa must have known him well enough to let him in her apartment. Which made him wonder why the man hadn't called or simply rung her doorbell. Why lurk around the corner, running the risk of being shot?

Zach looked up at the apartment again. The light was on in the front room, and Zach could make out a silhouette of the man sitting at a table. A minute later, Raissa set glasses on the table and joined him. Surely, if the guy was a friend or boyfriend he wouldn't have been hiding in an alley. Which left business.

He looked down at his watch.

Kinda late for a business meeting. He watched another thirty minutes and finally saw them rise from the table. A minute later, the man slipped out the front door, scanned the street, then took off in the direction of a lone truck parked at the other corner. Zach hunched down in his seat so the man wouldn't notice him as he drove past.

He watched the rearview mirror until the man had turned the corner, then started his car and took off after him. The truck turned again at the end of the next block, and Zach pressed the accelerator. His quarry was entering the highway, which gave Zach the perfect chance to get his license plate without being made.

He followed the truck onto the highway and eased beside it in the next lane. Zach gave brief thanks that the license plate was clean and easily readable and jotted the number down before continuing on the highway past him. Two exits later, he merged right and exited the highway, heading for the police station. It should be almost empty this time of night. A great time to run a plate without someone looking over his shoulder and asking questions.

Only one cop manned the front desk when he walked into the station. Zach gave him a nod and went to his own desk. It only took a minute to open the database and plug in the truck's license plate. Another minute and he was looking at pages of information on one Hank Henry. He scanned the pages, shaking his head. This Hank was a piece of work, and stupid.

He seemed to have the uncanny ability to be involved with the wrong thing at the wrong time.

But for over a year, his record was clean as a whistle. Interesting.

He checked another database, but no prison system had a Hank Henry listed as a recent resident. So the question remained: what was a man of questionable background and character doing hiding outside Raissa's store? And why did she invite him inside for drinks?

Questions he couldn't answer. Not yet. But Raissa Bordeaux definitely required more looking into.

It was a bright and sunny morning in Mudbug when Raissa pushed open the door to the Mudbug Hotel. Little bells tinkled above, alerting anyone inside to her entrance. No one was at the front counter, but she'd barely stepped inside before she heard Mildred, the hotel owner, yell, "Raissa, we're in the office. Come on back."

Raissa stepped down the hall, wondering who "we" was. For whatever absurd reason, Helena had insisted Raissa meet her at the hotel to "discuss an action plan."

Since Hank's visit last night, Raissa figured she had much bigger things to deal with than forming an "action plan" with a ghost, but on second thought, she decided an invisible partner *did* come with some advantages. Raissa had assumed the ghost intended to meet her outside the hotel, but after several minutes of waiting, she decided to try inside, even though she had no good explanation for Mildred as to why she'd be visiting her hotel in Mudbug when Raissa should have been preparing to open her shop in New Orleans.

Based on Mildred's greeting, an explanation wasn't necessary. Which meant that Helena must have talked to Sabine or Maryse, or both, and they were waiting at the hotel to come up with a plan. At the end of the hall, she stepped through an open doorway and into Mildred's office. The hotel owner was perched in a huge office chair behind her desk, eating a muffin and playing cards. Even more disturbing was her opponent.

Helena Henry sat across the desk from Mildred, grumbling about her hand. "I see you three doughnut holes and raise you one muffin." Helena was dressed in a long, flowing, pink gown made of some type of gauzy material. On her head sat a wide floppy hat in the same shade of pink as the dress, with a ring of white and red roses around the top.

Mildred looked up at Raissa and smiled. "I'm making Helena earn her breakfast."

Raissa stared for a couple of seconds, not sure what to even think—*way* beyond having anything to say. "You can see Helena?" she asked Mildred.

"Oh, yeah. She turned up like a bad penny right after my car wreck." Mildred motioned to Raissa to take the seat next to Helena. "Already poured you a cup of coffee. Might as well have a seat and drink a bit."

Raissa slid into the chair, still a bit numb. "And you're okay with this? I mean, I always got the impression you didn't go in for anything remotely out of this world."

"Absolutely right, but what the heck was I supposed to do? You can't exactly refute the evidence, especially when it's loud and eating you out of hotel and home." She disposed of two cards and pushed some doughnut holes and a mini-muffin into the stack of food in the middle of the desk. "Call."

Raissa looked over at Helena, who studied Mildred's face, most certainly trying to determine if her doughnut holes and muffin were now at risk. "What in the world are you wearing, Helena? Yesterday you just had on jeans and a T-shirt."

Helena waved a hand in dismissal. "I take Mondays off."

"Off from what?"

"From my wardrobe-through-the-ages adventures. Oh, it sounds like fun when you start, but it's actually a lot harder than you think to come up with something creative every day. Last month, I did music through the ages MTV-style. This month is classic movies through the ages."

Raissa started to understand, and wasn't sure whether that made her feel better or more confused. "So this is..."

"Gone with the Wind," Mildred supplied. "My suggestion. I wasn't about to allow her in my hotel with what she had on before. I don't care if no one else can see her. I can, and that's enough."

Raissa looked over at Helena. "What movie were you dressed like before?"

"Boogie Nights," Helena replied.

Raissa laughed. "*Boogie Nights* is a classic?"

Helena huffed. "It is if you've watched the last scene."

Raissa grinned and looked over at Mildred, who was frowning at Helena. "I can see where the problem might have come in."

"So," Helena went on, "that's why I'm wearing the pink flying-nun dress. I wouldn't want to offend Mildred's delicate sensibilities, even though those traveling salesmen she rents rooms to watch stuff that make *Boogie Nights* look like *Scooby-Doo.*"

Mildred shook her head. "Well, since I'm not walking through walls and spying on customers when they darned well think they're alone, I don't have issues with what they do in their rooms, as long as I don't know about it. Sophia bleaches the sheets when people leave anyway."

"Gross," Raissa said. "I think I'd rather talk about my impending doom."

Mildred laid down her cards and nodded. "That's why we asked you here. I've spoken to Sabine and Maryse. They both had other obligations that kept them from being here this morning, but we all agree—you've got trouble coming. No one sees Helena who doesn't live to regret it, but the good news is, so far, everyone's *lived.*"

Raissa sat back in her chair and sighed. "Only by the skin of their teeth. You were all very lucky."

"Yes, that's true, but we also heeded the warning—the Helena kind—and we took care to know that something serious was in the making, even if none of us could understand it all at the time."

"I know you took precautions," Raissa agreed, "but the reality is, if someone wants to kill you, they most likely will. The only way to stop that train is to either eliminate the killer or the reason he wants you dead."

Mildred nodded. "Exactly. So that's what we're gonna do. With Sabine and Maryse, it was harder to pin down because they weren't even aware of some of the things they'd gotten into. So we were off looking for an enemy without a clear view of the situation from the beginning."

Raissa looked at Mildred. "And you think somehow that's different with me?"

"Well, yeah. At least that's what we're hoping. I mean, after everything that happened last month and your involvement with it all, Maryse, Sabine, and I thought maybe Helena should shadow you for a bit and make sure you couldn't see her. We were just starting to think we'd gotten it all wrong when someone shoved you in front of a bus."

"And then I could see Helena," Raissa finished.

"Right," Mildred said. "But the only thing in your life that changed from that moment to an hour before was you talking to the police about that missing girl. Helena was there when you talked to that detective, but you couldn't see her then. So we know it has something to do with the missing girl and your talking to the police. We just need you to tell us what."

"What makes you think I know?" Raissa asked.

Mildred glanced over at Helena, then back at Raissa. "I've always known you were hiding from something. I figured it was an abusive husband or the like, which is why I never pressed you for answers. But after knowing you as long as I have, I've decided you're too strong to have been abused. Which means that whatever you're hiding from is a lot worse than one angry, vindictive man."

Raissa nodded. "You're right. It's not one man."

Mildred narrowed her eyes at Raissa. "You were a cop, weren't you?"

Raissa felt a wave of anxiety pass over her. She shifted in her chair and looked down at the floor, millions of denials already forming in her mind. Finally, she looked back up at Mildred and in an instant, she knew.

It was time.

Time to stop running. Stop hiding from her past. From the truth.

"I was an FBI agent."

Helena sucked in a breath and stared at her, wide-eyed. "Holy shit! You were a supercop. No wonder nothing fazes you. You've got balls of steel."

"Ha!" Raissa spit out that single word. "If I had balls of steel, I wouldn't have spent the last nine years hiding behind scented candles and tarot cards. If I had balls of steel, I'd have taken out the entire Hebert family so I could have my life back."

Mildred put one hand over her mouth. "The Hebert family... as in Sonny Hebert, the Don Corleone of southern Louisiana?"

"Yeah. As in, not one man—but a 'family.'"

"Holy shit," Mildred repeated Helena's words, then downed her entire cup of coffee. "Okay, this is far worse than I had imagined."

Helena nodded. "That's not the kind of family that does barbecues and beer."

"No," Raissa agreed. "They're more into extortion, and money laundering, and God knows what else."

Mildred refilled her coffee cup, pulled a bottle of scotch from the bottom drawer of her desk, and poured a generous amount into her coffee. She handed the bottle to Helena, who took a huge gulp straight from the bottle, then doctored her own coffee and passed the bottle to Raissa. Raissa, who had never been one to drink after another person, wasn't quite sure the ghost counted, but it still bothered her on too many levels, so she passed on the whiskey altogether.

"Okay," Mildred said, "so there's a bit of a setback in our original thinking, but there's no cause to panic."

"Are you fucking kidding me?" Helena said. "Hell, I'm panicked, and I'm already dead."

Mildred frowned. "Well, at least they can't kill you twice."

"That's not entirely true," Raissa said. "I died nine and a half years ago when one of the Hebert clan put a bullet through my chest. They resuscitated me in the ambulance. On paper, I've been dead ever since. So in this case, if the Heberts get me, then technically they have killed me twice."

"We're not going to let that happen," Mildred said, her voice growing strong again. "I promise you, Raissa, we will see you through this. The first thing we have to do is find you someplace safe."

Raissa laughed. "I know you mean well, and I love you for it, but I'm trained to hide, and they still found me."

"I didn't say you should hide, since you're right, that's obviously not going to work. But I *do* think relocating to a more defensible location would help."

"You mean move? No, I can't move. I have a business to run—"

"*Which,*" Mildred interrupted, "you've already offered to cut down to part time to cover Sabine's store for her honeymoon. Sabine will be at Beau's place in New Orleans to night, and they fly out tomorrow. There's no reason for you not to move here temporarily."

"I don't know," Raissa said, her mind racing with all the reasons that involving more people in her mess was a really bad idea.

"You should do it," Helena urged. "It's not like just anyone can come and go in Mudbug without being noticed. And you could stay at the hotel."

Raissa struggled to come up with a good argument, but had to admit that the idea wasn't the worst one she'd heard. In fact, it came with the advantages Mildred had mentioned and a few that she hadn't thought about. Finally, she nodded. "Okay. I'll move, but just for the rest of the week, and I'll still have to commute to my store a couple of times. I can reschedule my readings, but I don't want to cancel on my regular customers."

Mildred frowned, and Raissa knew she'd wanted a full-time commitment, but it was something that Raissa just couldn't offer without lying. One, because remaining in Mudbug wouldn't allow her to do the investigating she needed to do in New Orleans, and two, because if her situation even came remotely close to putting her friends in danger, then Raissa was out of Mudbug like a gunshot.

"What about your family, Raissa?" Mildred asked. "Do they know where you are?"

"My parents are both dead, and we weren't really tight with any relatives. So there's no one missing me, if that's what you're asking."

Mildred nodded and studied her for a couple of seconds. Finally, she sighed. "You're not going to bow out until you find that missing girl, are you? It's somehow tied in to your past and the Heberts'."

"I think so," Raissa said, "but I've never had any proof."

Helena's eyes widened. "There have been others…other little girls that were taken?"

"There were others before Melissa."

Mildred swallowed, then cleared her throat. "What happened to them?"

"They were returned a week later without a mark on them and no memory of what happened to them after their abduction. There's a very narrow window of opportunity to catch this guy and stop this from happening again." Raissa rose from her chair, already mentally packing a bag of necessities for her stay in Mudbug. "I have to go home and get some things. One of my conditions for staying here is that you let me rig the hotel with security. It can all be done with fingernail-size lenses and infrared. I won't install anything in the guest rooms, except for my own, but I insist on rigging at least the outside of your quarters, Mildred, or I won't stay here at all."

Mildred nodded. "Whatever you think is best."

"Good," Raissa said, "because as much as I want to find out what happened to those girls, I'd prefer it not be firsthand. Abduction is not on my list of things to do, and it's doubtful I'd come back without a mark on me…if I came back at all."

Mildred narrowed her eyes at Raissa. "I don't suppose you really are psychic, right? I mean, not that I wouldn't find that a bit creepy, but, well, we already have a ghost. I guess I'm willing to consider any edge we might have, even the strange ones."

"I wish I were," Raissa said, "but it's all a very clever front. Or at least, I used to think it was."

"But all those things you knew...How did you guess all those things and get them right? No one's that lucky."

Raissa smiled. "It was never luck. I'm a highly skilled computer hacker and an expert at surveillance. Someone asks me what's wrong with their marriage, I follow the husband and find the girlfriend, or the doctor's office. Then I hack the girlfriend's computer, since usually women don't destroy the evidence, like mushy e-mails, that the cheating husband asks them to. Or I hack the doctor's office and find out what he's being treated for. I feed them enough information to sound like a vision but send them off on the right track for exposing whatever is going on."

"No shit." Helena stared at Raissa in admiration. "That whole psychic gig is a genius way to use those skills. I take back every time I called you a nutbag."

Raissa laughed. "Thanks, Helena. Coming from you that means...well, damned near nothing, but I'll take it anyway." Raissa rose from her chair. "Are we done here? Everyone satisfied with the master plan?"

Mildred looked over at Helena who nodded. "I'm as satisfied as I'm getting," Mildred said. "But I really wish you'd reconsider staying here full-time."

"No can do, Mildred. I'm not trying to upset anyone, but this whole thing is far bigger than just me."

Mildred straightened up in her chair and stared at Raissa, her eyes wide. "You're going to try to catch that guy, aren't you? You have no intention of lying low or leaving this to the cops."

"This may be my last chance," Raissa said. "Think about those girls. Think about their mothers. And then tell me what I should do."

Mildred was silent for a couple of seconds, and Raissa knew her mind was racing to find an argument, anything that would hold up to Raissa's logic. Raissa also knew that Maryse and Sabine, Mildred's surrogate daughters, would be lodged in her mind, too. Finally, Mildred slumped back in her chair and nodded. "I don't like it, but I shouldn't expect anything less from you." She rose from her chair and surprised Raissa by giving her a hug.

"I don't even know if you have any family or if they even know you're alive," Mildred said as she released her, "but I want you to know that I consider you my family, another one of my girls. I'm not going to ask you to promise not to do anything dangerous, but I *am* going to make you promise not to die on us."

Raissa's eyes moistened and she rubbed her nose with one finger, sniffling. "That's a promise I'll be happy to make." She gave Mildred's hand a squeeze, then hurried out of the hotel before she embarrassed herself by becoming just another weepy woman.

Chapter Four

At two thirty P.M., Raissa closed the door to her shop after her last appointment and put the CLOSED sign in the window. There were a million things that had to be done before she could commence her part-time-living adventures in the Mudbug Hotel, but one absolutely couldn't wait.

She entered her upstairs apartment and opened the closet, scrutinizing her choices. This excursion wasn't exactly a jeans-and-T-shirt sort of call, not unless she wanted to stick out by a mile. She made her selections, then began a mid-afternoon transformation.

Twenty minutes later, she peeked through her shop blinds, scanning the street for Detective Blanchard's unmarked police car. Clear. Thank God. She left her shop and drove to a corner bar on a seedy side of town. Unlike most bars, this one was always open and always had clientele. It tended to cater to people who didn't keep regular business hours—drug dealers, hookers, petty thieves, and not-so-petty thieves—just the kind of people she was looking to see.

She was certain she made quite a picture walking down the sidewalk to the bar. The whistles and catcalls confirmed her choice of the short, tight, black leather skirt and blue sparkly top with a plunging neckline. Her six-inch stilettos put her right at six foot two, and the platinum wig put the finishing touches on the entire getup.

Satisfied that she looked like any other working girl, she opened the door and walked into the bar. The man she was looking for was sitting at the counter and he gave her a mental undressing as she walked in. She gave him the ole come-hither smile and walked to the back of the empty bar, shaking her hips as she strolled. She slid into a high-backed booth in the corner and waited for her prey to take the bait.

It didn't take long.

Spider, as he was called by the Hebert family, was predictable, if anything. And creepy, hence the nickname. A minute later—just enough time for her to slide her 9-millimeter from her handbag—he rounded the corner and peeked into her booth. Raissa was ready.

She reached up with one hand and pulled him into the booth by his hair. Spider screeched a bit but then leered over at her. "You like to play rough, do you? I can get into that."

Under the table, Raissa shoved her weapon into Spider's crotch. "Rough is my favorite," she whispered, "but I don't think we're talking about the same thing."

Spider's eyes widened with shock or fright, or both. He had always been a coward. "Wha—what do you want? I ain't done nothing to you."

"I want information, Spider," Raissa said in her normal voice and had the pleasure of watching the blood drain from the man's face.

"Taylor?" The man stared at her. "No fucking way. You're supposed to be dead. They told me you was dead."

"I'm sure they did, and likely things would be much more convenient if that were true, especially for you. But I'm sorry to tell you that I'm very much alive and still have a bullet scar on my chest from your nine." She pressed the gun a bit harder into his crotch. "I owe you, you know."

"C'mon now," Spider begged, sweat forming on his brow. "We can work something out. What do you need? ID, passport? I can get you a new life."

Raissa laughed. "You think I've been walking around for the last nine years as Taylor Lane? I had a new identity the moment I got released from the hospital." She smiled at him. "We're going to work something out, though. I want information."

"What kind of information?"

"Where can I find Monk?"

Spider swallowed. "Ain't nobody seen Monk in at least six months."

"Bullshit." Maurice Marsella, aka Monk, was Sonny's right hand. "Is he in the joint?"

"No. I swear, ain't nobody seen him. I pay Lenny now. He said I wasn't gonna ask no questions about the change, and I ain't gonna."

"You must have heard something." She pressed the gun harder against his jeans until he flinched. "What's the word on the street?"

Spider leaned in and whispered. "You gotta promise you won't say this came from me."

"I'm hardly going to pay Sonny a visit. I think your secret is safe with me."

Spider looked around the empty bar, then back at Raissa. "Word is that Sonny had him offed, that Monk's at the bottom of the Mississippi."

Raissa frowned. This didn't fit into her suspicions at all. "You're sure?"

"All I know is, Lenny's taken over all of Monk's territory. Ain't nobody seen Monk in half a year, and ain't no one mentions his name in front of Sonny."

"So who's got his stuff—you know, from his house?"

Spider shrugged. "Sonny, I guess. What didn't burn. Whole place went up in flames…well, I guess it's been about six months ago."

Raissa looked Spider directly in the eyes. "You wouldn't lie to me, would you?"

"Hell, no. I ain't heard exactly what happened to Monk, and I ain't likely to. Nothing to lie about." Spider licked his lips and glanced over at the entrance to the bar. "Does Sonny know you're back?"

Raissa nodded.

Spider let out his breath in a whoosh. "Thank God. I mean, I wouldn't want to be the one carrying that news. As far as I'm concerned, I never seen you, okay?"

"Not exactly. I still have enough on you to put you away for a long time. I can pull that evidence out if I want to."

"What do you want from me? I already told you I didn't know nothin'."

Raissa reached into her bra with her free hand and pulled out a card with her cell number on it. She handed it to Spider. "You don't know anything *yet.* But if you hear anything at all about Monk or that little girl that's missing, you'll call me. Right?"

The blood rushed from Spider's face. "You don't think Sonny has anything to do with that little girl…Oh shit, you do. I ain't got nothing to do with hurting kids, and I never would. I got some standards, even if you don't believe it."

"Just keep your eyes and ears open. If you come across anything out of the ordinary, then you give me a call. The phone's unregistered, so no one will ever track it back to me."

"Out of the ordinary?"

"Anything that's not business as usual. And I mean *anything.* If Sonny wears a white suit or calls his mother on any day other than Sunday, I want to know."

Spider nodded but still looked confused. Raissa could hardly blame him. The last time she'd seen Spider, he'd put a single bullet through her chest. Raissa had still threatened to kill him while she was standing there bleeding.

"Go on," Raissa said and nodded toward the door. "I need to leave, and it's probably better for you if we're not seen together." Spider jumped up as if he'd been shot, and Raissa realized she'd never removed the gun from his crotch. What a shame.

She slipped the gun back into her bag and had started to slide out of the booth when Zach Blanchard slid in beside her.

He gave her the once-over, and Raissa could feel a blush starting on her very-exposed chest. "Ms. Bordeaux," he said with a smile. "That's an interesting outfit for a psychic."

"Well, psychics are rarely boring."

"It was even more interesting when you threatened that man with castration by Glock."

Shit!

"He owed me for a tarot reading." She shrugged. "I have this *thing* about old debts."

Zach raised his eyebrows. "I bet."

"Well, if you don't mind, I've got a ton of things to do."

Zach studied her for a couple of seconds. "You know, I could haul you in for assault on that man."

"Well, now, that would be your word against mine, and I'm not going to admit to being that close to Spider's crotch any more than you're going to admit looking at it."

Zach blanched. "You really know how to hurt a man." He glanced at her hands, then the empty table. "Barehanded, and there's not a thing I can take with me to run a print. You're sharp, but you're not going to be able to avoid me forever."

An idea flashed through Raissa's mind, and before rational thought took over she ran her index finger along her lips, coating the tip with bright red lipstick. Zach's eyes widened as he followed her finger along the sexy pout of her mouth and sweat began to form on his brow. She leaned close to him and rolled her finger on his cheek, leaving a perfect print.

She slipped up from the booth seat and perched on the edge of the table, looking down at him. Giving him a wink, she spun around on the table and slid her long legs onto the floor. She pulled her skirt down to a barely legal level and leaned over the booth, placing her lips next to his ear.

"When you come to question me later," she whispered, "wear a uniform, and definitely bring handcuffs."

Unable to speak, Zach watched Raissa walk out of the bar, her curves swaying with every step in the sexy, spiked heels. His body had responded to her in all inappropriate manners, especially considering he was on duty. Especially considering she was a suspect.

His face still tingled where she'd left her print, and he tried to block his mind from recalling the way she'd run that finger across her lips and the look in her eyes as she'd done it.

Too late.

He groaned and waved a hand at a waitress at the far end of the bar. What he wanted was a scotch. What he was going to settle for was a piece of Scotch tape to remove the fingerprint from his cheek. No way was he walking into the CSI unit sporting a lipstick print on his face. There were some things a man could never live down.

He wondered briefly where he'd stashed his old patrolman's uniforms and if they still fit.

She's a suspect.

He blew out a breath. The sooner he ran that print, the better. God forbid he came up with nothing, because he was certain his spare handcuffs were in his glove box.

Hank Henry pulled the business card from his pocket and checked the address once more. This was the place. He parked his truck and walked across the street to the construction site, scanning the workers for the owner, a guy named Chuck. He finally located the man on the side of the building and introduced himself.

Chuck gave him the once-over, then lit a cigarette. "Pauley says you do some damned fine cabinet work."

Hank nodded. "I'm glad Pauley's happy with his cabinets."

"Pauley also said you do some damned fine drugs and some not-so-fine petty crimes."

Hank gritted his teeth and counted to three. *You have to expect this given your past. Don't take the bait.* "Well, sir, that would have been absolutely correct if you'd spoke to me a year ago."

The foreman blew out a puff of smoke and squinted at Hank. "Got clean, huh? I can respect that." He crushed out his cigarette on the side of the building and motioned Hank inside. "Place is gonna be some sort of clinic. Every room in the place is going to need cabinets, and they didn't want those cheap white prefab jobs. Said it was 'too clinical,' whatever the hell that's supposed to mean. The place *is* a clinic, after all."

Hank nodded and poked his head into a couple of different rooms. After rehab, Hank understood exactly what *too clinical* meant. The center he'd been in was a restored Colonial mansion, and the people running it had taken a "home" approach to getting clean and their counseling. For the first time in his life, Hank had felt like a member of a family, right down to the chore list and sharing dinner every evening.

"Looks nice," Hank said, wishing he had the clout to actually score the job.

"Think it's something you can handle?"

Surprised, Hank looked at the foreman. "You're serious?"

"Of course, I'm serious. Did you think I had you come all the way down here just for me to smoke a cigarette and run my mouth?"

"Yes...no...I mean, I figured you were talking to me as a favor to Pauley. I guess I didn't figure you were serious about hiring me."

"Hell, I like Pauley, but not enough to hire any ex-con or reformed druggie he tosses out to me. My reputation's good in this town, and I want it to stay that way. Truth is, I saw the work you did at Pauley's bar, and it's some of the best I've seen in years. I like that you took the time to customize those cabinets particularly for the same feel as the bar, but higher scale. Really classed the place up, but without making the rest of it look shabby in comparison."

Hank smiled, pleased that Chuck had latched on to the very thing Hank had been attempting to do with Pauley's bar. "Thank you, sir. I really appreciate that, especially coming from you. Pauley says you're pretty well sought after for this sort of work."

Chuck nodded. "Stay pretty much booked." He pointed his finger at Hank. "If you're serious about being straight, I can help you make a name for yourself. You got the talent. If you have the discipline, you could have a hell of a career."

Hank stared at Chuck, feeling almost dizzy over his words. A second chance at life. And not just any life—a great life, doing something he loved to do. It was almost too good to be true, and before he could stop himself, he started mentally calculating all the ways he could screw it up.

Stop it.

He forced his whirling mind to a stop. This was a golden opportunity. Some people never got one at all. He'd been given plenty and pissed them all away. If he didn't make this one work, then he'd have to put a hit out with the Heberts on himself. "You really think I could make a living doing this?"

Chuck laughed. "Are you kidding me? With your talent, you could get rich doing this. So what do you say? You interested in this job?"

Hank smiled until his jaw ached. "Damn straight."

Chuck stuck his hand out, and Hank shook it. "Be here tomorrow morning around nine, and we can go over the plans and the owner's 'vision' for the clinic. The owner will want to be here for that. She's nice, though—doesn't pick things apart and ask a lot of questions like most women." He elbowed Hank in the ribs. "She's cute, too."

Hank shook his head. "I just got divorced from a great woman who I wasn't even married to for a month before I ran out on her. I'm not looking to ruin anyone else's life."

Chuck laughed. "Sounds like what I told my wife twenty years ago, but she did okay."

"I'll see you tomorrow at nine."

Chuck gave him a nod and walked off through the building, calling for one of the workers. Hank took one final look around and exited the building, doing his best to contain his excitement. His new boss might fire him if he looked outside and saw Hank skipping. Men probably didn't skip unless they were high, so no use giving the man any reason to worry. But still, his step was lighter as he crossed the street.

He'd already slid into the driver's seat before he realized he had a passenger. The blood drained from his face as he looked over and saw Rico Hebert cleaning his fingernails with a razor blade.

"What's up with the construction?" Rico asked, still focused on his fingernails. "You know this is my territory. If you're hitting them up for anything, you gotta cut me in."

"I'm not hitting them up for anything. The man hired me to build some cabinets."

Rico looked up at Hank. "Straight work? Why would you want to go and do something like that? Work a shitload of hours for pennies. Break your fucking back and put stress on your heart. A workingman's life ain't no picnic, Henry."

But being a Hebert was. Right. "I told you I was straight now," Hank said, trying to keep his voice strong and steady. "I meant it. I'll work all the hours in the world if it means I'm not looking over my shoulder for cops all the time. *That's* stress on your heart."

Rico shot him an amused look. "It's stressful if you're a pussy, but then I guess that's where this conversation is over, right?" He laughed at his own incredible humor. "So what about the job I asked you to do with the magic lady?"

Hank felt sweat begin to form on his brow. "I already told you no, and the answer's still no. Get someone else."

"But no one else knows the broad."

"Hell, I don't know her, either! I've only seen her a time or two and that was at a distance."

"Hmmmmm. That's a shame. Sonny was really hoping you'd have the inside track on her. Sonny's real interested in knowing what she's up to. And you know how Sonny can be when he's really interested."

"She's my ex-wife's friend, not mine. And in case you've forgotten, I haven't lived anywhere near Maryse in over two years. I don't even know what *she's* up to, much less her friends."

Rico nodded. "Yeah, I guess I can see that. But you see, Sonny's real interested, and you know how he can be. So what do you say you do a little asking around, maybe to that pretty little ex-wife of yours, and find out what the magic lady is up to."

"And if I don't?"

"It wouldn't be that hard to put some drugs in your toolbox, make a call to that new boss of yours. Or maybe in your truck. Maybe even somewhere on the job site. Hard to know what I might come up with. I'm a creative motherfucker when I want to be."

Hank felt despair wash over him. He knew Rico was capable of everything he'd just threatened to do and much, much more. "I'll make a phone call, but I'm not promising anything. My ex may not know the woman's personal business."

"Let's just hope for your sake, she does." Rico opened the door and stepped out of the truck, then leaned back in the passenger-side window. "I'll be here tomorrow to see what you found out. And every day after that until Sonny's satisfied. Understand?"

Hank clenched his teeth and nodded. The last thing he needed was Rico Hebert at his job site every day. Chuck would immediately know that something was up, and it wouldn't take much to find out who Rico was and what business he was in.

He was royally fucked.

Chapter Five

Raissa pulled into the dimly lit parking garage and slipped through the shadows to the back door of her store building. Her mind raced with all sorts of things, none of them good. What Spider had told her was the absolute opposite of what she'd expected to hear. If Monk Marsella was really at the bottom of the Mississippi and had been for six months, then there was no way he could have kidnapped Melissa Franco. Which meant either that she'd been wrong nine years ago when she'd pegged Monk for the kidnapper, or someone had picked up his work with the exact same MO nine years after the fact.

Neither were very plausible explanations.

She gave the alley and garage a quick scan, an old habit but a practical one, and was relieved to see that neither Zach or any of Sonny's guys were lurking around corners or trash bins. She unlocked the back door and hurried up the stairs to her apartment. No way had she been wrong about Monk. She'd seen the evidence firsthand in Monk's house, and the only person besides her with a key to that closet was Monk. If only she'd been able to get the evidence out before he came back and caught her snooping.

That proof that she'd pursued but not collected had cost her two years of undercover work and nine years of her old life. But if Monk hadn't kidnapped Melissa Franco, then who had? It couldn't possibly be a coincidence that the MO was exactly the same. Certain details of the case had never been released, so an unrelated copycat wasn't likely. The only other answer was that

Monk had a partner. Someone who'd been in from the beginning and knew how to create the same setup.

But who, and why wait nine years between kidnappings? It made no sense.

Neither did hitting on Detective Blanchard.

Raissa unlocked the door to her apartment, trying to block her mind from the earlier scene at the bar. The fingerprint wasn't an issue. Sonny was well aware of where she was, so hiding was no longer a concern. The FBI would likely perk up considerably when Zach ran the print through the database, especially as Raissa knew the bureau had presumed her dead years ago when she'd fled protective custody and they'd been unable to find her.

I told him to bring handcuffs.

Raissa groaned and stepped into her apartment, a cold drink and a cold shower the first two items on her to-do list. She stopped short when she realized she had company. Maryse and Sabine sat at her kitchen table, staring at her as if they were waiting for her to pull a rabbit from a hat. Or maybe her cleavage.

"Do you give tarot readings in that outfit?" Maryse asked. "Or do you have *another* occupation you forgot to mention to your best friends?"

Her friends' obvious disapproval at her less-than-forthcoming behavior washed over her as if she'd been doused with a bucket of cold water. The good part was, she didn't need the shower any longer. The bad news was, it looked like the drink was going to have to be a triple. She tossed her keys on the kitchen counter, pulled a bottle of scotch from her refrigerator, and set three glasses on the table. Maryse raised her eyebrows at Sabine, but neither of them said a word.

Raissa poured a splash of scotch into each glass and added a couple of ice cubes, then slid into a chair at the table with her friends. She pushed a glass across the table to each of them and downed a good portion of her own. "I was a bartender in college," she said finally. "Got big tips for pulling the caps off beer bottles with my teeth. Took me two years of working at the FBI to pay for all the dental work I needed."

"You know that's not what we mean," Maryse said.

Raissa shrugged. "I might also do a little security work for corporations."

"What kind of security work?" Sabine asked.

"Companies hire me to test their system's security."

Sabine's eyes widened. "Companies pay you to hack their computer network? How do they even know how to find you?"

"Word of mouth on the Internet. Word goes out that a company is looking for me. I contact them on a secure computer with a new e-mail address, so I can remain anonymous. I get the particulars, hack their system, and point out where the weaknesses are."

Maryse leaned forward. "That is too cool, but how do you get paid if you have to remain anonymous?"

"Wire transfer to an offshore account."

Maryse stared. "You're kidding."

"I never joke about money."

"Just how much money are we talking about?" Sabine asked. "I mean, if I'm not being entirely too nosy."

Raissa smiled. "Anywhere from ten to fifty grand a job. Don't worry—I pay taxes on all of it. God knows, I don't need any more trouble with the government."

"So what happens if they don't pay?" Sabine asked, clearly fascinated with the entire thing.

Raissa laughed.

"Oh," Sabine said, her face clearing with understanding. "I guess if you just hacked their system, that wouldn't be a good idea, right? Talk about guaranteed payment."

"Holy crap." Maryse sighed. "Nine years, Raissa. In nine years of knowing us, you never once thought you could trust us with all this?"

"Hell, yeah. Jesus, all of this had nothing to do with trust. I didn't want to get people involved—especially with something that might put them in danger. Why do you think I keep my security testing anonymous? Even corporations can be convinced to provide information if the right person is asking. Surely, the two of you can understand that." Raissa frowned, knowing she was hitting below the belt a little. Well, a lot.

Maryse and Sabine had both recently gone through their own life-threatening crises and had tried in the beginning to get through it without involving anyone they cared about. In the end, it had taken everyone to make things right, but both still carried the guilt of how badly things could have turned out.

Maryse lowered her eyes to the table, and Sabine's face flashed with a look of guilt, then sympathy. "When you put it like that..." Sabine said.

"Bitch," Maryse said, and gave Raissa a small smile.

Sabine swatted at Maryse. "That's not polite. My God, you are never going to learn manners, are you?"

Maryse put on an innocent look. "Hey, for all I know, that could be her real name."

Sabine frowned and looked at Raissa. "Did Beau know who you really were?"

Oh shit. Raissa's mind raced for a way out of this one. Beau, ex–FBI agent and Sabine's new husband, had finally remembered seeing Raissa talking with an FBI assistant director in Washington, D.C. Despite the plastic surgery she had to change her appearance, he'd still recognized her, but promised to keep her secret. Apparently, he was a man of his word, but that might not score him many points with the woman he'd just married.

"Raissa?" Sabine prompted.

"Uh-oh," Maryse said, and scooted her chair away from Sabine's.

"Well," Raissa began, "he didn't remember me at all...at first."

Sabine narrowed her eyes at Raissa. "But then he did?"

"Yeah. That night at the hospital with Mildred, something made him remember, but I made him promise not to tell."

Maryse laughed at Sabine's frown. "Kind of a catch-22, huh? Your man has honor and integrity, but since he was FBI, that means he'll always be keeping things from you. Welcome to my world. Could be worse. At least you knew what Beau was when you met him."

Sabine's frown relaxed. "That's true." Maryse's husband, Luc, an agent for the Department of Environmental Quality, had been working undercover when Maryse met him. In fact, he was undercover investigating Maryse. Not the smoothest way to start a relationship, for sure.

"So," Maryse said and grinned at Raissa, "is that your official FBI undercover investigating sort of outfit? Because I have to say, it's kinda hot."

Raissa smiled. "Actually, I was at a confession."

Maryse hooted. "And what did they confess to?"

"Nothing I was hoping to hear, unfortunately."

Maryse sobered and nodded. "You're looking for that little girl, right? Have the police been giving you trouble since you handed them information you shouldn't have?"

"Just one," Raissa replied, and felt a blush creep across her chest and up her neck.

"Oh, no," Maryse said and poked Sabine in the side with her elbow. "I've seen that look. What exactly does Just One look like?"

Raissa sighed. "Hot enough to melt rubber."

"That sucks."

"You're doomed."

Maryse and Sabine spoke at the same time, shaking their heads in sympathy. After all, they'd already been there, done that.

"You can't let him find out who you really are, right?" Maryse asked.

"Well…since Sonny knows who I am, there's really no use hiding any longer." Her mind flashed back to the bar—her fingertip pressed against Zach's face and every square inch of her body screaming for her to make it more.

Maryse snapped her fingers in front of Raissa's face and brought her back to reality. "Earth to Raissa," Maryse said. "Where did you fade off to exactly? Oh, no, you like him."

"I barely know him."

Maryse and Sabine gave each other knowing looks. "But you'd like to jump him," Maryse said.

"Jeez," Raissa said, "you're not long on meaningless conversation, are you?"

Sabine laughed. "Especially not when she happens to be right."

Raissa groaned. "Nine years of avoiding men because I can't afford to get anyone involved with my situation—for my sake and theirs—and my body's in overdrive for a man I should be avoiding like the plague. Not to mention, I find out that the very people I thought I was hiding from know exactly who I am and probably have for a while, which adds to my general confusion in about a million different ways."

Maryse nodded and wrinkled her brow. "It *is* strange. I mean, if the Heberts know who you are and where to find you, I'd figure you for keeping Helena company, you know?"

"I know. That's the part that confuses me the most. There is no love lost between me and Sonny Hebert, and as soon as the FBI gets a line on me, they'll rush him to trial and have me testify. There's a ten-year statute of limitations on racketeering, which is the biggie. The limit runs out on what I know in six months."

"Wow!" Maryse said. "So do you think them asking Hank to kill you was your cue to get the hell out of Dodge? Why bother now?"

Raissa frowned. "I'm just guessing, but there's only six months left that my word is any good in court, unless I turn up dead. If the government can prove conspiracy, then the statute would start on the date of the last conspiracy act. I put the police on my track when I told them about the girls. The FBI won't be far behind, applying pressure as only the FBI can do."

"I get it. No statute of limitations on murder, and they might crawl all the way up Sonny's butt, especially over an agent."

"Exactly."

"Still, that's not going to stop the feds from coming to collect you as soon as they know where you are. How much time do you have before Just One sets off the alarms?"

"My fingerprint is going to hit the national database—it's probably going in as we speak—and before you know it, this building will be surrounded by local FBI, all wanting to lock me up or spirit me off to Kansas to be a chicken farmer."

"Is that such a bad thing?" Sabine asked.

"It is if I want to catch Melissa Franco's kidnapper," Raissa said. "I know I'm close. I can feel it, just like last time. If Sonny hadn't made me as an agent when he did, this would all be over already. The FBI can't force me to do anything, but I'm sure they'll send someone to try anyway."

Maryse looked over at Sabine, who nodded. "All the more reason to get you out of here and hidden in Mudbug," Maryse said. "I don't suppose it will take the FBI long to track you down there, but it might buy you a day or two."

Raissa downed the rest of her scotch. "I'm hoping the presence of more FBI in New Orleans, especially around my shop, will spark whoever took Melissa Franco to make a move they hadn't planned. I'm sure someone will be checking there. I just have to hope that they report to Sonny, and that Sonny is somehow involved, and that he gets word to whoever...What a mess."

"And you didn't even mention the part where you can see Helena. Not sure which is worse, her or Sonny Hebert."

Raissa sighed. "Thank you for reminding me. I guess the least of my worries is a sexy detective?"

Sabine shook her head. "The understatement of the century. But the first thing we're going to do is get you out of here and into the Mudbug Hotel, where at least you'll have people around looking out for you, and hopefully it will take the feds a while to catch on."

"And your choice of many, many hotel beds, just in case the sexy detective finds you first," Maryse said and winked at Raissa. "You'd better get to packing. Throw in something slinky, just in case."

Sabine wagged her finger at Maryse. "You are supposed to keep her out of trouble, not get her in more." Sabine looked over at

Raissa. "Give me a hug and wish me well. I'll be going straight to Beau's place from here, so this is the last time you'll see me before I get back."

Raissa rose from the table and gave Sabine a hug. "Have a wonderful time. And don't worry about anything here. I've got it handled."

Sabine released Raissa and nodded, but didn't look convinced. She gave Maryse a hug and left the apartment.

Raissa headed to her room to pack a bag. This might be her last chance to catch the kidnapper. Her last chance to stop another family from going through the agony and grief of losing their child, then the hundreds of unanswered questions that had followed every return. Hiding in Mudbug wasn't her first choice, but Maryse and Sabine were right. She wasn't going to get much done with the FBI—or Zach Blanchard—hounding her.

Maryse's comment about beds flashed through her mind. Who was she kidding? If anyone was going to hunt her down in Mudbug, she couldn't help hoping it was Zach.

Maybe it would be easier if Sonny Hebert just killed her.

Zach paced impatiently behind the computer, and the tech, Casey, glared at him for at least the hundredth time. "This isn't going to go any faster with you pacing," Casey said. "Don't you have someone to arrest...a doughnut to eat?"

Zach stopped pacing and shot Casey a dirty look. "I'm trying to avoid processed carbs, and I *might* have someone to arrest, if I had the results from that fingerprint trace."

"It's a national database, Detective, not internal."

"Damn it, I know what it is. Do you think I don't know? This is important, is all, and there's a lot of pressure right now."

Casey's expression changed to one of sympathy. "You working the kidnapping?"

Zach sank into a chair next to Casey, watching data whirl by on the monitor in front of them. "Yeah."

"I think the captain's got the whole department on overtime." Casey shook his head. "That case sucks all the way around. Little kid missing. Mayor's granddaughter. Makes me glad I'm a techno-geek. If I did your job, I might just shoot someone who kidnaps little girls."

Zach nodded. "Don't think it doesn't cross our minds, especially on the kid cases. But if we did, then we'd be no better than the criminals."

Casey didn't look convinced. "I got a five-year-old, and I'll tell you here and now, someone hurts her, and the judge won't even be able to give me bail."

"I hear ya," Zach agreed, and rose from his chair. "I guess I'll get some coffee. You want anything?"

"Nah, I drink coffee after seven p.m., and I've got a night of no sleep ahead."

"That's the point," Zach said, but just as he was about to leave, there was an audible click, and the data on the monitor stopped moving. In the center of the screen was a link with the words *100% match.*

"Hey," Casey said, "we got something here." He reached for the mouse and clicked on the link. The screen flashed for a couple of seconds, then brought up a picture of a woman that resembled Raissa, except that wasn't the name on the screen. There was only one other line of text on the screen: *Wanted for questioning by the FBI.*

Zach bit the inside of his lip. As if he needed any more trouble, and he'd likely just brought the feds down on the department by running that print. Damn it to hell. Casey looked up at Zach, the look on his face mirroring the way Zach felt.

"FBI?" Casey said. "The captain's going to shit."

"You think?" Zach ran one hand through his hair and paced the tiny office a couple of times. "Send me that link," he said finally. "I better get upstairs. I'm sure it won't be long before the bureau is knocking on the captain's door."

Zach hurried out of the office and down the stairs to his department. Of all the things he'd been expecting to find, this one hadn't been on the list. What in the world was Raissa mixed up in? He knew little more about her now than he did before he'd run the print, and the last people he expected a straight answer from were the feds. He fought the urge to drive over to her apartment and question her immediately, but he knew better. Department policy was clear. When the feds wanted someone, they had to be contacted first. Local PD could not get involved with a federal case unless asked.

And the chances of the feds asking for favors was slim to none.

Which meant Zach was back to zero on Raissa Bordeaux and her magical, mystical visions. He sat down at his desk and opened his e-mail. Casey had already sent the link, so he clicked on it and opened the page again. It was definitely her, he decided as he studied the picture more closely. Her hair was different, and she'd obviously had some surgery done, because the nose and cheekbones were different. But he had no doubt it was the same woman. He leaned back in his chair, remembering the scene at the bar.

There was something about the man Raissa had talked to that was familiar, but he couldn't place it exactly. He leaned forward and accessed recent arrest records. Maybe the guy was someone he'd seen being processed in the precinct. Thirty minutes later, his eyes were watering and he still hadn't located the man from the bar. He was just about to try another tactic when his captain stuck his head out of his office and yelled at him, his angry voice booming across the office.

"Blanchard, get your ass in here now!"

Detective Morrow looked over at him, eyebrows raised. "Uh-oh. Looks like someone's in trouble."

Zach clenched his jaw and managed to walk past Morrow without saying a word. He stepped into the captain's office, expecting a spectacular reaming, but was surprised to find that the captain wasn't alone. One look at the man and Zach knew exactly what he was—the dark suit, starched white shirt, perfectly knotted tie, sunglasses (worn inside), and the fact that he stood in front of the captain's desk rather than sitting in one of the chairs. Definitely a fed.

"That was fast," Zach said. "What did she do, steal your personality?"

"Zip it, Blanchard." The captain shot him a warning look. "This is Special Agent Fields with the local office of the FBI. He wants to know where you got the print you ran. And so do I."

Zach hesitated for a moment, not wanting to give away his information, but he couldn't think of a single way around it that didn't involve his going to jail. Which wouldn't exactly help his quest for a promotion. "I got it off a suspect."

"What suspect?" the captain asked. "The only case you better be working is the kidnapping, and I haven't been made aware of any suspects."

"Maybe *suspect* is too strong a word. *Person of interest* is probably better."

"And just how did you come up with this person of interest, and why haven't I been informed?"

"She came into the station yesterday and claimed to have psychically received information on the kidnapping."

"And you believed her?" The captain stared at him as if he'd lost his mind.

"Of course not. But when I ran the case through the national database, I realized that she was right. She'd given me information on all the previous kidnappings with a similar MO. Things that were never released to the papers."

The captain's face turned red. "Jesus H. Christ, Blanchard! And you didn't think that was something the rest of us should know? That woman either took those kids or knows who did." The captain looked over at Agent Fields. "Someone better start explaining. Why does the FBI want this woman?"

"That information is confidential," Agent Fields replied.

"Confidential, my ass!" The captain rose from his chair and glared at Fields. "If that woman was involved with kidnapping the mayor's granddaughter, I want to know why."

"She wasn't involved with the kidnapping," Agent Fields said.

"Says who?" the captain asked.

"Says the Federal Bureau of Investigation," Agent Fields replied, a bored look on his face. "Now, if Detective Blanchard would provide me with this woman's alias and her address, you'll be free to go about your business."

"And if I don't?" Zach challenged.

Agent Fields smiled. "It wouldn't be very good for your career to refuse. Federal prison is generally not a pleasant place for cops."

Zach clenched his fists and fought the urge to clock the condescending butthole. "Her alias is Raissa Bordeaux. She owns a shop on Landry Street."

Agent Fields removed a BlackBerry from his front pocket and tapped the keys. "Address?"

"I don't have it memorized, but you can't miss it. It's the only shop on the street with tarot cards and a crystal ball painted on the window."

"Great," Agent Fields said. "This department is under orders not to contact Ms. Bordeaux in any way. Is that clear?"

"Now, hold it one minute," the captain argued. "This woman is the only lead we have in a kidnapping, and you're telling us to step off but giving us no good reason why?"

"Exactly," Agent Fields said. "I'm so glad you understand." He slipped the BlackBerry back in his pocket and walked out of the office without another word.

Zach stared at the captain. "He can just leave like that?"

The captain stared after Fields and muttered something that sounded like "worthless motherfucker," but since Zach wasn't completely sure whether the captain was referring to Agent Fields or himself, he didn't comment.

"Yeah," the captain said, "he can leave just like that." He pointed at Zach. "You are going to sit down and tell me everything you know about this Bordeaux woman."

Zach sighed. "I could tell you everything I know before I even finished sitting."

Five minutes later, the captain was convinced that whatever Raissa was into, it probably wasn't going to help their case. Or he just didn't want to admit that they would be in deep shit if they talked to her again. Either way, Zach had his walking orders from the FBI and his captain: no contact with Raissa Bordeaux.

It was a shame he had no intention of listening to either of them.

Chapter Six

Maryse looked over at Raissa, tapping away on her laptop, and bit her lip. "Are you sure this is a good idea?"

Raissa opened the glove compartment of Maryse's car and tucked a black box with a wire inside, hoping her hastily rigged equipment worked as planned. "Of course it's not a good idea. Why do you think we're here at midnight?"

Maryse stared out the driver's window at the mansion across the street. Sonny Hebert's mansion. "Trying to get ourselves killed?"

"God, you're such a whiner," Helena bitched from the backseat. "All that shit you went through in the last couple of months, and you're getting all worried about sitting in a car on a public street."

Maryse turned around and glared at Helena. "Do I need to remind you that all the 'shit' I went through the last couple of months was *your* fault, and I never did anything to put myself in the middle of it? And that I'm still taking antacids?"

"When you put it that way..." Helena grumbled. "Maybe you should double your dose, just for tonight."

"I'd love to, but the pharmacy was out...again."

"The pharmacy is always out of medicine. Call Dr. Breaux and ask for samples. I don't think I paid for medicine the last three years." Helena looked over at Raissa. "You want to help me out here? I'm sorta getting killed on this one."

Raissa smiled. "Don't worry about your stomach, Maryse. We're not getting any closer than this, and his security cameras don't scan farther than the curb in front of his house. Besides, it's not like we're going to walk up to the door and ring the bell."

Maryse turned in her seat to face Raissa. "Do you honestly believe sending Helena in there is a better option? The Harbinger of Death? The Master of Disaster?"

Raissa laughed and handed Helena a little round piece of plastic. "All she has to do is hide this somewhere in Sonny's office, preferably not a plant, as they are prone to being watered, and take a peek in a storage closet. Piece of cake."

Helena tucked the plastic piece in the front pocket of her black leather jacket, then took the second piece Raissa handed her and popped it in her ear. "Are we ready to go?"

"One second." Raissa tapped more keys on her laptop. "Say something, Helena."

"Something."

"Smart-ass," Maryse mumbled as Helena's voice screeched from the laptop.

Raissa adjusted the volume and gave Helena a thumbs-up. "All set. When you get inside, turn right, then let me know when you're in the big hallway. I'll guide you from there. And everyone pray that Sonny hasn't rearranged his house since last time I was there, or it's going to be a long night."

Raissa gave Helena the once-over. "So what's with the outfit? You still doing the classic-movie thing?"

"Yep," Helena said and climbed out of the car, tugging her spandex pants out of the crack of her butt as soon as she hit the sidewalk.

Raissa grimaced. "Should I even ask?"

Helena rolled her eyes. "*Grease 2.*" She crossed in front of the car, the neon blue of the pants creating a glare from the streetlight.

Raissa studied her for a minute. "She's wearing a T-Birds jacket and motorcycle boots. Is she supposed to be a guy or a girl?"

Maryse shook her head. "I don't even want to know. Just be glad that lately her outfits cover most of her body. The MTV years were far less kind on the rest of us."

"Yuck." Raissa fitted a microphone around her ear and positioned it to the side of her mouth as Helena walked through the front wall of the house. "Helena, can you hear me?"

"Loud and clear," Helena replied. "I'm in the hallway. There's five doors on the right and three on the left. Jesus, this guy's house is bigger than mine."

"Try the third door on the right. That should be the office."

"Hold on...yeah, office furniture, computer. This is it."

"Great. Now find somewhere you can slip the device. A central location is better." There was a second of silence, then rustling.

"Let's see...plant, no that's real...might need the paper clips... crystal bowl of bullets—What the hell? Why can't he keep mints like the rest of us?"

"Just find a place. And not the bullet bowl. It's probably used a lot."

Maryse paled and made the sign of the cross.

"Yeah, yeah...there's a little flowerpot with a sad, fake flower in it. Looks like something a kid made. Will that work?"

"Perfect," Raissa said. "I remember that vase. Sonny's daughter made it."

"Well, he really ought to pay for some lessons. Kid can't even spell correctly."

"I'm sure he'd be happy to, but she died when she was five. Leukemia."

There was a pause on the other end. Then Helena said, "Oh shit, now I'm really going to hell, with that statement. Making fun of a dead kid's spelling. You could warn me about these things before I go putting my eternal soul at risk, you know?"

"I'm pretty sure God will overlook your anal-retentive spelling issues. Just stick the device in there and check that closet. Sonny's guys walk the grounds several times a night. I don't want them to see us sitting here for very long."

Maryse shot Raissa a dirty look. "That's information that might have been good to know. I could have borrowed someone else's car or something."

"And put someone else at risk instead?" Raissa asked.

Maryse crossed her arms and slumped down in her seat, looking warily across the street at the house. "I would have picked someone I didn't like."

Raissa grinned. "Well, that would narrow down your selection to human beings as a species. We can always drive around the block and pick someone at random."

"You know, you were a lot less scary when I thought you talked to spirits."

"Helena," Raissa directed, "check the closet."

"Yeah, yeah, I've got my head stuck in there. There's a bunch of file boxes and a trunk with a padlock on it. Has letters on the front...hold on...says 'Monk.' Hey, you ain't got me breaking into some preacher's shit, do you?"

Raissa felt her pulse quicken. "The trunk. Can you look inside? I mean, through the side or something?"

"I can try. It's awfully small and dark, so no guarantees on what I can see. I can pull the whole thing out—"

"No! Sonny is beyond anal-retentive. If anything is out of place, he'll sweep the office and find the bug."

"Okay, okay...hold on...It's dark in the closet and even darker in the trunk. I'm going to have to open the closet door and get some light in somewhere. I'm no vampire."

"Be careful."

"Yeah...okay, I got some light in here and I'm peeking through the top of the trunk. What the hell...I don't know...Are you sure I can't pull this stuff out for a better look?"

Raissa bit her lip, wondering if it was worth the risk, when Maryse grabbed her sleeve and pointed. "Lights! Someone is awake and coming down the stairs."

"Shit! Helena, close the closet door and make sure everything is perfect. Someone's coming downstairs."

Raissa heard the squeak of the closet door and held her breath, hoping the lights in the house continued in the direction of the kitchen and not the office. Seconds later, a light beamed on at the opposite end of the house, and Raissa let her breath out in a whoosh. "They're in the kitchen. It's probably Sonny. He has problems sleeping."

"You think?" Maryse grumbled.

"Helena, I think you should get out of there. Unless things have changed enormously, Sonny will grab something to eat and go to his office. I know he can't see you, but I'd really feel better if you were out of there before he gets in."

"No problem. I'm leaving now. Okay, I'm in the hall. Holy shit, Sonny Hebert is walking down the hall toward me. Crap, crap, crap."

"Don't panic. He can't see you."

"But it's Sonny Hebert. How the hell can I not panic?"

"Breathe in and out and ease by him."

"This is not good," Maryse said. "When Helena panics, things tend to go very wrong. Maybe I should start the car. Hey, maybe we should just leave now. She can find her way home."

"Sit tight," Raissa said, trying not to let Maryse and Helena's nerves affect her own. "Everything will be fine."

And that's when a crash echoed through the laptop.

"What the fuck!" Sonny Hebert's voice boomed.

"Damn it to hell," Helena said. "I hit that table and the vase and oh, shit, here he comes. Think fast, something to do, think fast, the cat—" There was a piercing wail, and more cussing from Sonny, but no clear indication of what was happening in the house.

Maryse sat frozen in her seat, and the thought flashed through Raissa's mind that her friend might have had a heart attack right where she sat. "Get the hell out of there," Raissa said to Helena, and grabbed Maryse's shoulder with her hand and shook her friend.

Maryse seemed to leap into consciousness and started the car just as Helena burst through the front wall of the house and ran across the lawn as fast as hot pants, motorcycle boots, and sixty pounds of excess, ghostly flesh allowed. Lights flashed on all over the mansion, and Raissa knew it was only a matter of minutes before the house, grounds, and street were covered with Sonny's men.

Helena jumped through the car door and crashed into the backseat as Maryse pulled away from the curb. "Don't speed," Raissa cautioned. "Make it look like we were just passing by. Don't draw attention."

Maryse's knuckles were white on the steering wheel as she eased the car down the block and around the corner. When she'd made it another block away, she took a hard left and floored the accelerator, pushing the car onto the freeway as fast as she could possibly go.

"What happened?" Raissa asked.

Helena huffed and wheezed in the backseat, far more than someone who was already dead should. "When I get nervous, sometimes I touch things when I don't mean to. It's a pain in the ass, I tell you. Normally I have to concentrate to touch stuff, but when I need to be transparent, it just happens."

"I tried to tell you," Maryse said. "When it comes to being a ghost, Helena is an amateur."

Raissa shook her head, trying to absorb the concept of a ghost having to learn how to be a ghost. "Okay. That's weird and something I'll definitely remember going forward, but it will have to wait. What happened, Helena?"

"I hit a table in the hallway and it had a vase on it. The whole thing crashed to the ground, and Sonny was getting closer. Then I saw a cat in the bedroom next to the table, so I grabbed the cat and threw it at Sonny."

A clear mental picture of what had happened flashed through Raissa's mind and she began to laugh. "Oh, my God. You threw a *cat* at him? The biggest mob boss in the state, and you attacked him with his own cat. Priceless."

"Well, I figured he'd think the cat did it all," Helena defended as Maryse began to chuckle along with Raissa.

"Oh, it was a brilliant move," Raissa agreed, "but just not the normal plan of attack for someone like Sonny."

Helena pouted for a couple seconds more, then started to grin. "Okay, so it might have been a little funny. Well, a lot funny. If you could have seen the look on his face."

Raissa tapped on her laptop. "We can at least hear it."

She hit a key and Sonny's voice resounded through the speakers, "That fucking cat! I swear to God, if my wife didn't love that animal, I'd kill it now."

"You're sure it was the cat?" one of Sonny's men asked.

"Yeah, the alarm is on, and nothing's out of place, except the vase, which I never liked anyway."

"So maybe the cat did you a favor."

"Yeah, maybe. But still. Damn cat usually spends all its time sleeping. I can't imagine what got into it."

"Maybe something spooked it. We'll take a look around, okay?"

"Yeah, yeah. That's a good idea."

Raissa clicked on the laptop and the voices stopped. "Cool. It's coming through great."

Maryse glanced over at her. "How are you getting a signal this far away?"

"I put a receiver in the abandoned building across the street this afternoon. It's recording everything and I can stream the audio anywhere I can get a decent satellite connection."

Maryse shook her head. "I'm not sure if I was more impressed with your alleged psychic ability or your computer genius."

"Ultimately, it's all the same thing." Raissa turned in her seat to look at Helena. "Were you able to see anything in the trunk?"

Helena shrugged. "Yeah, sorta. I mean, I guess. Hell, I saw something, but I don't think I saw it right. It doesn't make sense."

Raissa's skin began to tingle. "Tell me."

Helena frowned. "That fancy trunk and high-tech lock, and all that was inside was a broken crucifix necklace and a Halloween costume. A gray alien suit."

Zach stared out of his windshield and shook his head. Almost midnight. Four hours outside Raissa's shop and no sign of the voodoo princess. Oh, but he'd seen plenty of signs of Agent Fields. If the FBI's finest had been trained at the art of surveillance, it certainly didn't show. Agent Fields had parked his car directly in front of Raissa's shop hours ago, and every fifteen minutes or so, he got out of his car and banged on the shop door.

Stupid. Raissa knew Zach would run her print as soon as he could get it done, so he seriously doubted she was out on a hot date or tossing back beignets and coffee. No, if he had to guess, Raissa had flown the coop—whether permanently or temporarily remained to be seen—but he wasn't going to waste any more time watching Agent Fields doing nothing.

Zach tapped the keyboard on his laptop once more and got the name he was looking for—the owner of Raissa's building. He entered the name into the police database and finally came up with a phone number for the man. He was obviously asleep when Zach called but woke right up when Zach identified himself and asked about his building. It took him a couple of minutes to assure the man that the building was fine, and as far as he knew the tenant was fine, but she was a possible witness to a crime and he needed to speak with her as soon as possible.

The owner was only too happy to provide him with Raissa's emergency contact—Sabine LaVeche.

Zach hesitated for a moment, then told the owner that there was a bum outside Raissa's shop banging on the door, and if he moved a bit to the left, the owner might end up replacing that plate-glass window. He hung up before the owner could ask for details.

A few more minutes of laptop whirling and one more rather enjoyable round of watching Agent Fields make yet another pass on assaulting Raissa's door, and he had the information he was looking for. Sabine LaVeche, Mudbug, Louisiana. And unlike her friend, Sabine had pages and pages of information. He scanned the info for anything that might be able to help him find Raissa, even if it was only something he could threaten Sabine with.

Another psychic. Great.

And apparently a psychic with a death wish, he decided as he read the police report on what had to be one of the strangest and most convoluted cases he'd ever heard of. Faked deaths and war crimes and crazy aunts and people buried in the backyard of some of the wealthiest people in the parish. Zach would bet anything that Sabine regretted the day she'd decided to go on a manhunt for her family. He imagined that all the inheritance in the world wasn't going to erase that trauma from her mind.

He continued to scan the screen, hoping for a weak link, something he could use to his advantage. The last couple of sentences made him groan. Cancer. Jesus H. Christ! How was he supposed to strong-arm a dying woman who'd discovered dead bodies in her newly found family's backyard? That was a level of asshole even he wasn't going to be able to manage.

He shut the laptop and took one final look at Agent Fields pacing the sidewalk and yelling at someone on his cell phone. Enough of this. Cancer and dead-body-finding aside, he was going to locate Sabine LaVeche and tell her he had an emergency. It wasn't exactly a lie.

A little less than an hour later, he pulled into the town of Mudbug, what there was of it. It was tiny, just a single row of buildings and a neighborhood that stretched in front of the bayou, the houses there the sort that only old money could buy. He had no trouble locating Sabine's shop and parked in front. The building was dark, but then that hardly surprised him, as midnight had come and gone over an hour before.

He peeked in the store window, but all he saw was a replica of Raissa's store in New Orleans. This building had been listed as her home address, so he pressed the doorbell, hoping if she was asleep upstairs she'd hear it. He waited for a while, staring up at the second story to see if a light came on, but the building remained black and silent. He pulled his cell phone from his pocket and was just about to dial Sabine's home phone when a car turned onto Main Street, tires squealing as it rounded the corner.

The car slid to a stop in front of the hotel, and the driver jumped out, looking frightened and frustrated all at the same time. Zach felt his skin tingle and ducked behind his car, peering over the roof. The passenger finally stepped out, and he smiled. He knew it—Raissa Bordeaux. And whatever her middle-of-the-night adventure had been, it apparently required a laptop and an unhappy getaway driver.

He watched as the two women entered the hotel, then hurried across the street, careful to stay out of the glow of the streetlamps. The blinds were closed on the hotel windows, so he slipped by and stopped at the door. Locked. But then, that wasn't really unexpected. He bent down for a closer look at the handle and realized it was an old model and one easily opened with a credit card.

He pulled his driver's license out of his wallet and slipped it down the crack between the door and the doorframe. It hung in the frame for just a minute, and Zach mentally cursed himself for choosing his license instead of his grocery-store discount card. At least that didn't have his name printed on it. He wiggled the license a bit and pressed it down again. There was an audible click and he froze, listening for any noise inside the hotel. When several seconds passed with no reaction from inside, he eased open the door and slipped inside.

There was a dim glow in the room created by a lamp tucked behind a desk in the corner. Zach blinked twice and, after a scan of the room, decided he was in the lobby. The place looked more homey than corporate. With any luck, that desk in the corner would have a nice old-fashioned registration book. He eased over to the desk and pulled out the first drawer. Jackpot. He opened the book and flipped to the last page.

Eighteen fifty-six. What the hell?

He scanned the other entries on the page, then closed the book and shoved it back in the drawer. Obviously it was an old record used for display. He checked the remainder of the drawers but came up empty. Looking over at the computer tucked in the far corner of the desk, he sighed. Hacking wasn't exactly in his skill set, but it was either that or knock on every door in the building, which would only draw a bunch of attention he was trying to avoid.

He sat in the office chair and turned his attention to the computer. What was a good password?...*room service, mudbug, hotel, california.* Okay, so maybe he needed a better plan. He sat back in the chair and stared at the blinking password box.

"I never figured you for a breaking-and-entering kind of guy," a voice whispered in his ear.

Chapter Seven

Zach knew it was Raissa by the way his body responded. Her soft breath on his ear set his skin on fire, and he felt stirrings in places that had no business stirring over a suspect. He turned around in the chair and was certain his heart had stopped beating.

Raissa stood in front of him wearing a black silky tank with lace trim, black spiky shoes that had to be five inches tall, and from the looks of it, not much else. "I see you're not in uniform," Raissa said, her voice low and sexy. "Did you at least bring the handcuffs?"

Zach felt his blood rush to one part of his body, which didn't need the additional confusion, and down to another, which definitely didn't need the additional stimulation. His mind raced with all sorts of possibilities that had nothing to do with police work but everything to do with the discovery phase—starting with what she was wearing under that silk nightie. Agent Fields had said they couldn't question her, and by God, Zach couldn't think of a single question he needed answered at the moment.

Except maybe what she was wearing under that silk.

She smiled down at him, sexy, hot, and so clearly issuing a challenge. Zach rose from the chair and locked his lips on hers in a single fluid motion that made her gasp. He pushed her back against the wall, enjoying the momentary surprise that crossed her face before she grabbed his head and lowered his lips to hers once more. He brought his hands up to cup her face as their mouths parted and their tongues met each other in wild abandon.

Then something struck him on his neck and he dropped to the ground, certain he'd been hit by lightning.

"Got him!" he heard a woman shout. "Cover me, Mildred."

"Wait!" he heard Raissa yell in the frenzy.

His entire body screamed in pain, and when he turned to see what had happened, he got a blast of spray right in his face. "Shit!" His hands, still numb from the initial blast, covered his eyes, but it was too late. He felt the burning of Mace and hoped to God that the woman who had attacked him had a bigger weapon to use, because as soon as he could see again and move, he was going to shoot her.

"Are you all right, Raissa?" the woman asked. "We saw him strangling you."

Zach managed to get one eye partially open and saw Raissa staring down at him, her face a mixture of amazement and amusement. Two other women stood in front of her—an older woman with the Mace and a younger one with a stun gun. Jesus, what kind of hotel was this?

"Sabine had Beau hook up your security system to portable monitors and gave one to me and Mildred," the younger one explained. "We figured that way you'd have backup if anyone tried to sneak in here. And since Luc left this morning, I thought I'd stay here and help."

Raissa filled a plastic cup with water from a cooler next to the front desk and handed it to Zach with a smile. The other two women looked at each other, clearly confused, then at Zach, then back at Raissa. Then the younger one paled.

"Oh, shit," the young one said. "Here I was thinking you dressed pretty damned hot to sleep alone, and oh, shit." She looked down at Zach and bit her lower lip. "He's Just One."

"The one and only," Raissa confirmed.

The young one looked down at him, a pained expression on her face. "I am so sorry. If I'd known you were him, I wouldn't have tased you, I swear." She tugged on the sleeve of the older woman's robe. "Let's get out of here."

The older woman put her hands on her hips and gave them all a stern look. "Not until someone explains to me what is going on in my hotel."

"He's not here to kill her," the young one said, then paused and gave him the once-over. "Well, on the other hand..." She grinned at Raissa and pulled the older woman out of the lobby. "You're in big trouble, Raissa," she called over her shoulder as she trekked up the stairs with the hotel owner. "Huge. Enormous." He could hear her laughing all the way up to the second floor.

Zach struggled up from the floor, trying to appear anything but mortally embarrassed. "Friends of yours?"

Raissa smiled. "Why, Detective, you don't think perfect strangers would attack a man over me, do you?"

Zach cast a glance at the staircase. "Maybe not. The young one was scary."

Raissa laughed. "Oh, you have no idea. Maryse is a scientist."

"Let me guess...a mad one?"

Raissa gave him a sexy smile and stepped so close to him that he could feel the heat coming off her body. "I assume you didn't spend time tracking me down just for some night action. Might as well come up to my room. You can use my bathroom to clean up and tell me why you broke into a hotel and risked assault by two crazy women."

Zach hesitated, knowing being alone with Raissa in a hotel room...with a bed...was about the worst idea ever. He's already completely lost control and paid for it with his eyesight and a burn mark on his neck, but as she walked past him and up the stairs, he realized he was walking slowly behind her.

Raissa's room was quaint and homey, as he'd expected it would be, but he was surprised with the size and the equipment. What was likely once a sitting area contained two folding tables lined with computer monitors. He took a step toward the tables and glanced down the row of monitors. Different views of the street and alley outside the hotel and the lobby inside the hotel displayed on the screens.

He looked over at Raissa, who was, unfortunately, slipping a silk robe over her skimpy negligee. It was just as well. Being electrocuted hadn't been on his list of things to do, but it was probably far less painful than the mistake he had been about to make.

Raissa reached for a bottle on the dresser and poured two glasses of scotch. "The bathroom's through the far door if you need to flush your eyes more."

Zach shook his head. "I think I'll see again. Hopefully not blurry." He pointed to the row of computers. "What the hell is going on here? You've got more security on this hotel than we have at the police department."

Raissa handed him a glass and motioned to two chairs pushed over to the side of the tables. She dropped into one and took a long drink of her scotch. Zach slid into the chair beside her, hoping he was finally going to get an answer to the question of the enigmatic Raissa Bordeaux.

"I'm expecting company," Raissa said. "And I'm not really interested in visitors at the moment."

"I can tell," Zach said, and rubbed his neck.

Raissa reached for a backpack next to her chair and rummaged through it for a minute. Finally, she pulled out a tube of aloe vera cream and handed it to Zach. "I'm sorry about the burn. I honestly didn't know that Maryse and Mildred had their own closed-circuit system hooked up. Heck, I didn't even know Maryse was here. I thought I was the only one who knew you were in the hotel."

Zach squeezed some of the cream onto his fingers and rubbed a bit onto his neck. "So why does a psychic need so much hardware? If you were for real, you should have known I was coming here before I did, right? So why the Fort Knox routine?"

"I don't mean to offend your manliness, but you're not the reason all this hardware is here. Right now, you are actually the least of my worries." Raissa tapped one finger on her glass and stared at the wall behind him. Finally, she looked directly at him. "You're not supposed to be talking to me, are you?"

"Well, no. Not exactly."

Raissa sighed. "Who did they send?"

Zach didn't bother to play dumb. Clearly, Raissa knew the drill. "Some prick named Fields."

Raissa laughed. "You gotta be kidding me. Hell, Fields couldn't find me if I was sitting on top of him."

Zach couldn't help feeling pleased that Raissa had the same opinion of Agent Fields. "Yeah, I liked him about that much myself. The idiot's parked in front of your shop, beating on the door every ten minutes. I told your landlord a bum was banging up his property. It should distract him for an hour or so."

Raissa smiled. "Fields is going to be royally pissed that he's stuck at my house. He's sorta an early-to-bed guy."

Zach sobered and looked her directly in the eyes. "So are you going to tell me why you're wanted by the FBI and hiding out in a hotel room with Pentagon-level security? You wouldn't have given me that fingerprint if your secret still mattered. I knew that at the time. Something changed, but what?"

"What did Fields tell you?"

"Nothing, except that it was FBI business and the New Orleans PD was forbidden to contact you. Given the tip you provided on the Franco girl, my captain is about to have a coronary over that directive. I figured I'd just go ahead and ignore it and likely pay for it later."

"Unless you can find Melissa Franco."

"Yeah, there is that angle."

Raissa stared at him for a couple of seconds, then sighed. "The FBI wants me to testify against a mob boss, but they had some trouble keeping me safe. I left protective custody nine years ago and never looked back. Well, not for the FBI, anyway." She tapped one of the monitors. "I keep the mob boss in my sight on a regular basis, which is probably why I'm still alive."

Zach nodded. What Raissa said made complete sense, given her lack of background history. "Were you an informant?"

"I was an agent."

Zach straightened in his chair, unable to control his surprise. "Shit! I mean, I knew you could handle a weapon, but lots of criminals can, too. Not that I'm saying I thought you were a criminal…Oh crap, I'm messing everything up."

"It's okay. You'd have been stupid not to think I was a criminal. I would have." She smiled. "Although that does bring into question exactly why you were caught in a compromising position with a woman you thought was a crook."

"I didn't think that, exactly. Not really. Oh, hell, the reality is that all the evidence pointed to you being a criminal, but for some reason it never felt right. Intuition sounds stupid, but I guess that's all I've got."

"Intuition is far from stupid. It's kept me alive more times than I can count."

"Yeah, but still. An FBI agent? Wow. Sorry, but that's really not what I was expecting to hear—" He jumped up from his chair and stared down at her. "Holy shit. You investigated the other abductions. That's why you know so much."

"Actually, I fell into the investigation by accident when I was undercover on another case. In fact, investigating those abductions is what blew my cover. The bureau wasn't thrilled."

Zach sat back down. "What did you find?"

Raissa sighed. "You're going to think I'm crazy again."

"Maybe. But I'm not going to think you're lying. This case isn't exactly normal."

"I saw an alien suit in the closet of one of the people I was investigating. Not hanging, like you would a costume, but in a trunk by itself. A padlock was on the trunk but not fastened all the way, so I took a look inside. I had no idea what to think about something so weird and dismissed it, figuring I didn't want to know. Then a friend of mine told me about this abduction case he was working where the MO matched some previous cases. I asked about dates and times. Every time an abduction happened, this particular guy was 'unreachable.'"

"And the other girls had already been returned, so you knew about the alien part."

"That's the thing that really got me. I mean, why else would that suit be locked away like that unless it was something that could create a lot of trouble? It was too much of a coincidence to ignore."

"Why didn't you follow him?"

"He wasn't my primary, and he didn't live in New Orleans. So the next time he told my primary he was going to be off the grid for several hours, I went to Baton Rouge to follow him."

"And got caught," Zach finished.

"Yeah."

"And your primary…who was he?"

Raissa hesitated for a couple of seconds, then finally said, "Sonny Hebert."

Zach felt his heart pound in his chest. He stared at Raissa, at a complete loss for words the first time since he'd met her. "You were undercover in Sonny Hebert's organization?"

"Yeah, for almost two years."

"As what? I mean, what did you do that you got that close to him?"

Raissa gave him a small smile. "Can't you tell?" She pointed to the row of equipment. "I'm a computer whiz. I could move money in ways that even the banks holding it couldn't trace. And I dabble a bit with security systems. I'm probably indirectly responsible for the alarms being bypassed at the kidnapping scenes."

"Jesus. I can see where that might make you a valuable commodity in Sonny's world."

"Oh, you have no idea. Sonny paid me a quarter million a year. Not that I got to keep it."

"Holy crap! I think I'm playing for the wrong team. Damn my conscience."

Raissa nodded. "I damned mine a time or two when I was moving millions to tax-free shelters overseas. Or driving around in my 'company' car—a Bentley, by the way."

Zach whistled. "So Sonny caught you following up on his guy?"

"No, the guy did. Monk Marsella. He was Sonny's cousin and ran the Baton Rouge side of things."

"And you think this Monk is the guy who took Melissa Franco?"

Raissa frowned. "I did, but now I'm not so sure."

"Why not?"

"You remember that guy in the bar? You know, the one I was going to castrate with my nine-millimeter?"

Zach felt his heart beat stronger for a beat or two, but his mind had flashed firmly back to Raissa's lipstick-coated finger pressed against his cheek. "Yeah," he said, and cleared his throat, hoping it might clear up his mind. "Hard to forget."

"Spider hasn't likely forgotten, either. I picked Spider to question because he's a weak link, a real pansy compared to the others. He says no one's seen Monk in six months. I've asked around, and he's not lying, as far as I can find."

"So what happened to him? Somebody's got to know."

"I'm sure someone does, but I'm guessing he's not in rehab or taking a leave of absence in Bermuda. Even if someone suspected what happened, they're not going to say. It's not exactly safe to have an opinion on the boss's cousin coming up missing, especially if the boss is the only one with the rank to make that call."

"Yeah, I guess not." He tapped his fingers on the table for a minute, then asked, "So what do you think happened?"

"It doesn't matter what I think. I can't prove anything."

"It matters to me. I trust your instincts. You've been right about everything. In fact, you've been one step or ten ahead of me."

"Well, I did have the advantage of a historical point of reference, but you're right, I do have an idea. I think Monk is vacationing at the bottom of the Mississippi River."

"Then who kidnapped Melissa Franco?"

Raissa stared at him, her expression mixed with frustration and fear. "I have no idea."

She rose from her chair and put her glass on a tray on the dresser. "So, do you still want to pin me to a wall and frisk me?"

Her tone was light, but Zach could tell it was anything but sexual. He didn't blame her one bit. "Between being electrocuted, going partially blind, and finding out my main suspect is a damned

FBI agent—who I've been forbidden to contact—and my new main suspect is likely dead, I think I'm too overwhelmed to perform."

"Isn't that the truth." Raissa sat down next to Zach with a sigh. "Besides, I figure I've got another hour or so before Agent Fields shows up here looking for me. It would be best if your car's not parked out front, I imagine."

"He's going to be a problem."

"Who, Fields? Hardly. Fields is lazy. He'll come here once, find out Sabine's out of town. Mildred will tell him no one's seen me and that will be the end of it. Hell, he'll run from a town like Mudbug. The man thinks camping out means a four-star hotel instead of five."

Zach laughed. "Then you might have found a home base. I just hope you packed well. Your apartment is likely off-limits." He rose from his chair. "I guess I better get my car off the street, but I'm coming back tomorrow. I want to check a couple of things, and then I want to pick your brain."

"Next time, call first."

"Next time, I'll come in with police lights flashing and wearing a cowbell."

Raissa placed her hand on his arm. "That might be enough."

Chapter Eight

Hank Henry glanced up and down the street in front of the construction site and breathed a sigh of relief when he didn't see Rico Hebert's car anywhere. He was in the clear, at least for the moment. He had no doubt that Rico would turn up sometime that day. The man was a thug but completely reliable. If Rico said he was going to do something, you could bet on it.

Hank got out of his truck and saw Chuck waving at him from the doorway of the building. A young woman stood behind him. As Hank crossed the street and approached the building, his felt his pulse shoot up. He knew the woman, and that might not be a good thing at all.

"Hank Henry," Chuck said, "I want you to meet Lila Comeaux. Lila will be running this facility when it's open, and she's got some specific ideas about the look and feel of the place."

Lila smiled and extended her hand to Hank. "It's good to see you again, Hank. You look well."

Hank felt relief wash over him as he shook her hand. Apparently, she wasn't going to make an issue of his past. "It's good to see you, too."

"You two know each other?" Chuck asked.

Lila froze for a moment, and Hank knew she was struggling with exactly how to answer the question without betraying a confidence. He quickly decided to take the decision off her plate. "Yes, sir," Hank said. "Lila worked at the rehab center I stayed at in Mississippi. She was a huge factor in me getting straight. I'm glad to know you're opening your own place. I know you wanted to move back home, and I think you'll be able to help a lot of people here."

Chuck looked over at Lila. "Are you okay with Hank working on this job? If there's any discomfort, I can make other arrangements."

"I'm thrilled Hank is going to work here," Lila reassured him. "Hank was a huge success for the clinic. He really has the determination to make his life something of merit." She smiled at Chuck. "And I'm very pleased to know that you're the kind of man that gives people an opportunity to do something worthwhile for themselves, despite their past. It makes me even more certain of my decision to hire you."

Chuck blushed a bit and looked down at the ground. "Well, hell, we all made mistakes. Youthful indiscretions and the like. Some of us were just lucky enough to pull our head out of our ass before getting caught. Don't mean you can't do things right going forward." He looked up at Lila and grimaced. "Oh, hell, now I've gone and said 'ass' in front of a lady. My wife will have my hide."

Lila laughed. "You said 'hell,' too, but I won't tell if you don't."

Chuck looked pained for a moment, then laughed along with Lila and Hank. "Guess I did at that. Well, if the two of you are finished with the reunion talk, I guess we best get to talking about cabinets." He pulled a notepad from his pocket. "Let's start with the reception area."

An hour later, Hank walked Lila to her car, unable to contain his excitement about the job before him. "Your ideas are fantastic, Lila. I think people will really feel comfortable with the environment you're creating."

"Thanks," Lila said and brightened. "You have some pretty good ideas yourself, and I was very impressed with the photos of your prior work. You have a rare gift." She placed one hand on his arm. "I'm so glad you're pursuing a great life for yourself, Hank. I look forward to working with you."

Hank's arm tingled at her touch and he felt a blush creep up his neck. Lila smiled at him, a warm, sweet smile that made him feel good all over. "I'll see you sometime tomorrow with those color swatches," she said, and slipped into her car.

Hank watched her car until it turned out of sight at the end of the street, and that's when he heard whistling behind him. He felt his spine stiffen and turned around, already dreading what he knew he would see behind him. Sure enough, Rico Hebert was half a block up, leaning against his car.

And he didn't look happy.

"Pretty piece of work," Rico said as Hank approached. "Girl like that might be worth making some time for."

"Don't even go there. She's my boss, nothing else."

Rico stared at him for a couple of seconds. "Looked awfully friendly for a boss, but hey, maybe you got one of them jobs with perks. Might be the reason you went straight."

Hank clenched his jaw and struggled against clenching his hand. Hitting Rico would be instant gratification and long-term suicide. "What do you want?"

"You know what I want."

"I already told you, I don't know anything about that psychic woman. And my ex won't talk to me since our divorce," Hank lied. "She's not going to give me information on her friends, especially given our past."

"That's a shame, because you see, we got sorta an issue on our hands now. And the boss would really like it solved, you know?"

"What kind of issue?"

"That woman took a powder. Ain't no one seen her since yesterday."

Hank put up his hands. "I don't know nothing about that."

Rico studied him for a couple of seconds. "Maybe not. Still, if someone told the woman that we was looking for her, that person might be in trouble, you know?"

"I haven't been anywhere but this job site and my house." He pulled his cell phone from his pocket and held it out. "Check my phone. You can see every call in and out the past week, and I don't have a home phone. I can't help you."

Rico looked down at the phone, then back up at Hank and nodded. "Maybe you should ask that ex of yours again. You know, as a special favor to Sonny." He walked back to his car and pulled away.

Hank watched until Rico's car rounded the corner; then he crossed the street back to the job site. "Hey, Chuck," he called to his boss when he walked in the clinic. "Can I borrow your cell phone for a minute? Mine's dead and I need to make a quick call to my ex-wife. There's some legal business I need to get settled up with her."

Chuck pulled his cell phone from his pocket and passed it to Hank. "No problem. Come see me in the back when you get done. I want to put together a plan for building the cabinets and need to talk to you about when to order the supplies."

"Sure," Hank said, and waited until Chuck was halfway down the hall before he punched Maryse's number into the cell phone.

Maryse looked away from her computer and down at her phone, frowning when she didn't recognize the number. She answered on the second ring.

"Hello?"

"It's Hank. Don't hang up."

"What do you want?" Maryse asked in the exasperated tone she reserved only for her ex-husband.

"Your friend, Raissa...she's got trouble."

"Tell me something I don't know."

"Okay, how's this? For two days now one of Sonny Hebert's guys has shown up at my job site wanting to know where Raissa is. He says that the reason she left is because I warned her about Sonny. He thinks I should find out where she is from you."

Maryse felt her pulse quicken. "What have you told him?"

"That you hate me and won't even talk to me."

Maryse blew out a breath. "I don't hate you, Hank. I honestly don't know how I feel, and I'm sure you understand that now is not exactly the time to explore that."

"I get that. I'm just afraid that when he doesn't get the answer he wants from me, he might decide to go straight to you. You need to watch your back, Maryse, and tell Raissa to do the same. These guys don't mess around."

Maryse swallowed and stared out the front window of her and Luc's new home. "I know. We're being careful. I mean, as careful as we can be."

"Damn it." Hank sighed. "It's times like these I'm almost grateful that Mom's not around to see just how big of a mess I made of my life. I know she was a hard woman to love, but she still deserved a better son than me, and you deserved a better husband."

"We all make mistakes. It's what we do afterward that defines us. Thanks for warning me. And Hank, you watch your back."

"Yeah."

Maryse disconnected the call and leaned back in her chair, a tinge of guilt running through her. She still hadn't told Helena that Hank couldn't be her biological son—hadn't told Hank, either. After everything she'd been through in the past couple of months, Maryse knew better than most that you never knew when your last conversation with someone might be. And where Helena was concerned, that was doubly true, as no one really had a clear grasp on why she was here to begin with.

She pressed in Mildred's number on her cell phone. It was time for them to come clean to Helena.

"Damn it, Blanchard!" the captain yelled, his face flushed red. "Can you explain to me why the FBI was in my office first thing this morning blaming this department for that woman disappearing?"

Zach put on his best blank look. "I have no idea what they're talking about, sir."

The captain stared at him, but he never averted his eyes. Finally, the captain sat back down and threw up his hands. "I've got the mayor's son calling me every hour on the hour about his daughter. I had to call the police to get the media off *my* front lawn. One of those reporters snapped a shot of me through my bathroom window. I was taking a pee, for Christ's sake. Can you just see the headline? MAYOR'S GRANDCHILD STILL MISSING WHILE POLICE CAPTAIN HOLDS HIS CRANK."

"Captain, I promise you I didn't warn the Bordeaux woman off. I had nothing to do with her leaving." Technically, it was all true, so Zach managed to deliver it with a straight face.

"That better be the case." The captain tapped a pen on the desk and stared out the window for a moment. Zach waited, then wondered if he'd been dismissed. He was just about to rise when the captain looked back at Zach. "That wasn't the only reason I called you in here," the captain said.

Zach remained seated, but sat up straight. Something in the captain's tone was off. "Sir?"

"I have a problem, Blanchard. I know you have zero propensity for bullshit and even less tolerance for political positioning, so I want to ask your opinion on this."

Zach stared at him. "You want *my* opinion? Uh, yeah, I mean, if I can help with anything, certainly I'll try."

"You said that Bordeaux woman is who gave you the tip on the other missing girls, right?"

"Yes, sir."

"And then the FBI comes storming in here to claim her, which tells me she's probably an informant who saw something she wasn't supposed to see."

"That would be a logical guess, sir," Zach hedged.

The captain pulled a folder from his desk drawer and slid it across the desk to Zach. "Then can you tell me why it took that Bordeaux woman to bring those other cases to our attention when the mayor took part in a kidnapping seminar two years ago that discussed those very abductions?"

Zach stared at the captain, certain he'd heard incorrectly. "You're kidding me. Then why isn't the FBI taking over the case? If they released the facts for a workshop, why wasn't a public plea ever made?"

"Because after the girls were returned unharmed, the cases went cold. No point in spending a lot of time on healthy girls when they get new cases every day. If I had to guess, the last thing the FBI wants the public to know is that they did little to nothing about this in the past, and now it's happened again." The captain pointed to the file and Zach opened it.

The first page was an itinerary with a list of workshop attendees. The mayor's name was third on the list. Zach flipped through the rest of the pages. Surely, there had to be a mistake. Maybe he'd been invited and hadn't been able to attend.

But the paperwork said differently.

Notes from the meeting clearly outlined the mayor's opinions on the subject of child abduction and the steps law enforcement should take when it occurs. There was even a picture of some of the attendees at the back of the file, and the mayor's smiling face was front and center. Zach slowly closed the file, his mind whirling with a million different thoughts, but not one of them any he felt like telling the captain.

There was no way the mayor had forgotten the information presented. It was too unique, too outlandish for one to forget. And there was the glaring fact that Melissa had been taken out of a home with a high-tech security system. A security system that someone obviously had known how to disarm. That either meant a pro or someone on the inside. But what in the world did the captain expect him to say?

"I'm sorry, sir," Zach said finally. "I can't even begin to imagine..."

"Yeah, you can. And so can I. The problem is that neither one of us can come up with a good, *moral* reason for a man who has information pertinent to the kidnapping of his own grandchild to keep it quiet. That's why I'm asking you what you think, before I make a move that's career suicide."

Zach blew out a breath, the captain's position overloading his mind with dire consequences—for all of them. "It could be he's hiding something else and doesn't want us poking into his private life, particularly that seminar."

"But you don't think so."

"I don't think it's the best bet," Zach said.

"So what is?"

"Next year's an election year, and according to the polls, the mayor's popularity is waning. Something like this could create a huge sympathy vote."

"Motherfucking shit."

Zach nodded. "That pretty much sums it up."

"So, what do I do with this?"

Zach shook his head. "Either he knows something about the kidnapping, or he's keeping his mouth shut to hide something else. And I gotta say, captain, that if it's option two and this isn't some political maneuver, then you're not going to like whatever it is that's so important he's willing to risk his grandchild."

Zach studied the captain as he pulled at his tie. His face was an interesting mix of wanting to throttle someone and the precursor to a heart attack. "We're not going to get anything out of him," the captain said.

"No, sir."

"Then who might we get something out of? Someone's got to have suspicions."

"You want to know who would roll on the mayor?"

"Yeah. Blood isn't always thicker than water, and he's got a shit-load of relatives working for him. Which one do you think will talk?"

Zach considered the long list of relatives that he was aware of. "I think my bet would be on the little girl's mother."

The captain sat stock-still, and Zach could tell he was rolling that idea over and over in his mind, playing out every possible out-come—good and bad—of pumping the mayor's daughter-in-law for family secrets. Finally, he gave Zach a single nod. "Do it."

Zach rose from his chair and headed to the door. Before he opened the door, the captain's voice sounded behind him. "And not a word to anyone."

That kinda went without saying.

Raissa, Maryse, and Mildred sat in Mildred's office, all looking at Helena, waiting for the bomb to drop. Helena stared back at them in disbelief, her mind not even capable of processing the information they'd dumped on her.

"But that's not possible," Helena said finally, looking far more pale than even a ghost should appear. "I gave birth to Hank. I know he's my son. Giving birth's not the sort of thing you forget all that easily."

"We're not doubting that part," Maryse said. "But your blood types are completely off. There's simply no way you and Harold could have produced Hank."

Helena's eyes widened. "I never cheated on Harold. It was Harold who made a habit of running around. Hell, I should have cheated on Harold, but I didn't, I swear. In fact, I hate to admit it now that I'm dead and don't even have a chance at another go, but Harold's the *only* man I've ever slept with."

Raissa glanced at Maryse and Mildred, who were both grimacing. It was pretty horrific, if one knew Harold Henry. And very, very sad. "There has to be an explanation," Raissa said.

Helena shook her head. "I can't imagine what. Are you sure, Maryse?"

Maryse nodded. "I double-checked with the doctors I'm working with in New Orleans, just to make sure I hadn't forgotten anything about blood types. They all said it's not possible for a combination of your and Harold's blood types to produce Hank."

Helena stared at her, a lost look on her face. "I don't understand. Hank was my miracle baby. I'd had problems, cysts removed, and Dr. Breaux said it was unlikely I'd be able to get pregnant. When I got pregnant with Hank, I was so surprised and excited. And now you tell me he's not even my son. I know he's done a lot of things wrong, but I still love him. What could have happened?"

"I'm so sorry, Helena," Maryse said. "The only thing we can think of is that someone mixed the babies up at the hospital."

"But then…oh God…that means my real baby is wandering around somewhere out there, and I never knew him." Helena looked ready to cry. Maryse looked over at Raissa, the plea for help written all over her face.

Raissa took the cue and stepped in. "Are you certain you gave birth to a boy?"

"Yes," Helena said. "I remember the doctor saying so as soon as he came out, and Harold grinning like an idiot. Probably the only damned time the man was happy."

"That helps," Raissa said. "I'm going to do a little computer work and see what other male births happened at the hospital at the same time. We'll get to the bottom of this."

Maryse bit her lip and nodded. "I'm really sorry we had to tell you. I guess we were hoping there was some logical explanation."

"Like my having an affair?" Helena asked. "That's a great thing to think about a person."

"It's not like anyone who's ever met Harold would blame you," Maryse pointed out.

"That's true," Helena allowed. "I don't know what to make of all of this. First, I wind up killed. Then I find myself wandering around the earth and causing trouble most everywhere I go, and now you tell me the baby I raised isn't even my biological child. I guess that should relieve me some, given how he turned out, but it's just sorta sad."

Maryse blew out a breath. "I know he's done some bad things in the past, but Hank is getting better and he's still your son, Helena, no matter what the tests say. No one can take that away from either of you."

Helena rose from her chair and nodded. "I guess not," she said, and walked through the exterior wall of the hotel.

"That went well," Maryse said. "This sucks."

Mildred nodded. "It's a very odd and hurtful situation, but you were right to tell her. She'll come around in a bit. I imagine this is a shocking blow, on top of everything else."

"What else is there?" Raissa asked. "I mean, besides being murdered and roaming the earth, then finding out your child isn't yours?"

"Helena was dying," Maryse said. "The autopsy showed cancer all over her lungs and a rare form of leukemia.

Raissa frowned. "Why didn't she tell anyone?"

"She didn't know. Apparently, her symptoms were very mild and confused with her asthma. No one thought anything of it, including Helena. It's weird, but not impossible, according to the scientists I talked to."

"That is a lot to absorb, especially on top of being dead and still here."

"I know you've probably got things to do today," Maryse said to Raissa, "but do you mind meeting me for breakfast tomorrow morning? I've asked Dr. Breaux for coffee. I thought maybe he'd be able to shed some light on some of this…or not. But he *was* Helena's doctor and he did deliver Hank. I figure if anyone's going to be perturbed enough by all this to dig into it, Dr. Breaux will."

Raissa nodded. Whatever happened to their normal lives?

"There's something else," Maryse said, and bit her bottom lip. "Hank called me yesterday and again this morning in a panic. I didn't get a chance to tell you this last night, because I didn't hear you come in, and afterward…well, I figured you had your hands full, or I hoped you did…"

"No such luck," Raissa said. "Electrocution tends to lower the libido."

Mildred started chuckling and Maryse flushed red. "Oh, shit. I'm so sorry. I didn't mean to ruin your night."

Raissa waved a hand in dismissal. "You didn't. It was going to be ruined anyway as soon as he found out the truth. That's not exactly an erotic teaser. So what did Hank have to say?"

"He said one of Sonny's guys was at the construction site hassling him. Sonny knows you're gone, and the guy was pushing Hank to see if he warned you off."

"Shit. I hope my leaving doesn't put Hank in a bad position."

"Hank said he can handle himself, but he wanted to make sure you knew they were looking for you. I guess I'm hoping they'll think the FBI got to you, but that's probably too much to ask, right?"

Raissa sighed. "Since the FBI agent assigned to bring me in was parked outside my shop all last night and thinks banging on my door is the way to locate me, then yeah, it's too much to ask. Sonny's men only need a glance at Fields to know he's a fed. They probably already know Fields doesn't have me. I'm sure they were watching my shop if they know I didn't go home last night."

"Sonny knows you're friends with Sabine and me. They're going to look here next." Maryse looked over at Mildred, who nodded. "Mildred and I don't think you should open Sabine's store. You'll be on the other side of a plate-glass window. Might as well be a sitting duck. They'll know you're here, and it wouldn't take a genius to figure out where you're staying once they find Sabine's apartment empty."

Raissa nodded. "Or just sit at the end of the street and watch me walk to the hotel. I know they'll find me, but I can't back out on Sabine."

"Sabine wouldn't want you to do this," Mildred said. "I promise you that. If Sabine knew how this was going, she'd be on the first plane back."

Raissa shook her head. "It's really something, you know? Here I thought all these years I was hiding from life and people, trying to keep my distance, and I end up with the best friends a person could ever ask for. You guys are truly amazing."

A flush crept up Mildred's neck and onto her face. Maryse nodded. "I agree. We are amazing."

Mildred tapped Maryse's leg with her hand. "Stop bragging. I'm the only one who can brag about my girls." She looked over at Raissa. "Think about it, please. Maryse can sit in that store, same as you, although I shudder to think what she'd make of reading tea leaves or whatever else you do. The appointments can wait. Sabine is only gone a few days and her regulars already know that."

"Okay," Raissa agreed. "Maryse can store-sit, but that doesn't mean I'm hiding out here like a thief."

"I was afraid you were going to say that," Maryse said. "I suppose you're going to do some snooping?"

"This may be my last chance to catch a kidnapper, and time is running out. In five days, Melissa Franco will likely be returned to her parents with no memory of what happened. I can't let him get away with it again."

"Have you heard anything from Sonny's house that can help?"

"I wish. He was only in his office for ten minutes or so this morning, and I could only hear typing. I'll keep checking, though. He's bound to talk to someone sooner or later."

"Do me a favor," Maryse said. "I know she's sorta a pain, but take Helena with you. There's a lot of advantage to having a lookout that no one else can see. And even though things don't always turn out so great when Helena's involved, they could have been worse if she hadn't been there." Maryse looked around and lowered her voice. "But don't you dare tell her I said that."

Raissa smiled. "My lips are sealed. But I need to find her first."

"She'll probably be sitting on the dock at her house," Maryse said. "She goes there when she needs to think."

"And we've given her plenty to think about this morning." Raissa frowned. "Speaking of which, if a stupid man in a well-pressed suit comes around here asking for me or Sabine, that's Agent Fields. I half expected him to turn up last night, but he probably thought Mudbug would have dirt roads and it would mar the paint of his pristine car. He'll be here today, though. He won't have a choice."

"He won't get anything out of us," Mildred said.

"Actually, I want you to tell him that Sabine is on her honeymoon. Likely he'll leave as soon as he hears Sabine's not home."

"Then we'll be sure he gets the message," Mildred said. "In the meantime, I took the liberty of parking your car in the garage behind the hotel, and pulled mine up front. I figured it wouldn't do for them to see your car parked here."

Raissa nodded. “I figured as much when we raced in here last night and I didn’t see it out front. Thanks, Mildred. You’re getting good at this cloak-and-dagger stuff.”

Mildred sighed. “I’ll just be happy when I can get back to running my hotel and pestering Sabine and Maryse for grandchildren. I’m too old for this crap.”

Chapter Nine

Zach stood in the living room of a townhome that probably cost more than he made in ten years and looked from Susannah Franco to her husband, Peter. "So there were no issues with Melissa?"

"What kind of issues?" Peter Franco asked.

"The typical sort, like a fight, maybe?"

"Absolutely not," Peter said. "I hope you're not suggesting something foolish, like Melissa ran away. Nothing could be further from the truth, and the time you're wasting here is time you could spend looking for my daughter."

Susannah Franco placed her hand on her husband's arm. "He's just doing his job." She looked at Zach. "My husband's right. Melissa is a very happy child. I know all parents think their children are special, but Melissa truly is. She never has a harsh word to say and always finds the fun and joy in just about anything. She loves her life."

Zach nodded. "What about illness? Sometimes if a child is sick, they behave differently, or if they're running a fever, it can affect their memory."

Peter shook his head. "She wasn't sick. In fact, Melissa is never sick. She has allergies but a mild case at that. My wife is right. She is a very special child. Perfect, almost. Sometimes frighteningly so."

"Why do you say that?" Zach asked.

"I don't know," Peter replied. "It took us so long to conceive and we'd just about given up hope. I guess I just always had this feeling that I got something I didn't deserve with Melissa, and one day it would be taken from me." He gave Zach a bleak look. "I guess I was right."

"We're going to find her," Zach assured him. "When I called earlier I asked about the instructions for your security system. Were you able to locate those?"

"Oh, yes," Peter said. "They were filed in my office. I'll get them for you." He exited the living room and hurried up the stairway. Zach allowed himself one second of relief that he'd managed to get Peter out of the room, but then he turned his best investigative techniques on Susannah. The townhome wasn't that big, and Peter would be back any minute.

"Mrs. Franco," he said in a low voice, "before your husband returns, there's something I need to tell you."

Susannah's eyes widened. "Okay."

"Two years ago, your father-in-law was a member of a panel on child abductions. The cases covered were identical to Melissa's, but when questioned, he never volunteered that information. Can you think of any reason why your father-in-law would intentionally withhold information that could help find your daughter?"

Susannah gasped, the fear on her face plain as day. "No. I don't believe it."

"I saw transcripts of the panel and photos. If you know something about your father-in-law, you need to tell me."

"Is he a suspect?"

"At this point, he's a person of interest, but all of you are. That's the way this sort of thing works. Your father-in-law knew how to disarm the alarm. Melissa would have gone with him without a struggle."

"No," Susannah shook her head. "I won't believe it. I can't. He's overwrought and he forgot. There's no way Martin would hurt his granddaughter or Peter."

"Not even for a reelection win?"

Susannah's mouth snapped shut and she stared at Zach for a couple of seconds. "I don't know why he didn't give you the information, but there must be a good reason."

Zach looked her directly in the eyes. She met his gaze for one second, two, three—then she couldn't hold it any longer and looked away. "Are you sure about that?"

"I have to be," she said, her voice barely a whisper. "The alternative is not an option."

Helena sat in the passenger seat of Raissa's car, wearing a black leather outfit and dark sunglasses. Raissa wasn't sure whether she was going for Lara Croft or *The Matrix*, but she'd missed the mark on both counts. Raissa found herself longing for the days that she could only communicate with Helena through writing or holograms. Maryse may have been dead wrong about the MTV years being worse.

"I don't understand why you have to do this in New Orleans," Helena complained. "You're supposed to stay out of sight. And while I'll give you that the disguise is good, it's still not safe."

"It's not safe to do what I have to do in Mudbug, either."

"Why not? I thought you were some sort of computer whiz. They have the Internet in Mudbug."

"I am a whiz, but it would take time to create a diversion good enough to cloak the origin of the Internet signal. I simply don't have the time. So the safest way is to do my hacking at a public site and toss the computer when I leave. That way, no one can trace it to me."

Helena's expression cleared in understanding. "And no one will show up in Mudbug."

"Exactly. The last thing I want to do is put anyone in Mudbug in jeopardy, especially Mildred or Maryse."

"Well, I still think it's dangerous, but I guess that's what I'm here for, right? Lookout extraordinaire."

Raissa didn't miss the sarcasm in Helena's voice. "You're a great help. Maryse and Sabine wouldn't be around if not for your help. Your methods may be questionable, but your heart is usually in the right place."

"I suppose you're right." Her face brightened and she turned in her seat to face Raissa. "I don't suppose you'd stop at the grocery store on the way home and buy me a cheesecake?"

Raissa laughed. "What happened to the diet?"

"Hell, I didn't diet when I was alive. What's the point now?"

"Maybe the point is you're expensive to feed and don't need to eat, so it's a waste of money."

"Yeah, yeah." Helena waved a hand in dismissal. "So are wine, cigarettes, and gym memberships, and there's still plenty of those around."

Raissa glanced in her rearview mirror and frowned. There was a black car about a hundred yards behind them. It was tucked in behind a van, but Raissa caught a glimpse of it as the driver edged the car over, probably trying to see around the van. The thing that bothered Raissa was that the lane next to the van was completely clear. The car could easily pull around.

"What's wrong?" Helena asked. "You've got this weird look on your face, and you keep looking in the rearview mirror."

"I think someone is following us."

Helena spun around in her seat and peered out the back window of the car. "The van?"

"No. There's a black sedan behind the van, but it won't pass. It's been there for the last three miles."

"Do you recognize the car?"

"No, but I'm getting a bad feeling."

Helena turned around and fastened her seat belt. "That's not good."

"Why are you fastening your seat belt? You do know you're already dead, right?"

"God, everyone is always saying that. You're like a bunch of broken records. Of course, I know, but I'd still duck if someone was pointing a gun. It doesn't matter if it's irrational. Fear is fear."

Helena's logic never ceased to boggle Raissa's mind. So many variables with ghosts, and boy, did Hollywood have it all wrong. She glanced in her rearview mirror again and saw the blinker flashing on the van. She felt her stomach tighten. "The van is exiting." Raissa checked her mirrors and the highway in front of her, but there was no other car for miles.

Helena sat frozen in the passenger's seat. "Is the car following?" She clenched her eyes shut. "I can't look."

Raissa watched as the van eased off the highway at the last exit Raissa had passed. The black car slowed and Raissa felt her breath catch in her throat, but then the car sped back up and remained on the highway, now exposed. "Shit."

"They didn't exit?"

"No." Raissa pulled her pistol out of her purse, turned the safety off, then clutched the gun in her right hand. She checked her mirror again and realized the car was picking up speed. They were half the distance from her now that they had been just seconds ago. "This is bad."

Helena bit her bottom lip and Raissa could swear the ghost grew paler. "How far away is the next exit?" Helena asked.

"Five miles. We're sitting ducks. I should have taken the last exit and tried to shake them. Stupid! I'm losing my edge." She checked the mirror. Another thirty yards and the car would be on top of them, and it showed no signs of slowing.

"Hold on, Helena. This is about to get ugly."

She'd barely finished her statement when the other car struck them from behind, then dropped back. Helena curled up in a ball with her head between her legs and arms wrapped over her head. Raissa gripped the steering wheel with her free hand and just managed to keep the car on the road. "Damn it, Helena, I need help here."

Helena peeked out from under her arms. "What kind of help?"

"I have a plan. I need you to be ready to read the license plate off the other car."

Helena sat up and glanced in the passenger-side mirror. "There's no plate on the front."

"I know that. I'm hoping there's one in the back. Are you ready?"

Helena looked completely confused but nodded. "Go for it."

Raissa lowered the driver's side window and shifted her pistol to her left hand. She watched in the rearview mirror as the car built up speed behind her for another hit. Just before the car reached her, Raissa yanked the wheel to the left and slammed on the brakes. The other car shot by them on the right side. Raissa strained to see the driver, but the windows were tinted so dark, she could barely make out a silhouette inside.

Before the other driver got any bright ideas, like braking himself, Raissa held her gun out the window and fired a shot into the trunk of the other car. The driver swerved, but managed to maintain control. Raissa waited a couple of seconds to see what the driver would do. She prayed he'd take the warning and move on. The shot had been a warning. If she had to kill the man, things would get really sticky, and she couldn't afford to waste time sitting in a jail cell.

"Shoot him again!" Helena yelled. "Make it count this time."

The other driver, apparently realizing his mistake, leaped forward. Raissa pressed the accelerator as far down as it would go, but the other car kept inching away from them. Her finger twitched on her pistol, and she warred with herself over shooting out the tires. But then she'd be on the hook for whatever happened afterward. Damn it!

Raissa's chest and stomach hurt from the seat belt, and she brought her hand in the window, placed the gun in her lap, and loosened the belt. She took a deep breath, trying to control her racing heart.

"You're letting him get away," Helena complained.

"I'm not letting him. His car is a lot faster. There's a V-8 engine in that Cadillac."

"It's still not as fast as a bullet."

"I know. But I couldn't afford to waste a day or two in jail explaining myself to the police, and the FBI would be right there ready to expedite things as long as I agreed to be on the first bus out of here."

"Yeah, okay," Helena groused. "I guess I see your point, but I don't have to like it."

"I don't like it, either. I would much rather have put a bullet through his head. Did you get a look at the back of the car?"

"There was no plate on the back, either," Helena said, huffing like a freight train.

Raissa looked over at Helena, who was struggling to loosen her seat belt. "Are things supposed to hurt ghosts?" Helena asked. "Because this seat belt is killing me. What the hell?"

Raissa watched as the black car disappeared over the next rise in the highway. *What the hell?* was a really good question.

Working on her best pout, Helena sat in a secluded corner of Starbucks across from Raissa. "I can't believe you're going to drink that caramel, whippy-doodle thingie in front of me."

"You can't exactly drink one in here," Raissa whispered. "I'll get you one when we leave."

"Promise?"

"God, you're worse than a three-year-old. Don't worry. You'll have your coffee in twenty minutes or less. That whole run-in on the way here has made me change my plans. I don't have time for the hacking I had planned, and it might not be the best idea, when I can convince someone else to do it for me."

Helena winked. "Must be nice having a cop on the side."

Raissa laughed and pressed in some numbers on her cell phone. "Zach, I need a favor."

"What kind of favor?"

"Can you track down the other missing girls? I thought that if we could find where they are now, we might be able to ask if they've remembered anything about their kidnapping, or if anything's happened to them since."

"Sounds reasonable," Zach said. "Just let me run it by the captain. He's been watching us like a hawk. We're not supposed to do anything unless it advances the investigation."

"Great. And, um, there's one other little thing."

"What kind of thing?" The suspicion was evident in his voice.

"Well, I got into a little trouble, and I was hoping you could—"

Zach didn't even let her finish. "What the hell happened now?"

"A car followed me from Mudbug and tried to run me off the road. I might have taken a shot at them in a *Top Gun* sort of maneuver."

"Damn it! I told you to stay put."

"Yes, but I had things to do."

"Like what?"

"Like get a coffee. So can you help me do a DMV search or not?"

He sighed.

"Now, see, this is exactly what the captain doesn't want us running off on," he said. Then after a pause, "Did you get the plate number?"

"No plates, but I have a make and model. Black Cadillac DTS—current year."

"You want me to do a search for every Black Cadillac DTS in New Orleans? Seriously?"

"It's a sixty-thousand-dollar car. There can't be that many."

"Fine, but if I lose my job over this, I'm sending you my mortgage bill."

Raissa smiled. "I'll make it up to you. Give me a call when you have the info."

"So why do you want to know about the other girls?" Helena asked as Raissa hung up.

"I don't know. It's just a feeling that they're all connected in some way other than appearance, but it's a strong feeling. Do you know what I mean?"

Helena nodded. "Yeah. Kinda how I felt right before I died. I knew it wasn't just another asthma attack or something simple. It was too late by then, but it's almost like carrying a wet blanket around on your shoulders. I've been carrying it ever since."

"Exactly. And it's the one thing that's nagged at me for years. There has to be some reason these girls were chosen. I simply can't believe it's random."

Helena nodded. "You think any of them remember something?"

"It's possible. Maybe nothing with extreme clarity, but they could be experiencing dreams or reactions to certain stimuli. Unless the brain cells containing information are completely removed or damaged beyond repair, there's always the chance that a memory can surface."

"But if that's the case, wouldn't they have said something?"

Raissa shook her head. "Not necessarily. I know it seems like they would want justice, but I found with victims that the more time had passed after the crime, the less interested they were in justice than in just trying to forget."

"Makes sense. So you think maybe they wouldn't have raised a flag, but if questioned directly they might fess up?"

"That's what I'm hoping."

"So do you think the guy in the Cadillac works for Sonny?"

"It's certainly possible. Sonny liked Cadillacs and he never had a shortage of automobiles. He had twelve when I worked for him."

"Jeez," Helena said, "what the heck does he need all those cars for? You can only drive one at a time. Does he have fifty kids or something?"

"No. he only had the one kid."

"The one that died?"

"Yeah. His wife had complications with the birth and had to have a full hysterectomy afterward. The one thing I can say for Sonny is that the whole time I was with him, I never saw him cheat on his wife. Most of the guys figured he'd cut her loose when she couldn't give him a son, but they're still married."

"A mobster with family ethics? Weird."

"His daughter's death really affected him. I've never known a man to grieve that way. Despite everything I knew he was into, I felt sorry for him. His daughter was his light. After she died, he never really seemed to snap out of it. I was afraid he was setting himself up for takeover, being weak and all, but I soon realized that I was the only one that noticed. I think the rest of them are missing the empathy gene."

"Probably a good thing for Sonny," Helena said.

"Definitely a good thing for Sonny. Well, since I'm deadlocked until I hear from Zach, what do you say we get you the biggest latte they make and get out of here?"

Helena frowned. "Um, I wasn't going to bring this up, but seeing as how you're probably light-years smarter than me, I'm going to go ahead and ask. How did they know it was you in the car? I mean, you're wearing an awesome disguise and your car's the same, but you switched plates with Maryse, and well..."

"They had to be watching. It wouldn't have taken a genius to see me having breakfast at the café with Maryse or walking back across the street to the hotel. All someone had to do was watch the back and they would have seen me leave and get the car out of the garage." She tapped one finger on the laptop and stared out the window. "Or maybe it was something else."

"I don't see what. Even if they were in Mudbug looking for you, no one would have recognized you in that getup."

"Even without this getup, I still don't look like I did when I was in the FBI. I've had facial reconstruction done."

"Shit," Helena said. "Maybe we should get that coffee now?"

"I think that's a great idea, and I'm going to call Maryse and ask her to pick you up, okay?" Raissa said, an idea already forming in the back of her mind. And if she was right, it wouldn't take long to prove it.

Ten minutes later, they were perched on the top level of a parking garage half a block down from the Starbucks. Helena was panting after walking up the stairwell. "You didn't tell me I had to hike for my coffee. What are you trying to do, kill me again? And what the hell are we doing here? This isn't where you parked."

"I know, but I wanted a good view of everything, and this is the best view around."

Helena pulled the lid off her coffee and continued panting in the cup. "No need letting good air go to waste. This is a little too hot."

Raissa shook her head and looked back at Starbucks.

"So why are we playing eagle eye up here?" Helena asked.

"Because I want to see who else shows up." Raissa pointed across the street at the parking garage where she'd left her car. "Look on the third level. You can see my car where I parked it on the end."

"Yeah, but there's no way that guy followed us after the exit. You would have seen him."

"I know. Just wait. If nothing else happens in the next ten minutes, we'll leave."

Raissa leaned back against a cement wall and watched Helena savor her coffee. Five minutes later, she pushed herself off the wall and pointed. "Look."

Helena looked down the street from the garage where a black car with dark-tinted windows had pulled to the side of the street. The car was parked with a clear view of the garage exit. Helena turned to Raissa, her eyes wide. "Is that the same car?"

"Same type, but it's not the car that hit us earlier. There's no bullet hole in the trunk of that Cadillac."

"So how did they find you so fast?"

"I think there's a GPS tracker on my car. See how they parked to have a clear view of the garage? They're not sure where I went, so they parked where they can see the garage, for when I return."

"I'll be damned. So that's how they found you."

"That's my bet."

"Then that means they put something on your car before you ever came to Mudbug."

"Yep."

Helena's eyes widened. "Which means that Sonny already knew how to find you, assuming it's him, of course."

"I think so. I've thought so since Hank paid me a visit."

"Then why wait all that time and try to kill you now, when it's harder? You got the FBI looking for you, a new buddy with the New Orleans Police Department shadowing you, and an assortment of crazy women in a hotel rigged with better security than the White House. Seems stupid to make a move now."

"It's very stupid. That's what makes it so interesting. Sonny Hebert may be a lot of things, but stupid isn't one of them. He's very deliberate, almost methodical, about everything. It's why he's made it this long without going to prison or being bumped off by another family member looking to take over."

Helena frowned and looked back down at the black Cadillac. "So what the hell?" Helena asked for the second time in less than an hour.

Raissa looked down at the black car and shook her head. The question was just as pertinent now as before. And just as unanswerable.

Chapter Ten

Zach stood on the top level of a parking garage, staring at Raissa over the top of his unmarked police car. "I don't like it." His captain had given him the go-ahead to pull information about the other missing girls, but hadn't thought there was anything there to warrant questioning them. Raissa, of course, thought different.

She shrugged. "There's a tracking system on my car and someone tried to kill me earlier. I don't like *that.*

"So are you going with me to this girl's house, or do I need to get a new car and do this with my fake police ID?"

Zach groaned, the ten million things that could go wrong with Raissa's plan racing through his mind. "I still think this is a horrible idea."

"No, you don't. You just don't want to get caught doing it." She gave him a critical look. "You know, with a laptop and a printer, I could make you a new police ID."

Zach placed his hands over his ears. "I'm not hearing this."

"C'mon. There's only one girl in New Orleans. She lives with her aunt. It's not like I'm asking you to round them all up for a lineup or the Spanish Inquisition."

"Yeah, that's what you say now." He opened his car door. "Get in before I change my mind."

Twenty minutes later, Zach pulled up in front of a neat townhome in a quiet area of town. "I will introduce myself. Follow my lead, but don't say anything if it can be helped. Nice wig, by the way."

Raissa patted down her long brown curls. "Thanks. I have a blue silk nightie that goes perfect with this. If you're interested in seeing some of my other costumes."

Zach turned away, trying to block the mental picture of Raissa in blue silk and those sexy brown curls. He walked up to the front door of the townhome and could practically feel Raissa smiling behind him. He took a deep breath and rang the doorbell. He waited a couple of seconds and was just about to ring the bell again when he heard footsteps inside.

A second later, the door opened and a pretty young blonde woman peered out the door, safety latch firmly in place. "Can I help you?"

Zach opened his badge and held it up to the crack in the door. "I'm Detective Blanchard with the New Orleans Police Department. Are you Jennifer Warner?" he asked, giving the girl's new name.

The girl stared at him, a wary expression on her face. "Yes."

"I'm sorry to bother you, but I need to ask you a few questions. Do you mind? You can step outside if you're not comfortable with us being inside, or you can answer them through the door. You can have my badge if you want to call in my number." Zach held his breath that she wouldn't take that last option. He wouldn't even have time to clean out his desk, especially if Jennifer described the female partner that he didn't exactly have.

She looked at the badge again, then up at Zach. Finally, she closed the door and Zach heard the lock sliding back. The door opened a second later and she waved them inside. "I was just making some coffee," she said as she walked down a hallway into a kitchen. Zach and Raissa trailed behind.

Jennifer lifted the pot. "Would you like any?"

"No, thank you," Zach said. "We don't want to take much of your time."

Jennifer poured a cup of coffee and sat on a stool at the end of a bar, nervously fiddling with the handle on her mug. Raissa tugged on Zach's sleeve, and he took a seat along with Raissa across from the girl. As soon as he slid onto the stool, the girl relaxed. He glanced at Raissa. That woman could definitely read people.

"I guess I don't have to ask if you know who I really am," Jennifer said. "Is this about the kidnapping? It's been all over the news."

"Yes, but why do you assume that?" Zach asked.

Jennifer shrugged and stared into her coffee. "I don't know. I guess 'cause the missing girl sorta looked like me."

Zach studied her for a couple of seconds and decided that Jennifer was right. There was definitely a resemblance. "You do favor each other, but that's not the only reason. There are similarities regarding the disappearance that make us think it might be the same person or persons involved."

Jennifer looked up at him, her expression bleak. "What do you want from me? I told the police everything years ago."

"I know. I guess I was hoping that maybe after all this time you might have remembered something. Something you didn't mention before."

Jennifer stared at him for a moment, then shook her head. "I wish I could remember. I can't even walk down the sidewalk without wondering 'Is that the guy who took me—is that the guy?' Or maybe it was a woman. I'm scared of them, too. I thought changing my name and moving in with my aunt would help, and it did, but only barely. I've been homeschooled since I was returned. I graduated high school last semester with top scores. I already have offers from Ivy League schools, but I'm afraid to go. I've been through seven counselors and no telling how many drugs, and I still won't leave this house without an escort. Trust me, Detective, I would love to remember." Her hands shook as she stirred her coffee.

Raissa reached across the bar and placed her hand on Jennifer's arm. "Your fear is real and valid. Counselors usually try to tell you otherwise, which is where they go wrong, in my opinion, anyway. What they don't tell you is that because of your experience, your senses are finely honed. You are far better suited to recognize danger than the average person."

Jennifer looked at Raissa, her expression wavering between wanting to believe and wanting to run for cover. "I'm a quivering mess. I'm not finely honed."

"Not yet. You've tucked yourself away for so long that when you go out now, you're on sensory overload. If you increase your public time slowly, even by five minutes a day, you'll find the anxiety will start to fade. Then you'll be left with an awareness, almost a sixth sense, about what's going on around you."

"Did someone attack you?" Jennifer asked.

"I was stalked and shot. And I learned to trust that feeling in my gut and when the hair raises on the back of my neck. Fear is a gift. A gift far too many of us have forgotten how to access."

"Wow." Jennifer's expression cleared in understanding. "That makes sense." She gave Raissa a shy smile. "You're the first person who's made me feel anything but neurotic. Thank you."

Raissa smiled. "You're welcome. So how does knowing you have an advantage make you feel? Strong?"

Jennifer thought for a couple of seconds, then nodded. "Yeah. It does. This is so cool. Now, I can go out in public a little at a time, and I'll remember that my being hyperaware is a good thing. I could get better, right?"

"Yep, maybe even in time for college registration next spring."

Jennifer's smile widened, and Zach could see how Raissa had opened a whole new world in the girl's mind with just a few sentences. He liked to consider himself tough and hard, but he couldn't help being moved.

After a couple of seconds, Jennifer's smiled faded and she looked over at Zach. "I don't know if this means anything, but I started having dreams right after I saw the kidnapping on the news."

"What kind of dreams?" Zach asked, feeling his pulse quicken. Buried memories often started surfacing in dreams or in states of semi-consciousness.

Jennifer frowned. "Weird. Like it's me in the dream, but I'm watching it from the outside, you know?"

Zach nodded, but didn't reply, not wanting to interrupt her thought process.

"I'm in this room, but all I can see is bright light. The first time I had it, I thought I was dreaming about dying, you know, with the white light and all. But the next time I heard voices…regular voices, not God or anything."

"Do you remember what the voices were saying?" Zach asked, pen and paper ready.

"A man says, 'We're running out of time.' Then another man says, 'I won't have what we need until Wednesday. The blood wouldn't do any good now. It's too thin.' Then the first guy says, 'I hope that's soon enough.' And the other guy says, 'Of course it will be. I can make anything happen.' "

Jennifer stared at the wall behind Zach for a moment, then shook her head. "And then I woke up." She looked directly at Zach. "I tried to remember more. I tried going back to sleep, hoping more would come, but finally I just decided it was my imagination working overtime after that news story." She bit her lip and looked at Raissa. "What do you think?"

"I think something in that news story triggered a memory that's been buried for a long time."

"So you think that really happened?"

"Maybe," Raissa said, "or it might be something similar, but your recall is fuzzy because you were drugged at the time."

Jennifer crossed her arms across her chest. "I wish I knew what they did to me. The doctors said there was no…you know." She blushed and looked down at her coffee. "But why would someone take me for no reason? And why would they need blood? And if my mind's confused and it wasn't blood, then what was it?"

"I can't imagine how hard it is for you," Raissa said. "At least I saw my attacker and can easily identify him. I know why he shot me. To have no answers has got to be hell."

"Do you think I'll remember more?"

"I don't know. It's impossible to know what triggers buried memories. You may have opened the door, and your memory will start unfolding. Or it may be another ten years before it happens again. Or..."

"Or it may never happen again," Jennifer finished. "And I'll never really know what happened to me."

"There is another way," Zach said, more determined than ever to make the kidnapping son of a bitch pay. "If we catch the people who did this, I'll get everything out of them. I promise you."

Jennifer gave him a small smile. "You know, Detective, I believe you're telling the truth. I'm going to hold you to that promise."

When they climbed back in the car, Zach handed Raissa a stack of printouts with DMV information. "You were good in there," he said.

"Thanks," Raissa said. "It's hard not to feel for her. Knowing what you're hiding from is hard enough, even for an adult. I can't imagine living in constant fear of an enemy you don't know and whose purpose is a mystery." She flipped through the papers.

"Anything?"

"Yeah. There's a corporation listed on here that owns several of the same make and model—all black. It's one of Sonny's companies."

Zach blew out a breath, the desire to protect the woman beside him overriding all his other emotions. "If he tracked your car to Mudbug, he knows where you're staying. What's he waiting for?"

Raissa shook her head. "I don't know, but Sonny never does anything without a reason. How much trouble did you get in over pulling the information?"

"Let's just say that what the captain doesn't know won't hurt him."

"Oh, really? Mr. Anal-retentive Rule Follower was less than forthcoming with the big boss? Might cost you your job, you know?"

"Damn it, Raissa, there are things you don't know."

Raissa immediately lost her teasing tone.

"So tell me. We're in this together."

"It's a long story," Zach replied.

"Then give me the Cliffs Notes version, and don't worry about the ending. I've probably heard a lot worse."

Zach took a breath, not sure how to condense what some considered the biggest screwup in his career. Not sure if he wanted to share something that personal with a woman he barely knew, regardless of how attracted to her he might be.

"Several years ago, I screwed up on a case. I'm still digging my way out."

"What kind of screwup?"

"There was a guy we had our sights on for killing an eight-year-old girl, and all indications were she was hardly the first. The lab screwed up the chain of evidence and he walked."

"Shit. That sucks, but a lab screwup is not your fault."

"No, but I leaked who the guy was to the victim's father."

Raissa frowned. "But the father still had the right to file a civil suit, even if you couldn't make a criminal one. I still don't see the problem."

"I didn't give him the information for a civil suit. I knew what he would do."

"How could you possibly know what someone would do?"

Zach looked over at her. "He was an ex-marine sniper. His wife died a couple of years ago in a car accident and that little girl was the last of any family he had. He had connections in all parts of the world and the training to disappear without a trace."

"So, what happened?"

"They both disappeared—the father and the perp. We never found bodies."

Raissa was silent for a couple of seconds. "And you took the heat for telling him. He could have gotten the information anyway, and from the way you've described him, he definitely would have been the kind that went looking for it."

"Yeah, but that's not how Internal Affairs saw it, so they put me on notice. From that point forward, I was supposed to do everything by the book. No exceptions."

Raissa sighed. "And then you met me. Why are you risking everything, Zach? You barely know me."

"I know you're a tough, strong, intelligent woman who has sacrificed a third of her life to do the right thing. I know there's a little girl missing who might end up a recluse like the one we just left if I can't get some answers. I know this could happen again if we don't catch the guy now." He paused for a minute and took a breath. "I know I have to sleep at night, and sometimes things aren't black-and-white."

Raissa placed one hand on his thigh. "In our line of work, things are rarely black-and-white."

"So how do you keep from crossing the line?"

Raissa shook her head and stared out the window. "I don't think some of us can."

Maryse looked up from her laptop as the bells above Sabine's shop door jangled, then frowned when she saw the man standing there, stiff as a board, clad in a business suit, and still wearing his sunglasses inside. Definitely not a customer. She grabbed Helena's box of Moon Pies and tossed them into the break room, then motioned for Helena to make herself scarce. "Welcome to Read 'Em and Reap," Maryse said as she walked over to the man. "Can I help you find something?"

The stiff pulled a pad of paper from his pocket and glanced at it for a second. "Are you Sabine LaVeche?"

"No. I'm Maryse, but I'll be happy to help you if you'd tell me what you're looking for."

The stiff frowned. "I'm looking for Sabine LaVeche."

"I'm sorry, Sabine isn't available."

"I need to speak with her—now. Tell me where she is."

Maryse bristled. "If you'd give me your name, I'm happy to tell her you stopped by, but there's no way in hell I'm giving out her personal information."

Maryse saw his jaw clench and his face flush a bit. She stared him directly in the eyes until he finally understood that she wasn't intimidated now and wasn't going to be later. Finally, he gave her a disgusted look and pulled his wallet from his pants pocket, then flipped it open to show her his FBI identification.

She barely managed to hide her utter relief that the stiff was merely a fed and not one of the Hebert clan. "Agent Fields?" Maryse gave him her best confused expression. "Why in the world would the FBI want to talk to Sabine?"

"That's confidential. Can you tell me where to find her?"

"She's in the Bahamas on her honeymoon. There's no way to get in touch with her."

Agent Fields blew out a breath of frustration. "When is she returning?"

"In three days."

"And when did she leave?"

"Yesterday."

"I'm looking for a friend of hers, a Raissa Bordeaux. Do you know Ms. Bordeaux?"

"Yes." It was all Maryse could do to hold in a smile. Agent Fields was so frustrated with her clipped answers, his expression looked pained.

"Do you know where I might find her?"

Maryse gave him her wide-eyed innocent look. "At her store in New Orleans?"

Agent Fields threw up his hands. "Obviously, if Ms. Bordeaux was at her store, I wouldn't be looking for her here."

Maryse shrugged. "Then I can't help you. I have no idea where she is." At that very moment, the statement was entirely true.

Agent Fields pulled a card from his pocket and shoved it at her. "If you see her, please give me a call. It's a matter of utmost urgency." Agent Fields spun around and exited the shop.

"What an ass," Helena said.

Maryse nodded. "A matter of utmost urgency? Is that even English?"

"Pompous, stick-up-your-ass English. I'm not clear on the grammar part, though."

Maryse walked to the front window and watched as Agent Fields got into a tan Honda Accord, adjusted his mirrors, checked his blind spot, then pulled onto Main Street and headed out of Mudbug. "That guy is wound way too tight." She was just about to turn from the window when a glint of sunlight flashed in her eyes. She looked farther down the street to see where the reflection had come from and saw a black sedan with dark tinted windows parked at the far end of Main Street.

"Helena," Maryse said and waved at the ghost. "Come look at this car. Is that the car that ran you and Raissa off the road this morning?"

Helena peered out the window. "It looks like it, but then all I know is it was a black Cadillac. Seems like the front would be damaged if it was the one that hit us, though."

"Yeah," Maryse said, "but when Raissa called earlier, she said Sonny had several of that make and model, right?"

"Four is what you said, I think."

Maryse backed away from the window. "I need you to do something."

Helena gave her a wary look. "You? You hate it when I 'do something.'"

Maryse glanced back outside and walked to the cash register before she could change her mind. "I know, but this is different. We have to find out who the guy in the car is. If I walk down there, he'll leave. Well, best case, he'll leave."

"Worst case, he'll shoot you."

"There is also that." Maryse pulled a disposable camera from beneath the cash register and handed it to Helena. "Which is why I'm not the one who's going to walk down there."

Helena stared at her as if she'd lost her mind. "You want me to take a picture of him? Won't that be a little noticeable?"

"Yeah, for a minute, maybe. Hide the camera in your pocket until you get to the car. I'm still working on this ghost-logic stuff, but that should keep it fairly concealed. If you can't get a clear shot of them through the driver's window, then take a picture through the front windshield."

"Let me get this straight. You want me to stand in front of a killer's car and take a picture."

"All he'll see is the camera. You take the picture, and by the time he jumps out of the car, assuming he even does, it will be too late. You tuck the camera in your pocket and stroll back to the store."

Helena shrugged. "What the hell. Probably be more interesting than watching you type." She slipped the camera into her pocket and walked through the wall of the shop and onto the sidewalk.

Maryse moved behind a display of colored rocks so she had a clear view of the street without the driver seeing her in the storefront window. She peered over the top of the display and watched as Helena strolled down the sidewalk, then crossed the street to the black Cadillac. She bent over and peered into the driver's-side window, but apparently the tint was too dark for her to get a good picture, so she moved to the front of the car. Maryse sucked in a breath and clutched the top of the display.

This is for Raissa, God. If you could just help Helena get it right this one time.

Helena stood in front of the car, studying the windshield. She looked behind her, then moved one step to the right, apparently trying to cut out the glare. She glanced back at the store and gave Maryse a thumbs-up. Maryse tightened her grip on the display. *Please God. Please God. Please God.*

Helena pulled the camera out of her pocket, but it got stuck on the way out and flipped through the air, seemingly in slow motion, then landed directly in the middle of the hood of the car. Helena froze for a moment, then scrambled onto the hood and grabbed the camera. The car rocked with her weight, and Maryse could see frantic, shadowy movement inside. Helena kneeled on the hood and directed the camera at the driver's seat as the car roared to life and lurched in reverse.

"Oh, no!" Maryse gasped as Helena rolled off the hood of the car and into the street. She lay there for a second, completely still, and Maryse was certain she had somehow died again. Then she was up and running.

Clutching the camera in one hand held high above her head.

Maryse felt the blood drain from her face and she had to lean against the display for support. The display gave way, and Maryse and a million colored rocks spilled onto the floor of the store. She managed to pull herself up on her knees and peer outside, but the situation was dire. Helena was running as fast as she could, the camera still in plain sight. The car had stopped backing up and was now coming down the street after the floating camera.

Maryse managed to crawl to the front door of the shop and open the door a crack. Surely, the driver wouldn't hear her yell over the car engine. "Hide the camera," she yelled as loudly as she could, then slammed the door shut, rose from the floor, and peeked between the mini-blinds on the door.

Helena stopped dead in her tracks, which wasn't exactly smart. The car came to a screeching halt, but not before it bumped Helena and sent her rolling down the street.

Dazed, Helena jumped up from the ground and tucked the camera in her pocket just as the car door opened. Maryse strained to see the driver, but he had his back to her as he scanned the street for the missing camera. Helena staggered down the street to the shop. The driver took one final look in the street, then jumped in his car and tore out of town.

Maryse waited until the car had turned at the far end of Main Street, then opened the door of the shop to allow Helena in. "Are you all right?"

Helena leaned against the wall and slumped to the floor, wheezing. "I guess so. I mean, what could happen to me, right? I'm glad you opened the door. I don't know if I could concentrate enough to walk through a wall right now." Helena reached into her pants and pulled the camera out. "I don't think it got damaged when I fell, or when the car hit me, or when I fell again."

Maryse took the camera and studied Helena. "You know, I hate to say this, but you're white as a ghost. I know it sounds stupid, but normally you have color."

"Of course I'm white. That scared the shit out of me."

"It doesn't seem fair, you still feeling fear when there's really nothing that can hurt you. Kinda a rip, if you ask me."

"Tell me about it." Helena looked behind Maryse at the mess on the floor. "What happened?"

"Scared the shit out of me, too." Maryse looked at the mess and sighed. "I guess I better call Raissa."

"Think this will scare her?"

"No. And that's what worries me the most."

Chapter Eleven

Raissa snapped her phone shut and stared out the windshield of Zach's car as they drove down the highway back to New Orleans. Zach looked over at her, and Raissa knew he was waiting to hear what was said in the phone call, but she wasn't sure how to relay the information without his going ballistic. And then there was the whole Helena angle. He definitely wasn't ready for Helena. No one was.

"Was that Maryse?" he asked finally.

"Yeah. Fields showed up at Sabine's shop earlier."

"Was there a problem?"

"Not really," Raissa said. "Maryse deflected him by saying Sabine was out of the country. He left his card. My guess is, Fields is done with Mudbug."

"So what's the problem? And don't even try to say there's not one. I saw the expression on your face, and that conversation was far too long to just be chatting about Fields."

Raissa rolled the story Maryse had told her around in her mind. How the hell was she supposed to explain it to Zach when a key component was a photo-snapping ghost? Finally, she blew out a breath and told him about the black car at the end of the street.

"Did Maryse get a look at the driver?" Zach asked.

"No, but she might have a photo."

Zach raised his eyebrows and Raissa shook her head. "It's a long, complicated story going back months, and I'd rather explain the details when I can show you myself. Maryse is on her way to a drugstore in New Orleans right now to get the film developed.

One of those one-hour joints, so she can meet us somewhere in the city or back in Mudbug."

"What are you going to do about your car?"

"Nothing, right now. It's obviously not safe to drive." She waved her cell phone. "I'm glad I maintained an untraceable cell phone, or they'd likely be tracking me that way, too."

Zach shook his head. "This is all a bit much. I made detective five years ago, and I've never seen such cloak-and-dagger stuff in my life. I don't know how you've lived this way for so long. Hell, my captain's on the verge of a stroke and he's not even facing an opponent like Sonny Hebert." Zach sighed. "But in his defense, this case could cost him his job if it goes wrong."

Raissa looked over at Zach. "What do you mean? I know there's pressure on the department because it's the mayor's granddaughter, but that's status quo for this sort of situation."

"Not exactly." Zach hesitated for a moment, then decided that given Raissa's deductive skills, she might be able to help. He told her about his talk with the captain that morning and his subsequent visit with the Francos.

Raissa listened to the story, her eyes widening until he got to the part about talking to Peter Franco, and then she frowned and shook her head.

"Why are you shaking your head?" Zach asked.

"That's not right."

"What part?"

"That Melissa wasn't ever sick. Once a month, her mother took her to a specialist who has an office across from my shop. They usually stopped in my shop and bought Melissa candles."

"You're certain?"

"Of course, I'm certain. I've seen them once a month for probably six months or more. That's why I was so upset when I saw the details of the kidnapping on the news. This one was almost personal in a way, because I knew the victim."

"Why would the father lie?"

"I have no idea. Maybe we should ask?"

"If he's lying, he's not likely to tell the truth just because I ask him to."

Raissa shook her head. "Not him. The doctor."

Zach frowned and started to speak and she waved a hand to cut him off. "I know doctor privilege and all that, but this is the mayor's daughter who's been kidnapped. If the doctor knows something, he might tell us."

"No way. You're not going anywhere near your shop. One of Sonny's guys is probably watching it, not to mention the Agent Fields problem."

"I can handle Fields, and the FBI can't make me do anything. I'm not under arrest."

"Sonny's guys can probably make you do plenty, starting with giving up breathing."

Raissa turned in her seat to face him. "Who do you think stands a better chance against them—me or Melissa Franco?"

Zach rolled the options around in his mind for half a second. "Shit." He turned at the next red light and headed toward Raissa's shop. Raissa pulled off the wig and tried to fluff her hair into some semblance of normal.

A couple of cars were parked on the street outside of Raissa's shop, but none was a black Cadillac. She pointed across the street. "That's the office."

Zach pulled over close to the building and parked at the curb. A man in his sixties with black and silver hair stepped outside the door and turned to lock it. "That's him," Raissa said, pointing at the man locking the door. She checked the street, then jumped out of the car.

"Dr. Spencer," Raissa called as the doctor slipped the keys in his pocket. He turned around and gave her a wave.

"Hello, Raissa. I haven't seen you in a while. Did you finally take a vacation?"

Raissa walked over to the doctor, Zach close behind. "Hardly," she replied. "But a friend did—her honeymoon, in fact—so I'm filling in at her shop."

The doctor smiled. "That's nice." He gave Zach a curious look, then looked back at Raissa. "Well, my wife has dinner on the table, so I better run."

"Actually," Raissa said and pointed to Zach, "this is Detective Blanchard with the New Orleans Police Department. He'd like to speak with you about Melissa Franco."

Dr. Spencer's eyes widened. "The kidnapped girl? Why would you want to speak to me?"

"Because," Zach said, "you treated her, but her father clearly stated to police that his daughter had never been sick. I want to know why he would think that."

Dr. Spencer shook his head. "You're mistaken. Melissa Franco was never a patient of mine."

"I saw her here," Raissa said. "Once a month. She and her mother always stopped in my shop after they left your office."

Dr. Spencer appeared flustered. "I'm sure if you check my records, you'll see I'm telling the truth. I've never treated Melissa Franco. I didn't even know the name until it was on the news."

Zach narrowed his eyes at the man. It was so clear he was lying, but about what part? "Dr. Spencer, there are other eyewitnesses who put Susannah Franco and her daughter in your office," he lied, "so you can either tell me what's going on now, or I can drag you down to the station, and we'll take all night to go over it." Zach pulled the handcuffs from his waist. "Your choice."

Dr. Spencer paled. "You don't understand."

"That's exactly my point," Zach said. "And I need to understand. Rest assured that I don't care what you were doing here as long as it had nothing to do with Melissa Franco's kidnapping, but I do have to know what you were doing. So what was it—were you having an affair with Susannah Franco?"

"Good Lord, no," Dr. Spencer said. "I'm a happily married man, and Susannah is young enough to be my daughter."

"That's never stopped 'em before," Raissa said dryly.

Zach shot her a warning look and turned back to the doctor. "Good. See, this isn't so hard, is it? So you weren't sleeping with Susannah Franco. Were you treating her?"

Dr. Spencer sighed. "No. I was treating Melissa, but I swear I didn't know that was the child's name until I saw her on the news. Her mother gave a fake last name. Paid cash."

"Isn't that unusual?"

"Yes and no. Susannah said their church took up a collection each week for Melissa's visits. It's not that uncommon among some of the churches here."

"And you never noticed that their clothes or jewelry didn't match the charity claims?" Zach asked.

"Well, no. They were always clean and tidy, but never overdressed or even dressed fancy. The mother always had on jeans and a top. The child had on the type of cotton clothes that children wear. I never saw any expensive rings or other jewelry."

Zach looked over at Raissa for confirmation and she nodded. The doctor was right. There was nothing about them that automatically made one think "wealthy." Even Raissa had never caught onto their status during the shop visits.

"I apologize, Detective," Dr. Spencer said, "but the reality is, if Ms. Franco was carrying an eight-hundred-dollar handbag or wearing a two-hundred-dollar polo shirt, I'd be the last to know. My wife does all the shopping for our household."

"So let's just say you didn't know," Zach said. "Melissa's picture has been plastered all over the news. Why didn't you come forward then?"

"What could I possibly know that could help the police?"

"I find all this secrecy disturbing. You've never met Peter Franco?"

"No. Ms. Franco claimed she was a single mother. She didn't wear a wedding ring, so I had no reason until recently to suspect otherwise."

Raissa stared at the doctor. "But, Doctor, this is the part that I don't understand. It's one thing for Susannah Franco to hide her identity, but Peter Franco told the police that his daughter has never been sick. Are you trying to tell us the man doesn't know his own daughter is ill? How can that be? Why wouldn't Melissa tell him about the treatment herself?"

A hint of red crept up Dr. Spencer's neck. "Because we didn't tell her what was really wrong with her."

Zach threw his hands in the air. "Well, why the hell not?"

Dr. Spencer took one step back, clearly unnerved by Zach's obvious exasperation. "Her case was mild. Even the treatments weren't making her sick. Her mother said as long as the disease remained that way there was no use scaring her."

"So what, exactly," Zach asked, "did you claim you were treating her for?"

"Allergies. It's something that requires some blood drawn, regular care, and daily medication."

"And it doesn't bother you in the least that this woman obviously used you for her own purposes?"

Dr. Spencer gave Zach an apologetic look. "I wasn't trying to create a smoke screen for a crime spree, Detective. I only wanted to save a little girl a lot of worry, if it wasn't necessary. I know it's not the most ethical thing to do, but the mother really had the final word on the matter since Melissa is a minor. I was certainly unaware of all the other subterfuge."

"You said she takes medicine daily," Raissa said. "How much damage will be caused by her going without it?"

Dr. Spencer shook his head. "There's no way to know for sure, but the medication seemed to curb newly developing symptoms and relieve previously developed others. The longer she goes without the medication, the greater the chance she'll suffer a lot for it." Dr. Spencer pulled a card from his wallet and handed it to Zach, clearly worried. "If you need anything else, or when you find her, please call me. She'll need special care."

Raissa shot Zach a grim look. No further explanation was necessary.

Maryse flipped through the photos at the drugstore counter, then shoved them back into the envelope. "They look great," she told the woman behind the counter, who scanned the envelope to ring her up. Maryse passed the woman some money, picked up the envelope, and headed to the back of the store for the restroom. Helena was already waiting inside.

"Well?" Maryse asked.

"There's a black sedan parked across the street. Dark tint on the windows, but no bullet holes."

"Shit." Maryse said. "I was hoping Raissa was being melodramatic worrying about me, but apparently she wasn't. And the film counter is in clear view of the street. I'll bet black-sedan guy knows exactly why I'm here, even if he can't figure out how I managed to take the pictures."

Helena nodded. "It would be too much of a coincidence for him to ignore."

"Okay, so he probably won't kill me right there in the street, right? I mean, it's the pictures he wants, and the negatives."

"I guess," Helena said, but didn't look completely convinced.

"We'll go with that for now." Maryse pulled the photos out of the envelope and pulled out the spare copies. "I had duplicates made. I guess I was expecting trouble of some sort."

"God knows why, since your life has been a cakewalk for over a month now."

"Oh, you mean since you showed up?"

"You can't blame all this on me. Hell, if I had that much power and control, I'd run the world."

"There's a frightening thought." Maryse handed Helena the duplicate photos. "Hold on to those and do not lose them. Regardless of how scary things might be, remember that the bad guy can't see you. Keep those photos under your clothes, and try not to crease the heck out of them."

Maryse stuck the other set of photos back into the envelope along with the negatives and closed the flap. She looked at Helena and blew out a breath. "Okay, I'm going to leave the store and get mugged or jacked or rolled—whatever the hip, trendy term is for getting your butt kicked by a picture-stealing thug. *You* are going to get in the car and wait for me."

Helena raised her eyebrows. "You sure about this?"

"No, which is why we have to leave now. Otherwise, I'll spend the night in this restroom." Maryse opened the door and stepped outside. "Get ahead of me and let me know if the car's still there. It might have been a fluke."

Helena hurried out the drugstore ahead of Maryse, then rushed back inside. "The car's still there, but it's pulled up right behind your car now. Are you sure you want to do this? We can call Raissa and Zach—have them pick us up."

"That just puts Raissa in his line of fire and Zach on his radar. I don't think he'll shoot me. The street's well lit and lots of people are there. Besides, if this goes as planned, he'll think he got what he wanted and go away, right?"

Helena gave her a skeptical look. "Okay, but just in case things don't go as planned—which always seems to happen, by the way—why don't you give me your cell phone? I can call Raissa if something goes wrong."

Maryse frowned. "Do you think she would be able to hear you through the phone?"

Helena shrugged. "She heard me when I was putting the bug in Sonny's house."

Maryse's expression brightened. "You're right. I'd forgotten about that." She pulled her cell phone from her pocket and handed it to Helena. "Raissa's number is the fourth one on the favorites list."

Helena slipped the phone in her pocket. "Are you ready to do this?"

Maryse took a deep breath and blew it out. "As ready as I'm getting." Helena walked out of the drugstore ahead of her. Maryse said a silent prayer and followed the ghost onto the sidewalk.

The black Cadillac was parked ten feet or so behind Maryse's car just as Helena had reported. It looked like the car that had been in Mudbug that morning, but Maryse had no way of knowing for sure. She tried to appear nonchalant as she walked to her car, clutching the photos in her hand. No use making them harder to steal, or she'd likely show more bruises for her effort than necessary.

She pulled her keys from her pocket and unlocked the car door, then stepped to the driver's side and reached for the door handle. So far, there was no movement from the black car, and Maryse was beginning to think they'd made a mistake. After all, Sonny and his men couldn't be the only drivers of black Cadillacs, or there wouldn't be a reason to manufacture them.

She peered into the car to make sure it was empty, but she only saw Helena inside, clutching the cell phone with one finger poised on top, ready to dial at any moment. Letting out a sigh of relief, she pulled up on the door handle, and that's when she felt a hand on her shoulder and something cold and hard press into her back. Serious miscalculation. The man must have been hiding in the alley next to the cars.

"Give me the photos," the man whispered, "and you can drive off with all your body parts intact."

Maryse felt a rush of fear like a tidal wave, and then did what she always did at the wrong time—she got sarcastic. "Well, when you put it that way. I'm hungry and could really use my stomach." She lifted the envelope of photos above her shoulder. "I'll probably need my colon later."

The man removed his hand from her shoulder and grabbed the photos. "Smart-ass bitch," he said, and clocked her in the back of the head with his gun. Maryse remembered yelling once before she fell against the side of the car and slumped down on the sidewalk.

Maryse had no idea how long she'd been sitting on the sidewalk next to her car, but when she opened her eyes, she saw three people hovering above her.

An older lady bent over and peered down at her. "Are you all right, dear? Do you need us to call an ambulance?"

Maryse struggled to rise, feeling a bit dizzy. "No, I think I'm okay. Just a little woozy."

"Did that man steal your purse?"

"No. Just the things I bought at the drugstore. I wasn't even carrying a purse."

"A smart idea, with all the tomfoolery that's going on these days. Shall I call the police, then?"

"No, don't bother. They're busy with much worse things than this, and it seems there's never enough of them to go around."

"That is so true. You should still go downtown when you're feeling better and file a report. Likely they won't be able to do anything about your purchases, but they do keep a record of problem areas and try to patrol more often."

"I'll do that," Maryse said. "Thank you for stopping. I think I'll drive home now and soak in a hot bath."

The lady nodded. "Excellent plan. Lord only knows what kind of grime is on that sidewalk. Are you okay to drive, dear? Can I call someone to come get you?"

"No. I think I'll be fine. I'll just sit here for a minute, then drive. If I have any problems, I'll call my friend to come get me."

"Well, okay. You be careful, now." The lady gave her a nod walked down the sidewalk, the other pedestrians trailing behind her now that the show was over.

Maryse slid into the car and clutched the steering wheel, trying to steady herself. The dizziness was mostly gone, but the fear still raged. "Holy shit!"

"Are you okay?" Helena leaned over, peering anxiously at her. "I didn't know what to do. It all happened so fast."

"I'll be fine as long as I don't have a heart attack." She ran her fingers lightly over the bump that was already forming on the back of her head. "Did you call Raissa?"

Helena nodded. "As soon as I saw him put a gun in your back. She could hear me fine. She and Zach are on the way, but we should get outta here, just in case that guy's still around."

"Good idea." Maryse started the car. "There's a restaurant a couple of blocks over, Wally's Seafood Place. It's well lit and probably crowded. Text Raissa to meet us there."

"I grew up with manual typewriters. What in the world makes you think I know how to send a text message? I was doing good to make the phone call."

"Never mind," Maryse said, and took her phone from Helena's hand. She sent the text, then pulled away from the curb.

"I wonder how Raissa's explaining my call to Zach," Helena mused.

"Probably the same way she explained my taking pictures of the man to begin with."

Helena's eyes widened. "I hadn't even thought about that. So what are you going to say if he asks?"

"Damned good question."

Chapter Twelve

Zach looked across the restaurant table at Maryse and wondered what she was hiding. Ever since Raissa told him there "might" be photos, he'd wondered how on earth someone had managed to take a picture of the guy without him noticing. Obviously, the answer was she hadn't gotten away with it, or she wouldn't have been attacked. But how she'd gotten all the way to New Orleans to have them developed was another mystery. It seemed to Zach that the guy could have run her over in the street right there in Mudbug and saved himself the trouble.

Which meant something wasn't exactly right about her story. The only thing Zach could come up with that made sense is that it wasn't Maryse who had taken the pictures. But whom was she protecting? Obviously someone close to her, or no one would have followed her to New Orleans to begin with. And someone with a death wish, assuming they'd walked up to the car of a potential killer and snapped a photo. Whoever it was, it appeared to him that Raissa was also in on the secret. She'd maintained a fairly straight face, but Zach got the feeling Raissa was reading information between the lines in Maryse's story.

"And then I came to on the sidewalk," Maryse finished up her story, "with some lady looking down at me. I couldn't have been out for long, but the guy was long gone."

"With the pictures," Zach finished.

Maryse nodded. "And the negatives, but I had a contingency plan." She pulled a set of photos out of the front of her shirt. "I had duplicate copies made and hid one on my body."

Zach narrowed his eyes at her. "Why would you even think to do that?"

Maryse took a sip of her beer. "I peeked outside and saw a black car at the corner. I was afraid they'd followed me."

"So you hid a set of photos in your bra and went strolling outside, knowing full well you were probably going to be mugged."

Maryse frowned. "When you put it that way, it doesn't sound so smart, does it?"

"Ignore him," Raissa said and took the photos from Maryse. "It was very smart and very brave. Besides, you called me and put the phone in your pocket on the way out of the store so I could hear what was going on, so you were sorta covered."

"Yeah…I guess that was pretty smart." Maryse took another drink of her beer.

"By the way, if you do something like that again, I'll kill you myself."

Maryse rubbed the back of her head. "Don't worry. From now on, I'm leaving all the Jane Bond stuff up to you."

Zach smiled. It was hard not to like a spunky woman, even if she had electrocuted him. And was lying.

"You did a great job," Raissa said as she flipped through the photos.

"Do you recognize him?" Zach asked, leaning over to view the photographs with Raissa.

"I think so, but I'm not certain. He looks sorta like the son of one of Sonny's guys. But the last time I saw him, he was a teenager, so I can't be sure."

Zach pulled out one of the photos that offered a clean view of the man's face. "I'll take this one and run it through the database."

"Don't you need a reason to do that?"

"I'll make something up." He tucked the photo in his shirt pocket. "I'm more concerned about getting you two back to Mudbug. There's a lot of long stretches of road between here and there." He nodded at Raissa. "If your car has a tracking bug on it, Maryse's may, too. Anything can happen on your way there."

"Don't worry," Maryse said. "I've got that part covered."

Zach looked at Maryse, trying to hide his amusement. "Do you, Ms. Bond? And just what do you have in mind?"

"I talked to Carolyn, the lady who owns the seafood restaurant in Mudbug, before you got here. She's expecting a delivery of seafood this evening. Fred, the seafood-truck driver, always makes Mudbug his last stop because he lives there. He's agreed to park behind this restaurant and give us a lift."

"You trust these people?" Zach asked.

"With my life," Maryse said, "or I would never have asked." She looked a bit guilty, then looked at Raissa. "There is one little catch, though."

"Uh-oh," Raissa said. "I don't like that look."

"The cab of the truck was modified for Fred's paperwork. There's only room for the driver, so we'll have to ride in the back."

Raissa's eyes widened. "With the fish?"

Zach chuckled, unable to hold it in. "Well, it's the safest form of sleeping with the fishes that you two could have. You probably shouldn't complain."

Raissa looked over at him and raised one eyebrow. "I'm so glad our predicament amuses you. Keep in mind, if you were planning any more midnight visits to the hotel, that the back of that truck is refrigerated. It could take days for *me* to thaw out."

Zach ceased chuckling, but Maryse took over for him.

"If you could see the look on your face," Maryse teased. "Don't worry. I'll put her in a hot shower as soon as we get to the hotel. Trust me, Mildred will insist on it, or the whole place will smell like the shrimp house."

A vision of Raissa in the shower flashed through Zach's mind, and suddenly the restaurant felt overwhelmingly hot. He was really going to have to do something about his feelings for Raissa, but the one thing that came to mind was probably the worst thing, given their situation. Then, on the other hand, he was already lying to his boss and harboring a fugitive. Having sex with her wasn't exactly a stretch.

Zach looked over at Maryse. "So, if I happen to show up for a midnight visit, you're not planning on electrocuting me again, are you?"

Maryse gave him a sly wink. "Not unless you want me to."

Zach laughed. "I have to ask, what does your husband do for a living?"

"He's an investigator with the DEQ."

"The Department of Environmental Quality, no shit? That's great. And an investigator. He must love your side activities. They're somewhat unusual for a scientist."

Maryse reached over and patted Zach on the arm. "When all this is over, I'll tell you the story of how Luc and I met. Or you could run me through the police system when you run that photo. A little light reading while you're waiting." She grinned at Raissa, who smiled.

Lord help him, now his curiosity was in overdrive. On the other hand, if Maryse had a police record, it might give him an idea of what she and Raissa were hiding. If not, he planned on getting it out of Raissa later that night. Through whatever means he deemed necessary.

It was close to midnight before Zach managed to get away from the police station. The captain had been understandably unhappy over his take on Susannah Franco, and Zach hadn't even told him about the conversation with Dr. Spencer. He couldn't figure out a way to get around to it without revealing his contact with Raissa.

The captain had considered everything Zach had given him, and they'd tossed around a couple of outlandish thoughts, but neither of them had been willing to commit to anything more than checking into the mayor's past and keeping a closer watch on the movements of all the immediate family members. Zach was tasked with doing the digging. The captain would tap some other discreet detectives for the closer-watch detail.

Zach turned onto the highway and headed toward Mudbug. He'd been relieved when he wasn't placed on watch detail. There was no way he could have continued his investigating with Raissa if he'd been parked in a fake cable installer's van outside the mayor's house. He also needed to be extraordinarily careful about being seen with Raissa from this point forward. Questioning Jennifer yesterday had been a big risk, and he wasn't certain what they'd gotten from the girl had been worth it, except for the help Raissa had managed to provide her.

The stark fear in Jennifer's expression when she had recalled her dream still bothered him. That someone's life could be so derailed by another was beyond unfair and made him even more determined to catch the kidnapper and see to it that he could never hurt another girl again. Always looking over your shoulder, not knowing when an enemy might strike, was enough to render even the strongest person immobile.

He shook his head, amazed that Raissa had not only managed to live that way for nine years but had done so right under the nose of the very men she was hiding from. Unfortunately, all indicators pointed to the end of her charade. There were far too many black Cadillacs around Raissa and her friends. He smiled for a moment, thinking about Maryse.

He'd called her bluff and pulled her file. He had to admit that it wasn't at all what he'd been expecting, and it made him rethink his position on her lying about how she took the photo. For all he knew, she may have strolled down the street and asked the guy to pose. Maryse's escape from death was a story that belonged in a Hollywood movie, if they could even get an audience to buy it, which he doubted. If there was one thing Zach had learned long ago, it was that truth is definitely stranger than fiction. Still, he couldn't help admiring the way Maryse had handled a seemingly impossible situation, and he said a silent prayer for the man brave enough to marry her. Her husband, Luc, must have nine lives.

It was almost one A.M. when he parked his car behind the hotel. Maryse had been kind enough to provide him with a key to the back door so he could slip in unnoticed. He unlocked the back door and slipped inside. Raissa's room was on the third floor, so he hurried up the stairs and down the hall, hoping she was still awake.

Light shone underneath her room door. A good sign. He lifted his hand to knock and stepped back in surprise when the door swung open before he had even touched it. It took him only a split second to remember the security cameras. Raissa had probably been tracking his movements since he'd first driven down Main Street.

She was wearing a black silk negligee with a plunging neckline and a sexy smile. "About time you got here." She reached out with one hand and pulled him inside.

As he followed her into the room, he checked out her backside and realized the nightie ended just below the curve of her rear. He felt his pulse quicken. *Get a grip. You can't jump the woman as soon as you walk in the room, regardless of how she's dressed.* He laid his keys on one of the tables and turned to face her.

She was standing close to him, and when he turned, she ran her hands up his backside and bit him playfully on his neck. "Fun business now. Boring business later."

Zach felt a rush of heat throughout his body and he grew hard immediately. "You get no argument from me." He lowered his lips to hers in a crushing kiss, their mouths mixed in a frenzy of pure animal attraction. He ran a hand across her breast, feeling the engorged nipple through the thin fabric, and she groaned.

"I know this is going to sound really bad," Raissa said, "but I'm not really interested in foreplay."

Zach hardened even more and was certain he'd split the zipper on his jeans. "My God, you're perfect."

He pushed the nightie's thin straps over her shoulders and the silk slid to the floor. There was nothing else in the way. He ran his hands down her body and stopped at a scar in the center of her chest, just below her breasts. It was perfectly round, a shape he'd seen before. He looked up to ask, but she shook her head, unzipped his jeans, and pushed them down.

He almost lost control when she wrapped her hand around the hard length of him. Never had he wanted something so badly, knowing with every ounce of his being that it was a stupid thing to do. But damned if he was going to worry about that now. He slid his hand down and felt wet heat. He touched her with light, feathery strokes. She gasped and stroked him faster until he was on the edge.

"No foreplay," he reminded her. He pulled his jeans off his feet and retrieved a condom from his pocket. A couple of seconds later, he was ready for action. He pushed a pile of paper off the table with one arm and lifted Raissa onto it.

She pulled him to her and he entered her fast and hard. She ran her hands down his back, and he could feel her nails pressing into his skin. He lowered his lips to hers, kissing her deep and long while he thrust. She wrapped her legs around him and he felt himself being absorbed completely by this woman. Mind, body, and soul.

He felt the rise coming and he could tell she was on the verge, just like him. He thrust once, twice more, then one final thrust that sent them both over the edge.

He thought his mind would explode. Heat rushed over his body, but the last thing he wanted to do was cool off. He didn't want to let her go, but he wasn't sure how much longer he could stand without collapsing from sheer pleasure. The bed was at least ten steps away, so he yanked a spare blanket off the dresser with one hand, lifted Raissa off the table, and laid her down on the floor beside him, directly under the cool air of the ceiling fan. She leaned over to kiss him lightly on the lips, wearing a satisfied smile, then nestled her head in the crook of his arm.

Zach had been right earlier. Raissa was perfect.

When he'd gotten his breath back a bit, he rolled on his side and traced a finger down her chest and to the scar. "Nine-millimeter?"

"Yeah."

"Was it Sonny who shot you?"

"No. Spider."

"Spider? I thought you said he was a pansy."

"He is a pansy, which is why he shot me instead of bringing me in so Sonny could do it himself. Lucky for me he ran after the first shot."

"And you lured him into a booth in a seedy bar and shoved a gun in his crotch." Zach laughed. "You're my kind of woman."

"And you didn't arrest me for doing it." Raissa lifted one hand and placed it on the side of his face. "You're my kind of man."

Pounding on the room's door brought Raissa out of her satisfied haze. "Raissa," Maryse said in a loud whisper. "There's somebody out back. I'm opening the door." Raissa heard the key turning in the lock and looked at Zach, who was frozen, staring at the door as if he were headed for the chopping block. It was far too late to do anything about clothes, or blankets, since the only one within reach was the one they were laying on. So Raissa did what any other woman would do in that situation. She smiled.

Maryse opened the door and slipped inside. She looked toward the bed, but when she found it empty she looked the other direction and gasped. "Holy shit." She put her hands over her eyes. "I am sooooooo sorry. I had no idea you two were…um…working? On the floor? In the nude?"

She spread the fingers on one hand and took a peek. "Okay, well, maybe I'm not completely sorry."

Raissa laughed as she sat up and tossed Zach's clothes to him. "The bathroom's behind you. Put on some clothes before she gets any ideas."

Maryse lowered her hands as Zach slipped into the bathroom, and leaned slightly to the side so she could watch his backside. "You mean any more ideas." She grinned at Raissa. "Wow. Nice butt, but don't you dare tell Luc I said so."

All of a sudden, the grin dropped from Maryse's expression. "Holy crap—I completely forgot. The monitors. There's a guy out back." She grabbed a pair of jeans and a shirt from the dresser and tossed them at Raissa. "Would you mind?"

Raissa slipped into the jeans and shirt as she studied the monitors. "Where did you see him?"

Maryse pointed to a monitor showing the alley behind the hotel. "He was behind the hotel at the back door. He tried the door handle, and I figured he was going to try to break in, so I hauled butt down here."

Raissa studied the screen and frowned. "Then where is he now? The alarm never went off, so he's not in the hotel."

"Maybe we should have Helena look. She's in the room next to mine. I could send her outside."

Raissa nodded. "Do that, but get right back in here afterward. I don't want us separated if we don't have to be. Where's Mildred?"

"She had three glasses of wine at dinner tonight, so she's sleeping like the dead."

"Good, then tell Helena to keep this quiet so we don't panic her."

"Gotcha."

"Who's Helena?" Zach asked, and they both jumped. Maryse stared at him, her eyes wide, then rushed out of the room, shooting a fearful glance at Raissa on her way out.

"Who's Helena?" Zach repeated. "Another friend?"

"You could say that." Raissa frantically searched her mind for a rational way to explain Helena Henry. Finally, she decided to avoid the topic for the moment. "She has special abilities."

Zach raised one eyebrow. "Can she make herself invisible? Because I can't think of a good reason to send someone outside the hotel to look for this guy unless you want them dead." He stared at Raissa for a moment. "You don't want her dead, do you?"

"Of course not!" *Because she already is.* "I would never intentionally put another human being in danger." *Not a live one anyway.*

Thankfully, Maryse slipped into the room again and saved her from any more Helena questions. "Well?" Raissa asked.

Maryse shot a nervous look at Zach, then looked back at Raissa. "She was asleep, but she's headed downstairs now. If she sees anything, she'll come back up."

Raissa nodded and looked at the screen displaying the back of the hotel just in time to see Helena walk through the hotel wall and into the alley. She tapped the screen and Maryse stepped closer to look. Zach looked at the screen, then at Raissa and Maryse, wondering what the hell they found so interesting.

Raissa knew she was holding her breath as she watched Helena stroll across the alley to the garage. Neither Raissa's nor Maryse's car was in Mudbug, much less in the garage, but the intruder had no way of knowing they'd arrived by way of a fish truck. Helena walked through the wall of the garage, and Raissa looked over at Maryse.

Maryse's eyes were wide as saucers, and she inclined her head toward Zach. Raissa barely shook her head to let Maryse know that Zach was not in on the Helena connection. With any luck whatsoever, he'd never have to be. Raissa looked back at the monitor.

But her luck had run out.

A man burst out from the front door of the garage and right behind him came Helena. Raissa might still have been able to swing an explanation if it weren't for the trash-can lid and crowbar Helena was wielding like one of King Arthur's knights. The only blessing was that Zach couldn't see what she was wearing. Unfortunately for Maryse and Raissa, they could, and full body tights with a family crest on the front was not Helena's best look.

"What the hell!" Zach stepped in between Maryse and Raissa and leaned forward until his face was only inches from the monitor. "What is that?" He looked from Raissa to Maryse, neither of whom were speaking. "You both know something, and I want you to tell me what it is right now."

Raissa considered what it must look like from Zach's point of view and understood his disbelief. After all, floating garage articles chasing an intruder down an alleyway wasn't something you saw all that often.

Maryse gave the monitor one last panicked look. "I better head downstairs. I mean, there's no chance he's coming back to the hotel, right?"

"I seriously doubt it," Raissa said. "Go intercept."

Maryse nodded and hurried out of the room. Raissa watched the monitor until she saw Maryse open the back door and poke her head out. Helena appeared a couple of seconds later and slipped into the hotel with Maryse, dropping the crowbar and trashcan lid next to the back door. Raissa let out a sigh of relief that the excitement for the night hadn't involved injury or death.

"I want an answer," Zach demanded, "and I'm not leaving here until I get one."

"An answer to what?" Raissa tried on her best innocent look. "He was obviously looking for my car or maybe Maryse's and something spooked him, so he ran."

Zach's face flushed with anger. "You know damned good and well what spooked him. The man was being chased by a crowbar—a crowbar without a human being attached. Damn right he was spooked. I'm spooked, and I'm three stories up in a hotel room. It's like a B horror movie. What the hell is going on, Raissa? I know you and Maryse are keeping something from me. That whole picture-taking story never added up."

Raissa sighed and sank into one of the folding chairs in front of the monitors. "How open-minded are you?"

"In what way? Religion? Politics? Equal rights for cats?"

"To...um...paranormal things."

"You're telling me your friend, this Helena, *can* make herself invisible? I'm not buying it."

"No, she doesn't make herself that way. Man, this is hard. The paranormal realm has so many avenues that we really don't know that much about. I'm learning every day, and it's been my business for over eight years."

Zach stared at her, clearly uncertain of what to say. "You told me you hacked information to convince your psychic reading clients you were the real thing."

Raissa nodded. "And that's true, but...uh...that part where I told you I talked to dead people...Well, it's actually only one dead person, and I didn't ask to talk to her, but she's there anyway."

There was complete silence in the room. Raissa was sure neither of them was breathing. Zach stared at her with a mixture of horror, confusion, and a touch of fear. His expression clearly said he'd not only bought into the ravings of a madwoman, he'd slept with her, too. He was probably mentally processing his severance pay as he stared.

"I know," Raissa said, "it's a lot to buy—"

"It's impossible to buy. I don't know what kind of game you're playing, but you're not going to play it with me." He shoved his wallet and keys into his pants pocket and turned to leave the room, but before he could walk out, Maryse stepped in.

"I thought there might be a problem with, well, you know," Maryse said, "so I came back to help."

"Oh, there's a problem all right," Zach said. "You two are crazy. And from now on, you're on your own."

Maryse shook her head. "We're probably crazy, but not in the way you think." Maryse looked to Zach's side and nodded. "Show him, Helena."

Zach looked to his right as Raissa's lipstick rose from the dresser.

Chapter Thirteen

Zach stared in amazement as the cap came off the lipstick and the dial on the bottom spun round, pushing a glossy burgundy color out the end of the container. The lipstick connected with the mirror and swirled out sprawling lettering.

Sorry I missed the show earlier when Maryse walked in on you two.

Zach was certain he hadn't blinked since the lipstick left the dresser, and he was pretty sure he wasn't breathing, either. "Who are you?" he asked.

Helena Henry.

Zach's mind raced. That name was familiar. He whirled to face Maryse. "Your mother-in-law?"

"Ex-mother-in-law, but yes."

Zach slumped into a chair, completely overwhelmed and exhausted from the day. Of all the things in the world he had seen, this was by far the most outlandish. Never in his life would he have believed it was possible. Hell, he still didn't believe it was possible, and he was looking straight at it. "I don't understand."

Maryse snorted. "You think *you* don't understand. I've been able to see Helena since the day of her funeral. The woman I hated the most in the world, and I was the only one who could see or hear her for a long time." Maryse sighed and looked over at the mirror. "Don't get your panties in a bunch, Helena. You know I don't hate you anymore. I'm just giving him the four-one-one."

I don't wear panties. The words appeared on the mirror.

Zach grimaced. He had, after all, seen a picture of Maryse's mother-in-law in her police file. "That was far more information than I ever needed to know."

"All right," Maryse said. "Show's over, Helena. It's time for you and me to go back to bed." Maryse mouthed *Sorry* to Zach and opened the door, then glared at the air, apparently willing the ghost to leave. "No, I don't think he's getting naked again," he heard her say as the door shut behind her.

Zach stared behind them, still unable to form words.

"Sorry to hit you with it like that," Raissa said, "but there's really no simple way to explain."

"Yeah. I guess not." He studied Raissa, who sat calm and collected on the edge of the dresser. "None of that bothers you?"

"No. I mean, not in the ways you might think it should. I learned a long time ago to never close my mind to possibilities. Every time I did it made a fool of me."

"But you and Maryse can actually see her?"

"And Mildred and our friend Sabine, although I wasn't able to until recently."

"So you did what, exactly, to make that happen? Dance naked with lit candles...?"

"Well, Maryse has this theory that you develop the ability to see Helena when you've been targeted for murder. We've all come pretty close to biting it at some point fairly recently."

"Are you serious?"

"It's hasn't failed as a theory for over a month now."

Zach ran one hand through his hair, trying to make sense of everything. Trying to make *normal* out of anything. "So when did you first see her?"

"The night I left the police station, after I told you about the other girls. Someone pushed me in front of a bus on the corner. Helena pulled me out of the street just in time."

"Jesus!" Zach rose and started pacing the small room. "That means someone was following you before you ever came to the station. Your cover was already blown."

Raissa nodded. "Yeah, I tried to dismiss it at the time, but Helena was sitting in my car across the street. I knew it wasn't a coincidence."

Zach stopped pacing and stared at her. "Do you realize what you're asking me to believe? In ghosts...curses...whatever you think is going on here? Damn it, Raissa, you'd already stretched my mind to the limits with your past as an agent and your undercover work, not to mention your theories on the abductions, but this... this is something I can't buy into."

"I'm not asking you to buy into anything," Raissa said gently. "You know what you saw. You're a sane, rational, intelligent man. There's no other explanation than the one I gave you."

Zach sat back down again with a sigh, unable to get control over his warring emotions. "I don't know whether to be amazed, or scared, or worried."

"I think all three is a safe bet." She sat down next to him and placed one hand on his leg. "I know how you feel—well, maybe not exactly, but sorta. It's going to be fine, Zach. Think of Helena as another form of weapon. She's a pain in the rear a lot of the time, but she has her usefulness."

"So the pictures Maryse had developed—provided by Helena, the ghost photographer?"

"I told you she had her usefulness. If she'd tucked the camera in her pocket and then managed not to get run over, the entire thing might have gone off without a hitch. You can't always depend on Helena for the best judgment or to keep her cool."

Zach shook his head, still trying to wrap his mind around everything. "Yeah, I guess I can see that, especially after that garage escapade. That guy probably won't sleep for a week. Which reminds me, did you recognize him?"

"No. It was too dark, and the feed wasn't clear enough for me to make out a face. I'll do some work on the footage and see if I can clean it up, but the most we're probably going to get off it is height, weight, and an estimate of age based on movement."

"I figured as much." Zach looked over at Raissa. "So is there anything else you're keeping from me—a husband, five kids, a cat? Because I don't think I can take any more surprises."

Raissa opened her mouth to answer, when one of the laptops at the end of the table started beeping. A loud, persistent, annoying beep. Raissa rushed over to the laptop and looked at the screen.

"What now?" Zach asked. "Don't tell me you've set a timer to brush your teeth or paint your toenails at two A.M."

Raissa motioned him over, so he rose from the chair and walked over to stand beside her. "There is *one* more little thing. This audio is from earlier tonight."

"Oh, no." Zach looked down at the laptop as Raissa clicked on a speaker icon. A man's voice, yelling and cursing at the top of his lungs, bellowed out of the laptop.

"I had Helena put a bug in Sonny Hebert's office."

Zach stared at the laptop, listening to the mob boss rant about his desire to kill his "demon" cat and bury it in the backyard. For the second time that night, Zach was totally speechless.

Raissa slid into the booth across from Dr. Breaux and signaled to the waitress for a cup of coffee. "Morning," she said, and nodded gratefully to the waitress when she slid a mug in front of her.

Dr. Breaux looked at her over the top of his newspaper, an amused expression on his face. "It's not even eight o'clock. It can't already be a bad morning."

Raissa poured a ton of sugar in her coffee, stirred, and took a long swallow. "Because it's not even eight o'clock is exactly the problem."

Dr. Breaux laughed. "So you're not a morning person."

"Not much. I'm more of a night owl, which tends to catch up with you when you agree to coffee with the chickens."

"If I'd known you weren't a morning person, I would have suggested seven just for a change of pace. It's good for the heart, you know?" He put down his paper and gave her his full attention. "So what was so interesting that it kept you up last night?"

Raissa felt the flush at the base of her neck and hoped like hell Dr. Breaux would think it was only the coffee heating her up. There wasn't anything interesting, really, unless you counted hot sex, an intruder, introducing a ghost, listening to an hour of Sonny Hebert cussing, more hot sex, and maybe thirty minutes of sleep. "Nothing much."

Dr. Breaux raised one eyebrow. "The young man would probably be crushed to hear that."

Raissa groaned. "It can't possibly be that obvious. It's because you're a doctor, right? I'm emitting some pheromone. Or I have a tic. Please tell me everyone else cannot just look at me and tell I spent last night with a man."

"Well, I don't know about all that pheromone stuff, but in all the years I've known you, I've never seen you flustered over anything. I realize that coffee you're drinking is hot, but it's probably eighty degrees in this café, and that coffee is not hot enough to make you blush."

"Maybe you could give me something to throw people off track. Poison ivy would be a good start. Then people wouldn't know."

Dr. Breaux laughed so hard he shook the booth. "Lord, Raissa," he said, wiping his eyes with his napkin. "I don't think you have to go to such extremes. Why, if I were you, I'd be happy to have spent a night worth blushing over. It's been a lot of years since my wife passed, but I'm not so old I can't remember one or two of them enough to wish she were still here, and that we were both a lot younger."

Raissa took another drink of coffee. "You're right. It's normal. It's natural. Everything in nature does it." She looked over at him. "Then why doesn't it feel natural to me?"

Dr. Breaux cleared his throat. "If you're having…female issues…I'd be happy to see you in a professional capacity."

"If only it were that simple. It's not the plumbing. That part is natural and exciting and everything it should be. It's the emotional side of things that's a problem."

Dr. Breaux shook his head. "Matters of the heart I cannot help with. Unless of course, you're having a heart attack."

Raissa laughed. "Not yet. But I'm not ruling it out." Raissa looked up as the bells over the door jangled and Maryse rushed in.

"Sorry I'm late," Maryse said as she slid into the booth beside Raissa.

"No, you're not," Raissa joked.

Maryse blushed a bit. "I picked Luc up at the airport this morning. We had some catching up to do, so you're right, I'm not sorry I'm late."

Dr. Breaux gave them a wistful look. "Ah, to be young and in love again. I envy you girls."

"It's never too late," Maryse said. "There's a couple of eligible women in Mudbug I can think of."

"No, my time has passed. I'm married to my work right now, and in a year or so, I'll likely retire and spend the rest of my life sitting in a fishing boat off the Florida coast."

Maryse nodded. "Probably a lot more relaxing than a relationship. And definitely cheaper. Do you have any idea how much furniture costs? Luc and I looked at couches for the new house last week, and I swear I think I'm going to sit on the floor. Ridiculous."

Raissa laughed. "Says the woman who will pay thousands for a magnifying glass."

"That's a Meiji Epi-fluorescent microscope and is serious laboratory equipment. But I guess I see your point."

"Well, ladies," Dr. Breaux said, "I'm not senile enough to think two beautiful young women got out of bed early to have breakfast with an old codger like me just for fun. I have to assume something's on your mind, and I have to admit, I've been itching to find out what. I've simply drawn a blank trying to figure it out."

Raissa gave Maryse a nod. They'd already agreed that what they had to say would probably work better coming from Maryse, as she'd known Dr. Breaux her entire life. Raissa had suggested Maryse question him alone, but given her investigative background,

Maryse wanted Raissa there to see if she caught things Maryse might miss. Raissa hoped he'd be forthcoming with his responses and there wouldn't be anything to miss.

Maryse laid a file on the table and pushed it over to Dr. Breaux. "You know after everything that went down last month with me, the police got permission to autopsy Helena Henry."

"Yes," Dr. Breaux said and picked up the file. "Is this it? They gave you a copy?"

"I have my ways," Maryse said, "and I'd really rather not explain them. The autopsy didn't prove anything as far as Helena's being murdered, but it clearly shows she had cancer. No one who knew Helena, including Hank or Harold, was aware of that. I was hoping you could explain."

Dr. Breaux frowned and opened the folder. He flipped the pages over one at a time, his brow scrunched in concentration. Finally, he placed the file on the table and shook his head. "I had no idea. The tests clearly show lung cancer and a rare form of leukemia, but Helena's complaints were the usual sort for someone with asthma. I never even thought. My God. So many people in this town lost to that disease. I guess it shouldn't surprise me so much, with her house sitting right on that polluted bayou."

"All we can figure," Maryse said, "is that she wasn't in a lot of pain and was dismissing it as age or whatever. You said she complained about something before she died?"

"Not just before she died—chronically. Her asthma always bothered her, and she aggravated the situation with her weight and constant exposure to plants and flowers with her gardening."

"So did she come to see you any time right before her death?"

Dr. Breaux frowned. "No, but she might have seen the nurse. I could check my records if you think it's important."

Maryse sighed. "It probably isn't." Maryse looked over at Raissa. Raissa gave her a nod to move on to the next topic. So far, Dr. Breaux had been forthcoming, not that it had gained them any ground. They might as well hit him with the doozy.

"There's more," Maryse said. "In looking over some of that information I got, I noticed something odd. When I looked into it, I got more confused."

"What's wrong, Maryse?" Dr. Breaux asked. "You sound so troubled by this."

"There's no way Hank could have been Helena and Harold's son. The blood types rule it out."

Dr. Breaux stared at her, his mouth partially open. "I…well… that really doesn't have any bearing on anything, does it?"

"It might for Hank." Maryse narrowed her eyes at Dr. Breaux. "You already knew, didn't you?"

"I was the family doctor, so of course, I'd requested blood work on all of them at times, especially Hank, since he was prone to be anemic. The irregularities were hardly something a good doctor should miss."

"Stop hedging. His mother is dead, and his father is in prison. Hank might need to know his real medical history."

Dr. Breaux sighed. "I noticed the discrepancy, but I never asked about it. I always assumed that Helena had another man while Harold was in the service. I'm afraid many of the men I served with arrived home to children that weren't their own." He paused for a minute. "I have to say, I never saw signs of it, though. If the other man was still around when Harold came home, no one in Mudbug was aware. I figured as long as it was in the past, no good would come of letting anyone think any different than that Hank was Helena and Harold's son."

"So the babies couldn't have been switched at the hospital or anything like that?"

"Heavens, one wouldn't like to think so, although we hear about it in the news. I guess anything's possible, but that is far less of a possibility than a lonely woman seeking comfort."

Maryse looked over at Raissa, looking for advice on how to proceed. Raissa gave her a small shake of her head. There was nothing else to be done here. Helena had already been clear about her lack of outside relationships, and Raissa believed her. The ghost simply had no reason to lie and was obviously distraught over the entire mess.

"Dr. Breaux," Raissa began, shifting topics. "I wondered if you might know someone."

There were a couple of seconds' pause before he responded, but finally Dr. Breaux looked over at Raissa. "Who would that be?"

"A Dr. Spencer."

"I know two Dr. Spencers, as a matter of fact. Husband and wife pediatricians. Have a large practice in Miami."

"No, this Dr. Spencer is in New Orleans. He's a cancer specialist and works only with children."

Dr. Breaux frowned for a moment, then brightened. "Yes. Dr. Spencer was a guest speaker at a medical seminar I attended earlier this year. He did a very interesting panel on the increased rate of leukemia in children near manufacturing plants."

"But you don't know him personally?"

"No, can't say that I do. Why? Has he done something wrong?"

"Not that I know of. He was treating that little girl that was abducted on Monday."

"Really? They never said anything on the news about her being ill. Why, that's horrible. I hope she's found before her treatment is compromised." He shook his head, his expression sad. "I wonder what her prognosis is." He gave Raissa a curious look. "Did they say that on the news? I watched this morning, but I don't remember them covering anything like that."

"No. Dr. Spencer's office is across the street from my shop. The girl always came into my store with her mother after the appointments. She looked very healthy, if that makes you feel any better."

"Yes, that's good news. I guess we'll just have to pray that she's found before things worsen." Dr. Breaux looked over at Maryse and shook his head. "What interesting lives the two of you lead. You seem always to be right in the middle of the action." He gave them both a stern look. "Be certain you don't put yourself in a bad position with all this. There are lots of people who don't relish their secrets being exposed. You should both be well aware of that after the last couple of months."

"We'll be careful," Maryse said, and Raissa nodded.

Dr. Breaux stared into his coffee, his expression both confused and troubled. Maybe Maryse was right. Maybe he'd check into things. Things that happened twenty-nine years ago with the birth of Hank Henry.

Raissa still intended to do some checking on her own.

Chapter Fourteen

Zach sat across from Captain Saucier, trying to figure out the best way to lie to him and still not cause a heart attack. The man was clearly suffering from the strain. He kept running his fingers across the top of his bald head, probably wishing he still had some hair to pull out.

"Nothing," the captain complained, and banged one hand on his desk. "Four days and not a damned thing. Please tell me you've got something, Blanchard. Our futures here may depend on it."

"I might have something, but it's thin, and you're not going to like where I got it."

"I don't care if Satan himself showed up with a tip. I'll take anything at this point."

Zach took a breath and blew it out. "It wasn't Satan, but it could get us a one-way ticket to hell if anyone finds out."

The captain stared at him for a couple of seconds, then shook his head. "Shit. That Bordeaux woman."

"Yeah. She sorta called me. I gave her my card and—"

The captain waved a hand, cutting him off. "I know I'm likely to regret this, but I don't even care. Do you know where the woman is now?"

"No." At least that part was absolutely true.

"Could you track the call?"

"No." Since she'd told him the phone wasn't traceable, that part was technically true, also.

"Then fuck it," the captain said. "What did the woman have to say? Did she bother to explain why the FBI is after her? Or what she had to do with the kidnappings? Please tell me she knows something."

"She knows something, but I'm not sure what to make of it."

"I need to know that the information she provides is credible, so let's start at the beginning. What does the FBI want with her? Was she involved with the other kidnappings?"

"Sorta, but not in the way you're thinking. She claims she's former FBI."

The captain sat straight up in his chair. "Is she rogue?"

"No. She's the key witness in a huge case, but she fled protective custody when it was clear the bad guys could get to her anyway."

"And you believe this?"

Zach tried to appear nonchalant. "I can't see much reason not to. The FBI's looking for her, sure, but all they sent was that dick Fields. If she were wanted for criminal activity, especially kidnapping, wouldn't they have sent in a squad with guns blazing?"

"You have a point. Unless she voluntarily surrenders and puts on a set of handcuffs herself, Fields isn't likely to apprehend her. That guy must be related to somebody important to keep his position. He's useless. So was she on the kidnapping case?"

"No, but while she was undercover, she stumbled across something that made her think a member of her primary target's family was part of it."

"Undercover, huh? Please tell me she wasn't a secretary or something in the mayor's office. My ulcer is already killing me."

"No, it wasn't that kind of family, exactly."

The captain frowned. "Then what kind of family was it?"

"The Hebert kind of family."

Captain Saucier stared at him, a stunned expression on his face. "No shit. This broad claims she was undercover in the Hebert clan? No wonder she's been hiding. I'm surprised she's not hiding at the bottom of the Mississippi."

"Me, too, but apparently Ms. Bordeaux is much more resourceful than the FBI or the Heberts ever imagined."

"Unbelievable. Well, that's a twist I didn't see coming."

"Me, either, sir."

"So this Bordeaux woman thinks one of the Hebert family is involved? Did she say which one?"

"Yeah, but word is he hasn't been seen for some time now. She doesn't think he's vacationing. At least not alive."

"Shit." The captain picked up a pen and tapped it on the desk. "So what do you make of this? It could be a different Hebert now, but what the hell? There's never been a ransom request, so what's the angle? The Heberts aren't known to participate in not-for-profit activities."

"I was thinking the political angle," Zach suggested.

"With the mayor." The captain dropped the pen and sat back in his chair. "Okay. So the question is, did they take the girl to strong-arm some favor or did they take the girl per mayor's orders, to boost his reelection ratings for future favors?"

"I couldn't say."

"Did the Bordeaux woman give you anything else?"

"Yeah. A Dr. Spencer. Apparently Ms. Bordeaux knew the girl. Used to see her go to a doctor's appointment across the street from her shop. The mother and girl used to stop in her store afterward."

"And did you talk to Spencer?"

"He's a cancer Specialist and says the girl is sick, but apparently the mother lied about her identity, and even the girl doesn't know what she's being treated for."

"Does the father know?"

Zach shook his head. "I don't think so, and the mother's definitely hiding something. She looked scared to death when I mentioned the mayor's connection to the other kidnappings."

"Please don't tell me this kid's going to die."

"Dr. Spencer doesn't think so, but the longer she goes without her medication..."

"Shit. Can you find this Bordeaux woman?"

Zach shrugged. "I don't know. Are you telling me to go against FBI orders and look for her?"

The captain stared out the window for a while, then looked back at Zach. "Yeah, that's exactly what I'm telling you to do."

Zach rose from his chair, holding in a smile. He'd just been officially given permission to be in Raissa's company, and God help him, that was something he wanted badly. Plus, he tried to tell himself, it would make things much easier going forward...for the investigation.

"And Blanchard," the captain said as Zach stepped out of the office, "keep this between the two of us."

Zach nodded. It went without saying.

Maryse rang up a candle purchase in Sabine's store and handed the woman her change and a bag with the candle. "Thank you, and please come again. Sabine will be back this weekend. I'm sure she'd be happy to schedule a reading for you."

The woman smiled. "Thank you. I look forward to meeting her."

Maryse watched until the woman left the shop and crossed the street before hurrying from the counter to the break room. Raissa was perched on a chair at the break-room table with a laptop in front of her. Maryse pulled a chair next to her and took a seat. "Did you get in yet?"

Raissa nodded. "Piece of cake."

Maryse looked at the screen that prominently displayed the hospital's medical records and felt her pulse quicken. "You're sure no one will track it back to you?"

"Someone would have to know I've broken in to even begin a trace. Mudbug General has simply horrible security. A high-school student could hack their system and never leave a trace."

"That's great to know, considering all my medical records are stored there."

"Don't sweat it. No one bothers with hospitals unless they're looking for something to blackmail people over. And since most people go to clinics and pay cash for the blackmailable sorts of health issues, hospitals aren't exactly hopping with hackers."

"Okay," Maryse said, not completely convinced. "So did you find anything?"

"There were five babies born during the time Helena was in the hospital having Hank. Three were girls, so that leaves only baby Frederick Agostino."

"What a mouthful."

"Tell me. Take a look at that birth weight." Raissa pointed to a line on a birth record. "Surely if Hank had been an eleven-pound baby, Helena would have mentioned that."

"Are you kidding me? If Helena had given birth to an eleven-pound baby, we'd have heard about it every day of her life, and she'd still be complaining after death. No one does persecution drama like Helena."

Raissa closed the program with the hospital records and accessed a Web browser. She typed in a search for Frederick Agostino, and Maryse was surprised when a number of hits were returned. Raissa laughed and Maryse leaned in to read some of the results.

"A family-owned Italian restaurant. That explains the birth weight. Mama Agostino probably ate them out of restaurant and home while she was pregnant."

Raissa clicked on one of the links and a news article about the restaurant appeared, complete with a picture of the Agostino family. It was obviously taken with a wide-angle lens.

"Well, that blows another theory," Maryse said with a sigh. "Frederick is the spitting image of his mother."

Raissa shook her head. "That is truly frightening, but you're right. There's no way Frederick isn't Mrs. Agostino's son."

"Which means we still don't know what happened to Helena's baby," Maryse said.

"Or where Hank came from."

"Maybe when those aliens take one person, they leave another."

Raissa shrugged. "It's as good a theory as any other. You think Helena will buy that her son's from another planet?"

Maryse sighed. "I would."

Hank walked Lila to her car, anxious over what he was about to do. It was a risk. A huge risk, and Hank Henry was not the risk-taking kind of guy, not anymore. But Lila was standing there in her yellow sundress, her long brown hair falling in gentle waves across her shoulder, and Hank was mesmerized.

He opened her car door for her and stood there with his hand still on top of the door. She placed her notebook inside and turned to smile at him. It was a smile that turned his insides into jelly and other places on him into something far less squishy. In all his years on earth, Hank had never met a woman who left him so unbalanced.

"Thanks," she said. "That first set of cabinets looks fabulous. I can't believe you got them built so quickly."

Hank blushed. "I might have worked a little overtime. I wanted to have something for you to look at when you came today."

"It's so exciting. Everything is going to look even better than I imagined, and the rooms are going to look like home and not a clinic." She placed one of her hands on top of his. "I'm so glad you're working here, Hank. You understand how important all this is. I'm very proud of you. And I have to say, I told you so."

Hank looked down at the ground. "Thanks, but I can't take all the credit." He looked back up at her. "You made a huge difference in my life, more so than anyone else ever has. You were a stranger, and you still believed in me. I didn't trust that at first. Didn't think it was possible for me to be anything other than what I'd always been. Probably still wouldn't if I hadn't met you."

Lila squeezed his hand and sniffed. "That's so nice, and it means a lot to me." She rubbed her nose with one finger and sniffed again. "My father was raised in harsh circumstances. He got into all sorts of trouble when he was a teenager, and people figured it was a given that he was going to spend most of his adult life in prison. But my mom saw something in him that no one else did, and she brought it out in him. He owns his own CPA firm and does really well."

"Wow. He must be really smart."

Lila grinned. "He was a bookie before that, so he said it just fit."

Hank laughed. "That's cool. Your mom must be a special woman. I guess that explains where you get it." He looked down at the ground again and fidgeted, trying to build up the courage for what he wanted to do. Finally, he took a deep breath and looked back up at her. "Would you like to have dinner with me sometime? I understand if you say no, since I was a patient, and now I'm an employee, and well, I know you have a reputation to protect—"

Lila placed a finger on his lips to stop his rambling. "I'd love to have dinner with you. I'm free on Friday." She leaned over and kissed him on the check. "I've got to run to my next appointment, but I'll see you tomorrow morning at eight for the walk-through with Chuck. We can make plans afterward."

Hank nodded, unable to speak, as Lila got in her car and pulled away from the curb with a wave. His cheek tingled where her lips had touched his skin, and he watched her car until it turned the corner at the end of the block and he could no longer see it.

"How touching." The voice sounded directly behind Hank and he spun around to face Rico Hebert.

"What do you want, Rico?" Hank asked.

"I want what Sonny wants."

"I've already told you I don't know anything. My ex-wife doesn't know anything, and her friend that might know something is out of the country getting married. I'm a dead end."

Rico nodded. "That's what you say, but that psychic woman's still missing. Her shop's closed. She's not at home, and Sonny would really like to find her."

"Yeah, well, tell Sonny to get in line."

"Sonny doesn't wait in line. Why should he?"

"Because according to my ex-wife, the New Orleans Police Department and the FBI are looking for Raissa, too. My ex has already gotten the shakedown from all of them and told them the same thing she told me—no one knows where Raissa is."

Rico frowned. "That's very unfortunate."

"Look, unfortunate or not, apparently the woman's good at not being found. If the FBI can't find her, my guess is Sonny's not going to, either."

Rico studied Hank for a couple of seconds. "Maybe your ex-wife knows more than she's saying."

Hank shook his head. "No way. If my ex knew anything, she would have told the cops or that new husband of hers, and *he* would have told the cops. She's got some damned code of ethics that men like you and I simply wouldn't understand. Raissa's gone, Rico, and no one that cares about her knows where. My ex and her friends are frantic. They're not faking."

"Maybe not, but that would be unfortunate. You know, you not being able to find out and all." Rico inclined his head toward the clinic. "All kinds of accidents happen on construction sites. Bad electrical wiring and such. Some of these places are known to just go up in flames. Least that's what I hear."

Hank clenched his hand into a fist and gritted his teeth, trying to control himself. Hitting Rico was a surefire way to bring down the house of cards. "That's what insurance is for, I suppose," Hank said, trying to sound as if he didn't care.

"Yeah. Unless, of course, insurance thinks the guy building the clinic did it himself. I hear insurance fraud is a real problem for business owners."

Hank felt his blood start to boil. He was going to blow it. He was going to throttle Rico Hebert to death right there in the street, and God help him, there wasn't a thing he could do to stop it.

"Hank." Chuck's voice sounded behind him.

Hank spun around and saw Chuck getting out of his truck just a few yards away from where he stood. It momentarily unnerved Hank that he'd been so focused on killing Rico that he hadn't even heard Chuck's truck pull up behind him. "Hi, Chuck."

Chuck glanced over at Rico, and Hank could tell he didn't like what he saw. "Is there a problem?" Chuck asked.

"No problem," Rico said. "I was just asking for directions." He nodded at Hank. "Thanks for the help."

Hank watched as Rico jumped in his car and drove away, then turned to face Chuck. "Sorry about that. Guy was a little weird. I think he was hopped up on something."

Chuck studied Hank's face for a couple of seconds, and Hank could tell he wasn't completely convinced. Finally, he nodded. "I just came by to drop off the rest of the front-office designs." He handed a tube to Hank. "Might as well give them to you. It's the front-desk layout and the ideas you came up with for furniture in the lobby. Great stuff, by the way."

"Thanks. It's hard to believe I actually get paid for this. This is fun."

Chuck nodded. "Shows in your work, too. I tell you, it's a rare person that finds they can make a living at something they love. You and me are lucky men, Hank." He looked over at the clinic. "You done for the day?"

"Not quite yet. I have one more cabinet to stain. I wanted to get one coat on all of them today, so I can finish them tomorrow."

Chuck clasped one hand on Hank's shoulder. "Sounds good. I'll see you tomorrow morning for the walk-through with Lila."

"Yes, sir," Hank said as Chuck walked to his truck and hopped inside.

Hank waved as Chuck pulled away from the curb, then crossed the street to the clinic. Maybe another hour and he'd be done for the evening. Then he could go home and figure out what the hell had motivated him to ask Lila on a date. If he couldn't come up with any reasonable explanation for canceling besides being scared, which wasn't exactly something a man liked to admit, then he was going to have to call Maryse and ask for a restaurant recommendation. And what to wear. Jesus, dating was filled with difficulty.

He closed the front door to the clinic behind him and locked it just in case Rico was lurking anywhere nearby. He didn't doubt the thug would plow right through a locked door if he really wanted what was on the other side, but at least Hank would hear him coming. He headed down the hall to the last room in the clinic. He'd been using that room to assemble and finish the cabinets, and his first masterpiece was resting in the center of the room, all stained except for the corner unit. He grabbed his can of stain and paintbrush and got to work on the cabinet facing.

Hank heard the intruder as soon as he entered the building. He probably thought he was being quiet, but the click of the front door lock releasing echoed straight through the silence of the clinic. Hank grabbed a screwdriver from his toolbox and slipped behind the row of cabinets he was working on. He paused one second, two seconds, trying to figure out where the person was, but there was only silence.

He edged away from the cabinets and pressed himself flat against the wall, then crept down the hall until he reached the doorway. He peered around, but the hallway was empty, and he couldn't detect the sound of another person moving around inside the building at all. But he knew what he'd heard, and the hair standing up on the back of his neck told him he hadn't been wrong. He was a lot of things, but fanciful wasn't one of them.

For the first time in a long time, he wished he'd broken the law and bought a handgun. He'd hoped it wouldn't be necessary, but that had been a foolish thought. Battling whoever was out there with a screwdriver didn't seem like the best option, but he couldn't think of another one.

He waited a couple of seconds but didn't see or hear a thing. Finally, he slipped out of the room and down the hall, careful to avoid stepping on anything that would give away his position. He peeked into each room as he passed, but they were empty. When he reached the lobby, he peered around the corner from the hallway and scanned the room. The door was shut, but he could see it was unlocked.

Had the intruder been a common thief, looking for construction-site tools? Maybe he'd left after hearing Hank in the back. That must be it. Hank crossed the lobby and opened the front door. The lawn and street in front of the clinic was empty, and the only cars on the street were those he'd seen earlier in the day. Absolutely nothing seemed out of place. Letting out a sigh of relief, he closed the door and locked it.

When he felt the sting of the needle, he immediately knew he'd grossly miscalculated.

The intruder must have been hiding behind the frame for the front desk, and whatever he'd been stuck with was making him woozy. Hank turned, trying to get a good look at his attacker, but the last thing he saw before crashing to the floor was two huge eyes and a bug-shaped face staring back at him.

Chapter Fifteen

Raissa closed the folder she'd been studying and tossed it onto her hotel-room bed. Maryse looked up from a set of paperwork. "Frustrated?"

"To say the least. Six hours of combing these files, and nothing. There has to be something those girls have in common besides looks. Why would anyone go to such lengths to abduct them and return them for no good reason?"

Maryse nodded. "There's a reason. We're just not seeing it. I keep waiting to hear about a ransom note, given the last girl was the mayor's granddaughter, but if there's been one, it's being kept really secret."

"Zach would have told me if there had been a ransom request. It would change everything."

Maryse cocked her head to the side and studied Raissa for a couple of seconds. "So, you want to talk about your relationship with Just One, or do I have to leave it all to my very vivid and creative imagination?"

"It's not a relationship, so there's really nothing to talk about."

Maryse raised her eyebrows. "Looked relationshippy to me when I walked in on you two naked. I couldn't help but notice the cleared area on one of the folding tables *and* that the bed wasn't rumpled in the least. That says something."

"*That* says hot, wild sex, and that's all there is to it."

"You sure?"

Raissa sighed. "How can I not be? Even if this all turns out for the best, and Melissa is safely back with her parents—even if the kidnapper is caught and jailed—that doesn't remove my biggest threat. As soon as this is over, I'll have to leave, whether the FBI takes part in it or not. I'm not safe in New Orleans any longer, and if I stay, I put everyone I care about at risk."

Maryse frowned. "So can you just not testify?"

Raissa shrugged. "They can subpoena me anyway. Then the price of freedom would be lying under oath, and that's *if* I manage to make it to court alive, which is questionable, given the FBI's inability to protect me in the past."

"That sucks, but it's only for another six months, right? I mean you could hide out until the statute of limitations has passed, and then you're in the clear."

"If Sonny lets it go. Remember, I was his confidante for two years. He chose me. He trusted me. This isn't just business for him—it's personal."

"But wouldn't your death just bring the heat on him all over again? I mean, if you've passed the time limit on what you could testify to, doesn't it make more sense to just leave you alone?"

"Mob business isn't always about common sense, although I have to admit that Sonny's more controlled than most. But six months is still a long time. Long enough for people to realize what they had was a flash in the pan due to a highly emotional situation. Six months after the fact, all that emotion and stress is gone. Things are normal."

"So what makes you think you and Zach can't do normal?"

Raissa laughed. "I don't know the first thing about normal, and I get the impression that Zach is trying to manage it but failing dreadfully. My less-than-conventional ways of handling things would only make things tougher for him, especially given his job. His captain is already watching him closely and if he knew half of the things Zach's already done for me against orders, he'd be fired in a heartbeat. I'm a huge liability, no matter what."

"Do you think you'll ever go back to law enforcement?"

"I will never go back to the FBI, and based on Zach's description, the police department appears a bit too stringent for my methods, too. But I have to admit that even though this entire situation with the abductions is very serious, I find myself enjoying it on some level."

Maryse nodded. "It's like my research. Even though I've lost people I love to cancer, I can't help getting excited when I'm working. The disease is still out there, and it's still killing people, but I get a personal thrill from things that would appear very minor to anyone else. A guilty pleasure, almost."

"Exactly. And don't get me wrong, between my business and the security gigs, I still got to use some of those skills—the hacking, surveillance. It was all part of the game, but it's not the same as doing it full-time and in the open."

"Maybe you should go solo, like Beau. Heck, he may even consider a partnership of some sort. You two would be a deadly combination."

Raissa momentarily considered Sabine's husband, Beau, and his private-investigation service. It wasn't the worst idea she'd ever heard, even if she did it alone in another state with another name. Despite what was logical, Raissa still doubted her ability to remain in New Orleans much longer or to ever return. It was simply too dangerous for everyone around her, but the last thing she wanted to do was press Maryse to accept that when they were up to their neck in things. "It's a thought."

"Did you ever have anyone to rely on, or who was dependent on you before? I mean, I figured if you did, they'd either have to go into protective custody with you or you'd have to leave them, right?"

Raissa nodded. "Those are the choices, but fortunately for me, my parents were already gone before I went undercover. I was so focused through high school and college, I didn't give men a second thought." She stared past Maryse and looked out the hotel-room window. "There was a guy once. We met at the FBI Academy."

"What happened?"

"He died."

Maryse's eyes widened. "Oh, wow. I'm sorry. I didn't mean to bring up anything bad."

"You didn't. My relationship with him was all good. He was a great guy—dedicated to his job and an assortment of nieces and nephews. Sturdy, but not in a boring way, you know?"

Maryse nodded.

"He was interesting and funny and I really enjoyed spending time with him. He always made me laugh, even when the academy training was getting the best of me."

"What happened?"

"He was on a special task force for missing kids."

Maryse gasped. "The missing girls…that's how you knew about the cases. He was the agent on them."

Raissa nodded, her mind flashing back to the night Ben had told her about his case. "We met at an all-night diner, in a part of town that Sonny's men wouldn't be likely to enter. Ben had flown in from D.C. for the day—that's all the time he could afford to take off. The latest kidnapping had happened two days before, and he wanted my advice."

"And he wanted to see you."

"Probably. I'd been under over a year and a half by then. We'd only seen each other four times since I'd gone undercover, but I still wanted to jump him right there on that table in the diner."

Maryse smiled. "You two were good together."

"I'd like to think so."

"So did he get killed investigating the kidnappings?"

"No. That's the worst part of the whole thing. A drunk driver hit his taxi on the way home from the airport. That cheap, greasy dinner in a rundown café was the last time I got to spend with him."

Maryse placed her hand on Raissa's arm. "I am so sorry."

"One of life's ironies, right? He spent every day of his life putting himself at risk, and everything was cut short by a drunk. What a waste."

Maryse nodded.

"It just makes you think twice, you know? About how no matter what, you're never really safe. And then with our job, we were at risk even more than regular people. Makes you think hard about getting involved again."

"If Sabine could take that risk, then you can, too."

Raissa sighed. "Fortunately, I don't have to think about it. I can't say for certain how Zach feels, but I seriously doubt he's mentally picking out matching luggage. I'm a temporary distraction during a temporary situation, and soon I'll be gone. No risk at all." She picked up another folder and started to read.

"Your parents...were they still alive when you went into the FBI?"

"No. My dad died when I was eight. He was a fighter pilot and died in a training accident testing new aircraft. My mother passed my last year of college. Congestive heart failure. It ran in her family, and after my dad died, she never really took care of herself. She just sorta faded away."

"That sucks, but at least you have some good memories." Maryse stared down at the folder in her hands.

"I do," Raissa said, her heart going out to her friend. Maryse had never known her mother. She'd died when Maryse was too young to remember her. So, despite all the regrets and blame Raissa might fling at her mother, Maryse was right—there were still years of good memories she could draw on.

Maryse looked up at Raissa, her brow scrunched in thought. "What about the parents?"

"I just told you about my parents."

"No, sorry. Not your parents, the girls'. Maybe it's the parents who have something in common."

Raissa thought about all the families. "Well, they all live in different states. Until now, there were no political affiliations."

"Professions?"

Raissa slowly shook her head. "All your basic blue-collar type work. A mechanic, a fireman, a fisherman...I can't see how that has anything to do with—"

Maryse waved a hand. "Before. What about before they were firemen and fishermen and all that?"

Raissa picked up a file and scanned the history. "All I've got here is a couple of years before the kidnappings. I don't know that anyone went back further, as kidnappers rarely need that long to plan. Why? What are you thinking?"

"I don't know. I mean, it's not likely they met in college, given the professions, but what about the military? Did anyone ever ask them if they knew the other families?"

Raissa stared at Maryse. "I don't think so. There's no record of it, anyway."

Maryse frowned. "I suppose we'd go directly to jail if you hacked the military, right?

Raissa smiled. "Oh, yeah, but don't worry, I've got a better idea."

"What's that?"

"The Social Security Administration." Raissa reached for a spare laptop and Mildred's car keys.

Maryse sighed. "Yeah, much safer."

"Actually, it is. They have simply horrible security."

"There's a pleasant thought." Maryse placed a hand on Raissa's arm. "Let's try it my way first."

"Your way? Maryse, you've been holding out on me?"

Maryse grabbed one of the spare laptops and plopped back on the bed. "Hardly," she said, and started typing. "Give me the father of the first girl."

Raissa picked up the file and read the name.

Maryse tapped on the keyboard, hit enter, scrolled a bit, and clicked the mouse. She looked up at Raissa with a triumphant smile and turned the laptop toward her.

Raissa leaned over and stared in amazement. "Facebook? Your big investigative trick is Facebook?"

Maryse nodded and tapped the screen. "Look at the history. He's listed everyplace he ever worked, including his military service. When his wife got pregnant, they were stationed in North

Carolina." Maryse turned the laptop around and waved a hand at Raissa. "Give me another name."

Raissa grinned and picked up the file. The young dog had just taught the old dog a new trick. She'd opened the file to read off the name when the computer next to her started beeping.

Maryse looked up in alarm. "What is it?"

"It's the bug in Sonny's house." Raissa tapped some keys on the keyboard and Sonny's voice boomed out of the laptop.

"Damn it!" he yelled. "Why haven't you brought me anything? What the hell are you waiting for?"

"Taylor or Raissa, whatever she calls herself now," another guy said.

"Forget her," Sonny said. "Have any of you found out anything at all about that kidnapping?"

There was silence for a couple of seconds, then finally another guy said, "There's no word on the street, Sonny. That kid wasn't taken by anyone we know or have business ties with. Maybe it's just some perv, you know?"

"Get out," Sonny said. "Except you, Rico."

They heard the door click shut and then someone sighed.

"I don't like this," Sonny said.

"Neither do I, but the guys are right. This wasn't any of our associates or competitors. They're baffled we're even asking."

"I want to know what Monk Marsella involved this family in."

"Does it really matter, now? I mean, Monk's been gone for months now."

"Yeah, it matters," Sonny said, "because I want to know what was so important that it got him killed, and why it's happening again. Don't tell me the cases aren't related."

"I'm not saying that. Our sources indicate the police are looking into the old cases as well. They've made the connection. Probably from Taylor. She's a problem, you know. I think you ought to let me take care of her."

"No. If anyone can figure out what's going on, it's her. She's brilliant, or she'd never have fooled me. Leave her to work with the police. They'll never figure this out without help, and time's running out."

"You going soft, Sonny? This really ain't none of our business."

"Watch what you're saying, Rico. I ain't soft, but this is a kid we're talking about. We don't deal in wives, and we damned sure don't deal in kids. You know the rules. You want this family associated with whatever perverted shit is probably being done to those girls?"

"No, I suppose not."

"What about Hank Henry?"

"Ain't nothing going on there that I can see," Rico said. "I've been watching him close like, but he only goes to work and home. Ain't nobody else hassling him or anything."

"Keep watching. I'm sure that's the name Monk said before he died. If Hank isn't doing anything, then he must know something."

"Maybe, or maybe Monk just thought he did. The guy wasn't all that bright, you know?"

"Yeah, but it doesn't take smarts to run up on something bad," Sonny said. "Keep checking on Taylor, too, but you do not have authority to move on her, got it?"

"I got it, for now. But afterward…when this circus is over?"

"I'll deal with it then."

There was some shuffling and the door opening and closing, then silence. Maryse looked over at Raissa, her eyes wide.

"What in the world is Hank involved in now?" Maryse asked.

"I don't know, and I'm willing to bet Hank doesn't know, either. Apparently he's mixed up in something to do with Monk, but even Hank doesn't know what."

"Are you sure?" Maryse asked, drily.

Raissa nodded. "Yeah, I'm pretty sure. He was spooked that night we talked. I can usually tell when someone's holding back, but Hank just looked clueless. Whatever he knows, he doesn't realize how important it is. Or maybe he doesn't know or remember at all. Either way, he's not safe. I need to call and warn him."

Maryse nodded. "So if the Heberts didn't take that girl, who did?" Maryse asked.

Raissa looked at Maryse, a million thoughts—mostly bad—rolling around in her head. "I have no idea, but apparently Sonny thinks I can find out."

"I don't understand. If Sonny told his guys to leave you alone, then who's been trying to kill you?"

"That's a really good question."

It was close to midnight when Zach let himself into the Mudbug Hotel. He half-expected to find Raissa already in bed—or at least he hoped—but when he pushed the door open, it wasn't exactly the scene he'd envisioned on the forty-five-minute drive to Mudbug. Raissa was in bed, but she was wearing more clothes than he'd imagined, and he hadn't counted on her being surrounded by paper, either.

"Am I interrupting?" he asked, realizing she was so engrossed in whatever she was doing that she hadn't even heard him open the door.

"Crap!" Raissa jumped up from the bed at the sound of his voice. "Why are you sneaking up on me?"

Zach laughed. "Are you kidding me?" He waved one hand at the rows of computer equipment. "You could have seen what I was wearing as soon as I drove into town if you were watching your security. Unlike your ghostly friend, I cannot walk through walls, nor am I invisible."

"That's a good thing, or you'd be dead."

"True. Speaking of dead people, she's not in here, right?"

"Helena? No, why?"

"Well, I was sorta hoping you'd have on fewer clothes, so I thought maybe she was here."

Raissa laughed and jumped up from the bed. "I promise to have on fewer clothes later, but first I have to show you what Maryse and I found."

Zach's mind immediately shifted from carnal thoughts to the case. No way Raissa was this excited over nothing. "What did you find?"

Raissa grabbed a bunch of papers off the bed and sat at the table, spreading them out in front of her. Zach pulled up a chair next to her, ready for the show. "Maryse and I spent the afternoon going through the FBI files, trying to make a connection among the girls."

Zach placed his hands over his ears. "I'm not hearing anything about hacking."

"Wimp." Raissa said and pulled his hands down. "I wanted to find the common denominator in the abductions. I've never believed it was on looks alone. It just doesn't feel right, you know?"

Zach nodded. He thought there was far more to it than they had been able to discern. "So you found something about the girls?"

"No, their parents."

"Like what? They lived in different places, had different jobs... No reason their paths would cross."

Raissa smiled and handed him a stack of papers. "Unless they were all in the military. Check those papers. Three of them were stationed at Myrtle Beach."

Zach looked down at the first sheet. "Facebook? You're hinging a kidnapping investigation on Facebook."

Raissa shrugged. "I wanted to hack the Social Security Administration. Maryse's way was safer."

Zach gave a silent prayer of thanks. "And legal. Remember legal?"

Raissa waved a hand in dismissal. "Forget that. Don't you see—they were all at the same base. The last guy doesn't have a Facebook account, but what do you want to bet he was stationed there, too?"

"Were they all there at the same time?"

"No, but within the same year, seventeen years ago."

"And the FBI never caught that before?"

Raissa shook her head. "They wouldn't have looked that far back initially, and when the lead investigator died, it got shuffled around a bit. There was a lot of terrorist activity going on then and most of the agents were redirected."

"Then it went cold."

"Yeah. They probably figured whoever did it was dead or in prison, and the reality is, the predators who don't return kids alive are a higher priority than the one guy who returns them all seemingly unscathed."

"So he got conveniently off radar and no one noticed a connection."

"Until now. And guess who else just happened to be present on the base during that time?"

"Please don't tell me it was the mayor."

"Okay, I won't tell you, but you need to check this bio we pulled off the City of New Orleans Web site. The mayor spent his last year of service as an instructor…"

"…in Myrtle Beach. Shit."

"Guess who else was there?"

"I'm afraid to ask?"

"Our friend Dr. Spencer."

Zach ran one hand through his hair. "Did he have that listed on his Facebook page, too?"

Raissa grinned. "No. We called and asked."

Chapter Sixteen

Zach stared at Raissa, unable to wrap his mind around everything she'd just told him, much less what any of it meant. "You're sure?"

"Yep. Dr. Spencer is ex-military and did a part-time stint on the base when they were short on medical personnel. A lot of the boys had returned from the Gulf War and needed care. He flew up there two weeks a month for over a year."

"And the military just gave you this information because you asked?"

"Not me, Maryse. She explained who she was and the project she's working on—she has government funding, you know—and besides, the officer who worked in records is from New Orleans."

"So he gave out information over the phone to a stranger because she has government funding and he used to live in New Orleans."

Raissa nodded. "I was impressed with Maryse, too. She explained that she was considering him for work on her project, as he's a cancer specialist, but wanted to make sure he was telling the truth about his work with the military, since she has the utmost respect for military personnel and didn't want him sneaking in the door with a lie. She didn't ask for details, more like job-reference sort of stuff—what he was there for and when."

"You think Spencer knew the victims' parents?"

"I can't prove anything, but I think it's far too big a thing to be a coincidence."

Zach shook his head. "I agree, but what does it tell us?"

Raissa sighed. "I have absolutely no idea. That's why you found me sitting in bed with stacks of paper—my back hurt from the chair. But I still haven't made sense of it. It's all fascinating and can't possibly be irrelevant, but for the life of me, I can't come up with anything that fits."

"This case just keeps getting stranger."

"And that's not all." Raissa told him about the conversation between Sonny and Rico.

"Do you know this Hank?"

"A little. More secondhand than anything else. Apparently he owed the Heberts money and did a few jobs to pay off his debt."

"But you don't think he's involved with the kidnapping?"

"I don't see how. He's not the kind of guy you'd trust with delicate work."

Zach nodded. "I don't like the Hebert angle of this one bit. I don't care what Sonny said to night. He could just as easily change his mind about you tomorrow morning and alert his guys by cell phone. You won't have any idea he's coming."

Raissa waved a hand at the computers. "That's why I'm always prepared."

Zach ran one hand through his hair, his emotions warring inside of him. Finally, he said, "Maybe you should talk to Agent Fields. See what the FBI is offering."

"No way."

"But—"

"I'm not cutting out of here until this is over."

Zach could have sworn his heart stopped beating for just a moment. *Moron. You always knew she'd have to leave.* But had he? Had he really given any thought to what would happen to Raissa when the case was over? And when had it become important? He was attracted to her, and he admired her, and worried about her, but that was all. Right?

"Zach?" Raissa's voice broke him away from his thoughts.

"Huh." He looked at Raissa. "Sorry, I was thinking."

"Obviously. You didn't hear the last two things I said. Well, did you figure anything out during all that thinking?"

"No," Zach said, "not really." Except that he'd complicated his personal life right along with his career, all with the same woman. It had to be some kind of record.

"Well, I say we call it a night and start on this again tomorrow when our brains aren't fried."

"Sounds good to me."

Raissa gave him a sexy smile and started unbuttoning her shirt. "So let's see what I can do about that 'fewer clothes' thing you mentioned earlier."

"Raissa, what exactly are we doing here?"

Raissa stopped unbuttoning her blouse and looked directly at him. "I thought it was obvious."

He stared at her—the black lace of her bra peeking out the top of her partially unbuttoned blouse—and his mind warred with other parts of his body that were far more powerful. "You're right," he said, and took over on the buttons where she'd left off. Raissa knew exactly what he was asking, but she'd intentionally avoided the question. For that matter, he'd allowed it. He opened her shirt and pushed it over her shoulders.

But they were going to have to talk about it sometime. Sooner would probably be better than later.

Bright and early Friday morning, Chuck and Lila stood in front of the clinic. Chuck punched in Hank's cell-phone number for the fourth time in the last ten minutes, but Lila could hear the call go straight to voice mail.

"I'm sorry," Chuck apologized. "I just don't know what's keeping Hank. He's usually so punctual, and he always calls if anything comes up."

Lila frowned, trying not to think of all the wrong reasons for Hank to be late for their meeting. She didn't want to believe his change was temporary. Surely, something had delayed him, and he'd be there soon. "That's okay. Maybe we should just start the walk-through without him. I'm sure he'll be here soon."

Chuck nodded and reached for the door. He stopped short when he realized it was already unlocked. "What the heck?" He turned the knob and pushed the door open. "Hank? You in here?" He looked back at Lila. "Let's go check."

They stepped inside and Chuck called out again, "Hank? Where are you?" Nothing. Chuck walked down the hallway of the clinic, checking in the rooms as he went. Lila followed behind.

"Chuck?" A voice yelled from the front doorway.

Chuck turned around and saw his assistant foreman, Jimmy, standing in the doorway. "Yeah, Jimmy, we're back here. Looking for Hank. You seen him?"

Jimmy walked down the hallway to join them. "Nah, but I just got here. Had a flat on the truck this morning. Musta picked up a nail." Jimmy pointed to the back of the clinic. "Hank was working on a set of cabinets in the last office when I left yesterday. He's probably got his iPod playing and can't hear you."

"Maybe so," Chuck agreed, and headed for the back office.

Lila hurried after him, hoping the explanation was that simple and that benign. Chuck stopped short in the doorway. Lila inched to the side of him and peered into the room. It was empty, but something was wrong. She took it all in—the tools left out on the floor, the table saw that was still plugged in. She started to take a step into the room and her foot brushed against something on the floor. She looked down and realized it was an open can of stain.

"This isn't right," Lila said.

"No. It feels all wrong," Chuck agreed. He nudged the can of stain with his boot. "That stain has been open for a long time." He pointed to the top of the ladder in the corner. Hank's wallet and keys were perched on top where he always placed them. "Jimmy," Chuck called out. "You see Hank's truck out there?"

Jimmy opened the back door and looked outside. "Yeah, it's here. Same exact place it was yesterday. Weird."

Chuck backed out of the office and motioned for Lila to follow him. "We're going outside, and I'm going to call the police. Don't touch anything, okay?"

"Chuck, what in the world is going on?" Lila felt the blood drain from her face and she stumbled in the hallway. Chuck grabbed her arm and steadied her, guiding her out of the clinic and onto the front lawn. Lila took a deep breath, then looked at Chuck. "What is it? You know something."

Chuck pulled his cell phone from his pocket and dialed 911. He told the dispatcher he wanted to report a break-in and possible missing person. "They said someone will be here shortly," he said and closed the phone. "There was a guy parked across the street yesterday talking to Hank. It didn't look like a friendly sort of conversation."

"What did he want?"

"I don't know. Hank tried to play it off that the guy wanted directions, but I didn't buy it. And I didn't like the look of the guy. Now this. There's no way in hell Hank Henry left this clinic with power tools plugged in, stain uncovered, and his wallet and keys still on that ladder—not voluntarily, anyway."

Lila covered her mouth with her hand, worry and fear washing over every square inch of her body. "Oh, no."

Chuck looked Lila in the eye. "I know about all that doctor-patient-privilege stuff, but if you know what Hank was involved in before he went into rehab, I think I need to know. I think the police are gonna need to know."

Lila nodded, not concerned in the least about the ethics of the situation. All she wanted was Hank, safe and sound and staining cabinets at her clinic. "He got into trouble gambling. Owed the wrong people money. He worked it off, but never gave me details as to how, exactly. He only said that work is what sent him to rehab."

"What people?" Chuck asked, the fear in his eyes clear as day.

"The Hebert family."

Chuck closed his eyes and blew out a breath. "Dear Lord," he whispered.

Even though it was every bit of eighty degrees outside, Lila shivered.

Zach was still sound asleep when his cell phone started ringing. He reached for the nightstand, but all he found was air. Confused, he opened one eye, and that's when he remembered that he wasn't home—he was in a hotel with the hottest and most dangerous woman he'd ever met.

He hopped out of bed and dug through a pile of hastily discarded clothes scattered across the hotel-room floor. Finally, he located his pants and pulled the phone from the pocket, managing to answer the call just before it went to voice mail.

"Damn it, Blanchard!" the captain yelled. "What the hell took you so long to answer? It's eight thirty, and your ass was supposed to be at the station at eight. You got ten minutes to get here before I demote you to dogcatcher."

Shit! "Uh, that's not going to be possible..."

"It's possible from anywhere in New Orleans."

"I'm not exactly in New Orleans."

"Well, where the hell are you?"

Zach paused. "Uh...following up on a lead?"

He heard Raissa laugh and covered the speaker part of his phone.

"Did that lead require you to spend the night? Oh, no, do not tell me that your 'lead' involves crystal balls."

"Of course not, sir." His balls were absolutely not made of crystal. "I'll be there in forty minutes. I promise."

He snapped his phone shut and shoved it in his pocket along with his wallet. Then he grabbed his keys off the dresser. "I can't believe you let me sleep this late."

"Late? Good Lord, please don't tell me you're a morning person."

He looked over at her lying back in the bed, all rumpled and sexy. "I could probably be persuaded in that direction, but not today. The captain's in one of his yelling moods. I need to go take some abuse." He gave Raissa a quick kiss. "I'll call you as soon as I run Spencer through the database."

It was forty-two minutes later when Zach pulled up in front of the police station and hurried inside. He'd deal with parking in a tow zone as soon as the captain got done yelling.

"Blanchard!" the captain sounded off before he'd even gotten completely through the doorway. "My office—now!"

Zach saw Detective Morrow smirk as he rushed past his desk, but for once, he didn't even care. He had far bigger fish to fry. Hell, he had the whole Atlantic Ocean of fish to fry. He hurried into the captain's office and closed the door behind him.

The captain was pacing the length of his office and Zach almost ran into the man when he entered the office. "We've got trouble."

Zach felt his pulse rise. The captain's voice was different from when he'd talked to him at the hotel. Something was up. "What kind of trouble?"

"Another missing person."

Zach felt a rush of blood to his head. "You're kidding me. That's not the MO."

"It's not another girl. This is an adult male."

Relief washed over Zach. "Then it's probably not related."

"I know. Likely this has nothing to do with the Franco case, but it's the second goddamned missing person in a week. I'm catching hell all the way around here, Blanchard. I hope that psychic woman was able to give you a lead."

"Nothing solid yet, but there's a couple of things I want to look into."

The captain nodded. "You tell me as soon as you have something. First, I need you to check out this other case. Make sure it has nothing to do with the Francos."

"I don't think that's a good idea. I'd be wasting time when I could be looking into those leads."

"I know that, but you're also the only one in contact with the Bordeaux woman. I want you to see the crime scene so you can relay the details to her. Make sure there's not something in the FBI files that was missed or that we weren't given. I don't want that information second- and third-hand."

"No problem, sir. I'll get on it right away."

He took the sheet of paper with the crime-scene address on it from the captain and hurried through the station and back to his car. At least he hadn't been there long enough to get towed. He pulled away from the curb, his tires squealing. This was a colossal waste of time. If the captain hadn't been insistent, he'd have found some way to get out of it. He glanced down at the address and turned right at the red light.

Ten minutes later, he pulled up in front of a construction site. An older man and a woman stood out front with a patrolman. They both looked worried. Zach crossed the lawn, displaying his badge as he approached. "I'm Detective Blanchard. What's going on here, B and E?"

The patrolman shook his head. "No sign of forced entry, and nothing missing but the cabinetmaker."

"Maybe he's sick or didn't want to do the job any longer."

"No way," the older man said. He extended his hand. "I'm Chuck Daigle. I own the construction company building this clinic." He waved a hand at the worried woman. "This is Lila Comeaux. She's the owner of the clinic. We both know the man who's missing, and neither of us thinks this is in character. In fact, we'd swear to it."

Zach held in a sigh. He'd heard that all too often. "Any signs of a struggle?"

"No," the patrolman answered, "but there are some irregularities that make me think these two might be right. Let me show you."

Zach followed the patrolman into the clinic and down the hall, Chuck and Lila trailing behind. They stepped into the last room, and the patrolman pointed to a ladder in the corner of the room. "The guy's wallet and keys are on top of that ladder. His truck's out back and hasn't moved from where it was parked yesterday."

"There's more," Chuck said. "The table saw was still plugged in. There was an open can of stain right there in the middle of the floor with the brush right beside it, and from the way the stain was set on top, it had been open for a while. There's no way he just left things like that."

Zach walked around the room, studying the area. Considering it was a construction site, the room was pristine, but then, since he was staining cabinets in this area, it needed to be. He took a look at the cabinets and decided it was probably some of the best workmanship he'd ever seen. Everything about this guy said orderly and dedicated. As much as he hated to admit it, something was wrong with this picture.

"Anyone check where he lives?"

The patrolman nodded. "I sent a guy by there as soon as I saw the scene here. Apartment manager let him in, but the place looks fine. No sign of forced entry and no sign of the guy."

Zach blew out a breath and lifted the wallet from the ladder. "I'll take his wallet and keys, run him through the system...see if we can come up with anything. So who is this cabinetmaker?"

"His name is Hank Henry," Chuck said. "He's really been doing a fine job here. Something must be wrong."

Zach froze. Surely, it wasn't the same Hank that Raissa had mentioned last night. The one that Sonny Hebert's men were "watching." He flipped the wallet open and pulled out the driver's license. It was a lousy picture, like most licenses. He needed to run the guy as soon as possible.

The patrolman nodded his head toward Chuck. "Chuck tells me Hank's had some trouble in the past but nothing to speak of since being on-site, until yesterday."

"What happened yesterday?"

"There was a guy," Chuck said. "Looked like he was hassling Hank."

"Did you ask about it?" Zach asked.

"Yeah, but the guy said he was asking for directions, then took off. I don't think it was the truth. The guy…well, I don't know how to say this without incriminating myself, but he reminded me of some of the ilk I had to deal with when I first got started in construction. You know the type."

"The type that shake you down for money if you want to stay in business?" Yeah, Zach knew the type, and it was hitting far too close to home.

"Yeah," Chuck said. "I'm not saying that's what was going on, but I don't believe the guy was asking for directions, either."

"Would you recognize the guy if you saw him again?"

Chuck nodded. "I'm pretty sure I would."

"Good. I'll send someone over with some pictures…see if you can help us with another angle to investigate. Will you be here all day?"

"Until five or so." He reached into his pocket and handed Zach a card. "Give me a call. If I'm not here, I can meet anywhere to look at the pictures. Doesn't matter what time."

"Great," Zach said, and slipped the card into his pocket. "If there's nothing else I need to see here, I'm going to head back to the station and get working on this." He pulled his cards from his pocket and handed Chuck and Lila each one. "If there's anything you can think of that you forgot to tell me, please call me anytime."

As soon as Zach got into his car, he reached for his laptop and connected with the police database. He typed in Hank's information and waited while the system searched. A couple of seconds later, a clear picture of Hank Henry appeared on the screen. Shit.

He stared at the screen, hoping his initial reaction had been incorrect, but even with a closer look, he knew he wasn't. This was the guy he'd seen going into Raissa's apartment that night. The one she'd met in the alley. He'd completely forgotten about it, with everything else going on. And then it hit him where he'd seen the name before—in the police records on Maryse's many adventures.

Hank Henry was Maryse's ex-husband, son of a murdered ghost.

Knew him secondhand, my ass. Raissa Bordeaux had a lot of explaining to do.

Chapter Seventeen

Raissa walked into the coffee shop in downtown New Orleans wearing blue jeans, a polo shirt, and a black bob. She ordered her usual latte and took a seat in a far corner nearest the exit, where she had a clear view down the street of her shop, and more importantly, Dr. Spencer's office. She saw Helena huff down the sidewalk, then look back and glare. Because Raissa had refused to drop an invisible passenger off in front of the building and wouldn't buy Helena a latte until they left, Helena was pouting.

Raissa grinned at the agitated ghost and wondered if Helen would find anything of interest in Dr. Spencer's office. She rather doubted it. Surely he wasn't stupid enough to keep information on whatever he was mixed up in right there, where a search warrant could find it. But criminals weren't always smart, and Helena was invisible.

Despite Zach's assurances that he'd do a thorough check on their friend Dr. Spencer, Raissa was pretty sure he didn't have clearance for military records. Having Helena check out his office was a long shot, but you never knew what a long shot might turn up.

She opened her laptop, intending to make a list of all the items they'd discovered that didn't add up. Sometimes seeing the facts in print made her mind turn in a different direction, find a connection she hadn't seen before. Instead, she stared at the blank document, her thoughts drifting off to the night before, and Zach.

She'd been stunned when he asked what they were doing. She knew exactly what he wanted to know, but the reality was, she didn't have an answer. At least not one that made it seem anything but cheap and tawdry, and that's not at all how she felt. Zach brought out feelings in her that she'd never felt before. She'd never met anyone else who agonized with what was right and what was policy the way she did. He struggled with everything, as she had before her stint with Sonny.

That stint had changed everything. That and the kidnappings. The bad guys weren't all bad. The good guys and the rules weren't all good. And for the first time in her life, Raissa had had to learn how to live in shades of gray. Some people managed it easily, but Raissa felt it said a lot about a person if they struggled with creating a balance.

She let out a sigh. Not that any of it mattered. The reality was, Raissa's time in New Orleans was fast drawing to an end. One way or another, time was up in two days, assuming the kidnapper stuck to his MO.

Melissa Franco would be back at home with no memory of what had happened and unable to provide them a single lead. And Raissa would quietly disappear.

Again.

Raissa blew out a breath and stared out the plate-glass window across from her table. She'd run before, many times. There had been six other towns, six other identities, and countless other jobs before she'd landed back in New Orleans as Raissa Bordeaux. But this was the first time she'd felt she belonged. She had a job she enjoyed, that challenged her on some level even if it wasn't the thrill ride she was used to. She had all the money she needed from the security gigs, a comfortable apartment, and some of the best friends anyone could ever ask for.

And she had Zach.

Well, *had* was too strong a word, but Raissa liked to believe that if things were different, they might have made a go of it. It had been a long time since Raissa had allowed anyone that close to her. It scared her and excited her and depressed her all at the same time. It was going to be hard to let go…of everything.

Her cell phone's ringing yanked her out of her thoughts and she glanced at the display. Zach. That was fast. She opened the phone. "You got information on Spencer already?"

"No," Zach replied, his voice tight and hard. "I have another problem. One I'm hoping you can help me with."

Raissa felt her heart rate speed up. "What's wrong?"

"I was watching your apartment one night, and I saw you with a guy. He was hiding in the alley, but you brought him up to your apartment. I need to know what your relationship is with him."

Raissa frowned, completely confused. "You're in the middle of a kidnapping investigation and you're calling me about some jealous, macho stuff?"

"Give me a break. I'm calling because there was another kidnapping last night, and that guy I saw go into your apartment is the one missing. The same guy you claimed to only know secondhand, remember?"

Raissa clenched her phone. "What happened?"

"Looks like someone snagged him from his work site yesterday evening or last night. He came to see you damned near in the middle of the night, Raissa, and I already ran a check on him. I know all about Hank Henry's past. The construction company owner said some guy was at the site yesterday. He thought the guy was hassling Hank. Who's tailing him?"

"Rico Hebert."

"Damn it! You told me he wasn't involved in the kidnappings."

"I don't think he was."

"Then what did they want from him? The fool didn't learn the first time?"

"It wasn't Hank they wanted. Rico was shaking down Hank for information on me. He told me about it immediately after it happened."

"So that night he came to your place…"

"Was the first time I'd ever met him."

"And he thought it would be smart to accost you in an alley? What in the world did he tell you that couldn't wait until the next day?"

Raissa took a deep breath, knowing Zach wasn't going to like that she'd kept this from him. "He told me that one of the Heberts asked him to kill me."

There was dead silence on the other end of the line, and Raissa could practically feel Zach's anger over the phone. "Why didn't you tell me?"

"Because if they'd wanted me dead, I already would be. I think they were sending a warning, hoping I'd pack and leave. They knew Hank was no killer and probably figured he'd tell Maryse, who'd tell me."

"And that's why this Rico kept hassling him? You *did* leave. Why stay on the guy?"

"I don't know for sure. All I can figure is that since Monk mentioned Hank's name before he died, Sonny thinks he knows something about the kidnappings. I think he's got a tail on him to see if it leads anywhere."

"Like figuring out what Monk was into?"

"Exactly."

"And what do you think?"

"I think Hank is clueless. If he saw or heard something he wasn't supposed to, he has no idea what it is. I covered that ground with him already. He's not faking, or I would know."

"So maybe he just owed this Monk money, like he did everyone else in the state."

"Maybe, but then why was he kidnapped? Easier to just put a bullet through his head to leave a message for others who are thinking about banking with the Heberts."

"Shit. This situation is getting out of hand. A missing girl, a missing gambler, a lying doctor, a mayor with a shaky background, and far too many black Cadillacs for my taste."

"I know, I know. I'm trying to make sense of it, but then something else happens and I get even more confused than before. There has to be something we're missing. Did you get the check on Spencer yet?"

"No. I'll run it as soon as I get to the station and tell my captain about Hank. Not that I have any idea what I'm going to say."

"Just tell him what you got from the crime scene and witnesses. We'll figure it out, Zach, I promise. I need to call Maryse. I need to warn her and Mildred to be extra careful."

"Good idea. I'll call as soon as I can. Worry about keeping *yourself* safe, while you're at it."

Raissa disconnected with Zach and dialed Maryse's number. No answer. Damn. She didn't want to panic Mildred or Maryse. This might all amount to a bunch of nothing, even though she had a very bad feeling. Finally, she sent Maryse a text message asking her to call as soon as she got a chance.

She'd use the time in between to get everything down in writing, including this latest bit of trouble. And she'd figure out how to tell Maryse that her ex-husband was missing…again.

Ten minutes later, she shut her laptop and looked up to see Helena exiting Spencer's office. She glanced down at her watch. That was fast. She shoved the laptop in her bag and bought a coffee for Helena before leaving the shop to meet her on the street. How in the world was she supposed to tell the ghost that her son was missing? Raissa quickly ran through all the facts she had on Hank and potential scenarios, and finally decided to hold off for now.

They could be wrong. Hank could have fallen off the wagon and gone on a gambling bender and would show up in a day or two. Then she would have worried Helena for nothing.

And if the Heberts have him…

Her gut clenched. But it didn't change her decision. If the Heberts had gotten to Hank, then telling Helena now or later wasn't going to change the outcome. She tried to look normal as she hopped into the car. Helena was already sitting in the passenger's seat, gazing longingly at the latte. Raissa passed the cup over and pulled away from the curb.

"You weren't there very long," Raissa said. "Did Spencer show up or something?"

"No. There wasn't a lot to look at."

"What do you mean?"

"The place is almost bare. There's still a receptionist area with all the décor and computers, and the exam room looks like an exam room, but his office is almost wiped clean. No files, no books, no pictures. Did he say anything to you about moving?"

"No. In fact, he told me a couple of months ago that he'd renewed his lease for another three years."

Helena took a huge gulp of coffee and sighed with contentment. "You think he's making a run for it."

"It certainly looks that way."

"But what's he running from?"

Raissa shook her head. "If we had the answer to that, I think we'd blow this whole case wide open."

Maryse looked up as the bells over Sabine's shop door jangled, hoping it was Mildred or Raissa, but instead a petite, pretty blonde woman stepped hesitantly inside. The store had been swamped with business that morning, and the last customer had left only seconds before. Maryse had been hoping to return a call to Raissa, who'd sent her a text message earlier, but so far, there was no sign of a break in store traffic.

Maryse plastered on a smile and walked over to the woman. "Good morning. Can I help you find anything?"

The woman clutched her purse. "I hope so. Are you Maryse Robicheaux?"

Maryse studied the woman's face, trying to figure out if she was supposed to know her, but absolutely nothing came to mind. "Yes, I'm Maryse."

"My name is Lila." She extended her hand. "We've never met, so don't worry about offending me."

Maryse shook her hand. "Was it that obvious?"

"You're Southern. It's sorta a given."

"What can I help you with, Lila? If you're interested in a reading, Sabine will be back next week."

Lila's expression grew serious. "I wanted to talk to you about Hank."

"You know Hank?" Of all the things in the world Maryse figured the woman may want, information on Hank was the last thing that she would have thought of. "You don't look like a bookie, loan shark, or cop."

Lila blushed. "I'm not any of those things. I'm his boss."

"I thought his boss was some guy named Chuck?"

"Chuck is the owner of the construction company, but I'm the owner of the clinic that's being built. Hank's building the cabinets." Lila tucked a strand of hair behind her ear, her hand shaking.

Maryse placed her hand on Lila's arm. The woman was clearly distressed, and if it had anything to do with Hank Henry, she probably had good reason to be. "Let me put out the closed sign and we can talk in the break room. I have tea and coffee and might even be able to stir up something stronger."

Lila gave her a grateful nod. "That would be great."

Maryse flipped the sign in the front window and locked the door. She motioned to Lila and headed to the back of the store to the break room. "Have a seat," Maryse said, and waved a hand at the tiny table and chairs squeezed into one corner of the room. "I'll get us something to drink."

"Oh, I don't want to trouble you." Lila said, and slipped onto a chair in the corner. She sat completely upright, and Maryse could see the stress on her face.

"It's no trouble," Maryse said. "I'd just put on a pot of coffee before you came in. Would you like some? If not, there's soda, water, and tea. Anything stronger and I'd have to make a trip upstairs to Sabine's apartment."

"Coffee would be great."

Maryse poured two cups of coffee and sat them on the table along with a caddy of creamer, artificial sweetener, and sugar. Lila opened a packet of artificial sweetener and added it to her coffee, then began to stir the life out of it.

"You said you wanted to talk about Hank," Maryse prompted.

"Yes, but I really shouldn't bother you. This was a mistake. I just thought...But now that I've met you, there's no way..."

Maryse placed her hand on Lila's arm. "No way, what? Is something wrong with Hank? Is he in some kind of trouble?"

"He's missing," Lila said, her voice barely a whisper.

"Oh, well," Maryse struggled for the right words since it was clear that the woman was distraught. "Hank's not exactly proven to be reliable in the showing-up-for-things category. In fact, you might say he made a professional career of coming up missing for a couple of years."

Lila nodded. "I know about your relationship—how he ran off and left you to deal with everything alone."

"Really? I didn't know you could get that kind of information in a job interview."

Lila blushed. "I shouldn't tell you this, but I was Hank's counselor when he was in rehab. Please don't let anyone else know. It's not ethical for me to talk about things he said to me at the center."

Maryse leaned back in her chair, her mind trying to process what Lila had said. "Rehab? While I was hunting for him under every cypress tree on the bayou, he was in rehab?"

"Part of the time, yes, and I can tell you that he has a lot of guilt over what he put you through. He stated clearly from the first day of therapy that he was wrong, and you were a wonderful person who didn't deserve to be saddled with someone like him. I know it's hard to believe, given the way he treated you, but Hank has great respect for you. I think that's part of the reason he couldn't bring himself to contact you."

"So it had nothing to do with all his gambling debts I got stuck with, huh? I find that hard to believe."

Lila nodded. "I understand. When Hank first left you, he had gotten in with a rough crowd. Some of them you met when they were trying to collect, but that wasn't the worst of them. He finally realized that his life was headed to an early end, and he checked himself into rehab in Mississippi. It's probably what saved his life."

Maryse sighed. "I guess I don't really have any room to complain anymore, as he sorta took a bullet that was meant for me a month ago."

Lila shook her head. "You have every right to complain. The Hank Henry that you knew wasn't a worthy enough person to have a relationship with anyone, but you have to believe me when I tell you he's changed. He's really trying to do the right thing, and this job is the start of a real future for Hank."

Maryse turned up her hands. "Then if he's really changed and the job is great, why did he take off again? And how do you think I can help you?"

"Chuck and I think Hank was kidnapped."

"What?" Maryse sat straight up in her chair.

"We called the police. They looked things over and agree that it looks suspicious."

"Holy crap. Are there any suspects?" Maryse shook her head. "What am I saying? This is Hank. The list of suspects is the same as his list of creditors."

"There was a guy at the site one day that Chuck didn't like the look of. Hank was talking to him, and Chuck said Hank looked aggravated, but when Chuck asked about it, the guy said he was just asking for directions. Chuck didn't really buy it. He said Hank looked nervous after talking with him, but Chuck didn't press him. He wishes he had pushed, now. He's blaming himself, which is wrong."

"What did the guy look like?"

"Chuck said he had dark hair, dark sunglasses, and drove a black Cadillac."

Maryse felt the color wash from her face. "A black Cadillac? Chuck is sure?"

"Yes. He said he remembers specifically because he looked at the car to buy one, but ultimately he didn't want to pay for it. Why? Is that important?"

"It may be." Maryse studied Lila for a second. The woman was clearly worried. She'd stirred her coffee during the entire conversation but had yet to take a single sip. "I'm just wondering why you're here telling me all of this."

Lila blushed. "Um, well, one of the days before that, when Chuck thought he saw the Cadillac, Hank came in and asked to use his cell phone. He claimed his was dead, and he needed to call his ex-wife. I guess maybe we just thought he might have told you something."

"Did you tell the police about that call?"

"No." Lila frowned. "What's going on, Maryse? Do you know something about Hank that you're not telling me? I saw your face when I mentioned the black Cadillac. Is Hank in trouble? Is there anything I can do?"

Maryse stared at her, finally understanding why Lila was talking to her. "You care about him."

Lila looked down at her coffee. "Well, of course I'm worried when anyone I know comes up missing."

"That's not what I meant, but I won't push you." Maryse sighed. "Hank *did* call me that day, but it's not him that's in trouble, or at least we didn't think it was. He was stuck in the middle of a situation involving a friend of mine, and he called to warn me so I would warn her."

"What kind of situation?"

"I can't really tell you much without breaking a confidence, but suffice it to say that some very bad people are looking for her. I promise you, *she's* above reproach, but the people who are looking for her are some of the same people that Hank was involved with before. They know he was married to me and that she's my friend, so they've been trying to shake him down for information."

"But Hank wouldn't give them what they wanted."

"No, and in all fairness he doesn't know the answers to their questions. We all thought it better if he didn't."

Lila nodded. "That makes sense. You're certain your friend is telling you everything?"

"I'm positive. I can tell you that the local police and the FBI are trying to protect her. This is huge, Lila. She's in a life-threatening situation, and the fallout reaches far beyond her. She's just as unhappy about that and feels guilty as hell, but I promise you, there's nothing she can do about it that is not already being done." Maryse sighed. "I'm sorry I have to be so cryptic, but the police have really forbidden me to talk about anything."

"Please, don't apologize. I understand completely. Well, not really, but I understand why you can't provide me with details. The FBI? Wow. I shudder to think what your friend's gotten in the middle of that rates that kind of attention."

"It's been kinda hairy. That's for sure."

"And the New Orleans police are also aware of this situation?"

"Yes." One of them, anyway.

"Then they'll be able to connect the dots to Hank's disappearance?"

"I will call my contact and make sure that they do, if they haven't already."

"Thank you." Lila opened her purse and pulled out a business card. She wrote a phone number on the back of the card and handed it to Maryse. "The woman that's in danger—if there's anything I can do, please let me know. I have connections with several safe houses."

"Thank you. That's really kind, but you don't know my friend. She doesn't exactly duck things well."

Lila nodded. "If you hear anything that you can share, I'd really appreciate a call. That's my cell number on the back of the card. Call anytime."

"Of course," Maryse said.

Lila rose and Maryse followed her to the front door of the shop and drew back the dead bolt. "It was nice to meet you," Lila said. "I only wish it were under different circumstances."

"Me, too," Maryse said as Lila slipped out the door. At the last minute, Maryse tugged on her sleeve. "He's doing a good thing for my friend. Hank, that is. I want you to know that. You're not wrong in believing he's changed. I believe it, too, and I'm definitely the last person to say something good about him unless it's warranted."

Lila smiled. "Thank you. I'm glad I haven't been wrong."

Maryse closed the door behind her and turned the lock in place. She was officially closed for the day. She pulled the pay-as-you-go cell phone Raissa had gotten her from her pocket and punched in Raissa's number. Things were getting much, much worse.

Chapter Eighteen

It was noon before Raissa and Zach met up at a café in downtown New Orleans. Zach looked stressed, and Raissa couldn't blame him. Ever since he'd told her Hank Henry was missing, she'd only thought the worst. She'd managed to reassure Maryse when she called hours before that Zach was in charge of the investigation and knew everything they did about Hank and the Heberts. Which was practically nothing. Both of them had already agreed to delay telling Helena until they knew something more concrete.

Raissa took a bite of her chicken sandwich, even though food was the last thing on her mind. "So did you get anything on Spencer?"

"Nothing good. Guy's clean as a whistle when it comes to the police database. I figured as much."

"I may have something."

"Oh, yeah? What?"

"I had Helena do a search of Spencer's office. She didn't come back with much."

"How does that help?"

"I mean she *really* didn't come back with much. The place is almost empty."

Zach's eyes widened. "You think he's getting ready to cut out?"

"If he hasn't already. He knows you're looking at him, since you questioned him the other day. He might figure it's only a matter of time before someone connects the dots between him and the parents of the other kidnap victims."

"Damn it. What good does the information do us if we can't use it? I can hardly get a warrant from his home based on military personnel giving Maryse confidential information, and I have zero way of explaining how I know his office is cleared out."

"Maybe we should question Dr. Spencer again. The police could have gotten a subpoena for information, for all he knows, and if he's guilty of something—and it sure as hell looks like he is—the last thing he'd do is go running to the police to tell them about his suspicions that we broke into his office."

"Maybe, but it's a huge risk. If this whole case shakes loose over that information, how am I supposed to justify knowing what to ask him?"

Raissa frowned. He was right, and that frustrated her. Mainly because she hadn't thought that far herself. She was so focused on finding Melissa that she'd forgotten anything that might happen afterward. And while she could probably get away with taking a hit for it, she didn't want to ruin Zach's career.

"I did find something I wanted to run by you," Zach said.

"What's that?"

"You know how the captain has me checking into the mayor's family's background? Well, an interesting thing happened when I tried to get information on Susannah Franco."

"What?"

"She didn't exist until she was eighteen. I find that a little strange, and way too familiar."

Raissa's mind raced with possibilities. "Could have been in witness protection with her parents and taken on another identity when she turned eighteen. Or she could have changed her name for any number of reasons."

"Changing your name doesn't get you a new Social Security number."

"No. So what does her Social Security card say?"

"Susannah Forrester."

"She never changed it after she married. I wonder why."

"I think I can guess," Zach said. "Because Susannah Forrester died thirty years ago."

"Then who is Peter Franco married to?"

Zach shook his head. "I have no idea, and I wonder if Peter Franco does, either. They met in college, and all I can get from teachers and other acquaintances is that she was an only child and the rest of her family is deceased."

"So what are you going to do?"

"The real Susannah Forrester lived in a bayou town on the outskirts of New Orleans. I figure Mrs. Franco had to know her to assume her identity. I'm going there as soon as we finish lunch to poke around. Do you want to ride along?"

Raissa bit her lip, trying to decide. Heck, yeah, she wanted to go, but she'd promised Maryse she'd head back to Mudbug after lunch to check for any Sonny recordings and fill Helena and Mildred in on the situation with Hank. Maryse had sounded panicked when Raissa talked with her earlier, so she knew her friend was hanging on by a thread. "I can't. I've got to get back to Mudbug and handle the Hank issue with Maryse. And Mildred needs her car."

Zach narrowed his eyes at her. "You aren't thinking about questioning Spencer yourself, are you? Because that would be the dumbest thing in the world to do."

Raissa blushed, as it had crossed her mind that Spencer's office was only a couple of blocks from the café. "No, I'm not thinking about doing that."

Zach stared at her.

"Okay, so I thought about it, but I can't come up with a good enough excuse to do it. I promise I'll go straight to Mudbug."

"And call me when you get there."

"I promise."

"I mean it, Raissa." Zach rose from the booth and leaned over to kiss her hard on the mouth. "You're already taking enough risks. I want you around to see the end."

"The end is what I'm afraid of. We're running out of time."

"We know more now than the FBI ever did. I know it's a jumbled mess, but I'm just as certain that it's all relevant. We'll make sense of it in time to catch them."

Raissa watched him through the plate-glass window of the café until he drove away, then reached for her wallet, tossed some bills on the table, and left. The only good thing so far was that between the stress and giving all her sweets to Helena, she'd lost a couple of pounds.

She'd just gotten in Mildred's car when her cell phone began ringing. She looked at the display. Zach? She flipped open the phone and answered.

"Are you still at the café?"

"No. I just got in my car, why?"

"We have a huge problem."

"What happened?"

"I just got a call—homicide."

Raissa felt the blood rush from her face. "Oh, no. Not Hank."

"No. Dr. Spencer."

Shit. Raissa banged one hand on the steering wheel. "There goes our best lead."

"That's not the half of it. His body's in your store. I'm headed over there now. I know you don't want to run into Fields, and I can't promise you they won't ask me to hold you in custody until they figure this out, but I think you should get over there."

"I'll be there in a minute." She started the car and pulled onto the street, tires squealing. What the hell was Spencer doing in her shop? Who had killed him? And how? The questions outweighed the answers by a mile. It seemed that the closer they got to the truth, the more convoluted everything became.

The usually calm street was filled with vehicles, most of them with flashing lights. Raissa parked a block away and started up the sidewalk to her shop. A patrolman stopped her at the end of the block. "This is a crime scene, ma'am. No one's allowed past at this time."

Raissa pulled out her license to show the patrolman. "Your crime scene is in my shop. I got a call from a Detective Blanchard."

The patrolman checked her license and nodded. "Right this way, Ms. Bordeaux. I'll take you to the detective."

The patrolman waved at another officer to take his position and escorted her to her shop. There was a crowd of people outside, and as they stepped to the door, the paramedics came out, pulling the gurney. The body was completely covered.

"Wait," she said and stopped the paramedics. "May I?" She motioned to the body.

The patrolman nodded, and the paramedic pulled back the sheet to expose Dr. Spencer, with a clean bullet hole in the middle of his forehead.

The paramedic pulled the sheet back over Spencer's body and wheeled it onto the ambulance. The ambulance driver turned off the lights and they pulled away. No sense in hurrying on this one. Raissa turned and followed the patrolman into her store.

Zach stood next to the counter, talking to a member of the forensics team. He saw her come in and broke off his conversation to walk over. He thanked the patrolman, then pulled her to the back of the store to a section with the shape of a body taped on the floor. "He had a screwdriver, so we figure he was trying to open this door. That's the stairs to your apartment, right?"

"Yeah." Raissa shook her head. "But what was the point? Why come after me? You're the police. I'm just the nut who owns the psychic shop."

"Yeah, but you were with me when I questioned him, so he knows you're involved, and that's not all. We found his car in the parking garage behind his office. A black Cadillac."

Raissa stared at him. "No way. It's Sonny's guys following me. We know that. And besides, Spencer's name wasn't on the DMV list."

"It's registered to his wife." Zach glanced around and leaned his head toward her. "It has a bullet hole in the trunk," he whispered.

Raissa didn't know what to think. "Dr. Spencer tried to run me off the road? How did he even know to find me in Mudbug? He doesn't know any of my friends. He'd never know to look for me there."

"That is a damned good question, unless it was Spencer who put the tracking device on your car."

"But why? We questioned him after he tried to run me off the road. After I'd already figured out the trace was installed."

Zach shook his head. "I don't know what's going on here, but I don't like it. It smacks of a professional hit, which smacks of your friends the Heberts. Maybe you're wrong about Sonny being involved. Or maybe some of Sonny's family is into business he doesn't know about. All I know is that witnesses said the shot was fired from the driver's side of a black Cadillac driving down the street. Now, how many people do you know who can land a bullet right between a guy's eyes while driving?"

"Not many. What are we going to do? Spencer was the best lead we had."

"Which is probably the main reason he's dead. I'm going to call the captain about getting a search warrant for Spencer's office and home, but it won't happen immediately. Meantime, I'm calling in Morrow to cover this."

Raissa frowned.

"I know, he's a dickhead, but he's also an idiot. With any luck, he won't find any evidence that incriminates you in all this."

"So what are you going to do?"

"I'm going to continue with my original plan to check up on Susannah Franco. Someone close to the Francos bypassed that alarm system. I originally thought it was the mayor, but now I wonder. Anyway, get the hell out of here before someone else decides to question you."

"Okay, wait," Raissa said, confused. "Won't your captain have a stroke if you let me get away?"

"He sorta sanctioned contact with you in order to get leads on the kidnapping case."

"Sorta?"

"Yeah, as in, I'm allowed to contact you as long as I don't get caught. Then, my guess is, he wouldn't know anything about it."

"Then I guess I'll sorta get the hell out of here before I make things even messier."

"Get back to Mudbug and close yourself in somewhere safe. I'll call you as soon as I have some information on Susannah Franco."

Raissa hurried back down the block, her head low so maybe no one would remember what she looked like and associate her with Zach, at least not right away. None of this made sense. Why had Spencer tried to kill her? Was he tied to the Heberts? And who had taken Hank Henry and for what reason? Even more important, where was he now?

The first thing she needed to do was check the feed from Sonny's. If Sonny's men had anything to do with Spencer's murder, she'd be able to hear all about it, provided they were in Sonny's office. She got into her car and headed back to Mudbug as fast as Mildred's ancient sedan would allow.

Zach's phone rang the instant he climbed into his car. He knew it was the captain without even looking at the display. He could swear that even the ring had a desperate, angry sound to it. He pressed the button to answer and the captain's voice boomed out, making him wince.

"Damn it, Blanchard! What the hell is going on? You tell me this morning that you don't have any leads to speak of, then the doctor you questioned about Melissa Franco turns up dead in the psychic woman's shop. I guess you've got plenty of leads now. What I want from you are some answers."

"I wish I had them, Captain. All I can tell you is that it looks like Spencer's been stalking Ms. Bordeaux, but neither of us know why."

"How do you know that the Bordeaux woman didn't kill him herself? Maybe they were having an affair. Maybe she thought he'd kidnapped the kid, and she's lost it from so many years of hiding out."

"I'm sure that's not the case, sir."

"How can you be sure?"

"Because when Spencer was shot, I was sitting in a café with Ms. Bordeaux having lunch. And witnesses saw a black Cadillac, not an old tan sedan. It wasn't her, but it has all the signs of a hired hit."

"Which puts us right back to the fucking Heberts."

"It looks that way."

"So would you like to tell me why you called Morrow to take over for you on the hottest piece of evidence that we've got so far?"

"Please don't tell me the mother has anything to do with the disappearance of her own child."

"Okay, I won't tell you that, but I have to wonder."

"Wonder about what?"

"Why the Social Security number Susannah Franco's been using belongs to a woman that died over thirty years ago."

There was dead silence on the other end of the phone, and for a moment, Zach wondered if the captain had finally had that heart attack he kept threatening the department with. "Sir, are you still there?"

"Yeah, but I'm starting to wonder for how much longer. Jesus H. Christ, Blanchard. You call me as soon as you have any information on the Franco woman. I'll make sure the detail watching her doesn't let her out of their sight. Is there anything else that can pile onto this case?"

"As a matter of fact, remember that kidnapping you sent me on this morning?"

"Yeah, the adult male. So? Probably out on a bender."

"I don't think so."

"Do I even want to know?"

"The guy was a friend of a friend of Ms. Bordeaux's and an ex-associate of the Heberts. He warned Ms. Bordeaux earlier this week that one of the Heberts asked him to kill her."

"Blanchard. I've changed my mind."

"About what, sir?"

"Don't call me again. When I can handle it, I'll call you."

Forty minutes later, Zach was perched on a hard chair covered in hideous fabric and sipping tea from china cups with Magdalena LeBlanc, Susannah Forrester's old friend and neighbor. Zach took a sip of the tea and tried not to grimace. Why in the world did people actually like that crap? "So, Ms. LeBlanc, did Susannah have any children?"

"Oh, heavens, no. Susannah was an old maid, like me. That's why we were such fabulous friends. Neither of us had others to answer to once our parents passed away. Why, we were fancy-free and living the life."

Zach smiled. "Sounds like a good life."

"Oh, it was the best, up until Susannah got sick. Breast cancer. Wasn't testing then like there is today. Why, she just wasted away. It's such a shame."

"I'm very sorry to hear that. I'm sure you miss her."

"Every single day. So tell me, what's a New Orleans detective doing all the way out in the boonies asking about Susannah?"

"Her name came up in a case I'm working on as a possible relative to a suspect. I thought maybe if she had kids...But looks like I'm out of luck."

"She never had her own kids, but she had a niece she was very fond of. Used to send her money from time to time."

"Do you remember the niece's name?"

"Annabelle was her name. Annabelle Forrester. Her father was Susannah's brother, who died in the war."

"Did Annabelle have any children?"

"Oh, I don't know. After Susannah passed away, I never saw her again. She'd just recently married before Susannah's death, but I don't recall anyone telling me the young man's name. I'm really sorry I can't be more help."

Zach rose from his chair and took her hands in his. "You've been a great help, Ms. LeBlanc. Thank you for your time and the tea."

Zach left the house and hopped into his car. If Annabelle Forrester had married and had a child, she might have named that child after her favorite aunt. He'd passed the court house on the way into town. He'd try to find a marriage license and birth record there.

Chapter Nineteen

Raissa burst into her hotel room and ran straight to the laptop linked to Sonny's house. She sat down at the table and clicked to start the audio file. Sonny's voice was the first thing she heard.

"How the hell could you let this happen, Rico?" Sonny yelled. "You were supposed to stay on Hank Henry until I said otherwise."

"I *was* on Hank. He went back inside the work site. I had the GPS on his truck, so I drove around the block and picked up something to eat. I wasn't even gone ten minutes."

"Apparently, ten minutes is all it took for him to disappear. You are going to make this right, Rico."

"How am I supposed to do that?"

"You're going to put out word to every family member, bookie, prostitute, and bum in New Orleans that we're looking for Hank. Someone had to see something. If anyone gives you information that leads us to Henry, I'll pay ten g's."

"Ten grand for Hank Henry? You gotta be kidding me."

"Just do it, Rico."

The sound of the door shutting echoed over the computer; then Raissa heard Sonny slam his hands down on his desk, as she'd seen him do so many times. And that was all of the recording.

She checked the time—four hours before. Sonny's guys had a four-hour jump on trying to locate Hank. Not that it mattered. Raissa didn't have the network that Sonny had. But why did Sonny want him so badly? There had to be a reason, but damned if Raissa could come up with anything that made sense.

She needed her files, and they were in the trunk of Mildred's car. Surely there was something in those files that would connect the dots. They were so close. Raissa could feel it. She checked the monitors, but all she saw in the alley was the city garbage truck, making its weekly pickup. She grabbed Mildred's car keys and headed out the back of the hotel, pulling the door shut behind her. The sun was already setting behind the row of cypress trees on the west side of town, reducing the sunlight to a dim glow on the alley between the hotel and the garage.

She hurried across the alley in front of the garbage truck and slipped the garage key into the lock. The garbage truck passed and she heard the footsteps behind her, but before she could reach for her weapon, a hand grabbed her shoulder and spun her around. Looking directly at Sonny Hebert, Raissa realized she'd made the miscalculation that might cost her her life.

"Don't yell," he said in a low voice. "I can't afford for anyone else to notice me. I'm sure the garbageman already thinks I'm crazy for following that stinking truck down the alley, but I knew if you were staying here you'd have cameras."

Raissa nodded, her heart pounding as if it would beat out of her chest. She wondered if this was how it was all going to end—in an alley behind the Mudbug Hotel.

"I hear a friend of yours is missing," Sonny said. "He's in a warehouse on Canal Street. A brown building with blue stripes. You've got about two hours before he's removed."

"Removed?"

Sonny glanced nervously over his shoulder. "Yeah, and I'm afraid this time might be permanent."

"This time?"

"Shhhh. I can't tell you everything, because I don't know all of it. What I do know is if you want to see him again, you better get over there now." He whirled around, hurried down the alley. A couple of seconds later a nondescript late-model sedan passed the end of the alley, with Sonny at the wheel. He barely slowed and cast one glance at her, then drove away.

Raissa dug into her pocket for her cell phone. She didn't realize her hands were shaking until she pressed in Zach's name. "I'm going to a warehouse building on Canal Street. One with blue stripes. I just got a tip that Hank Henry is being held there, but we have to move fast to get him." Raissa jumped into her car and fired up the engine.

"What the hell?" Zach said. "Where did you get this tip?"

"Sonny Hebert," Raissa said as she hopped into her car and pulled away from the curb, her tires screeching. "And since I'm still alive I can only assume he's not interested in killing me. At least not right now."

"How do you know the whole thing isn't a setup to get you somewhere that he can kill you?"

"I don't, which is why I need you to meet me there. I'll be there in forty-five minutes."

"No fucking way! I'm more than forty-five minutes away. Don't go there, Raissa."

"Too late, I'm already on my way. Your choice, Detective." She disconnected the call and pressed the accelerator. Her cell phone buzzed at her from the passenger's seat, but she let it ring, choosing to concentrate on driving well beyond the speed limit without killing herself. Zach would be there. He wouldn't let her walk into something she might not walk out of.

She hoped.

Zach cursed when Raissa disconnected, and it was all he could do not to fling the phone against a wall. Not that he could afford to do that at the moment. Likely he was going to need it soon to call for backup, an ambulance, or the coroner. He was about an hour outside of Baton Rouge, which put him at almost the same distance from the warehouse as Raissa, but already behind her in travel time.

The county clerk who'd been helping him locate documents slid a couple of sheets of paper across the counter toward him. "These are the records you were looking for, Detective Blanchard.

Do you want to pay the fifty cents or would you like me to bill the New Orleans police department?"

Zach punched in Raissa's number and waited until it went to voice mail. "Damn it!"

The clerk stared at him in surprise.

"I'm sorry," he apologized, "but I have an emergency." He tossed a five-dollar bill on the counter for the copies, grabbed the papers, and ran out the door, yanking his keys from his pocket as he crossed the street. He tore out of the parking lot and was doing eighty miles per hour by the time he hit the interstate.

He dialed the station. "Captain, I need backup to a warehouse with blue stripes on Canal Street. I got a tip that Hank Henry is being held there."

"Where on Canal Street?"

"I don't know."

"Damn it. That street's miles long."

"Tell them to start on the north side. I'll start on the south." He dropped the cell phone into the passenger's seat, and only then did he remember the copies. He grabbed them from the passenger's seat and looked at them. The first was a marriage license for Annabelle Forrester and Franklin Marsella. The second was a birth certificate for Susannah Forrester Marsella. Too much of a coincidence not to somehow be related to the missing Monk.

Zach felt his blood run cold. The mayor's daughter-in-law was the Hebert connection, not the mayor. He reached for his cell phone, ready to call the captain back with this bit of information, but stopped. The captain had already made it clear he didn't want more clues with no connecting dots, and right now, keeping Raissa safe was his priority. He'd tell the captain about his suspicions concerning the mayor's daughter-in-law once he'd made sure Raissa was okay and they'd found Hank Henry. He pressed the accelerator down even farther and prayed that he got to the warehouse in time.

Thirty-five minutes later, he turned the corner on the south end of Canal Street, frantically scanning the street for any sign of

Raissa. He felt a wave of relief when he saw Mildred's car parked in front of a warehouse building just like the one she'd described, but Raissa was nowhere in sight. He jumped out of his car, pulled out his weapon, and hurried toward the warehouse entrance, scanning the street as he went. There were no other cars in sight and the entire area seemed completely abandoned.

The perfect place to commit a crime.

He slipped through the open door and looked down at the dusty floor. Prints led in different directions, but the majority broke off to the right. He crept down a long hallway, following the footprints, checking each room as he passed an open doorway. At the end of the warehouse, he looked into the last room and felt relief wash over him when he saw a very alive Raissa. Then a closer look revealed her hovering over a not-so-alive-looking Hank Henry, and his pulse began to race again.

Raissa looked up as he entered the room. "I've already called an ambulance. They should be here any minute."

Zach looked down at the pale man laid out on what appeared to be a hospital gurney. "He's alive?"

"Yeah, but I think he's drugged or something, and he looks really weak. Give me your handcuff key."

Zach looked confused for a moment until Raissa lifted Hank's right hand. He was handcuffed to the bed. Zach passed his key ring to Raissa and began to walk the room. "Did you see anyone when you got here?"

"No one. The street was as empty as the warehouse. But he didn't get here, chained to a hospital bed, by himself."

"No. Definitely not." Zach ran one hand across a window seal, then looked down at the floor and frowned. "This room has been cleaned. Spotless, as a matter of fact."

Raissa nodded. "Yeah, I noticed that. They're careful."

Zach shook his head. "You don't have to disinfect a room to remove prints, and I doubt even the best forensics team would find much, given the dust in the rest of the building."

"I don't think it was to erase evidence."

Zach looked over at her. "Why else then?"

Raissa looked down at Hank and bit her lip. "I think he's in a hospital bed for a reason. I think maybe they were going to do something to him. Medically."

Zach stared. "You think someone sterilized this room to perform a medical procedure? Jesus, does he have any incisions?" Theft of body organs was fairly rare, but it still happened.

"No incisions. It's the first thing I checked. It looks like everything is intact." Raissa looked up at Zach, a grim look on her face. "Maybe they hadn't gotten to the surgery part yet. Maybe that's what Sonny meant when he told me Hank would be removed."

Zach felt his face flush with anger. "Sonny Hebert has some explaining to do. I ought to go arrest him, now."

"Don't."

"Give me one good reason why not."

"I overheard a conversation between Sonny and Rico. Sonny's men put word out on the street this morning that Sonny would pay ten grand if anyone could tell him where Hank was."

"Why would he offer the money, then tell you?"

"I don't know. But I get the impression that Sonny knows or at least suspects something about what's going on here, though he isn't involved. Not directly, anyway. Even if that's the case, he took a big risk telling me where to find Hank, which tells me that whatever is going on is too reprehensible for even Sonny to let pass. He may be the only person who can lead us to the answer. If you lock him up, he won't be able to instruct his men."

"I can damn well demand the answer."

Raissa shook her head. "Strong-arming Sonny is the fastest way to get him to dig in his heels. He has to think he's running the show. It's the only way he operates. If you put the pressure on him, he'll back out of this whole mess, and I don't know what might happen then. To Melissa."

"Yeah, that's the part that worries me the most." Zach told Raissa about the marriage license and birth certificate.

Raissa stared at him, stunned. "Susannah Franco is related to Monk Marsella? So Monk was kidnapping the girls, and Susannah is related to Monk. But now Monk's gone and so is Susannah's daughter. What are we missing here?"

"I don't know. Damn it!" Zach paced back and forth across the room. "Do you think Sonny knows what happened to Melissa?"

"I think he has suspicions, but I don't think he knows where to find her. Sonny would never tolerate someone hurting a child."

"Great. A mobster with morals."

"I know how much you hate it, Zach, but you have to trust me on this one. I *know* Sonny Hebert, better than most people. You can't force him into anything or you'll lose. For whatever reason, he's looking into this kidnapping, and I have to tell you, he's likely to get results faster than we can."

Sirens sounded outside the warehouse and Zach glanced outside to see the paramedics hurrying into the building. "Back here!" he shouted, and waved them to the back room.

He looked over at Raissa, who stood to the side while the paramedics loaded Hank onto the gurney. Her expression was filled with fear and worry. Not that he blamed her. This case had thrown him more curveballs than opening day at Yankee Stadium.

Alien kidnappings, fugitive FBI agents, unauthorized medical procedures, and Sonny Hebert being helpful.

What the hell had they gotten involved in?

Dr. Breaux was leaving Hank's room as Raissa and Zach made their way down the hall. Raissa closed her cell phone, having just finished telling Maryse to spread the word that Hank had been found and was safe, and that she'd call back as soon as she'd spoken with Dr. Breaux. Zach flashed his badge and Dr. Breaux nodded and motioned them over to the side.

"I'm Dr. Breaux," he said, and extended his hand to Zach. He nodded at Raissa. "Good to see you again, Raissa. I hear Sabine returns tomorrow."

"I'm looking forward to it. How's Hank?"

"Fine. In fact, he's in excellent condition. I can't find any indication of trauma—his vital signs are perfect. I don't understand what's going on here. Can you tell me anything?"

Raissa hesitated. She looked over at Zach, who took over. "All we really know, sir, is that Hank was reported missing from his job this morning but was likely taken sometime yesterday evening. As for what happened after that, we were hoping you might give us a clue."

"His medical condition doesn't tell me anything at all. There's a small puncture mark on his left arm, but that could be anything. Where did you find him?" Dr. Breaux asked. "All the paramedics could tell me is that he was unconscious when they picked him up. Was he on another job?"

"No," Zach replied. "He was found in an abandoned warehouse. The room Hank was kept in was totally sterilized, and I found him handcuffed to a hospital bed. He wasn't conscious."

Dr. Breaux stared at him, then glanced at Raissa. "But that's just crazy. You're serious about this?"

"Yes, sir. I would never joke about a kidnapping."

"Well...I guess I just don't know what to say. I mean, I've heard of organ harvesting, of course, but it's one of those things you never think you're going to actually come in contact with. Especially among your living patients."

"So you think that's what was going on?" Zach asked.

Dr. Breaux frowned, obviously confused. "What else could it be? Why sterilize an area? Why chain a healthy man to a hospital bed? That puncture mark on his arm makes a lot more sense now if you assume someone kept him drugged or on an IV."

"You've got a point," Zach agreed. "Someone went to Hank's job site prepared to abduct him without a fight, which means it was all planned. The question is, who planned it and why Hank Henry?"

"How did you happen to find him?" Dr. Breaux asked.

"An anonymous tip," Zach said. "One of those things that rarely works out but this time turned out to be true."

"But you have no way of tracing the source?" Dr. Breaux questioned. "Surely, the police have methods of identifying that sort of thing."

"If it's a phone call or e-mail, sometimes, although technology still allows for the high-tech person to work around the system. But this was a note delivered by a kid on the street. He couldn't identify the man who gave it to him."

Raissa's eyes widened at Zach's story, but she had to admire his ability to make up something believable on the fly. The less anyone knew about Sonny Hebert and Raissa, the better.

Dr. Breaux shook his head. "Well, I wish I could help more, but there's simply nothing about Hank that can tell me what might have happened to him."

"Is he conscious?"

"Yes, but he says he doesn't remember anything."

"Damn," Zach said.

"You've got your work cut out. I understand."

Zach nodded. "Can we talk to him?"

"Sure. I'm keeping him overnight for observation just because of the circumstances, but there's not really anything wrong with him that I can find, except he's a little woozy from whatever they gave him. Should have the tox screen back in a couple of hours."

Zach pulled one of his business cards from his pocket and gave it to Dr. Breaux. "When you get the tox screen back, please give me a call."

"Of course," Dr. Breaux said, and slipped the card in the pocket of his hospital coat. "If that's all you need, I have a couple more patients to check on."

"Yes, thank you," Zach said, and motioned Raissa toward Hank's room.

Hank was propped up in bed when Zach and Raissa entered the room. Raissa was relieved to see the color was back in his face, and Hank looked equally relieved to see her.

Raissa walked over to the bed and sat on the side. "I'm glad to see you in one piece."

Hank nodded. "Same goes for you." Hank looked as if he wanted to say more, but he cast a nervous glance at Zach, then back at Raissa.

"Oh, sorry," Raissa said and point to Zach. "This is Detective Blanchard. He's a friend of mine. You can trust him."

"Then I guess he'll do." Hank gave her a small smile. "Would you mind passing me a bit of water? I wasn't in the mood to be waited on when the nurse was in earlier, but she says I need to take these." He lifted a disposable cup with two pills in it.

"Sure," Raissa said, and poured water from a pitcher into a paper cup. "Pain meds?" she asked as she passed the cup to Hank.

Hank tossed the pills in his mouth and drank the cup of water. "No. I don't have any pain to speak of. Just kinda weak. They gave me a vitamin B shot and some iron pills. Said it should perk me back up in a bit."

"That's great news. I was really worried when I saw you unconscious. I had no way of knowing what they'd done to you."

Hank nodded. "That makes two of us. When I came to, here in the hospital, I was afraid that the men who were looking for you had gotten to you. I haven't told Sonny's men anything, but they haven't let up with the questions."

"I know you haven't said anything," Raissa said, "and I honestly think Sonny has those men asking questions just to keep me on edge. They've known where to find me all along."

"How do you know?"

"Because Sonny and I had a little chat in the alley behind the Mudbug Hotel."

Hank's eyes widened. "Holy shit! How are you still breathing?"

Raissa shook her head. "I think Sonny has a bigger problem than me, but for the life of me, I can't figure out how it all ties together. He's the one who told me where to find you."

Hank sat up straight in bed. "No way!"

"Yeah, I thought it was crazy, too." Raissa thought about the scene with Sonny outside of the shop and shook her head. "It was weird, Hank. He was alone, I'm sure of it, but he was jumpy, like he was afraid somebody was watching. I've never seen Sonny jumpy. Not even the possibility of the feds watching him made him flinch in the past."

"Until now. We need to figure out what's going on. Dr. Breaux said you couldn't remember anything. Did you even see your attacker?"

Hank looked down at his lap, a blush creeping up his neck. "I remember one thing, but I didn't want the doc to think I was crazy."

Raissa felt her pulse quicken and would have bet money that she knew exactly what Hank was about to say. "Who was it, Hank?"

Hank looked up at her, his expression completely bewildered. "I was abducted by an alien."

Chapter Twenty

Mildred, Maryse, Luc, and Helena were waiting for Raissa and Zach at the Mudbug Hotel. Zach was introduced to Luc, and with the pleasantries out of the way, they all crowded into the kitchen in the back. Mildred passed around coffee, water, and anything stronger if someone wanted it. Zach chose stronger. It wasn't as if he was driving afterward, and the things he'd seen that day warranted a stiff drink.

"Somebody say something," Helena complained. "I want to know what happened to my son."

"Helena's getting restless," Maryse said. "Can someone please give her the four-one-one on Hank?"

Zach started for a moment before he realized Maryse was talking about the ghost. He looked around at the group of people, but no one else seemed fazed. "Can all of you see her?" he asked, unable to help himself.

"Everyone but me," Luc said. "At least, not anymore. I was able to see her for a week. That was enough."

"I don't understand a bit of this," Zach said, "but my mind's too full to absorb it all. Raissa, why don't you fill them in."

"For starters, as I said to Maryse when I called, Hank is fine. He's a little weak, but he wasn't hurt. The New Orleans police are grilling him now, but you should be able to see him in an hour or so." Then Raissa went on to tell the crowd about Sonny's tip and how she found Hank, the conversation with Dr. Breaux, and lastly, their conversation with Hank.

"Aliens?" Luc stared at Raissa. "What the hell have you and my wife been up to? I swear I can't leave for a couple of days."

Everyone laughed except Zach, who sorta knew how he felt. He couldn't even leave Raissa alone for a couple of *hours* or things went sideways.

Raissa and Maryse took turns filling everyone in on the investigation and the alien connection. There were many gasps and dropped jaws, and a fair amount of cussing.

"It's so outrageous," Mildred finally said. "I just hope it all ends soon. I pray for normal every night when I go to bed."

Maryse tugged at Luc's sleeve and said, "Helena wants to go to the hospital and see Hank. Let's take her now, then go home. I'm exhausted."

Zach and Raissa made their way upstairs to Raissa's room. "I was thinking of picking up a couple of shrimp sandwiches from the restaurant, okay?" Raissa asked as they walked into the room.

"That's great. I'm starving." Zach pulled his cell phone from his pocket. "I need to call the captain and tell him about Susannah Franco."

"You're doing that tonight?"

"Yeah. He'll send someone into the office tonight to make the family tree add up first, but he'll want to put the screws to her in the morning. He'll just have to figure out an angle to use, as no one but you ever suspected Monk Marsella as the original kidnapper."

"All he really has to say is that there were discrepancies in her background and they want answers."

"True. I'll suggest that. I told her they were all 'persons of interest' as far as the investigation went, and that it was standard protocol. She shouldn't be surprised."

"Probably not. I'm going to hop in the shower, then go get the sandwiches. I want to go over the girls' files again after that. There's something at the back of my mind, but it's not clear."

"Did Hank's situation make you remember something?"

Raissa frowned. "No, but I just have this feeling that there's something I should know, and it hasn't clicked."

Zach nodded. "Then we'll go over the files until it does."

"Two more days," Raissa said, and sighed before heading into the bathroom.

Two more days to find Melissa Franco or the kidnapper would get away with it again.

Lila knocked softly on Hank's hospital-room door, not wanting to disturb him if he was sleeping. There was no answer, but the door was ajar, so she pushed it open and peeked inside. The room was dim, with only a night-light shining at the side of the bed. She started to walk inside, then realized there was an older woman sitting at the side of the bed, her hand over Hank's. Lila heard faint singing that sounded like a lullaby.

She stepped back, not wanting to interrupt, and almost collided with Maryse. "Oh, I'm so sorry," she said.

"No problem. Are you here to see Hank?"

"Yes, but I didn't want to disturb him. I peeked in, but he's sleeping, and there's another woman in there."

Maryse frowned. "There's no one else here that I know of." Maryse stepped by her and pushed open the door. She looked back at Lila. "There's no one here."

Lila stepped into the room and looked around. Maryse was right—it was empty except for Hank. Lila sighed. "I must be losing it."

"Trust me, I know the feeling. The lighting in here's not all that great, either."

"Is it all right to see him? I mean, I'm not interrupting anything..."

Maryse waved a hand in dismissal. "Not at all. My husband's waiting for me in the car outside. I just checked in with the nurse and everything's fine." She smiled at Lila. "I'm sure he'll be happy to see you. I've got to run." She walked down the hall with a wave over her shoulder.

Lila took a deep breath and stepped into the room. As she approached the bed, Hank stirred and opened his eyes. "I thought I heard something. Were you singing?"

Lila shook her head. "I just got here, but I heard singing, too." She looked around the room but didn't see anything that could have created the noise.

"Probably in another room or something," Hank said.

"You're probably right." Lila stood at the side of his bed, fiddling with the bottom button on her blouse. "You don't know how happy I am to see you."

Hank reached up and took her hand in his and pulled her toward the bed. "Have a seat and relax." He smiled at her. "It's hard to see you so far away. Everything's still a little fuzzy."

She sat on the side of his bed and studied him as he pushed himself up to a sitting position. "How do you feel? Did they catch the guy who did this? Maryse called, but she didn't have any details, other than that you were fine."

Hank felt his heart leap into his throat at the concern in Lila's face. He swallowed once and tried to keep his emotions from his voice. Lila was his client and used to be his therapist. Even though she'd agreed to go to dinner with him the last time he'd seen her, the fact that she was visiting him in a hospital after his kidnapping was a clear indication that he had no business involving someone like Lila in his sordid life. At least, not on a personal level.

Keep things professional. "I feel fine, just a little tired. I don't think they've caught the guy. I don't know how they could, as I have no earthly idea who did it."

Lila gave him a worried look. "Chuck said a guy had been hanging around the site. He thought he saw him hassling you the night you disappeared, but said you passed it off as nothing. Based on his description, it sounded like someone from your past."

Hank sighed. "It *was* someone from my past, but I don't think that's who took me. The guy who took me bypassed a locked door and managed to creep up behind me without me hearing. He stuck me with a needle. I got the impression that he was taller than me. The other guy is shorter and not sneaky at all."

Lila bit her lip. "But he was hassling you? And he has friends, right?"

"Yeah, I guess he could have gotten someone else, but I'm not involved in anything. I swear."

"I went to Mudbug and talked to Maryse. Chuck said you called her one day with his phone, and I guess we hoped she might know something that could help. I hope you don't mind."

"I don't mind at all. It's nice that you and Chuck were trying to help. So what did you think about my ex?"

Lila laughed. "I think you were right saying you were crazy to let her get away. I think she's great."

Hank nodded. "She is, just not great for me. I see it now, but at the time, I guess I thought she could save me. I was wrong for using her that way. I'm still hoping she forgives me someday."

"I think she already has. So do you think this was about her friend?"

"I don't know. The guy Chuck saw had been trying to get information on Maryse's friend, especially after she turned up missing from her apartment and business."

"Why does he want her?"

"I honestly have no idea," Hank said. "I warned her after the first visit, and she disappeared afterward. I called Maryse when Rico started coming around the job site. I borrowed Chuck's phone for the call in case they were tracing mine. I never asked why they were after her, and I don't want to know. It's safer that way."

Lila nodded but still looked worried. "That's what Maryse said. But even though you didn't know anything, the guy kept coming back. Why didn't he just look somewhere else?"

"That's not the way these guys work. They think if they put pressure on you, you'll figure out a way to get them what they want, even if you don't have it. They like shortcuts."

"This woman is still in danger then. Is there any way I can help?"

Hank looked at Lila, unable to keep the smile from his face. "You're really something, you know. You know the kind of guys I'm talking about, and here I was kidnapped right after a run-in with them, and you're worried about the woman they're after. You're a wonderful person, Lila. Probably the most wonderful person I've ever known."

Lila blushed and stared down at the floor. "I'm just trying to do the right thing. It's no more than anyone else would do."

Hank used one finger to lift her chin until he was looking her eye to eye. "It's more than most people would do, especially for a stranger, and you know it." He looked at her a moment longer and tried to command his racing heart to still. He knew what he was about to do was a horrible idea, but for whatever reason, his mind simply couldn't convince his body to agree.

He leaned forward and pressed his lips to hers, fully expecting her to pull away. Instead she lifted one hand to his cheek and kissed him back, a soft lingering kiss that made him warm all over. He pulled back a bit and looked at her.

She sighed and smiled. "I thought you'd never kiss me."

Hank stared at her. "You wanted me to kiss you?"

"Of course. I would have liked to have dinner with you, too, but it looks like you're going to have to take a rain check, as I'm not really fond of hospital food."

Hank stared at her in disbelief. "I just never figured...I'm sorry, but I don't think you should be involved with me. Look at all the shit—stuff—that just happened, and I don't even know why." He shook his head. "No, that's wrong. I know why. It's because of who I was. If I'd never been that person, these things wouldn't be happening to me now. It still all comes back to my bad choices. I'm not an innocent."

"You can try to run me off, Hank Henry, but you'll find I'm tougher than you think. What about the woman in danger? Does Maryse know if she's safe?"

"She's not only safe, she's the one who rescued me."

Lila gasped. "Then it did have something to do with her."

Hank shook his head. "We don't know. That's the really weird part. This guy who's been looking for her is the one who told her where to find me, but he was all secretive, like he didn't want anyone to know."

"So his men took you, then he changed his mind?"

"I don't think so. I mean, I could be totally wrong, but I think there's something major going on here. Like I said, I don't ask questions, and I'm guessing I wouldn't get many answers even if I did."

"I asked Maryse about her. All Maryse would say is the woman was above reproach and that the right people were trying to protect her."

Hank nodded. "Yeah, she came to the hospital courtesy of a New Orleans detective who was looking at her like anything but a suspect. I think she's in good hands."

"Maryse said the feds were looking into things, too." She sat up straight and stared at Hank. "Do you think she's a fed?"

Hank stared at Lila in surprise. "You know, she's tough and smart and clearly not under arrest. And she knows how to handle a weapon. I've seen that firsthand." He shook his head. "Damn if you're not onto something. Her being a fed would explain everything."

"Well, maybe not everything, but probably a whole lot."

"A fed. I bet that's it. No wonder everyone's tiptoeing around her. That cop with her looked like he was guarding the Hope Diamond."

Lila smiled. "Maybe he thinks he is."

Raissa closed her cell phone and tossed it on the dresser.

"Maryse?" Zach asked.

"Yeah."

"How's Hank?"

"Good. Helena got to see him, so she's stopped panicking." Raissa frowned. "There was something strange, though."

"What's that?"

"Maryse said when she went back to Hank's room to check on Helena after talking to the nurse, that she ran into the woman, Lila, Hank's boss that I told you about. Lila was standing outside Hank's room and said she didn't want to go in because there was a woman already in there. But the only woman who could have been in Hank's room was Helena."

Zach stared at her, eyebrows raised. "Maryse thinks Lila saw Helena?"

Raissa shrugged. "She can't think of any other explanation."

"The whole thing is just weird. So Luc used to see her but can't now? What's that about?"

"Luc's a different story than the rest of us. Helena's not the only dead person he's seen. He's part Native American, and apparently ghost-seeing runs in the family. But after Maryse was out of danger, he ceased being able to see or hear Helena."

Zach shook his head in dismay. "Now that's a hell of a thing to inherit. Maybe he and Maryse should consider adopting."

Raissa froze at Zach's words, her mind racing.

"Oh, hey," Zach said, apparently noticing her lack of response. "I didn't mean that seriously. They can have a dozen kids if that's what they want."

"No. I have an idea." She jumped up from her chair and pointed at the files. "Grab those files. We have to get to the hospital. I need to check something."

Zach gathered the files and grabbed his car keys. "What are you thinking?"

"It's only an idea, but I think I can get proof."

"Of what?"

"What those girls had in common. And why Hank Henry was abducted."

Chapter Twenty-One

"Why the hospital?" Zach asked as he drove out of Mudbug toward the hospital. "Do you need to talk to Hank?"

"No. The hospital has a weak security system. It's easy to hack their Internet access. And I'll be less likely to be caught hacking medical records at other hospitals if the signal is coming from this hospital."

"You want me to help you hack medical records?"

"Trust me, Zach. If I'm right, I'm going to blow the lid off all of this."

Zach shook his head, knowing he was making a big mistake. A career-ending, prison-sentence sort of mistake. But if Raissa was right…if she really could wrap this up with a couple of pieces of paper, Zach was almost to the point of risking it. He'd figure out a way to get to that point before he pulled into the hospital parking lot.

The lot was sparsely populated, but then, it was eleven at night. This was it, he thought as he parked in front of the building and turned off the car. He either followed Raissa into the hospital because he had no doubt she'd go in with or without his help, or he backed out of the parking lot and kept his record clean. Sort of.

Raissa hopped out of the car, then looked back inside when he didn't follow her. "Are you going to sit here and wait to be discovered by security?"

Zach pointed through the glass front of the hospital to the security guard, flirting with the nurse at the front desk. "Do you have a plan?" Zach asked. "Or are you just going to hijack the front-desk computer when they're not looking?"

Raissa laughed. "I have a plan, but I need to find Helena. I'm hoping she's still here."

It was crazy—a plan to help an FBI fugitive hack a hospital's computer system, with a ghost as the primary advantage. And it was a plan that he'd never, ever be able to tell to anyone else. Essentially, if he was caught, there was no way out of this. No rational justification for his actions. But it was also the last option they had, and time was running out.

He hopped out of the car and flashed his badge at the security guard, who nodded. With all the traffic in and out of Hank Henry's room, the security guard wouldn't suspect anything was out of order. Raissa pointed at the hallway to Hank's room, and they headed down it. They were halfway down the hall, when Raissa stopped short. Zach looked back, wondering what was going on.

"What's wrong?" he asked.

"Nothing," Raissa said. "Helena's right here. She's leaving Hank's room." Raissa quickly explained to Helena that she needed to get into the medical records of several hospitals, then turned to Zach. "She knows just how to help us."

Zach squinted, staring at the air in front of Raissa, wishing he could make out something...anything...that would prove he wasn't crazy for believing in ghosts. "Help us do what?"

"Break into the medical-records room. Listen, if you'd rather stay out of this, I understand. It's not exactly the sort of thing you want on your record."

"Of course I'd rather stay out of this, but it's too late now. Worst case, I'll say you're a suspect in an investigation, and I followed you into the hospital to apprehend you. I will have to arrest you, though, if we get caught." *And no one's likely to believe it, but what the hell.*

"Fine by me. C'mon. Helena says the medical-records room is this way."

"Why medical records?" Zach asked as they walked. "Can't you use a computer somewhere else?"

"Yes, but the IP address of every computer is unique, so when I dial into another hospital asking for medical-records information, the security system is going to see the request coming from a medical-records-department computer at this hospital. I'm hoping it's enough to avoid setting off alarms. At least long enough for me to get what I came for."

"Which is? You still haven't covered that part."

Raissa turned down another hallway and stopped in front of the door to the medical-records room. A couple of seconds later, Zach heard the door unlock from the inside and it opened. He looked inside, but couldn't see a thing.

"Hurry up before someone sees you," Raissa whispered, motioning him inside.

Zach hurried into the room and shut the door behind him. Raissa had already slipped behind a desk in the far corner of the room. "Sorry," Zach said, "but that ghost shit still gets to me."

"As soon as I solve the mystery of Melissa Franco, I'm going to help Helena leave."

Raissa motioned for the folders, and Zach handed over the stack. "Help her leave?"

"Yeah, didn't I tell you? Helena was murdered. We're pretty sure that's why she's still hanging around. So the general consensus is that if we can figure out who murdered her and why, she'll be able to cross over."

Zach shook his head, trying to absorb all of that into anything that resembled rationality.

Raissa picked up the first file and handed it to Zach. "You read. I'll type. That will be faster. Give me the town the first girl lives in."

"Orlando, Florida." Zach pulled a chair next to Raissa and watched the screen flicker as she worked her magic. Finally, the screen stopped whirling and Zach looked at the header at the top left. "I hope I don't regret this."

Raissa laughed. "Don't worry. I've been doing this for years for my fortune-telling clients. Why do you think I'm so accurate?"

Zach placed his hands over his ears and hummed. "I am not hearing this."

Raissa swatted at him. "Give me the first girl's name with exact spelling. Middle name, too."

Zach read from the file and Raissa typed the girl's information into the hospital medical-records database. "All the girls came from families with moderate incomes and lived in outlying areas of small towns, sorta like Mudbug. I'm hoping they used a local doctor who worked out of the hospital."

"Is that common?"

"Yeah. It cuts out the doctor's office overhead and gives the hospital a doctor on-site a great majority of the day."

"So you're thinking their medical records would be at the hospital?"

"Yeah. Worst case, I'll get the emergency records, which might still tell me what I need."

"Okay." Zach didn't even pretend to understand where Raissa was going with this and apparently she was a show, not tell, kind of person.

"Bingo!" Raissa said. "Her records are here."

He leaned in to watch as Raissa opened the first girl's medical records. "Stomachache, vomiting, fever," he read. "Twice in the four months preceding her abduction." He looked over at Raissa. "So what? She ate something bad...had a virus...nothing that screams 'kidnap me.'"

"Not yet," Raissa said, and reduced the record to her desktop and opened another search. "Next name."

Zach shook his head and read off the name from the next file, wondering how one bridged the gap between a tummy ache and a kidnapping.

"Look," Raissa said, excited as she pointed to the next girl's record. "Stomach trouble three times in the six months preceding the kidnapping."

"Okay. So kids get sick. Maybe there was some big strain of the flu going around that year."

Raissa turned from the screen and stared at him. "I'll bet you twenty bucks that every single one of those girls went to the hospital complaining of stomach problems within six months of abduction."

Zach shrugged. "You're on. That's too big of an anomaly."

Raissa lifted the files from his lap and started typing. One by one she pulled up the girls' records, and one by one, the facts were right there for Zach to see. When she finished, Raissa looked at him.

"Okay," Zach said, still bewildered by the similarities in the records and the time line to abduction. "I owe you twenty bucks. Now, would you like to tell me what's going on? Obviously this proves your theory."

"I think every one of those girls was sick. I think the reason they were abducted has something to do with what was wrong with them."

Zach frowned. "But after they were returned, there's no record of illness."

"Exactly! And there was no record of illness earlier than six months before they disappeared."

Zach stared at Raissa, amazed. "Seriously? I didn't even notice. What the hell?"

Raissa jumped up from her chair and began to pace back and forth across the room. "Don't you see how extraordinary that would be? The oldest victim is seventeen. I know from my other research that she still lives with her family, in the same home, and they are still in the same income bracket, yet she's never visited the doctor again after her abduction."

Zach struggled to wrap his mind around what Raissa was saying. "So you think...what? They cured her?"

"Not then. Remember, they weren't sick until right before the abductions."

Zach ran one hand through his hair. "Jesus, Raissa. That sounds a little crazy, even for you. Even for this case, which is anything but normal."

"Melissa Franco was the same way. Remember, her dad said she was never sick, but Dr. Spencer said the medication they were giving her had curbed some symptoms that were beginning to form. What do you want to bet those symptoms included stomach problems?"

She slid into her chair again, tapped on the keyboard, then pointed to the screen.

"Cancer. And would you like to take a guess at how cancer usually presents itself in the early stages?" She tapped one fingernail on the monitor. "Take a look."

Zach read the screen that provided a list of the symptoms of leukemia in children. "Initial symptoms are usually attributed to the common flu," he read. "Damn." His mind whirled with the possibilities of everything Raissa had said. "But why these kids? And how did the abductors know when to take them? I'll admit this is fascinating, but it creates more questions than it answers. And it doesn't prove anything."

"I think someone's been carefully watching these girls since they were born."

"Spencer?"

"Most likely. But I bet there's more."

Raissa pulled up the first record. Her fingers flew across the keyboard, pulling up one record after another until she had three hospital records side-by-side on the screen. "Look." She pointed to the records of the parents of the first girl. "Look at the blood types."

She turned and looked directly at Zach. "Don't you see? There's no way she's their daughter. And I'd be willing to bet that we'll find that's the case with all the girls who went missing, including Melissa Franco."

"Peter Franco said they had trouble conceiving. Could be that Melissa was conceived in vitro."

"And the others? All blue-collar families, but they managed to pay the cost of in vitro while in the military? No way. Every one of those children except Melissa was conceived while the father was stationed at the military base in North Carolina."

"So what? Someone made a mistake with meds, or gave them the wrong babies. I don't know what you think this is, Raissa."

"I'm not sure, either. But let's go over what we know. Someone helped these parents conceive babies that were not biologically their own, and Spencer was present on the base when every one of those babies was conceived."

"You think he gave them in vitro—without them even knowing?"

"Could be. The actual insertion of the egg wouldn't require much more than an extensive exam. Spencer could have said their Pap was irregular in order to do more 'tests,' " Raissa answered. "So, continuing with what we have so far, someone was keeping tabs on the kids and arranged an abduction around the time the girls started showing symptoms of a stomachache."

"A possible precursor to cancer," Zach chimed in.

"Right. The girls are taken for a week, then returned—perfectly healthy and with no memory of what happened."

"Okay, even if I buy that Spencer impregnated these women against their will, where did the eggs come from? They had to be the same person, right? There's no way they'd develop the same disease at the same age otherwise. Wouldn't that imply a genetic similarity?"

Raissa nodded. "I think so."

"But that doesn't explain Melissa Franco. Why start all this again after nine years had passed?"

"My best guess is that when Susannah Franco couldn't get pregnant, she talked about it with her family. I'm certain Monk Marsella is the one who kidnapped those other girls, and he must have known enough about what was going on to convince whoever he was working for to do it for Susannah."

"You think Monk Marsella strong-armed Dr. Spencer into impregnating Susannah with a bionic baby?"

"Monk could've threatened to expose the other girls, so he agreed to the procedure."

"Then why wait almost six years after creating Melissa to kill him?"

"I don't know for sure, but it looks like someone's eliminating all liability associated with this mess. That would also explain why Dr. Spencer's car has a bullet hole, likely from my gun, in his trunk. He must have seen Melissa going into my shop after the appointments. He knew I could expose his relationship with Melissa and her mother."

"And on the day of the kidnapping, you went to the police station. It must have been Spencer who pushed you in front of the bus." Zach was beginning to think that in a bizarre, out-of-this-world sort of way, things were starting to make sense. "That would explain why Susannah lied about Melissa's medical condition, and why I got the feeling she wasn't as worried as her husband. She already knew where Melissa was and why. She knew they were going to do something that would kill off the cancer. She knew Melissa would return to her, the perfect child."

"Exactly. And I think that treatment involved a blood transfusion from Hank Henry."

"Whoa, you lost me here." Zach shook his head. So much for things making sense. "Why Hank? Because he was abducted?"

"Because he was abducted by an *alien*, like the others, and because he had a needle mark in his arm and was anemic when he was brought into the hospital. They were giving him iron pills, remember?"

"Okay, I'll bite—why Hank Henry?"

"We know Hank couldn't have been Helena's biological son," Raissa explained. "But he's obviously tied up in this mess, because Monk mentioned his name to Sonny in connection with the kidnapping—Sonny just didn't know why. And from everything Maryse told me, the man's never been sick a day in his life. I think Hank is the original version of the bionic baby, and a successful one. He supposedly had periodic problems with anemia, but what if it was because they were harvesting blood from him? Doing a transfusion to save the other girls?"

"But Hank's never been kidnapped before."

"No. Because he's always been available, and I think that's why Helena was impregnated. So they could keep an eye on their work. Until the last couple of years, at least, when Hank pulled a disappearing act."

"But the only person who could have gotten that much blood from him without anyone suspecting something is—"

"Yes," a voice sounded behind them. Raissa and Zach whirled around to find Dr. Breaux standing in the doorway, a 9-millimeter in his hand.

"I'm really sorry you had to push the issue," Dr. Breaux said. "We'd stopped our work here because it was too dangerous, but then Monk insisted we start again. I knew impregnating Susannah would be a mistake, but we couldn't afford to kill her. We weren't sure how much her cousin had told her, and with her husband's connections..."

He motioned to both of them with his gun. "Put your hands up and step out from behind that desk."

Raissa glanced at Zach, who barely shook his head. There was no way to get to their weapons in time. They stepped out from behind the desk and walked toward the doctor until he told them to stop, about ten feet in front of him. "You"—Dr. Breaux waved his gun at Zach—"take out your gun. Slowly, or I shoot her right now. Slide it across the floor to me."

Zach slid his pistol out of his hip holster and pushed it across the floor toward the doctor.

"Now you," Dr. Breaux said, and motioned to Raissa.

Raissa removed her pistol from the back of her jeans and slid it across the floor. She made no move at all for her ankle holster and hoped the doctor had no idea she always doubled up on weapons.

Dr. Breaux shook his head. "I was hoping I was wrong about you, Raissa, but some things just never added up. And when Dr. Spencer told me you went to the police after the abduction, I was afraid my worst fears were right. You have a certain way of moving, of watching people, that's familiar to me from my war days. You're a well-trained machine."

"How long has this been going on?" Raissa asked.

Dr. Breaux kicked both of their guns into a corner, then studied her for a moment. "I guess it doesn't matter if I tell you. You'll be the only people left who will know everything, except me, and that will all change in another couple of minutes.

"It started after the war...during the war, if you want the real beginning," Dr. Breaux said. "I was captured in a village in Vietnam. There was an outbreak of influenza. Thousands of sick people and one doctor. When they found out I was a doctor, they put me to work in their makeshift clinic."

"This wasn't about the flu," Raissa said.

"No. We cared for flu patients all day long and well into the evening, but at night, a Vietnamese doctor worked his own magic in nothing more than a pop-up tent and not even five thousand dollars' worth of medical equipment. Pretty impressive, when you consider he made the first huge theoretical strides in building a superhuman race. He'd barely started work on human embryos, but if he'd had the equipment and more time, he might have been successful. His theories were mostly sound, and decades ahead of anything I'd ever seen."

"So you and Dr. Spencer re-created his research in the States after you were rescued and returned."

Dr. Breaux laughed. "I killed him for his research and escaped with all of it. Do you really think I was going to let someone beat me to this discovery?"

"You impregnated women without their permission. You genetically altered the embryos before implanting. You knew what you were doing was illegal on so many levels, not to mention morally reprehensible."

"We needed a test sample, and we couldn't afford for all the children to be raised in the same location or someone might clue in on complications. Mothers wanted children. And I had several potential investors lining up to make me a *very* wealthy man."

"I thought Hank was a success. You could've cut and run," Raissa said.

"Yes, Hank was a success, but no matter how hard I tried, I couldn't duplicate the results with girls. No girls, no deal with investors. With Melissa, I'd finally isolated the problem and was ready to move forward with a new round of babies, when Helena got cancer."

Raissa felt the blood drain from her head. "Oh, my God. It was *you* who killed Helena."

"I could hardly have her asking Hank for a bone-marrow transplant, then finding out he wasn't her son. She would've made things very messy."

"And then you kidnapped Hank," Raissa said.

"Of course. I knew where Monk had kept an extra alien suit, but never figured on having to use it. It was quite a bit of fun, though, the look on Hank's face."

"And Melissa?"

"She'll be safely home tomorrow—just like the others."

"Why kill Dr. Spencer?"

"He was a liability. He was in a panic, ready to confess everything, and had forgotten entirely what a crack shot I was in the military. I've always kept in practice. You never know when you might need to kill something."

Raissa stared at Dr. Breaux, his eyes cold and calculating, and realized this was the end. This man had been working toward a single-minded purpose for over half of his life. He believed he was God and wasn't going to let anything get in his way.

She reached for Zach's hand and held it tightly in her own, regret washing over her. "I am so sorry," she said.

Zach shook his head. "I'm not."

"Touching," Dr. Breaux said. His finger tightened on the trigger, and Raissa closed her eyes, waiting for the end.

Suddenly, the door to the records room flew open and Sonny Hebert burst in. Sonny fired one shot at Dr. Breaux and caught him in the leg, but the doctor managed to squeeze off one of his own and caught the mobster in his arm. Sonny dropped his gun and launched behind a bookshelf to protect himself from more fire. Raissa and Zach hesitated for only a moment, then dove behind the computer desk.

Raissa pulled her pistol from her ankle holster and fired off a shot at the doctor, who slipped behind a set of bookcases just in time to avoid her shot. "Checkmate," she whispered to Zach. "Two of us and two of them." Raissa had no doubt that Sonny would only delay coming after her long enough to kill the doctor.

Raissa peeked around the side of the desk and gasped in surprise. Helena Henry was dangling from a ventilation pipe, pushing as hard as she could against the bookcase Dr. Breaux was hiding behind. The bookcase rocked back and forth, almost to the tipping point. Raissa tugged at Zach and pointed to the bookcase. "Helena," she whispered.

Zach nodded and perched on the other side of the desk, prepared to dive for his weapon as soon as the bookcase toppled. Raissa held her breath as the bookcase tipped forward, then backward, then forward, and seemed to almost pause before it crashed into the bookcase in front of it, setting them off like dominos all the way to the front of the office.

The fallout was immediate. Sonny popped up from behind the desk, dove for his gun, and opened fire at the doctor, who in turn had opened fire at everything in the room. Zach grabbed his weapon and ran for the emergency exit at the opposite corner of the room, Raissa close behind.

She heard Helena yelling at her to hurry, when she felt the bullet rip through her thigh. She stumbled and tried to brace herself, but her head hit the side of a metal filing cabinet. The last thing she remembered seeing was Zach's horrified expression as he looked back at her, and then everything went black.

Chapter Twenty-Two

Raissa awakened to a burning pain in her leg and voices arguing above her. She opened her eyes, but everything was blurry. Finally, things sharpened a bit, and she saw Helena hovering right over her face, looking down anxiously at her.

"Are you all right?" Helena asked. "Say something if you are. Anything."

"I think so," Raissa said, a whisper all she could manage with her aching head.

"The emergency-room staff is on their way, although I have no idea how Zach is going to explain this mess." Helena said. "And those two have been going at it ever since Sonny dropped Dr. Breaux." Helena moved to the side and Raissa looked up at Sonny and Zach, squared off and equally pissed.

"I didn't shoot her," Sonny argued. "I was only firing at the doctor. And I'm not going to apologize for killing the bastard who messes with kids."

"*Your* guy kidnapped those kids," Zach pointed out.

"I suspected Monk was up to something, but I could never prove it until Raissa blew her cover. I got all over Monk and he told me some of it, but he said he didn't do another job for them after I found out. I didn't figure out the rest until today, after talking with Susannah Franco. Those doctor assholes convinced him to take that first girl by telling him she was going to die and they could save her. Monk said if they didn't return the girl to her parents, he'd blow the lid off everything. Monk thought he was helping the girls, the dumb son-of-a-bitch. He never should have gotten involved, and he damn sure shouldn't have gotten his cousin involved, especially after he'd been out of it for years."

Raissa sucked in a breath. Finally, things were making sense. After the years spent trying to heal his dying daughter, Sonny would be the last man alive to intentionally hurt a child, despite his many other destructive ways.

"What are you even doing here, Sonny?" Zach asked.

"I came to talk to Hank, then saw you two and figured you were here for the same reason. You went off a different direction, so I waited a bit, then saw that doctor go the same way. I could see the outline of his pistol in his pocket, so I followed. I heard everything that sick fucker said."

Zach shook his head. "This whole thing is unbelievable. Why in the world would Susannah Franco want to have a baby she knew would get cancer?"

"Monk told me the doctors said they'd fixed the problem," Sonny said. "My guess is that Monk never even told Susannah about the illness. I think they were just using Melissa as a last test case before cutting out to another country. When Melissa got sick, Monk knew they'd lied. He confronted Spencer and Breaux, and they killed him."

"You expect me to believe that?" Zach asked.

"I don't give a shit what you believe. I know what I know. I just couldn't do anything about it until I knew for sure Melissa was going to be all right. I've waited years to finally understand this, but it's over. Melissa is the last of them, so there's no longer a use for Dr. Mengele. Besides, he shot at me first."

"He barely nicked you. It's not even bleeding anymore."

"Yeah, well, he didn't just nick your girlfriend. I'd think you'd be thanking me instead of complaining."

Raissa struggled up to a sitting position, distracting the two men from their conversation.

Zach dropped down beside her. "Don't move. You hit your head and we need to make sure there's no damage. The nurse is coming with a gurney."

Raissa looked at Zach, his expression filled with worry and anger and love, and she felt her chest constrict. He really cared for her, and as much as she'd tried not to, she'd fallen for the surly detective in a big way.

The door to the office flew open and two nurses rushed in with a gurney. Zach barked orders, and the nurses made quick work of securing her to the gurney. As they wheeled her out of the office, Raissa looked back at the man who wanted to protect her, then at the other man, the one who wanted to kill her, and was suddenly overwhelmed with the hopelessness of it all.

Zach pulled out his cell phone and dialed Captain Saucier. This was one time his boss wouldn't mind having to get out of bed. He told the captain everything he and Raissa had discovered about the girls, and the captain started making things happen. A quick real-estate search turned up a warehouse in New Orleans owned by Dr. Breaux, and thirty minutes later, Zach got word that Melissa was alive and well and on her way to a hospital.

Susannah Franco broke down when questioned by the police and gave up everything she knew about Monk, the experiment, and the other kidnappings. The mayor had caught her in a lie the day of the kidnapping and she'd confessed everything to him. In a typical move, the mayor had kept it all quiet in the guise of protecting his son and granddaughter, but Zach suspected he just wanted to increase his popularity.

Zach, Sonny, and the two policemen the captain had sent relocated to an exam room just off the lobby of the hospital. The police officers were trying to get everything Sonny knew on record, but kept double-checking with Zach. Not that he blamed them. Sonny's story sounded more far-fetched than a Hollywood movie.

After ten minutes of disbelief from the officers and swearing and hand gesturing from Sonny, Zach stepped across the hall to the visitor's lounge to pour himself a cup of coffee. What a night. What a mess. Raissa had blown the lid off of one of the most bizarre and corrupt things he'd ever heard of in his life. And she'd taken a bullet for her trouble.

His heart clutched when he thought about how close he'd come to losing her. And as much as he knew that Sonny Hebert belonged behind bars, he couldn't hate the man who'd saved the woman he loved.

Holy shit.

He set his coffee down on the table and the liquid sloshed over the rim of the cup, burning his hand. He shook the coffee off his hand and grabbed a napkin from the counter to wipe off the rest.

You've really done it now, Blanchard.

He stepped up to a window and stared out into the darkness. How the hell had he allowed this to happen? He'd fallen for a woman who was going to disappear like the wind as soon as she checked out of the hospital, and the worst part was, there wasn't a damn thing he could do about it. Raissa would never be safe with Sonny still gunning for her. She'd move off and become a bank teller in Idaho or a waitress in Seattle, and he'd never see her again.

He'd just go on the same way he always had.

No. He shook his head. Things would never be the same again.

Raissa sat propped up against the pillows of her hospital bed, her head still throbbing. The only good part was, the pain in her head had caused her to completely forget the pain in her leg. Maryse and Mildred had arrived earlier, and Raissa had filled them in on everything. Now they sat at the side of the bed, listening to Helena, who was perched on the bed, telling them everything that had happened when the New Orleans police arrived after Raissa had been taken away.

"The police were confused as hell, but the long and short of the immediate situation is that the only bad guy in the mix was Dr. Breaux, who is dead."

Mildred shook her head, the dismay on her face clear as day. "I still just can't believe it. How could we have been so wrong? We never noticed anything at all."

Maryse patted her hand. "It's not our fault. Obviously he'd been at this for a long time. We had no way of knowing that he was someone completely different. How could we?"

"I'm dead proof of that," Helena said. "He admitted to Raissa that he killed me."

Mildred gasped. "Oh, my God. Raissa, is that true?"

"Yes," Raissa confirmed. "I'm sorry. With everything else going on, I left that part out. I accused him, and he said he couldn't afford Helena finding out Hank wasn't her biological son."

"And if she found out about the leukemia," Maryse finished, "then she'd have asked for a donor match and found out then. Shit."

"But he didn't say how he did it," Helena said, "so I still don't know."

Maryse frowned. "I have an idea, but we'll never be able to prove it."

"I don't care if you can prove it," Helena said. "Just tell me something that makes sense."

"When we were planting that listening device at Sonny's you said you hadn't paid for medicine in years—that you'd gotten samples."

"That's right," Helena said. "Damned pharmacy was always out of my inhaler."

"And Dr. Breaux gave you samples from his office."

"Yeah."

"I think the poison was in the inhaler. Try to remember, Helena. Did you use your inhaler before you drank the brandy?"

Helena's eyes widened. "Holy shit, I did. That must be it."

Raissa shook her head. "Genius. It evaporates into her system, and there's no record of where she got it even if anyone asked. It was the golden opportunity. I think you're right, Maryse."

"It makes sense, as much as anything does," Helena said, then sighed. "I want you all to know that I really appreciate everything you've done...for me and for everyone else. I can't believe this is finally over."

"Not quite over," Maryse said, "or you wouldn't still be here. But I have an idea about that, and I'm going to run it by Sabine tomorrow. I'll fill you in as soon as I know more."

"Thanks."

"So, Helena," Raissa said, "finish telling us what happened when the police got here. Did they arrest Sonny?"

"Oh, right," Helena said, growing animated again. "They didn't arrest Sonny for killing Dr. Breaux, because Zach backs his story that Dr. Breaux was holding you two hostage with the intent to kill when Sonny burst in, and that Dr. Breaux fired the first shot. Probably good for Sonny that Dr. Breaux at least grazed him with that shot."

Raissa nodded, then flinched as her head throbbed more. "Makes him more sympathetic."

"Exactly. And Sonny Hebert needs all the sympathy he can manage. Then the FBI showed up, all mad and everything. They told Sonny they want to question him, but I'm not sure if they can make anything stick, as he wasn't actually the one kidnapping the girls."

"Probably not," Raissa said. "Sonny can always claim he didn't know about the kidnappings until after the doctors killed Monk and he found the alien suit."

"Which he has in his closet," Helena pointed out.

Raissa shrugged. "Doesn't prove anything. Besides, I have a feeling that suit is long gone by now anyway."

Helena shook her head. "Sonny put himself in the middle of a big fat mess. How do you think he'll get out of it?"

"There had to have been other people in on this—doctors, nurses...Someone else knows what they were doing, and the cops are going to want their heads on a platter big-time, especially since Dr. Breaux is dead. They'll need Sonny to testify about what Monk told him of the kidnappings and Dr. Breaux's confession, so the cops will deal. That ought to kill them."

Helena blew out a breath and looked at Raissa. "But that means you're still on the hook as far as testifying for Sonny's other crimes goes. Shit. I was hoping the FBI could get Sonny on something else so you could live normally. I guess there's no chance of that, is there?"

"No. If the FBI can't get Sonny on the kidnappings, they're going to want me to testify on the racketeering. The time on that case is almost up."

"So you'll be gone again."

Raissa looked at their expressions, hoping there was another answer but not believing there was. "Gone or dead. There's really no other way. I'm sorry, guys."

"That's bullshit!" Helena said. "I know Sonny's a bad guy, but he was only trying to help those girls, and he told you where Hank was. It's not fair that the FBI leaves you in a position of having no life, and no future but running from Sonny and his family."

"I agree," Maryse said. "Surely something can be done."

Raissa shook her head. "I'm the only witness who can testify to the things I saw and did. No one else is qualified to provide that testimony. I'm all they have."

"Makes me wish you weren't so good at your job," Mildred said. "If you didn't know anything, you could marry Zach and live in New Orleans, or maybe even in Mudbug with Maryse and Sabine." Mildred sighed. "I guess that's just wishful thinking, huh?"

Raissa stared at Mildred, an idea forming in the back of her mind. It was risky in all sorts of ways. In fact, it was the biggest risk she'd ever taken, and that was saying a lot. But it just might work.

Her thoughts were interrupted by a knock on the door. Raissa looked up in time to see the doctor who had examined her earlier, Agent Fields, and Zach enter her room, followed by Sonny and two NOPD officers. Zach went straight to Raissa and kissed her on the lips. "How are you feeling?"

"My head hurts, but I think I'm okay."

The doctor gave her a critical look. "These people insisted on seeing you and asking some questions. I am totally against putting any more strain on you, given your head injury, but I was forced to give you an option." The doctor shot a dirty look at the police and

Agent Fields. "If you aren't up to talking, just say the word, and I'll clear the whole lot of them out of here."

"It's okay," Raissa said.

"You're certain? I don't like to think you're being intimidated."

Raissa smiled. "I promise, if any of them get out of line, I'll ask them to leave myself."

The doctor nodded, but didn't look convinced. He gave all of the men a frown and left the room.

Agent Fields stepped forward, followed by the two cops. "First off, we need to hear from you who shot you."

"I have no idea," Raissa said.

Agent Fields frowned. "You came to the hospital to get evidence against Dr. Breaux, and then Sonny showed up. Shots were fired, but you can't say who hit you?"

Raissa frowned. "I came to the hospital?"

Zach looked over at Mildred and Maryse, his face filled with worry. "What's wrong with her? Has she been talking to you?"

Maryse looked over at Raissa, her eyes wide. Raissa looked her in the eye, willing her to understand. Mildred started to speak, but Maryse took her hand and squeezed. "She's been talking," Maryse said, "but mostly about stuff we did months ago." Maryse bit her lower lip and shot a worried look at Raissa. "We were just about to call for the doctor when you guys walked in."

Raissa managed to look confused and made a mental note to talk to Maryse later about her superb ability to lie on command. The woman was a pro.

"I think maybe you should call the doctor now." Zach leaned in close. "Do you know who I am?"

Raissa laughed. "No, I let strange men kiss me all the time. Of course I know who you are."

Zach nodded. "We met because you were trying to figure out why those girls were kidnapped, remember? You figured it all out by looking at girls' records."

"Kidnapped...Melissa Franco. She was kidnapped." Raissa sat up straight. "Is she okay? Did they find her? She always made her mom buy blue candles."

"Melissa's mother confessed to her part in everything, and they found Melissa at a warehouse Dr. Breaux rented in New Orleans. All his notes are there—decades worth of testing. We'll be able to figure out everything he did. Melissa's on her way to the hospital but appears to be fine."

"Thank God. I'm glad to hear that."

"There were other girls...from years ago. Do you remember?"

Raissa frowned. "I don't know any other girls. Only Melissa."

"You investigated the cases when you were undercover in Sonny Hebert's organization." Zach nodded toward Sonny, who cocked his head to one side and studied her, a confused look on his face.

Raissa stared at Sonny for several seconds, then gave Zach a bewildered look. "I don't know that man."

"That's Sonny Hebert," Zach explained. "You were undercover in his organization when you were in the FBI."

"The FBI?" Raissa widened her eyes and looked from Zach to Sonny to the cops.

Zach sucked in a breath. "You left protective custody over nine years ago and have been pretending to be a psychic in New Orleans."

Raissa laughed. "Pretending? I'm not pretending. I have a lot of clients. You guys are kidding me, right? Really, what's all this about, Zach?"

The room went instantly silent, and Raissa was fairly sure no one was breathing. The doctor walked into the room and immediately checked Raissa's vitals. "Do you want me to remove your visitors, Ms. Bordeaux?"

"No," Raissa said. "They're trying to pull a prank on me."

Zach looked over at the doctor, his face panicked. "She doesn't remember things. Some recent events and anything from about ten years ago." He pointed at Sonny. "She worked for this man for two years, but doesn't know him. I don't understand."

The doctor shone a light in Raissa's eyes and felt her scalp. "The injury was to the section of the brain that stores memory. Memory loss is always a possibility, and long-term memory is the most likely to go."

"But it will come back, right?" Agent Fields asked.

"There's no way to know," the doctor said. "I think it's better if you all let Ms. Bordeaux rest, and no more questioning until *I* say she's ready. Is that clear?"

Agent Fields and the New Orleans cops didn't look happy, but they couldn't exactly argue with the doctor, so they trailed out of the office. Sonny, following behind them, looked the most confused of the lot. At the doorway, he paused and looked back at Raissa.

Raissa stared at him, held his gaze. Sonny's eyes widened and he barely nodded, then left the room. Maryse hopped up from her chair, pulling Mildred with her. "I think we ought to give you two some time," Maryse said. "We'll go get some coffee. Call if you need anything."

Helena hopped off the end of the bed and trailed behind them, giving Raissa a wink and a thumbs-up on her way out the door.

"Thanks," Raissa said. She lay back against the pillows and looked over at Zach, who was frowning at her.

"You're faking," he said. "Holy shit, Raissa! This is not a game. Why are you faking memory loss?"

"Between my undercover work and hiding because of my undercover work, I've lost eleven years of my life to Sonny Hebert. And the ironic thing is, if it weren't for him, I wouldn't have another eleven years to make things different. He saved my life, Zach. And probably Hank's, too."

"But the racketeering case—"

"I know Sonny's done some bad things, but he did help us find out who was taking those girls, and he found Hank. If the FBI has to have me to make a case against him, then it wasn't much of a case to begin with, was it?"

Zach nodded. "You know what? You're right. You've given more than your share. Let someone else take up the slack. I'm sure Sonny's not going legitimate anytime soon. They'll get him, eventually."

"Maybe, or maybe not. If they didn't make a case in the nine years I was hiding, I can only guess that Sonny's gotten a whole lot better at his job."

"And what about you?" Zach asked.

"What do you mean?"

"What are you going to do, now that you're free?"

Raissa smiled. "Well, I'm not going back to the FBI, that's for sure. Honestly, I don't know what I'll do. I haven't had the freedom to choose anything in a long, long time." She leaned toward Zach and whispered in his ear, "But I hear there's this detective who needs someone to keep him in line."

Zach smiled. "And just what makes you think you can do the job?"

Raissa softly kissed his neck once, then again, then his earlobe. He groaned and turned to her, crushing her lips with his. He gathered her in his arms, and in an instant, Raissa knew she'd made the right decision.

She'd seen the future, and it was very bright, indeed.

Epilogue

One week later

The party started at five that evening. Maryse had worked her magic with the historical society, one of the recipient's of Helena's massive estate, and they all gathered in Helena Henry's mansion, now a historical landmark. Maryse, Sabine, Mildred, and Raissa had done all the prepping and planning, baking, collecting premade trays from a caterer in New Orleans, and stocking the refrigerator with enough booze for New Year's Eve at a fraternity house. Helena, of course, was there to sample everything before it was deemed worthy of the festivities.

They joked and laughed and swapped tasks, helping each other that entire afternoon. Helena spent a lot of time just watching. It was beautiful, those girls and Mildred. Like a mother and her daughters. They'd endured so much to be here today. More than any thousand people would likely endure in a lifetime, and they'd persevered through it all. There was so much strength, so much love, that Helena got misty just thinking about it.

The men started arriving around five. Luc, with his big smile and enormous charm. Beau, with his big heart and quiet strength. Zach, with his brashness and fierce loyalty. So very different, but all so perfectly suited for the women they'd chosen to make a life with.

When the doorbell rang thirty minutes later, Helena peeked around the kitchen wall to see whom Raissa was letting in. She almost dropped her plate of nachos when she saw Hank walk through the door, holding the hand of that lovely girl Lila she'd seen at the hospital. She watched as Maryse crossed the room and gave the girl a hug. Then she said something to Hank, kissed him on the cheek, and gave him a hug.

Maryse pulled Hank and the girl into the huge, open living area and started introducing them to the people they hadn't met. Hank looked shy at first, but finally relaxed with the warm greetings he received from everyone. Lila watched him every second, her smile radiant.

Luc handed Hank a beer and Lila a glass of wine and waved his hand at the buffet along the wall. They filled plates and joined the others laughing and chatting...like a family. Helena rubbed away a tear and smiled. Finally, she took her plate and her drink and went up the back staircase to the second floor. The big spiral staircase in the main living area had a huge landing with a great view of the room. She took a seat above the action and enjoyed the interplay.

After an hour or so of festivities, Maryse directed the others to help her light candles that she'd placed all around the room. Maryse walked over to Hank, took his hand, and spoke to him. Hank nodded, his expression anxious and hopeful. Helena wondered what was up, but before she could sneak down and ask, Maryse looked up at her and waved her down.

"Get the lights," Maryse said, and Mildred turned off the lights to the room, leaving it doused in candlelight.

Helena rose from her seat and started down the spiral stairway. When she stepped into an area lit up by the candles, she heard a gasp. She looked over in the living room, and realized Hank was staring directly at her, as was Lila. "Oh, my God," Hank said. "I can see her. Mother?"

Hank took a step toward the stairway, and Helena hurried down. She stood just inches in front of Hank, his amazement clear. "I can't believe it," he said. "I mean, I knew Maryse wouldn't lie, but I never thought...Can you hear me?"

"Yes," Helena said. "I can hear and see everyone. It just doesn't always work the other way. Can you hear me?"

Hank nodded, his eyes filling with tears. "I am so sorry, Mom, about everything—being a lousy son, running off and leaving you to be murdered. I want you to know that it wasn't your fault. You gave me the advantages I needed to be successful. I threw them all away."

Tears formed in Helena's eyes as she looked at the man that wasn't her son, according to biology, but had been in every other way. "I wasn't a great mother. I know that. I didn't trust myself to show my love completely, not even with you. But I always loved you."

"And I always loved you," Hank said. He reached up with one hand to touch her face, and Helena was amazed when she could actually feel his fingertips gently brush her cheek.

"I feel your skin," Hank said, his eyes wide. "I didn't think..."

"I wondered," Maryse said, and stepped forward. "When you were in the hospital, Lila saw a woman in your room, singing. I thought she'd seen Helena, but I didn't understand why, as Lila wasn't in any danger." Maryse looked over at Luc and Zach, who nodded.

"Everyone can see you, Helena," Maryse said. "Something's changing, and I thought maybe tonight would be the height of whatever was happening."

"Why tonight?" Helena asked.

Maryse laughed. "Do you mean to tell me you've been so distracted that you forgot your birthday? Why do you think we bought six cheesecakes?"

Helena stared. "My birthday. My God. I had forgotten."

Helena walked with Maryse and Hank to the center of the living room. Helena stared down at her feet and hands. "It's almost like I feel the floor beneath my feet." She reached out with a hand to touch Hank's shoulder and gasped. "I can feel him. Without concentrating, I mean. Just like when I was...alive."

Helena looked around the room, all of them looking at her with love on their faces and tears in their eyes, and she felt her heart swell. No woman deserved this, especially her. "My family," she said, and began to cry.

She hugged them all, one at a time, taking care to whisper to them her thoughts, her hopes for their futures. Something big was about to happen. She could feel it coursing through her body like an electrical charge. Finally, when she'd given her last hug, whispered her last thoughts, she stood in the center of the room and clutched Hank's hand with one of her hands and Maryse's with the other.

"Seems only fitting," she said, and smiled at the two of them. "Since this is how it all started."

As soon as the words left her mouth, a light began to form above them. It was small at first, like a candle on the ceiling of the room, but then it began to grow wider, and it dipped down, lower, lower, until it was past the second-floor landing and entering the first floor. Helena stared at the light, amazed by its beauty, by the warmth inside, and she squeezed Maryse's and Hank's hands as it began to pour over her body.

"I love you all. Be happy and well," she said, then slowly faded away.

The End

Made in the USA
Monee, IL
31 December 2023